"*Manhunt* holds a unique nich........ ....,
mystery, and detective fiction. In fact, it ranks among the three or four most important and influential in its genre. The first issue was dated January 1953, the last April/May 1967, a 14-year run roughly parallel to that of *The Saint*, not an especially long life for a digest-sized magazine that claimed to be the world's most popular in its category . . .

"From its first issue, *Manhunt* declared itself different. For one thing, all the stories were claimed to be new and remained that way until near the end. And many of the early contributors were familiar names from hardcover publishing lists, including William Irish (a.k.a. Cornell Woolrich), Kenneth Millar (as himself and as John Ross Macdonald), Eleazar Lipsky, Bruno Fischer, Craig Rice, Harold Q. Masur, Leslie Charteris, William Lindsay Gresham, Henry Kane, and David Goodis . . .

"The essence of Manhunt was not the private eye story, though it published plenty of them. What set it apart was what is now called noir fiction, a term often thrown around very loosely but in its purest form concerning a flawed but not necessarily unsympathetic protagonist who will not have a happy outcome."

From the Introduction by Jon Breen

THE BEST OF
MANHUNT
2

Foreword by Peter Enfantino

Introduction by Jon L. Breen

Edited by Jeff Vorzimmer

STARK
HOUSE

Stark House Press • Eureka California
www.starkhousepress.com

THE BEST OF *MANHUNT* 2
Published by Stark House Press
1315 H Street
Eureka, CA 95501
griffinskye3@sbcglobal.net
www.starkhousepress.com

ISBN: 978-1-951473-05-1

Book design by *¡caliente!Design*, Austin, Texas

Stark House Press Edition: August 2020

Table of Contents

Forward: For The Love of *Manhunt* ....Peter Enfantino 7
Introduction...Jon L. Breen 11
On the Passing of *Manhunt*........................Jon L. Breen 15
Life and Death of a Magazine.......................Robert Turner.............17
A Stabbing in the Street ....Elezazer Lipsky 23
As I Lie Dead...Fletcher Flora.................36
So Dark for April ....Howard Browne.............49
Shakedown..Roy Carroll.................66
The Choice ....Richard Deming.............73
Confession...John M. Sitan.................85
The Empty Fort ....Basil Heatter 92
You Can't Trust a Man.................................Helen Nielsen.................127
Sylvia...Ira Levin.................136
Protection..Erle Stanley Gardner.......145
Blonde at the Wheel...................................Stephen Marlowe.............154
Vanishing Act ....W. R. Burnett.................166
One More Mile to Go..................................F. J. Smith 186
Key Witness ....Frank Kane 192
Puddin' and Pie ....De Forbes 229
Blood and Moonlight..................................William R. Cox 234
Shadowed...Richard Wormser...........244
Death of a Big Wheel ....William Campbell Gault..248
The Geniuses...Max Franklin 271
Kitchen Kill ....Jonathan Craig 285
The Crying Target ....James McKimmey...........299
The Girl Friend..Mark Mallory 320
Midnight Caller ....Wade Miller.................326
Arrest ....Donald E. Westlake.........329
Time to Kill ....Bryce Walton.................333
Absinthe for Superman...............................Robert Edmond Alter.......356
Wharf Rat ....Robert Page Jones...........333
The Safe Kill...Kenneth Moore 374
A Question of Values..................................C. L. Sweeney, Jr. 378
Shatter Proof...Jack Ritchie.................381
The Old Pro ....H. A. DeRosso.................385
Retribution...Michael Zuroy.................395
In Memoriam ....Charles Boeckman...........398
Bugged..Bruno Fischer 402
Interference...Glenn Canary.................412

Forward: For The Love of Manhunt

Peter Enfantino

April 2020

First published in January 1953, *Manhunt*'s reputation was built on the contributions of Mickey Spillane, Evan Hunter/Ed McBain, Harry Whittington, and David Goodis. That's why these digests are so collectible. Most of the *Manhunt* elite never had their short stories collected. That's why you'll pay big dollars for key issues. But there are those of us who collect the digests for more than just the beautiful cover art of Dick Shelton or Ray Houlihan, or a rare Harlan Ellison appearance, or just the general musty odor of the pages. For those of us who actually read the gritty crime stories between the covers, *Manhunt* is a treasure trove of great writing.

For all its esteem, *Manhunt* has been pretty much ignored through the years, but for the random reprinting of some of its more well-known contents and the remembrances of its most faithful followers. That all changed when Stark House published the first volume of *The Best of Manhunt*, lovingly selected by Jeff Vorzimmer. Now, a new generation of crime readers could learn just what it is about this title that's kept it relevant for seventy years. But, surely, Jeff used up all the great material in that first volume, no?

What strikes you when you read *The Best of Manhunt 2* is the fact that there are so many good stories by so many writers that *aren't* "household names" (well, at least hardboiled households). Fletcher Flora, whose "As I Lie Dead" is a brilliant tale of crosses and double-crosses. Robert Turner, writing as Roy Carroll, delivers an unflinching look at two soulless individuals in "Shakedown." Frank Kane, author of several stories featuring hardboiled PI Johnny Liddell, is often overlooked when great authors of the 1950s are discussed, perhaps because so many of the Liddells seemed jokey. Kane's "Key Witness" (included in this volume), a rare non-Liddell novella, is anything but comic. An innocent bystander turned good samaritan is terrorized by the punks he witnessed commit murder. His transformation from good citizen to victim is starkly portrayed. Richard Deming, writing as Max Franklin, contributes "The Geniuses," starring the two most ruthless "thrill killers" since Leopold and Loeb. If I had the time and space, I'd extoll the virtues of "Absinthe for Superman," a gripping ocean-set tale of madness by Robert Edmond Alter (one of the most overlooked masters of crime and suspense of the 1960s), or "One More Mile to Go" by F.J. Smith (directed by Hitchcock himself for his TV show), but both are contained herein so you can experience them yourselves rather than listen to rantings of a madman. There are just so many choices here.

My own personal *Manhunt* collecting odyssey began in 1993 after a conversation with author Ed Gorman. Ed was writing a piece on Gold Medal paperbacks for *The Scream Factory*, a magazine I was editing at the time, and *Manhunt* kept popping up in the conversation. Ed let on that *Manhunt* had been an important part of his formative years. That sparked an interest in me and when, while browsing through a used paperback store (Nightmares and Notions, Oakland,

CA—RIP), I came across a cheap copy of the January 1956 issue ("Seven Brutal Shockers!"), I took the plunge. Further help on the trail to bliss and a full set came via Bill Pronzini, who introduced me to a man who had several issues of *MH* and *Mike Shayne* to sell at a paperback show in Los Angeles. Bill led me out to this guy's car and we had a look in the trunk. If this had been a *Manhunt* story, the booty in the boot would have been the guy's wife, of course, but the treasure there was much nicer: boxes of *Alfred Hitchcock's* and *Mike Shayne's Mystery Magazine*s, and dozens of *Manhunt*s! Seven years later, I had the high bid on the September 1955 issue (one of the pricier digests because of its Charles Williams novel) and completed my set. I'd estimate a total price at about $1200.00.

Aside from a few bumps in the road, assembling a set of *Manhunt* is not an impossible task for the collector with enough patience and funds. Most issues can be found for $15-20 apiece. If condition is not a factor (who are we fooling . . . of course it is), you can find them for half that amount. Before the advent of the internet and eBay several years ago, collectors depended on mail order catalogs or the annual vintage paperback shows like those held in New York by Gary Lovisi and in California by Tom Lesser. Now, it's not uncommon to find two dozen issues of *Manhunt* on eBay on any given day. Of course, there are the issues that will cost a lot more than fifteen or twenty bucks. In addition to the aforementioned Charles Williams, who contributed three novels to *Manhunt*, expect to pay more for issues with work by John D. MacDonald (5), David Goodis (4), or Mickey Spillane (3), to name just a few. I also had a hard time finding the last couple issues (this might have been due either to poor distribution or a decline in print run) and the less desirable *Giant Manhunt*s (the publisher would bind three, sometimes four, recent back issues together and sell them for half-a-buck). The last couple (bedsheet-sized) issues of the *Giant* are the Holy Grail of *Manhunt* collecting.

Then there's the matter of those pesky bedsheets. Beginning in March 1957 and continuing through April 1958, *Manhunt* was published in standard magazine size, or "bedsheet", rather than as a digest, in an effort to boost sales. *MH*'s publisher, Flying Eagle, was convinced that *MH* got lost behind the larger magazines on the newsstand. Years later, this would cause innumerable problems for the collector. Because of its awkward size, the bedsheet wasn't to be found with its digest brothers. Chances are, you'd find them in a box of old *Saturday Evening Post*s in an antique store. The scarcity drove the price up. Though not as scarce as the similar *Alfred Hitchcock's Mystery Magazine* bedsheets, which can fetch upwards of $100 each, you're still going to shell out $50-75 each for the twelve *MH* bedsheets. But, when you consider the insane prices found in the comic book collecting world, it's still a fairly cheap hobby.

After returning to digest size, *Manhunt* just wasn't the same again. Though the *Manhunt* elite would make an appearance now and then, most of the authors were new, untested writers. Writers not heard of before and, in several instances, never heard of again after *Manhunt*'s demise. Evan Hunter and Charles Williams gave way to Robert Page Jones and J. Simmons Scheb. Not exactly esteemed names in a crime aficionado's book. The general look of the magazine began to suffer as well. The magazine's frequency was dropped first to bi-monthly and eventually quarterly and reprints (of both covers and the fiction inside) became a fact of life. The beautiful hardboiled paintings adorning the covers gave way to out-of-focus shots of women cringing against brick walls. If you're looking for the quality, stick to the first six years. But, as evidenced in the two volumes of *The Best of Manhunt* published by Stark House, oh, those six years!

Introduction
Jon L. Breen

April 2020

When I first began collecting adult mystery fiction as a teenager in the 1950s, Main Street to me was the classical detective story, the work of Queen, Christie, Carr, et. al., and it still is. In my periodical reading, comic books were replaced by *Ellery Queen's Mystery Magazine* (*EQMM*) and *The Saint Detective Magazine*. But I wanted to know the whole field of fictional crime, and when I discovered the harder-edged *Manhunt*, it helped broaden my horizons. I added it to my back-issue search in used book stores (fairly easy and economical to do at that time), and I remember buying every issue new when the magazine, along with its then-stablemate *Alfred Hitchcock's Mystery Magazine* (*AHMM*), temporarily went to a larger format in 1957 and 1958. When I began writing my own short stories, I don't think I ever submitted to *Manhunt*, but I certainly would have if I had started earlier or it had lasted longer.

Manhunt holds a unique niche among magazines specializing in crime, mystery, and detective fiction. In fact, it ranks among the three or four most important and influential in its genre. The first issue was dated January 1953, the last April/May 1967, a 14-year run roughly parallel to that of *The Saint*, not an especially long life for a digest-sized magazine that claimed to be the world's most popular in its category. *Black Mask* ran longer (1920–1951) in its original form; so did *Dime Detective* (1931–1953), *Mike Shayne Mystery Magazine* (1956–1985), and the two venerable titles still in business today, *EQMM* (1941–) and *AHMM* (1956–). And truthfully, *Manhunt's* glory days were confined to the first half of its run. It may have started with a roar but went out with elongated whimper. So what makes *Manhunt* so special?

Black Mask and its fellow pulp magazines published and developed some great writers, but essentially the pulps were regarded as speedily written, low-paying, formulaic, and sub-literary, directed at a broad and relatively unsophisticated audience, something like the dime novels that preceded them. When the digest magazines came to prominence in the 1940s, they upped the respectability quotient by featuring more familiar hardcover novelists and slick magazine writers; they also tended more toward traditional detective fiction than the tough and hardboiled stories featured in the pulps. Reprints outnumbered original stories in most of the digests of that time, and they (in common with radio, motion pictures, general magazines, and to a lesser extent popular fiction) had a family-audience sensibility that rendered some themes and plot elements out of bounds.

From its first issue, *Manhunt* declared itself different. For one thing, all the stories were claimed to be new and remained that way until near the end. And many of the early contributors were familiar names from hardcover publishing lists, including William Irish (a.k.a. Cornell Woolrich), Kenneth Millar (as himself and as John Ross Macdonald), Eleazar Lipsky, Bruno Fischer, Craig Rice, Harold Q. Masur, Leslie Charteris, William Lindsay Gresham, Henry Kane, and David Goodis.

But one writer certainly inspired more newsstand action than any of these and put *Manhunt* on the map: Mickey Spillane, whose novella "Everybody's Watching Me" was serialized over the first four issues. Much of the mystery world was horrified by the extreme (for the time) sex and violence of Spillane's work, and for years it was rumored that he was denied membership in Mystery Writers of America, though the truth (according to the late Edward D. Hoch, who was there at the time) was that he never applied. In memorializing *Manhunt* in an April 1968 issue of *The Armchair Detective*, I wrote, "Whatever the merits of Spillane's work, and there's no telling what future critical re-estimates might make of him, lovers of detective stories must thank him for that service," *i.e.*, aiding the launch of *Manhunt*. I was right to hedge my prediction for Spillane's future reputation: late in his life, he was awarded the Grand Master award by MWA, and after his death he actually appeared in *EQMM* (in posthumous collaboration with Max Allan Collins), which would not have happened in the 1950s under the editorship of Frederic Dannay.

Speaking of Dannay, he always rejected artificial distinctions between popular genres and serious literature and delighted in publishing stories (usually reprints) by famous mainstream authors not generally identified with crime fiction. *Manhunt* did the same, but with original material by some of the best-known novelists of mid-20th Century America, including James T. Farrell, Erskine Caldwell, Nelson Algren, W.R. Burnett, Meyer Levin, James M. Cain, Jerome Weidman, and Charles Jackson. And by a stroke of fortune, one of *Manhunt*'s regulars from the first issue in 1953 became a major bestseller and continued to contribute as his string of mainstream successes continued: Evan Hunter, whose *The Blackboard Jungle* (1954) made a sensational splash and was followed by a popular film version with Glenn Ford and Sidney Poitier. Hunter contributed to what seemed like every issue (and sometimes more than once), either as himself or under the pseudonyms Richard Marsten, Hunt Collins, and a name that would eventually become more famous than Hunter, Ed McBain.

The lineup of major mystery writers making appearances was equally impressive: in consecutive 1955 issues, Rex Stout and Erle Stanley Gardner produced rare short stories. Others included Brett Halliday, Aaron Marc Stein (as himself and as George Bagby or Hampton Stone), John D. MacDonald, Richard Deming, David Alexander, William Campbell Gault. and Hal Ellson. Given the tough-guy nature of the magazine, not many women turned up in its pages, but Craig Rice was a longtime fixture and Helen Nielsen and De Forbes (DeLoris Stanton Forbes) made frequent appearances.

The essence of *Manhunt* was not the private eye story, though it published plenty of them. What set it apart was what is now called noir fiction, a term often thrown around very loosely but in its purest form concerning a flawed but not necessarily unsympathetic protagonist who will not have a happy outcome. A prime example is "Key Witness," included in this book, a non-series story by one of those private-eye writers, the creator of Johnny Liddell, Frank Kane. Like many novelettes in *Manhunt*, it would later appear in paperback original as a full-length novel, but at least in this case stretching it out could only reduce the impact of its shocking but sadly believable conclusion, which has stuck with me since I read it a half century ago. The successful combination of cinematic noir and more traditional hardboiled mystery inspired a number of newsstand imitators that provided writers a place to go with stories *Manhunt* might have rejected.

Manhunt could often surprise the reader, and not just for its shock endings. Another story that sticks in my mind for its finishing twist is from a writer and genre I never expected to see in this market for hard-bitten realism, Ray Bradbury. "The Millionth Murder" (September 1953) is time-travel science fiction, more than worthy of its celebrated author, but I wonder how it landed here rather than in either one of the s.f. digests or in one of the slick magazines.

The magazine changed editors several times in its short life, more often than might be expected from such a successful enterprise. And it didn't really have an editorial personality.

Whoever was calling the shots was not a Frederic Dannay or John W. Campbell, Jr. or Anthony Boucher or Hans Stefan Santesson. In recent years, insiders have revealed the reason for this, which was that (to oversimplify) the magazine was essentially an in-house product of the Scott Meredith literary agency, making it the rare periodical whose inner workings are as intriguing and dramatic as the contents of its stories.

Manhunt was already going downhill when it managed its last major coup in the February 1960 issue: the first U. S. Publication of Raymond Chandler's only Philip Marlowe short story, "Wrong Pigeon" (previously published in Britain as "Marlowe Takes on the Syndicate" and later elsewhere as "The Pencil"). The practice of cannibalizing the back files for reprints began in early 1964, and the very last issue featured a Craig Rice retread and a story called "Bad Blood" by John Ross Macdonald. (The John had not been part of the pseudonym for years.) Very few of the other bylines in that last issue would be recognized by even the most deeply immersed mystery buff. But even in the waning years, new writers who would eventually become major names were developing their craft, notably Lawrence Block, Donald E. Westlake, and Joe Gores.

By the time my obituary of *Manhunt* appeared in the *The Armchair Detective* back in 1968, I noted that plenty of time had passed for the Mystery Writers of America to have noted its passing in their house organ *The Third Degree*. The demise of *The Saint* around the same time had been appropriately recognized with an item titled "The Saint Goes West" after one of Leslie Charteris's books. I surmised that "nobody seemed to care too much [about *Manhunt*] except for the writers who'd had their stories accepted, or even published, by the magazine and never had been paid for them." Now, with the perspective of time, we can see that *Manhunt*, extraordinary but flawed and certainly doomed, was very like one of those noir protagonists that peopled its pages.

On the Passing of Manhunt

Jon L. Breen

April 1968

When *The Saint Mystery Magazine* recently came to an end, it was given proper obituaries, both in *The Armchair Detective* and in the Mystery Writers of America organ, *The Third Degree* (where the item was wittily headed "The Saint Goes West", after one of Charteris' titles). Another giant among the digest-sized detective magazines also apparently breathed its last recently, but nobody seemed to care too much except for the writers who'd had their stories accepted, or even published, by the magazine and never had been paid for them. After all, *Manhunt* for all practical purposes had been dead for years—its contents pages no longer sang with great names, and it had taken to the cannibalistic practice of reprinting stories from its own glory days.

Once *Manhunt* could proudly boast of being the world's best-selling crime fiction magazine. And for good reason. Its policy of encouraging tough-minded fiction, sans taboos, made it, during its heyday in the fifties, one of the three or four most important detective magazines of all time. Among its contributors over the years were such important novelists as Erskine Caldwell, James T. Farrell, Nelson Algren, W. R. Burnett, Charles Jackson, James M. Cain, and Evan Hunter (probably the magazine's most prolific contributor, who also wrote for the magazine under his pseudonyms, Hunt Collins, Richard Marsten, and Ed McBain, and sometimes had as many as three stories in one issue). Also among *Manhunt*'s contributors were poet and suspense writer Kenneth Fearing, mystery critic Anthony Boucher (who conducted a review column under his alter-pseudonym H. H. Holmes), and science fiction greats Ray Bradbury, Charles Beaumont, Will F. Jenkins (Murray Leinster) and Ray Russell. The names of mystery writers who contributed also form an awesome list. One of Rex Stout's very few short stories first appeared in the pages of *Manhunt*, as did stories by William Irish, Leslie Charteris, Donald Hamilton, Brett Halliday, George Bagby (and Hampton Stone), Robert Bloch, John D. MacDonald, William O'Farrell, William Campbell Gault, Raymond Chandler (with the last Philip Marlowe story, "Wrong Pigeon", in the February, 1960, issue), Fredric Brown, Harold R. Daniels and Erie Stanley Gardner. Among the magazine's regulars were such as Craig Rice, Frank Kane, Henry Kane, Harold Q. Masur, John Ross Macdonald, Richard S. Prather, Richard Deming, Bruno Fischer, David Alexander and Hal Ellson.

The first issue of *Manhunt* is dated January, 1953. The first story in that first issue, the first installment of a serial (I believe the only serial in Manhunt's history) called "Everybody's Watching Me", begins in this ways

I handed the guy the note and shivered a little bit because the guy was as big as they come, and even though he had a belly you couldn't get your arms around, you wouldn't want to be the one who figured you could sink your fist in it. The belly was as hard as the rest of him, but not quite as hard as his face.

Then I knew how hard the back of his hand was because he smashed it across my jaw and I could taste the blood where my teeth bit into my cheek.

The style is unmistakable. In 1953, Mickey Spillane's name was more likely to sell magazines than any of those listed above, and it was the creator of Mike Hammer who got the magazine off the ground. Whatever the merits of Spillane's work, and there's no telling what future critical re-estimates might make of him, lovers of detective stories must thank him for that service.

Life and Death of a Magazine
Robert Turner

September 1970

It happened early in 1953. The old pulp magazines, from which I'd been making a living as a writer for nearly fifteen years, were futilely struggling to keep alive. There were very few "men's"-type magazines at that time. For a pulp writer, the future looked bleak.

I had come to New York City that winter to talk things over with my agent, Scott Meredith, and to try to weasel an advance out of him. He told me then about a new magazine that was about to break. It was called simply *Manhunt*. was originally published by a man named Archer St. John. It was a new and original venture in the magazine field. They were looking for the best mystery, suspense and crime fiction that could be written. There would be no taboos, no limitations on subject matter nor manner of presentation. They wanted tough, rough, shocking, realistic stories in all lengths. They could deal with sex, aberrations, narcotics, abortion—anything, so long as the yarns were written with finesse. They did not want the old-time pulp-type stories; these would be pallid by comparison with the type of thing they were looking for. They would pay 5¢ a word and would be a regular market for writers who could give them what they wanted. They would read and make decisions and pay fast. Very fast.

This was the story I got over the telephone from Meredith, who suggested that I try something for them. "But don't write pulp. It's got to be tough; it can even be vicious, but it has to be done smoothly and well."

I had been about to leave to go back to North Carolina, where I lived at the time. But this sounded promising enough to make me stay on for another few days. I then proceeded to write what I thought was a tough, rough, and nasty, smoothly written story, one that I didn't think would have made it with a pulp.

Manhunt bounced it but said it indicated that I *could* eventually come up with what they wanted; would I please try again. I was a little desolate, but Scott said not to worry about it, that they'd sell the story elsewhere and the next one I came up with would probably be right on the nose. He did eventually sell that first *Manhunt* try to one of Leo Margulies' pulps, which were among the few still being published. He also told me that perhaps I'd misinterpreted the violence angle; there should not be harsh violence for its own sake. In fact, he said, they didn't necessarily have to have violence *per se* in their stories at all, if they were off-trail enough in other ways.

The whole night of that day was spent at the typewriter. I wrote two stories, one about four thousand words called "Be My Guest," about a likeable but punchy fighter and his wife who were hiding from the Mob after the fighter had unwittingly crossed them up by winning a fight. I did it first person, from the punchy fighter's viewpoint. When I was finished, I wasn't exactly sure of what I had, but I was certain it was off-trail.

The other ["Shakedown"] was a thirty-five hundred word story about a young heel who gets a girl in his office pregnant and then tries to foist her off onto his boss, who in turn murders her and works it so that the young heel is eventually nailed for the murder.

I ran them over to the office the next morning and then fell into an exhausted sleep. Late that afternoon I was awakened by a call that told me *Manhunt* had liked *both* stories and was buying them both. Would I like to try some more?

Silly question. I did try more. Nine more. *Manhunt* didn't buy any of them, but they all sold eventually to other markets, some of them to the raft of lesser-paying imitations of *Manhunt* that soon began to show up on the newsstands, and some of them to the slick-type men's magazines that also were now all over the place.

Trying to write for *Manhunt* eventually led to my selling *Bluebook, Playboy,* and other slicks and semi-slicks. It made me bear down more on being different, on trying to write more smoothly and sparsely. I knew I had to do this to compete with Floyd Mahannah, Hal Ellison, Richard Deming, Charles Beaumont, W. R. Burnett, Evan Hunter, John Ross MacDonald, Richard Prather, Hampton Stone, David Alexander, Bryce Walton, Jack Ritchie, and all the other big names that were shooting stories at the magazines and filling their pages. *Manhunt's* first issues serialized a new novel by Mickey Spillane, to give you an idea.

They didn't buy another story from me until April of 1953. Meanwhile, the St. John company came out with another digest-sized magazine, this one a western, to be called *Gunsmoke*. The same idea would hold: unusual, tough, realistic stories of the old west. The type of competition from other writers would be the same. The magazine featured stories by Frank O'Rourke of *Collier's* fame, A. B. Guthrie, Nelson Nye, Jack Schaefer, Steve Frazee, and other bigwig western writing hombres. I was fortunate enough to be able to sell them two stories, both of which were later anthologized in hardcover and paperback.

As far as I can recall, only two issues of *Gunsmoke* were published, even though the writing in a great many of the stories was superb. It just didn't go, partly, I believe, because of what Don Wolheim of Ace Books once told me. He said that the general reading public that was hung up on westerns wanted the standard stories, the bigger-than-life western heroes. They didn't want stories about heels, stories from the viewpoint of a killer. They didn't want the West the way it *really* was, but as the fantasy world that western fiction had made it to be down through the years. In other words, western readers didn't *want* to know that the western gun-slinging folk heroes were often cowards who shot first and asked questions afterward, some of them out-and-out psychopaths. They didn't want to know that many of the so called dance-hall girls were ugly, smelly creatures with bad teeth and, all too often, venereal diseases. So *Gunsmoke* magazine died. In the current era, when so many realistic, sexy movie westerns are being made, perhaps it should be revived.

Manhunt, however, was doing great. Its circulation soared.

They were using a lot of fiction by a writer named Hal Ellison. They frequently ran a picture of him and a write-up about him in a back-of-the-book department called "Mugged and Printed." They never did use my picture or write anything but a few lines about me. I knew why this was, but still it bugged me. Hal Ellison had hardcover books to his credit, and they usually received good reviews. He was a "name." I wasn't. At the same time, I'm sure I sold *Manhunt* as many stories as Mr. Ellison, if not more.

He had, at least at that time, a very distinctive style, and he always wrote about the problems of ghetto kids and life within their street gangs. Not that there's anything wrong with it, but he frequently wrote his stories in the present tense, first person. One, picked at random, began like this: "I don't know what happened. I'm high on a bottle of wine and heading for the Pelican's territory. I'm going to blast the first I see."

You can see how it might not be too difficult to satirize a Hal Ellison story. I sprinkled a little acid on my typewriter keys, stuck my tongue way in cheek, and began to write.

It came out about fifteen hundred words, a little thing called "Zip-Gun Boys on a Caper," right off the top of my head; I intended strictly to be snide, hoping it would have a therapeutic effect and rid me of my unhealthy, unwarranted resentment of Mr. Ellison, whom I had never met and who I'm sure is as fine a gentleman as he is a writer.

I mailed it in to Scott with no explanatory note, sure that he would get the joke, say ha-ha, and promptly throw it in the wastebasket. To my amazement, he wrote back that "Zip-Gun Boys" was a fine job and had been sent to market. A few weeks later it sold to *Playboy,* and was later reprinted in the *Playboy* Annual.

Later I followed up with another satire to *Playboy,* this one kidding the characters and the writing style of *Catcher in the Rye.* This one was done because I admired Salinger but was annoyed all to hell by the many imitators who capitalized on copying his style.

There were some close calls, but I never did sell *Playboy* again. However, my numerous attempts sold for good money to a lot of its better imitators, such as *Escapade* and *Rogue.*

A *Manhunt* story at one time became a sort of inside joke with the Steve Allen TV show. Steve, as talented a writer as he is a musician and comedian, sold *Manhunt* some stories. One of them appeared in the same issue that carried a story of mine called "Repeat Performance." It concerned the murder of a frotteur who victimized teenage girls while jammed against them in the standing-room-only backs of theaters while rock and roll shows, so popular at that time, were playing. At the end of the story, a group of girls gang up on him in the crowd and stick long hatpins into him, killing him. It never occurred to me that there was anything funny about this, but several times "the hatpin story" was mentioned on Steve Alien's show and several of the crew broke up. Not that I mind, but I *am* curious. Some day it would be nice to meet Mr. Allen and perhaps he could explain it to me.

Two of my stories that were adapted for TV, the one for "Pepsi Cola Playhouse" and one of the Hitchcock shows, originally appeared in *Manhunt.* All of the stories I sold to *Bluebook* were written with *Manhunt* in mind. Perhaps hundreds of rejects from that magazine went to imitating magazines such as *Pursuit, Hunted, Mantrap, Sure Fire Detective, Trapped,* and *Guilty,* keeping me in beans and bacon money between the larger checks. Frequently these magazines would use more than one story in an issue. In one issue of *Hunted,* I remember, four of the six stories were by me, three under pseudonyms.

Speaking of pseudonyms, it seems that I have some kind of a thing for using names of places where I have lived. When I used to have short shorts appear in the Ace pulp detective magazines under a pseudonym because a longer story in the same issue bore my own name, I was living in an apartment called Glenwood Gardens. My stories appeared under the name "Glen Wood."

In Florida, I lived on a street called Crissman Drive. So when I had additional stories in *Guilty* and *Sure Fire Detective,* they appeared under the byline "D. R. Crissman." In Hollywood, I lived in an apartment known as Franklin Villa. When I had more than one story in an issue of *Chase* magazine, the second one bore the pseudonym "Franklin Villa." This, of course, brought a "funny" from one of my friends who wanted to know if Franklin was Pancho's brother.

In many of those same digest-sized magazines a young writer named Harlan Ellison appeared. He later went on to write for *Playboy* and other men's slick magazines, wrote novels, and finally wound up in Hollywood, where he now has many fine TV credits including one show that was either nominated for or won an Emmy, and has written several screenplays, including the one for *The Oscar.*

Although I'd never met Harlan, not too long ago I wrote to him asking him for a favor, hoping that he would remember me as a neighbor on many magazine contents pages years ago. He not only remembered but was very flattering about some of my work and gladly obliged with the favor I asked. Professional writers are like that, for the most part. We help our own whenever we can.

A story, "Don't Go Away Mad," which appeared in *Justice* magazine (a *Manhunt* imitation) and has since been anthologized, brought me my first movie sale. I hope you don't believe everything you read about the fabulous prices paid for film properties. For this one I signed a contract about twenty pages long, taking everything from me but an arm and a leg. Are you ready for this? I got three hundred and fifty dollars, and all I can say to them at this late date is *for shame!* I would have spit in their eye, but I was broke and needed the bread. The magnanimous buyer was King Brothers Productions, Incorporated.

Manhunt continued to be published up until a few years ago. If you have read any of the issues of their last year or so of publication, don't confuse them with what the magazine originally was. Only the title was the same. Toward the end, the magazine was using reprints and much amateurish stuff because they had practically stopped paying for material. They reprinted quite a few of my stories in those latter days.

The magazine kept going great guns up to about 1956 or '57. Sometime before that, Archer St. John passed away and a new editor took over the magazine. Things began to go wrong. In desperation, in 1957, they went into a large, flat format, and although they still featured big name writers such as Gil Brewer, John D. MacDonald, Evan Hunter, Helen Nielson, Frank Kane, and so on, they continued to flounder. Eventually they went back to the digest size.

All this brought on money problems. They began to be slow pay. The last story I did for them, a novelette called "Hooked," appeared in the February, 1958 issue.

I had to wait a long, long time for the money. Still, I can't complain. The magazine was lucky for me right up to the end. "Hooked" sold to the Hitchcock TV show.

When you've been with a magazine since it was born, it is a sad, sad thing to watch it slowly die. Perhaps somewhere, sometime, it will be resurrected. In the meantime, Rest In Peace, *Manhunt*.

Editor's Note:

"Life and Death of a Magazine" originally appeared as a chapter titled "Manhunt—The Life and Death of a Magazine" in Robert Turner's memoir, *Some of My Best Friends Are Writers, But I Wouldn't Want My Daughter to Marry One* (Sherbourne Press: 1970) and as a shorter version in the August 1968 (v.1, n. 6) issue of The Mystery Lover's Newsletter. It has been edited for continuity.

Stabbing in the Street

Elezazer Lipsky

The ringing telephone came almost as a relief. Wiley was lying in bed unable to sleep. The sheets were wrinkled and uncomfortable and his mind was going over his preparation for a murder trial still a month off. The telephone continued to ring. He threw aside the covers, fished for his slippers, and flapped into the living room where he picked up the instrument.

"This is Wiley," he said, yawning. "There's a call from the Tenth," the man down in Communications said. "Some kid got stabbed in a street brawl. He's a merchant seaman, I understand. English. One of those things. They say they've got witnesses."

"Who's on the case?"

"Ricca and Corbin."

"Well, that's good," Wiley said, "Now, what about a car?"

"Just a minute." There was a moment's silence in which Wiley could hear familiar sounds in the background, then the man returned. "It's on the way, Mr. Wiley."

"Say, Sergeant—"

"Yes, Mr. Wiley?"

"Do you know what all this is about?"

"Sorry, I just didn't ask. The victim is at the hospital, but the rest of them are all at the Tenth."

There was a click and David Wiley was left holding the telephone receiver. He returned to the bedroom to dress in working clothes, a sweater, jacket and an old Army trenchcoat.

Dorothy murmured and turned.

He sat down on the bed beside her and slid his arm under her shoulder. "It's just some stabbing, I've got to cover. I'm sorry."

"Oh, dear." She brushed aside a hair. "What time is it?"

Wiley looked at his luminous wrist watch.

"About five. It's near dawn."

"Just don't get tied up, darling," she murmured, and turned over in her warm bed. "We've got company tonight."

Wiley kissed his wife and went to the kitchen. He found some milk and bread and he was drinking a pair of raw eggs when he heard the hooting of an auto horn out in the street.

He left the dark apartment and went down to the street and got into the waiting sedan. They started off. It had been raining and they swept through the wet streets with the sound of drumming tires.

"I hear an English kid got it," the driver remarked, "a merchant seaman. Now why don't they watch out for themselves?"

Stabbing in the Street   23

"I don't know." Wiley closed his eyes. "They just get into trouble." He sank into a weary silence while the driver talked about the previous day's baseball.

"We're here," the driver said.

Wiley looked up. The green lights of the station house were shining in the darkness. Wiley dismissed the driver and turned into the building. As he passed the desk, the officer, a sergeant, nodded. Wiley went upstairs into the Homicide Squad offices.

A detective named Vincent Ricca came forward holding a meat sandwich and a mug of coffee in either hand. "You won't like me for this, Dave," he said. "There ain't much to this case, what I mean."

Wiley looked about with an expert eye and remarked, "I can see that." The few witnesses were lolling without spirit on the benches in the large chamber. In an inner room, a barracks, two men were sleeping on cots wrapped in woolen blankets. The naked light bulbs were garish. Wiley returned to the detective and said crisply, "Let's get through this fast, Vince. Suppose you sum it up for me."

Ricca took a large bite of his sandwich. "These four merchant seamen got into a brawl with a customer in this bar, they're all English. After it was over, the customer came up and stabbed one of them outside in the street, a kid named Eddie Porter. They're operating on him now at St. Vincent's. We don't know about his chances to pull through."

"What was the reason for the stabbing?" Wiley shook his head as he declined a share of the sandwich.

The detective licked away a trace of mustard. "This customer can't tell us that. Doesn't talk English, what I mean. We know what he did, we just don't know why or what he had in mind. The way we got the story right now, this thing came out of a clear sky. He was drunk or vicious or both."

"I'll settle for 'what'," Wiley said grimly. "Let's get on with this."

"Come on." The detective took Wiley's arm and described the crime. Ricca was a lean man with a dark face, dressed in good taste, with amusement in his eyes. He carried himself with a jaunty air. He was friendly and willing to help Wiley do a good job. He drew Wiley over to a prisoner seated on a bench and said, "Here's Juan Figueroa. He did the cutting. When we get a translator, he'll give us his story."

Wiley stared down at a picture of misery.

The prisoner was a stout man of forty, dressed in a foreign cut business suit. He looked up and pointed with an imploring gesture to abrasions on his temples. He portrayed the picture of innocence. His reddish eyes were inflamed and tears were rolling down his cheeks.

The detective said forcefully, "Figueroa, this is the district attorney! You want to tell him your side of the story? The district attorney—see?"

The prisoner broke into a torrent of choppy dialect, showing his wounds and protesting until Wiley cut him short. "I don't talk Spanish, Figueroa! Now stop trying to kid me. You talk English and I'll listen!"

The prisoner stared a hopeless moment, then threw his head back and applied a bloody handkerchief to his nose.

Wiley turned back to the detective and thrust his hands into his pockets. "What's he crying about? Did he get a beating somewhere along the line?"

"Not from any of us," Ricca grinned. "He got those marks in the brawl. He's bawling because he knows he's in trouble. That girl there told him the kid might die."

"What girl?" Wiley looked across the room to a thin girl hunched forward on a bench near an inner office and smoking a cigarette with a thoughtful manner. Her long dark hair was tumbled down her neck in disorder. As he watched, she pulled a man's raincoat close about her, concealing a loose glittering black evening dress.

"That's the one." Ricca finished his coffee and put the mug away. "She could make sense out of all this, but she won't."

Wiley frowned. "Who was fool enough to let her know that the kid might be dying?"

Ricca shrugged. "She was here when the news came in."

"Well, let's see." Wiley crossed the room and said in a severe tone, "What's your name, Miss?"

The girl looked up with calm. "I'm Jenny Ortega," she said, in a husky voice. "Now this time, who are you?"

Wiley returned her stare. "I'm an assistant district attorney for this county. I want to know about this stabbing. Did you see it?"

The girl made a gesture toward the weeping prisoner. "It wasn't Figueroa's fault. I saw the whole thing."

"Tell me what happened." The girl shrugged and Wiley repeated sharply, "Why did Figueroa stab this young seaman?"

The girl considered him thoughtfully and a sneer gathered. "Why don't you ask those men there? They'll give you a pack of lies. Isn't that what you're after?"

"I want your side of the story," Wiley said sharply. "I'm looking for the truth."

She shook her head with contempt. "No, mister, you're not after the truth. Whatever I tell you, you wouldn't believe me. You just want a story against poor Figueroa. Well, get that from the others."

"The others?" Across the room three men were anxiously conferring in low tones with a second detective named Tom Corbin, Ricca's partner. "All right, let's do that."

Ricca and Wiley went over. Corbin got up with a pleasant smile. He was a freckled blue-eyed man, taller than his partner and dressed with equal neatness. He shook hands and introduced his three witnesses to Wiley. They were short muscular men whose hands showed large callouses. They nodded politely. Their faces were all sunburnt but the tans were old and faded. Under their stoic manner, Wiley saw that they were deeply upset. Their names meant nothing to him.

One of the men asked in a cockney accent, "How's the kid, mister? These here 'tecs don't seem to know."

Ricca said to Wiley in a low voice, "Start off with this witness. He can give you the picture."

"Let's go inside." Wiley nodded the witness into the inner office. He took out a yellow form and placed it on the desk and put questions. The witness was Alexander

Goudy, aged 28, unmarried, a British subject, a resident of Cowper's Lane, London, England. Ricca and Corbin entered these facts in their notebooks.

"All right, Goudy." Wiley sat back and shaded his eyes. "Tell me what happened."

"Eddie did nothing. It was really the rest of us who had this trouble with the man." Goudy spoke with a stammer. "This man had no reason to knife the kid at all."

"When you say 'this man' do you mean Figueroa?"

"Yes, sir, the man outside, the prisoner." Goudy fumbled to light a cigarette with a shaking hand. "Eddie, that's Edward Porter, sir, he's just eighteen. His mother manages a little sweets shop back home. We're neighbors and I promised to look after him. The fact is I expect to marry his sister, Kitty, when I get home. Here, you can see what they look like."

He showed a photograph of a group seated around a picnic basket under a tree. Goudy was in the picture with his arm around a girl with yellow hair. A tired older woman gazed pleasantly at the couple while a youth in shirtsleeves stood behind them grinning in a boyish pose. Wiley studied the group as Goudy pointed each one out. "That's Kitty, Mrs. Porter, Eddie and me last summer."

Wiley put down the print.

"Eddie's a nice boy," Goudy said solemnly. "He's wanted to go to sea since he's been a kid. That's because of me. Not having an older brother, that made me one, in a way of speaking. I've been to sea all these years. I'm an oiler and Eddie liked the idea—"

"Get to the point, Alex," Ricca said impatiently.

Wiley said, "Let him take his time."

Goudy went on in a slow serious way. "Mrs. Porter let Eddie go to sea when I promised to take care of him. This was his first time. We shipped to Boston and then started the run back to Oslo. One day out we hit an old mine square in the shipping run. There was a big blowup. The whole bloody sky crashed down on us. There was just four alive when this Norskie freighter picked us up New York-bound. Eddie couldn't swim and he's just alive because we kept him afloat—me and Hughie Cartright and Johnny Barrow, taking turns—"

"Cartright? Barrow?" Wiley asked.

"The two men sitting outside, sir."

Wiley made a note and Goudy added, "I almost went under myself, but I kept thinking how it would be to face up to Mrs. Porter and Kitty if anything happened to the boy and I stuck it."

"Were you in the War?"

"I made three runs to Murmansk, sir." Goudy rubbed his hands and lapsed into staring.

Wiley could see the pictures in Goudy's mind—the flaming tower of spume, the crash of the deluge, the shock of icy seas, the screams of men, the rumble of the sinking vessel with its spine cracked, death in the gray North Atlantic. He opened the door to the waiting room. "Which is which?"

Goudy turned. "That's Cartright, the other's Johnny Barrow."

The two dozing men looked up expectantly. They were without overcoats and they shivered. Cartright's spectacles gave a mild cast to his eyes. Barrow's hairy face with its lantern jaw made a picture of respectability. Wiley closed the door. "You were lucky the War was over," he said drily.

Goudy stammered, "I thought of that. With any Nazi subs around, the Norskies would have passed us by. I saw that happen once. As it was, they found us praying and crying and balmy. The next thing, we were in a rest home here in New York. The company was quite good to us. I asked them not to notify Mrs. Porter that the ship had sunk."

Wiley brought him back. "What about last night?"

"Well, we were out for a bit of fun. That's not easy for merchant seamen, sir, since we draw our pay in pounds mostly. But we were to ship out today for home and we did our best. We got wind of a little Hallowe'en party and we went there, but it was just for kids, and we left. Then we saw a film and walked around Times Square. We passed up a few prosties who tried to talk to us. We didn't want that sort of thing. The kid was red in the face, blushing you know, and besides Barrow and Cartright are married men, and me engaged. We walked all over town and when it began to rain, we were outside this nightclub. We were hungry, and we went in."

"What time was this?"

"About two." Goudy started another cigarette. "It was a nice quiet place. We went down and there were tables. A man was playing the piano, something bouncey, and a girl was singing *Enjoy Yourself.* She looked full of fun. There were only two couples about—"

"What about Figueroa?"

"He was at a table near the door drinking heavily."

"Was there trouble then?"

"The girl was singing and that was all. We took a booth and then this man Blasco—"

"Blasco?"

Ricca gave the answer. "He's the owner. James Blasco, 847 Arlington Street, Long Island City. We're out looking for him now."

Goudy waited while Wiley made a note. "The owner, Blasco, came over smiling, a friendly looking man, nicely dressed. He was wearing a dinner jacket. I said, 'We'd like a pint of ale each and some sandwiches.' He laughed and said, 'You sound English! I like the English—a great race of people! My sister married an Englishman. They keep a flowershop in London.' We talked a bit about London, and then he had the kitchen do up some lamb chops for us. They came in sizzling and rare, proper good stuff, with little paper flowers for holding. We offered to pay, but it was his treat, he knew we were short dollars. And then suddenly he looked up and said something in Spanish and went off. He seemed disturbed suddenly."

Goudy's mind was on the cafe with its few customers, garish and cheap, but looking first class to his eyes. He shivered and clasped his hands between his thighs. "The girl had stopped singing and was at Figueroa's table. I said, 'Beauty and the Beast' and we laughed."

"He means the girl outside," Ricca said. "Jenny, the good looker."

"Suppose we come down to the trouble," Wiley suggested.

"That came a little later, sir. We heard loud voices and we all turned. Figueroa was talking fast to the girl in Spanish. I thought he was drunk. Then he was standing up screaming at the owner."

"Where were all these people located?"

"Blasco, the owner, was behind the bar. Figueroa had thrown his table aside. His face was red as blood. He was sweating and dancing about, quite excited. The veins were sticking out in his neck. The girl was scolding him. He threw a chair across the bar and smashed the big mirror."

"What made him do that?"

"I don't know, sir."

"Go on."

"I said, 'I expect Mr. Blasco needs help!' Figueroa was tearing his hair and shaking his fist, a big one, the biggest I ever saw. I went to him and said, 'Now then, now then, we can't have this!' The others were behind me. I remember thinking I sounded like a silly London bobby in an American film. The girl tried to get in the way. She kept saying, 'Keep out of this, you. Let them alone.' And a lot of other things, not all of them nice."

The witness paused, then went on. "We knew what to do, of course. Cartright and Barrow took him from the sides, an arm each, and I hit him twice. I'm a fair boxer, but his face was slippery with sweat and I couldn't connect. Then the owner came up with a heavy stick. It was a hell of a row. We broke a chair and some glasses, Barrow sprained a thumb, and I got this." Goudy solemnly showed the mark of large teeth matrixed in the flesh of his hand. "The girl kept pulling at us, shrieking in Spanish. We were fair winded when the owner got in a clear whack. Figueroa started to moan and roll his eyes. We got out into the street and the girl ran after. Then the owner bolted the door and we stood about to catch our wind."

"Tell me one thing, Alex." Ricca scratched his face dubiously. "What possible reason made you men all get into the fray?"

"What else could we do, sir?" Corbin said drily.

"Mr. Blasco, the owner of the pub, needed help. This fellow Figueroa was quite out of hand." Goudy was puzzled.

"Ah!" Ricca said. "That explains it."

"Did the owner of the pub explain all this?" Wiley asked.

"No," Goudy said thoughtfully. "Blasco just looked sick at the mess and began to get the place cleaned up. He offered us drinks for having helped out but we had enough. Then suddenly we heard Figueroa shouting outside, and all at once his fist smashed through the glass door—smashed right through and hung there, bleeding. I pulled the door open and shouted, 'Hoy, you there! Clear off!' Then he ran off and I lost him in the drizzle. I thought to call the police but Blasco said, 'No, I know that man. A bad customer but he won't come back. I'll put up the shutters now.'"

Goudy bit a heavy underlip and concluded. "Meanwhile, the kid gave the girl his jacket against the rain and he walked her down the street, talking. I didn't like it but he came back in ten minutes. He told me he had taken the girl to her flat down a bit. His shirt was wet."

Wiley put a number of questions to establish the details and Goudy went on. "We left and we split up to scout out a taxi. Barrow and Cartright crossed the street and walked the north side. The kid and me walked the south side. I scolded the kid about the girl but he told me he'd had a nice talk with her and he didn't mind the wet. It was dark and we almost fell over him again."

"Who was that?"

"Figueroa, sir. He'd come back for more. The girl was with him, carrying a heavy stick. We stood still and I said as quiet as I could, 'Eddie, don't move—the man has a knife.'"

"The kid said, 'Don't worry, Alex. It's all right.'"

"The man said something in Spanish and held up his hand. I looked for Barrow and Cartright. They were off a distance looking for a taxi. The girl shook the stick and said, 'Keep away from us, keep away.'"

Goudy stared at Wiley and tears welled up. "I shall never forget that the kid was smiling at the girl. He just opened his hands and said to her, 'It's all right, Miss. It's just us. We want to pass by.' He took a step forward when this man made a quick motion to the kid's belly and Eddie screamed and fell down to the pavement. I couldn't believe it. Then I looked up and smashed him as hard as I could. I hit him three times, I think, then he and the woman ran off. I shouted ahead, 'Cartright! Barrow! Stop that man! He's hurt the kid!' They cut him off and just at that moment the police came.

"I came back to the kid and I got sick. He was holding in his guts and asking like a baby, 'What made him do it, Alex? What happened?' Then the ambulance came and took him away and that was all. Except that I don't know what I shall tell Mrs. Porter if he dies, sir. Indeed I don't."

The little group was silent while Wiley studied the family picture. He knew England and he fancied he could see the little shop Mrs. Porter kept. The mother seemed tired and her children carefree and thoughtless. Wiley rubbed his eyes and said, "Your girl's pretty."

Goudy's body was shaking violently. "Thank you, sir."

Wiley frowned. "For a man with a clear conscience, you seem nervous."

The witness considered this seriously. "I caught that off Murmansk, sir, shellshock. I was torpedoed twice and strafed after. Couldn't sleep mainly. Kept hearing those awful bombs. This thing's brought it back." He was silent and the bitter tears returned. "I almost wish I'd had it then. What did I fight for? What good did the whole bloody mess bring me?"

Wiley handed back the photograph. "All right, Goudy, wait outside. It won't be long."

Goudy went out, sniffling and blowing his nose.

Wiley drummed the table dubiously. "Well?"

Ricca raised his shoulders. "The others tell the same identical story. I guess we got the facts."

Corbin said, "Three witnesses is pretty good."

"What about getting some sort of confession?" Wiley said.

Ricca scratched his jaw. "Well, you know, we got nothing yet, not from the girl, not from Figueroa. We're trying to get a Spanish cop down to translate, but we may not need him. This Blasco, the owner, he'll tell us when he comes in."

Wiley noticed the light of dawn. He stretched and stalked into the waiting room. The witnesses were dozing. He stood above the prisoner. "All right, Figueroa, do you want to tell your side now while you have a chance?"

The prisoner pointed to abrasions in his scalp. He unwrapped a handkerchief to show his gashed fingers.

"I know all about that," Wiley said impatiently. "You talk English!"

"He's scared, mister!" Jenny Ortega got up angrily. "Let him alone! Why not be fair about this?"

"Well!" Wiley looked her over. "Since you talk English, suppose you come inside." She looked Wiley over with her self-contained manner still intact and said coolly, "If that's what you want, mister."

Wiley held the door aside as she entered the inner office and took a seat. Wiley placed the yellow form before him and considered the girl. She was small-boned but her carriage was proud. He invited her to begin. "Cigarette?"

The girl threw back the raincoat calmly. "I smoke my own."

"All right." Wiley lit up and began. "What made this man stab the English kid?"

"Who says he did?"

"I've got three witnesses."

"Then why ask me?"

Ricca said, "This is no way, Jenny. Here's your chance to tell your side. This is the district attorney. If you help him, he helps you. If you make trouble, he makes trouble." He waited, then said strongly, "For God's sake, Jenny, he can throw you in jail for a material witness! Fifty thousand dollars bail! You want that?"

"Jail?" She tossed her hair and said harshly, "What about my baby? You going to put him in jail too?"

Ricca said strongly, "This is Mr. Wiley, Jenny, a square shooter."

Wiley said, "That's up to you. I need the truth. If you have a side to tell, now is the time."

"You'll listen?" she asked cynically. "You'll take our side? You'll believe us?"

"You've been saying that all night. Why shouldn't I believe you?"

"Why should you? We're just dirt to you, me and my kind."

"You don't know what I think at all, Jenny," Wiley said quietly. "But I'll tell you this, if you hold out on me, I'll have to hold you and the baby goes to the Foundling Home. But if you tell the truth, I'll believe you. Now suppose you drop this act and think of that baby a minute."

There was a long moment of silence.

The girl put out her hand. "I'll take that cigarette." She smoked thoughtfully while the white plumes curled from her nostrils, and Wiley saw that she was quite beautiful. Finally she looked up. "I've been telling these cops they got the wrong party. But no! They arrest poor Figueroa. The funny thing is he's a citizen and they believe those foreigners against him."

"Tell me something about Figueroa?"

"He's a good man," she said simply. "He runs a little business in the neighborhood, a grocery store. He keeps to himself, just a hardworking man trying to get along. He's no criminal."

"What was he doing in this bar?"

"He's been coming these couple of months. He wants me to stop singing there and to marry him."

"What did you say?"

"I wouldn't do it. I said I'd just live with him. He didn't want it that way on account of his mother. She's very religious and he respects her. He's like a baby, that way."

"Why not marry him?"

She said in a low voice, "It wouldn't be right."

"Why not?" She said nothing, and Wiley went on. "What happened tonight?"

"Figueroa came in while I was singing. He had good news and he smiled to me. When he wants to, he's got a nice smile. I saw him ask for whiskey, though normally he drinks beer. I smiled back. Fle's the one man never treated me like an animal. Meanwhile these four walked in like they thought to take over, loud voices and everything, troublemakers."

"What kind of trouble?"

"The regular thing. They give me the eye but I paid it no mind. I was just interested in Figueroa's news."

"What was that?"

"Figueroa had fixed it to send his mother to San Juan with his relatives. That meant I could move in. Then when we finally got to arguing and talking about it, Blasco horned in. He knew the deal. That's because Figueroa's got a loose tongue in the neighborhood. Can't keep a thing to himself. He never could. He's too excitable."

"Were you going to take that deal?"

She shrugged. "Why not? That way I could get my kid to live with me. He's only four and he's staying with my grandmother now." She added bitterly, "My mother don't talk to me, my own mother."

"Are you married?"

"No," she said.

Ricca said, "Tell Mr. Wiley about Blasco."

She said, "Blasco didn't want me to go. When he came over, he was looking mean. He knows my line isn't singing but I draw a certain steady trade and how many singers can claim that? He told Figueroa to forget about me and he said, 'You take this girl away, and I ruin you! Now you got your warning!' He made the sign for death and walked away."

"What's the sign?"

She paused to draw a finger across her throat. "Now, Figueroa's got a few drinks in him at this time and he kept getting excited. Then Blasco said in a mean way, 'Figueroa, I hear all about you and Esteban!'

"Figueroa said, 'What about Esteban?'

"Blasco said, 'The cops pulled a raid on him last night. Some pigeon tipped 'em off!'

"Figueroa got nervous and grabbed a chair. 'What are you telling me?' he yelled.

"Blasco came right back at him. 'I say we got a pigeon in the house! I got my idea who it is!'

"Then Figueroa screamed, 'You mean me? You calling me a pigeon?'

"Blasco bites his thumb and yells back, 'Don't make me stick a finger in your eye! You been pigeoning! I'm passing the word! We don't want your kind around! You ask Jenny herself, she knows the whole story!' Then Blasco talked some more against me and Figueroa began to turn purple. He could hardly breathe and I was afraid for his bad heart. Then he yelled like a wild man and threw a chair and the four sailors ganged him. I begged them to let the men fight fair, but no, they jumped him—four against one. They held his arms while Blasco busted his head open with a club. Then they threw him into a gutter like an animal. I found him there crying in the rain."

"He went back for trouble," Wiley suggested.

"No!" She shook her head. "He didn't know what he was doing, he was so mixed up. He just wanted to go back to get his hat. But by then he was so wild he put his fist through the glass and cut himself. Then these four men came out to help Blasco gang him again and he ran home. When I got there, he was bleeding bad. He had to get to the hospital but he was afraid to go on the street. He thought they might be after him, so I promised to go with him. He finally took his small knife for protection and I carried his stick. It was dark, but before we took two steps, he whispered, 'Watch out, Jenny, they're back!' I looked around. I got the picture right there. We were cut off on both sides. Two of them were right on top of us. Two others were circling us. They closed in and poor Figueroa had to defend himself. Then the big one gave Figueroa a beating before we could get away. The cops took us and they never once blamed the other side."

Wiley drummed the table, then said pointedly, "The one he cut was the kid, the same one who lent you his jacket. That kid meant no harm."

"How did we know that?" the girl said with a hard look. "We were just looking for the hospital. I warned them both to stay away. They just kept closing in. We wanted no trouble."

"Did you give this warning in English?" Wiley asked pointedly.

The girl sat back and there was a moment of silence.

"When I'm excited, I use Spanish," she said slowly. She knitted her brows and thought back. "I guess I made a mistake. I didn't think of that. Now that you tell me, I'm sorry about that kid."

Ricca coughed and moved his chair.

Wiley shaded his eyes. "Who is Esteban? Why should his name get Figueroa excited?"

"Esteban?" She laughed harshly. "He's Blasco's partner in this house the cops raided. That's who Esteban is. Why isn't he under arrest? How can he be operating? Esteban and Blasco!"

Wiley put the next question with care. "What did Blasco say against you just before the fight?"

The girl sat mute.

Ricca threw away a cigarette. "It's obvious what Blasco said. He told Figueroa that Jenny works in that whorehouse for him. That's why he was objecting to her going away. Am I right, Jenny?"

She said in a low voice, "Figueroa couldn't stand to hear that said about me," and turned to finish the cigarette.

Wiley asked, "Didn't Figueroa know all this?"

"Sure he knew, but he couldn't stand to hear it said." She stared. "You're a decent man. How would you feel?"

"If Figueroa feels that way about you," Ricca said, "why wouldn't you marry him? What's the point?"

She said cynically, "Since I was twelve, I know too much about men. I won't get tied to the best men alive. If he don't treat me right, I want to walk out. I knew a girl got killed once just because a man thought he owned her."

After a moment, Wiley said, "Stick around, Jenny. I'm sorry, but you're a witness if there's a trial."

"What's going to happen to Figueroa?" she asked huskily.

"I can't tell until I know whether the kid dies. But I'll do my best for him. You can tell him that much in Spanish."

The girl looked at Wiley as though she saw him for the first time. There were hard lines about the lawyer's mouth. Whether his eyes, cold and blue, had any sympathy, she could not tell. "Four against one!" she muttered. "The poor man!"

The interview was over and the girl left the inner office and gave the prisoner Wiley's message. The prisoner kissed her hand and pressed it to his cheeks. *"Pobrecito!"* she murmured and he responded in Spanish. The girl looked up at Wiley. "He wants me to say 'Thanks'."

An hour of formalities passed. Other witnesses were questioned, then Corbin took the weeping prisoner downstairs and booked him for assault as a temporary measure.

They all left the precinct house together. Outside on the steps of the station house, Wiley paused to ask, "How old are you, Jenny? Do you mind telling me?"

"Nineteen." She answered with a lurking hard smile as though she knew that he had expected her to say thirty.

The street was wet and steaming but the early sun was warm. The girl turned abruptly and walked off, her black evening dress attracting the gibes of urchins.

Wiley and the detectives got into the car and drove off.

At St. Vincent's Hospital they got permission to visit the emergency ward. They found the young seaman in a corner bed under a dim light, screened off from the other patients. His face, they saw, was nothing like his laughing photograph. His eyes and lips were blue outlines in a waxy mask. His breathing was stertorous and shallow.

While Ricca took notes, Wiley explained his mission. The nurse kept stroking the boy's damp hair with a soothing motion. His thin nose rose like a scimitar from the pillow.

"Do you want to talk, Porter?" Wiley asked.

The boy turned his eyes and his lips moved. "Will I die, sir?" he whispered.

Wiley did not answer directly. "Do you want to tell me how you got stabbed?"

The boy made an effort. His eyes were frightened. He managed a whisper.

"It hurts."

Wiley paused to rub his jaw. His eyes were bleak. He hated this but he had to make an attempt.

"How do you feel about your chances?" he asked softly.

The boy whispered, "I'm all right, sir. I'll be up soon. I've got to make my ship, you know."

"Just tell me what happened in your own way."

The boy said weakly, "A girl. I only meant to pass. I told her that. I was only—"

The whisper trailed off and the nurse intervened.

"He's in a coma," she said. "There's nothing he can say now."

The investigators trailed out, feeling relieved.

"That's that!" Ricca lit a cigarette. "You go ahead, Dave. I'll stick around, just in case."

Wiley left and went directly to court to dispose of a lengthy sentence calendar. The hospital ward was in his mind throughout the day.

Toward evening he received a call from St. Vincent's that the young seaman had died in coma. Wiley looked at his notes on the desk, then telephoned Goudy.

"I know about it, sir." Goudy's voice was remote and, it struck Wiley, all the more desolate for being quiet. "They called me first thing. Thank you for calling."

Wiley scrawled a change in his report to indicate that the assault had become homicide. "We'll charge Figueroa with manslaughter, perhaps murder, but I can't promise the result. A jury will probably acquit."

"How can that be, sir?" Goudy cried.

"He'll claim he was defending himself. He was afraid of you."

"But, sir!" Goudy protested. "The kid told him we just wanted to pass!"

"The kid told him in English. This man didn't understand." Wiley paused. "It seems neither side spoke the same language. Too bad."

In a small voice, Goudy asked, "What shall I tell Mrs. Porter, sir? That it was too bad?"

"Tell her it was just a street accident."

"That wouldn't be true," Goudy objected. "How can I say that?"

"It's true enough, and she won't feel so badly."

"I don't understand!" Goudy said stubbornly.

Wiley waited with a sense of exasperation.

"Do you want her to know the boy was stabbed to death in a gutter?"

There was no answer.

After a time, Wiley concluded that Goudy had forgotten to hang up.

That evening, Wiley was grateful to get home. The children were frisky and demanding of attention until he read them their comics. They were not to be put off until dinner guests arrived.

Wiley did more than his usual drinking but he was a silent host. As the talk went on about him, he was conscious of the warmth of his home and the affection of his wife's eyes.

The evening ended early.

Even when the guests had gone and the dishes were done, his wife did not ask nor did he tell her about the stabbing in the streets.

As I Lie Dead

Fletcher Flora

February 1953

I rolled over in the hot sand and sat up. Down the artificial beach about fifty yards, the old man was coming toward us with a bright towel trailing from one hand. He was wearing swimming trunks, and with every step he took, his big belly bounced like a balloon tied up short on the end of a stick. Dropping the towel on the sand, he turned and waded into the water.

"The old man's taking a swim," I said.

Beside me on the beach, Cousin Cindy grunted. She was stretched out flat on her belly with her head cradled on her arms and her long golden legs spread in a narrow V. Her white lastex trunks curved up high over the swell of her body, and the ends of her brassiere lay unattached on the sand. When she shifted position, raising herself a little on her elbows, my reaction was not cousinly. Not cousinly at all. "Hook me in back," she said.

I readied over and brought the loose ends of her brassiere together below her shoulder blades, letting my fingers wander off lightly down the buttons of her spine. She sat up, folding the golden legs Indian style and shaking sand from the ends of her golden hair. She was gold all over in the various shades that gold can take. Even her brown eyes, behind dark glass in white harlequin frames, were flecked with gold.

Out in the lake, Grandfather was swimming toward the raft that was a small brown square on the blue surface of the water. He was swimming breast stroke, as many old men swim, and the water bulged out ahead of him in smooth, sweeping undulations.

"The old man's strong as a bull," I said.

Cindy didn't answer. She just handed me a bottle with a white label and a white cap and some brown lotion inside. I unscrewed the cap and poured some of the lotion on her shoulders and back, rubbing it in gently with my fingers until it had disappeared and her skin was like golden satin to my touch.

Looking over her shoulder, past the soft sheen of her hair and out across the glittering blue lake, I saw that Grandfather had reached the raft. He was sitting on the far side, his back to us, legs dangling in the water. He'd made it out there in good time. For an old man, damn good time. He was strong, in spite of his fat belly. It didn't look like he was ever going to die.

"It's hot," Cindy said, her voice slow and sleepy like the purring of a kitten, "but it's not as hot as it gets in Acapulco. You ever been in Acapulco, Tony? It's beautiful there. The harbor is almost land-locked, with mountains all around, and the ships come right up against the shore."

I didn't say anything. My hands moved across her shoulders and down along the soft swells of flat muscle that padded the blades. The perfumes of her hair and the lotion were a strange, exotic blend in my nostrils. Out on the raft, Grandfather still sat with his legs in the water.

"I was there for two weeks once," Cindy said. "In Acapulco, I mean. I went with a man from Los Angeles who wanted me to wear red flowers in my hair. He was very romantic, but he was also very fat, and the palms of his hands were always damp. It would be better in Acapulco with you, Tony. Much better."

My hands reversed direction, moving up again into her hair, cupping it between palms as water is cupped. The raft, out on the lake, rose and dipped on a slight swell. Grandfather rode it easily, still resting.

"He just sits," I said bitterly. "He'll be sitting forever."

Her head fell back slowly until it was resting on my shoulder, and her golden hair was hanging down my back, and I could look down along the slim arch of her throat into the small valley of shadow under the white band she wore. Behind dark glass, her lids lowered, and she looked dreamily through slits into the brash blue of the sky.

"Acapulco, Tony. You and me and Acapulco. It's hot and beautiful there by the harbor in a ring of mountains, but it wouldn't be good unless you and I were hot and beautiful, too. It wouldn't be good if we were too old, Tony."

"He's strong as a bull," I said. "He'll live forever."

A shiver rippled her flesh, and the tip of her pink tongue slipped out and around her oiled lips.

"It's a nice day, Tony. A hot, dreamy day with a blue sky and white clouds drifting. If I were old and ugly, I'd like to die on a day like this."

She remained quiet a minute longer, lying against me with her hair splashing down my back, and then she slipped away, rising in the hot sand.

"I want a drink," she said. "A long, long drink with lots of ice and a sprig of mint. You coming, Tony?"

I stood up too, and we stood looking at each other across the sand of the artificial beach that had cost Grandfather a small fortune.

"I'll be up in a little," I said. "I think I'll swim out to the raft and back."

Her breasts rose high against the restraint of the white band and descended slowly on a long whisper of air. She wet her lips again.

"I'll have your drink waiting," she said.

I watched her walk away up the beach, her legs moving from the hips with fluid case, even in the soft sand, and after she was gone, I went down to the water and waded out into it to my waist. The water was cool on my hot skin and seemed to make everything clear and simple in my mind. Swimming with a powerful crawl, I was nearing the raft in almost no time. A few feet from it, treading water, I stopped and looked at Grandfather's motionless back. I wasn't worried about his hearing me. He'd been partially deaf for years and usually wore a little button attached to a battery. After a few seconds, I sank in the water and swam under the raft.

The first time I reached for his ankle, my fingers barely brushed it, and it jerked away. Reaching again, I got my fingers locked around the ankle and lunged down with all the force I could manage in the buoyant water. He came in with a splash, and even under the water I could see his veined eyes bulging with terror as my hands closed around the sagging flesh of his throat.

He was strong. Stronger, even, than I'd thought. His hands clawed at mine, tearing at my grip, and I scissored my legs, kicking up to a higher level so that I could press my weight down upon him from above. My fingers kept digging into his throat, but he put up a hellish threshing, and when I broke water for air, it was all I could do to hold him below the surface. It was a long time before he was quiet and I could let him slip away into the green depths.

There was a fire under my ribs. My arms and legs were throbbing, heavy with the poisonous sediment of fatigue. I wanted to crawl onto the raft and collapse, but I didn't. I lay floating on my back for a minute, breathing deeply and evenly until the fire went out in my lungs, and then I rolled in the water and crawled slowly to shore.

On the white sand where he had dropped it, Grandfather's towel was a bright splash of color. Leaving it lying there, I crossed the beach and went up through a sparse stand of timber to the eight room house we called the lodge.

Cindy was waiting for me on the sun porch. She had removed the dark glasses but was still wearing the two scraps of white lastex. In one hand was a tall glass with ice cubes floating in amber liquid and a green sprig of mint plastered to the glass above the amber. Her eyes were lighted hotly by their golden flecks. Between us, along a vibrant intangible thread of dark understanding, passed the unspoken question and the unspoken answer.

"Tell me more about Acapulco," I said.

She set the glass with great deliberateness on a glass-topped table and moved over to me. Still with that careful deliberateness, she passed her arms under mine and locked her hands behind my back. There was surprising strength in her. I could feel the hard, hot pressure of her body clear through to my spine. Her lips moved softly against my naked shoulder.

"Was it bad, Tony? Was it very bad?"

"No. Not bad."

"Will anyone guess?"

"I had to choke him pretty hard. There may be bruises. But it won't matter, even if they do get suspicious. It's proof that hurts. All we have to remember is that we were here together all afternoon."

"What do we do now?"

"We have a drink. We wait until dusk. Then we call the sheriff and tell him we're worried about Grandfather. We tell him the old man went swimming and hasn't returned."

"Why the sheriff?"

"I don't know. It seems like the sheriff should be the one to call."

"The will, Tony. Are you sure about the will?"

"Yes, I'm sure. It's all ours, honey. Every stick, stone, stock and penny, share and share alike."

It was only then that she began to tremble. I could feel her silken flesh shivering against mine all the way up and down. Her lips made a little wet spot on my shoulder. Under my fingers, the fastening of her white brassiere was a recalcitrant obstacle, thwarting the relief of my primitive drive. Finally it parted, the white scrap hanging for a moment between us and then slipping away. My hands traced the beautiful concave lines of her sides and moved with restrained, savage urgency.

Her voice was a thin, fierce whisper.

"Tony," she said. "Tony, Tony, Tony…"

2.

Out on the lake, they were blasting for Grandfather. All day, at intervals, we'd heard the distant, muffled detonations, and every time the hollow sound rolled up through the sparse timber to reverberate through the rooms of the lodge, I could see the bloated body of the old man wavering in terrible suspension in the dark water.

On the sun porch, Cindy stood with her back to me, staring out across the cleared area of the yard to the standing timber. She was wearing a slim black sheath of a dress without shoulders. Beautiful in anything or nothing, in black she was most beautiful of all. She was smoking a cigarette, and when she lifted it to her lips, the smoke rose in a thin, transparent cloud to mingle with the golden haze the light made in her hair.

"It's been a long time," she said. "Almost an hour."

"What's been almost an hour?"

"Since the last explosion. They've been coming at half-hour intervals."

"Maybe they've raised him."

"Maybe."

She moved a little, lifting the cigarette to her lips again, and the sunlight slipped up her arm and over her shoulder. I went up behind her and trailed my hands down the black sheath to where it flared tautly over firm hips and then back up to her shoulders. I pulled her back against me hard, breathing her hair.

"Nervous, Cindy?"

"No. You?"

"A little. It's the waiting, I guess."

She turned to face me, her arms coming up fiercely around my neck.

"Sorry, Tony? Will you ever be sorry?"

I looked down into the hot, gold-flecked eyes, and I said, "No, I'll never be sorry," and her cigarette dropped with a small sound to the asphalt tile behind me. Out on the front veranda, there was a loud knocking at the door.

I went in through the living room and on out through the hall to the front door, and there on the veranda stood Aaron Owens, the sheriff of the county. He was a short, fat little man with round checks and a bowed mouth, and it crossed my mind that maybe he'd been elected sheriff because the voters thought he was cute. Looking in at me through the screen, he mopped his face with a bright bandana and blew out a wet sigh.

"Hello, Mr. Wren. It's a hot walk up from the lake."

I opened the screen door and told him to come in. "My cousin's on the sun porch. She'll mix you a drink."

We went back to the sun porch, and Cindy put bourbon and soda and ice in a glass and handed it to him. He took the drink eagerly.

"We've been listening to the blasting," Cindy said. "We haven't heard any now for an hour."

He looked at her over the rim of his glass, his face and voice taking on a studied solemnity.

"We've brought him up. Poor old guy. I came to tell you."

Cindy turned quickly away, looking again out across the yard to the timber, and the little sheriff's eyes made a lingering, appreciative tour of the black sheath.

"He'll be taken right into town," he said. "Twenty-four hours in the water, you know. Didn't do him any good. We thought you'd prefer it that way."

"Yes," I said. "Of course."

He lifted his glass again, draining the bourbon and soda off the cubes. He let one of the cubes slip down the glass into his mouth, then spit it back into the glass.

"The coroner'll look him over. Just routine. An old man like that shouldn't swim alone in deep water. Maybe a cramp. Maybe a heart attack. Never can tell with an old man."

"Grandfather was always active," I said.

He looked wistfully at his empty glass for a minute and then set it down on the glass-topped table.

"Sure. Some old men never want to give up. Ought to know better. Well, time to be running along. Lucky to get him up so soon. Can't tell you how sorry I am."

"Thanks very much," I said.

I took him back to the front door and watched him cross the veranda and go down across the cleared area into the timber. Turning away, I went back to Cindy.

She was facing me when I came in, black and gold against the bright glass. Her lips were parted, and her breasts rose and fell with a slow, measured cadence.

"Everything's all right, Tony. Everything's going to be all right."

"Sure. They can't touch us, honey."

"He was an old man. We didn't take much of his life away."

"Don't think about that. Don't think about it at all."

"I won't, Tony. I'll just think about the time when we can go away. I'll think of you and me and more money than we can spend in a dozen lifetimes. You and me and the long, hot days under a sky that's bluer than any blue you've ever seen. Oh, Tony..."

I went over and held her tightly until she whimpered with pain and her eyes were blind with the pleasure of suffering.

"It won't be long, honey. Not long. After the will's probated. After everything's settled."

She snarled her fingers in my hair and pulled my face down to her hungry lips, and it must have been a century later when I became aware of the shrill intrusion of the telephone in the hall behind me.

I went out to answer it, and when I spoke into the transmitter my mind was still swimming in a kind of steaming mist. The voice that answered mine was clear and incisive but very soft. I had to strain to understand.

"Mr. Wren? My name is Evan Lane. I have a lodge across the lake. I see the sheriff's men have quit blasting. Does that mean they've found the old man?"

"Yes," I said. "They found him."

"Permit me to extend my sympathy." The country line hummed for a long moment in my ear, and it seemed to me that I could hear, far off at the other end, the soft ghost of a laugh. "Also my congratulations," the voice said.

A cold wind seemed to come through the wire with the voice. The warm mist inside my skull condensed and fell, leaving my mind chill and gray and very still. Inside my ribs, there was a terrible pain, as if someone had thrust a knife between them.

"I beg your pardon," I said.

The laugh was unmistakable this time, rising on a light, high note. "I offered my congratulations, Mr. Wren. For getting away with it, I mean."

"I don't understand."

"I think you do. You see, Mr. Wren, you made one small mistake. You made the mistake of acting too soon after your lovely friend had been sun bathing on the beach. A girl like that is an open invitation to a man like me to use his telescope. I have a clear shot from my veranda. Now do you understand, Mr. Wren?"

"What do you want?"

"I think you'll find me a reasonable man. Perhaps we'd better meet and discuss terms."

"Where?"

"Say the barroom of the Lakeshore Inn."

"When?"

"Tonight? At nine?"

"I'll be there," I said.

I cradled the phone and went back through the living room to the sun porch. Cindy was standing at a liquor cabinet in the corner, moving a swizzle stick in the second of two drinks she'd mixed. She stopped stirring and looked across at me, becoming suddenly very quiet. "Who was it, Tony?"

"He said his name's Evan Lane. He has a lodge across the lake."

"What did he want?"

"He wants to meet me at the Lakeshore Inn. Tonight."

"Why?"

"He has a habit of watching you on the beach through a telescope. He was watching yesterday. He saw me and the old man in the lake." She took two stiff steps toward me, her slim body rigid in its black sheath. Bright spots were burning in her cheeks.

"Blackmail?"

"It looks like it."

"What shall we do, Tony? What shall we do?"

"Find out what he's after, first of all. After that, we'll see."

"He'll bleed us, Tony. He'll bleed us white."

"No," I said. "It won't be like that. It won't be like that at all."

Then she came the rest of the way to me, but her body was cold and rigid in my arms, and it was a long time before it got back the way it was before the telephone rang.

3.

The Lakeshore Inn was on an arm of the lake that was almost at a right angle to the main body. In the barroom, they'd tried to make an effect with rafters. After they'd finished, the effect was just rafters, but you felt friendly because they'd tried.

I crawled onto a stool. A clock on the wall behind the bar said five to nine. I looked at my reflection in the mirror below the clock and was a little astonished to see that I didn't look any different from the way I'd looked yesterday or the day before. Same brown hair. Same eyes a little browner. Same face in general.

The bartender said, "Good evening, Mr. Wren," and cocked an eyebrow to show that he was tuned in.

"The usual," I said.

He put a couple of cubes in a glass and covered them with White Horse. Down the bar, around the curve to the wall, a heavy man with a bald head was drinking beer. The bartender went down to him and resumed a conversation I'd interrupted. At nine precisely, someone came up behind me and got onto the stool on my left. I looked up into the mirror.

The face I saw went on from where mine stopped. Thin and dark, with a clean, chiseled look, burned mahogany by wind and sun. Above it, black hair was feathered with white around the ears and almost mathematically divided by a single white streak. It was a head to make the ladies itch. The head of a man who might have been a heavy actor but thought he was too good for it. I sat and watched it until the bartender had done his job and gone back to his beer drinker.

"You don't look like a blackmailer," I said.

An incisive white smile flashed in the shadows of the mirror. "Thanks. You don't look like a murderer, either."

"It's a funny world," I said.

We drank in silence, two congenial guys, and after a while I said, "You're a little previous. Right now I'm a poor relation. So's Cindy. You know Cindy, don't you? She's the girl you peep at through a telescope. We're just a pair of lovable young parasites, Cindy and I. We won't have any money for blackmailers until the estate's settled."

The smile reappeared in the mirror, growing to a laugh, the soft, substantial embodiment of the ghost on the wire.

"You think I want money? My friend, I have more of the stuff than I can ever use. More, I imagine, than you'll get from Grandfather."

"In that case, what the hell are you after?"

Our eyes came together, locking in the glass, and his, I saw, were darkly swimming with the amused and cynical tolerance that doesn't come from compassion or conviction, but from a kind of amoral indifference to all standards.

"Nothing that need worry you, if you're reasonable. Believe me, I feel no compulsion to see you punished merely for killing a man old enough to die." He lit a cigarette, doing it neatly with a silver lighter. In the mirror, the light flared up across planes and projections, giving his face for a moment the quality of fancy photography. "I'm a tenacious man, Mr. Wren. I know what I want, and I'll use any available means to *get* what I want. In the light of yesterday's events, you should be able to understand that."

"You're talking all around it," I said. "The point, I mean."

The coal of his cigarette glowed brighter and faded. "I'm thinking about the girl. Cindy, I believe you called her."

I guess I'd known all along what was coming. I guess I'd known from the instant I looked into the mirror and saw that thin, patrician face with its ancient eyes. Strangely, there was no anger in me. There was only a cold, clear precision of thought: This time it'll be easy. This time it'll be fun. Not just a job, like it was with the old man.

"You can go to hell," I said.

His white teeth showed pleasantly. "My friend, you are the one in peril of going to hell. I can send you with a few words."

Killing the White Horse and turning to face him directly for the first time, I said, "You're lousy with dough. You said it yourself. Buy yourself a girl."

I got off the stool to go, and his hand came out to lie lightly on my sleeve.

"Since she's involved in this, it might be smart to let Cindy make the decision. She may not be as ready as you for that trip to hell. In case she isn't, I'll be here until eleven."

"You can stay forever," I said. "You can stay forever and to hell with you."

I went away without looking at him again, because I was afraid if I looked at him that I couldn't resist ruining his pretty face. Outside, standing by my convertible in front of the Inn, I felt the cool wind come up off the lake and hit me, and all the strength went out of me. My hands began to tremble, and I clutched the edge of the door. After a long time, I got into the convertible and drove back down the lake road to the lodge.

In the drive, I killed the motor and sat quietly under the wheel. Beyond the timber, a cold slice of moon was rising. In the lodge, all lights were out except the one in the room where Cindy slept. Cindy, Cindy, Cindy. Golden, sultry Cindy. The thought of her and Evan Lane brought the hot trembling back into my body, and I gripped the wheel until I was quiet.

I'd kill him, of course. I'd kill him, and it would be a pleasure. It would be the greatest pleasure I'd ever have on earth, except the pleasure that Cindy brought. Thinking of it clearly that way made me feel better, almost uplifted, and I got out of the convertible and went into the lodge and up to the room with the light burning.

Cindy was in bed with a book open, but I could tell she hadn't been reading. I stood leaning against the door, looking across at her, and pretty soon, she said, "I heard you drive up several minutes ago."

"Yes," I said. "I've been sitting down there thinking. I've been thinking about how to kill a man."

"No, Tony. Not again."

"It's the only way. I've always heard that one murder begets another, and I guess that's the way it is."

"We'll have money, Tony. Lots of money. We can pay."

"Like you said, he'd bleed us. He'd bleed us as long as we lived. Besides, he's got money. He isn't interested in getting any more."

"What does he want?"

"He wants you."

Her eyes dilated, and the breath rattled in her throat. I watched her lips come open and bright color creep under gold, and I thought again of the pleasure of killing Evan Lane.

"What do you mean, Tony?"

"Just what I said, honey. He wants you. The same way I want you. The same way any man who looks at you this side of eighty must want you. He's the guy with the telescope. Remember?"

She came out of the bed in a mist of white nightgown that barely existed, and I went to meet her. Against my shoulder, she said, "What now, Tony? What'll we do?"

"I told you, honey. I'll kill him before the night's over."

"No. We'll find another way, Tony. There is another way."

"There is, honey. The way he wants. Is it the way you want?"

"It'd be better than prison, Tony. Better than the death house."

I dug my fingers into her arms until she gasped with pain.

"Don't say that, Cindy. Don't."

"I'm thinking of us, Tony. You and me and the big dream. Are we going to throw it all away because some louse wants a cheap experience? We can't do that now."

"We won't throw anything away. If he wants an experience, he can die. Dying's the biggest experience of all."

"It'll point. Oh, Tony, can't you see? Two deaths like that, the location of his lodge, all the things together. Together, they'll point right back at us. They'll dig it all out. Besides, maybe he's already on his way to the sheriff."

I shook my head. "No. He's at the Inn waiting for you. He said he'd wait until eleven."

"I'd better go, Tony. I'd better go see him. Maybe we can work it out short of what he really wants."

"No. Not a prayer. If you saw him, you'd know."

"Give me a chance, Tony."

"There isn't any chance."

"I don't want to die, Tony. I don't want you to die. If we have to kill him, let it be later. Let it be when the time's exactly right. Oh, Tony, give me a chance to save us." Her golden flesh burned through the white mist, but I was suddenly spent and impotent, and I turned and went away to my own room and lay down in the darkness.

After a while, I heard the convertible come to life below my window and move off down the drive.

I kept on lying there in the darkness.

4.

There was no warmth in the sun, and the wind blowing in across the lake was very cold. The timber stood naked against the sky above its fallen leaves.

In her room, Cindy was packing. I went in and closed the door and stood leaning against it.

"Going somewhere, Cindy?"

"Yes. Back to town. Summer's over, and it's getting cold, and it's time to go back."

"Going alone, Cindy?"

"Please, Tony. We've been over it all so often. You know how it is."

"Sure," I said. "Like you said a long time ago, you're saving us. Two months ago, Cindy. A long time." She kept going back and forth between the closet and her bag, not looking at me. She was wearing brown velvet pajamas with six inches of golden skin between the pants and the top, and the effect of the brown velvet and the golden skin was a matter of shading that made my heart ache.

"You're going with Evan. Evan, the pretty blackmailer."

"It's for us, Tony. For you and me."

"I know. That's what I keep telling myself. She's making a big sacrifice, I keep telling myself. But now maybe it's time to let Evan Lane start sacrificing. Maybe it's time now to let him make the big sacrifice for us, the same way Grandfather made it."

She stopped halfway to the bag and turned toward me, holding in her hands a scarlet cashmere sweater that was like a great soft splash of blood against the brown velvet.

"He's got us, Tony. However much we hate him, he's got us, and you know it."

"I should've killed him the first night."

"He'll get tired of it pretty soon, Tony. I know he will. Then it'll be you and me again."

"Sure. You and me and Acapulco. You and me and the hot nights."

"It will, Tony. It will."

I went over to her fast and took a handful of her golden hair. I pulled her head back hard until her slender throat was a tight arch and her lips were pulled apart.

"Is that the truth, Cindy?"

"Yes. Oh, yes."

"Say it. Say it's the truth and the whole truth, so help you God."

"It is, Tony. It's the truth and the whole truth, so help me God." I let go of her hair, and her head came forward and down until her mouth was warm and alive on the base of my neck, and her arms came up around me.

"I love you, Cindy. I've murdered for you, and I'd die for you, and there's no place to go without you but hell."

"It won't be long now, Tony," she whispered. "Not long now." Then I went out of her room and downstairs. From a desk in the den behind the living room, I got a .38 calibre revolver and put it in the pocket of my tweed jacket. Outside, I angled down through the naked timber to the artificial beach and turned right along the shore.

The grass around the lake was dying, but it was still long and tough and hard to walk in, and in spite of the chill, the shirt under my jacket was soon wet with sweat. It was a small lake, but it took me well over an hour to walk around it to Evan Lane's lodge.

The lodge sat among the trees. I went up the slope and across the front veranda to the door and knocked, but there was no response. I thought at first that I'd come too late, but when I went around back, I saw his car still in its shed, so I returned to the veranda and sat down on the top step.

From where I sat, I could look at an easterly angle and see the timber growing west of our lodge across the lake. Swinging my eyes a little farther east, I saw more trees, but they were thicker and closer and growing on a kind of little peninsula that jutted out into the water from the end of the lake. I got up and went down to the west end of the veranda, where the angle of vision was sharper, but I still couldn't see anything but the heavy growth of scrub trees on the little peninsula. I went back to the top step and sat down again.

Except for the soft sighing of the trees, there was no sound. Under the pale sun, the lake was quiet. My mind was quiet with the quiet that comes when things are accepted.

Down by the lake, beyond the trees, there was suddenly the faint sound of whistling. The whistling grew louder as it came nearer through the trees, and pretty soon Evan Lane appeared on the slope, dressed in a bright plaid shirt, open at the throat, and corduroy trousers. When he saw me sitting on the step, the whistling broke for a moment and then resumed.

A few steps from the veranda, Lane pulled up, saying, "Well. Mr. Wren. Your neighborliness is appreciated, but it comes a little late. I'm returning to town tonight."

"I know," I said. "Cindy's home packing."

"Yes? I still have mine to do. I know you'll understand."

"Sure. I'll only stay a minute. I was just sitting here admiring your view. You could improve it, you know, by having the trees cut off that little peninsula. If you had the trees cut down, you could see our place across the lake. You could even see the beach and the raft."

He turned slowly to follow the direction of my gaze, and when he turned back, his eyes were alive with that swimming, cynical amusement I had seen in the Inn's barroom.

"Oh, yes. I did say I spotted you from the veranda, didn't I? But, of course, it no longer matters."

"Sure," I said. "It no longer matters. As far as you're concerned, nothing will ever matter again."

I took the gun out of my pocket and pointed it at him, and then I saw what I'd been living to see. I saw the smooth assurance go sick in his eyes and fear come flooding in. When I'd seen that, I'd had everything from him I'd ever want, so I shot him. I shot him where I hated him most. Right in his pretty face. The bullet struck him just under the nose, and he went down like an empty sack.

I sat there a little longer, looking with a kind of cold detachment at the crumpled body, and then I got up and went back down the slope and around the end of the lake. By the time I got back to our side and the beach, the afternoon was almost gone. Crossing the beach toward the timber in front of the lodge, I thought for a moment that I saw Grandfather's bright towel lying on the sand where he'd dropped it over two months ago, but of course the towel wasn't really there at all.

I went up through the timber and into the lodge, and Cindy was in the living room with a glass in her hand. She was still wearing the brown velvet pajamas, and when I looked at her, there was still in my heart, in spite of everything, the pain of my love and the sadness of a great loss.

"It's late, Tony. You've been gone a long time."

"I went around to the other side of the lake," I said. "I called on Evan Lane."

The glass moved sharply in her hand. "Why, Tony? Why?"

"He wasn't home when I got there," I said, "and I sat on the veranda until he came. I learned something while I was sitting there, honey. I learned that you can't see our beach or the raft at all from his place. He never used a telescope, as he said he did. He never saw me drown the old man. I kept trying to think how he could have known, and the only thing I could think was that you told him."

I waited a few seconds, and she tried to speak, but no sound could pass through her constricted throat. After a while, I went on talking in a quiet kind of way with no anger in my voice, because there was really no anger in me.

"Yes, honey. You told him. You told him because you were hot for each other, and he could move in with a new kind of blackmail, and there would be nothing I could do about it because he knew I was a murderer. You talked about the big dream. The dream was there, all right, but I was never in it. When the time came, you'd have gone away, all right, but never with me. He was the one, honey. He was the one from the beginning, but first you had to have Grandfather dead. You had to have him dead for his money, because you wanted his money in addition to Evan's. He didn't have the guts to do his own killing. He didn't have the guts, and you didn't have the strength. So you drafted me. Well, the old man's dead now, as you wanted him, and Evan Lane is dead, too. He's lying on the slope in front of his lodge, and he's dead forever."

She tried again to speak, but nothing came from her throat except a dry sob.

"I'm sorry," I said. "You'll never know how sorry."

I took out the gun, and the glass fell from her hand, and her voice came at last with a hot rush.

"I don't care if he's dead, Tony. Honest to God, I don't. We can still go away together. We can still have the dream."

"Yes," I said. "We'll go away together, honey. I've got our tickets right here in the gun. One way and a long way."

"No, Tony. For God's sake, no."

I pulled the trigger then, and there was only a little bang that wasn't very loud at all, and a black spot appeared as if by magic in the golden area of skin just below the place where her heart lay hidden. Her legs folded slowly, lowering her to her knees, and she pressed one hand, with the fingers spread, over the black spot. A thin trickle of blood seeped out brightly between two of the fingers. The gold-flecked eyes were wide with shock and terrible supplication.

"Please, Tony. Please, please…"

Then she lay quietly on the floor, and I turned and walked out onto the veranda. I leaned against the railing, looking off into the timber where night had come, and from one of the trees came the crying of a crazy-voiced loon. I put the barrel of the gun into my mouth until the sharp sight was digging into the roof, and even then, when there was no reasonable alternative, I was a little surprised to realize I was actually going to do it.

So Dark For April

John Evans (Howard Browne)

February 1953

When I got through telling the sergeant at Central Homicide about it, he said to sit tight and not touch anything, that somebody would be right over. I told him I wouldn't even breathe any more than was absolutely necessary and put back the receiver and went into the reception room to take another look at the body.

He was at the far end of the couch, slumped in a sitting position, with his chin on his chest and an arm hanging down. A wick of iron-gray hair made a curve against the waxen skin of a high forehead, his half-open eyes showed far too much white, and a trickle of dark blood had traced a crooked line below one corner of a slack-lipped mouth. His coat hung open, letting me see a circular red stain under the pocket of a soiled white shirt. From the center of the stain protruded the brown bone handle of a switchblade knife.

I moved over to lean against the window frame and light a cigarette. It was one of those foggy wet mornings we get early in April, with a chill wind off the lake and the sky as dull as a deodorant commercial. Umbrellas blossomed along the walks eight floors below and long lines of cars slithered past with a hooded look.

I stood there breathing smoke and staring at the dead man. He was nobody I had ever seen before. He wore a handsomely tailored suit coat of gray flannel, dirty brown gabardine slacks spattered with green paint and an oil stain across one knee, and brown bench-made shoes. His shirt was open at the throat, showing a fringe of dark hair, and he wasn't wearing a tie.

The rummage-sale air of those slacks bothered me. This was no Skid Row fugitive. His nails had that cared-for look, his face, even in death, held a vague air of respectability, and they didn't trim hair that way at barber college.

I bent down and turned back the left side of his coat. The edge of a black wallet showed in the inner pocket. That was where I stopped. This was cop business. Let the boys who were paid for it paw the corpse.

A black satin label winked up at me. I put my eyes close enough to read the stitched letters in it. A C G—in a kind of Old English script. The letters seemed too big to be simply a personal monogram, but then there's no accounting for tastes.

I let the lapel drop back to the way I had found it. The dead man didn't seem to care either way. Something glistened palely between the frayed cuffs and the tops of the custom-made shoes. I said, "Huh?" out loud and bent down to make sure.

No mistake. It made no sense but there it was. The pale white shine was naked flesh.

The dead man wasn't wearing socks.

2.

Detective Sergeant Lund said, "Right smack-dab through the old ticker. He never even had time to clear his throat. Not this guy."

His curiously soft voice held a kind of grim respect. He straightened up and backed away a couple of steps and took off his hat and shook rainwater from it onto the carpet and stared thoughtfully at me out of gunmetal eyes.

I moved a shoulder and said nothing. At the wicker table across the room the two plainclothes men were unshipping tape measures and flash-bulbs and fingerprint kits. Rain tapped the glass behind me with icy fingers.

"Your turn, Pine," Lund said in the same soft voice.

"He was like that when I came in," I said promptly. I looked at my strapwatch. "Exactly thirty-two minutes ago."

"How'd he get in here?"

"I usually leave the reception room unlocked, in case I have a client and the client cares to wait."

One corner of his mouth moved up faintly. "Somebody sure wanted this guy to wait, hey?"

I shrugged. He took a turn along the room and back again, hands deep in the pockets of his topcoat. Abruptly he said. "It says on your door you're a private dick. This a client?"

"No. I never saw him before."

"What's his name?"

"I don't know."

"No identification on him?"

"I didn't look. The sergeant at Central said not to."

He seemed mildly astonished. "A man dies in your office and you don't even show a little healthy curiosity? Don't be afraid of me, Pine. I haven't chewed off anybody's arm in over a week."

"I obey the law," I said mildly.

"Well, well," he said. He grinned suddenly, and after a moment I grinned back. Mine was no phonier than his. He snapped a thumb lightly against the point of his narrow chin a time or two while thinking a secret thought, then turned back to the body.

He went through the pockets with the deft delicacy of a professional dip. The blood, the knife handle, the sightless eyes meant about half as much to him as last week's laundry. When he straightened again there was a small neat pile of personal effects on one of the couch pillows and the dead man's pockets were as empty as his eyes.

The wallet was on top. Lund speared it, flipped it open. The transparent identification panels were empty, as was the bill compartment. Shoved into the latter, however, were three or four cards. Lund looked them over slowly and carefully, his thick brows drawn into a lazy V above his long, pointed nose.

"Credit cards on a couple Loop hotels," he said, almost to himself. "Plus one of these identification cards you get with a wallet. According to what it says here, this guy is Franklin Andrus, 5861 Winthrop Avenue. One business card. It calls him a sales representative for the Reliable Amusement Machine Corporation, Dayton, Ohio. No telephone shown and nobody listed to notify. Any of this mean anything to you, Mr. Pine?"

"Sorry."

"Uh-huh. You ain't playing this too close, are you?"

"I'm not even in the game," I said.

"Initials in his coat don't agree with the name on these here cards. That must mean something, hey?"

I stared at the bridge of his nose. "His coat and somebody else's cards. Or his cards and somebody else's coat. Or neither. Or both."

His mouth hardened. "You trying to kid me, mister?"

"I guess that would be pretty hard to do, Sergeant."

He turned on his heel and went through the communicating door to my inner office, still carrying the wallet. He didn't bother to shut it, and through the opening I could see him reach for the phone without sitting down and dial a number with quick hard stabs of a forefinger. What he said when he got his party was too low-voiced for me to catch.

Two minutes later, he was back. He scooped up the stuff from the couch and said, "Let's talk, hey? Let's us try out that nice private office of yours."

I followed him in and drew up the Venetian blind and opened the window a crack to let out the smell of yesterday's cigarettes. On the outer ledge four pigeons were organizing a bombing raid. Lund shoved the phone and ashtray aside, dumped his collection on the desk pad and snapped on the lamp. I sat down behind the desk and watched him pull up the customer's chair across from me.

I got out my cigarettes. He took one, sniffed at it for no reason I knew of and struck a match for us both. He leaned back and hooked an arm over the chair back and put his dull gray eyes on me.

"Nice and cozy," he said. "All the comforts. Too bad they're not all like this."

"I could turn on the radio," I said. "Maybe get a little dance music."

He grunted with mild amusement. All the narrow-eyed suspicion had been tucked out of sight. He drew on his cigarette and blew a long blue plume of smoke at the ceiling. Another minute and he'd have his shoes off.

He let his gaze drift about the dingy office, taking in the Vargas calendar, the filing cases, the worn tan linoleum. He said, "The place could stand a little paint, hey?"

"You drumming up business for your day off?" I asked.

That got another grunt out of him. "You sound kind of on the excited side, Pine. Don't be like that. You wouldn't be the first private boy got a customer shot out from under him, so to speak."

I felt my face burn. "He's not a customer. I told you that."

"I guess you did, at that," he said calmly. "It don't mean I have to believe it. Client getting pushed right in your own office don't look so good, hey? What the newshounds call bad press."

I bit down on my teeth. "You just having fun, Sergeant, or does all this lead somewhere?"

"Why, we're just talking," he said mildly. "Just killing time, you might say, until the coroner shows up. That and looking over the rest of what the guy had on him."

He stuck out an untidy finger and poked at the pile. Besides the wallet, there were several small square transparent envelopes, some loose change, a pocket comb, and a small pair of gold tweezers.

He brought his eyes up to stare coldly at me, his mellow mood gone as quickly as it had arrived. He said harshly, "Let's lay off the clowning around, mister. You were working for him. I want to know doing what."

"I wouldn't bother to lie to you," I said. "I never saw the guy before in my life, I never talked to him on the phone, or got a letter from him. Period."

His sneer was a foot wide. "Jesus, you must think I'm green!"

"I'm not doing any thinking," I said.

"I hope to tell you, you aren't. Listen, I can book you, brother!"

"For what?"

"Obstructing justice, resisting an officer, indecent exposure. What the hell do you care? I'm saying I can book you!"

I didn't say anything. Some of the angry color faded slowly from his high cheeks. Finally he sighed heavily and picked up the necktie and gave it a savage jerk between his square hands and threw it down again.

"Nuts," he said pettishly. "I don't want to fight with you. I'm trying to do a job. All I want is a little cooperation. This guy just don't walk in here blind. You're a private dick, or so your door says. Your job is people in trouble. I say it's too damn big a coincidence him picking your office to get knocked off in. Go on, tell me I'm wrong."

"I'm not saying you're wrong," I said. "I'm saying what I've already said. He's a stranger to me. He could have come in here to get out of the wet or to sell me a slot machine or to just sit down and rest his arches. I admit he might have come here to hire me. It has happened, although not often enough. Maybe somebody didn't want him spilling any touchy secrets to me, and fixed him so he couldn't."

"But you never saw him before?"

"You're beginning to get the idea," I said.

"Go ahead," he said bitterly. "Crack wise. Get out the office bottle and toss off three inches of Scotch without a chaser and spit in my eye. That's the way you private eyes do it on TV eight times a night."

"I don't have an office bottle," I said.

The sound of the reception-room door opening and closing cut off what Lund was about to say. A short plump man went past the half-open door of the inner office, carrying a black bag. Lund got up without a word and went out there, leaving me where I sat.

Some time passed. Quite a lot of time. The murmur of voices from the next room went on and on. Flash bulbs made soundless explosions of light and a small vacuum cleaner whirred. I stayed where I was and burned a lot of tobacco and crossed my legs and dangled my foot and listened to the April rain and thought my thoughts.

Thoughts about a man who might still be alive if I hadn't slept an hour later than usual. A man with mismatched clothing and no socks and an empty wallet. A man who would want to go on living, even in an age when living was complicated and not very rewarding. A man who had managed for fifty-odd years to hang on to the only life he'd ever be given to live before a switchblade knife and a strong hand combined to pinch it off.

I went on sitting. The rain went on falling. It was so dark for April.

After a while the corridor door opened to let in two men in white coats. They carried a long wicker basket between them. They passed my door without looking in. There was more indistinct murmuring, then a young voice said, "Easy with them legs, Eddie," and the basket was taken out again. It was harder to carry the second time.

Sergeant Lund walked in, his face expressionless. He sat down heavily and lighted a cigarette and waved out the match and continued to hold it. He said, "Andrus died between eight-thirty and ten. The elevator man don't recall bringing him up. What time did you get here?"

"Ten-thirty, about. Few minutes either way."

"You wouldn't happen to own a switchblade knife, hey?"

"With a brown bone handle?" I said.

He bent the used match and dropped it in the general vicinity of the ashtray. "Seven-inch blade," he muttered. "Like a goddam bayonet." He put the cigarette in a corner of his mouth and left it there. "This is a real cute killing, Pine. You notice how Andrus was dressed?"

"No socks," I said.

"That isn't the half of it, brother. New coat, old pants, fancy shoes. No hat and no topcoat. In weather like this? What's the sense?"

I spread my hands. "By me, Sergeant."

"You sure you wasn't work—"

"Don't say it!" I shouted.

The phone rang. A voice like a buzz-saw asked for Lund. He grunted into the mouthpiece, listened stolidly for nearly a full minute, then said, "Yeah," twice and passed back the receiver. I replaced it and watched him drag himself out of the chair, his expression a study in angry frustration.

"I had Rogers Park send a squad over to that Winthrop Avenue address," he growled. "Not only they don't find no trace of a Franklin Andrus; they don't even find the address! An empty lot, by God! All right. Hell with it. The lab boys will turn up something. Laundry marks, cuff dust, clothing labels. It'll take 'em a day or two, but I can wait. The old routine takes time but it always works."

"Almost always," I said absently.

He glowered down across the desk at me. "One thing I hope, mister. I hope you been holding out on me and I find it out. That's going to be jake with me."

He gathered up the dead man's possessions and stalked out. A little later one of the plainclothes men slipped in with his kit and took my fingerprints. He was nice about it, explaining they were only for elimination purposes.

By one o'clock I was back from having a sandwich and coffee at the corner drugstore. The reception room was empty, with only a couple of used flash bulbs, some smudges of fingerprint powder here and there and the smell of cheap cigars and damp cloth to remind me of my morning visitors. Without the dead man on it, the couch seemed larger than usual. There were no bloodstains. I looked to make sure.

I walked slowly into the other room and shucked off my trench coat. From the adjoining office came the faint whine of a dentist's drill. A damp breeze crawled in at the window and rattled the cords on the blind. Cars hooted in the street below. Sounds that made the silence around me even more silent. And the rain went on and on.

I sat down behind the desk and emptied the ashtray into the waste-basket and wiped off the glass top. I put away the cloth and got out a cigarette and sat there turning it, unlighted, between a thumb and forefinger.

He had been a nice-looking man. Fifty-five at the most. A man with a problem on his mind. Let's say he wakes up this morning and decides to take his problem to a private detective. So he gets out the classified book and looks under the right heading. There aren't many, not even for a town the size of Chicago. The big agencies he passes up, maybe because he figures he'll have to go through a handful of henna-haired secretaries before reaching the right guy. Then, not too far down the column, he comes across the name Paul Pine. A nice short name. Anybody can pronounce it.

So he takes a cab or a bus and comes on down. He hasn't driven a car; no car keys and no license on him. The waiting room is unlocked but no alert gimlet-eyed private detective around. The detective is home in bed, like a man with a working wife. So this nice-looking man with a problem sits down to wait . . . and somebody walks in and sticks a quarter-pound of steel in him.

That was it. That explained everything. Everything but what his problem was and why he wasn't wearing socks and why his wallet was empty and why his identification showed an address that didn't exist.

I got up and took a couple of turns around the room. This was no skin off my shins. The boys from Homicide would have it all wrapped up in a day or so. The old routine Lund had called it. I didn't owe that nice old man a thing. He hadn't paid me a dime. No connection between us at all.

Except that he had come to me for help and got a mouthful of blood instead.

I sat down again and tried the phone book. No Franklin Andrus listed. No local branch of the Reliable Amusement Machine Corp. I shoved the book away and began to think about the articles that had come out of the dead man's pockets. Gold tweezers, a pocket comb, five small transparent envelopes, seventy-three cents in change, a dark blue necktie. There had been a department store label on the tie— Marshall Field. I knew that because I had looked while Lund was out of the room. But Field's has more neckties than Pabst has bottles. No help there.

Is that all, Pine, I thought to myself. End of the line? You mean you're licked? A nice, clean-necked, broad-shouldered, late-sleeping detective like you?

I walked the floor some more. I went over to the window and leaned my forehead against its coolness. My breath misted the glass and I wrote my name in the mist with the end of my finger. That didn't seem to help any. I went on thinking. Maybe what *hadn't* come out of his pockets was important. No keys, for instance. Not even to his apartment. Maybe he lived in a hotel. Not even cigarettes or a book of matches. Maybe he didn't smoke. Not even a handkerchief. Maybe he didn't have a cold.

I sat down again. There had been initials in his coat. A C G. No periods and stitched professionally in fancy letters against a square of black satin. Rather large, as I recalled. Too bad I hadn't looked inside the pocket for the tailor's label. Unless . . .

This time I used the classified book. T—for Tailors—Men's. I ran through the columns to the G's. There it was, bright and shining and filled with promise. A. Cullinham Grandfils, Custom Tailor. On Michigan Avenue, in the 600 block. Right in the center of the town's swankiest shopping district.

I closed the window, climbed into my trench coat and hat and locked up. The smell of dime cigars still hung heavy in the outer office. Even the hall seemed full of it.

4.

It was made to look like a Greek temple, if you didn't look too close. It had a white limestone front and a narrow doorway with a circular hunk of stained glass above that. Off to one side was a single display window about the size of a visiting card. Behind the glass was a slanting pedestal covered with black velvet and on the velvet a small square of gray cloth that looked as though it might be of cheviot. Nothing else. No price tags, no suits, no firm name spelled out in severely stylized letters.

And probably no bargain basement.

I heaved back the heavy glass door and walked into a large room with soft dusty rose walls, a vaulted ceiling, moss green carpeting, and indirect lighting like a benediction. Scattered tastefully about were upholstered chairs and couches, blond in the wood and square in the lines. A few chrome ashstands, an end table or two, and at the far end a blond desk and a man sitting behind it.

The man stood up as I came in. He floated down the room toward me, a tall slender number in a cut-away coat, striped trousers and a gates-ajar collar. He looked like a high-class undertaker. He had a high reedy voice that said:

"Good afternoon, sir. May I be of service?"

"Are you the high priest?" I said.

His mouth fell open. "I beg your pardon?"

"Maybe I'm in the wrong place," I said. "I'm looking for the tailor shop. No name outside but the number checks."

His backbone got even stiffer although I hadn't thought that possible. "This," he said in a strangled voice, "is A. Cullinham Grandfils. Are you interested in a garment?"

"A what?"

"A garment."

"You mean a suit?"

"Ah—yes, sir."

"I've got a suit," I said. I unbuttoned my coat and showed it to him. All he did was look pained.

"What I came by for," I said, "was to get the address of a customer of yours. I'm not sure but I think his name's Andrus—Franklin Andrus."

He folded his arms and brought up a hand and turned his wrist delicately and rested his chin between his thumb and forefinger. "I'm afraid not. No. Sorry."

"You don't know the name?"

"I'm not referring to the name. What I am attempting to convey to you is that we do not give out information on our people."

I said, "Oh," and went on staring at him. He looked like the type you can bend easy. I dug out the old deputy sheriff's star I carried for emergencies like this and showed it to him, keeping the lettering covered with the ball of my thumb. He jerked down his arms and backed away as though I'd pulled a gun on him.

"This is official," I said in a tough-cop voice. "I'm not here to horse around. Do you cooperate or do we slap you with a subpoena?"

"You'll have to discuss the matter with Mr. Grandfils," he squeaked. "I simply am not—I have no authority to—You'll just have to—"

"Then trot him out, Curly. I don't have all day."

"Mr. Grandfils is in his office. Come this way, please."

We went along the room and through a glass door at the far end and along a short hall to another door: a solid panel of limed oak with the words A. Cullinham Grandfils, Private, on it in raised silver letters. The door was knocked on and a muffled voice came through and I was inside.

A little round man was perched in an enormous leather chair behind an acre of teakwood and glass. His head was as bald as a collection plate on Monday morning. A pair of heavy horn-rimmed glasses straddled a button nose above a tiny mouth and a chin like a ping-pong ball. He blinked owlishly at me and said, "What is it, Marvin?" in a voice so deep I jumped.

"This—ah—gentleman is the police, Mr. Grandfils. He has demanded information I simply haven't the right to—"

"That will be all, Marvin."

I didn't even hear him leave.

"I can't stand that two-bit diplomat," the little man said. "He makes the bottom of my foot itch."

I didn't say anything.

"Unfortunately he happens to be useful," he went on. "The women gush at him and he gushes back. Good for business."

"I thought you only sold men's suits," I said.

"Who do you think picks them out? Take off that coat and sit down. I don't know your name."

I told him my name and got rid of the trench coat and hat and drew up a teakwood chair trimmed in silver and sat on it. He made a quarter-turn in the big chair and his glasses flashed at me in the soft light.

"Police, eh?" he said suddenly. "Well, you've got the build for it. Where did you get that ridiculous suit?"

"This ridiculous suit set me back sixty-five bucks," I said.

"It looks it. What are you after, sir?"

"The address of one of your customers."

"I see. Why should I give it to you?"

"He was murdered. The address on his identification was incorrect."

"Murdered!" His mouth dropped open, causing the glasses to slip down on his nose. "Good heavens! One of my people?"

"He was wearing one of your coats," I said.

He passed a tremulous hand across the top of his head. All it smoothed down was scalp. "What was his name?"

"Andrus. Franklin Andrus."

He shook his head immediately. "No, Mr. Pine. None of my people has that name. You have made a mistake."

"The coat fitted him," I said doggedly. "He belonged in it. I might have the name wrong but not the coat. It was his coat."

He picked a silver paper-knife from the silver trimmed tan desk blotter and rapped it lightly over and over against the knuckles of his left hand. "Perhaps you're right," he said. "My coats are made to fit. Describe this man to me."

I gave the description, right down to the kidney-shaped freckle on the lobe of the left ear. Grandfils heard me out, thought over at length what I'd said, then shook his head slowly.

"In a general way," he said, "I know of a dozen men like that who come to me. The minor touches you've given me are things I never noticed about any of them. I'm not a trained observer and you are. Isn't there something else you can tell me about him? Something you've perhaps inadvertently overlooked?"

It hardly seemed likely but I thought back anyway. I said, "The rest of his clothing was a little unusual. That might mean something to you."

"Try me."

I described the clothing. By the time I was down to where the dead man hadn't been wearing socks, Grandfils had lost interest. He said coldly, "The man was obviously some tramp. None of my people would be seen on the street in such condition. The coat was stolen and the man deserved what happened to him. Frayed slacks! Heavens!"

I said, "Not much in his pockets, but I might as well tell you that too. A dark blue necktie with a Marshall Field label, a pair of gold-plated tweezers, several transparent envelopes about the size of a postage stamp, a pocket comb and some change . . ."

My voice began to run down. A. Cullinham Grandfils had his mouth open again, but this time there was the light of recognition in his eyes. He said crisply, "The coat was a gray flannel, Mr. Pine?"

"Yeah?"

"Carlton weave?"

"Hunh?"

"Never mind. You wouldn't know that. Quite new?"

"I thought so."

He bent across the desk to move a key on an intercom. "Harry," he snapped into the box. "That gray flannel lounge suit we made for Amos Spain. Was it sent out?"

"A week already," the box said promptly. "Maybe ten days, even. You want I should check exactly?"

"Never mind." Grandfils flipped back the key and leaned into the leather chair and went on tapping his knuckles with the knife. "Those tweezers and envelopes did it, sir. He's an enthusiastic stamp collector. Less than a month ago I saw him sitting in the outer room lifting stamps delicately with those tweezers and putting them in such envelopes while waiting for a fitting."

"Amos Spain is his name?"

"It is."

"He fits the description I gave?"

"Physically, exactly. But not the frayed slacks and dirty shirt. Amos Spain wouldn't be found dead in such clothes."

"You want to bet?"

"... Oh. Of course. I simply can't understand it!"

"How about an address on Spain, Mr. Grandfils?"

He dug a silver-trimmed leather notebook out of a desk drawer and looked inside. "8789 South Shore Drive. Apartment 3C. It doesn't show a telephone, although I'm confident he has one."

"Married?"

He dropped the book back in the drawer and closed it with his foot. "We don't inquire into the private lives of our people, Mr. Pine. It seems to me Mrs. Spain is dead, although I may be wrong. I do know Amos Spain is reasonably wealthy and, I think, retired."

I took down the address and got up and put on my coat and said, "Thanks for your help, Mr. Grandfils." He nodded and I opened the door. As I started out, he said:

"You really should do something about your suits, Mr. Pine."

I looked back at him sitting there like one of those old Michelin tire ads. "How much," I said, "would you charge me for one?"

"I think we could do something quite nice for you at three hundred."

"For that price," I said, "I would expect two pairs of pants."

His chin began to bob and he made a sound like roosters fighting. He was laughing. I closed the door in the middle of it and went on down the hall.

The address on South Shore Drive was a long low yellow-brick apartment building of three floors and an English basement. A few cars were parked along a wide sweep of concrete running past the several entrances, and I angled the Plymouth into an open spot almost directly across from 8789.

The rain got in a few licks at me before I could reach the door. Inside was a small neat foyer, complete with bright brass mail boxes and an inner door. The card on the box for 3C showed the name Amos Spain.

I pressed the right button and after a longish moment a woman's voice came down the tube. "Yes?"

That jarred me a little. I hadn't actually expected an answer. I said, "Mrs. Spain?"

"This is Mrs. Monroe," the voice said. "Mr. Spain's daughter. Are you from the post office?"

"Afraid not. I'm an officer, Mrs. Monroe. Want to talk to you."

"An officer? Why, I don't believe . . . What about?"

"Not from down here, Mrs. Monroe. Ring the buzzer."

"I'll do no such thing! How do I know you're a policeman? For all I know you could be a—a—"

"On a day like this? Don't be silly."

There was some silence and then the lock began to stutter. I went through and on up carpeted steps to the third floor. Halfway along a wide cheerful hallway was a partially open door and a woman in a flowered housecoat looking out at me.

She was under thirty but not very far under. She had wicked eyes. Her hair was reddish brown and there was a lot of it. Her skin was flawless, her cheekbones high, her mouth an insolent curve. She was long and slender in the legs, small in the waist, high in the breasts. She was dynamite.

I was being stared at in a coolly impersonal way. "A policeman you said. I'm fascinated. What is it you want?"

I said, "Do I get invited in or do we entertain the neighbors?"

Her eyes wavered and she bit her lip. She started to look back over her shoulder, thought better of it, then said, "Oh, very well. If you'll be brief."

She stepped back and I followed her across a tiny reception hall and on into an immense living room, with a dinette at one end and the open door to a kitchen beyond that. The living room was paneled, with beautiful leather chairs, a chesterfield, lamps with drum shades, a loaded pipe rack, a Governor Winthrop secretary, a fireplace with a gas log. Not neat, not even overly clean, but the right place for a man who puts comfort ahead of everything else.

I dropped my coat on a hassock and sat down on one of the leather chairs. Her lips hardened. "Don't get too comfortable," she said icily. "I was about to leave when you rang."

"It's a little chilly out for a housecoat," I said.

Her jaw hardened. "Just who do you think you are, busting in here and making smart remarks? You say you're a cop. As far as manners go, I believe it. Now I think I'd like to see some real proof."

I shrugged. "No proof, Mrs. Monroe. I said officer, not policeman. A private detective can be called an officer without stretching too far."

"Private—" Her teeth snapped shut and she swallowed almost convulsively. Her face seemed a little pale now but I could have imagined that. "What do you want?" she almost whispered.

"Where's Amos Spain?" I said.

"My . . . father?"

"Uh-huh."

". . . I don't know. He went out early this morning."

"He say where?"

"No." Whatever had shocked her was passing. "Tom and I were still sleeping when he went out."

"Tom?"

"My husband."

"Where's he?"

"Still asleep. We got in late. Why do you want to know where my father is?"

I said, "I think it would be a good idea if you sat down, Mrs. Monroe. I'm afraid I've brought some bad news."

She didn't move. Her eyes went on watching me. They were a little wild now and not at all wicked. She wet her lips and said, "I haven't the slightest idea what you're talking about. Bad news about what?"

"About your father. He's dead, Mrs. Monroe. Murdered."

"I don't believe it," she said quickly. Almost too quickly.

"He's been identified. Not much chance for a mistake."

She turned away abruptly and walked stiffly over to a lamp table and took a cigarette from a green cloisonné box. Her hand holding the match wavered noticeably but nothing showed in her face. She blew out a long streamer of smoke and came back and perched carelessly on an arm of the couch across from me. The housecoat slipped open slightly, letting me see most of the inner curve of a freshly powdered thigh. I managed to keep from chewing a hole in the rug.

"There's been some mistake, Mr. Pine. Dad never had an enemy in the world. What do you suggest I do?"

I thought back to be sure. Then I was sure. I said, "The body's probably at the morgue by this time and already autopsied. Might be a good idea to send your husband over. Save you from a pretty unpleasant job."

"Of course. I'll wake him right away and tell him about it. You've been very kind. I'm sorry if I was rude."

She hit me with a smile that jarred my back teeth and stood up to let me know the interview was over and I could run along home now and dream about her thigh.

I slid off the chair and picked up my hat and coat. While putting them on I moved over to the row of windows and looked down into the courtyard. Nobody in sight. Not in this weather. Rain blurred the glass and formed widening puddles in thin brown grass that was beginning to turn green.

I turned and said, "I'll be running along, Mrs. Monroe," and took four quick steps and reached for the bedroom door.

There was nothing wrong with her reflexes, I'll say that for her. A silken rustle and the flash of flowered cloth and she was standing between me and the door. We stood there like that, breathing at each other, our faces inches apart. She was lovely and she smelled good and the housecoat was cut plenty low.

And her face was as hard as four anvils.

"I must have made a mistake," I said. "I was looking for the hall door."

"Only two doors," she said between her teeth. "Two doors in the entire apartment. Not counting the bathroom. One that lets you out and one to the bedroom. And you picked the wrong one. Go on. Get out of here before I forget you're not a cop."

On my way out I left the inner door downstairs unlocked. In case.

6.

The rain went on and on. I sat there listening to it and wondering if Noah had felt this way along about the thirty-ninth day. Smoke from my fourth cigarette eddied and swirled in the damp air through the no-draft vent.

The Plymouth was still parked across from 8789, and I was in it, knowing suddenly who had killed Amos Spain and why Spain had been wearing what he wore and why he wasn't wearing what he hadn't worn. It was knowledge built piece by piece on what I had seen and heard from the moment I walked in and found the body on the couch. It was the kind of knowledge you can get a conviction with—if you have that one key piece.

The key piece was what I didn't have.

Now and then a car came into the wide driveway and stopped at one of the entrances to let somebody out or to pick somebody up. None of them was for the rat hole to which I was glued. A delivery truck dropped off a dinette set a couple of doors down and I couldn't have cared less.

I lighted another cigarette and crossed my legs the other way and thought about hunting up a telephone and calling Lund and telling him to come out and get the knife artist and sweat that key piece out in the open. Only I didn't want it that way. This was one I wanted to wrap up myself. It had been my office and my couch and almost my client, and I was the one the cops had tromped on. Not that the tromping had amounted to much. But even a small amount of police displeasure is not what you list under assets.

Another twenty minutes floated by. They would still be up there in that apartment wearing a path in the rug. Waiting, sweating blood, hanging on desperately, risking the chance that I had known more than I let on and was already out yelling for the cops.

I would have loved to know what they were waiting for.

When the break did come I almost missed it. An ancient Ford with a pleated front fender wheezed into the curb. A hatless young man in a rained-on gray uniform got out to look at the number over the entrance to 8789. He had a damp-looking cigarette pasted to one corner of his mouth and a white envelope in his left hand. The local post office dropping off a piece of registered mail.

And then I remembered Mrs. Monroe's first question.

I slapped open the glove compartment and got out my gun and shoved it under the band of my trousers while I was reaching for the door. I crossed the roadway at a gallop and barged into the foyer just as the messenger took a not too clean thumb off the button for 3C. I made a point of getting out my keys to keep him from thinking Willie Sutton was loose again.

He never even knew I was in town. He said, "Post office; registered letter," into the tube and the buzzer was clattering before he had the last word out. He went through and on up the steps without a backward glance.

The door was off the latch, the way I had left it earlier. By the time the door to 3C opened, I was a few feet away staring vaguely at the closed door to 3B and trying to look like somebody's cousin from Medicine Hat. The uniformed man said, "Amos Spain?" and a deeper voice said, "I'm Mr. Spain," and a signature was written and a long envelope changed hands.

Before the door could close I was over there. I said, "It's me again."

He was a narrow-chested number with a long sallow face, beady eyes, a thin nose that leaned slightly to starboard, and a chin that had given up the struggle. Hair like black moss covered a narrow head. This would be Tom Monroe, the husband.

Terror and anger and indecision were having a field day with his expression. His long neck jerked and his sagging jaw wobbled. He clutched the edge of the door, wanting to slam it but not quite daring to. The silence weighed a ton.

All this was lost on the messenger. He took back his pencil and went off down the hall, his only worry the number of hours until payday. I leaned a hand against the thin chest in front of me and pushed hard enough to get us both into the room. I shut the door with my heel, said, "I'll take that," and yanked the letter out of his paralyzed fingers. It had sealing wax along the flap and enough stamps pasted on the front to pay the national debt.

Across the room the girl in the flowered housecoat was reaching a hand under a couch pillow. I took several long steps and stiff-armed the small of her back and she sat down hard on the floor. I put my empty hand under the pillow and found a snub-nosed Smith & Wesson .32, all chambers filled and dark red nail polish on the sight. I held it loosely along my leg and said, "Well, here we are," in a sprightly voice.

Monroe hadn't moved. He stared at me sullenly, fear still flickering in his small nervous eyes. The girl climbed painfully to her feet, not looking at either of us, and dropped down on the edge of a leather chair and put her face in her hands.

The man's restless eyes darted from me to the girl and back to me again. A pale tongue dabbed furtively at lips so narrow they hardly existed. He said hoarsely, "Just what the hell's the bright idea busting in here and grabbing what don't belong to you?"

I flapped the envelope loosely next to my ear. "You mean this? Not yours either, buster."

"It belongs to my father-in-law. I simply signed for it."

"Oh, knock it off," I said wearily. "You went way out of your league on this caper, Tom. You should have known murder isn't for grifters with simple minds."

A sound that was half wail, half sob filtered through the girl's fingers. The man said absently, "Shut up, Cora." His eyes skittered over my face. "Murder? Who's talking about murder? You the one who shoved in here a while ago and told Cora about Amos Spain?"

"I wasn't telling her a thing," I said. "She knew it long before. You told her."

"You might like to try proving that," he said.

"You bet," I said. I put the gun on the couch arm and looked at the envelope. Yesterday's postmark, mailed from New York City. Addressed in a spidery handwriting, with the return address reading: *B. Jones, General Delivery, Radio City Station, New York, NY.* I ripped open the flap and shook out the contents. A plain sheet of bond paper wrapped around three odd-looking stamps. One was circular with a pale rose background and black letters. The other two were square, one orange and one blue, with the same crude reproduction of Queen Victoria on both. All three wouldn't have carried a postcard across the street.

Monroe was staring at the stamps and chewing his lip. He looked physically ill. The girl was watching me now, her fingers picking at the edge of the housecoat, her face white and drawn and filled with silent fury.

I said, "It would almost have to be stamps. I should have guessed as much two hours ago. How much are they worth?"

"How would I know?" Monroe said sulkily. "They weren't sent to me. I never saw them before."

I slid the stamps back into the envelope and put the envelope in my pocket. "You'd know, brother. If you'd kept a better eye on Amos Spain you might even have gotten away with the whole thing."

"You've got nothing on us. Why don't you just shove off?"

"I've got everything on you," I said. "Not that I deserve any credit. The Army mule could have done the job. I can give you the State Attorney's case right now."

I picked up the gun and swung it lightly between a thumb and finger and sat on the couch arm. Rain beat against the windows in a muted murmur. From the kitchen came the lurch and whine of the refrigerator motor.

"Somebody named B. Jones," I said, "gets hold of some rare stamps. Illegally. Jones knows there are collectors around who will buy stolen stamps. Amos Spain is such a collector. A deal is made by phone or letter and the stamps are mailed to Spain. In some way you two find out about it. After the stamps are in the mail, perhaps. No point in trying to get them away from Uncle Sam; but there's another way. So the two of you show up here early this morning and force your way in on old Amos, who is still in bed. You tie him up a little, let's say, and gag him, leave him on the bed and come out here in the living room to wait for the postman with the stamps.

"But Amos isn't giving up. He gets loose, dresses and goes down the fire escape. He can't be sure when you're going to open the door and look in on him, so he puts on just enough clothes to keep from being pinched for indecent exposure. That's why he wasn't wearing socks, and why his clothes were mismatched.

"But by the time he's going down the fire escape, you look in. No Amos, and the window is open. You look out, spot him running away without topcoat or hat, and out you go after him. Tackling him on the street wouldn't do at all; your only hope is to nail him in some lonely spot and knock him off. How does it sound so far, neighbor?"

"Like a lot of words," Monroe growled.

"Words," I said, "are man's best friend. They get you fed, married, buried. Shall I tell you some more about words?"

"Go to hell."

I put down the gun and lit a cigarette and smiled. "Like I told you," I said, "you've got a simple mind. But I was telling you a story. I wouldn't want to stop now, so let's get back to Amos. You see, Amos had a big problem at this stage of the game. He couldn't go to the boys in blue and tell them about you and Cora, here. Doing that could bring out the business about the stamps and get him nailed for receiving stolen property. He had to get the two of you thrown out of his apartment before the envelope showed up.

"How to do it? Hire a strong-arm boy who won't ask questions. Where do you find a strong-arm boy on a moment's notice? The phone book's got half a column of them. Private detectives. Not the big agencies; they might ask too many questions. But one of the smaller outfits might need the business bad enough to do it Amos's way. At least it's worth trying.

"So Amos gets my address out of the phone book, the nearest one to him, and comes up to hire me. He has no idea you're following him which means he's not too careful about keeping out in the open where nothing can happen to him. He comes up to my office and I'm not in yet. He sits down to wait. You walk in and leave a switch knife in him. But that's only part of your job. You've got to fix it so there'll be a delay in identifying him—enough of a delay, at least to keep the cops away from here until the mailman comes and goes. Lifting his papers may slow things down, but you want more than that. Being a crook, you make a habit of carrying around phony identification cards. You substitute these for his own, lift whatever cash Amos had on him, slip out quick and come back here. Right so far?"

The fear had gone out of Monroe's eyes and there was the first faint sign of a smirk to his thin bloodless lips. He said airily, "If this is your idea of a way to kill a rainy afternoon, don't let me stop you. Mind if I sit down?"

"I don't care if you fall down," I said. "There's a little more and then we can all sit around and discuss the election until the cops arrive. A little more, like Cora knowing my name the first time I was here this afternoon. I hadn't told her my name, you see; just that I was a private dick. But to Cora there was only one private detective—the one whose office you'd killed Amos Spain in."

Behind me a quiet voice said, "Raise your hands."

I froze. Cora Monroe's .32 was on the couch arm, no more than six inches from my hand. I could have grabbed for it—and I could get buried for grabbing. I didn't grab.

A slender stoop-shouldered man in his early forties came padding on stocking feet in front of me. He had bushy graying hair, a long intelligent face and a capable-looking hand containing a nickel-plated Banker's Special revolver. The quiet voice belonged to him and he used it again, saying, "I won't tell you again. Put up your hands."

I put them up.

He went on pointing the gun at me while knocking the .32 off the couch with a single sweep of his other hand. It bounced along the carpet and hit the wall. He said gently, "I'll take those stamps."

"You will indeed," I said. My tongue felt as stiff as Murphy, the night he fell off the streetcar. "I guess I should have looked in the bedroom after all. I guess I thought two people should be able to lift three little stamps."

"The stamps, Mr. Pine." The voice wasn't as gentle this time.

"Sure," I said. I put my hand in my coat and took out the envelope. I did it nice and slow, showing him I was eager to please. I held it out as he reached for it and I slammed my shoe down on his stocking foot with every pound I could spare.

He screamed like a woman and the gun went off. Behind me a lamp base came apart. I threw a punch, hard, and the gray-haired man threw his hands one way and the gun the other and melted into the rug without a sound.

Monroe was crouched near the side wall, the girl's .32 in his hand and madness in his eyes. While he was still bringing up the gun I jerked the Police Special from under the band of my trousers and fired.

He took a week to fall down. He put his hands together high on his chest and coughed a broken cough and took three wavering steps before he hit the floor with his face and died.

Cora Monroe hadn't moved from the leather chair. She sat stiff as an ice floe off Greenland, her face blank with shock, her nails sunk in her palms. I felt a little sorry for her. I bent down and picked the envelope off the floor and shoved it deep into a side pocket. I said, "How much were they worth, Cora?"

Only the rain answered.

I found the telephone and said what had to be said. Then I came back and sat down to wait.

It was ten minutes before I heard the first wail of distant sirens.

Shakedown
Roy Carroll (Robert Turner)

April 1953

She was a cute kid and I hated to do this to her, but it had to be. I couldn't fool around. I gave it to her straight, told her I couldn't afford to get married, didn't want to get married and that I wasn't paying for any operation, either. Those things cost two—three hundred bucks, today. I didn't have that kind of money. I told her, too, that if she tried to put the pressure on me, I'd just take off, fast. I didn't have to hang around this town.

It was while she was putting on the big sob act that I figured an out for her. I told her to shut up for a minute and then I said: "Vera, listen. I think I've got it figured what you can do."

She cut off the tears fast, but her big, brown eyes stayed full and glittery as she looked at me. "What is it, Van?"

"It's simple," I told her. "You know the boss is nuts about you, don't you? Absolutely nuts. So when he hears you and I have busted up, he'll ask you for a date. You give it to him. And you keep on giving it to him. Not only the dates."

She sniffled and dabbed at her nose with a little wad of handkerchief. Those cow-like eyes stared at me dumbly. She said: "Go out with Mr. Owen? I—I don't think I understand, Van."

"You don't understand." I went over to the dresser mirror and started combing my hair. I knew Vera was watching me, thinking what nice curly hair I had, and how handsome I was, and big, like a college football player. I knew that because she was always telling me. It got monotonous.

"What do you want me to do?" I said. "Draw you a blueprint? After a few dates the dumb old slob will want you to marry him. Okay, you marry him. Your troubles are over."

I turned away from the mirror and she was sitting very stiff in the chair, her usually round, pretty face looking drawn and shocked. "Van," she said. "Do you know what you're saying? I—I can't marry someone I don't even love. Especially a fat man old enough to be my father. Van, what do you think I am?"

I didn't tell her.

"Van, you can't be serious. I—What's the matter with you? What's got into you, lately?"

"Nothing's got into me," I told her. "You're the one in trouble. Remember? I'm telling you, that's your out. Your only out. It's simple. Easy."

She came flying out of the chair, squalling and sobbing again and flung herself at me. I held her for a minute. "Van," she said. "I thought you loved me. How can you do this to me? Van, I only want to marry *you*. I only love *you*."

For a minute I almost felt sorry for her. In spite of the fact that she was a good-looking kid, with a body that drove the guys in the office nuts, she was kind of shy and dumb. Maybe that was because she was all alone in the world, no folks or anything, lived by herself, didn't even seem to have any girl friends. I was the first guy she'd ever gone out with steady. I was the first guy, period. But what good does it do you to feel sorry for someone? What does it buy?

"Look, Baby," I said, softly. "It won't be so bad. Harry Owen is stinking with dough. He's a nice old guy. You'll have the best of everything. And maybe after awhile, you and I can still get together."

She thought about that and the weeps died down again. Finally, she murmured: "Suppose he doesn't ask me to marry him, Van? What then?"

"He will," I said. "If he doesn't, you make him. You tell him he's got to because you're—"

She yanked away from me, and for a long minute she stared at me, a funny look in her eyes. "You're really serious, aren't you?" she said, finally. "You're really asking me to do a thing like that!"

Then she turned and ran out of my flat, still crying, slamming the door behind her. For a minute I was going to go after her, try to talk her into it. But then I realized I didn't have to. She had the idea, now. When she calmed down, she'd go through with it. What else was there for her to do? I knew she was scared stiff of any operation, even if she could get the dough.

The next day at the Owen Advertising Agency where Vera and I both worked in the mail room, she didn't even speak to me. She acted sullen and pouty, all day. Other people in the office started noticing right away and soon they were kidding both of us about it. They stopped, though, when Vera burst out crying and ran out to the Ladies' Room. That was good. I knew now that Harry Owen wouldn't lose any time hearing about it.

The whole thing worked out smooth and fast after that. I called Vera in a couple of days and she told me she was dating him. She said it was being done on the QT, though, that Harry didn't want the rest of the employees to know about it. Then she said: "You know something, Van, the joke's on you. I'm already beginning to like Mr. Owen—Harry—a lot. He's not so old, after all, and he's not so fat, either. He's kind to me, too, Van. Can you understand what that means to me after going with you? He isn't cruel like you. He doesn't do the—the things you used to do. I think this was a very smart idea of yours, Van. I'm not having any trouble forgetting you, at all."

"Good for you," I said and slammed the receiver in her ear. I don't know what I got so damned sore about, but I did. Wasn't everything working out the way I'd planned? But it bothered me, somehow. I got mean drunk that night, the kind of drunk I don't like to get. The next day I was all right, though.

It was about a month or so later and I wasn't sure whether Vera was beginning to look a little chubby already or if it was just my imagination, when she called me one night, told me she had to see me. I tried to shake her off but she insisted. She came up to my place.

She looked terrible, her hair not fixed right, kind of ratty looking and her eyes too dark underneath and with a kind of haunted look. She sat there, twisting her hands in her lap and told me how she and Harry Owen had gotten real cozy together and he'd told her he loved her, wanted to put her up in a swanky apartment and like that. But he never even came close to asking her to marry him. Well, today, one of the other girls in the office made a funny remark to Vera and she knew she couldn't wait much longer. So tonight she gave Harry the business. She told him.

"Van, he went crazy," she Said. "He told me I'd have to get it taken care of, I'd have to. He'd pay for everything. I told him that was out. I told him I wouldn't go for an operation, no matter what, and he couldn't make me, and that my—condition was his responsibility and he had to marry me. Well, he really went wild, then. He cursed me and, all of a sudden, he grabbed me, and started choking me. Look."

She undid a little silken scarf around her throat and showed me the imprint of his fingers. I didn't know what to say, couldn't figure it. Harry Owen was one of these Man Of Distinction types, gray temples, clipped mustache, a little paunchy, but always well groomed. Always quiet and polite, too. Every inch a gentleman. I couldn't even picture him doing something like that. Something was wrong, somewhere. I'd never even heard him raise his voice in the office. I didn't get it.

"What am I going to do, Van?" Vera said. "I—I'm afraid of him, now. No kidding. Van, he wasn't fooling. His eyes were murderous. He would have killed me right then and there, but I managed to break away."

I said: "You go home and get some rest. Try to forget about it. Maybe he'll calm down and be sorry and change his mind after he thinks it all over. What else can you do? Forget this crap about being afraid of him. He was just trying to frighten you. Guys don't kill girls for things like this, today. What have you been reading, *American Tragedy* or something?"

I talked to her some more, calmed her down, and got her out of my place. But the thing kept bothering me, all that night. I didn't sleep much. I knew that these quiet, gentlemanly guys like Owen were the worst kind when they did finally flip about something. I wasn't really so sure Vera had nothing to worry about. But it wasn't my business any more. This was between the two of them.

The next day, I noticed that the boss was grouchy and irritable, the first time I'd ever seen him that way. He looked pale and drawn and about ten years older, too, as though he hadn't slept very well. But late in the afternoon, I met Vera by the water cooler. Nobody else was around. She broke out in a big smile.

"It's all right, Van," she whispered. "He apologized today. And he said he'd be glad to marry me. He said it was just that the shock of finding out about my—you know—condition, was too much for him. But he was sweet as pie, today. Tonight he's going to drive me up to show me his country place in Westchester. And next week we'll announce the wedding. Isn't that swell, Van?"

I said I guessed it was and then somebody came along and we couldn't talk any more. At five o'clock, going down in the elevator with Joe Harvey, the office manager, it came to me that something was wrong. A guy doesn't change just like that. Not from one complete extreme to the other. And this taking her up to see his country place sounded a sour note to me. Down in the lobby, I told Joe Harvey I had a big date tonight, and would he loan me his car? He said sure.

I drove right to the block where Vera had a room and parked there and waited and watched. About seven-thirty, Harry Owen's big Lincoln swerved to the curb in front of the building and he went in and got Vera and the two of them drove off. I followed them.

They drove up deep into Westchester before the Lincoln turned off into a lonely dirt side road. I cut the lights on Joe's car, eased in behind them, way behind, because Owen would have suspected something if he'd seen another car behind him on this lonely country lane. Then I saw him stop, about a quarter of a mile ahead. I slewed into the side of the road, cut the engine, quick. I got out and started to walk, keeping in the shadows, toward the red glow of the Lincoln's taillight, up ahead.

I was about ten yards from their car when I saw Harry Owen get out of the driver's side, walk around the car to the other door, open it and start to drag something out. I edged a little closer. What he was dragging out, I saw, was Vera. He was dragging her out by the legs and her skirt got hiked way up and the starlight gleamed on the whiteness of her thighs. Then Owen went around to the trunk compartment of the car and got out a spade. He held the spade under his arm while he dragged Vera's corpse into the woods. I followed him and saw the clearing where he was going to bury her, and then I got out of there, fast. I drove home.

All that night I was so excited I could hardly sleep, hardly wait for tomorrow. I knew it would be better that way. Be more of a shock to him. When nothing had happened by morning, he'd pretty well figure he was safe. I waited most of the next day, too, until the middle of the afternoon. Then I took some mail into Harry Owen in his private office.

"Hi, Harry," I said. "How's Vera?"

He took it nice. He just looked up quietly and said: "Vera? Oh, you mean that little brunette you used to go with?"

The one I used to go with. I had to admire this guy, the way he'd got control of himself, even though he did look terrible. I said: "Yeah, that one."

"She doesn't work here any more," he said, fussing with papers on his desk, not looking up. "I got a call this morning, said she was resigning, had another job."

"Yeah?" I said.

"Yes, Van. She was a nice girl. Too bad you two had a falling out. I'm busy, Van. Anything special on your mind?"

"Yes," I told him. "Vera. I'm wondering how she made that call this morning. Any phone booths up in those lonely Westchester woods? You know, where she's tucked in for the long sleep?"

He jerked almost out of his skin. His head went back so hard his neck snapped. I've never seen such a scared, sick look in anybody's eyes. His face looked like crumpled parchment. He didn't say anything. Just looked at me.

"She didn't quit any job, did she, Harry?" I said. "She just took a one way ride along a dirt road, off the Hutchinson River Parkway, with a guy who had her in some trouble."

"Van," he said. His voice sounded like a frightened child's. He tried to say something else but all he could do was keep saying my name over and over.

"Don't worry about it," I told him. "I won't be greedy. But I think it's about time I got promoted, got a big raise, don't you, Harry?"

He said: "Go away, Van, for a few minutes. Leave me alone. Let me think."

"There's nothing to think about. I've been here long enough to get promoted, get more pay. Nobody will think anything. Not like what they would think if they knew about that grave up there in Westchester. I could take the cops there easy. I know just where it is."

"Wait a minute, Van," he said. Some of the color was coming back to his face. He loosened his collar. His eyes narrowed a little. "You're forgetting a few things. Vera and I were very—uh—circumspect. Nobody knows about our relationship. Not anybody at all. There's nothing to tie her in with me. I went back to her place, last night, and got rid of all her stuff, left a note written on her typewriter, explaining to the landlord that she'd gotten a better job in L. A. That angle's well covered. Van, the way it's set up, *you'd* be the one the police would jump on. Everybody in the office knew *you* were going with her, then had a fight when she got in trouble. It will just look like she let it go for a month, then really went after you. You got panicky—and took that way out. That's the way the police would figure it. So, you see, you've got no real hold on me."

I stared at him, unbelievingly. That turned my guts over for a moment. But not for long. I laughed. "Nice try," I told him. "But police work is super-scientific these days. When they go over your car, they'll find proof that Vera was in it, last night. They'll go over that car with vacuum cleaners, with a fine tooth comb. There'll be plenty of evidence that you're the killer and you'll never in a million years get rid of it. The shoes you wore, the shovel." I grinned at him. "A nice attempt to pass the buck, Harry, but it won't work. Let's talk about that raise some more."

I got to be Supervisor of the mailing department that day. With a big raise. And from then on I began living it up. I got a better apartment, a lot of clothes. My boss was a real good guy. Whenever I ran short I could always borrow a hundred from him. He wasn't in any sweat about me paying it back, either. Especially since I didn't overdo it. Poor Harry Owen wasn't enjoying life so much, though. He began to drink a lot. Even in the office, during the day, you could smell it on him. It started some talk but not much. So maybe business was bad or something and he was worried.

Once, I got curious, and asked him: "Why did you do it the hard way? Why didn't you marry the kid? She wasn't so bad."

He told me, then, that he was already married, although separated, and that his wife was against divorce. I borrowed an extra fifty from him, on that.

During that next month, I began to take it easy on the job, too. When I felt like taking an afternoon off or something, I did it. If I felt like sitting around, reading for awhile, I did it. Who was going to say anything? Harry Owen? It griped a lot of people in the office. They got jealous. I didn't care. The hell with them! One wise guy even said:

"Who does this guy Van think he is, a privileged character or something? I never saw a guy get away with so much. He must know where the body's buried or something."

The funny part was, he wasn't kidding. He just didn't realize it, that's all.

This went on for a month. Then one morning, in front of the whole office, when I came in an hour late, Harry Owen told me: "Van, you come in late one more morning, take another afternoon off, or sluff on the job any more, and you're through. You're fired."

I looked at him as though he'd said something in Arabic. "What?" I said. "Are you kidding?"

He'd aged badly in the last month but right now his jaw was set firmly. His eyes looked sunken way into his head and bloodshot from drinking so much, but they held mine steadily enough. "Try it and find out," he said.

There was only one thing to figure. The guy'd gone crazy. He couldn't do that to me. For this, for humiliating me like that, I was really going to rub his nose in some dirt. Now he was really going to pay. I'd get ten grand out of him, or else. From now on I'd bleed him dry. But it was late afternoon before I got into his office to see him. By then he was pretty drunk. A kind of controlled drunk, so that he could still talk all right, and sit fairly straight in his chair. But he was loaded, no question, in spite of that.

He didn't even give me a chance. "Whatever you're going to say, skip it," he told me right off. "The honeymoon is over, Van. You have no more hold on me."

I got so mad I felt as though I was swelling, like a puff adder. My collar got too tight. "I haven't, huh?" I said.

"No, Van." He showed his teeth in a ghastly grin. "I moved it. It isn't where you saw me put it, any more. I put it where nobody'll ever find it. Never. So now what can you prove?"

It took me a moment to get it through my head. I said: "I can still go to the cops."

"Sure," he said. "And they'll go up there and find nothing, and slap you around for bothering them."

"Wait a minute. You couldn't have moved her. She's been there a month. She'd have been a mess."

He looked for a moment as though he was going to throw up. Then he got control, and said: "She was. Don't let's talk about it any more, Van. It's all over."

"You're bluffing!" I shouted it at him. "What do you think I am, a chump? There wouldn't be enough left of her to move."

"Okay," he said. "Have it your way. Now get out, before I call someone to throw you out."

I went back to the mail room but I kept thinking about it and the more I thought the more I knew he wasn't bluffing. Yet he *couldn't* have done what he said. I had to find out. I borrowed Joe's car again that night and drove up there. Along that same dark, dirt road, to the same spot. It gave me the creeps a little. I hadn't brought a flashlight and in the dark it took me a little time to find the clearing. But I found it. The only thing was, he was right; he hadn't been bluffing. The shallow grave was still there but it was all dug up. It was empty. She was gone.

"I'll be damned," I said, out loud.

"Yeah," someone said, and I whirled around to stare into the blinding beam of three flashlights. Three flashlights held by cops.

They took me back into the city and I told the cops the whole story. I had to. They thought I'd killed Vera, buried her out there, just as Harry Owen had first said that they would. They'd gotten an anonymous phone tip about the corpse and where it was buried, earlier in the day. They'd gone out and dug it up. The same tip told them to watch me.

I told them, of course, that their phone tip had been Harry Owen. They said they questioned him, after that, investigated him. He denied knowing anything about any of it. Apparently, as he had said, they weren't able to dig up any connection between him and Vera. They couldn't find anybody who'd ever seen them together, or knew they were seeing each other. They'd been circumspect, all right. He was clean. I wasn't, as far as the cops were concerned.

I knew what had happened. I'd pushed him too far. He'd finally decided to take a chance on winding the whole thing up, getting rid of me, by putting the cops on me. It hadn't been much of a chance. He'd realized that the police couldn't see anybody but me. It was cut and dried. They wouldn't investigate him, too much, Harry Owen figured. And he was right.

I couldn't talk the cops out of it and my lawyer couldn't convince the jury, either. After the trial he told me that he'd heard Harry Owen was drinking himself to death, had wound up in the Alky ward a couple of times, already. A lot of good that did me.

The stupid part about the whole thing, the Police lab worked on the remains. And like I'd heard it happens sometimes, Vera may have had all the symptoms, but according to those lab boys, it must have been something else, because they said she wasn't that way at all.

The Choice
Richard Deming

June 1954

The thing I want to get across is that I'm an honest man. In all my years of public service I've never accepted a dishonest cent.

In most other respects too I think I'm what society calls a "good citizen." I'm a kind father and a good husband. I'm active in church and community affairs. And even beyond that, I've devoted my whole life to public service.

At the moment I serve as district attorney of St. Michael County.

In case my stressing of my respectability gives you the idea I am building up to confessing some crime, I'd better explain that I'm not. I don't want to create a false impression. I merely have a choice to make.

No matter how I choose I'll remain a solid and respected citizen. If I choose one way, I can look forward to spending the rest of my life pleasantly but unexcitingly in private law practice, probably at a better income than my salary as district attorney. If I choose the other way, almost certainly I will be my state's next governor and possibly, though I admit improbably, even end my political career in the White House.

The only way I can explain my position is to say I drifted into it. Each compromise with my moral precepts seemed so small at the time, and the consequences of not compromising seemed so drastic, even now when I look back I can't honestly blame myself.

I can't really blame the System either, for that would merely be blaming all humanity.

My first contact with what I have come to think of as the "System" was over the Max Bloom case, when I was a green young assistant district attorney. I was twenty-six at the time, and the junior of eight assistants.

Max Bloom was a bookie, and there was nothing exceptional about the case. Two officers had raided his bookshop, caught Max in the act of accepting bets and placed him under arrest. Since there seemed to be no possible defense, I contemplated a single appearance in court, where the defendant undoubtedly would plead guilty and accept the usual fine.

Instead, Big Joey Martin dropped in to see me.

I knew who Big Joey was, though I had never before met him. He was political boss of the Sixth and Seventh Wards, and also reputed to have some sort of connection with organized gambling. He was a huge man, at least six feet four and weighing probably two hundred and seventy pounds. Some of this was muscle, but a good deal of it was plain fat.

He came into my cubbyhole office without knocking, carefully lowered himself into a chair, squirmed until he was comfortable and began fanning himself with his hat.

"You George Kenneday?" he asked when these preliminaries were over.

I nodded.

"I guess you know who I am."

I nodded again. "Joey Martin."

For a moment or two the fat man merely fanned himself with his hat. Then he said, "They tell me you got the prosecution against Maxie Bloom."

I nodded for the third time.

"Somebody slipped up. It ain't Maxie's turn for two more months, and he's sorer than hell about losing two weeks' business. I tried to tell him I'd get his next tumble postponed two months overtime, but I can't talk no sense into his head. He's kind of a psycho, you know. I'm afraid he'll blow his lid in court and start yammering to the judge about getting his protection money back. So I think we better work out a dismissal or something."

I looked at the man with my mouth open. "Are you asking me to drop charges against a lawbreaker?"

"A lawbreaker?" Joey Martin repeated in a surprised tone. "Maxie's a bookie, not no criminal." He eyed me narrowly, then said, "I ain't asking you nothing if you're going to get horsey about it. I guess I just took it for granted you knew the setup. Forget I bothered you."

Heaving himself to his feet, he nodded indifferently and ambled out of my office. And I was so flabbergasted by the whole performance, I just sat there open-mouthed and watched him go.

Fifteen minutes later I was called into the office of First Assistant District Attorney Clark Gleason.

"How are you, George?" Gleason said in a friendly voice, waving me to a chair. "Beginning to get the feel of things?"

I told him I was getting along fine.

"Reason I called you in, George, I'm taking over the Max Bloom case myself. Mind dropping the folder next time you pass my office?"

Carefully I folded my hands in my lap. "Has Joey Martin been to see you, Mr. Gleason?"

"Well, yes. As a matter of fact, he just left."

"I see. Mr. Gleason, only a few minutes ago Joey Martin practically ordered me to get Bloom's charge dismissed. He said something about protection money and that Bloom's arrest had been a mistake in timing on the part of the police. When I started to jump him, he seemed more surprised than alarmed, and walked out. Now I learn he's been to see you, and you're taking over Bloom's case. I think I'm entitled to an explanation."

Gleason examined me thoughtfully for a long time before answering. Eventually he asked, "Why do you think I'm taking over the case?"

I said with a mixture of caution and belligerence, "I must be mistaken, Mr. Gleason, but on the surface it looks as though this office takes orders from a two-bit racketeer."

Gleason's smile was rueful, but it didn't contain any anger. "This office doesn't take orders from anyone, George. But sometimes we have to do political favors. Do you know who Joey Martin is?"

"Sure. A professional gambler."

"A little more than that George. Joey is the boy who delivers the votes down in the Sixth and Seventh Wards. All the votes. Election after election he turns out a solid majority for the party. In return he occasionally asks a small favor. Never much of a favor and never very often. It's just practical politics to go along when he asks."

"Even if you have to violate your oath of office?"

"Oh, for cripes sake, George," Gleason said impatiently. "Max Bloom isn't a murderer or bank robber. Everybody knows bookshops are tolerated in St. Michael and what raids are made are only token raids. Two weeks after his trial Max would be back in business in the same spot even if we got a conviction."

I said, "What you're saying in effect is that this office knows the police deliberately protect illegal bookshops. Even that they accept protection money for it. Yet we condone it because it wouldn't be practical politics to crack down. Why doesn't the D.A. swear out warrants for everybody concerned, including a few crooked cops?"

"Because next election there would be a new district attorney. If you intend to follow a political career, George, now is as good a time as any to learn the hard facts of political life. We're aware that the police to some extent connive with Joey and his kind, and we don't approve of it. But attempting to stop it would be tilting at windmills. No one in this office has any direct connection with men like Joey and no one receives any payoff. But as a matter of practical politics we sometimes have to rub the backs of such men, because it's the votes controlled by ward leaders like Joey Martin that keep our party in power. Call it a violation of public trust if you want, but what's the alternative? Kicking Joey out of the office and having two wards refuse to back John Doud for D.A. in the next primary?"

"Your job and mine aren't elective," I said. "We're appointed."

"By the D.A.," Gleason agreed. "Whose job is elective. And you're only kidding yourself if you think your appointment was entirely on merit. Weren't you sponsored by someone?"

Reluctantly I admitted, "My Uncle Crosby is an alderman."

When I left Gleason's office there was no question in my mind that the whole system was wrong in spite of the first assistant D.A.'s glib argument about practical politics. But I couldn't think of anywhere to go with a complaint. It would have been silly to go to the police, who seemed to be a party to the arrangement. And just as silly to expect action from the D.A. or any other elected official who owed allegiance to the System.

In the end I did nothing, justifying myself by deciding I would have taken some kind of action if I had been asked to get Max Bloom a dismissal myself. But since the case had been taken out of my hands, there really wasn't any action I could take.

Looking back, I still can't see anything I could have done. I have come to regard the Max Bloom case as the first compromise with my principles, but in a way it wasn't a compromise at all. At least not in an active sense. All I actually did was accept a situation about which I could do nothing. How many sincerely honest men in the same position would have done anything else?

Would you have?

It was nearly four years before I was called upon to make the next big compromise, though in the meantime I found myself making more and more small ones. Even now I can't put my finger on any one point of my career and say, "Here is where I should have resisted," because it was a gradual process. The mere mental act of accepting the System as a necessary evil of politics opened the way for greater and greater departures from what I knew to be right.

Yet if I had the chance to live this period over, I know my reactions would be the same. There was no fighting the System. Either you conformed, or you retired to private life. And since the party had begun to regard me as a bright young man with a political future, I conformed.

My growing influence in local party affairs was largely the result of the reputation I was gaining as a prosecutor. Actually this reputation was based almost entirely on a single murder case which the papers seemed to think I handled with some brilliance, but the party didn't care about that. What counted was that I had the public's confidence. As a result when Clark Gleason resigned to accept a job in the State's Attorney's office, I was appointed first assistant district attorney in his place.

During this four years I learned a lot about how the System operated. For the most part what Clark Gleason had told me was quite true. Most elected officials were honest men who had no direct connection with the underworld-controlled political machine which maintained them in office. Yet the influence of ward leaders such as Joey Martin was tremendous. In return for the votes necessary to elect them, officials usually found it expedient to wink at the illegal side activities of Joey and his kind, and occasionally grant favors which came close to criminal conspiracy.

At the time I was appointed first assistant district attorney I hadn't held, or even run for, any elective office, but I was aware of hints within the party that I might make a good district attorney when old John Doud finally decided to retire. I kept these hints alive by actively engaging in party affairs, which brought me in frequent contact with local political bosses.

With an eye on my future, I deliberately cultivated friendly relations with these men, with the result that I was asked for a lot of minor favors. For example, Willie Tamm, president of the Dock Workers' Local and also party leader of the three wards in the dock area, routinely mailed me his traffic tickets to have fixed.

Many similar minor favors were asked of me, but the one big favor I performed was done tacitly without being mentioned by anyone. This was a passive favor. It was simply closing my eyes to the rackets going on in the districts run by the men who controlled the votes.

That is, this was my one big favor prior to the evening Timothy Grange called at my house.

Tim Grange ranked higher both politically and in the underworld than Big Joey Martin. He owned the wire service which brought horse race results into town from all over the country, and his business was leasing this service to individual bookies. He also controlled the party organization for the entire East Side, including the two wards run by Joey Martin.

Grange was one of the men whose friendship I had been deliberately cultivating, but aside from passing time with him at a number of political rallies, we hadn't had much contact prior to the Friday evening he unexpectedly showed up at my house.

He was a tall, slim man in his late forties with iron-gray hair. He arrived about nine o'clock, after both the children were in bed. When he rather nervously refused Mary's offer of a drink with a statement that he had urgent business with me, she went into another room and left us alone in the front room. Grange stated his business at once.

"My kid's in a jam, George. Tim Junior. He's killed a man."

The abruptness of it startled me. "My God!" I said. "Murder?"

He shook his head in nervous impatience. "A traffic accident. He ran over a pedestrian at Fourth and Locust about an hour ago. An old man named Abraham Swartz. I just checked with City Hospital, and the man's dead."

"Oh," I said, partially relieved that it wasn't as serious as I first thought. "Was it Tim's fault?"

Grange paced up and down a moment before answering. Then he said, "He says he wasn't speeding. At least not much. He claims he was going about thirty-five in a thirty-mile zone when this Swartz suddenly stepped from the curb right in front of him."

"I see. Then what are you upset about? It's unfortunate, but those things . . ."

"He didn't stop," George interrupted. "He raced home and hid the car in the garage. Fortunately I happened to be going out just as he came in, and when I saw how upset he was, I forced the story out of him." He paused, then added in a flat voice, "He was drunk."

For a moment I just looked at him. Then I walked over to stare angrily out the window. When I turned again, I said, "At the risk of hurting your feelings, Grange, young Tim is a damned fool."

"I knew that before I came, George. The kid panicked. What's he up against?"

"Manslaughter, probably," I said bluntly. "The combination of hit-and-run and drunken driving almost automatically means a manslaughter charge, no matter whose fault the accident was."

"He's not drunk now. I threw him in a cold shower, and when I left I had my wife pouring black coffee in him."

I said, "The police make a blood test for alcohol content. It's routine in hit-and-run cases. Even if you have him walking straight and talking coherently, they'll be able to judge how drunk he was at the time of the accident."

"Suppose they didn't find him till tomorrow?"

I looked at him. "He can't wait till tomorrow. He'll have to turn himself in at once. If he turns in voluntarily, he may just possibly scrape out of the manslaughter charge. But it's already too late for him to get out of the hit-and-run. The law requires any driver involved in an accident to stop immediately and identify himself either to the other party involved or to the police. The law allows the alternate procedure of reporting directly to the nearest police station, but young Tim didn't do that either. The kid is in a jam, and the longer he waits before turning in, the worse the jam is going to get."

"Suppose he reported to the station closest to Fourth and Locust now, George? It was only a little over an hour ago."

"It might as well be a year. The law says immediately."

"Couldn't the report be . . . set back a little?"

I said, "Are you asking me to get the police to falsify a report? This isn't like fixing a parking ticket. Manslaughter is a felony."

"But it's only technically manslaughter," Grange said in a reasonable tone. "If he'd stopped, he wouldn't be in any particular trouble. Manslaughter's kind of a tough rap just for getting panicky."

"Death is kind of a tough rap just for stepping off a curb."

"I'm not excusing the kid, George. But he *is* my kid. I know you're hounded for favors by every ward heeler in town, but I've never asked you for one before. I'll put it right on the line. Get my kid out of this and I'm your friend for life."

He didn't put it into words, but his tone meant I would have the solid backing of the entire East Side any time I wanted to run for any office at all. It also meant I could count on its solid opposition if I failed to help his son.

I think I would have thrown him out of the house if he had offered me money. Even if he had come right out in the open and used his political influence as a weapon, I think I might have turned him down. But he offered me nothing but his friendship, and let the rest dangle there by inference.

There wasn't any middle course I could take. I couldn't, like Pilate, wash my hands of the whole affair. For if I refused to help young Tim out of his jam, I was going to have to prosecute him.

I thought about the talk within the party about my replacing old John Doud when he finally got around to retiring, and realized that with Tim Grange behind me, I wouldn't have to wait for his retirement. I could have the job at the next election.

But not if I refused Timothy Grange. If I insisted on trying his son for manslaughter, from the moment of that decision I could forget all political ambition.

Going to the phone, I dialed the Fourth Street Precinct House, got hold of the night captain, who happened to owe me a favor, and arranged for the log book to show that Timothy Grange Jr. had reported there five minutes after the accident at Fourth and Locust and that he'd been checked and found cold sober.

Conspiracy to compound a felony? Of course it was. But you tell me what else I could have done.

In the nearly eight years that I have been district attorney of St. Michael County I've thought back on this incident often. From the standpoint of abstract justice I admit there is no defense for my action. I was pledged to uphold the law impartially, and in my own mind I know that if Tim Grange Jr. hadn't been the son of an influential politician, I would have prosecuted him for manslaughter.

Yet I can't blame myself for deciding as I did. Kicking the elder Grange out of my house would have accomplished nothing but ending my political career. It wouldn't have brought the dead man back to life.

I can't blame Timothy Grange Sr. for bringing pressure to save his son. What normal father wouldn't? I've decided that if anything is to blame, it's the bad luck which created an impossible situation.

Nevertheless I recognize my action as the first great compromise with my principles. I also recognize that once having made this major step, future compromises became easier and easier.

This was just as well for my peace of mind, for from the moment I was elected district attorney I found it necessary to make more and more compromises. But I was no longer under constant pressure to perform minor favors. This nuisance now fell to my new first assistant, a young man named Edmund Rowe, who as chief prosecutor for the county was in closer contact with both the police and those on the other side of the law than I was.

This was because the district attorney of a county including as large a metropolitan area as St. Michael is a policy maker rather than a courtroom lawyer. He has too many administrative duties to handle prosecutions personally. His concern is crime in a general sense. Specific crimes are the business of his assistants, and I had eight to relieve me of this responsibility. Even important cases were tried by Edmund Rowe.

The compromises I was now forced to make came from my policy-making power. And this power was considerable.

At any time after I assumed office I could have eliminated any racket I chose from St. Michael simply by issuing an order to the police. The police wouldn't have liked it, but even though they were to some extent in partnership with the racketeers, they wouldn't have dared to refuse cooperation. The constant dread of any crooked cop is a shake-up in the police department, and the moment a crusading district attorney turns on the heat, every cop, even on a crooked force, becomes a crusader too.

I was aware of my power before I ever assumed office, and I gave a lot of thought to just how I was going to use it. If I wanted to conduct a crusade, I had four years to do it and nothing but the next election could put me out of office. Undoubtedly I could clean up the city and keep it clean during that four years.

But just as undoubtedly I would never again be my party's candidate for any office whatever.

The alternative to fighting crime as I was sworn to do was no longer as simple as it had been when I was merely first assistant district attorney. Then I had been forced to close my eyes to many of the things going on around me, but my cooperation with the underworld had been merely passive. My role had been that of chief public prosecutor, and I lacked the policy-making power of the district attorney.

But now my cooperation had to become active if I was going to cooperate at all. As D.A. it was not enough merely to ignore the rackets controlled by local political bosses. I was now in a spot where I either had to fight racketeering or help cover it up.

For example I often met with volunteer citizens' groups formed to combat organized crime. Sporadically such groups rise in every metropolitan community, and since they usually represent segments of the independent group, they can't just be brushed aside. It's only practical politics to avoid arousing unnecessary resentment in representatives of the Chamber of Commerce, Rotary International and other business groups out of which citizens' committees arise.

Consequently it was necessary to go through the motions of running cleanup drives against gambling, vice and other rackets whenever such a group offered its services. I had a standard procedure for handling such groups.

First I would make a public declaration of war against racketeers. Next my office and the police jointly would release to the papers that citywide raids had taken place and large numbers of arrests had been made. Actually probably a half dozen bookies and an equal number of house madams, all thoughtfully tipped off in advance of the raids, would be dragged in and booked. But since about six cases in addition to the routine parade of drunks and traffic violators was all police court could handle in one day, this was enough to keep a steady stream going before the judge for at least two days. Any of the citizens' groups interested enough to follow up as far as the courtroom usually tired after one day of watching and went away satisfied that justice was being done.

The newspapers, too, occasionally ran editorial campaigns against organized crime in St. Michael, and again it would be necessary to simulate ruthless war against racketeers. In either event, I became so adept, I actually began to gain something of a reputation as a crusading district attorney.

Never once did Timothy Grange or any other racketeer openly ask for this sort of protection. And never once during my entire political career was I ever on the payroll of any racketeer. I cooperated solely to weld a solid voting force behind me.

I succeeded too. When I was elected for my second term as district attorney, I got the most overwhelming majority in the history of St. Michael politics. And that thumping majority put me in line for at least consideration as the party's gubernatorial candidate in the following election.

My hope was only for consideration up to the time Tony Manetti and Arnold Price got interested in me. It is one thing to have the solid political support of a single county, and a different proposition to get an entire state behind you. But after Tim Grange brought Manetti and Price to see me, I began to think of my nomination for governor as almost a certainty. Which, in our one-party state, is the same as election.

This meeting, like my previous one with Grange, took place at my home instead of at my office. Both men were from out of state, Tony Manetti from New York and Arnold Price from Chicago, but they both represented the same organization.

Their organization was the national crime syndicate.

Tony Manetti was a squat, swarthy man with heavy features and kinky, close-cropped hair which fitted his head like a skullcap. Arnold Price was tall and lean and slow moving, with gaunt features and the homespun manner of a backwoods farmer.

After the four of us were settled with drinks in the front room and Mary had gone off to another part of the house, Grange opened the conversation.

"I guess you know who Mr. Manetti and Mr. Price are, George," he said. "I been telling them about you, and they thought maybe we ought to have a little political conference." He laughed genially. "You know. Smoke-filled rooms and all that stuff."

Neither man smiled at the joke. Noncommitally I said, "I see."

"As you probably know," Grange went on, "the boys here have been quietly building a political organization throughout the state. Now they're looking around for a candidate to back for governor."

I felt my heart skip a beat. Here, possibly, was the one big break of my career. The backing of a new, but rapidly growing, statewide political machine.

I wasn't for a moment under the impression that syndicate interference in state politics would be a good thing for our state. But neither was I starry-eyed enough to believe anything I did could stop the syndicate's growth. I knew all about what was going on in the state politically, and had accepted it as an undesirable but inevitable development.

Before the arrival of Tony Manetti and Arnold Price in our midst, state politics had been far from clean, but there was little centralization. The two big-city machines, St. Michael's and Tailor City's across the state, were powerful but autonomous units. Numerous smaller but equally autonomous machines ran things in the lesser communities and the rural areas. Though they were all the same party, no one unit was strong enough to dictate statewide policy. State conventions were matters of give and take, with the small rural machines often forming combines strong enough to force through platforms and slates of candidates opposed by both big-city machines.

The syndicate was attempting to weld these divergent groups into a solid, statewide organization whose policy could be controlled from the top. It was common knowledge to the politically informed that Manetti and Price had been spreading huge sums in the form of campaign contributions in the rural areas. It was not so well known that Tailor City had joined forces with the rising new machine, but I happened to be one of those who knew it. And now the appearance at my home of the two men with one of St. Michael's strongest political bosses could only mean that the local machine was falling in line with the rest.

It also meant the syndicate undoubtedly would be powerful enough by the time of the next state convention to put into the governor's mansion the candidate of its choice.

All these thoughts skipped through my mind while Grange was talking. And while they were passing through my mind, I dispassionately considered just what the syndicate was.

It is, as anyone who followed the televised congressional investigation of crime knows, a nationwide federation of professional gamblers, procurers, dope peddlers and racketeers. No decent citizen could feel anything but abhorrence for all that Manetti and Price stood for.

On the other hand my refusal to deal with the syndicate would merely transfer its interest to some other candidate who was willing to accept its backing. And if it was inevitable that a syndicate-backed governor was going to administer our state, I might as well be it.

I asked, "What does this backing involve?"

Tony Manetti spoke in a slurred voice which still contained a trace of Sicilian accent. "We're willing to drop two hundred grand into the campaign kitty."

The amount startled me, for the dark man mouthed it as casually as I would mention a dime.

I said, "How did you happen to pick me?"

"I sold them," Grange said. "You're a natural. Who else in the state can pull in the independent vote and at the same time draw machine backing? With the rubes you have a reputation as a crusader. To the smart boys you have a reputation for . . . cooperation. How could we lose?"

I asked, "What sort of cooperation would be expected of me?"

Arnold Price drawled, "Nothing much, Kenneday. We might ask for a few appointments. The police commissioners of St. Michael and Tailor City, for instance."

"I see," I said dryly.

I toyed with the thought of refusing point blank, as my ability to compromise didn't extend to turning the state over to a gang of murderers. But I only toyed with it. The next instant I thought of a number of justifications for accepting syndicate backing.

The first was the argument that if I refused, some other candidate was bound to accept and the state would be no better off than if I accepted. The second was that any promises I made to a gang of killers I was not: morally bound to keep. I told myself I could never get into the governor's mansion without syndicate backing, but once there I could stop being a politician and start being a statesman. I decided I would administer the state government to the best of my ability if I managed to get elected, even if it meant being kicked out of office after four years.

I said, "I would appreciate your backing for the governorship very much, gentlemen. And you won't find me ungrateful."

After the three men left I felt rather proud of myself. It pleased me to think Manetti and Price would go to great trouble and expense to put me in office, only to discover after election that they had made the mistake of backing an honest man. Somehow the situation seemed to counterbalance all the moral compromises I had made in the past in order to gain votes.

But I might have known syndicate representatives wouldn't be naive enough to be satisfied with mere verbal assurance that I'd cooperate after election. I should have been prepared for the next move. My only excuse for being caught by surprise is that I underestimated Manetti and Price.

In the month since my meeting with Tim Grange and the two syndicate men, political forces have been whipped into line, and it's now a practical certainty my nomination for governor will pass on the first ballot at the state convention. Meantime, I still have my job as district attorney to perform.

I wish I could resign tomorrow, for finally I am confronted with a decision for which I can find no self-justification by calling it practical politics.

I've known all along, of course, that the syndicate's political maneuvering is merely a means to an end, and the end is opening wide the whole state to gambling, vice, narcotics and every other illegal racket into which it can get its fingers. Some local opposition by racketeers who preferred to remain independent was inevitable, and the syndicate's solution to such opposition is murder.

There's already been one gang killing in St. Michael County. My old friend, Big Joey Martin, who was my first contact with the System. The underworld rumor is that Big Joey refused to throw in with the syndicate, and his death was a warning to others who might be slow about falling in line.

It's only a rumor though. There is no evidence pointing at anyone, which might be expected in a murder arranged by so efficient an organization. We have a body, three .45 calibre slugs from a gun which is probably at the bottom of the river, and nothing else but the rumor.

But even though I haven't enough evidence to justify an arrest, I know why Big Joey died. It's been bad enough to carry that knowledge in my mind, but my present situation is impossible.

An hour ago I got a phone call from Tony Manetti, who asked a small favor. The publicity over Big Joey Martin's killing was a bad thing only six months before election, he said, and it would be smart to avoid any such future publicity. He wanted to know how well I knew the coroner.

When I told him Howard Jordan was a personal friend of mine, he said arrangements had been made with Jordan to find accident the cause of death in the case of Willie Tamm, president of the Dock Workers' Local. There was the matter of paying the coroner a small fee for his trouble, however, Manetti went on, and he wondered if I would be willing to relay this fee on if he had it dropped by my office.

The meaning behind his words was unmistakable. The syndicate is not satisfied with my verbal promise to cooperate. It wants me involved beyond backing out in the compounding of a murder.

For you see, Willie Tamm is not yet dead.

Manetti gave me one hour to think things over and call him back. But, in the face of the horror of the situation, I can hardly think.

The insidiousness of the thing is appalling. If I refuse, I'm certain Willie Tamm will not die, for Manetti could hardly afford to go ahead with a murder he'd discussed with an uncooperative district attorney. At the same time, he hasn't run any risk, since I can hardly charge him with a crime which remains uncommitted.

But if I refuse to cooperate, I know my hope for the governorship is gone forever. Without putting it into actual words, Manetti has served notice that I'll become governor on the syndicate's terms, or not at all. Almost certainly, arrangements have been made with Coroner Jordan for some kind of deposition confessing I paid him to cover up a murder. A deposition which they'll keep as a secret weapon to force my future cooperation.

I wonder how huge a sum the syndicate had to pay Jordan to get him to risk his own neck.

The thing which makes it impossible is that I'm an honest man. My moral precepts are probably as high as those of any other member who attends my church. Never in my life have I accepted a penny of dishonest money. My worst sin has been accepting the compromises any practical politician must make if he expects to stay in public life.

How could I possibly have drifted into such an untenable position? Obviously I can't be party to a deliberate murder.

On the other hand, until an hour ago the governorship was right within my grasp.

How can I turn it loose now?

Confession
John M. Sitan

July 1954

John Egan adjusted the rifle's telescopic sight again. It was quite easy to pick out the circle of light from the single lamp over the theatrical announcement plaque. The spot was a good target point. It was ten minutes after eleven and no one was about on the apartment house roof. He had counted eight persons crossing the circle of light. They had all been men. The ninth person was a woman. The white shoes and dress under a dark coat indicated she was a nurse. There was a young couple walking behind her. A policeman turned the corner.

When the nurse reached the circle of light her head flew apart.

John Egan detached the stock of his gun and fitted the barrel portion and the stock into a trumpet case that had been rebuilt to accommodate them. When he looked again to the street below the young couple and the policeman were beside the fallen nurse. John settled to watch; his German Army sniper rifle had a silencer and there had been no sound excepting a dull thud when he fired.

The policeman went to the corner and a police call-box. When he came back, John picked up his trumpet case and backed from the building edge. As he had been watching the scene below his hands had continuously opened and closed, the fingernails digging into the palms of his hands. Now that he was out of sight of anyone in the street he began running from roof to roof until he reached a building on the other side of the block. He let himself through a roof doorway and went quickly but quietly down the stairs until he was on the street. A tight smile of satisfaction was on his face.

The smile was still there when he got back to his two-room apartment. He put the trumpet case on the single bed in his bedroom and opened it. It took him half an hour to clean and oil the rifle. He then put the rifle in its trumpet case and put the case at the back of his closet. He took a black leather-covered notebook from his desk and made an entry. It took him twenty minutes of studied writing and then he put the notebook away. A moment later he went down the hall to the bathroom and took a hot bath and shower. When he returned he went to bed and slept very soundly.

The death of the nurse—her name was Edith Scarf—occupied the front page of the daily newspapers the next day. John Egan bought a newspaper on his way to work. When he saw the name of the nurse he wrote it down in a small wallet notebook and threw the newspaper away. The name was to be added to his records. He did not hear any more about the murder, as he did not have a radio in his apartment and never bought a newspaper unless he needed a name from it. He usually found what he wanted on the front page.

At work John Egan did not hear anything about the murder. The factory was noisy, which wasn't conducive to conversation while working. He worked for a company that made paper containers of all sorts. He had been there six weeks. It was his job to collect all the paper scrap and bale it in a giant baling machine. The scrap was sent back to the pulp mill for reprocessing.

When he had finished work John Egan went to the library, which he visited from two to three times a week. This time he returned two biographies he had been reading of Abraham Lincoln and checked out yet another biography of Lincoln. It would take him two days to finish reading it. His reading speed was good and he could scan a printed page quickly with full understanding. He had read biographies on Edison, Ford, Einstein, the great U. S. presidents and a host of other famous men. He kept a list of famous names (they were all men) and of the material he had read about each of them. His list was of quite formidable length. He was twenty-eight years old and had been keeping the list since he was twenty-two years old. He had not seen his parents since he was seventeen when he had run away from his father's house where his mother had left him when she divorced his father. He had always lived alone, except for a three-year interruption of Army service, and liked living alone. He had never gone out on dates with girls. He did not like girls.

Saturday afternoon John Egan went to the park. He spent the day there walking its many twisting pathways. Finally he settled on a grassy knoll that was lightly wooded but allowed unbroken vision of several pathways and of a children's playfield. He spent nearly an hour judging distances, and finally paced from his position to several points on the pathways. He decided at last on the juncture of three meeting pathways. From the knoll it took him four minutes of walking at a reasonable pace to reach the edge of the park. There he could catch any one of a number of busses that arrived and departed every few minutes.

Sunday at eleven o'clock John Egan walked to the grassy knoll in the park carrying his trumpet case. He sat down and then lay on his back for awhile and let himself relax completely. When almost an hour had passed he sat up and looked around to see that he was alone on the knoll. He opened his trumpet case and fitted together the German sniper rifle. It took a moment to adjust the sight on the junction of the three pathways. A number of people passed and he did nothing. He sighted on the junction again when he saw a woman and a little girl coming along. The girl was about five years old and wore a pink frilly dress. She was skipping a little ahead of the woman when she reached the junction. At that moment John Egan squeezed the trigger of his rifle. He watched the convulsive sideways jerk as the bullet thudded home. At his distance it appeared as if the child had stumbled. John did not look back until he had broken the sniper rifle down and put it in the trumpet case. When he did look back the woman was on her knees and screaming.

Two minutes later John was on the main pathway leading from the park. He reached the bus stop just as a bus arrived and got aboard. He dozed on the bus until it reached the business section of town and got off. He went to a motion picture theatre that had a double bill featuring two comedies, and enjoyed himself hugely. His laugh was high-pitched and piercing. It was late in the afternoon before he returned to his room. He bought a late edition newspaper on the corner before he went up to his room.

In his room John Egan cleaned his rifle lovingly and put it away. Then he opened the newspaper and found the name he wanted on the front page. The little girl's name was Kathy Lewis. It took John only half an hour to make the entries in his black leather notebook. After that he applied his attention to a sheaf of papers that were typewritten double-space from edge to edge and contained numerous penciled marginal notes and corrections in the body of the material. He pulled a portable typewriter from under his bed and rolled a sheet of paper into the machine. He worked on the typewriter for an hour and a half. He spent another half-hour working over what he had written, making additions and deletions. When he finished he again put the typewriter under his bed and the sheaf of papers back in their drawer. Before going to sleep he read some of the biography of Lincoln that he had on the stand beside his bed.

John Egan went to work as usual the next day. At noon he talked to his boss, who sent him to the main office. In the main office a secretary had him sign a company voucher. Before quitting work that evening he received a check from the cashier's window. It was a check for payment of his services in full. On the way to his apartment he stopped at the library and returned two books he had out on a library card.

When he left his room later he carried only a good-sized suitcase, his portable typewriter and his trumpet case. He stopped at the landlord's door and rapped. The week's rent he owed was seventeen dollars. A taxi was waiting at the entrance and took him to the railroad station. Five minutes later he had bought a ticket for Seattle, Washington. After a half hour's waiting he boarded a coach car of the train. It was ten o'clock, and he made himself comfortable in his seat. Before he put the portable typewriter case above him in the luggage rack he opened it. There was a small space above the typewriter in the case. John had packed his black leather notebook there. He now opened the notebook and thumbed through it. The notebook was divided into four sections, each headed with the name of a different city. San Diego, Los Angeles, San Francisco and Portland. Turning a page he started a new section—S . . . E . . . A . . . T . . . T . . . L . . . E—he wrote the city's name carefully. The notebook was repacked and John dozing as the lights of the Portland, Oregon, disappeared behind the train.

It was early morning when John Egan arrived in Seattle. Outside the train station he caught a cab and went to a hotel. In his hotel room he stripped down and took a hot bath. He soaked in the tub for some time. When he came out of the bathroom he towelled himself and looked at his watch on the bureau. He was thoughtful for a moment and then, making a decision, went over to the bed and pulled back the bedspread. He got into the bed nude and was asleep almost immediately. He had always been able to go to sleep quickly and easily.

It was close to noon when he woke up. He lay looking at the ceiling for awhile and then finally got up and dressed and opened his typewriter case. He spent some time in reading from his black leather notebook. It was one o'clock when he lay the notebook down. Hunger was beginning to bother him, as he hadn't eaten since the evening before. Before leaving the hotel room he took a heavy manila envelope from a secret pocket in the suitcase. In the envelope was nearly six hundred dollars. Money that he had saved from the numerous jobs he had had in the past six years. He nodded in satisfaction over the horde, and took three twenty dollar bills from the envelope and put them in his wallet. On the way downstairs to a restaurant he stopped at the hotel's desk and paid for his hotel room for two weeks.

After eating he walked around the city streets for awhile and then returned to his hotel room. He bought a daily newspaper in the hotel lobby but did not read it when he got to his room. On his walk about town he had bought a ream of typewriting paper and an envelope of carbon paper. He worked until very late at night over the sheaf of papers that bore many alterations and corrections. At two o'clock in the morning he stopped working. Before he went to bed he read the theatre section of the paper. When he finally got into bed he fell asleep immediately and slept soundly.

John Egan awoke at ten the next morning and went down for breakfast. When he returned to his room he went back to work on the sheaf of papers. He worked on them the remainder of the day and only paused to go out for a late dinner. The next day and the three following were spent on the growing sheaf of papers. He now had a respectable manuscript of over seventy thousand words. At last he was satisfied and began reading the manuscript over to make more corrections. The title he had affixed to the first page was: "The Autobiography of John Stevenson Egan."

It took John Egan a week of constant and careful work to complete the final copy of the autobiography he had written. He had one carbon copy. The manuscript was finished up to the last chapter. It was early evening when he finished the final copy of the manuscript up to that point. He went out for dinner and, as usual, brought back with him the evening paper he had been buying every day. He again read only the theatrical section. This time he took particular notice of a movie that was going to premiere in Seattle in two days' time. That evening he went to bed early. He needed the rest that the extra hours would afford him.

The next day John Egan located the theatre he wanted to find. It was on a corner facing a busy intersection. The three facing corners housed two department stores and a jewelry store with the floors above it rented out to doctors and lawyers. He found that he could reach the roof of the building housing the jewelry store quite easily. The surrounding buildings were all taller than the one he had picked. When he returned to the intersection at eight o'clock that night he was pleased to see that only one or two of the windows of the overshadowing buildings were lighted. When he had made certain of the hour the building's doors were locked he returned to his hotel room.

The next day John Egan hired a car for the day and took a long drive around Seattle's Lake Washington. He stopped along the shore and sat looking out over the water. It was a bright sunny day and many small sailboats were on the lake. He returned to his hotel room at six o'clock and opened up his trumpet case. It was the first time he had opened the case since his arrival in Seattle. He spent an hour in cleaning and oiling the rifle. When he had finished he took a carton of cartridges from his suitcase and poured ten shells on the bureau top. He lined the shells up on their flat ends and looked at them for a moment. Then he knocked the first one down which, in turn, upset the remaining nine in a chain reaction. He picked the shells up one by one and put them in a spring clip. He put the clip in the trumpet case with the rifle. When he finished he looked at his watch. He still had an hour before the building housing the jewelry store closed. He spent the hour in musing over his notebook. He had used the notebook extensively in writing the last part of his autobiography. The notebook had ninety name-entries in it. The greatest number of names came under the heading of Los Angeles. When it was twenty minutes to the closing of the jewelry store building he left his room. He entered the building without being noticed. Instead of using the elevator he walked up the stairs. When he reached the roof he closed the door quickly, stood near the closed door for a moment, and looked at the facing buildings overlooking the roof. There were no lighted windows excepting those of a stairwell. No one was on the stairwell.

It took John only a moment to set up his sniper rifle and telescopic sight. When he looked over the building edge he faced the theatre across the way. It was as it had been when he had entered the building. A long line of people snaked for about a hundred yards along the sidewalk. This was the premiered picture. John Egan sighted through his telescopic sight and made another adjustment. When he began firing he moved methodically from target to target and emptied the clip in less than a minute. The first target was the woman driver of a car waiting for a stop light. The car moved into the intersection and was smashed by two other cars . . . each going in opposite directions. John moved to the girl dispensing tickets in the glass booth of the theatre. The glass shattered as the girl was struck in the throat. In swift order eight other women were shot down. In one case a bullet passed through the woman and smashed a plate glass window behind. The crowd was beginning to panic and shoved three persons onto the broken shards of glass. Events had moved so quickly that many people in the crowd had not reacted at all. John Egan did not pause to watch events developing below but hurriedly took the sniper rifle apart and packed it in the trumpet case. When he reached the street below women were screaming and the sound of approaching sirens wailed over the scene. A lone policeman was at the wrecks of the three cars in the intersection, trying to bring some sort of order to the scene. When John rounded a corner away from the intersection a police car had arrived.

In his room John cleaned his rifle. He fondled it lovingly for a moment. He had long ago had his name engraved on the barrel. After he had put the rifle in its case he sat for a moment in silence. Finally he smiled. He sat for a moment longer and then got ready for bed. He fell asleep immediately after climbing between the blankets.

The next morning John Egan was up early and down to the hotel lobby. He went to the cigar stand and bought a paper. The front page was alive with bold-face print, pictures and dark headlines. Up in his room he read the paper with care. His notebook was to one side of him and every now and then he jotted a name and some data down. There were twelve names in the paper of those who had died. Eleven were women and one was a man who had been shoved into the broken window and bled to death. One woman had died in the accident in the middle of the intersection. She had suffered from a bad heart condition. The remaining ten had all died instantly from John Egan's well-placed bullets.

When he had completed the notes in his notebook he rolled a fresh sheet of paper into the typewriter and began typing. As he composed he consulted his notebook frequently. He was working on the last chapter of his autobiography.

It was late afternoon before John had a draft that satisfied him. Then he began a final copy and made a carbon copy. It was ten o'clock when he finished. He then typed out a short letter. The letter was to the publishing company he was sending his manuscript to.

Dear Sirs:

I am a murderer. I have killed one hundred women and children directly and several persons indirectly. This is not a hoax. You will see the truth of my statements when you read this autobiography I intend you to publish. When you receive this manuscript I will be in the hands of the Seattle, Washington, police. You will be readily able to check the validity of my statements.

Yours truly,

John Stevenson Egan

When he had typed the letter he enclosed it with the manuscript and addressed the package. He went to bed and slept. His sleep was sound and he did not dream.

In the morning John Egan got up early and went downstairs for breakfast. When he was again back in his room he rolled a piece of paper into the typewriter and started composing what he titled "Press Statement." At noon he went to the Post Office and sent his manuscript to the publishing house, airmail express. He finished his "Press Statement" at two o'clock. It took him an hour to pack his belongings nearly. He was careful to fold all his shirts and roll his socks. He wanted his things to be neat when they were unpacked. He put his suitcase and typewriter centered on the bed. He had made the bed up carefully. Taking his trumpet case, the carbon copy of his autobiography and his black leather notebook he left the room. At the police station he stepped into the press room and looked around; no one was there. He saw a bulletin board in a corner and, clearing the board, pinned his "Press Statement" in the center of the board. The papers he had removed from the bulletin board he straightened and left on a table.

PRESS STATEMENT

My name is John Stevenson Egan. I have shot and killed twenty-four children and seventy-six adults. I was further responsible for the death of two persons by heart failure, one person by crushing in an automobile accident and another who was shoved into a shattered plate glass window and bled to death. I used a German Army sniper rifle brought from Germany where I saw service with the U. S. Army during World War II. All the persons I have shot and killed with my rifle have been women.

My motive in this action is to insure the inclusion of my name in man's history and memory. Further details of my case can be found in the autobiography I have sent to the Bismark Publishing Company for publication. The police will have my notebook in which I have kept a record of the place, names and conditions under which I killed each person. Bullets fired from my rifle can be compared with those that undoubtedly have been recovered from the bodies of my victims.

I thank you gentlemen in advance for placing my name in newspapers and magazines across the country. You will find my story a sensational and unusual one. I will cooperate in any way with anyone wishing information about myself . . . serious biographers are especially welcomed. I am sure I will be a quite interesting and important subject for psychiatry journals. Few have their names remembered long after their death. I intend to be one of the few. I have made sure of it. My name will be remembered.
Signed,
John Stevenson Egan

The police sergeant was busy when John Egan came up to his desk. John wasn't noticed until he put the trumpet case, black leather notebook and manuscript on the sergeant's desk. The sergeant frowned and was about to speak when John Egan opened the trumpet case.

The Empty Fort
Basil Heatter

September 1954

There was the hot blue sea and the scrubbed white coral and on top of that the fort. There was sun-blasted brick spattered with bird droppings and an overgrown parade ground and the long, civil- war-type cannon that had rusted away without having been fired. The gun emplacements stared out at the sea like empty eye-sockets and the warm rain blew through it all and the sun nibbled the mortar away from the bricks. The roofs had crumbled away but the six-foot thick walls remained hunched and waiting for an enemy that had never come.

No one could remember now just why or how they had come to build it in that place that was dry as dust, where they had to bring the water in kegs from the mainland over two hundred miles away. In Key West you can hear about how the bricks were brought down from Boston in lighters and were six months traveling. And of how the men who went out to build the fort and to live there came from God knew where. And of how most of them died. The story is that for every brick there was a life. That would be an awful lot of lives but they might be about half right at that.

In the end they had to abandon it because of the yellow fever, and there it stands.

2.

I got to stop sleeping in the street, Cruze told himself. It's cold now. It's getting on to be winter and even here in Key West it's damn cold. And the nights are long. I bet you if I opened my eyes I'd find the sun isn't up yet. In the summer it comes up early and you can feel the heat on the stones but the way it is now you can't hardly tell the difference.

Maybe you think I can't open my eyes if I want to but I'll tell you right now you're wrong, buddy. I can open my eyes any time I want to. I got perfect control over my eyes. But why the hell should I? Just to please you? What have you ever done for me? I'll keep them shut. You can go to hell, buddy.

He hunched up tighter in the doorway and hugged himself but there was no warmth in his arms. He was all bone anyway. The whiskey had eaten the flesh off him.

He dozed a little and then somebody was kicking him and without opening his eyes he said, "Yes, sir. Just resting, sir. Moving on right now."

"Wake up," Flake said.

Cruze opened his eyes. The sun hurt them and he closed them. When he opened them again Flake was still standing over him.

"Get up, rummy," Flake said.

Cruze sighed and pulled himself together. He got up in sections, unfolding his stiff-legged length like a collapsible toy.

"What do you want, Flake?"

"I'll buy you a cup of joe."

"Well, I don't know," Cruze started to say but Flake took him by the collar and dragged him off down the street. Cruze was a head taller but Flake could have carried him easily under one arm.

They went down the street to the Cuban place in back of the turtle pens and there were ten drunks sitting on the bench like chickens on a roost. They were sitting there soaking in the sun and holding each other up. They had been there all night or maybe forever. Flake could not remember when they had not been there.

He put his wide shouldered bulk through the sagging doorway and dragged Cruze after him. He ordered coffee for two and eggs and sausage for himself. The rummy made an effort to drink his coffee; he held the cup in both hands but it was no use; he shook uncontrollably.

"Give him a beer," Flake said to the girl.

"What kind?"

"Any kind. Schlitz."

The girl brought the bottle. Cruze picked it up in both hands and let the cold beer pour down his throat. His skinny neck worked on the beer and his adam's apple bobbed up and down. He drank the whole thing without stopping. When he had finished he wiped his mouth with the back of a grimy hand and pleaded, "Lemme have another one, Flake."

Flake was eating. Without looking up he said, "No."

"Just one more."

"Goddamit, I said no."

Cruze muttered to himself.

"You want some eggs?" Flake asked.

"No. If I can't have a beer I don't want nothing."

"Then that's what you'll get. Nothing."

They sat in silence while Flake finished his breakfast. After he had cleaned the plate he bought two cigars for fifteen cents and put one in his mouth and lit it and blew a cloud of smoke into Cruze's face. The rummy wrinkled his eyes and coughed.

"What did you do that for?"

"To wake you up."

"I was awake."

"You want your coffee now?"

"Yes."

The girl brought another cup of coffee and this time Cruze was able to drink it.

"What did you want me for, Flake?"

"I'm going out this morning and I need a man."

"You already got a crew."

"I lost Benninger last night."

"How?"

"He got in a knife fight over some tart on Duval Street."

"Is he dead?"

"Not yet."

"You know I can't work. I got the shakes too bad."

"Shakes or no shakes, you can still make a diesel run."

Cruze shook his head. "I think I'll stay ashore."

Flake turned and with a short jolting motion hit him hard on the side of the face with his open hand. The hand was like a piece of wood and made a flat hard sound on the rummy's head.

Cruze fell off the stool and lay on the floor. There were tears in his eyes. His mouth worked. "What did you want to do that for?"

"Get up."

"We don' wan' no fight in here," the Cuban girl said. "I call the cops."

"This isn't a fight," Flake said.

He picked Cruze up and guided him out into the sunshine. "Here's a dollar. Get whatever you need. Meet me at the Gulf docks in half an hour. If you're not there I'll come and get you. You know what that means."

"Okay, Flake."

"You better be there."

"I'll be there."

Flake left the rummy and walked two blocks west and came out on Duval Street. Although the sun had only been up for half an hour they were already playing the piano in Sloppy Joe's and half a dozen sailors were drinking at the bar. The place smelled of whiskey and smoke and sweat.

"Shut up a minute," Flake said to the piano player. "I got to make a phone call."

He called the police station and talked to the duty sergeant and asked about Benninger.

"We just got a report from the hospital," the sergeant said. "He's dead."

Flake didn't say anything.

"Who're his people?" the sergeant asked.

"I don't know. He didn't say."

"Where was he from?"

"He didn't say."

"You didn't ask him?"

"Look," Flake said. "All I know is he was a good man. He worked hard. He didn't give me no trouble. He's dead."

"Okay. Okay," the sergeant said.

Flake hung up. As he was going out the bartender, a thin tubercular man with sideburns and a mustache, said, "Hi, Flake."

"Hi, Johnny."

"How's it goin'?"

"All right. How you doin'?"

"Livin'."

"That's good."

He went on up the street to the marine hardware store and bought three orange colored floats for the nets and a square of copper mesh for the intake strainer. The boy who waited on him was a new boy. Flake had to tell him the name of the boat twice. "Jezebel. Owner, Mangio. Captain, Flake."

"Anything else you need, Captain? How about charts?"

"I got my charts."

"For the whole area?"

"For all the way to Mexico."

"You don't fish off Mexico any more, do you?"

"Not any more," Flake said, remembering the leg irons and the rats and the rotting stones in the rotting cell. In bad weather he could still feel the irons. He had been thirty-two days in jail in Campeche for fishing in Mexican territorial waters. That was before they had discovered the Tortugas beds, when the shrimpers were starving, when they had to run to Mexico to try to make a living. The gunboat had caught him six miles out of Campeche. They had let the crew go but they had put Flake in irons and hauled him off to jail. In the end it had cost him a thousand dollars and the flesh off his ankles. He didn't fish Mexican waters any more.

He took the bundle the boy gave him and put it under his arm and bought a carton of cigarettes in the drugstore and a fifth of Irish whiskey at Joe's and went up the stairs to Mangio's office above the Chink place.

He sat there waiting for Mangio, smelling the Chinese cooking and listening to the distant rumble of the bull horns on the destroyers in the navy yard. Through the window he saw a girl come out of Freddie's. She was a blonde girl and she was a little drunk, teetering unsteadily on her high heels. She went off down the street and he admired the way her bottom moved under the tight blue skirt. He had never seen her before. He wondered if she was the new girl at Mom's.

Mangio came in and said, "What do you know, Flake?"

"I'm ready to sail."

"You get another man?"

Flake nodded.

Mangio was short and plump and wore a pink silk shirt with pearl cuff links. He had started as a bus boy at the Casa Marina. Now he owned three shrimp boats, an icehouse and a big new sea food place out near the Bight. He had pale unhealthy-looking skin and even at this hour the sweat was running down his neck.

"Too bad about the boy who died."

"Yeah."

"He should of stayed away from niggers. They cut you for nothing."

"That's right."

"Who you get to replace him?"

"Cruze."

"The rummy?"

"Yeah."

Mangio shook his head. "That's no good. Rummies bring trouble. He be drunk the whole trip."

"Where else can I get a man on a half hour's notice? He knows them engines as good as anybody."

"I don't like it."

"I'll handle it," Flake said flatly.

Mangio belched loudly. He rubbed his hand over his paunch. "My stomach is killing me."

"You ought to quit eating that Chink food."

"You think it's bad?"

"Anything you get too much of is bad."

Mangio grinned and examined the saliva wet end of his cigar. "Except one thing."

"Even that."

Mangio closed his eyes and hugged himself. "Last night . . ." he began.

"Save it till I got more time. I came to see the books."

Mangio opened his eyes. "Books? What books?"

"Account books. I want to know how much dough I got riding."

"Nobody sees the books but me and Uncle Sam."

"All right," Flake said carefully. "Then tell me. How do I stand?"

"I don't know. A couple or three thousand. I ain't looked lately."

"Then look now."

Mangio grinned and belched again. "What's the matter? You don't trust me?"

"Not particularly."

Mangio stood up. "We go over it when you get back."

"Now."

"What's the matter, Flake? You don't like your job? I can get another Captain."

"And I can get another berth. Hunchy has been after me all season."

"You won't get another boat like the Jezebel."

"Don't give me that. All shrimp boats are the same. Frig you and your boat." He threw down the package of floats. "Here. These belong to you. You know what you can do with them."

Mangio didn't say anything.

"And I still want to see those books."

"Go to hell," Mangio said.

Flake shot a thick arm across the desk and grabbed the owner by his pink silk collar. Mangio wheezed. His face turned purple. He was trying to get something out of his hip pocket. Flake pinned his wrist and ground the bones together. Mangio tried to scream but there was no wind in him. The knife fell out of his hand. Flake released his grip and shoved the owner back into his chair.

"The books," Flake said.

Mangio was unable to speak. He pointed to the filing cabinet and to the keys on his desk. Flake unlocked the cabinet and found the ledger he wanted. It was an accounting of the Jezebel's voyages and the boxes of shrimp she had brought in each time and the market price and the various shares. The rest of the crew had been paid in cash but Flake had let his credit ride. He took a slip of paper out of his pocket and compared it with the book.

"You stinking bastard," he said. "You're eight hundred short."

Mangio started to protest but one look at Flake's face shut him up.

"I want a check for thirty-eight hundred and I want it now."

Mangio wrote out the check. Flake folded it carefully and put it in his ragged black leather wallet.

"And another thing. From now on my share is an extra five per cent."

"There's no other captain gets that much. Why should I pay you more?"

"Because I bring in more shrimp."

Mangio hesitated but then thought better of it and nodded.

Flake picked up his packages. "I guess we understand each other," he said, going out of the office without bothering to close the door.

3.

The sixty-four-foot motor sailer Irydia rode to her anchor in the mouth of the government channel. Her sail covers were neatly furled and her teak decks newly scrubbed. Her white topsides shone in the morning sun. Her sheets and halyards were carefully flemished. Her windows, which had been streaked with salt after her voyage from Miami, had now been washed clear with fresh water. She was a tribute to her owner and master, Allan Chambers the second. But that gentleman derived neither pride nor joy from his ship; instead he sat on his bunk with the tears running down his face.

Oh God, he was saying to himself. Oh God help me. Get me off the bloody hook. Make me stand up like a man and throw her out. Don't let me go crawling back to her. She promised. And now you see. She's rotten. And I'm even more rotten because I know in my heart that when she comes on board I'll take her back.

Chambers howled like a dog. A seaman working on deck stood transfixed for a moment listening to the tide of grief welling out of the ventilator and then moved away. He had heard it before.

The cause of Chambers' anguish was the namesake of his boat—Irydia. Irydia was a tall dark girl who had been living with Chambers for a year. She was not Mrs. Chambers. Mrs. Chambers was at this moment attending a dog show in Westchester and feeling the flanks of an Irish terrier. Mrs. Chambers did not know where Mr. Chambers was and did not care. For a long time she had been more interested in dogs than men.

Chambers was a tall man who looked substantially the same as he had when he had rowed stroke in the Princeton shell fifteen years before. His shoulders were still very good although his legs were going a bit thin. He wore his hair cut close to the skull and what with the tan and the J. Press clothes you had to look twice to see that he was no longer a college boy.

In the past few years he had developed a passion for boats. Soon after his wife became interested in dogs he became interested in yachts and he would go off on these ocean races to Bermuda and Nassau and Cat Cay on sixty or seventy foot yawls or ketches and all he talked about was roller reefing and genoas and Merriman hardware.

It was a good life and it kept him healthy and the last thing he ever had to think about was Allan Chambers. He might have gone along that way for years except that he had been struck by lightning in the form of this dark-haired girl Irydia.

Irydia had been married twice. Her first husband had committed suicide by shooting himself in the liver with an incredible amount of Vat 69. The second, after receiving his mail from home, had volunteered for a patrol through a mine field and they had not even found any pieces of him. All that should have been a warning to Chambers but it was not.

She was a great girl. Everybody who met her was crazy about her. She was pretty and vital and intelligent and warm-hearted and loving and wide-bosomed. But she had one failing—Every so often she liked to spend a night out.

She and Chambers would be sitting at a bar and she would excuse herself and go to the ladies' room and out the back way and that would be the last he would see of her until the next day. He never knew where she went nor whose bed she had been in.

It had happened in Paris and in New York and in Bar Harbor and in Southampton and in Palm Beach and now in Key West. Each time they had a terrible fight about it and Chambers swore to kick her out and she promised that it would not happen again but each time it did and he did not.

That was why he had bought the boat. He had thought that at least on the boat she would not be able to pull any tricks. But somehow she did. She always managed to get ashore. One time when they were anchored well out in the bay she had left him in the night and had taken the dinghy and had rowed half a mile to the city docks and he had not seen her for two days. In his fury he had pulled up the anchor and had gone fourteen miles out of the harbor before he turned back. And when she did return she had been as chic and smiling and affectionate as ever and had refused him any explanation. Underneath, way down, there was iron in her. Chambers had always thought of himself as a strong man but she had taught him that he was a miserable weakling.

He wiped his face and soaked his eyes with a wet towel and went up to the chartroom. The charts were neatly rolled in an overhead rack. He pulled out the one he wanted and studied it carefully. It was a chart of the area between Key West and the Dry Tortugas.

He had never been to the Tortugas but he had heard about it. There was a huge abandoned fort there, Fort Jefferson, that they had made into a national park. It was entirely dry, no water and no accommodations. And there was a lot of historical background, something about confederate prisoners and the famous Dr. Mudd who had set John Wilkes Booth's broken leg and had been imprisoned for his pains. But the best thing about it from Chambers' point of view was that so far as he knew it was completely deserted. Irydia would have a tough time finding a playmate there.

He took a bottle of scotch out of the mahogany side cabinet and fixed himself a drink. Then, holding the chart in one hand and the glass in the other, he went back to his bunk to wait for her. He was beginning to feel better already.

4.

Irydia was lying on the beach with the sun warm on her and her black hair spread out around her on the towel. She felt marvelous. The sun was always so good for her. She hoped no one would speak to her. She just wanted to lie like this with her eyes closed and the sun burning her bones.

She was thinking about the boy she had met last night, the naval aviator. What a nice boy. Fliers were sometimes difficult but this one was so nice. They were all nice. She loved them all. Allan was nice too. Moody sometimes and childish with his weeping but really very nice. She hoped he wouldn't start drinking again. He was always so proud of his condition and did those pushups and things on deck every morning and drinking would ruin that.

She wondered if the boat would be gone when she got back. There was always that chance. He had tried it once before and some day he would get really angry enough to do it. But not now. He was still too fond of her. Anyway there was not much point in brooding about it. The big thing now was to close her eyes and to let the sun do all these delicious little things to her legs and thighs and breasts and to taste again the business of last night. What a strange boy. At least she could say nobody had ever done that to her before. Such a nice boy.

5.

Mangio was not a very smart man but he knew about people. He knew instinctively who would do what and for how much. His world was peopled with whores. Every woman had her price and so did every man. That was why, for the job he had in mind, he thought of Cutter. Cutter handled the winch on the Jezebel and from the first time Mangio had seen him he had known that he would do anything for money.

There was not much time. Flake, walking swiftly, would be at the boat in half an hour. Mangio stood up and smoothed out his shirt. The shirt was torn at the seams. That was Flake's work. Hatred welled up as bitter as bile in Mangio's mouth.

He left the office and clashed the gears in the new light gray Buick and beat the light and went down Duval Street at forty miles an hour. He passed Flake and turned his head away and Flake did not see him. He went by the big place at the end of the street where they have the life- size colored posters of the strippers and it was the only time he ever went by that place without slowing down to look at the pictures. He turned in between the two big orange-colored fuel tanks and ground to a stop on the loose gravel.

The Jezebel was outboard of two other shrimpers. Mangio crossed the cluttered decks and high gunwales, regretting the smear of grease on the cream-colored gabardine pants but going on regardless. Cutter was busy on the winch with an oversize wrench. Cruze, the rummy, was sprawled on the fantail. His eyes were closed. He looked sick and pale in the sun. The third man, the negro Bush, was not in sight.

Cutter was a medium sized wiry man with light hair and cold flat eyes. He was wearing grease-blackened dungarees held up on his narrow hips by a wide leather belt, and shapeless shoes with no laces. Even in the open air there was a sour unwashed smell about him. He wore no shirt and his hairless chest and arms were covered with obscene tattoos.

"I want to speak to you," Mangio said. "Come ashore."

There was no curiosity in Cutter's eyes. He put down his wrench and followed Mangio across to the pier.

"Get in the car," Mangio said. "I'll bring you back."

They drove away from Duval Street and into an alley and Mangio stopped the car facing a brick wall. Even with the windows open Cutter's smell made him sick. A pig, he thought. An animal. Why can't he take a bath? Then he remembered that a man who bathed more often might not be interested in the proposition he was about to offer.

"Listen, Cutter. Is five hundred bucks a lot of money to you?"

Cutter rubbed his chin. "Yeah."

"What would you do for five hundred bucks?"

"I don't know."

"What do you think of Flake?"

Cutter shrugged. "He knows his business."

"You had a fight with him one time, didn't you?"

"Yeah."

"He beat you."

"He's a hard man."

Mangio took a deep breath and then came out with it. "I would like it if he did not come back from this trip."

Cutter didn't answer. He took a crumpled pack of cigarettes out of his pocket and lit one without offering it to Mangio and blew a cloud of smoke out of the window.

Mangio was aware of the sweat running down his neck. He mopped his brow with his handkerchief. There was a lump of nausea in his stomach. He wondered if it was his indigestion again or just sitting next to Cutter. In the end Cutter might be worse than Flake. He was beginning to regret the whole thing. But it was too late to stop now. And anyway he could still feel Flake's hands on him and the thirst for revenge came boiling up in him again.

Still Cutter said nothing.

"Do you understand me?" Mangio finally blurted out.

Cutter nodded.

Mangio was beginning to gain a little assurance. "It's easy for a man to be lost overboard when you're fishing at night."

Cutter looked as though he had not heard a word.

"How about it?"

"Not for five hundred."

"How much?"

"A thousand."

It's cheap, Mangio thought. Five hundred for revenge and five more that I will save out of Flake's extra share. A bargain. And suppose he had said five thousand? It would still be worth it. I want the gulls picking at his eyes and the fish eating his flesh.

"Only one thing," Mangio said. "Can you bring the boat in without him?"

"Easy. All I got to do is steer due east. I'm bound to pick up the lights."

"All right."

"I want the dough now."

"Half now. The other half when you come in."

Cutter nodded.

Mangio took out his wallet and pulled out five hundred dollars in hundred dollar bills and put it on the seat. He did not want to touch Cutter's hand. He was looking the other way when Cutter picked up the money.

Mangio dropped Cutter at the entrance to the docks and drove away fast. He felt good now. He felt excited. Maybe he would go by Mom's place. Was it too early? It was never too early for that. But first he would stop for a bicarbonate.

6.

Chambers, sweating out his anguish on board the yacht, waited for his lady love until noon and then, when his racking impatience had torn him to bits, determined to go to look for her. He had no idea of where he would look but he knew that any activity was better than sitting alone with his grief.

He climbed down into the dink and pulled for shore. The wind and tide were against him but he made good progress, putting his shoulders and trunk into it and making a smooth easy motion of it that shot the light boat over the surface.

And for a little while, if he closed his eyes, he could imagine that he was back in the Princeton shell and that the sweat running down his back was a boy's sweat and that around him were his good friends and that all you had to do in life was to pull and pull until you thought your heart might burst except that you knew it would not. And the way it was then you had the confidence of youth and strength and you had never been defeated in anything because there had never been a real test made of you, and so you did not live under any bloody cloud of frustration and fear.

All right now, he told himself. Stop it. It's daylight and you got through the night and somehow, if she's not back, you'll get through tonight also and all the ones after that. You won't kill yourself and someday, please God, it will be over. Someday the fever will stop and the sickness will have gone and you'll wake up and look at her and know her for the rotten treacherous bitch she is and she'll put her hand on you and nothing will happen and she'll put her lips on you and you'll turn away.

But until then you're helpless and you've got to live through it and go on walking and talking and eating and drinking like anyone else. And you can stand it or most of it except that time when you wake up in the night. That's the time when you're really alone and in the middle of a polar waste and the ice is cracking under you. Somebody, I guess it was Fitzgerald, another Princeton boy the poor bastard, wrote: "In the real dark night of the soul it is always three o'clock in the morning." He was tied up with one too and she must have given it to him right in the same place I'm getting it now. I remember reading about it. There was that time on the Riviera with that French aviator and God knows how many after that. And it busted him up altogether so that he was lost forever in darkness and died without ever really coming out of it.

He brought the dink in neatly in back of the icehouse, careful not to let it rub against the tar-blackened pilings, and pulled himself up onto the pier. A girl was sitting there with her feet dangling over the edge and she said to Chambers, "Have you got a match?"

"Certainly."

He flicked his lighter and extended the flame and she bent her head and put her hand on his and sucked in the smoke. She was blonde, except not really blonde because as she bent over his hand he could see the darker roots in the parted hair. She was young and wore a powder blue skirt and ridiculously high heels and even here in the daylight you got the odor of whatever she had been drinking.

"Thanks," she said.

"Not at all."

"Some tub," she said looking out toward the Irydia. "Yours?"

"Yes."

"Tough."

He managed a small smile. He was glad she had asked him for a light. It was good to talk to a stranger.

"Cigarette?" she asked extending the pack.

"Thank you."

"What's it like on a boat like that?"

"What is what like?"

"Just living. Just waking up in the morning and eating and sleeping and all of that. Tell me about it."

"Would you like to see her?" Chambers asked. He said it on impulse, without giving it any thought.

She gave him a long look and there was a peculiar expression of contempt on the young—not so young—face.

"It's all right," he said. "I won't give you any trouble. You don't have to worry."

"I wasn't worried."

"Then shall we go?"

"Why not?"

He got back into the dink and helped her down and rowed out toward the yacht. She sat in the stern with her feet tucked up under her and the blue skirt drawn tight over her knees. She wore too much powder and her lipstick was not on straight and her hands were blue- veined and cold looking.

"What's your name?" Chambers asked.

"Molly."

"Molly what?"

"Smith."

"That's a good name."

"Isn't it? And you?"

"Allan. Allan Smith."

She grinned and said nothing more. He helped her on board and again the high heels nearly tripped her. With a quick, charming gesture she reached down and pulled off the shoes and went barefoot along the deck.

"It's enormous," she said.

"Comfortable."

"A sea going hotel. From out there she didn't look nearly this big."

He was amused by the expression on her face when he showed her Irydia's cabin She stroked the silk coverlet and opened the pink cosmetic jars and sniffed happily. When she had had enough he took her back on deck and seated her in one of the varnished wicker chairs and mixed a drink.

"Where are you from, Molly?"

"I don't know. Here and there. Everywhere."

"Where are you going?"

"Just drifting."

"How did you wind up here?"

"This is the end of the line. This is where all the drifters come. You can't go any further."

She might have been a whore but he did not think so. She did not have the toughness of a whore. Maybe she was close to it or on the way but she had not got there yet. Anyway he didn't much care. He had no interest in her that way. All he knew was that he was pathetically glad to have someone to talk to and that there was a sort of I don't care quality about her that gave him some relief from his torment.

"Would you like to take a trip?" he asked.

"All right."

"You haven't asked where."

"What's the difference?"

"You really don't care?"

"I really don't care."

"How soon can you be ready?"

"I'm ready now."

"No baggage?"

"Nope."

"You're a remarkable girl, Molly."

"Oh sure."

"We'll leave this afternoon. I'm just waiting for someone."

"I thought you might be."

"And by the way, my name isn't Smith."

"Neither is mine."

He fed her lunch and then put her down below and she fell asleep. He had it all figured out.

"Darling," Irydia would say. "There's a girl asleep in my cabin."

"Is there?" he would answer.

"Who is she?"

"Her name is Molly," he would say, turning away, feeling very pleased with himself.

But in the end he weakened and was unable to go through with it. The thought of Irydia's displeasure frightened him. He woke Molly up and told her it was all off and took her back to the shore.

"I'm terribly sorry," he said.

"That's all right. It doesn't really matter."

"You understand, don't you?"

"Sure I do. But you know something?"

"What?"

"You should have gone through with it anyway."

She went off down the pier and he rowed back to the yacht and thought that she was absolutely right and that he had not even had the guts to do this one small thing and that having failed at it he was now really sunk.

7.

The Jezebel went out the northwest channel past the fortifications and the sunken barge and when they rounded the sea buoy Flake set her due west. There were half a dozen other shrimpers going out also and a big new destroyer looking as tall as a block of apartment houses in the clear air. The destroyer went by fast, throwing her wake all over the channel, and Flake cursed it steadily while he fought the wheel.

Rising out of the sea ahead was an abandoned concrete lighthouse set up on stilts. Every time Flake saw it he remembered the flak towers in the English channel and the Focke-Wulfs coming in hard and the towers keeping them up so that it was tough for them to strafe the Estuary and the ships huddled waiting and the thin nervous scream of the bombs. And every time he thought of it he felt the familiar fist in his stomach and wondered if he would go on feeling it all the rest of his life or if someday it would go away as everything else had gone away.

Toward sundown they were over the shrimp beds and had the nets rigged and the night lights ready, and as soon as it got dark they would begin to drag the nets in thirty fathoms. In the last red flutter of day he saw a pinpoint of light many miles off far behind the Marquesas and put the glasses on it and saw that it was some kind of yacht and wondered briefly where they were bound and then forgot about it.

Cruze came up to him, looking sick and unhappy, and said, "Let me have one, Skipper."

"No."

"I got to have one. I don't feel so good."

"Later."

"I need it bad. I need it right now."

"Get out of here."

The rummy stared at him and shook his head and went shambling off. Flake felt sorry for him but not sorry enough to give him the bottle. What the hell. Key

West was full of rummies and none of them would live very long and if you got to feeling sorry for them they would take advantage of you every time.

"All right," Flake said to Cutter. "Let her go."

Cutter gave him a dirty look and muttered something under his breath. Now what the hell's the matter with him? Flake wondered. I got a rummy and a nigger and a temperamental sonofabitch. Some crew. The nigger's the only one that's worth a damn. Cutter's getting too big for his britches. I'll have to cut him down again. And Mangio. That stinking Mangio. He was too quiet when I left. He should have been down at the pier. What's he cooking? You know damn well he's cooking something.

The weighted nets sank slowly down into the dark water. The ship lay motionless. The sun had hesitated for a moment over the horizon and then had plunged out of sight. The darkness reached out for them. Flake switched on his running lights.

The net was heavy now. He kept his hand on the cable and he could feel it pull.

"Take her up," he told Cutter.

"What makes you think she's ready?"

"Goddamn you, one more crack out of you and I'll beat your ears off and feed the rest to the sharks. When I tell you to move you better hop to it."

The winch groaned as the cable began to rise. The ship heeled to starboard under the weight.

"Put some oil on those winch bearings," Flake said to Cruze.

The rummy started forward with the oil can. He walked stiffly, as though his joints hurt. Suddenly Flake let go of the wheel and darted through the doorway and jerked Cruze away from the winch.

"Watch your hands, man. What the hell's the matter with you? That thing will chew you up like hamburger."

The rummy began to shake. Tears formed in his eyes and ran down his furrowed cheeks. "Give me one, Flake."

"All right. One."

"One's all I need. Honest. Let me have one and I'll be a good man. You know I'm a good man. If I wasn't you wouldn't of taken me."

"Shut up," Flake said.

He went back and got the bottle of whiskey and handed it to Cruze. When the rummy had had a good long pull out of it Flake forced his hands loose and took the bottle away from him.

Cruze grinned and wiped the back of his hand across his mouth. "You're a good man, Flake."

"Get back to work."

The first haul was a good one. The nets came up slow, alive and heavy with the weight of what was in them. The shrimp were thicker than a man's finger and pearly and glistening on the ice. Later, when they returned to Key West, the shrimp would be pulled out ice and all in the swinging bucket attached to the steam winch and there would be maybe fifty or sixty boxes of them and at fifty-four dollars a box that would be a lot of shrimp and a lot of money.

They dragged again and while the nets were down Flake went back to the wheelhouse. There was a cold stillness in the air that he did not like. The air was too quiet and there was a touch of north in it. It was always still at sundown and right after but there was something funny about it tonight.

He tapped the barometer and was surprised to see that the needle had dropped sharply. He turned on the receiving set but was unable to get a clear signal; the air was loaded with static. That means a northwester coming, he thought. What a lousy break. Here we are really hauling them in and we get a lousy northwester. Now it will blow for maybe three or four days and fishing will be out of the question and we'll be stuck with half a load and our ice going and what the hell. Damn.

He stepped out on deck and said, "Speed it up. There's a blow coming."

Cutter didn't answer.

"You hear me?" Flake demanded.

"Yeah."

"Then answer me, damn you."

"Okay."

Flake returned to the wheelhouse and flicked on the radio phone and let it warm up for a few minutes and then called the marine operator in Key West and asked for a weather report.

"Marine operator to Jezebel. A cold front is moving across the Gulf and will strike us sometime tonight. Winds will veer to the northwest and increase in velocity."

"What velocity?"

"Gust of twenty to thirty miles an hour."

"Great."

"I beg your pardon?"

"Nothing. Thank you."

Twenty to thirty. That meant forty to fifty down here. It always blew harder down here. There would be nothing for it but to run in behind the Tortugas and no one knew how long that would be for nor how much of their haul would go bail.

Around ten o'clock they were dragging for the second time and Flake was trying to get a later report when Bush put his head through the doorway and said, "You better do something about them two."

"What about them?"

"Old Cutter is about to kill that other fella."

Flake went out fast, thinking: This is definitely not my night. Some other night maybe but not this one. This night I should be in a room in the La Concha hotel in a big bed with the curtains open and the moon coming in and a bottle of whiskey and a soft, loving girl and to hell with shrimp and northwesters and Mangio and all of it.

Cruze was curled up on the deck holding his arms over his head to protect his face and Cutter was kicking him hard in the ribs. Flake took Cutter by the collar and spun him around and hit him solidly in the throat. His fist made a meaty sound and Cutter fell to his knees, his mouth working, groping for air.

Flake picked Cruze up and propped him against the winch and went back for the bottle. He poured whiskey down the rummy's throat and waited until the sick bewildered eyes opened and stared at him blankly. Cutter was still on his hands and knees shaking his head like a dog with the heaves, trying to suck the wind into his clogged throat. Flake capsized a bucket over the side and pulled it up dripping and spewed the water over Cutter's head.

Cutter glared up at him and Flake said, "Get up, you pig."

"Why you hit me?" Cutter managed to grate out.

"You're some boy. Beating up on a rummy. Some boy."

"I'll fix you."

"Sure you will. But not when I'm looking at you."

Flake took the rummy into the wheelhouse and stretched him out on one of the bunks. Cruze's long limbs rattled and shook like palmetto fronds in the wind.

"Sorry, Flake. Sorry I made trouble for you."

"Forget it. He's been asking for it all day anyway. What was it about?"

"I guess I got in his way. You told me to keep that bearing oiled and I guess I was in his way. He cussed me and then he hit me."

"You want another shot?"

Cruze shook his head. "Not now."

"Good man."

But the real trouble came an hour before dawn. It was blowing hard by that time; the ship was climbing into steep crests and there was black water spilling over her bow. Sheets of rain boiled out of the west and spattered the wheelhouse windows. Flake got into his foul-weather gear, boots and yellow oilskins. As he was buttoning the jacket he heard the winch scream and knew what it meant; the cable had fouled somewhere and was stripping the gears.

"Turn it off," he bellowed into the blackness and heard the shrill sound die away and with it the pounding of the donkey engine.

He got out his big four-cell flashlight and went forward along the slime-wet deck. Cutter was up on the bow peering over the side.

"Anchor cable slipped loose," Cutter said. "Net's fouled in it."

"What do you mean slipped? How the hell could she slip?"

"Look for yourself."

"Where's Bush?"

"Down below. On the engine."

"Here," he said to Cutter. "Hold the light."

He went over the gunwale and held himself with one hand while he groped with the other along the cable. She had slipped all right. Some mess. Maybe they would lose the whole rig. How the hell could she slip? In all his time at sea he had never heard of an anchor rope slipping. It was goddamn funny. Had that sonofabitch Cutter . . . ? He raised his head to look at Cutter and as he did so Cutter clubbed him hard on the side of the skull with the flashlight.

He saw the light coming at him looking as big as an aircraft beacon and then there was a brighter light that exploded inside his head and then there was no light at all. He did not know that he had fallen away from the boat or that the oilskins were dragging him down or that Cutter had left the bow and gone back to the wheelhouse. He did not know that his slowly sinking body was alone in the dark sea and that the Jezebel was thrusting away from him at full speed.

The first he knew of anything was that he was dreaming and in his dream they were back on that run to Murmansk and they had gotten it for fair this time right in the engine room and she was going down fast and he was fighting the suction and trying to keep the oil out of his lungs and the cold was scissoring him up the middle and the destroyers were dropping their bloody charges and if they got any closer they would blow out his guts and leave him floating like a dynamited fish.

Then he was fighting his way up and kicking off the boots and trying to get out of the jacket and knowing now that it was not a dream but that he was really in the water and his head hurt and something had happened to him but he could not remember what.

8.

Cutter severed the cables with half a dozen blows of the fire axe and then ran back to the wheelhouse and put the throttle full ahead. He swung the boat in a wide circle, wallowing in the trough, thinking he might sight Flake's body and that if he did he would run it down. But in the black water and against the spray and rain he could see nothing and anyway there was no reason to suppose that Flake had not gone directly to the bottom. He put the wheel over and began to run to the westward, quartering the seas.

Bush came up from the engine room, a rag tied around his neck and the sweat running down his arms and looked surprised to see Cutter at the wheel.

"Where's the captain?" Bush asked.

"Gone."

"What do you mean gone?"

"Washed over."

Bush stared at him. "How could that be?"

"We fouled the net and he went over the side to break her loose and a big one caught him and he was gone. I've been running in circles for an hour looking for him but you can't see a damn thing in this weather. He's gone."

"It don't sound like Flake. It sounds mighty strange."

Cutter turned his head and looked directly at him. Bush lowered his eyes.

"I got to make a report," Cutter said. "You better get back on that engine."

Bush went back through the hatch to the engine room. Cutter lashed the wheel and moved aft to Flake's bunk. On the way he passed Cruze. He stood for a long moment staring down at the rummy but there was no sign that Cruze was awake or had been awake at any time.

Cutter reached under Flake's mattress and took out a short nosed .38 calibre Smith & Wesson wrapped in a green plastic bag, and a small metal box. He smashed the lock on the box with the butt of the revolver and then put the gun inside his shirt and opened the box. There was more there than he had figured on, most of it in hundred dollar bills. He did not bother to count it. He stuffed the bills into his pocket and went back to the wheelhouse and called the operator in Key West and told her that the captain of the Jezebel had been washed overboard in heavy weather and that because of the storm he was taking the boat into the Tortugas. The operator acknowledged his signal and he flicked off the set and brought the boat back onto course.

9.

Flake had gotten rid of his oilskins and was swimming easily, not trying to get anywhere, just staying afloat. The big seas heaved him up and dropped him down and when he rose again he saw that a gray watery dawn was chewing away at the blackness.

He knew that he would drown after a while but still he kept swimming. His head hurt and he put his hand up to it and brought it away bloody and thought how much easier it would be to quit and let it go at that. But there was a stubborn core in him that kept his arms and legs moving slowly in spite of anything his brain might have decided.

He had been in the water before and he knew that if a man nursed his strength he could stay afloat for a surprisingly long time. He knew also that in the end it would not make any difference but still he wanted to stretch it out as long as possible. He was not terribly afraid of dying but he wanted very much to live. He wanted more than anything else to get his hands on Cutter. That need alone would sustain him. And he wanted his own boat. He did not want to work any more for Mangio or anyone else. With this last check that he had cashed and with his cut from this trip and with what was already in the box he could have done it. He had been working toward it for a long time and now he was ready and that was when they had taken it away from him. It was like one of those crooked crap games where you're going good and you let everything ride and it looks like you've got it made and then on the last pass they switch the dice on you and it's all over.

Where was the sense in it? Where was the sense in the war and the fighting and the women and the money if it was to end this way? One lousy boner and they had finished him. He should have known better than to turn his back on Cutter but he had forgotten and now he was through.

He rose again on a crest and this time there was something white a long way off, looking as far oft as the moon but definitely there. And at first he could not believe it because it was an incredible piece of luck and then when he did believe it he thought what a lousy trick it was to show him a ship now when it was too far off or too late or maybe going the wrong way with him struggling to reach it and not being able to and dying struggling.

But even while he was thinking about it he had started toward it and it seemed bigger and he was able to judge its course. And he was remembering the glimmer of white he had seen the night before and wondered if this was the same one and decided it could be no other.

He knew that they would not see him in these big seas unless they were right on top of him and so he swam straight out toward them not saving anything any more, using it all up, knowing that if they missed him the rest did not matter.

And when he was very close he was absolutely finished and did not remember much of anything after that except that she was some kind of big white motor sailer and there were hands on him and then darkness and then nothing.

10.

It was close to noon before Chambers picked up Loggerhead Key. He had been moving slowly because of the heavy weather, trying to ease his ship as much as possible. The man they had fished out of the water was wrapped in blankets and asleep down below. Irydia had been there with him most of the morning. She was very good about that sort of thing. She had immediately taken charge of the half-drowned man and had undressed him and bandaged his head and put him to bed. Now she was sitting beside him, waiting for him to wake up, wanting to reassure him when he opened his eyes. Isn't she marvelous? Chambers thought. Why did she have to turn out such a bitch? Why did al! that warmth and tenderness have to turn into some kind of crazy nymphomania that could only end in destruction?

He could see the fort now and studied it carefully through the glasses. It was a bad day for a landfall. The. water would be milky and he would not be able to see any variation in depth and he would have to be right on top of the markers before he picked them up. He slowed his speed and studied his chart again and this time when he looked up he saw that there was a boat ahead of him. It was a shrimper going down the channel and all he had to do was to follow it. Except that as he watched it he saw that it was not going anywhere; it was fast on the reef and pounding hard and beginning to break up. At least I know where not to go, Chambers thought.

Irydia came through the open hatch and with her was the man they had taken out of the water. He was a short dark man with heavy arms and tremendous hands. He had close cropped hair and a dark intent face. He might have been thirty-five or forty and would probably look younger when rested.

Chambers glanced at Irydia and she shrugged and said, "I couldn't keep him down there. He insisted on getting up."

"She told me you were heading for the Tortugas," the dark man said. "Maybe I can help."

"Have you been in here before?"

"Sure," Flake said. "There's nothing to it in good weather but in a blow like this it's tricky because sometimes a northwester will shift the bar. But if you hold her as she goes you'll be about right."

"I think one of the markers is gone. According to the chart there should be a nun out there but I don't find it."

"Let me see your glasses."

Chambers handed him the Seiss 7 x 50's and Flake studied the entrance carefully. Suddenly his face changed and Chambers knew what he was looking at—the ship on the reef.

"How long has the wreck been there?" Chambers asked.

"Not long. Maybe a couple of hours."

"How can you be so sure?"

"Because she's my ship."

"What about the marker?"

"It's gone, but I can take you in without it."

With Chambers at the wheel and Flake up on the bow piloting, they made the entrance and came abeam of the wreck.

"I got to go aboard her," Flake said.

"How do you expect to do that?"

"Swim."

"Are you crazy? You came within a minute of drowning last night. Do you want to finish the job?"

"I'll make it. If you want to wait for me I'll be back in ten minutes. If you don't wait I'll go anyway."

"He seems a very determined man," Irydia said.

"What about it?"

"You don't leave me much choice," Chambers said.

"You're in good water here. You've got a hundred feet on either side. Just hold her into the wind and I'll make it as fast as I can."

Chambers shrugged. "I guess you know what you're doing but even if you don't I can't stop you. Suit yourself."

Flake mounted the rail and went over the side without hesitation. He was under water a long time and then they saw the dark cropped head looking like a seal's head moving steadily. He was swimming breast stroke, not wasting his strength.

"Quite a man," Irydia said.

Chambers looked at her. Is it starting already? he wondered. "Yes," he said.

They saw Flake seize a line trailing over the stern and go up it hand over hand. Then he was gone into the wrecked ship. Five minutes later he let himself down and started back toward them. Chambers had put down a swimming ladder for him and Flake grabbed it and pulled himself up. His back muscles stood out in sharp relief under the wet shirt and his face showed ridges of strain. His eyes were red rimmed from salt. Irydia handed him a towel and one of Chambers' dry shirts.

"Did you find what you wanted?" Chambers asked him.

"No, but I know where to look."

"What do we do now?"

"This is Hospital Key. That's Bush Key dead ahead and then Garden Key where the fort is. There are markers between Bush and Garden and that's where the channel lies. Keep her as she goes."

The wind was on their quarter now, pushing them toward the massive domination of the fort. The fort occupied almost the entire key. ft was a huge six-sided affair with a tower in the middle. Sheets of spray were beating up against the great brick walls. Another line squall sent hard driving rain slashing at the yacht.

"When you get in the lee you'll find a pier," Flake said. "You can pull right up to it. There's plenty of water."

Chambers was dividing his attention between the channel and the big following seas that came boiling up astern, letting the yacht fall off every now and then to avoid the danger of being pooped. Flake watched him with approval. He was not sure yet what kind of a man Chambers was but if nothing else he was a seaman.

11.

When the Jezebel had struck Cutter had known at once that she was through. The coral had taken the bottom out of her. You could tell by the way she settled into it, the kind of easy relaxed way she gave herself to the coral, that it was all over. By the time Bush came bounding up from the engine room Cutter was already sliding the raft over the side.

"What did we hit?" Bush demanded.

"The bloody reef."

"Man, man. Couldn't you see the channel?"

"Save the talk. Give me a hand with this raft."

"You leaving her?"

"Damn right I'm leaving. She'll break up fast in these seas."

"What about Cruze?"

"The hell with him."

"You can't leave him here."

"What's the difference to a lousy rummy? He's better off dead."

"You got to take him."

It was not so much the way Bush said it as the realization that with two men missing he would have to answer too many questions that decided Cutter. "All right. Get him out here."

Bush helped Cruze out on deck. The rummy staggered on rubber legs.

"What happened?"

"She's on the rocks. We got to get off her."

"Where's Flake?"

"Overboard."

Cruze started to protest but Bush took him firmly by the shoulder and said, "Come on now."

"Listen," Cruze said shaking his head. "I don't understand it. What's going on ?"

"Never mind. You come along."

"But where's Flake?"

"Never you mind."

Bush got an oilskin jacket out of the wheelhouse and put it over Cruze's shoulders and buttoned it around him. The rummy had a breath on him that was enough to knock down a mule. Bush was not a drinker himself and the stale smell of the whiskey sickened him. He felt sorry for Cruze and at the same time a little angry with him.

"You come on now," he said.

Cruze allowed himself to be led to the rail and pushed down into the raft. Cutter was there already, cursing at them to hurry. Bush saw that Cruze was stowed where he would not fall out and then pushed them away from the side of the boat. There were two paddles in the raft. Bush took one and Cutter the other and they set out for the fort.

The seas took them and beat them back. The white flecked crests spattered over them. Cruze was shivering, his jaws rattling like those of a spring-wound doll. Then they were in the lee and out of the worst of it and making it to the beach. They grounded in the shallows and Bush took the rummy by the shoulders and dragged him up onto the shore.

"Is there anybody on this island?" Bush asked Cutter.

"No."

"Then what do we do for food and water?"

"I don't know," Cutter said.

"If you wasn't in such a hurry to get off the boat we could of took something with us. And if you wasn't in such a hurry to get away from where Flake went over we might of found him."

"What do you mean by that?"

"You're a smart man, you figure it out."

Cutter stood up. Bush watched him carefully. Cutter reached inside his shirt and took out the plastic bag with the revolver. Bush's face changed, It did not reflect fear but intense caution.

"For a lousy nigger you talk too goddamn much," Cutter said.

"Yes, sir," Bush said.

"I don't want no more talk."

"Yes, sir."

"Don't forget it."

"I'll remember."

I got to get rid of him, Cutter was thinking. He talks too much. He smells something about Flake. If he puts his mind to it he'll begin to talk about it. I can get rid of him and say he was lost trying to swim ashore. The way it's blowing it will be a couple of days yet before the Coast Guard comes after us and that will give me time to figure it all out.

Bush was looking over Cutter's shoulder. Suddenly his face brightened. "There's a ship coming," he said.

Cutter looked up and saw a large white yacht working its way to the pier. There was a man, a heavy- backed dark-headed man, up on the bow. Even at a distance of five hundred yards it was unmistakably Flake. For a moment Cutter felt as he had when Flake had hit him in the throat; he could not breathe. Then, without a word, he turned and ran toward the walls.

12

After they had come ashore and Flake had seen his crew Irydia asked him to show her the fort.

"There's not much to see," he answered. "Nothing but ruins."

"But that's the wonderful part. I think it's marvelous. Fantastic. Come and walk with me."

"What about your husband?"

"What about him?"

"He might not like it."

"Surely there's nothing wrong in our taking a little walk together."

"If I was your husband I'd think it was plenty wrong."

"Well, I'll tell you a little secret.
He's not my husband."

"Whatever he is, he's still the guy who pulled me out of the water."

"Really now. You're making a tremendous production out of nothing. All I wanted to do was to take a walk."

"Where I come from a girl doesn't go walking with a man unless she's got a pretty good reason."

"Where do you come from?"

"Key West."

"Such a strange town."

"Maybe so. I don't pay much attention to it."

"What do you pay attention to?"

"Shrimp."

"Oh my, she thought. This one is a dilly. You've known all kinds but this is a real strange one. Awfully attractive though. Sort of brooding and difficult and terribly tough looking but probably very nice underneath. Look how sweet he was with that ghastly drunk on the beach. And the negro. He was terribly nice to that negro.

"Why are you so nervous, you poor little man?" she said. "You look as though you expected to meet someone."

"I do."

"Here?"

"That's right."

"But I thought the place was abandoned."

"It is."

"Oh, stop being so difficult. I don't know what you're talking about at all. And I don't think you do either."

"There's a man in there somewhere. His name is Cutter. I'm looking for him and I guess maybe he's looking for me."

"Then why don't you find him?"

"Maybe I will."

"What's it all about?"

"Attempted murder."

"You're joking."

"Do I look like the kind of man who makes jokes?"

"No," she said. "I can't say that you do. Is that why you were in the water?"

"That's right."

She put out her hand and touched his forearm lightly with her fingertips. "I don't think I like Mr. Cutter."

"That makes two of us."

"I'd better change that dressing for you. Or are you planning another swimming party?"

Flake shrugged. "It feels okay."

"Well, it won't if it becomes infected. And I imagine you'll want to be in reasonably good shape when you meet up with this friend of yours."

Cruze and Bush were fishing off the end of the pier. Cruze had his eyes closed and was dozing. Bush was working at the fishing and beside him was a pile of pink and yellow grunts.

"You see any sign of him?" Bush asked Flake.

"No."

"He's in there all right."

"Sure he is. There's no other place he could go."

"Don't forget he's got that gun with him."

"I'm not forgetting."

"What a shame Allan doesn't have a rifle or something on board," Irydia said. "Isn't it?"

"He never thought he'd have any use for a gun. Anyway, he hates them."

"Sure."

"What do you mean by that?"

"He's the kind who would hate guns."

"And you like them?"

"I don't feel either way about them. Only that they're necessary."

"Why couldn't we just sail out of here and leave Cutter on the island?"

"Because right now it's blowing about forty miles an hour out there. You don't feel it here in the lee of the fort but as soon as you got out of the channel it would knock you flat."

"If we called the Coast Guard wouldn't they come to pick him up?"

"I want to take him myself."

"But he has a gun."

"I'll take him."

"Are you really so tough or just stupid?"

"Both."

The long watch of the night before had exhausted Chambers and he had been asleep in his cabin for most of the day. Now, in the late afternoon, he awakened to find Irydia and Flake sitting on the fantail with a bottle of whiskey and a bucket of ice between them.

"Hello, darling," she said. "Mr. Flake was bashful about staying for a drink but I insisted."

"Of course. Perfectly welcome."

"And then too I wanted to change the dressing. Doesn't he look beautiful with a turban around his head?"

"I don't know if that's exactly the word."

"Of course it is. All sort of glowering and dark and beautiful. Do you always scowl that way, Mr. Flake, or do you do it just because you know it's so lovely?"

What a bitch, Flake thought. If she was mine I'd boot her into the street so fast. Why does he take it? She's a hot looking piece all right but there are plenty of others just as hot or hotter. She's got the knife in him and she's twisting it. Poor bastard. I better stay clear. After all he did pick me out of the drink. I guess I owe him that. But nothing more. Let each man defend his own. I'll keep away but if she chases after me it's up to him to do something about it. If he doesn't want to do anything about it then to hell with him. To hell with both of them.

Flake stood up. "I better go and see how my crew is making out."

"But you'll be back for dinner, won't you?" Irydia said.

"No. Bush has got him a mess of grunt. We'll eat on the beach."

"That might be better," Chambers said.

"Sure," Flake agreed. "Better all around."

After he had gone Chambers turned to her and said, "You can't wait, can you?"

"For what, darling?"

"You know for what."

"You're not going to start that again, are you, sweetheart?"

"I'm not starting anything. I'm trying to finish something."

She gave him a loving smile. "You will, sweetie. But in the meantime we're here to have some fun so let's relax and be gay."

"It's all so simple for you."

"Not really. But what good does it do to stew about things?"

"I would like just once to understand what goes on in that head of yours."

"So would I," Irydia said.

13.

Towards sundown the wind increased. And with it came the sharp rainsqualls. Flake and his crew huddled behind the dripping walls. They kept a fire going but the rain-wet wood gave off more smoke than heat. The peculiar tropic cold that is somehow colder than northern cold bit at them out of the bricks.

Flake stood up and walked down to the beach and began to collect another load of driftwood. In the last glimmer of day he could see the Jezebel on the reef. From where he stood she looked almost intact but he knew that she was completely destroyed underneath and that in another few hours the pounding would shake her apart and there would be nothing left of her but bits of wood on the beach.

It made him sad. It was true that she was not his boat and he certainly didn't give a damn what happened to Mangio's property but, still, he had been her skipper and no skipper likes to lose his ship. He knew her quirks and vagaries and virtues. In a way, he reflected, it's like a marriage between a captain and his ship. A ship develops personality—some are sweet and gentle, others tricky and uncertain— and a man learns to accept that personality and to live with it and to believe that he alone of all men is qualified to cope with it. When he turns over his ship to another captain it's a little like watching a woman he has loved go off with another man. The destruction of the ship then was something more to add to the score against Cutter.

His head was a brute now, pounding like a drum. He thought of going to the yacht and asking for aspirin but decided against it. He did not want to become involved. He hated trios. A relationship between a man and a woman should be a simple proposition but this business between Chambers and Irydia was unhealthy. He did not want any part of it. She was a whore and he felt nothing but contempt for whores. Whores had a hard masculine quality that repelled him, and whether they were peddling their wares along Duval Street or on board a fancy yacht they were all the same.

He gathered his wood and walked back to the fort and found that in his absence Bush had been down to the yacht and had borrowed a tarpaulin with which to protect Cruze from the cold. Flake felt guilty about Cruze. The rummy was obviously ill. A series of chills racked his skinny body. His face was flushed and dry looking.

"How are you doing?" Flake asked him.

"Okay."

"Feel bad?"

"No, sir."

"I should of left you in Key West. I never should of dragged you out on this trip." Cruze grinned. "What's the difference? Nobody lives forever."

"Now what do you want to go and talk that way for?" Bush said.

"Did he eat anything?" Flake asked.

"Nope."

"Rummies don't eat much anyway."

"How about giving me a shot, Flake?" Cruze called, "One for the road."

"If I had it I'd give it to you."

"They've got it down there on that fancy boat, haven't they?"

"Yeah, I guess they have."

He hated the thought of going down to the yacht to ask for anything. Because of the woman there was a wall between himself and Chambers and he did not want to have to climb over it. But he owed it to Cruze.

"Wrap him up," he told Bush.

"What do you aim to do with him?"

"He's sick. I'm taking him down there. They'll find a place for him."

Bush nodded his approval and wrapped the canvas around Cruze. Flake bent down and picked the rummy up and cradled him on his arms. He was astonishingly light. I bet he doesn't weigh over ninety pounds, Flake thought. What keeps him alive? It must be the whiskey. There's probably a lot of nourishment in whiskey only in the end the alcohol burns you up to nothing.

"Where are we going?" Cruze asked.

"To get a drink," Flake told him.

There was no one on deck and the hatchway was closed. I probably picked the wrong damn time, he thought. She's probably earning her board and keep.

He knocked on the hatch cover and a moment later it slid open and Chambers was there wearing gray flannel beltless slacks and a navy blue jersey shirt and holding a glass in his hand.

"I'm sorry to bother you," Flake said.

"Not at all," Chambers answered stiffly.

"I've got a sick man on my hands and this is bad weather for him to be outside. I thought maybe you could find a place for him up forward."

Chambers frowned and examined his drink carefully and then said, "Of course."

"Can I bring him through?"

"There's a hatch up forward. If you don't mind I'd rather have you use that."

He doesn't want me to see her, Flake thought. That's all right. He doesn't have to worry. I don't want any part of her.

He carried Cruze down into the crews' quarters and stowed him in an empty bunk and wrapped a blanket tightly around him. In spite of himself he stared aft through the galley thinking he might see her, but her stateroom door was closed and she did not come out.

"You said you'd give me a drink," the rummy whispered.

"I'll see what I can do."

He put his head into the main cabin and said, "Maybe you'd do me one more favor."

"Certainly."

"This guy I brought down is in a bad way. He's got the shakes. Maybe you could spare some whiskey for him."

"Of course."

A bloody little gentleman, Flake thought. If he found her in the hay with some joker he'd say 'I beg your pardon' and go quietly away. But I don't know. Maybe it takes more guts that way. I can see what a row he has to hoe.

"Take the bottle if you like," Chambers said.

"No. Just a shot in a glass. That will carry him."

Chambers gave him the glass and Flake thanked him and took the whiskey back to Cruze. The rummy clutched at it and tossed it off in one gulp and burst into a fit of violent coughing.

Flake waited until Cruze had caught his breath and then left him and went up on deck through the forward hatch. As he crossed to the rail he was able to look down through the glass hatch cover into Irydia's brightly lit cabin. She was lying on her bunk wearing tight blue silk pajamas that emphasized her full bosom and outlined her hips. She was not reading, just lying there with her eyes open. He thought she might be able to see him through the glass but her face did not change nor did her eyes move. He stood there for a long moment staring down at her and then realized that because the light was from below she was unable to see him after all. He turned away and jumped over the rail onto the pier.

Bush was nursing the fire. "You get him fixed up?" he asked.

"Yeah."

"It won't be for long. He'll be dead soon."

"How do you know?"

"I can smell it on him. You can smell death a long way off. I smell it stronger on him all the time."

"Maybe he'll be better off."

"Maybe."

"What do you smell on me?"

Bush stirred the fire. His face was serious. "I don't know. Not death. Money."

"That's not a bad smell."

"No, sir."

"What about Cutter? What do you smell on him?"

"He just stinks all the time."

"You can say that again "

"What you fixing to do about him?"

"I'll go and get him."

"When?"

"When I'm ready."

"He'll kill you if he can."

"He's already tried that. Next time I won't give him the chance."

"Maybe he's looking for you right now."

"I don't think so. There's too many witnesses now. If he killed me out here in the open he'd have to kill all the rest of you too, and that would be a big job even for Cutter. No, he's holed up there waiting for me to come at him. I'll let him sweat a while."

"What about you? Don't you sweat?"

"All the time."

Bush yawned. "It's going to be a long cold night."

"We got enough wood to last us."

Bush lay down by the fire and was almost instantly asleep. Flake moved a little further away, into the darkness. He hated to give up the warmth but on the other hand he did not want to be too close to the light. It was always possible that Cutter might get some bright ideas.

Once, above the roar of the wind, he heard angry voices from the yacht. What a pair, he thought. What does he get out of it? No dame is worth all that fuss. Then he was asleep and did not awaken until he heard steps dragging on the sand and the dry whisper of leather on the courtyard paving. He sat up quickly and got his legs under him and crouched there waiting.

A figure came into the firelight and he saw that it was the girl. She had a blanket wrapped around her shoulders and her long black hair was loose down her back and blowing in the wind. She bent over Bush for a moment and then straightened and stood irresolutely by the fire. She looked small and childlike standing there with the blanket around her and her hair loose. Then she was moving toward him and he stood up and she said softly, "Oh, there you are."

"Yes."

"It's terribly cold, isn't it? You have no blanket. I brought you a blanket."

"Thanks."

"How is your head?"

"Fine."

There was a long silence and she shivered a little and hugged the blanket tighter. "Do you want me to go?"

"Suit yourself."

"I wanted to talk to you."

"All right."

"You don't make it any easier, do you?"

"No," he said. "Do you?"

She turned and started away. He stood and watched her. When she had gone beyond the fire she stopped and came back. Her eyes were very large and black in the yellow light. She came up to him and let go of the blanket and kissed him hard.

"Be kind to me," she said.

14.

Chambers was awake when she left the ship. They had quarreled for two hours and finally she had said, "I can't stand any more of this," and had gone into her cabin and slammed the door. He sat alone for a long time finishing the bottle and thought of going in to her but decided against it and went instead to his own bunk. He was drunk but not as drunk as he wanted to be. He was not drunk enough for his brain to stop functioning or for sleep to ease his unhappiness.

When he heard her door open and the hatch sliding back he raised his arm and looked at the luminous dial on his watch. It was after two. She's only going up on deck to get some air and smoke a cigarette, he told himself, but even while he said it he knew that it was not so and where she was really going and what she was going for. He knew too that if he went after her he could stop her but that once he had done that the whole thing would be out in the open and everything would be finally dead. As long as he did nothing she would return and they could go on a little longer. The big thing, the great thing, was to do nothing.

He got out of his bunk and went up on deck and stood there in the wind looking at the yellow point of light that was Flake's fire. The dirty thing, the rotten thing, he thought was that he did not really hate either one of them. The only absolutely solid hate he had was for himself. And the worst part, the most absolutely contemptible part, was that right now he wanted her more than ever.

15.

Next day the wind blew stronger. The sky was hard and clear, as if it had been carved out of some bright blue metal. The sea had been churned to a milky gray and yellow clots of foam spattered the beach. The birds were down on the water in the lee of the fort, riding it out, facing up into the wind. Chunks of purple jelly trailing poisonous streamers came drifting ashore and died in the sun. Chambers ran spring lines fore and aft and the yacht rode comfortably beneath the sheltering walls.

Irydia stayed in her cabin. Once Chambers tried the door and found it locked. He knocked gently.

"What is it?" she asked without opening the door.

"I want to talk to you."

"Please, sweetie. Let's not have any scenes."

"No scenes. I just want to talk to you."

"Later, darling."

Her voice was husky as though she had been crying. He felt very sorry for her.

16.

Flake paced the beach. He was worried. Not about Chambers and the girl and what had happened last night; it had been up to Chambers to stop her and he had not. He was worried about himself. He should have settled matters with Cutter by this time. He should have gone right into the fort and taken Cutter immediately. He had said he would let Cutter sweat a while but that was not the real reason. The real reason was that he had not the guts for it. A man with guts doesn't sit around making explanations; he goes ahead and does what he has to do and when he isn't doing it he shuts up about it.

Maybe he had been in the water too long. Something had taken the starch out of him. In a way it was like Chambers and his girl—always on the defensive, always waiting for her to make the move. What he needed was a drink. The old giant killer. His shield and his armor. Some hero.

And what about the girl? He had to do a lot of thinking about that girl and some time he would get around to it but just now he was putting it off like everything else.

"He got to come out for food and water," Bush said.

"Sure he does. But not yet."

"When he comes he'll use that gun."

"You afraid of him?"

Bush thought it over. "Yes, sir. I am."

I haven't even got the guts to admit it, Flake thought. It was the one thing I was always sure of, the one commodity I could always trade on, and now that's gone.

In the afterglow of sundown the wind dropped. The sky was brassy and there was a haze over the water. Then the sun was gone and the wind came pushing up bigger than ever. It howled through the cannon emplacements and across the parade ground. It was blowing a full gale now. And with the wind came the moon, throwing gaunt shadows across the walls.

Flake stood up and went over to Bush and shook him gently and said, "Lend me your knife."

The negro was instantly awake. "What's the matter?"

"I just want your knife."

"Why do you want a knife in the middle of the night?"

"None of your damned business. Give it to me."

Bush pulled the big clasp knife out of his pocket and handed it to him.

"All right," Flake said, moving quickly away into the darkness.

He had removed his shoes, and made no sound crossing the quadrangle or in the passageways. Once something exploded in an angry flutter beside him and he leaped back with the knife open in his hand and saw that it was only a pelican going up black against the moon.

Back in Key West they said this place was haunted. They said the ghosts of the prisoners who had died here still roamed among the ruins. If so this was a great night for them. Between the moon and the wind a man could see almost anything on a night like this.

It occurred to him that Cutter might not be in the fort at all; he might be down on the tip of the island where he would have clear ground to see across and room in which to shoot. Flake went over the wall and dropped down onto the sand and ran crouching low across the moon-washed space. Out here the wind was even stronger. Particles of sand stung his face and gritted against his teeth

There was a patch of palmettos and he got into them and crouched there waiting, the breath pounding in his chest, the blade held across his bod) , waiting, not seeing anything, expecting at any moment the thunder of the gun and not hearing anything but the scrabble of the wind through the bushes.

There was a dank cold lump in his stomach and it kept him crouched there motionless when he should have been moving on. Go ahead, he told himself. You started it and you got to finish it. Keep moving. Keep it simple. What could be simpler than a man with a gun? You're thinking too much. Keep moving. Come on.

He jumped out of the palmettos and forced himself down to the heaped coral tip of the island and saw that there was nothing there and some of the coldness went out of him so that, coming back to the fort, he was able to keep himself from crouching or running.

Working systematically he began to explore one turret after another and it was while he was in the third turret that he heard the steps. At first he was not quite sure but then they came closer and they were steps all right. He froze against the wall and loosened his grip on the knife handle and unclenched his cramped fingers and tightened them again. Then the shadow that was more than a shadow came through the archway and without any further hesitation Flake propelled himself off the wall and had the man's wrist in a hammerlock and the point of the knife digging into his back. Except that even as he did so he knew the wrist was too thin and the back sagged too limply and the smell of whiskey was like a cloud around him.

Cruze giggled. "Fooled you." His voice was slurred.

Flake released him and said, "What the hell are you doing here?"

"Looking for you."

"Are you crazy? I came within an inch of killing you."

"So what?"

"How did you get off the boat?"

"Walked. Me and my old friend Johnny Walker. We carried each other."

"Did you steal Chambers' hooch?"

"Careless man. Left it lying around."

"Get back where you belong."

"Can't. Came to help you."

"I don't need any help."

"Cutter has a gun. Takes two good men to handle guy with gun."

"Clear out, damn you."

Cruze made a sound that could have been laughter but was more like strangulation. "No savvy," he said.

Flake's open palm shot out and took him across the cheek and under the impact of it Cruze's head jerked back and he slid down the wall. Flake took him by the collar and hauled him erect and said, "Do you savvy that, you rum-dumb bastard?"

"Okay, Flake."

"Now get back to the ship."

"I only wanted to help you."

"Get going."

"But listen, Flake . . ."

"Move."

The rummy shambled off, his long legs throwing grotesque shadows across the moonglow. Flake watched him until he was out of sight. He felt lousy about hitting Cruze but what else could he do? And anyway he was furiously angry. The fact that he had come so close to knifing the rummy had left him thoroughly shaken.

He went through the archway to the next turret. He was out of the lee now and the wind leaped at him, tugging at his shirt, pulling his hair. Electric ripples of tension were traveling along his spine.

What was it Bush had said about smelling death? It had sounded like just nigger talk at the time but it didn't sound that way now. It was in the air all right. You could smell it all around. That Bush was some nigger all right. A hell of a lot smarter than most white men . . .

The sound of the shots, hollow and long thudding on the wind, brought him up short. He listened to the first two and by the time the third was reverberating among the walls he was racing toward the sound.

He burst out of the corridor into the moon bright quadrangle and saw the man with the gun and flung himself directly at him, knowing it was coming but not waiting for the spurting blossom of flame nor the sharp thunder nor the whine of the ricochet.

Then he had him by the throat and was bending him backward with his thumbs going in right up to the joints and the man flopping like a stranded fish. This time there was no mistake about it; it was Cutter all right and he was trying to get his knee into Flake's groin and Flake was squeezing him all the time and pushing him back. Cutter arched his wiry body and managed to free one arm long enough to punch Flake in the face and Flake growled and took the arm that had punched him and began to bend it steadily back, feeling the bones grating and hearing Cutter howl and then feeling the stiff point beyond which it would not go and making it go even further so that there was a snapping sound like a dry twig breaking and

Cutter let out a little yelp that might have come from a kicked dog and then was still.

Flake stood up, aware for the first time of the sweat soaking through his shirt and the blood running out of his mouth, and remembered the knife and wondered why he had forgotten to use it. Then he thought of Cruze and began to search for him and found him a dozen yards away slumped against the wall. It was a familiar position for Cruze except that now he was not drunk anymore. As soon as Flake touched him he knew he was dead.

He lit a match and held it over the dead man for a moment and saw where the bullets had gone in and then the wind blew it out and he let it drop.

Cutter was groaning. Flake went back to him and chopped him across the face with his fist. He was getting ready to kill Cutter with his hands but he wanted to do it slowly. He hit Cutter on the nose with the edge of his palm and felt the cartilage break and the nose go sideways and saw the blood, black in the moonlight, burst out.

Cutter tried to scream but was unable to and what came out instead was, "Mangio . .

"What about Mangio?"

"His idea."

"What idea?"

"Push Flake over."

So that was how it had been. He might have guessed that Cutter lacked the initiative to start things on his own. With Mangio behind him it began to make sense.

"For how much?" Flake said.

"A thousand."

And that was all he was worth. A lousy grand. This scum had been willing to murder him for a lousy thousand bucks.

He hit Cutter again and brought his hand away wet with blood.

"My arm," Cutter moaned.

"Wait till you see what I do to the rest of you. Where's the dough you took out of the box?"

"My pocket."

Flake backed off and kicked him hard in the ribs. Cutter's body jerked and the breath whooshed out of him. Flake kicked him again and turned him over and took out the roll of water-soaked bills. Killing Cutter now would be a mistake. He would take him back to stand trial for the murder of Cruze and to testify against Mangio. That way it would work out all right. It was lousy about Cruze getting it but at least it was over for him and maybe it was better than freezing to death in an alley.

He took Cutter by the collar and hoisted him roughly to his feet. Cutter's knees buckled and Flake straightened him with a slap in the jaw. Cutter's broken wrist hung twisted at a peculiar angle. Flake dragged him across the quadrangle toward the beach. He didn't fancy the idea of leaving Cruze lying on the stones but he would have to take Cutter in first. The stones hadn't made too much difference to the rummy when he was alive and certainly wouldn't bother him now.

17

The Coast Guard PBY plowed a furrow across the lagoon and taxied up to the pier. Flake was standing waiting for them and took their bow line and secured it to one of the pilings. The hatch opened and a tall thin lieutenant came out. It was Huckins. Flake had known him for a long time.

"Hello, Huck."

"What's all the ruckus? We got word you were drowned."

"Not quite."

Flake told him about Cutter and Cruze and the lieutenant looked at Cutter and said, "What ran over him?"

"We had an argument."

Huck sighed. "All right. There isn't much of him left but we'll take what there is."

They handcuffed Cutter to a galley stanchion and carried Cruze's body, still wrapped in the tarpaulin, back aft.

"I'll need statements from the people on the yacht," Huck said to Flake. "You wait here."

Flake sat down on the pier and stared out at the reef. During the night the Jezebel had broken up. There was nothing left but a small section of her bow. He no longer felt any regret about her. She had been Mangio's and Mangio was finished. The whole thing was finished.

Then Huck was coming back toward him and with him was Irydia. She was carrying a small plaid suitcase.

"I'm afraid it isn't very much," she said pointing to the suitcase. "But then how much do we really need?"

Flake didn't answer. Huck stood there waiting for them to say something and when nothing happened he shrugged his shoulders and stepped down into the plane.

Irydia took Flake's hand and held it tightly. "What is it, darling?"

"Nothing."

"Don't you want me?"

"No."

"Do you mean that?"

"Yes."

She let go of his hand. Her face had gone very pale. "Then say it."

"Get away from me," Flake said.

"Say it again."

"Get away from me, you whore."

"All right. That's enough."

She picked up the suitcase and began to walk very fast back toward the yacht. He watched her go. She had extraordinarily fine legs.

Huck put his head out of the pilot's window and said appreciatively, " That's a lot of woman."

"Let's get out," Flake said.

18.

Chambers had been watching. It was killing him but he kept watching. It was like pressing on an aching tooth, he had to savor every last bit of pain. But from the expression on her face it was clear that it was not going the way she had planned.

Then he saw her start back to the yacht and he saw Flake get into the plane and his heart stopped pounding and the sweat began to dry on his hands. By the time she reached the yacht he was sitting in his chair with a magazine on his lap and managing to look cool and disinterested.

"Changed your mind?" he asked easily.

She gave him a small, utterly charming smile. "He changed his."

"What did he say?"

"Do you really want to know?"

"Yes."

"He said, 'Get away from me, you whore'."

"I remember that morning we picked him up you said he was quite a man."

"Did I?"

"You were absolutely right, you know."

"All right, Allan."

He stood up and began to examine his face in the small mirror behind the liquor cabinet. "Do I look different to you?" he asked.

"I don't know."

"I feel different. I ought to look different."

She looked at him carefully then and saw that he was indeed different. In the last five minutes his face had changed very much. It was quite astonishing.

"Let's not talk about it now," she said. "Later on. Not now. Please?"

"Do you know something?" he said cheerfully. "I don't think there's anything to talk about at all. Not ever."

He went out on deck and stood there enjoying the cold, bright air. The plane was a long way off now, small and black against the sun. He watched it until it was gone. Then he smiled.

He wondered if that girl Molly Smith was still sitting on the pier in Key West.

But then he decided that the first thing he had to do when he got back, the most important thing, was to buy a drink for his good friend Flake.

You Can't Trust a Man
Helen Nielsen

They were a couple of very special jobs—the convertible and the woman. Blonde, streamlined, and plenty of firepower under the hood. The convertible was a later model, at least twenty-five years later, but it didn't have any more pickup and not nearly as much maneuverability in traffic.

She came across the parking lot like a stripper prancing out on the runway, a healthy, old-fashioned girl who believed that whatsoever the Lord hath cleaved asunder no Parisian designer should join together. She was wearing the kind of gown that's called a creation and carries a three-figure price tag, and over it hung a pastel mink stole that could feed a family of six for a couple of years. She opened the door of the convertible and slid in behind the wheel over red leather upholstery as soft as a lover's caress, and was just touching a gold-tipped cigarette to a jeweled lighter when the opposite door opened and a thin man in a shabby suit and a battered hat crawled in beside her.

For just an instant the flame in the woman's gloved hand brightened her face like candlelight before a Madonna, and then the flame and the illusion died together.

"Faithful Tony," she murmured. "I knew you would come."

A spiral of smoke sought the open window like a released soul; then the motor throbbed alive and twin eyes bored holes in the darkness. The woman barely glanced at the shabby man. She was too busy steering on a street that was a lot more crowded at other hours, when the little shops and the big markets were open for business. Now, only one place was still open, and business was fine. You could see the colored neons and hear the wail of a clarinet being tortured by an orgy of jungle drums, and out in front of a chocolate stucco building without windows you could see the bigger-than-life photo of a full-mouthed blonde who didn't look at all Madonna-like under floodlights.

"Featuring Crystal Coe and her intimate songs," the shabby man read aloud, as they wheeled past the billboard. "You're big time now, baby. Real big time."

There was no enthusiasm in the words. He didn't sound like a press agent, or an MC, or a kid with an autograph book in his hand.

"Is that why you wanted to see me?" the woman asked.

"Did I want to see you?" A twisted smile slid across the man's dark face. "I thought it was the other way around. I thought it was Crystal Coe who phoned my hotel and set up this cozy reunion."

"*After* I read your threatening note."

"Threatening?" The smile was wider now. "You've been imagining things, baby. That was just a fan letter."

He wasn't going to be offered one of those gold-tipped smokes, so the man poked around in his pockets until he came up with a crumpled pack of his own. The lighter

You Can't Trust a Man   127 on the instrument panel worked fine. Any time it didn't, this job would be traded in on a newer model.

"Just imagining things," he repeated. "You always did have a big imagination. Remember that story you told me back in Cleveland seven years ago? It was a real heartbreaker . . .. 'I can't take the rap, Tony. I can't have our baby born in prison!'"

A deep drag on the cigarette and the man leaned back against the deep-cushioned seat. The way he did it, it was as if he hadn't been so comfortable in a long time. It was as if he'd like to take off his shoes and stay a while.

"I never did get a birth announcement," he added. "What was it, Crystal—a boy or a girl?"

"A girl can make a mistake," the woman said.

"That's right, baby. She sure can."

His voice was as cold as the night air. The woman pressed a button with her left hand and the window hummed upward. Everything automatic. Press a button and the red carpet rolls out . . . as long as nobody turns off the ignition.

"No birth announcement, no letters," the man mused. "Seven years is a long time to sit in stir without letters, but then I guess you were busy. Broadway . . . Hollywood . . . Hell, baby, I never knew you could sing. I always thought you had only one talent."

Up ahead, a light turned red and the convertible stopped with a lurch. Gloved fingers snuffed out a gold-tipped cigarette in a tray that was already overloaded and then tightened on the steering wheel. It was so late the streets were like eyeless sockets in the face of the city. A diesel trailer job thundered up in the next lane, and a black and white prowl car sniffed past the intersection, but that was the only traffic in the time it took for the light to turn green.

"All right, Tony," the woman said, as the convertible leaped forward, "what do you want?"

"Seven years . . ."

It might have been an answer, or it might have been just a man talking to himself. He wriggled down against the soft leather until the battered hat tipped down over his eyes.

"For me they were empty years, Crystal. For me no bright lights, no big time. At first I nearly went crazy wondering why you didn't write. I thought maybe that stupid gin-mill operator got wise that it was your fingers in his till instead of mine. Then I thought maybe something went wrong with the baby. That's a laugh, isn't it? I'll bet you've split your sides over it more than once."

The gloved fingers tightened even more on the steering wheel, but still the woman didn't turn her head. She was driving slowly and carefully. She never took her eyes from the street except to glance at the instrument panel now and then.

"Empty years," the man continued. "Then, all of a sudden, they weren't empty anymore because one day I saw a newspaper and guess whose picture? I didn't recognize you right off, not with the blonde hair and the fancy clothes and that name—Crystal Coe. But the paper said you'd just changed your name by marrying that band leader. Whatever happened to him, baby? Was he the one who turned alcoholic, or was that the Hollywood agent?"

The light from the instrument panel caught the man's twisted smile, but Crystal Coe's face was like marble, cold, hard, and silent.

"No, I remember now," the man reflected, "the agent was the one who shot himself. I read all about it in a fan magazine. 'Crystal Coe's Tragic Loves'—that was the name of the story. But then it went on to say that you'd found happiness at last with an older man . . . old enough to own a few dozen oil fields."

"All right, so we've had the story of my life!" Crystal snapped.

"Not quite, baby. I was thinking about that when I read that magazine story. They left out a few things. Maybe I should do a sequel: 'Crystal Coe's Secret Love.' How do you like that for a title?"

"It'll never sell!"

"Why not? Because I can't swim in oil?"

"Because you can't prove anything!"

Marble shouldn't get hot so quickly; it was liable to crack. The man shook his head sadly.

"You know better than that, Crystal," he said. "No matter how many little pieces of paper you destroy, there's always a piece left somewhere."

Outside the wind was rising. It howled up from the desert a hundred miles away, whipping the dry fronds of the skinny palms and flapping out the rhythm of the canvas top against the steel frame. Inside, everything was cozy. Any time it wasn't, there was another button to press.

The man stretched out his legs and leaned back his head so he could take it all in. All the chrome, all the leather, all the buttons . . .

"Nice," he murmured. "Real Class. Not like the old days."

"You don't have to remind me," Crystal said.

"I'll bet I don't! Some things you would like to forget. That cheap apartment with the garbage smell in the halls—that lousy saloon where I found you talking the boys into buying another drink. You always were a good talker, Crystal, especially when you kept your mouth shut . . .. That's something else the story in the magazine got wrong. It said you started out as a waitress."

He reached out and pressed one of the buttons. In a couple of seconds the radio began to give out with a jump tune from somebody's all-night platter show. An old jump tune. Seven years old, anyway.

"Remember that one?" he asked. "Remember how we used to feed nickels in the jukebox so we could kick that one around? Takes a dime now. Seems like everything's a lot more expensive than it was seven years ago."

"How expensive, Tony?"

If the woman had been looking at him, she would have seen how his mouth twisted upward at the corners. But she didn't look at him, and he didn't answer her. The brasses took a chorus and then the piano came up strong. Whoever was playing it must have had ten fingers on each hand. Then the bass came in like the amplified heartbeat of a bad case of hypertension.

"You can't beat the old tunes," Tony said. "The old tunes, the old days . . . the old loves. Sometimes, when I was sweating out those seven years for you, baby, I'd wake up in the night and forget where I was. I'd reach out for you in the darkness and grab an armful of air, and then lie awake all night going crazy with memories. We did have some good times in the old days. Even you must remember that."

"I stopped remembering," Crystal said, "a long time ago."

"Before you knew me?"

There was no answer but the whine of the tires as they took the turns. The street was developing curves now. The little shops and the markets had been replaced by neatly clipped lawns and geraniums.

"It must have been before you knew me," Tony said. "You must have started forgetting early to be such an expert so young . . . .But I couldn't forget. I'd keep remembering how I used to feel whenever I worked the late show and came home to find you out at that dive again. It's in the blood, I guess. Once a saloon tramp, always a saloon tramp. But it didn't matter. That's the crazy part of this whole thing, baby. Whatever you did, I made excuses. Even when you took that money, I blamed myself because I was just a lousy movie projectionist and couldn't make enough to give you the things you wanted."

Suddenly the man threw back his head and laughed, high-pitched and humorless.

"Remember how I used to tinker around in the basement trying to invent something that would make us rich? Always something. Always some new idea I was going to run into a fortune so I could dress you in mink . . . .."

He reached out and stroked the soft fur where it rested close to her throat. There was no pressure in his feeling fingers, but she trembled slightly at the touch.

"Always something," he murmured. "I used to think about that whenever I read about one of your divorce settlements. I guess no invention is ever going to improve on nature."

"A girl has to live!" Crystal snapped. "She can't wait around for some tinkering fool forever! She has to live!"

"Are you sure of that, baby? Are you real sure?" The laugh came again, thin as the distance between his fingers and her throat. "I could have saved those suckers a lot of money if I'd sounded off, couldn't I? Me, the jailbird Crystal Coe couldn't acknowledge even to a judge . . . .. But that would have spoiled everything."

"For both of us, Tony."

"For both of us," he echoed. The fingers touched her skin, now, slowly, carefully, they barely touched her skin. "Now you're getting the idea, Crystal. That's what I've had in mind all these years. So Tony kept his mouth shut and just went on remembering and tinkering. They have places for that even in stir. Always something. Always figuring something . . . .."

"How much, Tony?" she asked.

"You're not the only one who likes expensive things, baby. Seven years of hunger can sure give a man an appetite for expensive things."

"I asked you, how much?"

"For what I want, you won't need your checkbook."

"Then what?"

The crooked smile sliced across the man's face again, and the fingers were real busy now.

"I just told you," he said. "Seven years is a long time to live on memories . . ..
What do you think I want, Crystal? After all, I'm still your husband."

When the record stopped playing on the platter show the announcer started
selling used cars and Crystal's hand plunged him into silence. For a few blocks it
was terribly quiet. All that horsepower under the hood barely whispered at the
darkness, and the street elbowed in close to the hills where even the wind was
subdued. The lawns were wide and deep now, and the night had that lush hush of
a neighborhood where nobody worries in public.

. . . Silence, and then a woman's voice speaking as unemotionally as if the man
in the shabby suit had suggested stopping someplace for a nightcap or a cup of
coffee.

"I'll have to stop for gas," she said, glancing at the instrument panel again.
"The tank's nearly empty."

"And then what?" the man asked.

"There won't be anyone at the beach house tonight. We never use it in winter."

Just like that. No argument at all. The smile lingered on the man's face. The
specialty of the house wasn't so expensive after all if you had a membership. Just
ahead the white glow of a twenty-four-hour service station came into view like an
actor responding to cue, and the little green arrow on the instrument panel clicked
the left-hand warning for all the traffic that wasn't in sight. As the convertible slid
alongside the gas pumps, the man began to laugh again. He was laughing like a
fool by the time the station jockey poked his head in the window.

"Fill it up," Crystal said, and whirled about to meet the laughter. There wasn't
a trace of that marble face makeup now. She was wearing a colorful blend of
bewilderment and anger.

"Where are you going?" she demanded.

Tony's hand was on the door handle. "That's my business," he said. "This is
where we part company."

"I don't understand—"

"I'll bet you don't! Nobody ever walked out on you, did they, baby? Nobody ever
turned down such an invitation! That's what I figured while I was giving you the
big buildup about the hungry years. I wanted you to learn how it feels to have the
only thing you can offer thrown back in your face . . .. Don't you get it, baby? I'm
the chump who sweated out seven years in a cell because I loved you. You were in
my blood, even when I knew about all those other guys. I used to rip your pictures
apart, pretending they were you! A thousand times I've smashed your face until it
wouldn't look good to any man; a hundred times I've killed you in a hundred ways!
All these years I've dreamed of what I'd do when I got out and found you again . . .

"Last night I did find you. I went to that club where you sing, if that's what they
call it now, and I saw the woman I'd gone through so much hell for—just a cheap,
overdressed saloon tramp, that's all. Seven years is enough to give any saloon
tramp. I went back to my hotel and wrote you that note just so you'd know I was
out again, so you could do the sweating for a change; but I never intended to see
you again. I've had it, baby. I'm cured. I don't need your dirty money, and I don't

want you in that beach house or anywhere else. I wouldn't touch you if this was the coldest night of the year!"

It wasn't cold at all. In the last few moments the temperature had gone high in the front seat of the fancy convertible, and there was no button to press that would cool it off. Anger, surprise, and something else livened Crystal's face—something like excitement. Her package had been delivered COD, but she wasn't ready to let the delivery man go.

"Wait. Not here!" she commanded. "Don't get out yet!"

Tony drew back from the door. "I get it," he said. "The station man—you're known here."

"Yes, I am."

"And you wouldn't want a shabby bum to be seen getting out of your car under all these lights any more than you wanted him calling at your dressing room. A parking lot is darker."

She didn't answer. All this time the automatic pump had been whining out gallonage; now it stopped and she leaned across to open the glove compartment. She could have reached without rubbing so close to him, but this was her routine and she played it her way. He got the treatment again as she drew back with the coupon book.

"Nice try," Tony murmured, "but I'm not aroused . . ."

Not by the routine, maybe, but by something else. He never finished his speech because suddenly he was too interested in what he saw inside that lighted glove compartment. It was a gun—a small, snub-nosed revolver . . .

"That'll be four-ninety, lady," the station jockey said at the window.

Crystal scratched her pen across the coupon and handed it to the man. "Here, you finish filling it out," she said. "I can never remember the license number."

. . . A small, snub-nosed revolver. When she looked around it was resting in Tony's hand.

"Go ahead, take it," she said. "It's yours."

"You've kept it all these years," he murmured.

"They're difficult things to get rid of."

"You bet they are—especially if you happen to be an ex-con! No thanks, baby, I don't want this gift either."

He started to put the gun back in the glove compartment, but Crystal intercepted the attempt. She seemed to feel better when it was tucked just inside the open handbag in her lap. She sighed as if something had been too tight and now it was loosened.

"Here's your book, lady," the station man said at the window again.

"Did you get the number?" she asked.

"I sure did, lady."

She was relaxed now. Not cold, not marble at all. "I wonder if Sunset's open all the way out?" she asked. "They were working on it last week."

"Working on it?" echoed the station jockey. The bright overhead light made his face look as white as his uniform. "Oh, sure. It's okay now, lady."

"Fine. Then I'll just stay on Sunset."

She was smiling, actually smiling. The convertible cleared its throat and swung back onto the boulevard. Within a few seconds the bright white glow of the all-night station had been swallowed up in a blackness punctuated only by an occasional streetlamp marking the curving sweep of a road that climbed and dipped on its way to find the sea.

"It's always nice to know where to find a station open at this hour," Crystal murmured. "I usually have the chauffeur get the tank filled every morning, but this morning I didn't. It's easy to get careless, isn't it, Tony?"

There was such a thing as being too relaxed. Some people shouldn't be friendly.

"You must have been really scared," Tony said, eyeing her face in the glow of the instrument lights. "How come you set up this intimate little rendezvous if you thought I wanted to kill you? Did you think I'd be sucker enough to try something at that station?"

"As you say, Tony, there's always a piece left somewhere."

"A piece?"

"A record, a proof of our marriage. Fortunately, you're the only person on this earth who would ever think to look for it."

"Fortunately?" Tony didn't laugh anymore; he didn't even smile. "Look, I told you," he said, "I want no part of you, and I wouldn't dream of ruining your 'career.' The chump who marries Crystal Coe deserves all the grief he gets, even if it isn't legal . . .. You can let me off at the next bus stop."

"You'll never get a bus at this hour."

"Then I'll walk!"

"You don't have to walk, Tony. I'll take you where you're going."

She meant what she was saying, whatever it was. The accelerator moved closer to the floorboards and the convertible took the hills as if they were gulleys.

"What's the pitch?" Tony demanded. "Is your pride wounded? Do you still think you can stir up the embers at that beach house?"

"Maybe that's it, Tony."

"And maybe it isn't? . . . What the hell's that?"

One minute there was nothing on the face of the earth but that big white convertible gouging a tunnel through the blackness, and then they had company. A pair of bright headlights were bouncing in the rearview mirror, and a red spot was flashing a signal that meant trouble in anybody's neighborhood . . . especially to an excon who suddenly felt a little conspicuous among all the gilt.

"The police!" he gasped. "Damn you, what is this? What are you trying to do?"

It was such a jolly ride. The man had his laugh at the service station and the woman had hers as she bore down on that foot pedal. "I'm trying to shake them, Tony," she said, "trying to outdistance them, like the man told me."

"Man?" he yelled. "What man?"

She laughed again. "Why, the man who's holding the gun on me, of course! The man who crawled into my car back at that parking lot and was too busy enjoying his big joke to worry about why I wanted his fingerprints on his own gun . . . or to notice what I wrote on a gas coupon. Do you want to know what I wrote, Tony? I wrote, 'This man is going to kill me . . . call the police!' Don't you get it, Tony? Don't you understand?"

Understanding always took a little time, a few seconds, maybe, a fraction of a second. Time enough for the convertible to make a sudden turn off the boulevard, barely miss a row of brooding pepper trees, and go roaring down a dark side street that stretched like an empty corridor to nowhere. Time enough for a passenger, without a steering wheel to use as a brace, to pick himself off the instrument panel and make a lunge for that gun in the open handbag . . . and come in second.

"Too late," Crystal said, without laughter. "You should have killed me back at the station when you had the chance . . . but I knew you wouldn't. You never had that kind of nerve, and it takes nerve, Tony, to get what you want . . . and keep it!"

"You're crazy!" he yelled. "I told you I was clearing out!"

"If I believed that, I would be crazy! Nobody walks away from a sure thing! If I let you live, you'd bleed me white—"

"But I don't *need* your money! You don't understand—"

Shout at the stars . . . shout at the wind trying to pull loose from the nodding pepper trees . . . shout at death, it was all the same now. Those headlights were in the rearview mirror again, and the lights of the convertible had picked up a row of red buttons on the dead-end barrier ahead. It was time to hit the power brakes and brace against the steering wheel once more, because every ride had to end sometime . . . .

The man plunged forward. He was clawing at the door as he came up, but it was much too late. The snub-nosed revolver had been in the woman's hand ever since the turnoff, and she wasn't going to let him go without a farewell present.

"The first lesson I ever learned was that you can't trust a man," she said. Then she pulled the trigger. Once . . . twice . . .

A frantic hand grabbed at her, ripping away the front of that three-figured creation . . . . Three times . . .

He was dead when the police reached the convertible, dead and bleeding all over the soft red upholstery.

The woman was sobbing hysterically over the steering wheel.

Crystal Coe sobbed for a long time. Nobody asks questions of a sobbing woman; they just stand around looking miserable and wait for her to tell her own story in her own way . . . and in her own time. The time was almost dawn. The window behind the police lieutenant's head had begun to show a foggy gray, and the white ceiling light was starting to pale from competition. In the anteroom outside the lieutenant's office, the representatives of the press were waiting for another front-page spread that would crowd the minor problem of world survival back to the obituaries, where it belonged, and inside the office Crystal Coe was waiting for an annoyance to end. She sat small and helpless in her chair, her face drawn and her eyes appropriately red. At her side stood a paunchy old man with a sweaty bald head and an accumulation of chins. In one hand he held a white Stetson hat; with the other he caressed her bare shoulder. Crystal restrained a shudder and smiled bravely.

"I guess the good Lord was riding with me," she said, in a husky voice. "I knew from the moment the man climbed into my car that he meant to kill me . . . or worse." She paused to draw the mink scarf tighter across her de-bosomed gown. The lieutenant dropped his eyes, and the hand on her shoulder tightened. "All I could do was drive slowly and try to keep him talking—"

"You're a brave woman, Miss Coe," the lieutenant said. "Most women wouldn't have had the presence of mind."

"But there was no choice, Officer. I had to take a chance on a prowl car being near that station . . . . I had to swing off on that dead-end street so he wouldn't make me lose it when it came. That's when he fell against the instrument panel and dropped the gun. That's when I—Oh, it was so terrible!"

Crystal Coe buried her face in a handful of damp linen and smothered one last sob. "My wife's been through enough for one night," the paunchy man said. "I'm takin' her home right now!" It was the voice of a man who didn't expect an argument when he spoke, and he didn't get one now. There was a gun on the lieutenant's desk that was covered with a dead man's fingerprints—there was a coupon from a gasoline credit book covered with a frightened woman's message. There was no argument at all.

Behind the damp linen, Crystal Coe smiled. She was safe now. Nobody would have any curiosity about a crazed ex-convict. She could pose for the photographers outside and wait for the afternoon editions to finish up the story . . . . "Crystal Coe Slays Attacker" . . . "Singer Escapes Rapist." She could go into seclusion for a week or two to rest her nerves, and then go shopping for a new convertible. The old one had bullet holes in the upholstery.

"The man must have been crazy," the lieutenant muttered, "just plain crazy. That station attendant said he was laughing like a maniac."

He couldn't know, of course, what brought the flash of anger to Crystal Coe's eyes. Not knowing, he mistook it for something else.

"Now, don't you trouble yourself because you had to kill a man like that," he said quickly. "He'd have done the same to you—and worse. But his death is going to cause a big headache for somebody. I'm just glad it isn't in my department."

Crystal came to her feet slowly. She didn't want to ask. She didn't want to do anything but get out of this awful place fast, but she had to know.

"A headache?" she echoed.

"A big headache," the lieutenant said. "You see, Miss Coe, we had a report on this man a few days ago. He was an ex-convict, a parolee from another state, but he had special permission to leave that state and come here to close a business deal. Seems he'd invented something while he was in prison—some kind of equipment for showing motion pictures. Signed a contract yesterday that's supposed to guarantee a quarter of a million dollars, cash, for his patent."

"A quarter of a million!"

"Just plain crazy," he repeated, "but can you imagine the kind of investigation it's going to entail to dig up this man's past and find his beneficiary?"

Sylvia
Ira Levin

April 1955

Shortly before noon on the day of his scheduled departure for the Italian Riviera, Lewis Melton searched his daughter's room for a letter she had received a few hours earlier. This secret violation of Sylvia's privacy was performed with reluctance. Like every act it was the result of a somewhat involved set of circumstances and motivations.

A month before, Sylvia had been granted a divorce. Her husband, Lyle Waterman, had been a fortune hunter—a fact which, though obvious to everyone else, had not been demonstrable to Sylvia until he was caught red-handed tracing her endorsement onto an intercepted dividend check. When this happened Melton made a bargain with his son-in-law; Melton would not press a charge of forgery and Waterman would not contest a Nevada mental cruelty divorce. Melton, who was retired, then accompanied Sylvia to a dude ranch outside Reno, where in the usual six weeks the divorce was accomplished.

Back again in Connecticut Melton succumbed to the idea of a few weeks on the Riviera, a suggestion of Sylvia's. The year before, returning from two months abroad to find Sylvia married to Waterman, Melton had been forced to recognize that despite her thirty-two years it was unwise to leave her alone for long periods of time, and he had resolved to avoid doing so in the future. But his relief at Sylvia's freedom, coupled with her expressed desire for solitude, had erased his resolution and lulled him into booking air passage, renewing his passport, contacting acquaintances in San Remo—and now, on the very day of departure, Mrs. Redden, bringing the coffee into his bedroom, had said, "Redden thinks I should tell you, sir, that Miss Sylvia just got a letter addressed in Mr. Waterman's handwriting"— and immediately the whole trip was subject to cancellation.

A letter from Lyle might be harmless; a request, perhaps, for the forwarding of some clothes he had left behind. But it might also be the first step in a brazen campaign to reestablish his influence over Sylvia, undertaken in the knowledge of Melton's planned absence. If that were the case the trip was certainly out of the question, for Sylvia was as easily led as a child's pony. Furthermore, Melton suddenly realized, her habitual demeanor of withdrawn silence, which had deepened since the moment when she learned the truth about Lyle, had effectually masked what emotions might lie within her, and he really had no way of knowing whether her love for Lyle had turned to bitterness, as he had assumed, or whether there might not linger an inclination to forgive, an eagerness to accept any explanation . . .

Desultorily he began his packing, almost certain that the suitcases would have to be unpacked before the day was over. At eleven-thirty, when Sylvia retired to her garden at the rear of the estate, Melton entered her room and began to search for the letter.

In the course of the search he came upon a gun. He had opened a quilted satin box in the top drawer of her dresser and had riffled the edges of the handkerchiefs stacked within it. They parted in mid-pile. He lifted off the upper stack and there it was; a small nickel-plated pistol with a black bakelite grip, incredible upon the soft cushion of Sylvia's flowered handkerchiefs. Melton looked at it, his right hand blindly de positing handkerchiefs on the dresser, thinking: *It must be a joke or a cigarette lighter or something.*

He picked it up. It was heavier than it looked; certainly no cigarette lighter. He held it disbelievingly on the flat of his palm. The bakelite grip was milled in a pattern of tiny diamonds. The short barrel gleamed with an oily sheen, smooth to the fingertips, the whole having an indefinable smell of newness. Where had she gotten it? Reno? The fool! a gun. . . . Events of the past month suddenly sprang into a new and frightening significance. "You really do need a rest," she had said. "The Mallinsons are still in San Remo, aren't they?"

"Well . . . yes. I suppose we *could* leave on the—"

"Not we. You go alone. Honestly, I think being here by myself for a while would be the best thing."

And he had let her talk him into it!

"About the Reddens," she had said later. "We might as well give them their vacation while you're away. I can fend for myself, and then you won't have to put up with a few weeks of canned food later on. I really think that being completely by myself . . ."

Knowing that each of his previous absences had been the occasion for some sort of irresponsible behavior on her part, he had still let her talk him into it! So lulled, so blind!

He found the way to open the gun; the bakelite plaque on the right side swung clockwise, revealing within the handle a vertical metal rack holding five small bullets ready to be pushed up in turn into the firing chamber. Melton shuddered and swung the plaque back down, wishing he could as easily replace Sylvia's mask of stolidity which, penetrated, had disclosed such unsuspected depth of feeling, love warped into such pathetically intense hatred.

The letter from Lyle . . . Melton set the gun carefully upon the dresser and, with an aggrieved headshake, returned his attention to the handkerchief box. He found the letter almost immediately; it was beneath the uppermost handkerchief, the one on which the gun had lain. The envelope, ripped open at one end, was addressed to Sylvia in Lyle's bold, affectedly masculine hand.

Melton drew out a single sheet of paper and unfolded it. It was the stationery of an unfamiliar hotel on West 54th Street in New York. Dated the day before, it read :

Syl darling,

How can I tell you how happy your sweet letter has made me? I can't—not on paper. But when I see you, darling!

Lewis's plane leaves at midnight, so I suppose the train you are driving him to will be the 9:01. I will take the 8:00 from N. Y. which will get me into New Haven at 9:35, so you will only have to wait in the station half an hour.

Until tomorrow night, darling—

Always your loving

Lyle

Melton read the letter twice, then folded it back into its envelope. He picked up the gun and stood with the letter in one hand and the gun in the other, staring at them, thinking that Lyle, poor Lyle, with his scheming and conniving, wasn't truly dangerous at all; but Sylvia, slow, quiet Sylvia . . .

He put the letter back on the handkerchiefs in the box, covered it with the single one, and put the gun on top of that. He replaced the other handkerchiefs, closed the box and closed the drawer. With his hands braced on the top of the dresser, he leaned forward, resting his suddenly tired weight upon them. Slow, quiet Sylvia . . .

He straightened up and stared unseeingly at his reflection in the mirror. After a moment he turned and walked quickly from the room.

He went back into his own room and to the telephone beside the bed. A call to Information supplied him with the number of the hotel on West 54th Street. He relayed it to the operator along with his own number and stood waiting, his eyes on Sylvia's photograph on the bedside table, until a female voice small in his ear slurred the name of the hotel into an unintelligible syllable.

"Lyle Waterman, please," Melton said. Again he waited, searching for words that would not sound melodramatic. After a moment there was the sound of a receiver being lifted and Lyle's voice said, "Hello?"—thick, cut out of a yawn.

"Lyle? This is Lewis."

"Well. What a *lovely* way to start the day."

"Lyle, I have to speak to you." There was a moment of silence. "You mustn't come up here tonight. Sylvia—"

Angrily Lyle said, "Been reading Sylvia's mail?"

"Lyle, she's—"

"Let me speak to Sylvia."

"She isn't in the house. She—"

Lyle hung up.

Melton jiggled the crossbar and got the operator back. He told her he had been disconnected and she put the call through again.

"Mr. Waterman doesn't answer," the girl in the hotel said.

"This is a matter of life and death," Melton said. "Literally of life and death."

"I'll try again," the girl said nervously.

She tried again, but there was no response. "Should I send one of the boys up?"

"No. Never mind." Melton hung up.

He rang for Redden and took off his sport shirt. He put on a white shirt and was knotting his tie when Redden came in. Melton told him to bring the Lincoln around front. He ran a comb through his white hair and took a tweed jacket from the closet.

When he descended the stairs into the hall, Mrs. Redden was on a stepladder polishing the mirror with a ball of wadded newspaper. Melton said, "Tell Sylvia I was called into New York on some business. I'll be back at five or so." He straightened his tie in the mirror. "I want you to take all the phone calls this afternoon, Mrs. Redden," he said. "If Mr. Waterman calls—you'll know his voice, won't you?"

"Yes, sir."

"Tell him that Sylvia's in New Haven. He's been bothering her."

"Yes, sir," Mrs. Redden said.

Melton went briskly out into the graveled drive, where Redden was holding open the driver's door of the Lincoln.

At a quarter past two Melton parked the car in a lot on West 53rd Street and walked around the block to Lyle's hotel. It was a shabby building with a blue neon *sign—Transients—glowing* dispiritedly in the bright sunlight. The lobby was dim, with sagging leather chairs and the smell of rubber floormats. There was a quarter-circle desk in one corner and behind it, in a nest of pigeonholes, a round-faced man with no facial hair whatsoever and an embarrassingly obvious wig. Melton asked him for Lyle Waterman.

"He's out," the man said.

"What room is he in?"

"Three-fourteen, but he's out. You can't go up."

"Did he tell you to say he was out?"

"He's out," the man said. He pointed to the 314 pigeonhole; a brick-colored key tag hung from it. "He went out about an hour ago."

"Did he leave any word as to when he'd be back?"

"No word," the man said. "He just went out."

Melton sat down in one of the leather club chairs, across from two dark-skinned men speaking machine gun Spanish. The chair was too deep for comfort and there was a fetid cigar butt in the pot of sand beside it. After a few minutes Melton pulled himself up, went to the newsstand and bought a *Journal-American.* In a different chair, which was just as bad, he sat skimming the newspaper, glancing up at each sibilant push of the revolving door.

Lyle came in at twenty after three, his finger hooking a paper-sheathed clothes hanger over his shoulder. Melton stood up. Lyle paused for a moment, staring at him, and then he continued on his way towards the desk, his lips clamped and his thick-lashed eyes narrowed, like a spoiled child going up to bed without his dinner. Melton intercepted him and caught his free arm, gripping it tight in a sudden burst of hatred. "Let go of me!" Lyle whispered.

Melton took a deep breath and, with urgent emphasis, said, "I have to speak to you."

"Let *go* of me."

Melton released his arm.

"Go on," Lyle said, not looking at Melton, "speak. I can hardly wait."

"Not here," Melton said.

"Look, if you—"

"I drove all the way for this, Lyle. Not for my sake; for yours."

Lyle's mouth worked peevishly, and finally he said, "Oh, hell," and went resignedly to the desk to collect his key. Melton followed him. Waiting for the elevator Melton saw that Lyle had just had a haircut; bits of black hair clung to the back of his shirt collar.

They rode up to the third floor and walked along a narrow corridor whose floor creaked under thin carpet. Lyle unlocked 314. "The presidential suite," he said wryly, pushing open the door and going in. Melton followed him and closed the door. Lyle hooked the clothes hanger on a partially opened closet door. "*House Beautiful* is taking pictures next Tuesday," he said.

The room was small and crowded. There were a bureau, a writing table and a sink squeezed together against one wall, and jutting at them from the wall opposite, twin beds separated by a night table with a spindly white lamp. The single window, in the central wall, had a buff shade and a green one, but no curtains. The beds were metal, painted to look like wood. On the one nearer the window lay a gray leather suitcase with white whipcord stitching and L.W. in small gold letters.

Lyle sat down on the other bed, then swung himself out full length, his hands cupping his head on the pillow, his heels pushing ripples into the faded peach bedspread. He lay looking at the ceiling, blinking occasionally, as though he were completely alone.

Melton drew a chair from the writing table, turned it to face the beds, and sat down.

"Before I tell you what I have to tell you," he said, "I want you to bear in mind that Sylvia is thirty-three years old, that she was thirty-two when you married her, and that she had never been in love before."

Lyle closed his eyes.

"You should also know," Melton said, "that her face, when she was shown your little penmanship exercise on the back of her check, was not a very pleasant face to behold. It was like watching a human being turn into a statue. And she's remained that way. She holds a book in front of her but she doesn't read. Or she goes into her garden and presses earth around flowers that are already dead."

A deep breath lifted Lyle's chest and sighed out from his nostrils.

"I think she has it in her mind to kill you tonight," Melton said. "There's a gun in the top drawer of her dresser."

Lyle's eyes opened.

"I assume she bought it in Reno."

Lyle raised himself on his elbows and looked at Melton. After a moment he said, "You're making this up."

Sharply Melton said, "Oh, yes. I go around telling people that my daughter is contemplating murder." He stared contemptuously at Lyle, and then sank back in his chair. "This trip of mine," he said. "It was Sylvia's idea. And the Reddens are leaving for Vermont tonight. Immediately after dinner. That was Sylvia's idea too."

Lyle said, "She didn't tell me the Reddens would be away. . . ." He swung his legs off the bed and sat leaning forward, his elbows on his knees and his hands clasped in space.

"What *did* she tell you?"

Lyle rubbed the heels of his clasped hands together.

Melton said, "For pity's sake, there's a *gun* in her dresser!"

Lyle unclasped his hands and sat up straight, palming his thighs rigidly. "I got a letter the day before yesterday," he said. He was trying to sound brisk and businesslike, but he sounded frightened. "She said she wanted to see me. She was driving you to New Haven and she wanted me to come up and meet her at the station after you left. Tonight. She wanted to give me a chance to explain. She told me—" his voice wavered—"she told me not to tell anyone where I was going because it might get back to you somehow and you might call off your trip."

Melton put his hands to his face and rubbed his eyelids with his fingertips. "Oh Lord," he said, "can you conceive of her plotting, planning . . ." He stood up and turned his chair back under the writing table. "It's my fault," he said. "I never should have let her talk me into taking the trip." He turned to the window and stared out into a gray courtyard. "Did she ever tell you about the gypsies?"

"Gypsies?"

"Eight, no, ten years ago. My wife was alive then. We went to South America for a couple of months. You would think you could leave a girl of twenty-three alone for two months, wouldn't you? With a houseful of servants? Well, we came back to find the servants gone—she'd paid them off and given them a holiday—and the house full of gypsies. Gypsies! She'd invited them in for tea, like a girl in a fairy tale." He shook his head dolefully. "There were two goats in the garage."

"Gypsies," Lyle said, smiling thinly.

"There are some people," Melton said, "who grow up without ever attaining a firm grasp on reality."

They fell silent for a moment.

"What are you going to do?" Lyle asked.

"I'm not sure," Melton said. "My trip is cancelled, of course. I'll tell her that there's been some trouble with my passport or something. I'd like to avoid humiliating her, manage somehow to smooth over this entire situation without ever letting her know I'm aware of its existence. I'll talk to her, tell her I can see she's still brooding about you. If I can make her realize you're best forgotten . . . ."

Lyle said softly, "Good Lord, she actually wants to kill me . . ." He stretched out on the bed again. "Good Lord," he said wonderingly. There was a faint, flattered smile about his lips. It lingered for a moment, then dissolved, his eyes growing thoughtful. He glanced at Melton's back.

"What if you can't?" he said. He was speaking more slowly now. "What if you can't make her see the light? Suppose she takes her gun and comes after me. Don't you think it would be a good idea if I moved to a different hotel?"

"Yes," Melton said, "I suppose it would."

"The only trouble is," Lyle said, "I can't afford to move to a different hotel."

Melton turned from the window.

"I would even leave New York," Lyle said, "if I could afford to. Then you wouldn't have *any* worries about Sylvia getting herself into trouble."

Melton looked at him.

"Where would you go?" he said. Lyle pondered.

"Dallas," he said. "Dallas, Texas." He thought for a moment. "Or is Houston the big city there? Oh well, Dallas or Houston."

Impassively Melton took out his wallet. Behind the bills he always kept a blank check.

Locked in the crawling traffic of the West Side Highway, Melton considered how best to temper Sylvia from her intended violence without revealing his own knowledge of it. He turned off onto the Merritt Parkway and as he did so he remembered that he had not eaten since breakfast. He stopped at a restaurant, ordered mechanically and ate without interest.

It was past seven o'clock when he guided the Lincoln between the stone posts and up the circular drive towards the front of the house. The Reddens' Plymouth was parked there, with Mrs. Redden in the act of pushing down the lid of the luggage compartment. Melton pulled up behind her and got out of the car.

"Good evening, sir," Mrs. Redden said a bit uncomfortably. "There's some dinner keeping warm on the stove."

"I ate on the road," Melton said .

Mrs. Redden brightened. "We offered to stay on till tomorrow, but Miss Sylvia insisted we shouldn't."

"Where is she?"

"Playing the piano."

Melton went up the steps and to the front door, stopping short as Redden came out with two umbrellas on his arm. "Oh, good evening," Redden said cheerfully. "I finished your packing and brought the suitcases down. There are two telegrams in your room."

"I . . . thanks." Melton caught the door, interrupting its slow swing closed.

"*Bon voyage,*" Redden said.

"Yes, *bon voyage!*" Mrs. Redden called from the car.

"Thanks. Have a good trip." Melton stepped into the house and pulled the door shut after him. He heard Mrs. Redden call out something about Italian food.

His three aluminum suitcases, tagged and labeled, were lined up in a corner of the hall. He looked at them blankly. From the rear of the house came the skipping notes of *The Spinning Song*. Sylvia had been given lessons as a child, but *The Spinning Song* was the only piece she remembered now. She played it rarely and not well. Melton went to the stairs. He listened as he climbed, thinking of all the lessons and practicing that had gone to produce this one awkwardly played selection, and thinking, beneath that, of what he would say to Sylvia.

He went into his room and found the two telegrams. They were from friends, wishing him a safe flight and a pleasant stay on the Riviera. He tossed them on the bed and went into the bathroom.

When he had washed up he came down the stairs again. The piano was silent now. "Sylvia?" he called.

There was no answer. He went into the living room and through it to the music room. She was not there. He returned to the hallway and called her name up the stairs, thinking that perhaps she had gone into her bedroom while he was in the bathroom, but the only answer was silence.

She was in her garden, of course. Melton went down the hall, through the pantry, and into the kitchen. He opened the back door. The sun had gone from the sky and the first blue of dusk was falling. Melton peered across the expanse of lawn, searching for movement behind the high shrubbery that fronted the garden. He moved forward. How like Sylvia, he thought—a walled garden . . . Birds were calling from the woods beyond. Melton was halfway across the lawn when there was a flutter of movement in the shrubbery and Sylvia came out. She was wearing her gardening smock.

"Sylvia," Melton called.

She gave a little jump. "Oh, hello," she said, smiling. Her glasses were askew and as Melton drew nearer he saw drops of perspiration on her white forehead.

"Working hard?" he said .

"I was beginning to worry. You're late, aren't you? The Reddens have left already."

"I know."

She looked at his jacket. "You're going to change, aren't you?"

"No rush," Melton said. He went over to a wooden bench built around the trunk of an old oak and sat down.

Sylvia followed and stood before him, looking at her watch. "It's twenty of eight," she said.

"I'm afraid the trip is postponed," Melton said.

"What?" She was staring at him.

"There's been some trouble with my passport."

"How could there be trouble with your passport? They renewed it. You showed it to me. How could there be trouble?"

He took her hands and drew her gently to the seat beside him. "Well, as a matter of fact, there *hasn't* been trouble. It's because of you that I'm going to put it off."

"But you told everyone you're leaving!"

"So I'll call them tomorrow and tell them I'm not leaving."

"But why?" she said. "Why?"

"Because you're still brooding about Lyle," he said. "I can't leave you this way, Sylvia."

She managed a nervous laugh. "No," she said. "No, I'm not. Honestly I'm not."

"You are, Sylvia," he said. "You know you can't fool *me.*"

Her gaze dropped to her lap.

"He's not worth it, Sylvia," Melton said. "Believe me, he's not worth brooding over, not worth hating, not even worth thinking about."

She looked up, suddenly smiling. She took his hand. "Come look at the flowers," she said childishly.

"All right, Sylvia."

They rose and went to the shrubbery and the narrow path that penetrated it. Sylvia parted the branches with her free hand, holding them as she went through so they wouldn't spring back at Melton.

Once on the other side she released his hand and moved forward quickly to a hill of earth at the far side of the garden. She pointed to the ground beside it. "Look!" she said proudly.

Melton came forward and looked. There was a large rectangular hole, very long and quite deep. In the bottom of it, inexplicably, lay Melton's three aluminum suitcases.

He looked at Sylvia wonderingly.

The gun was in her hand. She pushed a wisp of hair up off her forehead. "You ruined my life," she said softly.

Melton stared at her.

"You did," she said. "Ruined it. Thirty-three years. Snooping, spying, arranging things behind my back. Do you think I'm some kind of idiot who can't comb her own hair?" Tears welled up behind her glasses. "That's all there is, a person's life. And you ruined mine!"

"Sylvia . . ."

"Thirty-three years!" It was a scream, cords stretching in her throat. "But no more! Not the rest of it! He's coming back!" Tears were rolling down her flushed cheeks. "Lyle's coming back! Tonight! And he still loves me and this time you're not going to send him away!"

The gun in her hand spat brightness and shot a bolt of heat into Melton's chest. "Sylvia!" he cried.

Melton swayed, trying to speak, trying to tell her that Lyle was no good, that Lyle had been bought off, that Lyle wasn't . . . He stood swaying, staring at her, his hands to his wet chest, and for the first time in his life he saw that her eyes, which had always seemed a dull and empty blue, could burst on occasion to a vivid, gemlike intensity.

"Oh my God," he said, tumbling forward to the ground.

Protection
Erle Stanley Gardner

May 1955

The roadside restaurant oozed an atmosphere of peaceful prosperity. It was a green-painted building set in a white graveled circle in the triangle where the two main highways joined.

Five miles beyond, a pall of hazy smog marked the location of the city; but out here at the restaurant the air was pure and crystal clear.

George Ollie slid down from the stool behind the cash register and walked over to look out of the window. His face held an expression which indicated physical well-being and mental contentment.

In the seven short years since he had started working as a cook over the big range in the rear he had done pretty well for himself—exceptionally well for a two-time loser—although no one here knew that, of course. Nor did *anyone* know of that last job where a confederate had lost his head and pulled the trigger . . .

But all that was in the past. George Ollie, president of a luncheon club, member of the Chamber of Commerce, had no connection with that George Ollie who had been prisoner number 56289.

In a way, however, George owed something of his present prosperity to his criminal record. When he had started work in the restaurant, that bank job which had been "ranked" preyed on his mind. For three years he had been intent on keeping out of circulation. He had stayed in his room nights and had perforce saved all the money that he had made.

So, when the owner's heart had given out and it became necessary for him to sell almost on a moment's notice, George was able to make a down payment in cash. From then on, hard work, careful management, and the chance relocation of a main highway had spelled prosperity for the ex-con.

George turned away from the window, looked over the tables at the symmetrical figure of Stella, the head waitress, as she bent over the table taking the orders of the family that had just entered.

Just as the thrill of pride swept through George whenever he looked at the well-kept restaurant, the graveled parking place, and the constantly accelerating stream of traffic which furnished him with a constantly increasing number of customers—so did George thrill with a sense of possessive pride whenever he looked at Stella's smoothly curved figure.

There was no question but what Stella knew how to wear clothes. Somewhere, George thought, there must in Stella's past have been a period of prosperity, a period when she had worn the latest Parisian models with distinction. Now she wore the light-blue uniform, with the white starched cuffs above the elbow and the white collar, with that same air of distinction. She not only classed up the uniforms but she classed up the place.

When Stella walked, the lines of her figure rippled smoothly beneath the clothes. Customers looking at her invariably looked again. Yet Stella was always demure, never forward. She smiled at the right time and in the right manner. If the customer tried to get intimate, Stella always managed to create an atmosphere of urgency so that she gave the impression of an amiable, potentially willing young woman too busy for intimacies.

George could tell from the manner in which she put food down at a table and smilingly hurried back to the kitchen, as though on a matter of the greatest importance, just what was being said by the people at the table—whether it was an appreciative acknowledgment of skillful service, good-natured banter, or the attempt on the part of predatory males to make a date.

But George had never inquired into Stella's past. Because of his own history he had a horror of anything that even hinted of an attempt to inquire into one's past. The present was all that counted.

Stella herself avoided going to the city. She went on a shopping trip once or twice a month, attended an occasional movie, but for the rest stayed quietly at home in the little motel a couple of hundred yards down the roadway.

George was aroused from his reverie by a tapping sound. The man at the counter was tapping a coin on the mahogany. He had entered from the east door and George, contemplating the restaurant, hadn't noticed him.

During this period of slack time in the afternoon Stella was the only waitress on duty. Unexpectedly half a dozen tables had filled up and Stella was busy.

George departed from his customary post at the cash register to approach the man. He handed over a menu, filled a glass with water, arranged a napkin, spoon, knife, and fork, and stood waiting.

The man, his hat pulled well down on his forehead, tossed the menu to one side with a gesture almost of contempt.

"Curried shrimp."

"Sorry," George explained affably, "that's not on the menu today."

"Curried shrimp," the man repeated.

George raised his voice. Probably the other was hard of hearing. "We don't have them today, sir. We have . . ."

"You heard me," the man said. "Curried shrimp. Go get 'em."

There was something about the dominant voice, the set of the man's shoulders, the arrogance of manner, that tugged at George's memory. Now that he thought back on it, even the contemptuous gesture with which the man had tossed the menu to one side without reading it meant something.

George leaned a little closer.

"Larry!" he exclaimed in horror.

Larry Giffen looked up and grinned. "Georgie!" The way he said the name was contemptuously sarcastic.

"When . . . when did you . . . how did you get out?"

"It's okay, Georgie," Larry said. "*I* went out through the front door. Now go get me the curried shrimp."

"Look, Larry," George said, making a pretense of fighting the feeling of futility this man always inspired, "the cook is cranky. I'm having plenty of trouble with the help and . . ."

"You heard me," Larry interrupted. "Curried shrimp!"

George met Larry's eyes, hesitated, turned away toward the kitchen.

Stella paused beside the range as he was working over the special curry sauce.

"What's the idea?" she asked.

"A special."

Her eyes studied his face. "How special?"

"*Very* special." She walked out.

Larry Giffen ate the curried shrimp. He looked around the place with an air of proprietorship.

"Think maybe I'll go in business with you, Georgie."

George Ollie knew from the dryness in his mouth, the feeling of his knees that that was what he had been expecting.

Larry jerked his head toward Stella. "She goes with the joint."

Ollie, suddenly angry and belligerent, took a step forward. "She doesn't go with anything."

Giffen laughed, turned on his heel, started toward the door, swung back, said, "I'll see you after closing tonight," and walked out.

It wasn't until the period of dead slack that Stella moved close to George.

"Want to tell me?" she asked.

He tried to look surprised. "What?"

"Nothing."

"I'm sorry Stella. I can't."

"Why not?"

"He's dangerous."

"To whom?"

"To you—to both of us."

She made a gesture with her shoulder. "You never gain anything by running."

He pleaded with her. "Don't get tangled in it Stella. You remember last night the police were out here for coffee and doughnuts after running around like mad—those two big jobs, the one on the safe in the bank, the other on the theater safe?"

She nodded.

"I should have known then," he told her. "That's Larry's technique. He never leaves them anything to work on. Rubber gloves so there are no fingerprints. Burglar alarms disconnected. Everything like clockwork. No clues. No wonder the police were nuts. Larry Giffen never leaves them a clue."

She studied him. "What's he got on *you?*"

George turned away, then faced her, tried to speak, and couldn't.

"Okay," she said, "I withdraw the question."

Two customers came in, Stella escorted them to a table and went on with the regular routine. She seemed calmly competent completely unworried. George Ollie, on the other hand, couldn't get his thoughts together. His world had collapsed. Rubber-glove Giffen must have found out about that bank job with the green accomplice, otherwise he wouldn't have dropped in.

News travels fast in the underworld. Despite carefully cultivated changes in his personal appearance, some smart ex-con while eating at the restaurant must have "made" George Ollie. He had said nothing to George, but had reserved the news as an exclusive for the ears of Larry Giffen. The prison underworld knew Big Larry might have use for George—as a farmer might have use for a horse.

And now Larry had "dropped in."

Other customers arrived. The restaurant filled up. The rush-hour waitresses came on. For two and a half hours there was so much business that George had no chance to think. Then business began to slacken. By eleven o'clock it was down to a trickle. At midnight George closed up.

"Coming over?" Stella asked.

"Not tonight," George said. "I want to do a little figuring on a purchase list."

She said nothing and went out.

George locked the doors, put on the heavy double bolts, and yet, even as he turned out the lights and put the bars in place, he knew that bolts wouldn't protect him from what was coming.

Larry Giffen kicked on the door at twelve-thirty.

George, in the shadows, pretended not to hear. He wondered what Larry would do if he found that George had ignored his threat, had gone away and left the place protected by locks and the law.

Larry Giffen knew better. He kicked violently on the door, then turned and banged it with his heel-banged it so hard that the glass rattled and threatened to break.

George hurried out of the shadows and opened the door.

"What's the idea of keeping me waiting, Georgie?" Larry asked with a solicitude that was overdone to the point of sarcasm. "Don't you want to be chummy with your old friend?"

George said, "Larry, I'm on the square. I'm on the legit. I'm staying that way."

Larry threw back his head and laughed. "You know what happens to rats, Georgie."

"I'm no rat, Larry. I'm going straight, that's all. I've paid my debts to the law and to you."

Larry showed big yellowed teeth as he grinned. "Ain't that nice, Georgie. *All* your debts paid! Now how about that National Bank job where Skinny got in a panic because the cashier didn't get 'em up fast enough?"

"I wasn't in on that, Larry."

Larry's grin was triumphant. "Says you! You were handling the getaway car. The cops got one fingerprint from the rearview mirror. The FBI couldn't classify that one print, but if anyone ever started 'em checking it with *your* file, Georgie, your fanny would be jerked off that cushioned stool by the cash register and transferred to the electric chair—the hot seat, Georgie . . . You never did like the hot seat, Georgie."

George Ollie licked dry lips. His forehead moistened with sweat. He wanted to say something but there was nothing he could say.

Larry went on talking. "I pulled a couple of jobs here. I'm going to pull just one more. Then I'm moving in with you, Georgie. I'm your new partner. You need a little protection. I'm giving it to you."

Larry swaggered over to the cash register, rang up No Sale, pulled the drawer open, raised the hood over the roll of paper to look at the day's receipts.

"Now, Georgie," he said, regarding the empty cash drawer, "you shouldn't have put away all that dough. Where is it?"

George Ollie gathered all the reserves of his self-respect. "Go to hell," he said. "I've been on the square and I'm going to stay on the square."

Larry strode across toward him. His open left hand slammed against the side of George's face with staggering impact.

"You're hot," Larry said, and his right hand swung up to the other side of George's face. "You're hot, Georgie," and his left hand came up from his hip.

George made a pretense at defending himself but Larry Giffen, quick as a cat, strong as a bear, came after him. "You're hot." . . . Wham . . . "You're hot." . . . Wham . . . "You're hot, Georgie."

At length Larry stepped back. "I'm taking a half interest. You'll run it for me when I'm not here, Georgie. You'll keep accurate books. You'll do all the work. Half of the profits are mine. I'll come in once in a while to look things over. Be damn certain that you don't try any cheating, Georgie.

"You wouldn't like the hot squat, Georgie. You're fat, Georgie. You're well fed. You've teamed up with that swivel-hipped babe, Georgie. I could see it in your eye. She's class, and she goes with the place, Georgie. Remember, I'm cutting myself in for a half interest. I'm leaving it to you to see there isn't any trouble."

George Ollie's head was in a whirl. His cheeks were stinging from the heavy-handed slaps of the big man. His soul felt crushed under a weight. Larry Giffen knew no law but the law of power, and Larry Giffen, his little malevolent eyes glittering with sadistic gloating, was on the move, coming toward him again, hoping for an opportunity to beat up on him.

George hadn't known when Stella had let herself in. Her key had opened the door smoothly.

"What's he got on you, George?" she asked.

Larry Giffen swung to the sound of her voice. "Well, well, little Miss Swivel-hips," he said. "Come here, Swivel-hips. I'm half owner in the place now. Meet your new boss."

She stood still, looking from him to George Ollie. Larry turned to George.

"All right, Georgie, where's the safe? Give me the combination to the safe, Georgie. As your new partner I'll need to have it. I'll handle the day's take. Later on you can keep books, but right now, I need money. I have a heavy date tonight."

George Ollie hesitated a moment, then moved back toward the kitchen.

"I said give *me* the combination to the safe," Larry Giffen said, his voice cracking like a whip.

Stella was looking at him. George had to make it a showdown. "The dough's back here," he said. He moved toward the rack where the big butcher knives were hanging.

Larry Giffen read his mind. Larry had always been able to read him like a book.

Larry's hand moved swiftly. A snub-nosed gun nestled in Larry's big hand.

There was murder in the man's eye but his voice remained silky and taunting.

"Now, Georgie, you must be a good boy. Don't act rough. Remember, Georgie, I've done my last time. No one takes Big Larry alive. Give me the combination to the safe, Georgie. And I don't want any fooling!"

George Ollie reached a decision. It was better to die fighting than to be strapped into an electric chair. He ignored the gun, kept moving back toward the knife rack.

Big Larry Giffen was puzzled for a moment. George had always col lapsed like a flat tire when Larry had given an order. This was a new George Ollie. Larry couldn't afford to shoot. He didn't want noise and he didn't want to kill.

"Hold it, Georgie! You don't need to get rough." Larry put away his gun. "You're hot on that bank job, Georgie. Remember I can send you to the hot squat. That's all the argument I'm going to use, Georgie. You don't need to go for a shiv. Just tell me to walk out, Georgie, and I'll leave. Big Larry doesn't stay where he isn't welcome.

"But you'd better welcome me, Georgie boy. You'd better give me the combination to the safe. You'd better take me in as your new partner. Which is it going to be, Georgie?"

It was Stella who answered the question. Her voice was calm and clear. "Don't hurt him. You'll get the money."

Big Larry looked at her. His eyes changed expression. "Now that's the sort of a broad *I* like. Tell your new boss where the safe is. Start talking, babe, and remember you go with the place."

"There isn't any safe," George said hurriedly. "I banked the money."

Big Larry grinned. "You're a liar. You haven't left the place. I've been casing the joint. Go on, babe, tell me where the hell that safe is. Then Georgie here will give his new partner the combination."

"Concealed back of the sliding partition in the pie counter," Stella said.

"Well, well, well," Larry Giffen observed, "isn't *that* interesting?"

"Please don't hurt him," Stella pleaded. "The shelves lift out . . ."

"Stella!" George Ollie said sharply. "Shut up!"

"The damage has been done now, Georgie boy," Giffen said.

He slid back the glass doors of the pie compartment, lifted out the shelves, put them on the top of the counter, then slid back the partition disclosing the safe door.

"Clever, Georgie boy, clever! You called on your experience, didn't you? And now the combination, Georgie."

Ollie said, "You can't get away with it, Larry. I won't . . ."

"Now, Georgie boy, don't talk that way. I'm your partner. I'm in here fifty-fifty with you. You do the work and run the place and I'll take my half from time to time-But you've been holding out on me for a while, Georgie boy, so everything that's in the safe is part of my half. Come on with the combination-Of course, I could make a spindle job on it, but since I'm a half owner in the joint I hate to damage any of the property. Then you'd have to buy a new safe. The cost of that would have to come out of your half. You couldn't expect *me* to pay for a new safe."

Rubber-glove Giffen laughed at his little joke.

"I said to hell with you," George Ollie said.

Larry Giffen's fist clenched. "I guess you need a damn good working over, Georgie boy. You shouldn't be disrespectful . . ."

Stella's voice cut in. "Leave him alone. I said you'd get the money. George doesn't want any electric chair."

Larry turned back to her. "I like 'em sensible, sweetheart. Later on, I'll tell you about it. Right now it's all business. Business before pleasure. Let's go."

"Ninety-seven four times to the right," Stella said.

"Well, well, well," Giffen observed. "She knows the combination. We both know what that means, Georgie boy, don't we?"

George, his face red and swollen from the impact of the slaps, stood helpless.

"It means she really is part of the place," Giffen said. "I've got a half interest in you too, girlie. I'm looking forward to collecting on that too. Now what's the rest of the combination?"

Giffen bent over the safe; then, suddenly thinking better of it, he straightened, slipped the snub-nosed revolver into his left hand, and said, "Just so you don't get ideas, Georgie boy—but you wouldn't, you know. You don't like the idea of the hot squat."

Stella, white-faced and tense, called out the numbers. Larry Giffen spun the dials on the safe, swung the door open, opened the cash box.

"Well, well, well," he said, sweeping the bills and money into his pocket. "It *was* a good day, wasn't it?"

Stella said, "There's a hundred-dollar bill in the ledger."

Big Larry pulled out the ledger. "So there is, so there is," he said, surveying the hundred-dollar bill with the slightly torn corner. "Girlie, you're a big help. I'm glad you go with the place. I think we're going to get along swell."

Larry straightened, backed away from the safe, stood looking at George Ollie.

"Don't look like that Georgie boy. It isn't so bad. I'll leave you enough profit to keep you in business and keep you interested in the work. I'll just take off most of the cream. I'll drop in to see you from time to time, and, of course, Georgie boy, you won't tell anybody that you've seen me. Even if you did it wouldn't do any good because I came out the front door, Georgie boy. I'm smart. I'm not like you. I don't have something hanging over me where someone can jerk the rug out from under me at any time.

"Well, Georgie boy, I've got to be toddling along. I've got a little job at the supermarket up the street. They put altogether too much confidence in that safe they have. But I'll be back in a couple of hours, Georgie boy. I've collected on part of my investment and now I want to collect on the rest of it. You wait up for me, girlie. You can go get some shut-eye, Georgie."

Big Larry looked at Stella, walked to the door, stood for a moment searching the shadows, then melted away into the darkness.

"You," Ollie said to Stella, his voice showing his heartsickness at her betrayal.

"What?" she asked.

"Telling him about the safe—about that hundred dollars, giving him the combination . . ."

She said, "I couldn't stand to have him hurt you."

"You and the things you can't stand," Ollie said. "You don't know Rubber-glove Giffen. You don't know what you're in for now. You don't . . ."

"Shut up," she interrupted. "If you're going to insist on letting other people do your thinking for you, I'm taking on the job."

He looked at her in surprise.

She walked over to the closet, came out with a wrecking bar. Before he had the faintest idea of what she had in mind she walked over to the cash register, swung the bar over her head, and brought it down with crashing impact on the front of the register. Then she inserted the point of the bar, pried back the chrome steel, jerked the drawer open. She went to the back door, unlocked it, stood on the outside, inserted the end of the wrecking bar, pried at the door until she had crunched the wood of the door jamb.

George Ollie was watching her in motionless stupefaction. "What the devil are you doing?" he asked. "Don't you realize . . .?"

"Shut up," she said. "What's this you once told me about a spindle job? Oh, yes, you knock off the knob and punch out the spindle—"

She walked over to the safe and swung the wrecking bar down on the knob of the combination, knocking it out of its socket, letting it roll crazily along the floor. Then she went to the kitchen, picked out a towel, polished the wrecking bar clean of fingerprints.

"Let's go," she said to George Ollie.

"Where?" he asked.

"To Yuma," she said. "We eloped an hour and a half ago—hadn't you heard? We're getting married. There's no delay or red tape in Arizona. As soon as we cross the state line we're free to get spliced. You need someone to do your thinking for you. I'm taking the job.

"And," she went on, as George Ollie stood there, "in this state a husband can't testify against his wife, and a wife can't testify against her husband. In view of what I know now it might be just as well."

George stood looking at her, seeing something he had never seen before—a fierce, possessive something that frightened him at the same time it reassured him. She was like a panther protecting her young.

"But I don't get it," George said. "What's the idea of wrecking the place, Stella?"

"Wait until you see the papers," she told him. "I still don't get it," he told her.

"You will," she said.

George stood for another moment. Then he walked toward her. Strangely enough he wasn't thinking of the trap but of the smooth contours under her pale blue uniform. He thought of Yuma, of marriage and of security, of a home.

It wasn't until two days later that the local newspapers were available in Yuma. There were headlines on an inside page:

RESTAURANT BURGLARIZED
WHILE PROPRIETOR ON
HONEYMOON

BIG LARRY GIFFEN KILLED IN
GUN BATTLE WITH OFFICERS

The newspaper account went on to state that Mrs. George Ollie had telephoned the society editor from Yuma stating that George Ollie and she had left the night before and had been married in the Gretna Green across the state line. The society editor had asked her to hold the phone and had the call switched to the police.

Police asked to have George Ollie put on the line. They had a surprise for him. It seemed that when the merchant patrolman had made his regular nightly check of Ollie's restaurant at 1 A.M., he found it had been broken into. Police had found a perfect set of fingerprints on the cash register and on the safe. Fast work had served to identify the fingerprints as those of Big Larry Giffen, known in the underworld as Rubber-glove Giffen because of his skill in wearing rubber gloves and never leaving fingerprints. This was one job that Big Larry had messed up. Evidently he had forgotten his gloves.

Police had mug shots of Big Larry and in no time at all they had out a general alarm.

Only that afternoon George Ollie's head waitress and part-time cashier had gone to the head of the police burglary detail. "In case we should ever be robbed," she had said, "I'd like to have it so you could get a conviction when you get the man who did the job. I left a hundred-dollar bill in the safe. I've torn off a corner. Here's the torn corner. You keep it. That will enable you to get a conviction if you get the thief."

Police thought it was a fine idea. It was such a clever idea they were sorry they couldn't have used it to pin a conviction on Larry Giffen.

But Larry had elected to shoot it out with the arresting officers. Knowing his record, officers had been prepared for this. After the sawed-off shotguns had blasted the life out of Big Larry the police had found the bloodstained hundred-dollar bill in his pocket when his body was stripped at the morgue.

Police also found the loot from three other local jobs on him, cash amounting to some seven thousand dollars.

Police were still puzzled as to how it happened that Giffen, known to the underworld as the most artistic box man in the business, had done such an amateurish job at the restaurant. Giffen's reputation was that he had never left a fingerprint or a clue.

Upon being advised that his place had been broken into, George Ollie, popular restaurant owner, had responded in a way which was perfectly typical of honeymooners the world over.

"The hell with business," he had told the police. "I'm on my honeymoon."

Blonde at the Wheel

Stephen Marlowe

October 1955

It was a tomato-red convertible with cream colored leather fixings. I looked under the girl's tawny arm and saw the speedometer needle dance up around seventy, then glue itself there. The dash looked Buick.

"I don't know why I'm doing this," the girl said.

Sun-scorched asphalt shimmered on the highway with heat-haze. Scrub pine crowded the road on our right, fringed it sparsely on the left and shared the job there with palm trees, partially screening the beach and blue water beyond. I wondered how long we'd been driving like that. I wondered if I should know the girl's name. She wore a one-piece, strapless yellow bathing suit, tight across her tawny thighs, low and tight across her chest, where the cleft between her breasts was darker than the rest of her. Long yellow hair wind-whipped behind her, fluttering over the curve of neck and bare shoulders. Very white and very green against her tawny face, her eyes looked straight ahead at the road.

"You don't know why you're doing what?" I said.

The Buick slowed. The girl's thighs shifted around on the leather seat as she got her right foot off the gas pedal and on the brake.

"If that's your attitude," she told me, "we can stop right now. End of the line."

"I'm sorry. I don't remember."

"What do you take me for?" She'd set her lips in a straight line a crimson slash on the bronzed face.

"No. Sometimes I forget I try to remember so hard, but the more I try, The worse it gets. I don't know how long we've been driving I don't remember starting. I don't know who you are. I have a headache."

We crawled along at thirty. A black and white roadsign rolled up on our left Florida A1A, the Ocean Highway. "It's the truth," I said a little desperately. "I can't remember a thing."

"You begged me to give you a ride last night. We've been driving ever since. Are you trying to tell me you have amnesia?"

"No. They have fancy words for it . . . War neurosis. Battle fatigue. A lot of stuff like that. I was in South Carolina yesterday. Sumter. On business. I must have flown down here. I don't remember."

"You were in St. Augustine yesterday. I met you reading the Sunday paper on the beach."

"Sunday papers?" I asked foolishly. "My God, what happened to last week? Tuesday I was in Sumter. Tuesday. . . ."

"Have a cigarette, Fred." Her purse lay between us on the seat. She groped in it with her right hand, found a pack of Camels and tossed it to me. "Are you telling me the truth?"

I lit up with the dash lighter. "Damn it, yes."

"You were running away from something last night. I met you on the beach in the afternoon. We swam together, you took me to dinner: You took me to my motel. You came by later in the evening. You looked a mess. You'd been drinking. You still look like hell."

I glanced down at my clothing. T-shirt and khaki trousers. The T-shirt was torn and cake-stained with brown.

"That's blood I think. . . ." the girl told me.

"Blood? I don't remember anything." And I didn't. The medics had said war neuroses come in a wide variety. With me it was temporary amnesia, turning itself on and off at irregular intervals and leaving me with a headache and without memory. The cure was time, they said. Forget about Korea. See things. Do things. Live a normal life.

I crossed my arms down at the belt line and slipped the torn T-shirt off over my head. It looked like blood, all right. I balled the T-shirt up and tossed it away into the scrub pine, watching it open up, snag on a branch and flutter there, a tattered white flag. I felt better when the ocean highway curved and hid it from view.

"You were in a fight, you said. Had to get away in a hurry. It was dark. I should have asked questions. I didn't see the blood until this morning."

"Why didn't you say so? If I'm in some kind of trouble you shouldn't stick your nose into it."

"You don't remember anything, do you?" She smiled at me, taking her eyes off the road for the first time. The smile warmed her face and warmed me and I thought it was wonderful to have a friend when you're sick and need the kind of help doctors can't give. "Last night, after you took me home from dinner . . . well, if you don't remember. Try, Fred. . . ."

"I'm trying." Everything since Sumter, South Carolina, was a blank. "It's no good."

Her, eyes blinked and got all watery. She stepped down hard on the gas pedal. The Dynaflow roared under us with a new surge of power and she didn't look at me again. She said, without expression, "Then you don't remember anything?"

"Nothing," I admitted. "Better take me back. If I did anything wrong, I'm not going to run away from it."

"We're almost in Miami Beach. We could take the causeway over to Miami and have you on a plane for Havana in a couple of hours. You don't have to go back, Fred."

"I've got to. If I keep running away from things I'll never get well. Like throwing that shirt away. It was bloody, all right. It got me scared. Whenever I start remembering again, things get me scared like that. It could have been a bloody nose or something. What's a little blood? Happens all the time. I was drinking, I was in a fight. Big deal."

"Who are you trying to convince, me or you?"

"Big deal," I went right on. "No more running. If you can't take me back, I'll try to hitch a ride."

"I haven't any place to go . . . I thought you wanted to run away. I can take you back if that's what you really want."

"That's what I really want."

"You were talking in your sleep this morning."

"Was I?"

"Yes. I'm afraid it wasn't a bloody nose, Fred. You kept on talking and saying you were sorry and you had to get away and would I hurry. You were trembling and sweating and cursing. You said it was murder."

I ground the cigarette out in the dashboard ash-tray, then pulled the small metal box out and emptied its contents, watching the butts scurry against the side of the car before they tumbled away. I looked up at sun and it brooded sullenly over a hot smoky sky. I figured by the position of the sun it was almost noon and would get hotter and whoever brought the chamber of commerce story up north that Florida isn't a sweatbox in the summer was a damned liar. I'd said it was murder. I'd done some peculiar things when I got that way, forgetting. Told about them later and looked at people queerly, and my stomach used to tie itself in knots and I'd have to drink too much, to forget in a different way. I couldn't stay in one place long. I had to travel so people wouldn't know. But murder . . .

Back in Kingston, New York, the neighbors used to whisper and my folks would smile like it wasn't anything and the doc had said no, he doesn't have to be committed anywhere, but the way they looked at me made me want to run and keep on running. They didn't understand. How could they. I didn't want them to, because pity would be even worse and that was why I couldn't stay long in one place. It was part of the sickness. Before I was going to forget I would start to talk about it and the doc said that was fine, people could care for me then if they knew it was coming. But I thought it was like being a werewolf when the moon was full and if you just locked him up that night, that one night when the moon was full each month and only if there were no clouds in the sky, everything would be all right. So I'd run and I'd held more jobs in a year than an employment agency gets to see, over more territory than a travel agency cares about.

And now I'd, killed a man.

"You take me back, then," I said, lighting another Camel and throwing it away after the first puff because it tasted like punk and I was past the punk-smoking age.

2.

We got back to St. Augustine an hour before nightfall. Matanzas Bay glittered in the sunlight with the pleasure boats bobbing on it like painted corks. The bigger commercial fishing boats had pulled into the Municipal Pier and I watched tourists testing their legs on land again as the traffic snarled us near Lion Bridge. St. Augustine seemed more Spanish than Spain itself, except for the language. Overhanging balconies threatened to fall and block the narrow streets, but they'd stood that way, threatening, for generations. Wrought iron grillwork made you think of New Orleans.

The tourists chattered gayly, calling to one another and making plans for the evening. I wondered what it was like to be carefree and planning on fun for the evening, or the next day, or the rest of your life. I tried to think of me like that, but it was a long time ago and not easy to recall and Korea was in the way, and everything afterwards, which in a lot of ways made even Korea seem not so bad.

"Do you remember where . . . where it happened, Fred?"

"No."

"We could go to the police, if you'd made up your mind. We can still forget about it, though. Say the word and I'll turn right around and . . ."

"First thing you're going to do is get something to eat. But no, I won't be going to the police. Not yet. I want to reconstruct this thing if I can. There are newspapers to read, places to go. I'll work it out. I don't want you around, though. You've been swell . . . Now you've got your own life to lead. I owe you a dinner, but that's all." I gave it to her like that, short and choppy, because she'd been kinder to me than a person has a right to be under the circumstances and I didn't want her blowing my nose for me all the time.

Our Buick followed a Cad around the lighthouse and across Lion Bridge into the heart of the city. We found a small restaurant with its own parking lot and went inside. I picked up a newspaper at the counter before a waiter convoyed us to a wall booth and flipped a couple of menus on the table. *El Piscador,* the menu said. The fisher. I hadn't noticed outside. I'd been thinking of the newspaper and what I might or might not find in it. Now, when the waiter brought water I said, "Beer. Plenty of cold beer."

He came back with a frosted pitcher and two glasses and I said we'd order later. *El Piscador* was a third-rate eatery, with no air-conditioning, stale, uncirculated air, waiters who'd learned how to walk around in hundred-degree temperature and tattered monkey-suits without sweating, and a management that didn't mind its patrons wearing faded khaki trousers, tennis shoes and nothing else.

"I have no change," the girl said. "Give me a dime?"

I nodded, found one and shoved it across the table.

"Got to clean up. They might have one of those pay things, Fred. Be back in a minute."

I thought the odds against *El Piscador* making a tariff, on anything but food, were tremendous. I thought that and a lot of other unimportant things and I had been so eager to get my hands on a St. Augustine newspaper but now that I had it I was afraid to start reading. On the way back to St. Augustine the girl told me her name was Petey. I watched Petey walking to the rear of *El Piscador* in her tight yellow bathing suit, damp and dark with sweat because she'd been sitting and driving so long.

It was a beautiful thing to watch, but there was this newspaper in my hand. My hands were clammy and had soaked up some newsprint. They shook when I spread the eight-sheet paper out on the table, and I still didn't look. I poured some beer and let it caress my throat, then poured some more and thought, what the hell, if I killed someone I killed him and it will be here to read and not reading it won't make it any less true.

St. Augustine is a city of less than fifteen thousand, and a killing will get the headlines every time. It got a four-inch banner this time and now my hands were really shaking. I tried for some more beer but couldn't pour it. I wished Petey would come back from the jane in a hurry and suggest again I run away. I closed my eyes and tried to think myself back in Korea or anyplace. It was all no good, so I took a deep breath and wondered if they hung people in Florida or electrocuted them or what. Then I read.

MAN MURDERED IN
BUENA VISTA MOTEL
Knife Wound Proves Fatal
To Vacationing Tampa Resident

There was an amateurish photograph showing the sheet-draped body and three pairs of legs standing guard over it. An insert showed a switch-bladed knife framed by a neat white handkerchief on someone's hand and the cut-line proclaimed unnecessarily that it was the murder weapon. The article said the man, name of Walter Pearson, a wealthy cigar manufacturer who owned half of what made Ybor City a city, had been found at eight this morning when a cleaning girl entered an unoccupied room to prepare for the possibility of an occupant. It was already occupied. Walter Pearson, dead, a four inch switch-blade sandwiched between two of his ribs up to the hilt. There were no known suspects, no motive, no clues. Mrs. Pearson had been notified and had flown to St. Augustine during the early afternoon to identify the body. The newspaper promised an interview with the bereaved in tomorrow's edition. The chief of police promised he'd get his man; This was a blot on the escutcheon of this fair city of St. Augustine or some such thing and the murderer, in all probability an out-of-towner, the chief of police said and hoped, would be apprehended forthwith.

I took out a handkerchief and mopped the back of my neck. I'd sat still long enough for the sweat which driving had fanned away to collect on my skin and drip off onto the table. A ceiling fan rotated sluggishly, stirring the flypaper hanging not far from its lazy blades but cooling the air not at all. They had no suspects, no clues. They knew no motive, although robbery had been guessed at since Pearson was wealthy. . . . I'd done some strange things during my sick periods, but robbery and murder. . . The beer rumbled in my stomach and one of those piercing, throbbing headaches was threatening to sit down inside my skull and start twisting again. Petey's suggestion made sense. Even if I had killed Pearson, I didn't think of it as me. Not me, I wasn't the murderer. The sick thing which takes over inside my brain from time to time, that was the guilty one. But could they lift him out of my skull and hang him and say to me you're free, free and cured, so go home, friend?

I stood up. I gazed around at people sipping beer . . . and eating and making small talk. I heard some of it; I heard murder and kill and knife and motel in a kind of avid, eager flow of words. There was something thrilling, warped and table-talk stimulating, about having a murder in your home town. Almost like having a celebrity in your midst, putting your town on the map and making you feel suddenly important. And there was something just a shade dangerous about it, like kids getting up their courage and walking through a dark alley in some slum, half-expecting a hulking figure to dart out from the shadows and attack them. Here, in our town, St. Augustine, a killer is walking the streets, unapprehended. They'll get him. . . Oh, don't you worry, Charlie, they'll get him. Always do. Don't you go to the movies? But until they do, I think maybe the Missus will stay home at night with the kids and if there are any errands, I'll run them. I'll run them.

I thought of that guy in New Jersey who had brooded so long and so hard and had a different kind of war neurosis. It got all bottled up inside him and no one knew except maybe he was a little queer and kind of quiet, but he let it out all at once, both barrels, and kept on blasting with it until he was spent. And when he was through he left a trail of dead in his wake and he wasn't sorry, just puzzled and confused.

I got up and I started walking toward the door, not even remembering about the beer I hadn't paid for. I didn't know if I was going to the police and tell them I thought I was their man but couldn't be sure because I didn't remember or, instead, run away. I didn't know and I wouldn't until I got outside, but I couldn't stay there in *El Piscador* with the newspaper spread on the table and the four-inch banner headline and everyone talking.

3.

"Fred. Fred! Wait' a minute, please." I turned. It was Petey. She looked down at the newspaper and then stared at me and at this distance I wasn't sure, but I thought she bit her lip. She picked up the check on the table and brought it to me. "Okay, Fred. We'll go someplace else. Pay the check and take it easy. Everything's going to be all right."

"Yeah," I said. "All right."

"Fred. Please. People are looking' at you. You're dripping sweat and you've got the strangest expression . . ."

"Sure." I paid the bill with a fiver took my change and pocketed it. Petey steered me outside into the gathering dusk, fanned but not relieved by hot, sticky gusts of wind. She gripped my arm with long, tawny fingers. I felt sick and she must have known it.

The yellow one-piece bathing suit and my sun-tans attracted scowls at night. We were on display as we headed back toward Petey's Buick, and I said so.

"We could go to my place, Fred."

"You live in St. Augustine?" It was a rhetorical question. Right then I didn't care if she lived in Timbuctoo. I either had to give myself up or run. I could think of disadvantages either way, but not advantages.

"No. I'm staying in a motel. I'm not the world's best cook, but there's a little kitchen in my place. What say?"

It would give me time to think. It would take me away from the jostling crowds. If Petey had some whiskey as well as food, it might clear my head so I could think. "You talked me into it," I said, and tried to smile.

Petey grabbed my arm possessively and steered me to the Buick. I climbed in and stared straight ahead while the convertible rolled smoothly from the parking lot. Growing darkness had taken the daytime mantle off a few of the brighter stars and the clean night breeze sweeping in off the Atlantic rustled palm fronds as Petey pointed the Buick's grill northward on U.S.1. Palms surrendered to great old trees which formed a canopy of foliage and Spanish moss overhead. By the time night squatted on the Florida coast, scrub pine replaced both the trees and the stately residential streets of St. Augustine.

Far ahead on our right, neon lighting blinked on and off, punctuating the night with a lurid red glow. We got closer and Petey slowed down. If the convertible's top were up, I'd have hit the roof. The neon glowed and faded, glowed and faded. The neon said:

Buena Vista Motel—25 Cabins 25—10 with kitchens.

"Jesus," I said. "Jesus."

"What is it?"

"You read the paper."

"Only the headline. Oh." Petey looked at me. "Oh. This is where you. . . ."

"Yeah."

"I'm sorry, Fred. I didn't realize." She braked the Buick and pulled off on the right shoulder of the highway, craning her neck to watch the traffic flash up behind us. A Greyhound bus roared past us, faint illumination inside shining coldly through blue-tinted windows. A new Studebaker followed impatiently in its wake, lacking sufficient pick-up to pass the bus with a curve bending the highway out of sight just beyond the Buena Vista Motel.

"We'll go back," Petey told me, and started to swing the Buick into a U turn.

I shook my head. "Uh-uh. If this is your place, this is where we eat."

Petey eased the Buick off the highway and onto a gravel drive leading to the Buena Vista Motel, a long, rambling structure set two hundred yards back from the road, its brick units looking like parts of one continuous building because carports connected them. Most of the carports were not empty.

"I admire you," Petey said.

"What for?"

"Well, if this is where you . . . killed the man, and you're willing to come back as if nothing happened. . . ."

"I'm not sure I killed anyone. It still could have been just a bloody nose and a coincidence. Running won't get me anywhere, unless I want to keep running the rest of my life."

"That's what I mean. I admire you. What did the newspaper say the police thought?"

"Nothing much. They've drawn a blank so far."

"I only had a chance to read the headlines, then I had to catch up with you. I was wondering."

"So are the police."

4.

We swung in front of the Buena Vista office and the dining room, pale fluorescent light washing the gravel driveway through its windows. Petey pulled the Buick into a carport at the far end of the motel, but before it was sandwiched in the darkness between two of the sleeping units I noticed a white police car two ports down. A pulse began to hammer in my head. The police still had business at the Buena Vista.

"Here we are," said Petey. She reached into the top of her bathing suit and extracted a key with a little plastic tag attached to it. I wondered if the place would look familiar Sometimes I had vague memories of what had happened during those periods of forgetting, and the murdered man's cabin must have been a carbon copy of Petey's.

She fingered a light-switch inside the door, bathing the mom with the soft glow of fluorescents, recessed at the juncture of wall and ceiling. The Buena Vista was no fly-by-night motel, although most of its customers probably never stayed long enough to appreciate it. Petey's large room contained a double bed, a blonde chest and dressing table, a squat, modern easy chair, a writing table and a pair of pullup chairs. A small foyer led from it to the bathroom. The kitchen adjoined the bathroom, hardly more than a vestibule with stove and refrigerator in miniature, but it served the purpose.

Petey went straight to the refrigerator and got out an amber bottle of Schlitz. "You'd better start on this while I change."

"I was hoping you'd have something the same color but stronger."

"I've some bourbon." She convoyed me back to the bedroom bent from the hips to the bottom drawer of the chest, opened it and reached in. The yellow bathing suit rode up slightly on her thighs and stretched tautly on the flare of her hips. She looked dressed only because it was a different color.

Soon I was gulping bourbon gratefully from a tumbler and listening to the bustle Petey made in the miniature kitchen. I was hungry and the bourbon burned all the way to my stomach and raced with warmth clean down to my fingertips and toes. It filled my head with buoyancy and I thought I'd murdered a man, probably. Somehow, it hardly seemed so bad with the bourbon and I got to thinking I wouldn't have to run away at all, not if the police had no leads. I drank more bourbon and thought the same thoughts stronger. I found a pack of cigarettes on the chest and a book of matches. Inhaling long and hard I felt still better.

I commenced blowing smoke rings and popping a finger through them. Then I poured more bourbon and did more gulping. I use the cigarette up and lit another one from the butt and kept on drinking. Petey and her labors in the kitchen sounded far, far away and I hoped she wouldn't hurry because I'd found a chance to relax for the for first time the long, impossible day and, then I began to hope she would hurry because I remembered what she looked like bending over in the tight yellow bathing suit and there were all sorts of ways to relax, some of them better than bourbon.

Petey came in with a couple of plates of spaghetti, steaming hot. She placed them on the writing table, glanced at me, smiled, took the tumbler from my hand and finished the remainder of the bourbon.

"I have to change," she said, her voice struggling through all the bourbon in my head. "The spaghetti's too hot, anyway."

She touched my hand and that made me forget the empty bourbon bottle. "You've really tied into one," she said.

I leered the way you can leer only when you're drunk and don't mean it for a leer at all. Petey must have known I was higher than a box kite on a windy day, for she smiled and turned her back to me, finding a zipper on the bathing suit under her right armpit and pulling it down about eight inches. "You turn around too," she said.

I tried. But tomorrow I would give myself up to the cops if I had a change of heart and tonight at least there was Petey and lot of bourbon making my heart tick off half-seconds much too fast inside my skull. Instead of turning around I followed Petey to the closet and watched her select a robe, filmy and smoke-silver in color, with about the thickness of two or three spider webs plastered together. Then I placed my hands on her shoulders and turned her around.

She pirouetted slowly, the right side of her bathing suit hanging loosely away from her body where she'd unfastened the zipper. She was bronze and the suit was yellow but under the suit she was white, all creamy white and curving with a splash of rose-red on the whiteness, floating like a rose on an inverted cup of cream.

"You're beautiful," I said. "You're beautiful, and you've been so good when you didn't have to be and I don't know why. But I needed every word you said and every gesture and everything you did."

"You're drunk, Fred. Please." She didn't back away. She didn't push me away. I let my hands fall from her shoulders to her supple waist and I pulled her against me.

5.

"Fred. Oh, Fred. I'm not a good samaritan, I never was. I just felt this way about you all along. I'll do anything for you. Anything. I only want . . . what's good for you."

We sat together in the easy chair. Petey had draped herself in the spider-web robe and it tickled against my chest. I thought of the cops outside and the man who had been killed a few Buena Vista cabins away and how I went around forgetting and never knew what I did at those times or why and how I always talked about it because the doctors said not to keep it a secret. Then I figured that was a hell of a lot of foolishness to be thinking about. It could wait until tomorrow.

"The spaghetti must taste like spaghetti chewing gum by now," Petey said, and laughed.

"I'm not very hungry."

"Liar."

"You're beautiful."

"You said that."

"Very beautiful. Listen, Petey. I'm thinking out loud, see? I'm talking off the top of my head and not really planning, not for good and all . . . but, well, if I killed this guy when I wasn't myself, I . . ."

"You shouldn't get in trouble for it, is that what you mean?"

"I guess. We could do like you said. We could be out of the country by morning, and . . ."

"Fred. Fred, stop. I'd love to."

"Then why should I stop?"

"Just because of that. Because I'd love to, that's why you should stop. It isn't fair to both of us. We'd run away together and at first we'd like it because we're in love, brand new in love and new love has a way of making you forget everything else . . . But it won't last, not if we have to spend all our lives worrying and wondering if they'll ever find something which will lead to you. After a while we'd start to hate each other and not want to look at each other and . . . no, Fred. It couldn't work."

I smiled and watched her lips trembling. "You're right, I guess. Only now that we . . ."

"I know. It's hard. It isn't right. Yesterday was yesterday and now we have a whole life we want to live together." She got her hand up behind my neck and stroked my hair slowly. "If it hadn't happened, if this was two or three hours ago I'd have told you to run away, but not now. I'd have figured you're a nice guy and what the hell, you're sick. So run away. A nice guy who did something he wouldn't have done, except he was sick and couldn't help it. You killed Pearson and nothing could bring him back. I would have said to hell with it and run way.

"But not now. Now if you run I want to run with you. We can't have it that way. We just can't." She was talking softly, almost whispering, her lips brushing my ear. "We've got to find another way. This sickness you have, I don't know about it. I'm not a doctor. But if it can be proved you didn't know what you were doing and it won't happen when you're well. . . ."

"The best they'd do for me is lock me up," I said bitterly. "But maybe it is better that way. Jesus, Petey. If I went away with you and it happened again, you might wind up the same way as that guy—what's his name? Jesus, Petey, I wouldn't . . ."

"Pearson. Walter Pearson. You could never hurt me, Fred. But listen. What if you did give yourself up? Maybe they could cure you. Maybe it's only temporary and some time in a hospital would fix it."

"It's no good. Up north they tried everything."

"They might have something else down here that. . . ."

"What did you say?" I stood up. I stood up so fast that Petey rolled off my lap, hit the floor with a thud and sprawled there, the spider-web robe, floating open and spreading around her on the dark rug like foam.

She glanced at me in alarm. "I said they might have something else." She averted her eyes. "Fred, take it easy. If that thing is coming on again, I'm right here. I'll watch over you, don't worry. Don't worry, darling, I'm here."

"Before. You said his name. The dead man's name."

"I . . . well, yes. I read it in the paper."

"No. You only saw the headline. You said that twice. You looked at the paper for a couple of seconds and saw nothing but the headline."

I stood up. I crossed the floor and let Petey have a corner of the room to herself. The bourbon drained from me like water rushing to fill a vacuum. I felt cleaned and dirty at the same time and I wished I were a thousand miles away or in the police station surrendering or anyplace.

"I guess I must have seen more. What's the difference?"

"A lot of difference." I didn't want to look at her. I never wanted to look at her again. I'd get sick if I saw her or maybe I'd try to kill her, I didn't know which.

"I met you on the beach yesterday," I said. "We must have talked a long time, and gone swimming and got friendly. If one of these attacks was coming on, I must have talked about it." I stared at the closet, its door swung back against the wall. Most of Petey's clothing was sporty and casual, but some of the stuff in the closet she never wore at all. There were two men's suits and several pairs of slacks, and shoes.

"You'd already planned it then," I said. "If a fall guy came along, the better."

"What are you . . . talking about?"

"I don't have to tell you." I swallowed hard. She was beautiful, so goddamn beautiful, and she had been so good to me. I needed a friend, I'd cling to one. And she was beautiful I felt like crying and then maybe hitting her until my hands hurt and I couldn't hit her any more. But I didn't turn around . . . I stood there staring at the closet and almost wishing I'd gone right on thinking I'd plunged that shiv into Pearson. What the hell, I was sick. No one would be disappointed. No one would stare at a closet and a blank wall and feel like busting out and bawling like a baby.

"Me." I said. "Me. Your patsy. By late afternoon yesterday you must have seen the way I was. It was bad, huh? I walked around in a fog and you probably said that guy's crazy as a loon and boy, does he come in handy."

I heard her starting to get up,.' I could picture her, without looking, on all fours on the rug, the gossamer gown clinging like dew. I couldn't look. I said, "Stay there. If you get up I think I'll kill you."

"Fred." But she stayed put.

"I don't know why you killed Pearson," I said. "I don't give a damn. You killed him, and you had your reason. He's got a wife in Tampa. Maybe you were his mistress and getting plenty from him . . . Maybe you and your friend, or your husband or somebody—maybe you were blackmailing him and he said he'd go to the cops. I don't give a damn for the reason. You killed him and I was your patsy."

"Fred. You're sick. You're not thinking straight, darling. How can you say that after . . . after . . ."

"That's what hurts. But shut up. Don't talk about it. I won't touch you. I won't call you names. Just sit there. Don't move. Don't move, Petey. Please."

6.

Outside, I could hear laughter from one of the other cabins and the far sounds of music. I thought the sky would be peppered with stars and back on the beach in St. Augustine the palms would wave in the ocean breeze, serene and graceful and I wished it were raining or snowing and everything around here was ugly and not so beautiful.

"You killed him or your friend did. Someone, one of you, killed him. I was walking around in a daze. I was perfect. You smeared blood on my shirt and drove off with me and knew I'd get to think about it and want to come back, especially if you felt sorry for me and maybe made a little play."

"Fred. Stop it. You call what happened before . . . a little play?"

"Shut up, I said. That wasn't planned. You wanted to feed me and let me drink a lot and then maybe, after that, go into a clinch and convince me I'd better give myself up. You had all night, there wasn't any hurry. I should have known *El Piscador* wouldn't sport a pay toilet. Jesus, not that place. I should have known. I wasn't thinking. You called your friend here and told him to get the hell away from the cabin, you had to use it with me. But when I followed you to the closet you were afraid I might see his clothing and that would spoil everything. So you decided I might as well take the ball from there."

Everything was suddenly very quiet. Outside, the music and laughing had stopped and I could hear Petey breathing hard. I wondered what she would look like now and I didn't think I would like it. I almost turned around to look, but didn't. I wanted to remember her another way. I wanted to remember the best friend I ever had and all the wild dreams which had flitted through my thick, empty skull like confetti and thinking about it got me feeling sick. I headed for the door, then changed my mind and went back to the closet, taking out one of his shirts, whoever he was, and putting it on. Then I went to the door.

"What are you going to do?" Her voice was small, completely lacking in expression.

I opened the door. "Not a goddamned thing. I'm going away, that's all."

I heard a noise, a scampering. She was getting up. She was running toward me. Her arms came around my neck from behind and she was panting. She was trying to pull me back in to the room.

I swung my left arm behind me and drove her away. I heard her stumble and crash into some furniture and fall to the floor and whimper there. I didn't look back. I wouldn't.

"I'm not going to the cops," I said. "It's none of my business and I don't have any more proof than I said. You and your friend and the cops can fight this thing out yourself."

Outside, a quick tropical rain was falling, drumming on the roofs of the cabin and sending swift little torrents streaming down the sides of the gravel roadway.

I started walking north on U.S.1 and hoped I'd get a ride before too long.

I didn't look back.

Vanishing Act
W. R. Burnett

November 1955

Call it what you please: blind accident, predestination, luck . . . but the thousand-to-one shot meeting of Lou Jacks, taxi driver, and Bob Stuart, out-of-work police reporter, in an all-night restaurant which neither had ever visited before, defied all the laws of probability.

Stuart, a tall, spare rather glum-looking young man, was returning from a date. It was two A.M. He had spent thirty dollars in various bistros and he was mentally kicking himself for being a show-off and a blowhard. True, the doll was a nice one and was used to the best squiring. But who was he kidding—out of work, as he was, in bad, and with only two hundred-odd dollars in the bank?

Lou Jacks had dropped a fare at one of the big, swank apartment houses of the district. He hadn't eaten since five P.M. and his stomach was rumbling. He arrived first. Stuart came a few minutes later. Their eyes met in the glass beyond the counter as Stuart passed behind the taxi driver on his way to the rear of the place.

"Fancy seeing you up here," said Lou, snickering rather sadly.

Stuart hesitated, then sat beside Lou. "Oh, I know some high-toned people. Few, but some."

"Want a ride in?"

"On the company?" asked Stuart.

"I did my spending for the night."

"You going to walk?"

Stuart pulled out a few crumpled bills and a handful of change, counted it over slowly, then put it away, nodded and remarked: "It's a nice summer night."

Again Lou snickered sadly.

Their orders came, and they ate in silence. Lou, who was ordinarily full of small talk about boxing, baseball and allied subjects, seemed lost in a surly, ruminative dream of some kind. But as Stuart rose to go, Lou put a calloused hand on his arm.

"Sit down, reporter. I need help . . . or I need something, maybe advice."

Stuart resumed his seat but said: "In case you got a story to give me, I've been fired again. My old pal, Nolly, the city editor . . ." He broke off. "The hell with all that, but I'm in bad at the 30th Precinct, particularly with the Lieutenant. I sassed him, it says here; I'm uncooperative, I do this, I don't do that . . . you know how it is. And Nick, the Lieutenant, is a very big man, politically and horizontally. Don't waste your time on me."

Lou regarded him for a moment in silence. "Ain't this part of the 30th District, Bob?"

"Strangely enough, it is. Why?"

Lou hesitated, then asked: "Do you know Dan Polling?"

"Not personally. I know a good deal about him. Gunther and Polling. Hey! Gunther was buried yesterday, wasn't he?"

"Yeah," said Lou, "but that's got nothing to do with what I'm thinking about. Bob, ain't those guys kind of mob lawyers?"

"I wouldn't call 'em that. They take criminal cases. Why not? They're solid with the Bar as far as I know. Last time I saw Gunther it was in a courtroom. He collapsed after pulling one of the wickedest cross-examinations I ever heard—heart, high blood-pressure. Now he kicked off for good. What about Polling?"

Lou seemed to change his mind. Shrugging slightly, he rose, paid his check, and sauntered out of the place, followed by Stuart. "It's nothing, I guess," said Lou, as they stood outside on the deserted street. "I was born in a tough neighborhood where you keep your nose clean or else. I guess I'll keep it clean."

"Suit yourself," said Stuart, yawning; then he turned and started away. Lou stood watching him go.

2.

Stuart turned into the boulevard and walked toward the big, distant, towering buildings of the downtown area. "Good God, they seem a long way off," he thought—and *he* lived beyond them. So it might cost him two more bucks! He'd already spent thirty. Just as he began to look about for a taxi, one turned the corner abruptly and stopped almost in front of him at an intersection.

It was Lou. "Get in. Bob," he said. "I got to get this off my chest. Come on. It's on the house."

Stuart climbed in, and Lou started off slowly down a dark side-street. "It's like this," he began. "I picked this guy Dan Polling up on a street-corner downtown. He was drunk as a skunk. He told me to take him to the Union Station, he had to meet a train. I took him there. I was just letting him out of the cab when he climbs back in, like he's seen something that give him a start, and says to drive away, to hell with meeting the train. So I drove him through the park for a while. He gets drunker all the time, so pretty soon he says to take him home. I took him home. He couldn't even get out of the cab. I practically had to carry him in and he's as big as you are, and then I had to take him up in the elevator—no operator after twelve. He gives me his key and I unlock the door. He's already paid me. I open the door. There's a dim light inside. And I can see a great big monkey with his hat on standing in the next room—a real rough-looking boy. Polling goes in, seeing nothing. Then the door shuts with a slam—and that's the last I see. The thing is, somebody was standing behind that door and, as soon as Polling went in, this guy slammed it. I was took by surprise, see? Anyway, I had my money and I'd delivered my fare—he was on his own. But, Bob, I just don't like it. It don't smell right. Okay. Tell me to mind my own business."

If it had been anybody else but Lou Jacks, Stuart would have laughed at him, cursed him, maybe, for wasting his time. But Lou was the original Silent Joe on subjects that mattered. Stuart, in his work as police reporter, had often tried to pump Lou, who had grown up with some of the toughest boys in town, and besides, was single and played the tough joints on his nights off: he saw and heard plenty. But Stuart had never been able to get a peep out of him.

"Well," said Stuart, "this is nothing to call the police in about—yet. May be just a private matter."

"Yeah, and that poor drunk may be dead by now. It's just a feeling I got, Bob. I didn't like the looks of that big monkey I got a glimpse of."

"You want to report this at the 30th Precinct? I know *I* don't," said Stuart. "In the first place, the Lieutenant would think I was trying to pull a fast one on him—or a rib. He knows I'd just love to make him look like a hoosier, after the bad bill he sold Nolly about me—some of it true, however. Lou, if you want my opinion, they'd laugh you out of the Station. Tell you what. Let's you and me go back. Here's the gag. He meant to give you a five and he gave you a twenty; you are an honest Joe. You're returning the money."

"I'll go back," said Lou, "just so I can sleep. But who's going to furnish the money? Suppose everything's okay? So I'm out twenty bucks."

"All right," said Stuart. "Let's take it this way. He gave you a one instead of a five, and you've come back to collect."

"That's more like it," said Lou. He was silent for a moment, then he said: "Of course we may both get our heads knocked off."

"I doubt it," said Stuart. "I got a gun. Don't look at me like that. I got a permit."

3.

To their surprise a slender, well-dressed blonde woman opened the door at the sound of the buzzer and, looking them over with mild interest, said: "Yes?"

She had a coat and hat on and they could see a couple of traveling bags just beyond. Stuart and Lou exchanged a quick glance.

"What is it, driver?" the woman inquired. "Didn't I pay you enough?"

Lou looked blank. "I didn't drive you, ma'am."

"Well, what is it, then?" the woman demanded, showing some concern now.

"I brought a man here—Mr. Polling," said Lou. "He meant to give me a five and only gave me a one."

"I don't understand how that could be," said the woman. "He's not here."

"Are you Mrs. Polling?" asked Stuart.

"Yes, of course. Who did you think I was? And by the way, who are you?"

"I'm a friend of Lou's—the driver, here."

The woman looked from one to the other, then she took a five-dollar bill from her purse and handed it to Lou, who took it with a rather embarrassed air. "Was Dan . . . was my husband . . . had he been drinking?"

"I'm afraid he had, ma'am."

"Well, then . . . God knows where he is. He may be upstairs with friends—knows a lot of people in the building. I'll look for him. If you brought him home he must be around someplace."

"Have you looked through the apartment?" asked Stuart.

"Yes," said Mrs. Polling. "I thought he was going to meet me at the Station. But the fact that he didn't means nothing—not with Dan."

"Have you looked in the closets?" asked Stuart.

Mrs. Polling recoiled. "Why should I?" Now her face showed deep concern. "I think I'd better call the police. What are you men up to?"

Stuart hesitated, then got out his obsolete press card.

"Oh," said Mrs. Polling. "Newspapermen."

"As a matter of fact there's a story I wanted to discuss with Mr. Polling, so Lou and I rigged up this little gag."

With a deep flush of embarrassment, Lou handed Mrs. Polling back her five dollar bill.

"See him at the office tomorrow," she said. "He's not hard to get to. But, Mr. Stuart, what did you mean about the closets?"

"Excuse me for saying so, Mrs. Polling," said Stuart. "But according to Lou here your husband was very very drunk indeed, falling down, in fact. So where could he get to?"

They looked in all the closets and searched the place from top to bottom. Mrs. Polling assured both men that there was not even a knick-knack out of place.

They apologized at length and left.

Driving back, Lou said: "I still don't like the smell of this. Do you, Bob?"

"No," said Stuart. "But that woman's either the greatest actress in the world—or she knows nothing about whatever it is."

"You sure threw me a curve with that five," Lou grunted. "Embarrassed hell out of me!"

4.

Stuart couldn't sleep; he'd drunk too many cocktails and worries about the future kept repetitiously running through his mind. Besides, from time to time he'd remember Lou Jacks' story about the drunken Polling and speculate about it fruitlessly. He turned and tossed, switched his light on and off, smoked one cigarette after another. Finally he rose and paced the floor. The more he thought about the Polling business the more it intrigued him—and then a big story—if there was one—might be a real help at this uncomfortable juncture of his life. He was getting a bad reputation for insubordination and outspokenness. Things got around. Times were tight, jobs far from plentiful.

Just as it was beginning to get light there was a quick tap at his door, which startled him considerably, as he had heard no footsteps or creaking in the hallway. He hesitated, and then, not quite knowing why he did it, he noiselessly slipped his small automatic out of the night table drawer and tiptoed to the door.

He could hear breathing. The tap was repeated.

"Yeah? Who is it?" asked Stuart.

"Telegram."

"Slip it under the door," said Stuart, who was not expecting any telegrams or even a letter from anybody on this earth.

"Can't do that, mister."

The voice did not sound like the voice of one who delivered telegrams. Stuart, holding the automatic loosely in his right hand, put his ear to the door and listened intently.

"I said I can't do that, mister," the voice insisted.

"Why can't you?"

There was a pause. "It's collect."

"How much?"

Another hesitation. "Two thirty-five."

"Where's it from?"

"Look, mister—I haven't got all night to argue."

"Slip it under the door and I'll slip you the two thirty-five."

There was a brief pause. With his ear to the door, Stuart heard muffled curses, and his stomach muscles tightened. This was a phony, all right. But what was the big idea? The boy on the other side of the door had a voice as chilling as ice down your back.

"Look, mister . . ." came the voice. Pause. "Stuart, I got to see you for a minute."

But now a strange thing happened. The gun in Stuart's hand seemed to fire of itself, and Stuart jumped sideways, badly startled, at the ear-splitting crash.

Completely unstrung and shaking, Stuart heard heavy running in the hall, a distant slam, then silence. He kept muttering: "How did I happen to take the catch off? Was I that nervous? I better give up guns. How did I . . . ?"

He sat down heavily on the edge of the bed and stared at the windows which had a tinge of blue now as morning came on. Well, at least he was safe as long as he stayed in his room with the door locked. He was on the third floor; one window opened on a court, from the other there was a sheer drop to the pavement of the side-street and no house nearer than fifty feet.

But why? What? Stuart sat shaking his head. Finally he examined the gun to see that it was on safety, put it carefully away in the night table drawer, lay back on the bed and with his arms under his head stared up at the ceiling where the faint light of dawn was beginning to show.

Exhausted, he fell asleep almost at once.

5.

At a little before eight there was a heavy knocking at his door. He woke immediately, sat up and shouted: "Get away from that door."

"Police! Open up!"

"Don't try to kid me," Stuart said, hastily opening the drawer of the night table.

There was a brief silence, then a familiar voice chimed in: "Bob, it's me—Coogan."

With a heavy sigh of relief, Stuart jumped out of bed and opened the door. Coogan and an unfamiliar city detective were standing in the hallway.

"Well," said Stuart, "what's the beef—double parking?" Then suddenly he remembered that Coogan worked out of Homicide at the 30th Precinct, but he grinned, stifling this thought. "Selling tickets?"

"Lieutenant wants to talk to you, Bob," said Coogan, eyeing Stuart rather oddly—or at least Stuart thought so.

"Oh," said Stuart. "So he finally wants to apologize."

"I wouldn't know," said Coogan. Say, Bob, have you got a gun?"

"Sure. Permit gun."

"Where is it?"

Stuart indicated the night table, but when the unfamiliar detective—Smith—started to open the drawer, Stuart stopped him. "Wait a minute. What is this?"

Smith turned to Coogan, who said: "Bob, I'm your friend. You know that. I'm giving you a little advice. Cooperate this time. It might help."

Stuart studied Coogan's big tough face. "Might help who?"

"All of us."

Stuart was baffled. He stepped away from the night-table and let Detective Smith take the gun.

"Now get dressed," said Coogan.

6.

Lieutenant Nick Parshal seemed neither more nor less friendly than usual. He had a big, square, swarthy face and the shoulders of a wrestler. He regarded Stuart in silence for a moment, while Coogan, leaning against the office wall, looked on in assumed boredom.

"Just a couple of questions, Bob," said the Lieutenant.

"I thought maybe you got me down here to say you were sorry."

"I think for a long time before I take steps," said Nick, slowly. "So I'm seldom sorry."

"I'm the impulsive type, I guess," said Stuart.

"That was my thought," said Nick, glancing momentarily at Coogan. There was a brief silence; then Nick asked: "Where did you go last night?"

"Want to get the steno in, so we can have a record of this conversation? It's two to one now."

Nick flushed slightly and nodded. Coogan went for the steno, who came in pushing his machine ahead of him.

Stuart detailed his movements at unnecessary length, mentioning all the bistros he had frequented, and all the cocktails he had consumed—naming them and even explaining the ingredients of an unfamiliar one. Nick was not amused. He sat in glum, red-faced silence, listening.

"And the young lady's name?" he broke in abruptly.

"Not with the help of thumb screws," said Stuart.

"It's your neck," said Nick.

"It's my what?" asked Stuart, looking around.

"Go ahead. Go ahead," barked Nick.

"Well," said Stuart, "by now it's two A.M. and I'm hungry. So I walk from the doll's apartment—pardon me, the young lady's apartment—and I find a diner in a side street." Now Stuart hesitated briefly. Should he bring the Polling business up?

It was a fantastic, you might even say, silly story and would lead to endless questions. And then if he started telling everything, how about the guy with the telegram . . . good God! the whole business was like a nightmare . . . and what was happening, anyway? Stuart began to lose a good deal of his confidence. His neck, was it? What kind of a remark was that. He resumed, sweating now: "So I find this diner. I had a club sandwich and a cup of coffee. I was there maybe fifteen minutes. Then I walked home. That's it."

"When we get to the sworn testimony, you'll have to do better than this, kiddo," said Nick.

"Maybe you can help me out," said Stuart.

Coogan moved in. He looked worried. "Bob, don't hold out. Advice from a pal."

Stuart looked from Coogan to Nick, then lowered his eyes, but said nothing.

"This gun the boys picked up," said Nick, "has it been fired lately?"

"No," said Stuart, smiling slightly. "I keep it for laughs." Suddenly an odd expression crossed his face and he stared again from Coogan to Nick. "Yes! What am I talking about? It went off by accident last night. I was just holding it in my hand and . . ." His voice trailed off. What a feeble, lying statement that sounded like!

Coogan turned away and stood looking out the window.

"Where did this happen?" asked Nick.

"In my room."

"How?"

"I . . . well, I was putting the gun in the night table."

"So you had it with you last night."

"Yeah. I always carry it. I guess I've got a gangster complex or something."

"I guess you have," said Nick. "Where did the bullet go?"

"Go? How the hell do I know?"

"Well, did it make a hole in the wall? The ceiling? The chest of drawers? Where?"

Stuart thought this over, trying to remember how he'd been standing, how he'd held the gun. Vaguely he recalled that an open window had been facing him across the room.

"It might have gone out the window," he said, even his voice sounding dubious.

"Sure, sure," said Nick. Then he turned to Coogan. "Check it."

Coogan nodded and went out to make a call.

Nick was silent till Coogan returned.

"Bob," said Nick, lighting a cigar and puffing on it slowly, "let's go back. You had a bite to eat, then you walked home. Right?" Stuart nodded. "When did you meet Lou Jacks?"

Stuart started slightly. "You tell me."

Coogan groaned. "Bob, listen. This is no game."

"And I don't like it much," Stuart said. "Let's get the cards on the table. What do you want from me?"

"The truth," said Nick. "That's all."

There was a long silence. Finally Stuart said: "I assume, since Coogan's on the case, that somebody got the big bite put on. Right?"

"You can assume it."

"Look, Nick," said Stuart, "do me a favor. Question Lou Jacks first. He got me into this hassle—he knows a lot of wrong boys—and I don't want to get him in trouble. After he talks, I'll talk."

Coogan and Nick looked at each other for a long time, then Nick said: "It's a good idea, Bob. I like it. There's only one trouble. Lou's dead."

Stuart jumped slightly in his seat, and a horrible feeling of apprehension began to nag at his solar plexus.

"When? How?" he cried.

"We'll take that up later," said Nick. "Now, Bob—do you want to talk?"

"Yes," Stuart said, "and fast."

7.

Stuart told the whole story from beginning to end, leaving out not a single detail. But even to himself the story sounded like the worst and most preposterous kind of fabrication. He noticed during the recital that Coogan was sweating so heavily that he kept his handkerchief in his hand to wipe his face with. Nick's eyes got stonier and stonier. Finally Stuart finished.

"Bob," said Nick, after a pause, "if you don't mind me saying so, that is without a doubt the craziest goddamned story I ever had told to me."

"It's the God's truth," said Stuart.

"We'll check, we'll check," said Nick, wearily.

"We blundered into something," Stuart insisted. "I don't know what."

"You blundered into something all right," said Nick.

"Be sensible," cried Stuart. "Why would I kill Lou? What's the motive?"

"You're out of work," said Nick. "You pack a gun. Robbery."

"Was he robbed?"

"Yes," said Nick. "He was robbed. His pockets turned out. All his papers gone, his wallet, everything."

There was a long pause. "Well," said Stuart, "I hope I wake up shortly."

Nick got up and put on his hat. "Hold him," he called to Coogan as he started out.

"Detention room, okay? I don't want to throw him in the can, Nick."

"Just so he don't get away."

When Nick had gone, Coogan said: "Boy, boy—what a night you must have had! Are you crazy? Telling the Lieutenant about all the cocktails you drank! Let him build his own case."

"Coogan—Pat," said Stuart, patiently. "There's no case. I told you the God's truth."

The steno went out shaking his head. "After all those drinks, boy, how can you be sure?" Coogan asked sadly.

8.

At four o'clock that afternoon, Coogan came into the detention room, still mopping his brow. Rita, a young police woman Bob had known for some time, was sitting talking with him. Stuart did not know that Nick had assigned her to the case and that she was trying to pump him. Nick was well aware of Stuart's susceptibility in regard to good-looking girls. Rita was a cute brunette doll with a baby face and the cunning of a fox.

Coogan chased her away and sat down beside Stuart.

"Buddy boy," he said, "you've got to get yourself a lawyer and a new story."

"What's up?"

"Look, I'm your friend, Bob. I got a weak, sneaking hunch you got caught in a switch of some kind—I don't know what kind, mind you. Well, there's no trace of a bullet in your room. But this is worse. We checked the Pollings. They never heard of you or Lou."

"You mean he's home?"

"Sure, he's home. I talked to him myself."

"Did you talk to his wife?"

"Yes."

"How did she seem?"

"What do you mean?"

"First, let me describe her." He did so, and Coogan began to look at him with interest. Then Stuart described the whole apartment, even to some pictures he remembered having seen on the wall—excellent prints of modern masterpieces.

"That's the woman—and that's the apartment," said Coogan, his eyes showing hope instead of anguish for a change.

"Now about the woman. Did she seem calm—as if nothing was the matter?"

"No," said Coogan. "She seemed damned nervous and jittery to me."

"Look," said Stuart. "Let me give you a tip. Keep the Pollings under surveillance if it takes twenty men. Something big is going to break here. I can smell it. Do me a favor? Get Nolly Walters down here for me to talk to."

"The editor? Hell, he won't come."

"Tell him I'm going to drag his name into the case if he doesn't."

Coogan laughed hard, for the first time that day. "Okay, son. What a guy you are. Always in trouble."

9.

Stuart's ex-boss, Nolly Walters, was frothing at the mouth when he arrived, but Stuart soon had him calmed down. He explained at length about his hunch that something big was going to break—"we blundered right into it," he insisted—and that the *World* might just possibly have it exclusive if . . .

"If what?" snapped Walters.

"If you can get me out of here and put me back on the paper."

Nolly received this bizarre proposition with surprising calm. "I might get you out—depends on Parshal. But as for putting you back on the paper—I've got our respectability to think about, you jailbird. This is the *World,* you know, not a yellow sheet. How about under cover?"

"Just so the checks don't bounce."

"What checks? I'll pay you in cash out of a fund I carry."

Stuart looked at his ex-boss in silence, then: "You don't think I'm guilty, do you?"

Nolly made a sweeping gesture of disgust. "Of course not. You haven't got nerve enough to kill anybody."

"Thanks, Nolly," said Stuart. "You're a real understanding friend."

After Nolly had gone, Coogan came back in. Stuart grabbed him. "Pat—about that bullet. The window was open. I remember. It opens on a court. If the bullet went out the window it hit a wall, or broke a window across the court. Has to be. If it hit the wall, you'll find it at the bottom of the court. And if it broke a window . . ."

"We'll take another look, and I hope we find it. Jacks was killed with a thirty-eight—like yours."

"Great," said Stuart.

Coogan left. Pretty soon Rita came back with a couple of cokes.

"You find me irresistible, I see," said Stuart.

"Always did, honey," said Rita, handing him the coke, and taking a seat.

While Stuart was eating his supper alone in the detention room, Coogan came in with a letter in his hand.

"One of the boys picked it up at your apartment."

The envelope was filthy and creased as if carried around in a pocket for a long time before it was used; it was addressed in pencil and badly smudged. Stuart tore it open impatiently.

He gave a wild start. It was from Lou Jacks, apparently.

It read:

Dear Bob:

I had a flash on Polling.

Barek—Transco. Now you are on your own. I'm out, boy, and how! This ain't minor league. Goodbye.

Hackie

Stuart handed it quickly to Coogan. "It's from Lou. He must have mailed it just before he got knocked off."

"How do you know it's from Lou?"

"I assume it is. Get a handwriting expert. Dig up a sample of Lou's writing."

"Good," said Coogan. "But what does it mean?"

"I don't know."

"What's this word here? Looks like 'Transco.'"

"That's what it looks like."

Coogan grabbed up a phone. "Lieutenant there yet? Good. Tell him I'll be right in." Now Coogan turned to Stuart, beaming. "I knew you were in some kind of switch. A hunch. If I'd been wrong I might have lost my job."

"You're a sweet guy, Pat. I'll lose to you every night at gin rummy once this thing's over."

10.

Stuart slept fitfully on a cot in the detention room, with one dim, unshaded bulb burning over his head. From time to time he'd wake with a start and look at his watch. There seemed to be no end to the night.

At a little before five, the door opened and Coogan came hurrying in. Stuart sat up at once and reached for a cigarette.

"I'll give it to you fast," said Coogan. "The note was in Lou Jacks' handwriting but nobody can make any sense out of it, it's so badly written. Carson, handwriting, says he's not sure it says 'Barek' or 'Transco' . . ."

"That's a big help."

The interruption irritated Coogan, who wagged his big head impatiently. "Now hold on to your hat. The Pollings have disappeared."

Stuart jumped to his feet as if he'd suddenly been given a touch of the shock treatment. "What! Why, you dumb Irishman! Didn't I tell you . . ."

"I'm not in command," Coogan said. "I can only suggest. We were late with the stake-out. They blew. We checked with the manager. It was a slick job. Polling must have had a car parked in the alley back of the place, another car, I mean. His own is still in the apartment house garage. . . ."

"Or they were snatched," cried Stuart.

"No. They weren't snatched. Couldn't be. It was early evening. Place was busy. No way to get down except in the elevator. Boy took Polling down to the garage to get something out of his car, brought him up again to the lobby. Then the boy brought Mrs. Polling down to the lobby, and that's the last anybody saw of them. Plenty people round, too."

"Well, at least," said Stuart, "this proves my point. So let me out of here."

Coogan shook his head sadly, then he took a small roll of bills from his pocket and handed it to Stuart. "Here. From your boss. So you can have good food sent in."

"So I can what?" cried Stuart, taking the money.

"I'm sorry, Bob, but the Lieutenant just can't see his way clear to letting you go. Material witness. Your boss is working on it with a lawyer."

Stuart began to yell. "I want to make a deposition. Get that lawyer in here just as fast as you can. I've got rights. I'm a citizen. What is this, a Police State?" Stuart fumed and fretted up and down the narrow room, with Coogan trying to calm him.

Finally Coogan said: "All right, now. All right. Relax. I'll get the lawyer for you just as fast as I can."

"You'd better," yelled Stuart.

But as soon as Coogan had gone a curious change came over Stuart. He calmed down at once, counted the money Nolly had sent him—a lousy fifty dollars!—then he tiptoed to the door and glanced out into the corridor. Empty!

Now he transferred various items from his coat to his vest and trouser pockets, then he took off his coat, tossed it onto the cot with his hat, opened the door and started down the corridor to the private men's room. A uniformed policeman turned a corridor corner abruptly and they almost collided. The policeman looked at Stuart mildly—it seemed obvious he didn't know him from Adam.

"Okay to use this men's room?" asked Stuart.

"It's locked, I think," said the cop. "Who are you?"

"Reporter. *World.*"

"Here. I'll unlock it for you," said the cop.

He unlocked the men's room door, then passed on with a friendly wave of the hand. Stuart called thanks, entered the men's room, and locked the door after him. Then he examined the window; it wasn't barred, but it opened onto a parking lot where there were several radio cars and quite a few Station employees moving about. Hopeless in the daytime!

He returned to the corridor and walked calmly and leisurely to the front vestibule. A sergeant at a glassed-in desk was talking loudly on the phone. Stuart glanced at him mildly, then turned to his right, crossed the vestibule, went out the big, revolving front door, and down the worn granite steps to the sidewalk. Two cops passed him on their way in; they didn't even glance at him.

Stuart turned down a side street at once, then he crossed it diagonally and disappeared up an alley where commission-house trucks were already being loaded.

Two minutes later he was checking in at a cheap little hotel not three blocks from the Station. He signed the register as Nolly Walters, Jr. and said to the clerk, an old man who didn't seem to hear very well: "I left my coat in the car. I'll get it later. Been, driving all night. Got to make a phone call, then I want to sleep."

"It's all right with me," said the old man, vaguely and indifferently.

Stuart went to the pay-phone booth in the lobby and called No-Neck Creeden, an ex-cop, ex-private detective, ex-bookie, ex-proprietor of a tip-sheet . . . Creeden was largely ex, including ex-convict, having served time on an attempted bribery charge. Creeden cursed Stuart for waking him up, then chuckled in his beery bass voice. "Where y'calling from, bud?" he inquired. "I hear they finally stuck you in the cooler—where you belong."

Creeden was an odd character. With tried and true friends he was tough and honest; with others he was just tough. He said he'd be right over.

11.

Creeden listened in bored silence; but occasionally he smiled. Stuart was wearing an old coat of his he'd brought over. It hung on Stuart's rather spare frame like a flour sack.

When Stuart finished, Creeden asked: "What's in this for me?"

"A few bucks. My good will. I'm back on the *World* now."

"Think of that," said Creeden. "Why, you'll die rich. One question. Are you on the weed?"

"I know all this sounds pretty fishy. . . ."

"That is too weak a word."

"I know. Now listen. Find out everything you can about Mrs. Polling—especially where she came from. Give me that train schedule. I'll be checking. Get on the ball."

"I don't know how I get talked into these things," Creeden mumbled as he went out.

It was late afternoon before Creeden called in. He had quite a dossier on Mrs. Polling—but sadly enough all good. She was a highly respectable woman from a highly respectable downstate family.

"Hold the phone," cried Stuart, and for a few moments he studied the railroad time table; then he groaned. "No train from her home town at the time we're looking for. Wait a minute! What's the matter with me?" cried Stuart suddenly. "What about her husband? Know where Dan Polling's from?"

"Why didn't you ask me that in the first place, save shoe leather. He's from my hometown."

"Is there a train from there that gets in around one in the morning?"

"There sure is, and it's a beauty. Stops at every bird's nest on the way."

"Get up here as quick as you can."

Stuart's mind was working too fast to get much of any place; thousands of ideas occurred to him, all wrong. He sent out for a sandwich and a bottle of beer. Afterwards, he felt a little drowsy and lay down to rest. Just as he was beginning to doze off a word began to run crazily through his mind: "Transco . . . Transco," and then it evolved into "Cotrans . . ." and half a dozen other forms until it turned into "Cusco . . ." and Stuart sat up, still half asleep, and observed: "That's in Mexico, isn't it? Or maybe South America?" and then he came fully awake and grunted wryly: "What am I talking about?" and then suddenly out of no place the word came to him: "Taxco."

He jumped off the bed, hit by a sudden revelation, and at that moment there was a scratch at the door and Creeden came in with a paper in his hand. "You made print," he observed, pointing out a small item which read: *Witness in Taxi Driver Case Disappears.*

"I've been demoted from suspect, I guess," said Stuart; then: "What does the word 'Taxco' mean to you, Creeden?"

"That's it," shouted Creeden. "It's been running through my mind ever since you told me about it. The Taxco Armored Truck Robbery." Now Creeden sat down heavily. "Boy, oh, boy, do I have to tell you the rest? This friend of yours who got knocked off, he was just too nervous to spell, or even write straight, I guess."

"I'm afraid so," said Stuart with an odd expression.

"The guy he saw in that apartment must have been Maresh, also goes by the name of Merritt. He's been wanted for two months in that robbery—prime suspect."

"I had a real hunch this was a big one," said Stuart. "Got any ideas?"

"Yes. A big idea. I want out of this."

"Oh, come on now, Creeden."

"Well . . . I guess I've lived long enough, anyway—and to damn little purpose. But let's not forget what happened to Lou Jacks and almost what happened to you. When guys are playing for half a million dineros they play rough. Especially guys like Maresh, habitual—he'll go up for life if they catch him . . . so what's a few extra murder raps."

"Wait a minute. What do you mean, playing for half a million bucks? They got that dough two months ago."

"Yeah," said Creeden, crestfallen.

"Hot money though, wasn't it?"

"Yeah."

"What would be the procedure then?"

"Why," said Creeden, "they'd sell it to a fence, a passer. Or they'd stash it, if they were wise, maybe for a year or two, till things cooled off."

"Right," said Stuart. "Now we're getting some place. Can you give me a rundown on Gunther and Polling?"

"Yeah," said Creeden. "Roughly. Gunther used to be known to the top boys as the undercover Big Fix. I think he'd been slipping lately, sick man. Polling is just a big drunk. Gunther carried him. In the old days, it was 'see Gunther' to quiet a serious beef."

"Fine," said Stuart, rising. "Let's take a little Drive-Yourself trip to Dan Polling's hometown."

"Mine too, don't forget."

"Are you sentimental about it?"

"No," said Creeden. "Just scared."

12.

As they were passing through a distant suburb, Creeden sighed and glanced over at Stuart, who was driving.

"Kid, I don't like this one. This is once we ought to cooperate. The coppers ought to at least have all the information we've got—and also . . . maybe . . . know where we are—in case."

"Listen," said Stuart. "First place, I want to show Nolly what a whiz I am. You know he almost handed me the sports desk once? Second, don't underrate Nick Parshal . . . we don't get along but he is one very smart boy—shrewd as they come."

"Let's hope he's a genius," said Creeden, shuddering slightly.

It was night again when they arrived at the big sprawling upstate town on the lake. Stuart was parked on a dimly-lit side-street, waiting for Creeden, who was out on reconnaissance, to come back. It suddenly occurred to Stuart that he had no gun; visions of the newspaper pictures he had seen of Maresh, alias Merritt, began to rise before his eyes. What had Lou Jacks said? A big tough-looking monkey. And that was no exaggeration. According to the pictures, Maresh was a harsh, bleak-looking dark-haired man with an abnormally prominent chin that seemed solid as granite, and the unworried, penetrating but inward dark gaze of a large predatory animal.

"When No-Neck gets back," Stuart told himself, "we'll find a hock-shop and buy a gun."

The minutes passed slowly. Once a police car turned into the side-street and slid past him toward a big lighted boulevard. He ignored it and did not even throw a glance in its direction, so he had no idea whether he was being observed or not. Later he heard loud sirens on the boulevard, and another police car tore past him and disappeared.

He grew more and more uneasy, but finally he saw the dark but unmistakably bull-necked and barrel-chested figure of Creeden turning the corner and coming toward him.

"No real luck," said Creeden. "They haven't showed in town. Polling's father—he's an old man—still lives here in the house where Dan was born. Dan's pretty prominent around here. Used to be in the State Legislature, you know. However, I talked to a guy I know real well and can pump. He says if they don't want to be seen they might be out at a cottage Dan owns on the lake. He says that way Dan wouldn't have to have come through town; he'd just drive to Eliotsburg and cross over to Indian Point by motor boat, where the cottages are. Another thing. This guy hasn't heard anything about Mrs. Polling being here recently. So it sounds like the cottage."

Stuart nodded, then mentioned the hock-shop business to Creeden, who agreed.

"I know one," he said. "Always open. We better get some ammunition, too. We might need it. But I'd rather run than fight when it comes to guys like Maresh."

"We've got to defend ourselves," said Stuart, and Creeden laughed nervously.

The hock-shop was dark except for a nightlight, but a sad-looking middle-aged man let them in at once.

"Remember me, Charley?" asked Creeden.

"Sure," said Charley. "Where you been lately?"

"*Lately!*" cried Creeden. "I haven't been around here for over ten years."

"How time flies!"

Now a door creaked some place and Charley turned. A younger man, who might have been Charley's son or brother, stepped in from the back and whispered to Charley, whose jaw seemed to drop momentarily; then he said with averted eyes: "Would you fellows come into the back room? I'm supposed to be closed."

Creeden went through the portieres followed by Stuart. To their right in the dimness they saw two short, rather stocky young men with guns in their hands.

"Oh-oh!" said Creeden, sadly.

The young men ignored Stuart and Creeden for the moment, and one of them addressed Charley and his son—or brother—briefly: "We won't give you no trouble, Charley, if you don't give us none. We'll fade shortly. Just sit down and keep still."

"You boys are strangers," said Charley. "I'm solid in this town. Watch what you do."

"We'll watch."

Now the two of them turned their attentions to Stuart and Creeden and frisked them swiftly but expertly, extracting Creeden's gun.

"Don't you know me, No-Neck?" asked one. "I done a stretch with you."

"So did two thousand other cons," said Creeden.

"Do you know him?" asked Stuart, quickly.

"He's a young heavy," said Creeden. "Name's Whitey Goss."

Stuart started slightly but made no comment. Whitey Goss had been named a couple of times as a suspect in the Taxco Armored Truck robbery. They were getting close; maybe too close.

"I never did no time," said the other young thug, known as Speed. "I'm smarter than Whitey."

"Oh, sure," said Whitey. Now he turned Stuart around roughly and gave him a push. "What are you doing up here? We just seen you by accident-like and tailed you. What do you want in this town?"

"I might ask you the same thing," said Stuart. "You're from downstate, aren't you? Anyway, how did you know it was me? And what have I got to do with you?"

"You guys got no business in the big time, especially No-Neck here. He's strictly for the birds—yard birds. Look at Jacks."

"You look at him," said Stuart.

"He's not pretty now."

"I thought they had you in the can for the Jacks knockoff," said Speed.

"I climbed down a pipe."

"In Nick Parshal's jail? Oh, sure," exclaimed Speed.

"Is this straight you got canned off the *World* on Nick's say-so?" asked Whitey.

"Yes," said Stuart. "And he's trying to hang a bum rap on me, besides, and you know it's a bum rap."

"Hoosiers don't belong on the big time," said Whitey, severely. "You'll get yourself killed, Stuart."

"What are you talking about?"

Whitey looked at Stuart for a long time, then he took Speed aside for a conference. Finally Speed said: "There's only one thing to do. Keep 'em here. I'll go see."

Speed went out. They heard a car start up and leave. Whitey said: "Sit down, gents. We'll be here for a little while."

13.

Half an hour passed slowly. Whitey allowed Charley to wait on a couple of furtive, after closing-time customers. Finally Speed came back.

"Stuart," he called, "Come over to the door here."

Stuart walked over to the open door. There was a tall man standing just outside the door in the alley. The light was dim and Stuart could not see him very well. Besides, he had his hat pulled low and his coat collar turned up and he seemed to have a scarf across the lower part of his face.

"Stuart," the man said, "you've got a good chance to get your head blown off."

Stuart felt a distinct chill. This was the man who had tried to deliver the telegram and he was pretty certain that it was the big boy himself—Maresh.

"I know."

"This Jacks—he was in it with you?"

"Looks like it, doesn't it?"

There was a brief pause. "I guess we got the same idea, coming up here. Know where Polling is?"

"I can't find him," said Stuart. "He's not home."

"Know where he could be?"

"Holed up in the big town, I guess."

Another pause. "Tell me one thing sucker. How did you get on to this deal?"

"Word gets around when there's a thing as big as half a million."

"Yeah," said the man, "but the whole business was an accident. Gunther kicking off, I mean. He was solid. Polling ratted at the last minute. You a friend of his?"

"No," said Stuart.

"Well, the hell with that," said the man. "I'm just figuring what to do with you and that cheap crook you got with you."

"Don't be calling people cheap crooks," said Stuart. "You're not doing too good. You let Polling's missus get away with all the money, and plant it. And then you let the Pollings get away from you."

"We had problems," said the man, calmly. "We snatched Polling, but brought him back when you and Jacks got into the act. You put the heat all over us. You spoiled the shot, Mac; and I'm for dumping you in the lake with enough lead in you to make you sink." Now he turned to Whitey. "Get 'em in the car. What's the use of talking?"

"I don't like it," said Whitey, "dragging these guys clear through town. You're wanted bad, my friend. They may be looking here as well as other places."

"Why here?" cried the man, impatiently. "What would I be doing here? But okay—if you don't want to drag 'em around, knock 'em off here in the alley."

"And spoil it for Charley in this town?"

"Okay," cried the man irritably. "Knock 'em off your way. I'm getting fed up with all these bum angles."

"First thing is," said Whitey, "get 'em out of Charley's place."

Stuart and Creeden were herded out into the alley and Charley hastily shut the door on the whole party.

"Walk up the alley ahead of us," said Whitey, "and don't try to run."

"Why not?" asked Stuart with dry lips. "We get it anyway, don't we?"

"And I was dragged into this for peanuts!" muttered Creeden, dolefully.

There was a brief silence.

"Look," said Stuart, "maybe I'd better come clean with you."

"Maybe you had," said the man.

"Maybe I know where the Pollings are."

"Maybe you don't."

"Maybe I could take you there."

"You think this is square?" Whitey asked the man.

"No," said the man. "If he knew, he'd be there now. By the way, what were you doing in that hock-shop?"

"I went in to buy a gun."

"Why?"

"Before I called on the Pollings. I was afraid he might be sober for a change."

There was a long silence. Finally Stuart broke in, stalling. "You cut me in, I'll take you there."

The man laughed harshly. "He's making deals yet." He laughed again. "Okay, wise guy. You take me there . . . I'll see you're took care of."

14.

They drove north along the river, toward the lake road under Creeden's directions. They were all in one car, the unknown man and Creeden in front; Whitey, Speed, and Stuart in the back. Stuart sat in the middle.

He kept talking. "No reason why we can't all get rich. Five hundred grand is a lot of money, plenty for all. Don't you agree, boys?"

He went on and on. Finally the unknown man turned half around and cried: "Cut the yack—or we'll drop you off the next bridge."

"Unpleasant character," said Stuart, "all I'm trying to do is make us all rich. Lucky you guys ran into me." He began to talk at random.

"Please, Bob," begged Creeden, "keep it down a little. You're bending our ears."

Ahead of them now the far southern end of the big lake began to glimmer in the moonlight. Clusters of lights showed on the west bank. After a few hundred yards, the road took an odd turning and began to wind across marshy land. The road rose higher and higher on its steep embankments. Sheets of water could be seen on either side, and thousands of frogs were sending up a loud, continuous chatter.

Stuart started to yack it up again. Suddenly the unknown man turned and began to shout at him, wildly irritated; and at that moment, Stuart leaped forward, pushed the man roughly aside, grabbed the wheel and swung it violently over.

The tires shrieked piercingly; the car careened, almost went over on its side, then, with a sickening lurch it left the road, bounded down the embankment, and went into the marsh with a tremendous splash, and lay on its side, two wheels still spinning rapidly. Creeden was thrown clear, through an open window, but lay face down in the mud under a foot of water, unable to extricate himself for the moment. Stuart, lying on top of Whitey, kicked the back door open and crawled out. Speed, half-stunned, made a feeble effort to grab his legs, but was kicked in the face for his trouble.

"Creeden! Creeden!" cried Stuart, looking about him wildly.

Creeden rose at Stuart's feet like some water monster, Stuart grabbed him and they ran diagonally up the embankment. Behind them they heard cursing and splashing, then two shots were fired and bullets sang low over their heads, far too close for comfort.

But they had made the road now.

"Woods up to your left," gasped Creeden, through mud, water and marsh-weed.

But before they could get started, a spotlight sprang on and picked them up, blinding them. And a familiar voice called: "Halt! Police! Halt, or I'll fire."

They stopped. Stuart turned and shook hands with Creeden. "Did you notice the voice? My old pal, Nick Parshal."

A short while later the police fished three mud-soaked and cursing wretches out of the marsh.

Nick Parshal regarded them impassively. "Maresh, Goss, and a young punk I never saw before."

"His name's Speed," said Stuart, helpfully.

"Thanks," said Nick; then he turned to two radio cops. "You're to take all five prisoners back to town—in two cars."

"All five—*what?*" shouted Stuart.

"You heard me," said Nick; then he turned to the cops again. "But hold off with Stuart and Creeden till I question them. Get the other three started."

Later, Creeden and Stuart rode back to the big town in silence. The two young cops in the front seat kept smiling.

15.

Now they were all sitting in the Lieutenant's office: Stuart, Creeden, Coogan, Nolly Walters, and Nick.

Nick seemed more relaxed than usual, almost human, Stuart thought. "I was right up there on the second floor watching you make your getaway," Nick explained to Stuart. "We set it up for you. We knew you'd blow."

There was a general, goodnatured laugh, but Stuart did not join in.

Nick went on: "So . . . we just followed all your movements."

"What about the Pollings?" asked Stuart, suppressing his desire to have a row with Nick.

"You were right. They were at the cottage, playing the radio as if they didn't have a care in the world. Polling came clean. His wife didn't know what was going on. She just did as he told her. We got the money."

Noticing the expression on Stuart's face, Nolly Walters restrained his smiles and said: "Great job, Bob. Top news story. I always did say . . ."

"One more question," Bob broke in, interrupting his boss. "Why were you so sure I'd lead you into something, Nick?"

"What kind of a word is 'sure'?" Nick demanded. "Nothing's sure. I'm going to tell you the truth, Bob. I still hadn't made up my mind about you."

"Now look here, Lieutenant," cried Coogan, indignantly.

"I've seen guys go wrong before," said Nick, ignoring Coogan. "And they're almost always the impulsive type, like our friend here."

Stuart's face was red with suppressed rage. It was leave now or have a row with Nick. "Come on, Creeden," he said. "Let's lam out of here."

Just as they started out, Detective Smith, Coogan's helper, hurried in with an eager look in his eyes.

"Coogan," he said, "good news. We found the bullet."

"What bullet?" Coogan demanded, staring at him blankly.

"Why, the bullet Mr. Stuart fired from his gun. It was buried in some dirt at the bottom of the court."

Stuart patted Smith on the back. "Good work, Sherlock," he said. "This means promotion."

Stuart and Creeden went out. Coogan shook with laughter. But Nick, as usual, was not amused.

One More Mile to Go
F. J. Smith

June 1956

It was exactly nine-thirty when Jacoby walked quietly into the dark bedroom and strangled his wife. There had been no fuss or commotion. Earlier, she had complained of the heat and had gone to bed and fallen into a deep sleep. Before she had been able to as much as let out a startled cry, his lean, hard fingers had closed firmly about her windpipe blocking out her nagging voice forever.

Although he had planned the crime with painstaking attention to detail and figured every step of its progress from start to finish, it had required every ounce of his courage to see the first phase through. This was not surprising, for Jacoby was an obsequious, mild little man with a narrow, lined face and dull gray eyes that peered over sturdy, horn-rimmed glasses. He looked like, exactly what he was, an elderly small-town storekeeper.

After he had arranged the body and a box of iron weights in the luggage compartment of his car, he drove slowly along a series of dark, unpopulated streets to the highway, where he turned left in the general direction of New Orleans. He leaned back now and lit a cigarette. His gaze was divided between the yellow path of his headlights, the speedometer and the rear view mirror.

Jacoby was a cautious man who left nothing to chance. Even though he had a good ten mile drive ahead of him, he still kept well within the speed limit.

Lulled by the steady hum of the engine, he once more reviewed every step of the details that lay ahead. "Routine," he then told himself. "All routine." Any fool could handle the rest. The part that had required courage and determination was over and done with.

The turnoff lay about two miles beyond Fischer's Service Station. It was marked by a yellow crossroads sign so there would be no possibility of overshooting it. He would turn right at the sign and proceed along a seldom used dirt road for exactly one mile to a clearing that lay less than two hundred feet from a deep bayou. There he would park the car, carry Edna's body to the bayou's edge and return for the weights—one hundred pounds of iron sashweights, accumulated over the course of a month. After the weights had been fastened to the body with a quantity of wire he had brought—you couldn't trust rope in the water over a long period of time—he would dispose of the corpse. He knew from previous investigation that the murky water ran particularly deep in this location and that the bottom was composed of a slimy, grayish mud which would clutch and permanently hold any heavy object.

A thin smile of confidence turned to a scowl when his car hit a bad bump. Damn it, he thought irritably. The highway had been damaged by the heavy rain of a few days ago. Water had soaked under the road-bed, and the road had sunken in spots making deep depressions and sharp-edged holes. A man could break a spring or burst a tire. He wanted no mechanical trouble, tonight of all nights.

Jacoby slowed to thirty-five, and his closest-set gray eyes scrutinized the highway carefully while his thoughts moved to the next day.

In the morning he would go to work as though nothing had happened. He would eat lunch at the Traveller's Hotel, the way he usually did on Wednesday. Perhaps after he had closed the store at six, he would stop in the Monarch for a glass or two of beer and talk a while. He would arrive home about six-thirty or seven. About eight, he would start phoning neighbors and friends. After that, he would become very worried and call Sheriff Thompson. Let Thompson think what he wanted—if he was capable of thinking at all. For no matter what suspicions the Sheriff might have, he could prove nothing. There would be no clues: No poison to be traced; no blood stains to be analyzed; no blunt instruments to be discovered. Nor would there be any *corpus delicti*. And without a body there could, of course, be no crime. Edna had disappeared mysteriously. And that was all. Let them prove otherwise.

So deep in thought was Jacoby, that it required a moment or two for the deep-throated cry of the siren to reach him. With a start, he looked up at the rear view mirror and caught sight of the rapidly approaching patrol car with its flashing amber light. He eased over to the road's shoulder at once and stopped. The patrol car pulled up ahead of him. With a sinking heart, Jacoby watched the trooper climb out. Then the trooper sauntered over to Jacoby's car with a slow, easy gait, as though he had all the time in the world, and placed his elbow on the window sill.

"I was only doing thirty-five, officer," Jacoby said quickly, defensively.

"Did I say you weren't?" the trooper replied and poked his head inside to inspect the dark interior. "You've got a tail light out, Mac."

Jacoby's tongue moved across his lips and his fingers worked at the wheel, opening and closing like pale, restless tentacles. "Why—I had no idea. It was all right when I left the house. I'm very careful about those things. I'm a law-abiding citizen."

"It's your left tail light," the trooper said. "One sure thing, you're violating the law with it out. Something like that can cause an accident."

Next he carefully inspected Jacoby's driver's license and registration paper under the glare of a flashlight. He handed them back. "So you're from Edgetown."

"Yes, officer It's a little town, few miles down the road. I own a feed store there."

"I know where Edgetown is," the trooper said. "Where you heading to now?"

"Why—why I'm just taking a little drive." Jacoby smiled genially and blew at the perspiration beading his upper lip. "Just a little drive to cool off. Lord, it's hot! It does a man good to get out in the air and take a drive once in a while. Now take my wife," he added, shaking his head, "she's home reading. She's a great one for reading. Once she gets a book in her hand, you can't budge her from the house. She'll read 'til she falls asleep. She's probably sleeping by now. But me, I like fresh air. A man needs it after he's been cooped up in a feed store all day."

"Sure, sure," the trooper said with an impatient gesture. "Now about that tail light. There's a gas station up the road. You'd stop there and get a bulb for that tail light. If I wanted to be tough, I could give you a ticket. You know that."

"Well, thanks," Jacoby said, fairly groveling. "Thanks, officer I'll see to it right away Believe me, I will."

Swearing under his breath, he watched the trooper walk away.

Fischer's Service Station was small and neglected, attended by a lanky, freckle-faced youth who shuffled over to Jacoby's car and gaped in at him. "Fill 'er up?" he asked indifferently.

"I want a bulb for my left tail light," Jacoby said, drumming nervously on the wheel.

When the youthful attendant returned a few minutes later, Jacoby handed him a five dollar bill. It was the smallest thing he had. The boy studied it. Then asked, "Don't you want me to put that bulb in?"

Jacoby glanced into the rear view mirror in time to see the patrol car easing into the driveway "Yes. Yes. Certainly I do."

The attendant stuffed the bill into the pocket of his grimy, snug-fitting denims and walked around to the back of the car. Jacoby got out and watched him work clumsily removing screws and the glass which he placed on the concrete beside him. The young fellow then snapped out the old bulb and replaced it with the new one. Nothing happened.

"What do you make of that?" he asked jiggling the bulb with a greasy finger and looking up at Jacoby.

"Maybe the bulb you just put in is no good," Jacoby said and cast a sideways glance towards the trooper. The trooper's car was parked off to the side and he was working the coke machine. His back was turned to Jacoby.

"It's a brand new bulb," the attendant insisted loudly. "I just took it out of the wrapper. You seen me."

"It could be defective anyway."

"Nuts!" the boy exclaimed and removed the bulb.

He was holding it up to the light and squinting at the filament, when the trooper came over, smacking his lips and eyeing his coke bottle with satisfaction. "What's the matter, Red? What's all the noise about?" he asked good naturedly.

"Take a look at that bulb," Red said and handed him the bulb. "Tell me what you think. It looks okay to me."

The trooper took the bulb and rolled it between his fingers and held it up to the light. He tilted his head from one side to the other, examining it carefully. "There's nothing wrong with that bulb," he said. "Stick her back in and try jiggling her a little. Sometimes the sockets get rusted up."

"That's what I done," Red replied. "I just jiggled the hell out of it and nothin' happened." He replaced the bulb and shook it with his finger. "See what I mean?"

The trooper frowned in silent meditation; and then he stepped over and gave the fender a thump with the heel of his hand. The bulb blinked on, flickered momentarily and went out again. "You've got a bad connection there," he said and took a swallow of coke. "You've either got a loose wire inside or a frayed wire that's rubbing and grounded." He gave the bumper a tap with the toe of a polished boot. "What's in the trunk? Looks like she's pretty loaded down."

Jacoby felt his heart slow down and stop beating. Sweat gathered more profusely on his forehead, and his tongue felt fuzzy and incapable of forming words. "Two bags of fertilizer," he said. "I'm supposed to drop them off on the way to work tomorrow. Like I told you, I own a feed store."

The trooper finished his coke, belched comfortably, and removed his large Ranger's hat and ran fingers around the damp sweat band. His hair was short and thick and the impression of the sweat band encircled his forehead like a pale-red ribbon. "Fertilizer, eh?"

"Yes."

"That's what probably done it. You hit one of those bumps back there and one of those fertilizer sacks bounced against a bad wire and grounded it. It happens sometimes. I know My brother's a mechanic." He put his hat back on and held out his hand. "Let's have your key We'll open her up and Red can take a look. Probably a little piece of tape will fix it."

Suddenly Jacoby felt as though he were about to fall or faint. His knees were shaking, and he was forced to lean on the fender to brace himself.

"What's the matter?" the trooper said eyeing him curiously "You look sick."

"It's the heat," Jacoby said in a feeble voice. "I'm getting so I can't take this humid, hot weather any more."

The trooper looked up at the sky speculatively. "She's gonna rain again before the night's over It's always like this before a rain." He blew out his breath and tugged at his breeches. "Okay Let's have the key. We'll have a look."

"I don't have a key, officer," Jacoby said. "You see, I lost one of the keys. I left the other one home so my wife can have a duplicate made tomorrow."

"Didn't you say you had some fertilizer to deliver on the way to work?"

"I do. Yeah. Yeah. I'd forgotten all about that tonight when I removed the key from my ring." He laughed uneasily A croaking sound. "This heat. Sometimes it gets a man so he can't think or remember things. What I need is a vacation, I guess."

The trooper thought about this a while as though trying to arrange things in his head. "That light should be fixed," he said. "There's been a lot of accidents along this highway and they're clamping down." He compressed his lips and stared down at the luggage compartment lock. Then, before Jacoby actually knew what was happening, the man's short, strong fingers closed over the handle and he gave a vigorous pull upward. The lid held firm and Jacoby was forced to cling even harder to the fender to support himself.

The trooper was too busy frowning down at the lock to notice him. "Sometimes you can spring 'em open on these old cars. A hard jerk is all it takes."

He was about to try again, when Jacoby found his voice. "Can't you just give me a ticket and be done with it?"

"Why?"

"Well, it would perhaps be cheaper in the long run than ruining the lock," he pleaded. "I carry merchandise in the luggage compartment and I need a good lock."

The trooper braced his foot on the bumper and rested his arm on his knee. "Sure I could give you a ticket. But that won't fix the light, will it? Suppose some fella comes along and hits you in the rear He thinks you're a motorcycle or something. Or maybe he's half tanked. You both end up in the hospital. Is that cheaper than a new lock?"

"No, of course not," Jacoby said helplessly "But—"

The trooper chuckled, mildly amused. "Some of you fellas give me a laugh. You treat these old cars like they were old ladies. You get a scratch on the fender and you lay awake all night worrying about it."

He removed his foot and stepped over to the light and gave the fender another resounding thump with the heel of his hand. Nothing happened. He tried again and the light flashed on and glowed steadily. Then he smiled with satisfaction. "That's one way of doing it."

"Why that's wonderful," Jacoby breathed. "Just wonderful, officer."

"Don't count your chickens before they're hatched," the trooper said. "I can't say how long she'll stay that way You'd better get that light fixed tomorrow."

"I certainly will," Jacoby promised. "Believe me, I'll have it taken care of first thing in the morning."

The trooper flipped his coke bottle to his other hand and started to walk away "Okay You'd better make sure. Next time you'll get a ticket. No bones about it."

The instant the attendant finished replacing the glass and screws, Jacoby scurried in behind the wheel, started the engine and swung out into the highway. He was half crying, half laughing, trembling violently However, once the lights of the gas station had disappeared behind a tangle of trees, he rapidly gained control of his emotions and assured himself that his remarkable deliverance from near calamity had been only the result of his own ingenuity He complimented himself on his glib tongue, his presence of mind, his facility to think quickly and lie convincingly.

Smiling confidently, he treated himself to a cigarette. In a few minutes he would arrive at the crossroads sign. After that, there'd be a mile of dirt road. He would have to drive carefully and slowly on the rutted road, but it didn't matter for there wasn't a chance in ten thousand of meeting a car on that road at night. There were only several Cajun fishermen and trappers who used the road, and the nearest shack to the spot where he intended to park was a quarter of a mile away.

The smile remained on Jacoby's lips. He smoked tranquilly until his rear view mirror picked up the amber light of the patrol car once more. A sudden sinking sensation made him queasy as he lifted his foot off the accelerator and eased to a stop on the shoulder. Ahead, within range of his headlight beam, he could distinguish the bright-yellow crossroads sign.

The trooper pulled in ahead of him and climbed out and walked over to him shaking his head from side to side. Again he rested his arms on the window sill and looked in. "What's the big hurry?"

"I was only doing thirty, officer," Jacoby said meekly "That's the speed limit, isn't it?"

"I didn't say you were speeding. Why is it people always think they're being stopped for speeding?" He fished in his pocket and removed some money. "The way you pulled out of Fischer's, any one would of thought you were on fire. Red tried to call you back. Here," he held out the money, "you gave Red a five-spot and forgot your change."

Jacoby took the money and without counting it stuck it in his pocket. "Why, thanks. Thanks a lot, officer. I'm certainly obliged. It completely slipped my mind."

The Best of *Manhunt 2*

"It would take a lot to make me forget five bucks."

Jacoby laughed uneasily. If only the fellow would stop talking and go, his mind cried out. His eyes turned towards the crossroads sign.

The trooper rubbed finger tips across his smoothly shaven chin. "I got news for you. That tail light's out again. She went out just as you pulled off the road."

"What!"

"She's out like a light." He laughed at his joke. "But don't worry about it. I happened to think of something. Headquarters is about a half mile up the road. We've got a mechanic up there and he's got master keys. He can open that trunk in ten seconds. He'll fix the light and it won't cost you anything." He straightened up. "Follow me. I'll lead the way."

Key Witness

Frank Kane

August 1956

Fred Morrow stood on the corner of 110th and Park and looked around. It was almost twenty-five years since he had so much as passed through this neighborhood and he marveled at the changes that time had wrought. The houses themselves seemed to have degenerated from homes into rabbit warrens. He wrinkled his nose as he thought back to the squalor and filth of the buildings he had just gone through.

The vestibules were filthy, the mailboxes had been pulled from the walls. The walls themselves had been covered with scribbled filth, accompanied in some instances by illustrations. The hallways were permeated with odors of foreign cooking, unwashed humanity and inadequate toilet facilities, odors that would be more appropriate in a dump than in a human habitat. But then, maybe, it wasn't so inappropriate at that. The neighborhood had become a dumping place for human refuse.

He checked his watch, saw that it was almost 4:40. He debated the advisability of flagging down a cab instead of taking the bus. He decided a cab couldn't make any better progress in the stream of cars of all vintages that clogged the narrowed avenue, settled for the bus.

He studied the tide of pedestrians of all colors that ebbed and flowed the length of the avenue.

Suddenly, he had the impression his ears had clogged up. It couldn't be that, because he could still hear the roar of traffic. But it was as if a void, a tangible silence had settled on the street. The tide of walkers seemed to have been stopped, and what was trickling through was diverted around a small group that stood back against the buildings.

A thin, tall boy in a maroon satin jacket, across which was written in bold script "Black Aces" was struggling in the grip of two other youths, one light complexioned, the other dark, who stood on either side of him each holding an arm. A third stood facing him, his teeth gleaming in a grin.

Morrow had the impression of heavily oiled black hair, a pimply face with a scar that puckered the side of it. The third boy shuffled closer to the one being held by the other two. His arm flashed upward in three strokes, the boy in the maroon jacket reached up to his tiptoes, then seemed to sag in the grip of the two holding him.

When they released his arms, he slumped to the sidewalk, a loose bundle of arms and legs. The three stood over him for a moment, the scar-faced one contemptuously holding the blade of his switch knife for all to see. Then they sprinted for a nearby doorway.

It all happened so quickly, Fred Morrow stood rooted to the spot. By the time he had recovered, the three assailants had vanished, their victim lay squirming on the sidewalk. Morrow pushed his way through the small morbid circle that had formed.

The boy lay on his back, his hands laced across his stomach in a futile effort to stem the red flood that was seeping through his fingers. Red-tinged bubbles formed and broke between his lips, as his eyes rolled from side to side.

Morrow went to his knees. "Are you hurt bad, boy?"

The pain-filled eyes stopped rolling. The boy was young, Morrow noticed, light-skinned, probably Puerto Rican. He nodded. "He cut me bad. Real bad."

"There'll be an ambulance along soon." He looked up into the sea of faces around him. "Anybody send for an ambulance?"

The boy groaned, his legs jerked spasmodically. "It was Big Step. He do the cutting. He—" His jaw sagged, a film glazed his eyes. His head rolled loosely to the side, a thin red stream ran from the corner of his mouth. The eyes stared unblinkingly ahead.

Morrow looked up at the crowd that was pushing closer to stare at Death. One of the women was blessing herself; the others just stared in morbid fascination.

"Well, don't just stand there," Morrow thundered at them. "This boy is dead. Get the police."

There was a rustle of movement on the outer perimeter of the crowd, a patrolman pushed his way through. He was tall. His face gleamed with perspiration; he was breathing heavily. "All right, get back. Give the boy some air," he snapped at the crowd. They shuffled back a few inches, inched forward again when he knelt at the side of the dead boy.

"Air won't do him any good now, officer," someone said. "He's dead."

The cop turned the boy's face, examined the sightless eyes, then nodded. He reached down, caught the cuff of the boy's sleeve between his thumb and forefinger, lifted the hand away from the wound.

Morrow had the feeling he was going to be sick. He stood up, looked away as the cop let the hand fall back.

The cop pushed his cap on the back of his head, tugged a dog-eared leather notebook from his hip pocket. He looked around the crowd. "All right, now. Who saw it happen?" His eyes hop scotched from face to face in the crowd. None spoke. They met his glance blandly, no one stepped forward.

"They did. All of them. They just stood there and let it happen," Morrow protested indignantly.

The cop grunted, wiped his damp forehead with his sleeve. "Not them. They don't see nothing. They don't hear nothing. They don't know nothing." He looked around again. "Anybody know this boy?" Again, the bland silence.

"Well, if they didn't see it, I did," Morrow growled.

The cop rolled his eyes back to Morrow's face, raised his eyebrows, seemed to be seeing him for the first time. Morrow was a few inches shorter than the cop, made up in girth what he lacked in height. He was hatless. His thinning hair was streaked with grey and had receded from his brow, leaving a freckled pate. His face glinted with perspiration; anger had etched a white ring around his lips.

The cop brought a stub of pencil from his blouse pocket, wet the tip with his tongue. He flipped open the notebook, checked his watch and made a notation. "What was it you saw, mister?"

"There were three of them. Two of them held his hands while the other knifed him." He glared around at the faces that ringed them. "They saw it, too!"

"Three of them, huh?" The cop transferred the information to his notebook, looked up. "You don't live around here?"

Morrow shook his head.

"Then you wouldn't know who they were."

"One of them was Big Step. That's what the boy said before he died."

The cop drew his breath through his teeth, studied Morrow for a moment. "You're sure of that, mister?" Behind them the crowd started shuffling, muttering under its breath.

"Of course I'm sure. I was kneeling right alongside of him. He said it was Big Step who cut him."

The cop shrugged. "I'll have to have your name and address."

"Fred Morrow. 453 East Seventh Street, Brooklyn." He watched while the officer noted it in his book. "I was down looking over some houses a client of my firm owns. I was waiting here for the bus when it happened." He pointed to a doorway. "They ran in there after they killed him."

The cop wasted an incurious glance on the doorway. "That don't mean anything. They could go in there and come out a block away." He returned to his notes. "You're sure he said Big Step. You see the guy who used the knife?"

"Yes. He was facing me. He was young, sixteen or seventeen, dark. Had a scar alongside his mouth. Right about here." He touched his index finger to his cheek.

The cop looked up, nodded. Somewhere a siren moaned.

The cop flicked his notebook closed. "That'll be the Dolly Sisters," he grunted. "You better let them take you down to the house. The D.A. will probably want one of his boys to hear your story. Unless you change your mind."

"Why should I change my mind?"

The cop shrugged. "It's been known to happen."

A patrol car skidded to a stop at the curb, the crowd parted to make room for the newcomer. He was young, redheaded. He nodded to the other patrolman, glanced down at the body.

"There's a call in for the Harlem Hospital bus."

The other cop grunted. "Too late. This is a DOA."

The newcomer pursed his lips. "Too late to stop the bus now." His eyes flicked to Morrow. "Got anything on it?"

"Man here says he saw it happen." The first cop opened his book, flipped through the pages. "Was standing right here when it happened. Says the victim told him who did the cutting." His eyes rolled up from the book. "Big Step."

The redheaded cop raised his eyebrows, offered no comment. "I think you'd better have Dinty run him down to the house. The D.A.'s office will probably want to talk to him," the beat cop suggested.

"Okay." The redhead nodded for Morrow to follow him, pushed his way through the crowd. The faces that were turned to Morrow were sullen, unfriendly. They made no move to get out of his way, forced him to push his way through.

"It's a DOA," the redheaded cop told his partner. "Man here was a witness. Says he got the killer's name from the dead kid before he went out." He looked at Morrow.

"He's willing to testify to it. That right, mister?"

Morrow nodded. "That's right."

The driver of the car shifted the toothpick he was chewing from the left side of his mouth to the right. "What name'd he give you, mister?"

"Big Step," Morrow told him.

He watched the glance that passed between the two cops.

One of them said, "These spics've been spoiling for a real rumble and now they've got a good excuse."

The driver nodded, motioned Morrow into the car. "I'd better fill the skipper in. He may want to move some extra men in to break it up before they start chopping each other up. Not that it would be any great loss."

The redhead nodded, slammed the door behind Morrow. "I'll hold it down until you get back."

"Okay." The driver touched his siren, swung out into a hole in the traffic and headed downtown.

2.

Sol Robbins had been an ambitious, bright young boy just out of law school when he was tapped for the district attorney's staff. He envisioned a skyrocketing rise to prominence on the wings of publicity. Unfortunately, the only cases that had come his way had been routine, lacking in color or importance sufficient to warrant notice.

So—when he drew this case, he was determined to squeeze the last drop of publicity out of it.

Fred Morrow was sitting in a small cubbyhole office just off the squad room of the precinct house when Robbins arrived. The Assistant D.A. swung through the squad room, waved a salute to a man he knew, walked into the office.

He shoved a moist, pudgy hand at Morrow. "I hope I didn't keep you waiting too long," he panted. "I got down here as soon as I got the flash."

Morrow nodded, swabbed at his moist face with a balled-up handkerchief. "I don't think there was any necessity for you to come all the way uptown, Mr.—"

"Robbins. Sol Robbins." He walked around the desk, dropped into the chair. "Think nothing of it. I wanted to meet you personally." He picked up four sheets of typewritten paper, flicked through them, nodded his satisfaction at the signature on the fourth sheet. "They've got your statement all typed up, I see. Good. I can study it at my leisure. First, I'd like to hear the story from you first hand." He leaned back, tugged two cigars from his breast pocket, held one up to Morrow, drew a shake of the head. He bit the end off one, returned the other to his pocket. "Now, as I understand it, the dead boy—his name was Julio Rigas, incidentally—identified his killer to you?"

Morrow nodded. "He told me Big Step had knifed him."

Sol Robbins smiled, rolled the unlit cigar between thumb and forefinger in the middle of his lips. "You also saw the killer well enough to be able to identify him?"

"He was facing me when he stabbed the other boy. I wouldn't be very likely to forget his face."

"Very good, sir." The Assistant D.A. beamed his approval. "I want you to know that we all owe you a debt of gratitude for your public spiritedness in being willing to testify." He chewed on the cigar for a moment. "Do you have a family, Mr. Morrow?"

Morrow nodded. "A boy and a girl."

"We'll see to it that they have all the protection necessary until this matter is taken care of."

"Protection?" Morrow was uncomfortably aware of a cold finger of apprehension. "From what?"

Sol Robbins shrugged. "Just a routine gesture. Sometimes in a case like this, pressure is exerted to make a witness change his mind about testifying. We'll see to it that you're not bothered."

Morrow swabbed at his face again. "Maybe I ought to—"

Sol Robbins pulled the cigar from between his teeth. "There's only one way we can lick this lawlessness and that's for a few of us to be willing to stand up and fight." His eyes moved up from the cigar to the other man's face. "We can't afford to let ourselves be intimidated. All of us have got to be willing to make some sacrifice to make this city a safe place to live in. Am I right?"

Morrow nodded uncertainly. "I—I guess so, but—"

The man behind the desk pounded the desk with the flat of his hand. "Good. Then we'll depend on you." He replaced the cigar between his teeth, and chewed on it. "There are a couple of newspaper boys outside, I understand. I'd like you to meet them with me. All right?"

Morrow nodded. "I guess so."

The man behind the desk picked up the phone, pressed a button on its base. "Sergeant, you can let the press in now." He dropped the instrument back on its cradle, leaned back and laced his fingers at the back of his head. "If it's all right with you, I'll do the talking. I'm used to handling these boys."

Morrow nodded again, swabbed at his face.

The "boys" consisted of two wire service police reporters, a mannish looking female from the Standard and a scholarly looking young man in horn-rimmed glasses from the Advance. They filed into the room, nodded to Robbins and studied Morrow curiously.

"I've just finished interviewing Mr. Morrow, gentlemen—and ladies," he hastily amended. "We have a positive identification of the killer of Julio Rigas. The dead boy whispered his name to Mr. Morrow practically with his dying breath."

The mannish looking female fastened an embarrassingly direct stare on Fred Morrow. "I understand he was knifed three times through the stomach and hemorrhaged from the mouth. Yet he was able to tell you who killed him?"

"That's right," Robbins snapped.

"What's the matter with him? Can't he talk?"

Robbins colored slightly, started to retort, dug his teeth deeper into his cigar instead. He worked at a smile which didn't come off. "Of course." He turned to Morrow. "This is Fanny Lewis of the Standard, Mr. Morrow."

She turned back to Morrow. "Well?"

"I heard him, I saw the killer. He was a Negro. And I saw the two who held the boy for the killer."

"Even though you may not like our black brethren," the woman said, "you wouldn't deliberately swear one into the electric chair, would you?"

"Of course not," Morrow protested quickly. "I've got nothing against colored people."

Robbins gave Morrow an understanding smile. Then said, "We're all aware the Standard has very set editorial opinions maintaining that the District Attorney's office, the police department and practically everybody but the Standard discriminates against the Negro. Nonetheless, the fact remains that Mr. Morrow is performing a public service in cooperating with the police department in this matter and is deserving of more courtesy than is implied by Mrs. Lewis' question."

Fanny Lewis waited patiently until he finished, then, without giving any sign that she had heard, said to Morrow, "May I ask what you were doing in that part of town?"

"I was there on business."

The woman pursed her unpainted lips. "Oh, you don't mind doing business with them?"

"What do you mean, *them?* One of my firm's clients owns some property up there. I was looking it over for him."

"Pretty picture, wasn't it?" She fished a pencil and some folded copy paper from her bag. "What did you say your firm's name was?"

"I didn't say. And I don't intend to."

Fanny Lewis smiled at him sweetly. "We can find out, you know."

The AP man, a gray-haired veteran named Kiely grinned at Morrow. "Don't mind Fanny, Mr. Morrow. She sees an anti-Harlem plot in every thing that happens in or close to Harlem."

"You stay out of it, Kiely," the woman snapped at him. "You know damn well what they're trying to pull. The cops and the D.A.'s office have been getting hell about all these gang killings, so they've got to produce a killer. They get a guy who heard what was probably death rattles, put a name in his mouth until he thinks he heard it. So Harlem gets a bad name because it happened there."

"You try printing something like that, my friend, and you and your paper are going to find yourselves mixed up in the Goddamnedest lawsuit you ever ran into," Robbins roared at her. "I'm sick and tired of the way you start bleeding every time there's some trouble in Harlem. Talk about slanting evidence, you slant it so far it's almost on its back. This man doesn't care whether Big Step is white or black or in-between, merely that his—"

"Next election they might like to know that your boss appoints assistants who are violently prejudiced against the people whose skins—"

"Print whatever you like, but these are the facts. Three races mingle on the fringe of that area. Maybe four races—who knows how many. Today a young Puerto Rican was knifed to death on a crowded street. The police believe the knifing was the result of ill feeling between two gangs, the Black Aces and the Royal Knights. The dead boy was the war counsellor for the Black Aces and the police expect to announce at any moment the arrest of the killer who is believed to be a high ranking member of the Royal Knights." Robbins' eyes moved from face to face. "Mr. Morrow happened to be an eye witness to the killing, ran to the aid of the knifed boy and was told by him the name of the killer. He was also able to describe the killer to the police. Any questions?"

Fanny Lewis grinned at him. "No names?"

Robbins ignored her and spoke to the group. "Please no. Not at least until the arrest has been made. I've given Mr. Morrow my word on that. Any other questions?"

"A killing like this could start a real all-out rumble. Are the police doing anything to control it?" the scholarly-looking man from the Advance wanted to know.

"I understand additional men are being assigned to the area, and the foot men are being equipped with helmets. The precinct captain assures me that every possible step is being taken to avoid any violence. We feel confident that as soon as the arrest is made, the feeling will die down."

"Why all the secrecy, Robby?" Fanny Lewis wanted to know.

"Because my office feels that a witness as important as Mr. Morrow should get all the protection we can give him."

The sinking feeling of apprehension was heavy again in Morrow's stomach. "Look, I'm not looking for any trouble. I saw a boy killed today and I thought it was my duty as a citizen to try and have his killer caught. I'm beginning to feel like I was the killer."

"You could be—if you finger an innocent man into the electric chair," Fanny Lewis snapped.

3.

The rooftop was dark. Big Step sat with his back against the parapet, his legs stretched out in front of him. The girl lay with her head in his lap, with only the occasional gleam of white teeth to betray her presence.

His hand idly fondled her bare, hard nippled breast. His mind was back to the afternoon. He was reliving the three sharp thrusts that had elevated him to top dog in the Royal Knights.

"You sure are mean," the girl purred. She took his hand from her breast, gnawed at the knuckle. "You sure cut that boy for good."

Big Step grinned. "He like to die before I even cut him." He caught her by the back of the neck, pulled her mouth up against him.

Her arms were around his neck, her fingers digging into his shoulders. The door to the roof swung open. A triangle of yellow light spilled out onto the roof, spread to where they sat locked together. Big Step pushed the girl away, his hand flashed for his pocket, came out with the bare blade of the switch knife.

A figure stood framed in the doorway. "Big Step," it whispered hoarsely. "You out here?"

"Who that?" Big Step's voice was low, harsh.

The figure in the doorway shuffled out onto the roof. "Me. Stud. Where you at?"

"Over here," Big Step growled. "How come you go busting in on me and Ruby, Stud? How come?"

"Trouble. Big Trouble." Stud stopped in front of where Ruby sat, stared at her for a moment. He was tall, thin. His clothes seemed sizes too big, hung loosely from his shoulders. "Cops come looking for you."

Big Step chuckled. "Cops always come looking for Big Step."

"It in the papers. A guy seen you."

"A hundred seen me. Everybody knows who did it. But them cops, they can't prove nothing."

Stud shook his head. "They got an ofay who talked. He tell the cops he seen you. He tell the cops the spic finger you before he die."

The girl caught Big Step's hand. "Make him go away, Big Step."

Big Step pulled his hand loose. "Who this guy that talked? Where he live?"

Stud shook his head. "It don't say."

Big Step raked his fingers through his hair. "You stayed there, Ruby. You seen who might finger me?"

The light highlighted the girl's tip-tilted breasts, the long, graceful legs, the softly curved thighs. Stud watched her hungrily as she tried to put her arms around Big Step, got pushed away.

"There was a man," she said. "He go away with the cops."

"We got to find him. We got to let him know what happens if'n he fingers Big Step. How we going to find him, Stud?"

Stud scratched his head.

Ruby said, "The cop know. He take his name and address down in his book. Why don't you ask him?"

Big Step stared at her for a moment, then his wide mouth split in a grin. "Which cop?"

"Hurley." She grinned maliciously. "You go ask Hurley, he crack your head."

Big Step scowled at the girl. "You mean that cop all the time sniffing round Mae's place?"

Ruby nodded. "He like her girls. She let him do more'n sniff around and he don' bother her business none."

Patrolman Everett Hurley (Badge 16462) stood in the shadows of a store front, cupped his cigarette in the palm of his hand. He smoked surreptitiously, flicked the butt toward the gutter. He straightened his cap over his eyes, buttoned the top button of his blouse. His wristwatch showed the time to be 10:50, with a little over an hour left to his tour.

He watched the thinned stream of people out walking, scanned the front stoops loaded with sweating humanity. Across the street, a girl caught his eye. Her hair was cut in a provocative Italian gamin cut. When she walked, her full breasts strained against the thin fabric of her dress. As she passed the street light, he stared hungrily at the slow, languorous working of her hips against her skirt. He could tell from where he stood that she wore nothing under the dress.

He ambled down his side of the street, slightly to the rear of her. Near the corner, when she crossed the street, she almost ran into him.

"Hello." Her lips were thick, soft looking. Her teeth were even and white against the blackness of her skin. Her eyes were black and moist.

"What are you doing out alone?" Hurley wanted to know. He made no attempt to hide the fact that his eyes were taking inventory of her assets. "A pretty girl like you ought to be out on a date this time of night."

The smile faded, the girl pouted. "I got no man no more. We just bust up for good." She turned the full power of her eyes on him.

"Besides he a runt. I like my men big and strong."

Hurley eyed her speculatively. "I'm a working man. And when I quit working I've got to go straight home."

Ruby pouted again. "That too bad. I don't like sitting on that roof alone. I get scared of the dark. And there ain't nobody come on that roof."

"What roof is that?"

"Down the street. Four house from the corner. Ain't nobody come on that roof a'tall." She grinned at him, swung away, walked down the street swinging her hips with an exaggerated motion.

Hurley stood watching hungrily until she disappeared into the entrance to the fourth house from the corner. He knew why no one ever went on that roof. The house had been condemned, its occupants forcibly moved out. In a matter of days wreckers would be tearing it down.

Slowly he walked down the block. When he came abreast of the fourth house from the corner, he stopped, looked casually around. Certainly, if a house were condemned, it was his duty to investigate who might be trespassing. He tried the door, found it unlocked. Inside, the vestibule was dark, redolent with nose-offending odors. The door to the hallway hung crazily from one hinge, half open. He walked in, felt his way cautiously to the stairs.

He was just about to test the first step, when an arm encircled his throat, cut off his wind. Two other arms pinned his arms to his side.

The first blow knocked his hat off, started bells ringing. He struggled feebly, was dimly aware that the second blow had hammered him to his knees. The arm around his throat seemed to tighten; he could feel the perspiration break out in little bubbles on his forehead. Suddenly, there was a bright flash in the back of his head; his body went limp; he hit the floor face first.

The unconscious man didn't even feel it when Big Step brought back his foot and kicked him in the side of the head. From the cop's back pocket, Stud pulled the leather memo pad. Sam, who got down beside Stud, tugged away at the gun in the holster, couldn't get it loose.

"I want me this iron," Sam panted. "Then when them Black Aces come rumbling, bang-bang, they think I'm a cannon." He tugged again. "How come them cops let their gun get stuck?"

"That not stuck," Big Step growled. He reached over, stuck his thumb into the holster, eased the gun out. "That a special catch so's you can't steal no cop's gun."

Hurley moaned softly on the floor. Big Step lashed out again with the toe of his shoe. The moaning stopped.

"Let's get out of here," Big Step said.

4.

It was cool on the porch in Brooklyn. Fred Morrow sat in an old wicker armchair, sucked on his pet pipe as he finished telling his story. His wife, Ann, prematurely grey, and comfortably fat, had stopped rocking.

"I just happened to see the boy killed," he concluded, "and I saw the one who did it. That's all."

"They'll be after you," she said. "You read every day what they do." Her voice was concerned.

"They don't know my name or anything." Fred knocked the dottle from his pipe, dug a pouch from his hip pocket. He dipped the bowl in, started packing with his index finger. "What could I do? I couldn't just stand by and let the killer get away with murder."

"They'll find your name. It wasn't your affair, Fred. Why should you get mixed up in it, and have them come looking for you? How about Gloria or Freddy? Maybe they'll take it out on them!"

"Stop worrying, Ann." He stuck the pipe between his teeth, scratched a wooden match. "The police will see to it that we're not bothered."

"The police!" She ran her fingers nervously through her hair. "Can they be with us every step? They've got other things on their minds."

Morrow touched the match to the tobacco, sucked a mouth full of smoke, exhaled noisily. "Look, Ann, you're always saying something should be done about all the killing and the maiming these teen-age gangs are doing. Right?"

"Yes, but not by you. That's what the police are for."

"The police are handcuffed unless the public helps. We've got to make an example of one of these killers and maybe the others will think twice." He ground his teeth on the pipe stem. "It's not a pleasant thing to do, but it's my duty to do it, and I have to."

"But how about me and the kids? Is it fair to us to get a gang of murderers after us because you feel you have to do your duty? You weren't the only one on the street when it happened. Why didn't someone else step up and identify the killer? Why you?"

Morrow shrugged helplessly. "I don't know, Ann. Just because they don't doesn't say I shouldn't. The sooner these kids find out they're not beyond the law, the sooner decent people like you and me won't have to be afraid to stand up for their rights."

The woman dry washed her hands agitatedly. "I know, I know. But I can't help worrying. I wish you hadn't done it. I wish it hadn't been you."

"It's too late to wish now. I've already signed a statement giving the boy's name and his description. When they pick him up, I'll have to identify him." He blew a stream of murky white smoke at the ceiling. "They'll put him away where he can't do anybody any more harm."

"But he has friends. Those hoodlums travel in packs. You know that. His friends won't let you rest if you're the cause of him going to jail."

"Please, Ann. There's just no sense in arguing with me. It's too late to turn back now."

"You can refuse to identify him. Say you're not sure."

"And let him know we're knuckling down to him? Let him laugh at law and order with blood fresh on his hands?"

"What's the difference? At least they'll leave us alone. You can't bring the other boy back by sending this one to jail."

"Maybe not, but maybe we can save some other boy from getting what he got. Maybe our own boy. When they get so bold that they can commit a murder on a crowded street with no fear of being identified, then it's time we did something about it."

"But why do you have to elect yourself the hero? Don't you ever think of us, what will happen to us if anything happens to you?" She covered her eyes with her hand, fought back a sob. "Why did you have to get mixed up in it at all? Why?"

A wave of helplessness surged over him as he watched her shoulders heaving. He swore softly under his breath, got up from his chair, slid his arm around her shoulder.

"It'll be all right, Ann. You'll see. It'll be all right."

Later that night he lay in bed, stared at the dim smear of the ceiling above him. He was aware that in the other bed Ann too lay wide-eyed and sleepless. Both pretended to be sleeping.

The phone on the night table shrilled.

Morrow got up on his elbow, pulled on the night table lamp. The little clock on the stand showed two o'clock. He stared at the phone with a frown, looked over to where Ann lay, a knuckle between her teeth.

The phone continued to shrill.

"You'd better answer it. It'll wake the kids," she told him finally.

Morrow pulled the receiver off its hook. He held it to his ear. "Hello?"

The voice on the other end was low, muffled. "Hello, Big Mouth."

"Who is this?" Morrow tried to keep the fear out of his voice. "Who do you want?"

"You, Big Mouth. I want you and I'm goin' get you. Good night, Big Mouth. Sleep tight."

The receiver clicked in his ear. Morrow tapped on the crossbar of the phone. "Hello, hello."

The metallic voice of the operator cut in. "What number are you calling?"

"Operator, I just got a phone call. Can you trace it for me? I want the party back. Please."

"I'm sorry. I must have the number."

"I see. All right. Thanks." He dropped the receiver back on its hook.

Ann had swung her feet from under the covers, sat on the side of her bed. The color had drained from her face, leaving it white and old. "It was them?"

He nodded.

"I knew it." There was resignation in her voice, an acceptance of what lay in store. "You thought they didn't know where to find you, but it didn't take them long. I knew it wouldn't."

"But how?" He shook his head bewilderedly. "The police promised. They said they'd protect us, that—"

Ann got up, walked to the window, looked out on the quiet Brooklyn Street below their window. She pulled the shade. "They might be out there right now. I told you they wouldn't let you do it. They'll never let us alone." She slid her feet into slippers, pulled a robe around her. He could hear the slippered feet slithering down the hall to the boy's room.

After what seemed a long time, she was back. She sat wearily on the side of her bed. "What are you going to do, Fred?"

He shook his head, sank his face into his hands. "I have to go ahead with it, Ann. You know that. I can't turn back now."

The second call came at three o'clock, the third at four.

After he hung up for the third time, Fred Morrow dialed the telephone of Police Headquarters. He was routed through to the Detective Bureau of the East Harlem Division.

"Torno, speaking. Detective Bureau."

"This is Fred Morrow. I—I'm the witness in the killing of that boy in Harlem this afternoon."

There was a slight pause at the other end. "What can we do for you?"

"You've got to protect me. They've been calling me. Every hour on the hour. They've been threatening my wife and me, and my kids. You've got to protect us."

"Take it easy, Mr. Morrow. It may just be cranks."

Morrow shook his head. "It isn't. They mean business. They said they'll kill all of us. You promised they wouldn't get to me. You promised—"

The voice on the other end was soothing. "We didn't give out anything. It's probably somebody who knows you who thinks it's a real funny joke to throw a scare into you."

"They meant business."

A note of impatience came into the other voice. "How could they? You didn't give anything to anybody, did you?"

Morrow investigated the fine bristle along the point of his chin with the tips of his fingers. "No. I don't think—wait a minute, yes I did. That first cop where it happened—he took my name and address. Before he sent me to the precinct station. Yes. I remember now. He wrote it down."

"I see. Well, you get some sleep. I'll see to it that a guard is assigned to you and your family. Just get some sleep, we'll keep an eye on you."

"Thanks." He dropped the receiver back on the hook, walked over to the drawn shade on the window. He pulled it back, applied an eye to the side. The street was empty.

Ann sat on the side of the bed, speechless, white. She followed him with stricken eyes. "What did he say?"

"They'll give us protection." She laughed bitterly. "They'll give us protection? How? Can they spend every minute with us? Can they sleep with us? Can they stop that phone from ringing?" Morrow shook his head helplessly, dropped into a chair and stared at the clock. He was still staring at it when the hands showed five o'clock.

The telephone rang.

5.

Detective First Grade Marty Torno dropped his receiver back on its hook, glanced around the half empty bull pen, signalled down his partner. Torno was young, rangy. His face was sunburned a deep mahogany and when he smiled, dimples cut deep white trenches in the tan. He picked up a report he was working on, dropped it into his top drawer.

His partner, Al Doyle, was an old timer. He affected a rumpled blue suit, a battered and stained gray fedora. An ever-present wad of chewing gum kept his jaws in perpetual motion. He had the long nose and inquisitive eyes of a real ferret. He ambled across the room in a flat-footed stride that bespoke many years of pounding the pavement before some spectacular police work had brought him into the Bureau.

"What's the squeal?" he wanted to know.

Torno stared up at him, frowned. "The guy who turned up as a witness in the knifing this afternoon. They're bothering him with phone calls."

"Cranks."

Torno shook his head. "He don't think so."

The man in the blue suit shrugged. "They never do. Some screwball gets their name and address—"

"It wasn't given out."

Doyle stared at his partner's face. "If they didn't give out the address, how would the mob find it?"

"You know Hurley, the cop that got himself mugged just before midnight? He was the cop on the beat where it happened."

Doyle pursed his lips, squeezed at his nostrils with thumb and fore-finger. "He take the guy's name and address?"

Torno nodded. He picked up the phone, dialed a number. "Hello? Torno at the Detective Bureau. Put me through to the Property Clerk." While he waited he drummed on the edge of the desk, stared up at his partner. Then, "Torno, Lou. You got the stuff they took off the cop that got jumped on 110th?" He nodded. "His gun. Anything else?" He stared up at Doyle significantly, nodded. "Thanks, Lou." He dropped the receiver on its hook. "Two things missing, Al. His gun and his book—the book with the guy's name and address."

"What are you going to do?"

"Who's handling from the D.A.'s office?"

Doyle wrinkled his nose, shook his head. "It'll be on the sheet." He walked back to the little cubbyhole partitioned off for the lieutenant in charge. After a moment, he came out fingering a flimsy, walked back with it to Torno's desk. "Robby's got it. Sol Robbins." He flipped the report on the desk in front of his partner. "Now what?"

"I'll call Robby and tell him if he wants that witness delivered in court in one piece he better set up around-the-clock protection."

Doyle consulted his watch. "At this hour? You know what time it is?"

Torno grinned at him. "We're awake. Why should Robby sleep?"

In a few minutes he was outlining what had happened to a very sleepy assistant district attorney. When he explained how the address had gotten into Big Step's hands, Robby came wide awake.

"Thanks, Torno. I'll get in touch with downtown and have Morrow covered until we can lay our hands on Big Step."

Torno grinned at the mouthpiece glumly. "And then what happens?"

"What can we do? Put a guard on Morrow for the rest of his life?"

Torno dropped the receiver back on its hook. "What do you say we do a little calling, Al?"

"Any place in particular?"

Torno shrugged. "Just calling."

110th Street is a street that never goes to bed. The stream of strollers of early evening was now a dribble, but still there were continuous signs of life. Al Doyle drove the black department car slowly down the length of the street, his sharp little eyes flickering from side to side.

Tired little Puerto Rican girls shuffled their way homeward after a long hard night, their brightly colored clothes and heavy make-up scarecrowish in the early morning light. Finally, Doyle spotted a familiar figure, nudged his partner. The big car slid to an easy stop at the curb, near a man who stood leaning against a store front.

"Hey, Sugar," Doyle called softly. The man in the shadows stiffened, seemed undecided whether or not to run.

"Come here, Sugar," Doyle called him. "I just want to talk to you." The figure emerged from the shadows. He was short, fat. His black face shone in the light, he shuffled rather than walked.

"You hadn't ought to do this, Mr. Doyle," he complained. "It gives me a bad name they see me talking to a cop. You hadn't ought to do it."

Doyle pushed open the back door to the car. "Get in."

The black man's eyes rolled white. "I ain't done nothin', Mr. Doyle. You know that. I'm yoah frien'!. I ain't done nothin'."

"Get in. I want to talk to you."

The fat man slid into the back seat, got down low as the car picked up speed, headed west.

"I swear I clean, Mr. Doyle," Sugar protested. "I ain't done a thing."

"You hear about Hurley tonight?"

Sugar sucked a whistling breath through his teeth. "I don't know nothin'."

"Look, Sugar, we been pretty good to you. We let you operate a little bit. We never blow the whistle to the Feds on that powder you push. That right?" Torno swung around in his seat. "You want us to keep on being good to you?"

"Yes, sir, Mr. Torno. Yes, sir. I sure do." He wiped the wet smear of his lips with his sleeve. "But I'm tellin' it true. I don't know nothin' about Hurley."

Torno studied the man's face for a minute. "Where does Big Step hang out?"

The man in the back seat shook his head so vigorously, the jowls shook. "I don't know. Word o'God, I don't know."

"You better start levelling, Sugar. We know Big Step and the rest of his gang are hooked. And you're their source. Where does he pad down?"

Sugar continued to shake his head. "Not me, Mr. Torno. I take care of maybe a couple little girls who real dead beat after a hard night. Not them boys. No, sir, Mr. Torno. They real mean."

"Who's their source, Sugar?" Sugar licked at his lips with a thick, fat tongue. His eyes flicked from one side of the car to the other, finally came to rest on Torno's face. "You'll protect me, Mr. Torno?"

"Sure," Torno grinned. "We wouldn't want anything to happen to you, Sugar. Would we, Al?"

"Where would we get our information?" Doyle said.

"You know Cozy Jacks?"

Torno nodded. "Guy runs the pool room over on Lexington?"

"That's the guy, Mr. Torno. He got a real shooting gallery back there. He got a real big high power trade, not a chicken push like poor Sugar."

"Big Step hang out there?"

Sugar wiped the streaming perspiration from his forehead and upper lip. "If'n Cozy ever heard who tipped you, I be a dead cat before morning."

"He won't know. Maybe with him out of business you can spread out."

"Thank you, Mr. Torno."

Torno nodded toward the curb. "We'll drop you here, Sugar." The car pulled up to the curb, the rear door opened and the fat man scurried out. He headed for the building line, melted into the shadows. He waited there until the tail light of the sedan had blinked around the far corner. Then he started shuffling back to his regular stand.

6.

Fanny Lewis had no illusions about herself. She knew she was only a fair to middling reporter who drew the Harlem beat because she was tagged as a "bleeding heart nigger-lover" by the rest of the staff. She didn't resent it, because everybody on the staff who was anybody was a bleeding heart for some minority.

The Standard had once been an important paper in New York. Hidebound, ultra conservative, but important. But it never survived World War I and the revolution in morals and social customs. It staggered along during the late Twenties and early Thirties, a dreary ghost of its once important self. Little by little the tight little band of ultra conservatives who were its *raison d'être* died off leaving it with no support.

Then the business department started to scream. As revenue dropped off, so did the good staffers who could draw better pay elsewhere. And the Standard went on the block.

The new owners were faced with the dreary fact that there was no longer any reason for being for the Standard. The conservatives were ably represented by two papers, the liberals by two more and the middle of the roaders by still another. Advertisers could see no reason to stretch their too thin budgets to support still another.

But necessity is often the mother of inspiration. When Carleton Morris took over the Standard, he did it with the cold-blooded purpose of establishing himself and his wife as important figures in New York life. The project was an abject failure and he bowed out of active operation of the paper, turning it over to Leslie Hunt, his managing editor and former classmate, to be run as he saw fit.

It was then that inspiration entered the picture. Hunt decided to make his paper the mouthpiece and defender of minority groups, to such an extent it would make it seem the other papers bent over in maligning them. Fact was not important to Hunt. Whatever viewpoint the other papers took, The Standard took the other, whether it be defense or vilification. The Negro was Leslie Hunt's best bet to attract attention. Particularly, with the desegregation uproar now headlining the news.

At first it had been a sorry experiment, but as months went by, the department stores and advertisers who had stayed away from the Standard in droves started to discover that the minorities not only had money to spend, but were rabid about supporting the paper that fought their battle so one-sidedly.

So, the outcasts and the Fifth Amendment fringe of journalism started to drift toward the one paper whose policy they could adopt. Fanny Lewis was the forefront of this contingent.

No person working for The Standard, no matter what mud they previously helped mould into the printed word, so epitomized the rabble-rousing sheet as Fanny. She *was* the paper. Fanny had been born in New Orleans of a mother who was part Spanish and part Negro and of a white father who deserted them when the third child arrived. Fanny was as Caucasian-looking as her father and perhaps that's why she hated him, and felt so sorry for herself and her mother. She never permitted herself to question what her feelings might have been had her mother disappeared. A big, homely, raw-boned, lonely woman lost between two worlds, she found herself vehemently forced to take the side of one or the other. When Hunt hired her, she knew she had found what she'd been seeking for nearly forty years.

Fanny was getting ready for bed when the desk called her.

"Better get on down to the hospital," the night editor on the city side grunted. "Cop on the beat at 110th got half his brains kicked out in an empty hallway."

She nodded, dropped the receiver on its hook, started to dress. She looked around the dingy flat dispiritedly, her eyes came to rest on the clock on the dresser. Almost one o'clock and Benjy hadn't even bothered to call.

She walked into the bathroom, dashed cold water into her face, examined herself in the mirror. She tucked a wisp of hair back over her ear with her finger, stared at the drawn, angular features that glared back at her.

The only reason he had married her was because she could support him. She knew that and everyone else knew it. And now all he did was use her money to spend on other women, every kind of woman. She wondered why she didn't leave him, why she didn't walk out and go back to living by herself.

The sound of a key in a lock brought her out of the bathroom.

She rushed to the door, pulled it open. At least he was home! Benjy Lewis was tall, broad-shouldered, very good-looking and nattily dressed. He was ebony-skinned, his teeth square and white. Tonight his eyes were sunken behind black puffy sacs, bloodshot and watery. His nose was flat, broad at the base; his lips were thick and loose.

He stared down at his wife's street dress, pushed her aside and closed the door after him. "Where you think you going, this hour o'night?"

"I just got a call from the paper, Benjy. I've got to go out on a story."

He walked over to a chair, dropped into it. "I need some money."

She stared at him. "More money? But Benjy—"

"I said I need more money." He pulled himself out of the chair, walked over and caught her by the shoulder. "Where you got it?"

She winced as the thick fingers dug into her shoulder. "I don't have any more money, Benjy. Honest, I don't."

He pushed her back roughly, picked her bag up from the table, rummaged through it. He came up with a few rumpled dollar bills. "Where's the rest?"

She shook her head. "That's all there is." She walked to the table, started putting back the contents of the bag. "What'd you do with the money I gave you tonight?"

He grinned at her. "I been spending it, Sugar."

She wrinkled her nose at the strong smell of gin on his breath, the smear of lipstick on his collar. "Who on?"

He didn't answer, made for the door. He looked back at her. "You better start getting more money, Sugar. A lot more. I can't hardly get by on what you bring home."

She started to protest; he waved her to silence.

"You can't afford me, they's lots of women can. Get that money."

He slammed the door behind him. She could hear him stamping down the stairs. She stared dry-eyed at the closed door for a moment, then followed him.

The door across the hall was open, a heavyset Negro woman stood in the doorway grinning at her. She knew. Everybody knew. The only way Fanny could keep him was to buy him. And they despised her almost as much as she despised herself.

On the bus, she saw the whole thing again, felt it as she always would feel it.

Elvira was a beautiful colored show-girl. Benjy had been Elvira's friend. Fanny met him for the first time one night years ago. She was overwhelmed by his good looks, his broad shoulders, by his animal magnetism. A man like this and Elvira, she thought, belong together. They look so *right* together. But by the end of the evening Fanny had learned that Benjy couldn't afford Elvira. And Benjy saw something he could use.

She married him because she had never had a man and needed one and knew she should have one. She had no regrets in her initiation to sex. Benjy was all that he seemed to be, and more. But he was what he was, and there were no illusions left by now. All that remained, and in themselves they were sufficient, were the occasional nights when Benjy remembered he was her husband. It came as no shock tonight to realize that the way things had been going lately she would have to bid still higher to keep him.

She got off the bus, headed up the long flight of stairs to the hospital entrance. A nurse in a freshly starched uniform sat behind a small reception desk in the lobby. Fanny Lewis moved across the highly polished floor.

"I'm Lewis of the Standard. Anything new on the cop they brought in tonight?"

The nurse looked up at her incuriously, pulled open a small card file. She checked through it, brought out a card. "Officer Hurley?"

"I guess that's him. How is he?"

"Condition serious. Hasn't regained consciousness. They have him in the operating room. You can wait on first-floor reception, if you like."

The reporter nodded curtly, started down the long corridor to the reception room. A uniformed Negro policeman, whom she didn't know, two district men from the newspapers whom she did know and a taut-faced woman were in the room.

"Anything new?" Fanny greeted one of the reporters.

He shook his head, didn't raise his eyes from the paper-back he was reading. Fanny fumbled through her bag, found a rumpled cigarette, stuck it in the corner of her mouth. She touched a match to it, exhaled twin streams through her nostrils. She walked over to where the Negro patrolman sat twisting his uniform cap between his fingers.

"I'm Fanny Lewis," she told him. "From the Standard."

She was a little taken aback by the hostile look in his eyes. "There's nothing new yet. He's been in there over an hour," he told her.

"What happened?"

The cop shrugged. "We're not sure. He didn't check in at the end of his tour at midnight. We found him in a condemned house near the corner of 110th. Mugged."

Fanny stuck the cigarette in the corner of her mouth where it waggled when she talked. "What was he doing in there?"

The hostile look was more marked in the man's eyes. "He hasn't regained consciousness, so we don't know. When we find out, we'll tell you."

"Funny place for him to be, wasn't it?"

The woman who had been sitting silently, walked over. "What is that supposed to mean?"

Fanny Lewis looked the woman over insolently. She was nearing middle age, her face was prematurely lined, her hands big knuckled. "Who are you?"

"This is Mrs. Hurley, the officer's wife," the Negro cop told her.

Fanny shrugged. "I was just thinking it would be a funny place for him to be going—alone."

The other woman's lips split in a pitying smile. "I know who you are now. That paper. I heard all about you and your kind." She turned her back on the reporter and returned to her chair.

The color drained out of Fanny's face, she started to follow the older woman. The Negro cop caught her by the arm. "She has enough to do without having to slap you down," he told her in a hard voice.

"Who does she think she is?" Fanny raged. "Did you hear the way she talked to me?"

The cop nodded.

"You'd think I was dirt under her feet. Who is she that she can—" The cop didn't raise his voice. "Leave her be. Suppose it were your husband?"

7.

The door to the room was closed, the shades drawn. The sickly sweet smell of mezz perfumed the air. Ruby lay sprawled out on the unmade bed, her heavily lidded eyes following Big Step as he paced the small room.

Sitting in the corner, his back braced against the wall, Sam spun the cylinder of the Police Special he had taken from Hurley. He polished the long barrel on the leg of his pants then sighted down it.

"Hot damn," he grunted. "Them Aces come near me I blow a hole through 'em big enough you stick your head in."

Stud sat on the bottom of the bed, his eyes hungrily watching the soft rise and fall of the girl's breasts.

"When that Long Joe goin' get back with that car?" Big Step growled. He walked to the window, pulled back the shade, peered out.

He dropped the shade at the sound of the knock on the door. He motioned for Sam to cover the door with the gun, walked over and pulled it open. Long Joe scurried in, closed the door after him.

"I seen Cozy like you said. He say no soap on the car."

"Why not?"

Long Joe shrugged. "He say it crazy to go gunning cause they have your name. They know who if anything happen. That ofay seen it."

"He seen me, man," Big Step snarled. "He seen me real good."

Long Joe bared his teeth in a grin. "Sure, he seen you. But maybe when he see you again he say it ain't you he seen. If like Cozy say, you throw a little scare into him."

Big Step stared at him for a moment, comprehension dawning in his eyes. "That's a real gone cat, that Cozy. Real gone." He walked over to the bed, pushed

Stud off and sat down. "We tell that ofay what happen to him and maybe his wife and kids. Then maybe he ain't got such a good memory, huh?"

Long Joe nodded.

"Give me that cop's book again." He took the dog-eared notebook, flipped through the pages, stopped at the last page. "Fred Morrow," he read, "453 East Seventh Street, Brooklyn." He looked up. "What time is it, man?"

Sam consulted his watch. "Almost two."

Big Step nodded. "We take a little walk, do some telephoning." He motioned for Sam to come along. When Stud rose to follow, Big Step shook his head. "You stay here. She flying and I don't want her to get in no trouble where she might do some talking."

Sam cast an envious glance at Stud, followed Big Step and Long Joe out. As soon as the door had closed behind them, Stud walked to the window, held his eye to the shade, waited until they had gone down the steps.

He walked over to where the girl lay. Her heavy lidded eyes had difficulty focusing. He ran his hand up the soft curve of her thigh. She stirred and murmured. His mouth found hers, soft and wet. She snuggled against him. "Be nice to Ruby, Step," she murmured. "Be nice to Ruby...."

The Elite Billiard Parlor stared at the dwindling traffic along Lexington Avenue through two large, dusty, plate-glass windows set in the second story of a five-story brick building. A yellow light spilled from the windows to the dark street below, a lettered sign advertised "Open All Night."

Big Step led the way up the stairs and into the big room beyond. Shaded lamps hanging from the ceiling spilled triangles of light over the green felt tables; the clicking of pool balls was constant and muted. A thin man in a sleeveless sweater was perched on a high stool behind the cash register and was watching a hot game on table one.

Big Step walked over to him. "Cozy busy?"

The man turned rheumy eyes on him, wiped the tip of his long, thin nose with the side of his index finger. He seemed to have difficulty recognizing Big Step.

"Yeah, he's busy."

Big Step scowled at him, motioned the other two to follow him as he swaggered to the telephone booth in the far corner of the room. While Long Joe laboriously looked up the telephone number of Fred Morrow on East Seventh Street in Brooklyn, Big Step kept his eyes glued on the entrance. The telephone booth was close enough to the escape hatch Cozy used for his shooting gallery upstairs, for him to make a fast break if he had to.

He dialed the number Long Joe took out of the phone book. He got a big charge out of the fear in the man's voice.

He called again at three o'clock. At four. And five.

He could tell by the sheer panic in the man's voice on the last call that he had him on the run.

He dug a cigarette from his shirt pocket, stuck it in the corner of his mouth. He shook Long Joe who had fallen asleep on one of the big armchairs, and was ready to lead the way out when they came in.

There were two of them. One was tall, young looking and mean. The other was an old guy in a wrinkled blue suit and a gray hat. Big Step had them figured the minute he saw them. They were cops.

He headed for the escape hatch, a doorway in the back of the room with Sam on his heels. Long Joe was still drowsing in the chair when they disappeared through it.

Across the room, Detective Marty Torno was showing the thin man in the sleeveless sweater the muzzle of a snub-nosed .38.

"You push any buttons, friend, and you get a nice hole through your belly for resisting arrest." He watched while the thin man's finger froze inches from the button. "Come out from behind there."

The thin man skittered around the counter, came out into the open. "What is this, a stickup?"

"You know better than that, friend. Just an official visit, but we'd like it to be a surprise." He leaned over the counter, tugged the pushbutton loose from its wires. "Where's the gallery?"

"You gold?"

Torno shook his head. "No, we're not Fed. Just local. This is no raid. Where's the gallery?"

The thin man pointed to the rear of the room. "Upstairs."

"Show us," Torno urged. He followed the thin man to a concealed door set in the far wall. Beyond it a flight of stairs ran to the next floor. He wrinkled his nose at the familiar unpleasant smell of mezz, followed the thin man up the stairs. At the head of the stairs, a small landing was bordered by a railing.

A heavy dark blue drape had been hung across the doorway, effectively muffling all sound from the room beyond. Torno leaned over the railing, signaled to his partner by touching the tip of his index finger to the ball of his thumb. Doyle nodded.

"Okay, you. Downstairs," Torno whispered to the thin man. "And don't try anything fancy. My partner's a real nervous guy. Real nervous."

The thin man licked at his lips, nodded. He headed for the stairs, went down them swiftly.

Torno slid behind the heavy curtain, fumbled for the knob to the door. It turned easily in his hand. He pulled it open a crack, applied his eye to it. A cloud of heavily scented smoke rolled out at him, almost smothering him. He heard the soft moan of a saxophone, the thin whine of a clarinet supplemented by other instruments he couldn't identify. The music was wild, frenzied. He traced its source to an automatic phonograph in the corner.

The room itself was bathed in a subdued light; a heavy dark rug covered the floor. There was no furniture in the room, but a dozen or more men and women were sprawled around the floor. Some white, some black.

A tall blonde danced wildly in the middle of the floor, her hair flying, her body undulating in time with the music. Nobody was paying her much attention, although she was easily recognizable as a top line dancing star from a current Broadway show.

A slow cloud of sluggish smoke hung over the whole room, stirring lazily in the draft created by Torno's half opened door. He pushed the door wider, slid in. Nobody paid any attention to him as he walked around the room to another door at the far side. He stood outside it for a moment, pushed it open. It was a completely equipped shooting gallery, with needles soaking in alcohol, pads of cotton, all the necessary equipment.

He was looking around when suddenly a man appeared from a room beyond. The newcomer's eyes widened when he saw the man with the gun. His mouth opened and he let out one screech, "Raid!" but the menace of Torno's gun kept him frozen where he stood.

In the room behind there was a moment of shocked silence, then chaos broke loose as men and women alike rushed for the escape hatch. One moment the place was filled with starry-eyed couples, the next it was empty except for the moaning music of the phonograph—and the two men, one with the gun in his hand, the other with his eyes fixed on its muzzle.

"Take it easy, Cozy," Torno commanded. "You may have a lot of stuff around that puts you out of this world, but what I've got here could make it permanent."

Cozy Jacks licked at his lips. "I ain't goin' give no trouble, officer. I been up against the gun before. They ways of fixing it so's nobody got to have trouble. Ain't that right?"

Torno grinned. "Could be."

Cozy relaxed. "For a bad minute, you sure had me scared. I—"

"Im no Fed, Cozy. I'm local. You want out on this rap, you play with me. I'm looking for a punk named Big Step."

The black man licked his lips. "What makes you think I know him?"

"You must want trouble real bad. 'Cause I'm just the guy who can give it to you."

"You ain't Fed, you got no cause to give me trouble, mister." Cozy was beginning to feel sure of himself. "You ain't even got any call to come bustin' in here."

Torno grinned at him bleakly. He walked over to where the man stood, caught him by the front of his shirt, pulled him off balance. "Where is he?"

"I don't know who you talking about."

Torno's hand lashed out, knocked Cozy's face to the left, then he backhanded it into place. "You're his source. Where is he?"

Cozy started to retort, changed his mind. "I don't know. Honest. He don't come by hisself. He got a chick. She's real hooked. She come by."

"Who is she?"

Cozy licked at his lips, his eyes jumped around the room. "Ruby. Tha's all I know. Jus' Ruby."

Torno showed his teeth in a grin that didn't reach his eyes. "I'm looking for a good excuse to rough you up, Cozy. Keep talking and I'll forget you can't tell me what I want to know without teeth."

Cozy tried to meet his stare, dropped his eyes first. "She Ruby Steele. She a real gone chick. That Big Step he have her all for hisself in a room on 110th. Sixth house, third floor front."

"Sixth house, eh? Did you know a cop got mugged in the fourth house on that block?"

Cozy shrugged. "A man hears a lot of things, officer."

"Who did it?"

Cozy shook his head violently. "I don't hear that particular thing. I just hear this cop like girls. Maybe he followed one inside."

"Ruby?"

Cozy's face gleamed wet with perspiration. "She wouldn't be hard to follow." He watched Torno's expression anxiously. "Maybe you like—"

Torno's fist didn't travel more than a few inches. It caught Cozy on the side of the chin, drove him back against the table with the hypos and the set-ups. He crashed into it, hit the floor. He lay there in the wreckage blinking up at the detective.

"As soon as I hit the street, I'm tipping the Feds off to this setup. You better hit the road and keep going. Between the Feds and Big Step, when he hears you fingered him, this ain't going to be a very healthy neighborhood for you."

8.

Fred Morrow sat on the side of his bed, chain-lit a fresh cigarette from the inch-long butt which he added to the pile in the ashtray beside him. His face was gray and wan in the morning light.

Ann stood at the window, with her eye placed to the edge of the shade. On the street below, a broad-shouldered man in a fedora leaned against the front fender of a black sedan. Every so often he glanced upward at the second story window, then his gaze wandered from one end of the deserted street to the other. After awhile, he crossed the sidewalk, mounted the stoop and dropped into the big wicker armchair.

"Fred! He's leaving. The cop is leaving," Ann called.

He crossed the room, put his eye to the window, sought for the reassuring bulk of the plainclothesman.

"He couldn't leave. His car's there. Maybe he just went on the porch to sit down. He wouldn't leave his car there." He dropped the shade. "You better get some sleep, Ann. You haven't closed your eyes all night."

"How can I close my eyes when I don't know when I'm liable to have my throat cut?" she wailed. "And the kids, what are we going to do about them?"

Fred raked his fingers through his hair, dropped wearily on the side of the bed. "They'll be all right. Everything will be all right. You'll see." Nervously, his eyes sought out the clock. It was over forty minutes since the phone had rung. He pulled his eyes away, couldn't shut out the slow ticking of the clock from his ears.

The phone jangled with such a suddenness that both the man and the woman jumped. She plucked at her lower lip with a trembling hand.

"Th-they're calling more often now. It—it's not an hour since—"

Morrow ran the back of his hand down his jowls, stared at the phone with stricken eyes. "I—I won't answer it. Let it ring."

"You can't, Fred. The kids. It will awaken the kids."

A faint twitch had developed below the man's left eye. He had difficulty controlling it. He looked from the phone to his wife and back. Then, he shrugged helplessly and lifted the receiver.

"Morrow?" It was a new voice.

"Can't you leave us alone? What are you trying to do to us?"

"This is Torno, Detective Division, East Harlem. I've got some good news for you. We've picked up Big Step."

Morrow was speechless for a second. "You're sure?"

"It's Big Step, all right. We picked him up a few minutes ago. The boys are talking to him in the squad room. He admits his identity."

"Did—did he admit the killing?"

Torno's laugh was low. "Not yet. They never do—at first."

"Will—will I have to identify him?"

"Maybe not. Depends on how sure he is of himself. I just thought I'd let you know so you could get a few hours' rest."

Morrow nodded. "Thanks. Thanks a lot." He reached over, dropped the receiver on the hook. "They've got him."

Ann buried her face in her hands. "Thank God. Oh, thank God." She swayed gently. "It's been like a nightmare. Any minute I expected to see one of them coming through the window—" She broke off, stared at her husband. "They got him, but what about his friends? What about the others?"

"They're probably hiding. They know the cops mean business now." Some assurance was beginning to seep back into Morrow, warming the marrow of his bones like a stiff drink. "They're nothing but rats. Now that they know they can't get away with murder, they'll run and hide."

The woman walked to the window, pulled back the shade a bit, stared down into the street. "They didn't take away the cop. He's still down there."

Some of the assurance drained away. "Maybe they couldn't reach him. Maybe they're just letting him finish his tour. He goes off duty in a couple of hours."

The rest of the assurance drained out, leaving him limp and worn when the phone rang at six.

"They got Big Step. You know that mister?" the receiver told him. "They got Big Step and they expect you to finger him for them."

"Who is this?" he demanded weakly.

"Nem'mind that. I just figured you might like to know you ain't fingering nobody for nobody. You seen what happened to that spic yesterday. How you like somethin' like that, Mister Big Mouth? How you like that, eh?"

Cold perspiration broke out on Morrow's forehead and upper lip. "You wouldn't try anything like that," he blustered. "I signed a statement and you know it. Anything happens to me, and they'll have your friend for sure."

"Nothin' goin' to happen to you, mister. Nothin' at all. But how about your wife, mister? You got kids? Nothin' goin' to happen to you for sure. It's goin' to happen to them."

The phone clicked. Morrow sat holding a dead receiver to his ear.

"It was them?" It was more a flat statement than a question.

He looked up into his wife's face, nodded. "His friends. If I talk, they'll hit back through you and the kids." Morrow shook his head. "Things like that can't happen to us. Not in this country. These punks aren't God Almighty. They can't make their own laws and laugh at the whole world. They can't!"

"We could move," the woman said in a low voice. "We could just pick up and get out of here. Not let anybody know where we were."

The man looked around. "But this is our home, Ann. We've lived here over twenty years. Both the kids were born here."

"I don't want them to die here." There was a touch of incipient hysteria in her voice.

"But where can we go, Ann? Where can we go? I can't quit my job and leave everything we've worked for."

"What good is it, if we're afraid to turn around? If we never know when they're going to—"

Morrow shook his head. "We can't do it, Ann, they won't let us." He walked to the window, pulled the shade back, stared down at the black car at the curb. "We thought they put a man down there to keep anyone from getting in. Maybe they're keeping him there to keep anyone from getting out."

9.

Fred Morrow's children couldn't have been happier. Young Freddy felt like a conquering hero when the patrol car delivered him right to the school. He got out under the eyes of envious classmates, waved to the cop as the car pulled away. The joy was slightly tempered by the fact that Mr. Edwards, the gym teacher, came out and took him right into the principal's office. He had to sit there until it was time for class and he couldn't mix with the rest of the gang out on the playground. But he had had that moment of triumph, and there would be another this afternoon when his police escort returned to pick him up.

His sister Gloria was also the object of envy by her classmates at Abraham Lincoln High. The cop assigned to escort her was young, couldn't have been over twenty-one by Gloria's fourteen year-old figuring, and he was handsome. Besides, he just stood around and talked to her until it was time for her to go into classes. She didn't bother to explain what he was there for, hoped that some of her classmates might think it was a boy friend walking her to and from school.

Big Step sat huddled in a wooden chair on the far side of the desk. He glanced across at Torno, lifted the corner of his mouth in a snarl, looked away.

"A real tough cat," Torno grunted. "You ever hear one of those real tough ones crack, Al?"

Doyle nodded. "When they crack, they really crack. They sing like a stagestruck canary."

Big Step rolled his eyes up insolently. "Not me, cop. I got nothin' to sing about. You ain't got a thing on me. Not a thing."

"Let's find out." Torno turned to Doyle. "Take him down to Interrogation. I'll be right down, Al." He waited until his partner caught the manacled Big Step under the arm, led him through the door. Then he dialed a number. It rang several times before he got an answer.

"Larsen. Treasury."

"Swede, Marty Torno down at the Bureau. I got a hot one for you. A fully set-up shooting gallery."

The voice on the other end grunted. "Good. Got an address?"

Torno gave him the address on Lexington Avenue. "Name's Jacks, Cozy Jacks. Entrance is a door on the back wall of the Elite Billiard Parlor. We busted the place up a little getting some information, but we left enough for your boys."

"Thanks, Torno. We'll handle from here."

Torno dropped the receiver on its hook, turned off the lamp on his desk, headed for Interrogation.

Big Step lolled in a wooden chair in the center of the room, grinned at Al Doyle and two other plainclothesmen who ringed him in a semicircle.

"Go ahead, try beating it out of me," he jeered. "I'm under age. You know what that means? You can't lay a hand on me."

Torno nodded to the plainclothesmen. "I'll take him."

"He's a snotty little bastard, Marty. Just let me—" one of the plainclothesmen pleaded.

Torno shook his head, grinned down at Big Step. "He only thinks he's a big man. Wait'll the stuff wears off and his stomach gets weak."

Smirking amusement drained from the boy's eyes, leaving his parted lips a caricature of a smile. "You better not slap me around, mister. I yell so loud even the mayor hear me. Yeah, and the newspapers, too."

Torno walked behind the chair, caught a handful of Big Step's hair, pulled his head back until the overhead light beat straight into his face. "Start yelling, you cop-mugging bastard."

"I know my rights. Just because I a black boy—"

Torno bared his teeth in a mirthless grin. "Pulling that won't do you any good. All you punks get the same dose—white, black, yellow or red."

Big Step licked at his lips. "You just talk big, Mister Man. You think you scare me with that kinda talk, don't you?"

"I hope you keep on being tough," Torno told him softly. He tugged down on the hair, brought water to Big Step's eyes. "You read the wrong comic books. There's plenty of ways of breaking a punk like you. And without leaving marks."

Big Step stared up at the detective, the first signs of fear beginning to show in his eyes.

"How about Hurley?" Torno asked.

Big Step's face was gleaming wetly under the light. "I don't know nothin' about no Hurley."

"How'd you get him into the hallway?"

Big Step licked at his lips. "I don't know what you're talkin' about, mister."

Torno released his grip on the hair, shoved Big Step's head forward. "You made a mistake on that one. If Hurley goes out, you don't stand a chance. Maybe for cutting the Spic, some soft-headed judge will settle for a murder two. But nobody's going to stand still for anything but the chair, if the cop dies."

"I don't know nothin'."

Torno brought a cigarette from his pocket, stuck it in the corner of his mouth, touched a match to it. "That's not what Cozy says."

Big Step folded his hands in his lap, stared down at them.

"Cozy says you used a girl to get Hurley into the hallway." Big Step continued to stare at his hands.

Torno grabbed the hair, pulled the boy's head back, stuck his face inches away. "You wanted his book, didn't you? It had the address of the guy who was due to finger you for the cutting. That's why you tried to kill Hurley."

"I don't know nothin' about it," Big Step maintained.

Two hours later, Torno swabbed at his streaming forehead, swore at the wilted figure in the chair.

"He's a tough one to break," Doyle muttered. "But why get in a fever about it? Robby's on his way down here now with the witness."

"Morrow?"

Doyle nodded. "They're picking him up. Robby wants to sew it up good. He don't want anything to go wrong. So why should we sweat? He's going to grab all the credit anyhow."

Torno rolled down his sleeves, nodded to Doyle. "You're right. Let Robby do the work. Cuff him to the chair. I'll send a couple of boys in to make sure he don't cool off."

Outside in the bull pen Torno stopped at the first desk, where Connie Ryan was laboriously typing a report with one finger.

"Anything from the hospital on Hurley?"

Ryan shook his head. "They think it's a fracture. Bastards stomped him, looks like."

Torno growled in his throat. "We got the guy in the sweat box. I've been working him over. Want to keep him company awhile? Guy from the D.A.'s office is on his way over. Should be here pretty quick and I don't want the pigeon to cool off."

Ryan nodded. "Okay, Marty. This Morrow—he's a God-damned fool. Whatever happens to him he deserves. A white man shouldn't tangle with Harlem."

"Sometimes a guy talks too fast for his own good," Marty admitted. He sat down, laced his fingers behind his head. "Those neighborhood people didn't speak up because what the hell, one more spic dead—so what? But it's not whites and blacks,

Connie. Let's say a Long Island Negro had seen it and his name went down in Hurley's book. Would Big Step be after him or not?"

Ryan shrugged and headed for Interrogation. Torno rubbed at his eyes with the heels of his hands, swore under his breath. He had hoped to have Big Step broken and ready to sing by the time Robby arrived. A quick arrest and statement in a case like this could mean a lot, but now—hell, let Robby skim off all the credit.

He got up, walked over to where a water cooler was humming to itself near the window. Outside, the first signs of day had lightened the sky, painted the empty street gray.

A few minutes later, Sol Robbins skidded his car to a stop at the curb, pushed open the door. "Okay, Mr. Morrow. They'll have him ready for us."

Fred Morrow blinked red-rimmed eyes, shook his head uncertainly. "I don't know if I'm doing the right thing, Mr. Robbins. My family—"

Robbins took his arm. "Don't worry about your family. We're going to put this fellow where he can't harm anybody. Ever."

Morrow permitted himself to be guided from the car and across the sidewalk. The little Assistant D.A. kept up a happy chatter all the way up the stairs to the detective bull pen.

He pushed the door open, stuck his head in. "Torno around?"

Torno waved him in from his desk.

Robbins nodded for his witness to follow him into the big room. He walked down to where Torno sat, shook hands ceremoniously. "This is Mr. Morrow, Marty." He turned to Morrow. "Marty's the cop we've got to thank for such fast action."

Morrow shook hands. "H-how about his friends? Did you get them, too?"

Torno shook his head. "Not yet. We will."

"Morrow got a call at six from one of them. They're still trying to throw a scare into him." Robbins clapped Morrow on the shoulder. "But it'd take more than a couple of young punks to scare him off. Right, Fred?"

"I don't know. My family—"

"These punks do a lot of talking. Isn't that right, Marty?" Robbins appealed to the detective. "Ever know of a case where they made good their threats? I never did. I get 'em all the time."

"I wouldn't worry too much about 'em, Mr. Morrow," Torno said. "As soon as we nail this character for the cutting, he'll break. And that mob of his will forget him and you at the same time."

"I sure hope so."

The Assistant D.A. asked, "Where've you got him, Marty?"

"Interrogation. Connie Ryan's keeping him company."

"Might as well get it over with," Robbins said. "Okay with you, Mr. Morrow?"

"I guess so."

Robbins slapped him on the shoulder. "There's nothing to worry about. You just take a good look at him and tell us if he's the punk you saw knife the other kid."

Morrow nodded. "Then what happens?"

Robbins grinned. "Then it's my baby. We'll rush through an arraignment and an indictment. You'll be present, of course, to make the identification formally. After that, it's my job to put him in the Death House." He nodded to Torno. "Let's get it over with, Marty."

Big Step was still cuffed to the chair in the middle of the room. The bright light burned down mercilessly, rivulets of perspiration ran down the side of his face, dripped from the tip of his nose.

"You'll be able to see him," Torno explained, "but with that light in his face he can't see anything. I'll hold his face up for you, so just take your time. Okay?"

Morrow nodded.

They walked into the room, Torno nodded to Ryan. "He do any talking, Connie?"

The plainclothesman shook his head. "He's pretty stubborn."

"It doesn't matter. This is the man who saw him cut the Spic. A positive identification from him is all we're going to need." Torno walked behind Big Step's chair, caught him by the hair, pulled his face up. "Take a good look, mister. Is this the punk you saw cut Julio Rigas?"

With a sinking feeling, Fred Morrow stared at the young face. He could see it again as its owner wielded the knife that turned the other boy into a bleeding rag doll sprawled on a sidewalk. In his ears he could hear the threats, the obscenities its owner had mouthed over the phone. He could smell the perspiration, sense the fear that permeated the room. In his mouth was the bitter taste of his own fear, his own cowardice.

"How about it?" Robbins had difficulty keeping the anxiety from his voice.

Fred Morrow took a deep breath. "It's him. That's the one I saw stab the other boy to death."

10.

Fanny Lewis walked into the City Room of the Standard. She made her way through the organized confusion of the desks. Men and women were sitting in front of typewriters of varying ages and vintages, punching out stories on the keys for the next edition.

She made her way up to the slot where two men were chopping copy, two others leaned back and stared with bored eyes around the room. A thin man with tired, baggy eyes, a green shade pulled low over his forehead sat at a desk apart, checking the opposition papers for follows, throwing the mutilated copy into a barrel-sized waste basket at his elbow.

He looked up with no show of enthusiasm as Fanny Lewis stopped at his desk. Bristles glinted whitely on his chin, the side of his mouth was discolored from the tobacco he chewed. He didn't like Fanny Lewis and she knew he didn't like her, any more than he liked working for the Standard with its taboos and bias.

Ken Flint had once been a top flight newsman. His by-line had been featured on the front pages of top dailies all over the country. When he was riding high, managing editors and publishers were willing to put up with his losing bouts with the bottle. But as time slowed his reflexes and alcohol dulled his perception, they became less and less understanding. Jobs became fewer and harder to find. Soon no paper in the city would touch him.

Except the Standard. Only the Standard would touch a newsman of Flint's reputation, because not a newspaperman of Flint's innate ability would touch the Standard. But Ken Flint had found out that by-lines on clippings in manila envelopes in the basement morgues of even the best papers in the world are pretty thin fare. He swallowed his pride and permitted his new bosses to put him behind a desk where what was left of his genius could be used to sugarcoat their preachings into a semblance of news.

He stared at the plain, angular woman in front of him. He had to work with such as these, but he didn't have to like them. Or even pretend to.

"What's on your mind, Lewis?" he wanted to know.

"That cop. The one they found in that abandoned house uptown. He still hasn't recovered consciousness." She pulled some folded notes out of her bag. "Looks like he tried to take some girl in there and either her parents or her boy friend beat him up."

Flint curled his lip. "That's the way it looks, eh? The girl wouldn't have been a black one, by any chance?"

She looked up from her notes, tried to stare him down, dropped her eyes first. She hated herself, for not being able to stand up to this alcoholic wreck, but she couldn't face up to the disgust in his eyes. She went back to her notes.

"I also got a tip that they picked up a boy on suspicion in the Rigas stabbing during the night. I couldn't find out where they took him, but they've probably given him a bad time."

"You ought to see the other guy. He's in the morgue."

"You don't know this boy did it. Neither do the cops. They just needed a fall guy so they went out and grabbed the first kid they could lay their hands on. Just because he was a Negro, they—"

Flint reached over, pulled a page of typewritten copy from a spindle. "His name's Stepin Field. They call him Big Step, he's got a record as long as your arm." He flipped the paper at her. "D.A.'s office has a guy who saw the cutting—"

"I've already talked to that witness. I wouldn't take his word that today's Tuesday. He's obviously a Negro baiter and he wouldn't hesitate to swear away—"

"Save it for your story," Flint told her wearily. "I may have to turn those orations of yours into English for this rag's illiterates, but I don't have to listen to it."

Lewis' face was white with rage. "If the boss ever heard you talk about our readers like that—"

"He's heard me. He doesn't like me any better than you do. But he can't get anybody with a stomach as strong to work as cheap. And he feels the same way about our dear readers, so stop the crap and turn some out."

He watched her stalk back to an unpainted desk near the wall. She slammed her bag on the desk top, yanked some copy paper from her basket. In a minute her typewriter was rattling the whole desk under the fury of her punching.

Slowly, the tempo of the city room changed. Copy boys who had been ambling between the desks, stopping to exchange jokes and gossip with the men and women sitting there drinking coffee from cardboard containers, were now scurrying with copy in one hand and galleys in the other. Cigarettes lay smoldering on the edges of the desks, burning down to add new service stripes on what was left of the varnish. The coffee became cold in the soggy containers.

The Standard was getting ready to go to bed with its daily impassioned defense of the downtrodden everywhere.

Later, the bus dropped Fanny Lewis a block from her home. She dragged weary feet down the street to her house, an old converted brownstone that nestled anonymously in a row of identical brownstones on the fringe area in the lower 100's. She wished they could move away from this neighborhood where whites intermingled with blacks harmoniously, but where she was uncomfortable in either camp. She dismissed the thought with the knowledge that it would be the same anyplace. She never told anyone what she was unless they asked her point blank; and then she took a fierce pride in saying she was a Negro.

Wearily she climbed the stairs. The door to her flat was unlocked. She pushed it open and walked in. Benjy's coat had been tossed carelessly onto a chair, dragged onto the floor. She picked it up, brushed it off. This suit had cost her $125 and deserved better treatment. She hung it carefully on the back of the chair, walked to the bedroom door.

At the open door, she froze. Benjy lay unclothed in the bed. Next to him was the naked body of a tall, full-blown blonde who looked like a chorus girl or a model.

Fury turned Fanny's entrails to water. She ran across the room, grabbed Benjy by the shoulder, turned him over. He woke to lay staring at her stupidly for a moment, then anger twisted his face. "What you think you're doin', pushin' me around like that?" He reached up, put the flat of his hand against her, sent her reeling backwards.

The girl at his side moaned softly, squirmed sensuously. She opened her eyes, stared at Fanny who stood glaring at her.

"Get her out of here, Benjy!" Fanny spat through clenched teeth. "Get her out or I'll throw her out!"

The girl in the bed grinned. "That dried up woman going to throw me out, honey?" Her voice slurred from drink or dope, Fanny didn't know which.

Fanny went for her, her nails poised.

As Benjy watched, grinning, the girl in the bed laughed, rolled out of the way, sank her fingers into Fanny's wispy hair and pulled her down. They rolled off the bed onto the floor, biting, clawing. The blonde's youth made the difference. Her hand went up and down like a piston, each time connecting with the older woman's face with loud, sharp slaps.

Finally, the blonde stood up, magnificent, long-legged, high breasts heaving. Fanny lay on the floor moaning softly, her face buried in her hands.

Perspiration gleamed on the long flanks, the flat stomach, the lithe hips of the young girl. "Tell her, Benjy. Tell her how it's going to be," she panted.

Benjy, who had been enjoying the fight, reached for a cigarette. "This is Flora. She goin' to move in with us, Fanny."

The hands fell away from Fanny's face. She sat up, stared at Benjy with stricken eyes. "What do you mean she's going to move in with us?"

Benjy lit the cigarette, blew smoke at her. "You heard what I said. Flora, she's goin' move in with us." He reached over, pulled the gleaming body of the younger woman to him. "She got no place to stay so I thought she stay with us. Till she find a job anyhow."

Fanny pulled herself painfully to her feet. "If you think I'd ever let you get away with that—"

Benjy laughed at her. "I ain't gettin' away with anything. Just that Flora goin' stay with us." He made no attempt to hide the contempt in his eyes. "You don't like that, you jus' go ahead and move out. Flora stays."

Fanny's eyes hopscotched from her husband's grin to the smile on the face of the girl. "I wouldn't stay here for all the money in the world."

"You be back," Benjy told her. "You be back real soon."

She stared at him, then dropped her eyes. "Where could I sleep out there, Benjy? Where could I sleep?"

11.

Ruby sprawled on the unmade bed, watched the men from under half closed eyes. The lift from the last mezz was fading and she felt down.

Sam sat in his customary place on the floor, the wall supporting his back, polishing the Police Special with an old rag.

There was a soft knock on the door. Long Joe pulled the snub-nose .38, held it under the table. "Who that?"

"Stud."

Long Joe motioned for Sam to open the door. Stud came in, set the bag full of coffee containers and buns on the table.

"You hear the radio?" he wanted to know.

"How we hear any radio?" Sam growled. "You know we ain't got no radio."

"That ofay, he goin' to put the finger on Big Step today, 'bout two 'clock. In front of a judge."

Ruby sat up on the bed, swung her legs over. "I thought you cats scare that man so he don't finger Big Step. I thought you give him a real big scare."

Long Joe shook his head, swore. "That man put the finger on him, that the end for Big Step. Maybe for us, too. They get Big Step, they come looking for us. They know he didn' do it alone."

Sam scratched at the side of his head with the muzzle of the Police Special. "Where this all goin' happen, Stud?"

"Courthouse. Why?"

Sam shrugged. "We gotta get Big Step out'n there."

Stud curled his lip contemptuously. "How you goin' get Big Step out? You goin' walk in that courthouse with your popgun and take him away from 'em cops? You musta been sniffin' Cozy's powder when no one's looking."

"Cozy ain't there no more. Feds knock him off." Sam paused for a moment, thinking. "We gotta get Big Step out. An we don' need no gun to do it. That ofay got to finger him before they can hold him. Ain' 'at right?"

Stud started to deride, was waved to silence by Long Joe. "That's right, Sam. The ofay fingers him, Big Step's in trouble. He don' finger him, he ain't. But how we goin' fix it so's he don' finger him?"

Sam grinned. "We fix it."

Sol Robbins was walking on air. His boss, the Hon. Francis X. Corrigan, had personally spoken some kind words for the speed with which his office had arranged for the arraignment of the suspect in the widely publicized "Teen Age Murder Incorporated" killing. Corrigan, himself, had arranged for Judge Aaron Shapiro, a widely publicized foe of juvenile crime, to preside and plans were already under foot for widespread coverage by the press.

Sol Robbins already had visions of moving up into the number one assistant slot, with an office right next to Corrigan. All this on the wave of public applause, for a job well done.

He assigned Cliff Meyers, a former Police Department lieutenant, now attached to the district attorney's office, to the task of delivering Fred Morrow safely to the arraignment.

"Morrow's pretty skittish and scared stiff," Robbins told Cliff confidentially. "And he'd back out if he could. All we've got to do is get him to stand up in front of Shapiro and finger this punk and we're in. Your job is to make sure he gets there. I'll do the rest."

Meyers had a shock of silvery white wavy hair, startlingly blue eyes, a glowing pink complexion. His constant smile, which exposed a complete set of porcelain jackets over his front central teeth, disguised the fact that in his heyday Cliff Meyers was one of the ablest strong-arm men attached to the Central Office Squad. The bulk of his shoulders indicated that he could still be a dangerous man in a knock-down, drag-out fight.

"He'll get there if my boys have to carry him piggyback. What time do you want him delivered?"

Robbins took a moment to think that over. "No later than two-fifteen. Don't get him there too early. Try shooting for around two, on the head."

Meyers nodded. "He'll be there." Robbins slapped him on the shoulder. "I'm counting on you, Cliff. Frankly, our whole case hinges on his identification. If he backs out we haven't a thing to hold the punk on."

"He identified him this morning, you said."

The Assistant D.A. nodded. "Unofficially. I wanted to make sure there was no screw-up. I let him have a look at the punk in Interrogation. It's the right one, all right."

"So stop worrying. You don't think a handful of punk kids are going to stick their necks out trying to pull anything, do you?"

Robbins shook his head uncertainly. "I don't know. That's why I'm counting on you, Cliff. Those hopped-up kids, you can't figure from one minute to the next what they'll do. I think they're bluffing, but I'm taking no chances. Until I get my conviction, we carry this guy Morrow around on a silk pillow."

"And after that?"

Robbins shrugged. "What are we, his keepers? After that he's on his own. Strictly."

12.

Fred Morrow was apologetic when Cliff Meyers walked in.

"I've tried to talk her out of it, Mr. Meyers, but my wife insists on going along."

Cliff Meyers showed his porcelain jackets in a disarming grin. "Why not? How often does a citizen get an opportunity to get a ride in the District Attorney's own Cadillac? And get a front row seat when Judge Shapiro makes a speech?" He turned to Ann Morrow. "You get your hat, Mrs. Morrow. We'll wait for you."

"You're sure it's all right?" Fred Morrow sounded worried. "Mr. Robbins didn't say anything about Ann coming along."

"Take my word for it," Cliff winked. "It's okay."

In spite of herself, Ann felt a little twinge of pride as she walked down the porch steps to the big shiny Cadillac at the curb. She was aware of the tilted shades, the moving curtains on some of the houses, the franker curiosity of those who stood on their porches and watched her leave.

She had to admit that she enjoyed sinking back against the luxurious cushions, as the big car whisked her out Flatbush Avenue to the bridge. Traffic opened up for them as the driver touched his siren. She was comfortably aware of the two heavy set men in the front seat, of the quiet assurance and unquestioned capability of Cliff Meyers. She was beginning to wonder if maybe she hadn't been a little silly to try to talk Fred out of doing his duty.

Fred sat in the other corner of the back seat, watching traffic and houses fly by. He was wondering what they were saying back at the office. True, Lionel Simons, the big boss, had gotten on the phone and commended him for his public spirit in going through with this thing. He had even advised him to take a few days off. But he had sounded a little critical, when he asked Fred where the reporter for the Standard got the idea that he worked for an organization that was mulcting Negroes with substandard housing. He asked him to keep the firm's name out of the papers. Maybe that was the reason he told him not to hurry back to the office. Maybe he figured public curiosity would have died down by then. Silently, he cursed the reporter from the Standard and her bold-faced putting of words into his mouth. He resolved that if she had any questions today, he'd ignore her.

At the courthouse, the Cadillac pulled into a special garage. Cliff Meyers escorted them to a private elevator that took them directly to the second floor where the arraignment was scheduled.

Cut rate attorneys, anxious relatives, friends of those being arraigned milled around or held up the old, paint-peeled walls of the corridor. Cliff Meyers' experienced eyes ran over the crowd and he was relieved to note that, though he was ready for trouble, no one appeared to constitute a threat to his charge.

There were a half dozen Negroes interspersed in the crowd. Three he recognized as lawyers, one of them regarded as a criminal lawyer who thus far had failed to get the break he deserved; a fourth worked for a bondsman. The other two looked and acted like a young married couple.

As soon as the reporters spotted Meyers and his charge, they descended on him en masse.

"This the key witness, Cliff?" one of the picture snatchers asked.

"Take it easy, boys. Mr. Morrow can't talk now. Robby'll give you a chance to get all the pictures you want after he comes out." He cut a fast path through the small group, parried questions as he ushered the Morrows into Courtroom B, ignored the groans of the press.

Inside the courtroom itself, there was a sprinkling of spectators in the rows of hard wooden seats directly behind the railed off portion. To the left of the inside portion, a few reporters sat fingering through the early editions of the afternoon papers. Fanny Lewis was among them and vaguely Fred Morrow wondered about her newspaper and how it manipulated facts and justice.

Sol Robbins was sitting at a long table near the front of the room. Judge Shapiro hadn't as yet made an appearance and the prisoner had not been brought up.

"We're a little early," Cliff Meyers grinned. "I guess the Judge had a long lunch. Suppose we go up front and sit with Robby."

Fred Morrow nodded. His wife said to him, "I wonder—" Ann looked a little embarrassed. "I wonder if I could go to the little girls' room."

"Sure. But I'd better go along with you," Cliff Meyers offered. Ann looked perplexed.

"Not all the way," Cliff grinned. "I'll just walk down the hall with you, show you where it is."

It was almost a full minute before Fanny Lewis, the humiliation of the Flora incident bothering her, realized where they might be going and decided to follow. An interview with Mrs. Morrow, alone, with exactly the right questions posed, might be better than the account of what she had come here to report. She slid off the bench.

Cliff escorted Ann Morrow close to the door marked "Ladies" and stood there waiting. In a moment the corridor reporters and photographers were on him. Engaged in fending off their questions, turning good-naturedly to say "Nix" to a photographer who wanted to catch Cliff and the key witness' wife and the door with the "Ladies" on it in one overall shot, he did not see what had happened in the busy hallway.

Ruby had ambled over, turned the knob and walked in. The woman was standing in front of the mirror fixing her hat when the girl's face appeared in the mirror. Ann Morrow turned around.

When she saw the expression on Ruby's face, she started to scream. It came out a smothered moan as she tumbled backwards, fell against the basket for paper towels. Ruby moved in on her with a loaded handbag. She brought it down again and again on the head and face of the woman.

Ann could feel her senses reeling. She knew that only the arrival of someone could save her. She prayed that someone would come. The warm wet feeling on the side of her face she knew to be blood. She tried to protect her head from the heavy blows of the bag, only half succeeded.

Ann was dimly aware that her prayer had been answered. She saw the hem of another dress, shoes, silk stockings in heavy shapeless legs. The scream that had been lodged in her throat broke out. She screamed again, and again . . .

Outside, Cliff Meyers cursed and sprinted for the door. He pulled it open, saw Ann's face—a mass of blood. Blood was pouring from her nose and lips and from cuts over her eyes and above the hairline.

He caught Ruby around the waist, slammed her back against the wall. She stood there, panting, glaring at him.

To Fanny Lewis, in the fore part of the crowd jamming the restroom door, he said, "What?" The question was loaded with hot anger, with threat. Fanny's eyes hop scotched from Meyers to the girl to the woman on the floor.

"She say dirty things to me. She want me to do things," Ruby snarled. "Go ahead, arrest me. I tell them everything. I tell the court what she want me to do. She a dike! A lady lover!"

Cliff Meyers stared at her openmouthed. Then he said to the reporter, "All right, Lewis. You saw it. Walked in on it. What happened? Help a dirty little slut like this to ruin the name of a woman and her kids? Go ahead. It'll sell more copies of that filthy rag of yours."

Shocked at what she had walked in on, what she actually had been responsible for stopping, knowing the truth as this man knew it, Fanny Lewis gave no answer.

Meyers turned to Ruby. "You won't get away with this," he snarled. "I'll see that you don't."

The A.P. reporter kneeling on the floor, wiping some of the blood from Ann's face with a wet towel asked Ann, as he helped her to her feet, "What happened?"

Meyers pulled him away. "She can't talk now, boys. I've got to get this woman to a hospital."

"What about the girl?" the A.P. reporter wanted to know.

Ruby grinned at him insolently. "Lady lover. That what she is. Go ahead, Mr. Policeman. Arrest me. You do just that," she jeered. She spat at Ann. "I tell the whole world what she is. A dirty dike."

Ann caught Meyers by the sleeve. "Let her go. Don't make any more trouble. Let her go, let her go."

"Well?" Meyers' eyes fastened on Fanny's face. She felt the old familiar churning in her stomach at the look of revulsion in the man's eyes.

"You see?" Ruby said to the crowd. "Anybody get arrested, it better be her. Saying dirty things to me." She pushed her way through the small crowd clogging the doorway. No one tried to stop her.

Inside Courtroom B, the arraignment was already under way. Sol Robbins got to his feet, brushed an imaginary piece of lint from his lapel as he marshaled his thoughts, approached the bench. Suavely, he outlined the charges on which the defendant was being held.

Judge Shapiro scowled ominously at the sound of the disturbance in the hall, fixed Fanny Lewis with a baleful glare as she found her way back to her seat in the press section. He motioned for a bailiff to go out into the hall and quiet the perpetrators of the disturbance. Then he nodded for Robbins to proceed.

"Your Honor, because of the frightening disregard for law and order exhibited by this defendant and because of the threats made against the person of an eye witness to this slaying, I move that permission be granted to have the suspect identified by the witness here and now."

"It's a little unusual," Judge Shapiro said, "but if that's the way you intend to nail down your indictment, it's all right with the court." He looked up as the bailiff returned. "What was all that noise?"

The bailiff walked up to the bench. "Some woman was attacked in the ladies' room, your Honor. She got beaten up real bad. Cliff Meyers from the D.A.'s office is taking her over to the hospital."

Judge Shapiro frowned, failed to see that the key witness had risen in his seat, and reluctantly permitted Sol Robbins to pull him back down.

"Bring the suspect up to the bench, you men," the Judge ordered two uniformed patrolmen who stood on either side of the prisoner.

The night in jail had made Big Step look shrunken. His hair was mussed. His eyes were red-rimmed and bloodshot.

"Will you stand, Mr. Morrow?" Robbins said. "Will you take a good look at this man? Is he the man you saw stab Julio Rigas to death?"

Fred Morrow stared at the prisoner in front of him. He felt hate rising in his throat like gall. He could see his wife lying on the rest room floor, her face smashed. He could see the body of Julio Rigas twitch as Big Step sadistically plunged the knife into it three times. He thought of his son and daughter, no longer free to play and walk around like other kids. He thought of the phone calls, the nightmare of night, the abuse and obscenity.

He said, "I never saw him before in my life."

Puddin' and Pie
De Forbes (DeLoris Staton Forbes)

August 1956

I stood outside and watched them as they pranced before the small barred window, little children singing a twisted version of an innocent nursery rhyme. I had sent them away several times before, but they seemed to be fascinated even by the very dirt on which the jail stood. There they played their games of mumblety-peg, little girls brought their corncob dolls—and they sang:

> "Georgie Porgie, Puddin' and Pie
> Sliced up Mae and made her die.
> Tomorrow's the day he has to pay—
> Poor Georgie Porgie can't run away."

Once again I sent them off. As the childish prattle echoed up and down the heat-laden twilight streets, a pair of soft, pudgy hands clutched the lowest visible part of the barred window. The hands themselves were obscene—fat and soiled, yet white, like the under-body of an eel. To me they represented untold agony, expressing the torment within the creature who owned them. Torment that could never hope to be realized, much less expressed.

Murder had been committed, the trial held, and the verdict delivered. There was nothing the jury could do but find him guilty. But it was obvious to all that he wasn't responsible, that he had no idea of the enormity of what he had done. When I protested this they told me that their laws provided no alternative. "You folks back East," the sheriff said, "you got places to put ones like George here. Out here there's nothin'—just the end of a rope." I have vowed that I shall try and change this situation. But, as in the way of all reform, it will be too late for Georgie and his mother. Now it was time for me, as a servant of God, to try and bring some sort of peace to that poor body with the empty mind. It was the most difficult task I had ever faced in my long years of service. I knew in my heart that I would fail, but I had to go in—to try again.

The thing that was called George Finley hunched in the darkest corner of the sweltering cell. It resembled, at first, a massive pink spider clad in overalls. As I approached there was movement and a head emerged from the shapeless mass. The eyes were blank and the mouth moved, drooling slightly. The hair was sparse and the pink scalp made me think of hurt, new-healing flesh. The wet mouth stretched and I knew he was smiling. Georgie was glad to see me—a fact which made it all the harder. I did not know how to help him die tomorrow.

"Howdy, Mr. Ryson. Did you come to play with me? I know a new game." The voice was a man's, as was the grotesque body—but the thoughts were perpetually childlike. Each day I came he urged me to play some game or another that bloomed in the arid soil of his idiot brain.

"No games today, Georgie." I sat on the stool by the bed. "How do you feel?"

"All right, I guess. I don't like it much here, though. Ma will be comin' soon to take me home, won't she?" The bass voice quivered in childish concern.

"Very soon, Georgie, very soon," I soothed him. Then, hoping to divert his simple thoughts, I asked, "What have you been doing all day, Georgie?"

"Just sittin' here listenin'. I could hear them out there singin'. It's such a pretty song. Why can't I go out and play with them?"

It was a pretty song! Father in heaven! I wondered as I sat there and watched him how he had managed to live so long. Only because his mother was always with him from the very beginning. Except for that one day. She was his friend, his playmate and his protector. And one day she left him alone for just a little while. She went to a seamstress for a new dress. Now Mrs. Finley would wear that dress— at her son's hanging.

The first name I heard, I think, when I came to Dawsonville was that of Mrs. Finley, the doctor's wife. "She's a saint," they told me. I felt that they were right. Georgie was her cross—and the load was heavy. But if she was a saint and Georgie was the fruit of their union, did that make Doc the devil?

I sat in the abysmal cell and tried to find words to tell Georgie that God loved him regardless of what he'd done. As I fumbled with the seemingly unsolvable problem I heard the corridor door open and she appeared, her black-gloved hands welded in unspoken supplication.

"Georgie," she said and he wiggled like the whelp of some unspeakable animal. "Georgie, are you all right? How do you do, Reverend?"

"Ma," he cried. She went swiftly to him, her fingers smoothing the wrinkled clothing. She searched the faded blue eyes anxiously.

"Ma, I want to go home. I don't want to stay here any more. I'm tired of playing jail. Let's go home and play something else. Can't we, Ma? Please."

She turned toward me and the anguish in her eyes was such that I had to leave. I, whose purpose in life is to give solace, had nothing to offer this woman in her hour of need. They sat there together, mother and son—saint and sacrifice, stone and sand.

Sheriff Collins was reading wanted circulars at his desk. "Howdy, Reverend. Converted Georgie yet?" The remark was intended to be humorous, but the sheriff's eyes were not laughing. I read in them the puzzled anger of a man who has a job to do but has not the will to do it. George Finley had been the object of derision all his life—but no one wanted to kill him, in spite of the crime he had committed.

"Has Doc Finley been around yet?" I asked. Doc Finley had disappeared into the depths of his office the day of the murder and had remained there, not even coming out to eat, as far as we could tell. The scorn of the whole town was cast upon him. His only child convicted of murder and now would die, and his father had not even come to say goodbye. He had been a taciturn man, the doctor, a hard man and not really well liked, but he had done his job well and was respected, as suited his position, until now.

Of course, there had been rumors about him and Mae Miller. Mae Miller, who had been carved up like a Christmas turkey by her employer's idiot son. Rumors about Mae Miller-and the others before her, but the whispers had never seemed justified. The girls had just quit working and left town, never to be heard of again. Mae Miller wasn't as lucky as her predecessors. Mae hadn't been able to leave and begin again—Mae, with her pretty face and her starched white nurse's uniform.

No one knew the motive for Georgie's horrible crime—but then no one knows what battles occur between a child's mind and a man's body. He had done it, there was no doubt about that. He had stood there with the bleeding scalpel, pleased beyond reason with his hideous accomplishment. "That was fun, wasn't it, Mae? Let's do it again." He had protested when the mangled body didn't respond, he had protested when they had taken the knife from him. A razor-sharp blade stolen from his father's instrument bag. As I said, there was nothing the jury could do but find him guilty. And now there was nothing we could do but carry out the dreadful ritual.

I should have gone back to the parish house—I had a sermon to compose— but since the time was so near I somehow couldn't tear myself away from the proximity of the jail. Like the children who had returned again to sing their little song . . . *"Georgie Porgie, Puddin' and Pie . . ."* The lure was irresistible; I could only pray that my reason for remaining was not morbid curiosity, too.

Mrs. Finley came into the office, weeping silently. She was a big woman, typical of those who first came to this pioneer country. Doc, his wife and child showed up in Dawsonville when Georgie was a baby. It was before my time there, but they tell me Doc was a gay blade with a handsome wife. Time had aged them and marked them with sober faces and sad eyes. But time had passed Georgie by; he would never be more than that baby. I couldn't find a soul to whom they had complained. So we didn't know how they felt toward George or toward each other. We could only guess of the devotion—and watch George's mother's hands. They were the gauge to her feelings, sometimes the only gauge. She was strong and silent for the most part, though she seemed to talk often enough with Georgie. Many's the time I had seen them together, the big woman holding the big child's hand as they ventured forth into the surrounding countryside on some mysterious errand of their own.

Why, I wondered, hadn't Doc Finley come forth to comfort her? What sort of man could fail his family at a time like this? I didn't know Doc well, but then no one did. And he never attended my services. I sighed and looked through the window to the sky for some sign of help. But all I saw was the scaffold looming black and tall against the vivid sunset.

Perhaps, I thought, that was something I could do. I set out for Doc's office through the black desert heat. There was no light in the small building, but I pounded on the door. There was no answer.

"Dr. Finley," I called, "this is Reverend Ryson. May I please come in?" A stray breeze lifted a scrap of paper in reply.

I pleaded with him then. I told him in the best words I could choose how his family needed him. But words were not enough and in the hot silence of the night he answered, "Get out of here. I have no family!" And so it seemed that there was nothing I could do.

We sat the night out, Mrs. Finley, the sheriff and myself. We said very little, but toward morning she whispered, "It is, perhaps, just as well. Who would look after him when I am gone?" There seemed to be no answer.

With the sunrise she went in to Georgie, taking his breakfast. I went, too, still searching for something, anything, to make it easier for them. He ate happily and noisily, some of the food dribbling down his chin. His mother did not seem to care. She crooned to him and caressed his sparse fine hair. "We're going to play a new game today, Georgie," she told him, a strained smile on her bony face. "I'll tell you how it goes and we'll have a good time and when it's over—" her voice wavered— "when it's over, I'll take you home. Will you like that, Georgie?"

"Yeah, Ma. Sure. You know I always like new games. What is this one called, Ma?"

She stared at her hands a moment, then clearing her throat she began, "It's called Hanging, Georgie. Hanging. Reverend Ryson here, he'll play, too, and the sheriff and maybe some more of your friends will be there to play. You'd like that, wouldn't you? It won't take long and then we can go home afterwards like I promised."

"Aw right, Ma. You explain it to me so I'll know how to play. I wouldn't want to make a mistake." As I watched the two of them I knew I was not needed. I could do nothing she couldn't do. She was playing a game with her child and she was his whole world. Quietly I withdrew as she began to explain the "rules" of Hanging.

Back in the office several men sat staring at the tobacco-stained floor. Outside a false breeze stirred the dust faintly and then subsided in a hopeless fight against the inexorable desert. I joined the waiters. The door opened and more silent men entered. There were no more seats and they stood, blocking the windows, especially the one window framing the dark finger of death. We all waited . . . and soon she came.

"It's almost time, isn't it?" she asked as she wiped her reddened eyes. The sheriff nodded. She looked around at the silent faces. Her hands trembled slightly and clutched each other. "Has anyone—" her voice stumbled—"has anyone seen Doc yet?" No one replied. The answer was obvious. "It's all right," she said, "He'll come home soon." The hands were calm again as though she had forced their pose. "Georgie is ready, Sheriff . . ." You could hardly hear the last words, ". . . and so am I."

There was quite a crowd outside. An eerie, quiet crowd. I had never seen a hanging before, but I had some sort of idea that these vital, fighting people with their black and white ideas of wrong and right would feel a frightening emotion, almost of elation, at a time like this. I was wrong. They stood without a murmur, their faces stony, as he emerged. Georgie shuffled happily along between his mother and the sheriff, crooning the insidious nursery rhyme and greeting old acquaintances.

"Hi, Lennie. We're going to play a game. Isn't this fun? Did you come to play, too? Hello, Tex. I missed you lately. You ain't been in town for quite a spell. Hi, Slim. Don't forget you said I could ride your horse. Maybe after we play hanging, huh?" He greeted almost every one of the long row, but they could not answer. Most had never answered him in life, so he didn't seem to mind or even notice as he walked in the shadow.

They left her at the gallows steps and there she stood, a great rock of a woman who moved only her hands in meaningless gestures and looked upward as the final act was about to begin. Georgie wavered and tittered in childish amusement as the rope tickled his elephantine neck. I opened my prayer book and stepped forward.

Georgie was not through, however. He called from behind the red kerchief that served as a blindfold, "Isn't this enough, Ma? I don't want to play this game any more. I want to go home now, like you promised." There was no answer, just a muffled sob from somewhere deep within the crowd. "I been good, Ma." He tried to step forward, but the rope pulled him back. "I did just like you showed me. I played the game. But I'm tired now, I want to go home." The sheriff's hand reached for the trap lever, eager to shut off the childish pleading. "Come on, Ma, let's go home. You promised I could play Doctor again. That was the best game of all. You said I could operate again-like I did with Mae. You showed me just how to do it, remember, and you said I could operate again . . . on Pa. When are we going to operate on Pa?"

The sheriff's hand moved in fatal surprise and could not be stopped. The trapdoor yawned.

God's words were on my lips, but I could not speak.

Above the murmur of the crowd, the snap of the neck, the thud of the body, droned the dry rasp of the mother's voice: "The Lord is my shepherd. I shall not want . . ."

Blood and Moonlight
William R. Cox

October 1956

Langton parked the police car at the intersection of Bourne Street and Shyve Square. There was a patch of white moonlight and a dark hump of clean-smelling jasmine and he stopped a moment, looking up at the one lighted window in the cheap flats. Then he said, "The hell with it. It was a long while ago."

He went up to the fourth floor and into the dingy, close aura of poverty and death. Young Johnny Lee was there in uniform, waiting for him.

"Hi, Lang, they get you up?" Johnny was new on the Force and uneasy. "This ain't nice."

"She in there?"

"Uh-huh. The coroner's on his way."

Langton went into the bedroom. Betty Lou lay across the bed, her legs dangling awkwardly, her stockings twisted. She was wearing a slip, but she never had been one for underthings, he remembered. He felt he should put a sheet over her, only it was better the coroner should see her like she was. Everything would have to be as tight as they could make it if they expected to get a conviction. Which they would not get, he told himself.

It was a shame about Betty Lou. She had been real pretty before she married old, drunk Jake Harris, when Langton had been going with her. Too easy, but pretty and with a nice, pert way about her. There had been other moonlight nights he could remember, and he had almost married Betty Lou.

Then she ran away with Jake, who didn't last long, and then she had picked up with Harry Jay Wynne.

Then it was no use.

It wasn't that Harry Jay was married, though he was. It was the Wynne way with women that set them aside, put a mark on them. Many a time in many a bar, Harry Jay made his brag, "Any liquor, any gal. I got a strong stomach."

It was about all he had left. Everything else had been spent. The family money, his youth, most of his good looks, his own mother, all down the drain.

Old Miz Wynne had been a Hunter. A good woman and a proud one, she spent plenty money keeping Harry Jay out of jail and paying off the men after Harry Jay got the women. When she died, holding her son's hand, she was only worrying because she wouldn't be around to keep him safe, because the money was all gone.

Harry Jay knew the answer; he married the Croswell girl, the elder, not so pretty one, Elinor. The family fought it, but lost, and then they rationed him, just enough money for food and drink and clothing. He had a little real estate business and he was able to do business by exploiting the family names.

There was the city, to which progress had come in every other way, but not in this way. The old names hung on; you couldn't do anything to the Wynnes or the Hunters.

Langton reached out and defiantly dragged a soiled thin blanket over the slim legs and lower torso of the dead woman. There was a bullet hole beneath the plump left breast and he left that exposed where the slip had pulled away.

Langton asked, "He been picked up yet, Johnny?"

"On the corner. Drunk to the nines. Had the gun on him." Johnny Lee tried to make it sound routine. "Ran right into me. Sent him in with Jackson and come up here. I ain't touched anything. Figured it's open and shut."

"You ought to know nothin' is open and shut when there's a Wynne in it." Langton moved about the unkempt, ill-smelling flat. "It ain't like Betty Lou was anybody."

In the closet he found male clothing. There were pajamas and a spare white suite the men wore that year and a laundry bag hung on a rusty nail. He emptied it on the floor.

A shirt fell out. It was a white shirt with an attached semi-stiff collar. There was blood on it. Langton said, "Nobody but Harry Jay wears this kinda shirt."

"That'll do it," Johnny Lee nodded.

In a dresser against the wall there were underclothes, but no other shirt.

"Looks like he kept a change here. Stands to reason there oughta be another shirt. Or he's wearin' it."

"He wore a clean shirt. Seemed funny, him so drunk. Like he oughta be mussed up. But the shirt was spankin' clean."

Langton looked at Johnny Lee. "That's good police work, noticin' things like a clean shirt. I'll remember that, Johnny Lee." The boy flushed. "I hope we can hang him, Lang. The way he does, it ain't decent. His wife and everything. Why, he even cheated on Betty Lou. He was down to Mammy Todd's at least once a week, when he had the price and she had a new young whore."

Langton said, looking around the mean lodgings, "Hell, he didn't even keep Betty Lou good."

The coroner came then and they let him take over.

The gun, thought Langton, and the bullet and the bloody shirt all put together would hang anyone. Maybe this time Harry Jay wouldn't get away with it. Maybe this time there wouldn't be a woman to save his neck.

Langton sat uncomfortable in the hot, crowded courtroom. The State had sent down a prosecutor, a right bright man, and he was summing up the airtight case the police had handed him. Harry Jay Wynne was dressed in a quiet gray, some of the harsh lines gone from his arrogant, fleshy face, his hair slicked back, his confidence unshaken. Only his eyes were bad; astigmatic, bloodshot, watery. Maybe someone had slipped him a half pint to bolster him for the ordeal.

Their glances crossed for a moment and Harry Jay glared hatred for a moment. That was because they couldn't shake his testimony on the stand and because everyone in the court had known that Langton fully believed Harry Jay's guilt and people believed Langton.

The expensive defense attorneys had managed to dig up the old romance between Langton and Betty Lou, but when Langton admitted it and guilelessly stuck to facts, there had been no doubt in anyone's mind that he was telling the truth. Harry Jay, living or dead, would always hate Langton.

It looked like he might die, at that. Every item of evidence dovetailed, his defense of having found Betty Lou dead and blacking out through grief and rage fell apart on the matter of the bloody shirt that he had doffed before he left the flat on Bourne Street.

Langton stared at the jury. He did not like it, composed as it was of semi-professionals, the ones who turn up in every panel, the hangers-on whom clever defense attorneys always manage to select. Their unintelligent faces reflected nothing, they listened in somnolence, apathetically slapping away the summer flies which invaded the courtroom.

The evidence of expert bullet men, the big blow-up pictures of the bullet meant nothing to them. Only the prints of the nearly nude dead woman had brought them alive to lick their chops and breathe through their mouth for a salacious moment of thrill. They were a bunch of nothings—still he couldn't see how they might vote acquittal.

Elinor Wynne sat in the front row of spectators. She had not gone near Harry Jay, which was kind of funny, Langton thought. Every day she sat in her black and white costumes, cool and detached and neat, watching, her lined face expressionless. Langton couldn't figure her out. These people, the Croswells and Wynnes, might revile each other in private, but it was their age long habit to stick together in a crisis.

The prosecutor wound up his peroration in a blaze of forensics. He was shrewd; he knew he had to stir up the jurors and lift them out of lethargy. It seemed to Langton that he had got to them, that they were awakening to the fact that a crime of murder had been committed.

Harry Jay felt it. He moved restlessly, perspiration beading his high, white brow. He half-turned toward the jury box. The prosecutor impaled him with a quivering forefinger, opening his mouth to make a flat accusation.

The woman's voice was loud and clear, interrupting, "Stop this! It's all a mistake! I admit I killed her!"

Langton swore and rushed across the space between them and tried to get at her, but people milled about and he could not get past them. He saw Johnny Lee stumble and cursed savagely, shoving men from his path.

The emotionless voice went on, "She broke up my home, stole my husband. I shot her. Harry Jay took the gun to protect me. I can't let him go through with it."

Langton got to her. He seized her without ceremony, slapping his hand over her mouth. She did not struggle. She went quietly up the aisle, between the rows of staring, buzzing spectators.

In the detention room, Langton said, "That was somethin'. Did his lawyers put you up to it?"

"I'm ready to make a statement," said Elinor stonily. "I killed her."

She had never been beautiful. Years of living as Harry Jay's wife had given her a peculiarly aloof expression, as though she was an onlooker at life, never a participant. She had a certain style, something inherent in her family, but she was not sexually attractive, Langton decided. It was said she drank secretly and this he could believe.

"First his ma. Now you. How come he can get a woman to do for him every time?"

"I killed her."

"Seems like you'd want him hanged. You ain't old. You got life in you."

"She broke up my home. I killed her."

"You busted that trial all to hell, to save his neck. This county ain't about to go to the expense and trouble of another one and nobody is about to try you. For him, you did it."

"I'm guilty. Bring in your stenographer."

"What's he got? Why do women always save him? He treats you bad. He's no use under God's sun. Why don't you let him hang and be rid of him?"

She shut her mouth tight. He felt he was getting through to her, but it was like she was hypnotized or something. She would not look at Langton. She stared at the wall, her face showing nothing.

He heard the lawyers yapping outside and knew he was powerless. He said, "So that's the way it is. And I bet you if Betty Lou was here, alive, she'd testify for him, too."

Still she betrayed nothing. He opened the door and let the lawyers in. He went out and walked down to Bull's Tavern and sat in a booth in the back and ordered bourbon and water and after a moment Johnny Lee came in and sat across from him.

"Thought you'd be here."

Langton said, "Yeah. Have one."

"It ain't right. It plain ain't right."

"No. It ain't right. Lots of times you ain't sure. Maybe yes, most likely yes, but you could be wrong. Not this time."

"He beats up on the gals down at Mammy Todd's. I been checkin' around on him. He beat Betty Lou plenty."

"I wonder if he beats *her.*"

"Her? Oh, you mean Miz Wynne?"

"It's somethin' he's got. Somethin' that ain't any good to the world, but that gets the women."

Johnny Lee said youthfully, "Mebbe he'll meet one some day. One that'll really rap him. Maybe he'll get it from a dame some day."

"I want to be around when that happens." It wouldn't ever happen, Langton knew. It was something which would always baffle him. It was something he had no power to alter, a wall he could never climb. It would worry him always and he would try to do something about it, but he had a bad feeling about what the outcome would be.

Weeks went by. Langton failed to get a promotion he had earned and he knew the reason. Stubbornly he managed to keep an eye on Elinor and Harry Jay. He saw them around plenty, but never together. Elinor was out on bail, her trial docketed two months hence. It was doubtful in Langton's mind that she'd get much. Temporary insanity maybe—put away for a short while, and then out. Tough on stone-dead Betty Lou of course; but it was Harry Jay who needed the clobbering. Harry Jay went on as usual, doing the things he had always done, getting a little worse as he coasted down the hill. Mammy Todd barred him and made it stick through a bully boy she kept as bouncer. Langton protected the bully boy; he could do that much.

Elinor played contract bridge. There was a game which had been going on for ten years, all the same women from the old families, and sometimes they played twenty-four hours at a stretch, drinking whiskey and dealing the cards like female automatons. She never missed a session. Some of the other wives catted around on the side, but not Elinor. Just cards and whiskey for her and you never saw her drunk, either. She had a very straight back and her eyes were deep-set and hidden.

One night Langton met her on a deserted street. It was late, after a bridge session and maybe she had been drinking a lot. He said, "I'll walk you home, Miz Wynne. Been some muggin's lately. It ain't safe, walkin' alone."

She laughed. He had never heard her laugh before. It was a harsh brittle sound. "Thank you, Langton. You're a polite boy."

Their heels clicked on the paving. When they got to the old Croswell place with its mansard roof and the thick honeysuckle vines, the moon made the night mysterious. She paused and spoke again.

"Betty Lou—was she a nice girl?"

"I couldn't say what she was."

"You were in love with her once."

"Does that mean I knew about her? What does a man know about a woman?"

"You slept with her. You held her in the night and listened to her. What was she like then?"

He could not have been more startled if she had pulled a gun on him. He stammered, "It was long ago, ma'am."

"Yes. Long ago and now forgotten. Good night, Langton."

He stood in a daze, watching her straight back go up the walk. He could grasp no meaning from the strange conversation. Maybe, he thought, he was out of his depth completely. Maybe he ought to forget Harry Jay, forget Betty Lou's death, put it all out of his mind.

He could not. He was in the Bardsley Hotel on Saturday night because he knew that Harry Jay was there, upstairs in a room with the new Yankee manicurist, the redhead that all the bloods had been courting. He heard the commotion all the way down in the lobby and saw the red-faced anger of the clerk as he phoned the room and got no answer. There was no house detective in the ramshakle old Bardsley and the clerk turned to Langton.

"Sure wish I could do somethin'. He's been kickin' up a fuss in here ever since Mammy Todd ran him out."

"Who's he got up there?"

"The redhead."

"Thought she was choosey?"

The clerk looked puzzled. "I coulda sworn she was straight. You know what I mean? Maybe if she liked a guy a lot. But she fluffed off a dozen better men than Harry Jay."

"He did it again," muttered Langton.

"Huh? What'd you say, Lang?"

"Nothin'."

There was the sound of furniture being shoved around. Loud voices floated down to them.

"You know I can't make no complaint against him," the clerk said. "I'd be fired if I did. It ain't right people like him can have a man fired."

"It ain't right a lot of things." Langton's ear was cocked. He was off duty and his own position was precarious. He told himself he was an officer of the law twenty-four hours of the day and if an assault was taking place he had a right to interfere. It might hurt him in the end, but he had a right.

The woman screamed. A chair turned over. The woman yelled again and maybe she had yelled for help.

Langton went up the rickety stairs. The clerk called a panicky warning, then followed without haste, frightened but hopeful.

Behind the flimsy door, Wynne's voice held a note of high excitement which held Langton motionless, puzzled. It was like Harry Jay was having fun. "I told you I'd give it to you. Get up and I'll do it again."

"You louse," said a husky, angry girl's voice. "So that's the kind you are."

"I'll hit you again! Get up, I tell you."

"And I thought you wanted to play. You dirty, perverted slob."

"I'm going to hit you," Harry Jay said in that strained, happy tone. "I'm going to hit you harder and harder . . ."

Langton went in, breaking the door with his shoulder, slamming it wide. He stood a moment, taking in the scene.

The girl crouched on the floor. She had quite a lot of red hair streaming over her shoulders. Her blouse was in shreds and her skin was creamy white and youthful and nice. She had bright blue eyes with a lot of gray in them. There was a slight cut at the corner of her wide mouth, but when she looked at Langton she grinned, showing white, even teeth. She was not a beautiful girl, but she was young and healthy.

She said, "Am I ever glad to see you, copper."

She'd been around. She knew a cop when she saw one. She was, Langton observed, unafraid. She was angry, but she wasn't scared, not of Harry Jay, not of anything.

Langton said, "You want to make a complaint?"

She got up. She had long legs and arms. She tried to put her blouse together, failed, shrugged. "What do you think?"

Harry Jay had recognized Langton. "Persecution. Always following me. Hounding me. You're the one. Langton. I know you. Persecutin' me."

Langton explained to the girl, "I can't do nothin' if you refuse to sign the complaint. Mostly they say they will; then he talks 'em out of it."

"He would, he would," she nodded. "A real cute cracker boy. Talks up a storm. How do you think he got me up here? Booze and fast talk. Real cute."

"Persecution. You ain't going to let this crooked cop do anything to me, are you, honey?" Harry Jay took a step toward her.

The girl winked at Langton, asking a question with her eyes, and Langton nodded. He poised, ready to move, watching, great satisfaction in him as the girl stepped to meet Harry Jay.

She was too smart to hurt her knuckles. She swung one of her long arms. One breast came loose from the blouse, lifting as she cut with the edge of her hand. She caught him between the shoulders and the ear, a knifing slash. Harry Jay staggered. She pronged two long fingers and jabbed. She got him in the eyes and he gasped, sinking toward the floor.

She brought up her knee and nailed him on the nose and then stepped nimbly back before the blood could spatter her nylons. She said calmly to Langton, "Self defense, huh, copper? You saw him attack me."

She put her white breast back into her torn brassiere and re-examined her blouse. The clerk said excitedly, "I seen it. He tried to kill you. Okay, Lang?"

Langton said, "You got to go along with us to sign the complaint. If you do that, sister, it was self defense."

The girl stared at him. "What have I got here? A wheel?"

"Ma'am?"

"This jerk." She indicated Harry Jay with her toe. "He's a shot in this burg?"

"Yeah."

"He can cause trouble for me? And you?"

"Unless we rap him with a signed complaint."

"Then what happens?"

"Judge Haycock is kinda sore at him. I think we can get him thirty days."

"Whew! Now that's a stiff bit!" She surveyed Harry Jay contemplatively. He was mumbling and trying to stem the nose bleed. The girl took a quick step and kicked. Harry Jay went over backwards, clapping both hands to his mouth. The girl said, "I think I got a tooth. That'll help."

Langton said, "That's enough. I can't let you do no more to him."

The girl nodded. "Yeah, it wouldn't look good." She went across the room and picked up a light cloak. I'll just put this on. The blouse speaks for itself, huh?"

"Yeah," said Langton. He sent the clerk down to call the wagon. He looked at the girl and he had to grin.

She said, "This guy should be stashed away, you know. He's queer. You don't like him, huh?"

"I'm a cop. I just do my duty."

"You read the lines good," she laughed. Then she sobered. "This is a real grim deal. What's with this Harry Jay?"

He told her a little about it, as much as he could make dear. He ended, "It's always some woman, you see. They get him off, they protect him. Somehow he does it to them. He gets away with it, because of the women."

She stared at the man groveling on the floor. He was an unlovely, suffering animal toward whom no sympathy need be expended. She said, "No crummy queer is going to slug Minnie Barnes and get away with it."

Langton reached down and got hold of Harry Jay's collar. He hauled the glibbering figure upright and said, "You hear what the lady says, Harry Jay?"

Amazingly, Wynne spoke calmly, "Sorry Langton. You can go now. Won't be any further trouble."

Langton shook his head. "You didn't hear the lady."

Harry Jay turned to the girl. He smiled, oblivious of the fact that she had broken a tooth and so spoiled the effect. "I'm terribly sorry, honey. I was drunk. I'm all right now. Let's forget it, shall we? I apologize."

It was amazing the way he turned on a sort of charm. He was—What was the word? Debonair, that was it. Like in the old stories about his ancestors. Gay, debonair folk, Langton remembered. It almost sounded like he had made a slight error, the first of his life, and was truly sorry.

The girl said, "Listen to him."

"You'll forget it, won't you honey?" wheedled Harry Jay. "Just tell Langton you don't want to make charges."

She laughed again. "How about him? Come on, copper, let's get with it. This bum's got to learn."

They went down the stairs and into the lobby. They were going toward the street exit, with Harry Jay trying to keep his head and shake off Langton's steadying hand and the girl tall in her cloak, her red hair thrust back in a knot, when the clerk intercepted them.

In Langton's ear he whispered, "Miz Wynne . . . she came in, asked me about it. I hadda tell her. I hadda . . ."

Langton walked on, pushing Harry Jay out onto the street. The moon made it almost like day time. The wagon was always slow and tonight there was still no echo of its siren. Since the girl had laughed, Harry Jay had not said anything. He was emptier than Langton remembered, much emptier than in the courtroom when he had been on trial for murder.

There was a little traffic and no people about in this neighborhood and the moon cast black shadows against the buildings. They stood on the corner waiting and none of them spoke. Langton was admiring the girl with the unofficial section of his mind and thinking about Harry Jay with the other. It was Johnny Lee who had hoped for a woman who would turn him in and now it seemed that she had appeared.

Wynne made another effort, slowly, painfully. "I'll have your badge for this, Langton."

"You'll try."

"I can get it. I kept you from promotion. You can't do this to me."

"I hear you sayin' it."

"There's still a chance, Langton."

After waiting a moment, Langton asked quietly, "For Betty Lou?"

Harry Jay quit, then. The girl looked sharply at Langton, a question in her eyes. He could see her quite plainly, but he had nothing to communicate with her. He had a sudden disquieting memory of Betty Lou when she was young, when he had been going with her, a feeling of guilt, although he had not been the first to bed her down.

Outside the shimmering white glow of the moon there was movement. Langton, wrapped in his thoughts, did not perceive it. The girl, watching Langton, was oblivious. Only Harry Jay moved and said, "No!"

Then there was the flat report of a revolver and Harry Jay crumpled in Langton's arms, repeating, "No. Oh, no!"

Langton couldn't hold the dead weight and Harry Jay fell down and lay in a heap and if he had seemed empty before, now he was depleted as though he had never been alive. His blood mingled with dirt upon the paving and he kicked once, feebly, and was still.

Elinor Wynne came out of the shadows and dropped the revolver. It landed on the body of her husband and rested there.

"She shot him. That woman shot him," said the girl.

Elinor Wynne came close and her face hadn't changed any. When she spoke, it was in the tone she had used that night when Langton had walked her home. As though she were explaining something, scarcely believing anyone would understand.

"Not again. Not for anything past or present. Because there never was anything, you see, Langton. Not really."

"Yes, ma'am."

The girl said, "Walked right up and shot him. Holy cow, that took nerve."

"Be quiet," Langton said to her. He was beginning to understand. He knew Elinor Wynne would not talk later and he wanted to hear her out. The siren of the police wagon sounded at last. "They won't convict you in this country, Miz Wynne," he said.

"Convict me?" She did not seem to get the significance of this. "I just couldn't go to court again for him. Knowing everything."

"He'd have killed again, sooner or later."

She shook her head. "It is too much to expect of me. Sitting there in the courtroom, knowing they all were staring. Knowing he had never loved me. Never anything but the money."

She stopped talking and though standing there she was not with them any longer.

Langton said softly, "He played hell with women while he lasted. He sure played hell 'til his luck ran out."

He turned to the redhead. She was looking down at Harry Jay, who had turned so that the moon was on his dead face. It was a sorrowful face, now, the bad things erased, the weakness hidden by the fickle moonlight. One arm was upflung like he was a small boy warding off a blow.

There were tears on the cheeks of the red-haired girl. "The poor bastard," she murmured. "What'd she have to kill him for?"

Langton turned wearily, looked toward the approaching red light of the wagon.

Shadowed

Richard Wormser

March 1957

Gordon Harris fidgeted with his private checkbook, his fountain pen, a blotter. He was the fidgeting type. Finally he slid the check across the desk, and said: "I won't need you any more."

The man from the detective agency examined the check. He grinned a little. "This is the seventh day," he said. "The check's only for six and a half."

"It is now two o'clock," Gordon Harris said. "Since you have not had a man on duty until ten each morning, precisely one half of a business day has expired; no more."

The detective waved a good-natured hand. "Have it your own way, Mr. Harris. Who knows, you may have more business for us some other time."

"Hardly."

The detective got up, swinging his hat against his thigh. "You'd be surprised, pal. Once a guy gets to suspecting his wife, he goes on from there. Next thing, it's his partner, then his secretary, then the office boy. Plenty work for us."

Gordon Harris ended the conversation where it had started: "I won't need you any more."

The detective left . . .

Muriel Harris dressed with great care. The slip and panties were imported silk; the stockings were her sheerest. The dress was one her husband had never seen; the hat had an intriguing little veil.

It was necessary, if Gordon searched her room, that he know how much care she had taken. Very necessary.

As she came out of the house, she let her eyes slide sidewise, once. The battered series of cars that had been parked—with clumsy innocence—somewhere on the block every day for the last seven business days had ended. But just around the corner, she thought she caught the sparkle of the gold ornament on the front of a black Cadillac. She couldn't be sure, but she knew her husband well enough to be almost sure.

For all his money, he hated expenditure almost as badly as he hated the income tax. Seven days of paying a private detective would nearly strangle him; now that he was sure on which house she called every day, with whom she rendezvoused, he would cut the detectives off and take over himself.

She smiled a little as she opened the door to the garage, climbed into her own Cadillac convertible—Gordon was generous enough when it was a matter of show.

She smiled, because the thing about Gordon she hated most, his strict routine, his dry determination to do today what he had done yesterday and would hope to do tomorrow—this very thing was undoing him. He was not accustomed to pay money to private detectives, and—she knew him so well—he had been uneasy while paying that money. So he had stopped it as soon as possible, and taken over himself.

He would be sorry for that, Muriel Harris thought. The motor was warm now, and she backed gently out of the garage, touching the control to make the windows roll down.

She drove less than two miles, and three times she got glimpses of the other Cad in her rear-view mirror. But at that, Gordon was shadowing her as expertly as his hirelings had done.

Muriel Harris thought wryly that this was a mighty expensive shadowing job. The shadow car and the one it followed had cost nearly twelve thousand dollars, and they were less than four months old.

But now it was time to park and start walking, as she had done for a month; the same parking spot, the same walk.

Halfway there, she had to pass a supermarket. At this hour of the morning, all the shoppers were women, but even so she got admiring glances from some of them, and she completely stopped a clerk in his work of pyramiding oranges.

She walked very straight, careful not to let her thin hips roll. Her breasts were small, but well shaped, her legs long, and the frock she had on had cost enough for her to feel securely beautiful.

It was a lovely spring day.

The rest of the walk was through residential streets. The only persons she bothered were a gardener spading up a flower bed, a young mother putting a baby out in a playpen. She could read their thoughts: the gardener wishing he were twenty years younger, the mother wishing she had clothes like that.

Here she was. Muriel Harris took a key out of her French handbag, opened the door she had opened regularly for a month, let herself into the house. She paused at the front door long enough to see Gordon's black Cadillac go sweeping by. The reports, of course, would have told him which house she visited.

After the pause, she went to the hall closet under the broad steps that rolled upstairs. She opened the closet door, smiled again, and went into the closet. A high window showed her only the top of a newly-budded tree; when she had first hid in this closet, the limbs had been bare.

She settled down on the little boudoir chair there, and took up the book she had been reading.

At ten-forty-five—as on all other mornings—the front door opened and heavy footsteps banged into the house. She heard the rocking noise as Hervey Melton threw his topcoat and hat on the chair opposite the closet door.

He never hung up his hat and coat.

Men were such creatures of habit, Muriel Harris thought. Damn men!

Hervey Melton's heavy stride banged on her head as he ran up the stairs over the closet. Habit! He went downtown every morning, got the mail from his lock box at ten-thirty, brought it back and stormed up to his drafting room.

There he spent the rest of the day working at his profession, which was consulting engineer to a gun manufacturer. He never came out of the drafting room till four o'clock.

Gordon Harris sat behind the wheel of his Cadillac sedan, and sweat poured down his face. It was one thing to read dry reports from private investigators; it was another to see your wife—your own wife, dressed in the clothes you had bought her, driving the car you had given her—boldly open another man's door with a key from her bag, go to a rendezvous with him.

And in daylight. Gordon Harris, no man to scorn a cliché, called it bold daylight. She was without shame.

But worse than she was Hervey Melton. How that big devil must be laughing, as he—Gordon Harris's imagination was trite, but active—removed the shoes Gordon Harris had bought from Gordon Harris's wife's feet; slid the sheer silk stockings down, helped her with the dress—that had cost so much of Gordon Harris's money and—Gordon Harris forced himself to stop. Maybe she kept some of her clothes on. That was supposed to be stimulating . . . his mind became a panorama of photographs sold under the counter, of drawings from French magazines.

Sweat drenched his clothes. Slowly he reached for the glove compartment, took out the pistol he kept there.

He crossed the street on a long diagonal. He staggered a little, in his rage. Nobody had ever taken anything of his and not paid for it! Nobody was going to start now . . .

Muriel Harris heard the unlocked front door open again, heard it slam. She held her breath. The footsteps sounded like her husband's, but she was so anxious, it was possible that she was practicing self-deception.

Then they came closer, and she was sure.

Gordon knew his way about this house, she thought. The times they'd been here for dinner had usually ended up with the two men going off to Harvey Melton's drafting room, leaving her and Mrs. Melton to console each other in the living room.

Gordon knew this house and he knew Hervey Melton. He knew the big man slept in an alcove of the drafting room, seldom coming out of there except for his heavy meals, and that he was never disturbed by Mrs. Melton during working hours. And so Gordon would know where to look for his wife.

And now Gordon was tapping over her head, as he went upstairs. How much lighter his steps were than Hervey Melton's!

She waited another minute and then walked quietly out of the closet and back to her car. She did not follow her usual route, but took the next block over. The people along her new line of march felt it was a much better day for having a glimpse of such a beautiful, well-dressed woman . . .

"That's all," the police lieutenant said. "Jealousy." He snorted. "According to that private detective—and I wouldn't believe anything any of them said—your husband thought you were having an affair with Mr. Melton, Mrs. Harris."

Muriel Harris shook her head. "Ridiculous. Mrs. Melton and I have been doing our marketing, our shopping together. We were in that big supermarket when it happened, I guess."

The lieutenant said, heavily: "People ought to stay away from private detectives. They got minds like sewers . . . And citizens oughtn't to have guns around. A man has a gun long enough, he's going to shoot it at someone . . . It's against regulations, but if you want to see your husband, I'd let you."

Muriel Harris said: "That's kind of you, lieutenant. But, no. Maybe some time. But—a man who'd think that of me."

The lieutenant said: "Yeah, a shock for you. Want someone to drive you home?"

"I've got my car here. I'll take Mrs. Melton . . . She won't want to go back to that house."

Mrs. Melton was not as tall as Muriel Harris, but she was just as slim, except for her shoulders; they indicated that she might have once won a cup as a country club tennis or golf champion. She shuddered. "If I could stay with you, Muriel. Anyhow, I'm putting that house on the market."

The lieutenant politely got up and opened his office door; he stood in the door for a moment, taking a normal man's delight in watching two young, nicely-shaped women walking away from him.

Then he closed the door, but the sight stayed with him for another moment. Too bad he was married. Each of those dames stood to inherit more than he would make in a career of police salaries; the Melton gal right away, the Harris one when the court convicted Harris, as it was sure to do: the chair, life or at least twenty years.

The night had turned cool, after the lovely spring day. Muriel Harris touched the electric button, and the windows of the Cadillac slid closed, noiselessly. She drove out of the police lot, and then took one hand off the wheel to drop into Mrs. Melton's lap.

That woman grabbed the manicured hand convulsively, pressed it against her thigh. "Drive fast, Muriel," she said. "I'm cold."

And Muriel Harris drove fast, towards the house that had been Gordon Harris's, towards the double bed that had been his, too; drove fast, so that they could be warm, soon.

Death of a Big Wheel
William Campbell Gault

April 1957

It had been a hot and trying day and I'd come in for a quiet drink. I'd had the first and was contemplating the advisability of another, when the man took the stool next to mine.

His face was familiar, a worn face, sensitive and still virile. His clothes were a bit frayed, but he wore them well; his voice was a trained voice. He ordered a Scotch on the rocks.

I knew him now. He'd played in my favorite picture before the war. He'd starred in it, and registered a very fine performance.

The bartender said, "Palm Springs, Mr. Haskell? I see you've been getting the sun."

"I've been getting the sun," the man said mildly, "but not at Palm Springs. How is every little thing with you, Charles?"

"Fine, Mr. Haskell. I had Needles, yesterday."

John Haskell smiled. "I didn't even know you were on the stuff, Charles."

The bartender grinned and shook his head. "The horse, I mean, Mr. Haskell. Ain't you betting any more?"

John Haskell shook his head and sipped his drink. "Not betting the horses or taking blondes to Palm Springs. It's a monastic life I lead."

"I'll bet," the bartender said genially. He looked at me, "Another of the same, Mr. Puma?"

I nodded.

John Haskell turned. "Joseph Puma, the private detective?"

I nodded again. "The same, Mr. Haskell. Where have you heard of me?"

"In the *Examiner,* on the Engle murder. I'm addicted to murder stories, *true* murder stories. You did a beautiful job on that case."

"Thank you," I said. "And you did a beautiful job in *Man In The Street.* I think that's my all-time favorite picture and yours was my all-time favorite performance."

He looked at me without expression. "That was a long time ago. That was before the war."

I said nothing.

He said quietly, "I was very big before the war. I was so big I thought it would be smart to be independent. I turned down four duration contracts before I went into the service."

Here it comes, *I thought.* The detailed and lengthy story of John Haskell's fall. And all I meant to have was one drink.

I shook my head sympathetically, but said nothing.

John Haskell said, "The studios put all the boys to work who had signed pre-service duration contracts. They had to pay the lads anyway, so they put them to work. What keeps an actor alive is work."

I nodded and sipped my drink.

John Haskell chuckled. "Don't look so bored. I only told you all that to forestall the tedious question too many people ask me. They continually ask me, 'What happened to you?' Well, that's what happened to me."

"I wasn't going to ask you," I said with a smile. "I'm not a tourist, Mr. Haskell."

"Of course you're not," he said. "I should have realized. Now, tell me about the Engle case. What put you on the trail of the Pastore woman?"

The man was drunk, I realized now. He spoke carefully and held himself primly erect, but he was almost blind drunk and only a supreme effort of will was keeping him off the floor.

I said, "Why don't I buy you a dinner while I tell you about the Engle case? I'd like to tell my grandchildren, some day, that I bought a dinner for John Haskell."

His voice was very steady. "I don't need your charity, Mr. Puma."

"One dinner is hardly charity, Mr. Haskell."

Silence, while he stared at me. "Italian, are you?"

"That's right."

"My first wife was Italian. Very compassionate people, Italians. You were undoubtedly thinking that if I had some food in me, the alcohol would have something to work on besides the walls of my stomach."

"You're discerning," I said.

"And so are you. But of course, that's your business, isn't it?"

"Part of it," I admitted. "My size and my hunger help, too."

He looked at the bartender and talked to me. "Now, Charles, here, serves drinkers day and night. But he didn't know I was drunk. Charles is not discerning."

Charles smiled and said nothing, as good bartenders do.

"A steak," I said, "and some coffee, Mr. Haskell, and the story of Gina Pastore. There's a quiet booth over there in the corner."

He turned slowly to look at the booth and then swung back slowly to look at me. Finally, he said, "Fair enough. And you may call me John."

The bartender looked at me and shrugged. I ignored him.

Haskell swung around on his stool, his drink held steadily in his hand. I stood close to him, waiting for him to fall. He didn't. I walked alongside him all the way to the booth and he never wavered.

The waiter came, and I ordered a pair of steaks. Then I told Haskell the story of Gina Pastore who had asked Alan Engle to go on a picnic with her and had, during the course of the picnic, bashed in Engle's head with a rock.

It was a story even uglier than my resume, but it didn't affect the appetite of John Haskell. He ate the steak and all the rolls they brought and all the butter—everything, in fact, but the dishes.

Then he leaned back and looked at me contentedly. "A fascinating story. I knew Alan Engle in high school. He was always in trouble."

There had been some satisfaction in his voice. I said, "You sound as though you've had an opinion vindicated."

"A pattern," he said. "We're all victims of a pattern, don't you think?"

"No," I said. "That's defeatism."

He smiled. "A big muscular Italian like you would no doubt be a hedonist."

"Partially. I guess almost everybody is, partially. If I'd had a talent, though, nothing would have stopped me. And certainly not booze."

He looked at me curiously. "You're speaking of me, now, I suppose? You think I have a talent?"

I nodded. "And so did all the critics. How many actors can please *all* the critics? Name me five."

He smiled sadly and patronizingly. "Critics—They won't even pay to get in; that's what they think of the theatre. Joe, I hit my peak at the age of twenty-seven. Then I had four years in the service, three years of it overseas, two of them in combat."

"You enlisted, if I remember right," I pointed out. "Where was the pattern there? That was an act of your will."

He shook his head. "It was an act of my youth. Of emotional thinking, my enlisting." He gestured to the waiter and ordered a pair of drinks.

At a table on the other side of the room, we were getting a lot of attention. A blonde in a pale green cashmere sweater was pointing us out to her escort.

The escort was sitting, so I couldn't judge his height, but his shoulders were impressively broad.

Our drinks came, and Haskell lifted his. "To luck."

"You don't believe in it," I told him, "but I'll drink to it."

We drank, and I said, "Don't look now, but do you know that blonde across the room who's giving us the eye?"

Haskell swung his gaze that way and said, "I know her. Her name is Lira McCrea and she hates my guts."

"Who's the muscle with her?" I asked.

Haskell shrugged. "Never saw him before. He looks—malignant, doesn't he?" He sipped his drink. "I met her at a party. I was drunk and she was ready. I was too drunk to take advantage of that. At any rate, that's my memory of the thing. About a week later, at *Ciro's* she walked over to my table and really told me off. It was very vulgar."

I said, "I think you're due for an encore. She's on the way over right now. And the muscle is trailing her."

Haskell smiled. "I'll take her. You can have the big guy." He didn't look their way.

The blonde seemed younger than I had first imagined her. And the big man was not tall, only broad. He had the kind of a face that looks naked without a number under it. I was sure I had seen it before, if only on a poster in the post office.

The blonde said nastily, "Well, well, if it isn't drunken John Haskell. Have I told you what I think of you lately, John?"

He smiled and shook his head. Behind Lira McCrea, the muscle looked at us impassively.

I said, "Lady, we were having a serious conversation. Would you mind running along?"

Her gaze swung to me. "Don't get flip, big boy. I've got all the man I need behind me."

"Not quite," I said. "And I'll tell you something else. If I have to get up to pop him, I may also hand you one for luck. Beat it."

John Haskell's eyes were bright with interest. The muscle growled something I didn't catch and the blonde reached forward to slap at Haskell's face.

I put a hand out that pushed her off balance, and she stumbled against the edge of the booth.

Her escort came charging in, then, to join the fray. I came up out of the booth and brought the good left hand along.

It was a lucky punch. My body was in it and it caught him just exactly where it was supposed to. He went stumbling backward until a table got in his way. Luckily, it was an empty table. He took it over with him.

The blonde screamed and a waiter and the bartender started our way and John Haskell said, "Now might be the intelligent time to leave."

We stood up and I put some money on the table and we were out of the place before the resistance could get properly organized.

On the parking lot, John Haskell said, "Well, Puma, it's been a pleasure. We must do this again."

"You're not driving, are you?" I asked. "You're not in condition to drive."

"I'm not driving," he said. "I sold my car. I'll get a cab down at the corner."

"All right," I said. "Take care of yourself. If you ever crawl out of the bottle, you might make a comeback, you know."

He smiled. "Don't worry about me, Puma. I'm not that important. Nobody is."

I watched him as he made his way steadily and leisurely toward the corner. He certainly didn't look drunk from the back.

I went to a movie that night and the next day I put in on a hotel skip. I couldn't get Haskell out of my mind. He was faintly arrogant and soft on mysticism, but I'd liked him and I'd always thought of him as one of this town's really good actors.

Friday morning, his picture was on the front page of the *Times*. He had been bludgeoned to death. By a person or persons unknown.

2.

What was Haskell's death to me? Nothing. I'd enjoyed him as an actor and talked to him for an hour and now he was dead. There were ten thousand police officers in this town. So what was it to me?

According to the *Times,* there was very little that the police had to go on. John Haskell had no known enemies. Most of his old friends had lost track of him; he was living in a cheap motel in Santa Monica. The most logical theory seemed to be that he had been the victim of a prowler. That, of course, could have been the reporter's theory, not the Department's.

It was a bright and sunny morning and I had nothing to do. I could have run over to the Department and told them about the blonde, Lira McCrea, and her pugnacious boy friend. But that might be unfair to the blonde.

I phoned an agent I knew and asked him if Miss McCrea was an actress, and if he knew where she lived. He'd heard the name, he told me, but very little more. He would check and call back.

He phoned back in ten minutes and told me Lira McCrea was a starlet under contract to *Verital Films* and he gave me her address.

Verital was a small outfit, specializing in low budget pictures, and there was a strong rumor around town that Arnie Roman had a big piece of the firm. Arnie had come up through pandering, dope and gambling to Las Vegas and the big time. He was a highly respected citizen of that Nevada rat's nest now, and active in Los Angeles real estate speculation.

If a man can afford it, buying a small studio is a fine way to keep supplied with dames. The blonde could be one of those.

Not that any of it was my business, but I had liked John Haskell. And I wasn't busy at the moment.

I climbed into the flivver and drove over to Beverly Hills.

The apartment house was on the edge of that gilded village, a rambling, two-story stucco building filled with small units. The directory in the lobby informed me Lira McCrea had a second floor apartment.

She was without make-up this morning, wearing a lounging robe of brocaded red satin, and the natural brown of her hair was showing at the roots.

"What the hell do you want?" she asked.

I studied her. Her toughness was not inherent and it seemed recently acquired; she obviously wasn't thoroughly at home in the gutter yet. I said, "Information. I'm looking for enemies of John Haskell."

"Look somewhere else," she said. "You're not the law; you're a private man."

"How did you know that?"

"My friends know you."

"How well do you know them?" I asked. "Well enough to expect them to rush to your rescue if I tell the police about you?"

Her face was momentarily vulnerable and she looked at me doubtfully. I said quietly, "How long ago did you decide *Verital* was the studio for you? How long ago did you learn there were short-cuts in this acting game?"

Her young face showed scorn. "What are you, a minister? Crummy, angle-shooting private eye—"

"You've been watching television too much," I said. "I'm a respectable member of a dignified profession. You could probably use an ally like me."

"I've got friends," she said, "who could buy you with their cigar money."

"The man was never born who can buy me," I told her. "But it's your decision. I'll let you argue with the boys from the Department."

I turned, took two steps, and she said, "Wait."

I waited, looking at her quietly.

"I don't want any trouble," she said. "I don't know anything about John's enemies. My friends aren't his enemies."

"You looked like an enemy two evenings ago."

"That was—personal." She hesitated. "Come on in."

I went into a one bedroom apartment furnished in just-under-first-class modern. She said, "I'm making some coffee. Want a cup?"

"Yes, thank you."

I followed her to a small dinette.

"Maybe some toast, too?" she asked. "I've got some really special marmalade from England."

I chuckled. "Why the Dale Carnegie touch for a crummy, angle-shooting private eye?"

She looked at me bleakly. "Maybe you're not one. Maybe you're what you claim to be."

"Maybe. All is not lost, anyway, if you can still think like that. Why did you hate John Haskell?"

"Didn't he tell you? Weren't you a friend of his?"

"I met him only that evening in that bar. He told me you had made a play for him at a party and he hadn't been interested. He seemed to think your vanity was inflamed."

She stared at me blankly. "The lying son-of-a-bitch—"

"Easy, now. Let's hear your story."

She said quietly, "My best friend committed suicide because of John Haskell."

A pause, and I asked, "Unrequited love?"

"Yeah. If that means unreturned love." She went to the small stove to get the percolator. "After an abortion."

"John Haskell's child?"

"He claimed it wasn't. She claimed it was and I believed her. I knew her since we were seven and she *never* lied to me."

"Why didn't she get a lawyer?"

"Because she loved him and he could talk fast. He was a great talker, that bastard."

I asked softly, "Why do you use those ugly words? It's not really natural for you."

She put some toast into the toaster and sat down across from me. "It's an ugly world, isn't it? If anybody should know that, you should."

"I should. But you shouldn't. Not yet." I sipped my coffee. "Did Haskell know you were a friend of this girl's?"

"Of course he knew it. We used to double-date."

"Was she an actress, too?"

Lira nodded. "Only she had more talent than I have. And she was prettier."

"Did she consider Haskell a step in the right direction?"

Lira McCrea looked at me steadily and angrily.

I said, "I don't want an emotional answer. *Think* now, and be honest."

She took a deep breath. "She loved him very much. She knew knowing him would help her career, but I honestly think she would have given up her career for him."

"I'll buy all of that," I said, "but now let's think of it from his viewpoint. He had probably met dozens of girls as pretty and talented as your friend. And many of them were undoubtedly—available. A gent in—oh, say Cedar Rapids might consider himself very lucky to marry a girl like your friend. To John Haskell, there were too many of them; she was only one of many. We're all victims of our environment to a degree, you know. He simply had more chances to be immoral than his less fortunate brothers."

"Man thinking," she said. "You're all alike."

"That could be. But some of us are worse. How long have you been hanging around with the hoodlum element in this town?"

"Is there another element in this town?"

I didn't answer. I spread some toast with marmalade and took a bite. "It is good marmalade," I said.

She didn't look at me. "If you only met him two evenings ago, why are you here now? Did somebody hire you?"

"Nobody. I liked him. I hate murder and I wasn't busy."

Doubt was on her face.

"Nobody is paying me," I repeated, "and nobody is required to tell me anything. What was your girl friend's name?"

"Jean Morley. I've a picture of her, if you'd like to see it."

I said I would and she went into the bedroom to get some snapshots. Some of them were of the girl alone, a thin and attractive dark-haired girl. Two of the snaps showed her with John Haskell's arm around her. In one of these, she was wearing a bathing suit, and she wasn't thin any place it would hurt her.

I said, "Are her parents living?"

"No. The only living relative she has is a brother."

"Does he live out here?"

"He—" She paused. "Why do you want to know?"

"I'm looking for a killer, Miss McCrae."

"Well, it wasn't Jean's brother. He lives in New Jersey."

She looked at me candidly as she said this, but I knew she was lying. Lying, like her toughness, was too new for her to handle skillfully. I'd believed what she'd said about Jean Morley, but perhaps Jean Morley had lied to her.

And then I remembered Haskell's preoccupation with a pattern in lives and wondered if that was the way he was trying to absolve his conscience from the guilt of Miss Morley's death.

"Why so quiet?" Lira asked.

"I've been thinking about Haskell. It's hard to get a picture of a man from the newspapers, isn't it?"

"It is, if he has a good press agent. And John could be very charming when he wanted to make the effort."

"So can you," I said. I stood up. "Move warily among your new playmates, won't you? Keep your guard up."

"I'll get by," she said. "Are you still going to look for the man who killed John?"

I nodded.

"He wasn't fit to live."

"We can't decide that. Good luck, Miss McCrea."

The sun was still shining and there was a slight breeze from the east. I drove over to my office and phoned the agent again.

I asked him, "Do you remember a Jean Morley?"

"Sure do. She committed suicide. Great young talent."

"Do you know anything about her brother?"

"Didn't even know she had one."

"Could you find out about him?"

"For how much?"

"For nothing," I said. "It's a charity case; I'm working for the public. Don't you ever do public service work?"

"Not unless there's a promotion angle."

"All right," I said. "Good day. To hell with you."

"Wait," he said. "Don't let your wop temper get the best of you. Some day I may need a little free investigating. I'll tell you what I'll do. I'll ask around among a few of Jean's friends. Okay?"

"Fair enough," I agreed. "Is Arnie Roman really the big man at *Verital?*"

"Right. I hope you don't plan to tangle with him. He's got too many strings to too many places, Joe."

"I'm shivering," I told him. "You let me know about Jean's brother. I'll be here at the office."

I was going over some statements when the phone rang. I thought it was my friend calling back, but it wasn't.

A feminine voice said, "This is Arnold Roman's secretary, Mr. Puma. Would it be possible for him to talk with you this afternoon?"

"I'm sure I can squeeze him in," I said. "Where does he want to talk to me and about what?"

"Here, at his office, at two o'clock?"

"I can make it. Is it business?"

"I—I imagine so, Mr. Puma. He only instructed me to arrange an appointment for this afternoon." She gave me the address.

"I'll be there," I assured her. "Thank you for calling."

I went back to the statements, and had addressed and sealed the hopelessly past due ones when my agent friend called back.

Jean Morley's brother, he informed me, worked at an auto body repair shop on Lincoln Boulevard and lived in Venice, in an apartment over a four car garage. He had both addresses for me.

"You're a noble man," I told him. "I hope I can repay you in kind, some day."

"We both do," he said. "What are you hounding this kid for?"

"I'm not. How do you know he's a kid?"

"One of my—informants told me he was on the sunny side of thirty. That's a kid to me. He also told me he served with John Haskell in the army. And with Haskell murdered and all, I thought you might have something I can sell to *Confidential.*"

"Who served with John Haskell, Morley or your informant?"

"Morley. My informant served under Teddy Roosevelt. Is there a column item in this business, Joe?"

"Not yet," I said. "If there turns out to be, you'll be the first to know, of course."

"Good boy. Got to feed the dirt, you understand, if I expect to get plugs."

"I understand," I said. "Carry on."

On the sunny side of thirty? How could he be and still have fought in a war that had ended eleven years ago? If he had been only nineteen when that war had ended, he would be thirty now. Of course, there had been some young ones who had lied about their ages. And for combat, the powers that decide had preferred the young ones. John Haskell had had two years of combat.

One of John Haskell's patterns was forming.

3.

The fat bald man in the office said, "He's out on a call right now. He's due back soon, though, if you want to wait."

I said I'd wait. I sat on a bench in the bare office, listening to the pounding of the lead mallets on body steel from the shop and studying the three identical Monroe calendars that hung on the wall. Cigar smoke from the office mixed with the smell of acetylene from the shop and I thought about the war.

So you're a kid from nowhere and you meet a wheel from Hollywood in the service and get to be buddies and when the killing is over, you move out here and look up your old friend and even introduce him to your sister. And your sister falls for the big wheel and he is no longer the nice guy you knew. And your sister commits suicide, so you take one of those leaden hammers and look up your old, big wheel service buddy.

On the phone, the fat man was saying, "Sure, that's wholesale. What the hell did you think it was?

"So, go to Acme. I'm crying for your business? Yeh? Well, I didn't get fat off you. I got fat off my wife's cooking, and she can stretch a buck from here to Topanga." He banged the receiver down, looked at me and shook his head.

"Another lost account," I said.

"Him? Hell, I've been talking worse than that to him for eighteen years. He'd think I was sick if I talked any other way."

I lighted a cigarette to combat his cigar. I said easily, "Has Arthur Morley been working for you long?"

"Five years. Good man. Real good man. He's not in any trouble, is he?"

"Not to my knowledge. How old is he?"

"Around thirty. He looks a lot younger, though. Before his sister died, he looked about eighteen. You a cop?"

"Private investigator," I answered. "I—do a lot of insurance work."

"Oh? The suicide clause, eh?"

"Not exactly," I said. "Arthur's sister was a lot younger than he was?"

"Five, six years, I'd guess. Pretty girl, if you like 'em skinny." He looked out toward the shop. "Morley just came in. You want to talk to him in here?"

"No need. I'll see him in the shop."

Arthur Morley was thin, like his sister had been. But he was taller and had light hair in a crew cut. I told him who I was and that I was investigating the death of John Haskell.

"For who?" he asked. "Who'd pay to find that out? He didn't have any friends."

"Weren't you a friend of his?"

"Not since my sister died. I didn't kill him, if that's why you're here. I thought of it, but what would it prove? I had all the killing I wanted in New Guinea."

"You served with Haskell there?"

"Under him. He was a first looie, a platoon leader. He was one hell of a fine soldier, too, I've got to admit. He lost some men, but never foolishly."

"That's the first nice thing I've heard about him today," I said. "When was the last time you saw him? "

"Four months ago, in a bar on Wilshire."

"I see. Where were you last night?"

"Bowling and then out for beers. I got a raft of guys that'll swear to that."

"Better get them alerted," I said. "There's a line the police can follow from a bartender to John Haskell to me to Miss McCrea and then to you. She told me you were in New Jersey, but I didn't believe her and I'm sure the police will check it."

"I'm not worried," he said.

"Miss McCrea has some strange new playmates, hasn't she? You ought to give her a serious talking to."

Arthur Morley shrugged. "She's old enough to know what she's doing. And nobody would call me a first-rate judge of character, not any more."

I could have asked him who his alibi friends were, but I wasn't too sure I was going to continue the search for Haskell's killer. When I did charity work, I had to have my heart in it. Haskell's death seemed less important than it had that morning.

It was past noon now and I was hungry. I drove over to the Santa Monica Pier for some sea food.

Actually, if that bartender had read the morning paper, the police should be almost on the same trail I had followed, but it would have started with me. Unless the bartender knew Lira McCrea. In which case, they would have started where I had started, with her.

I ate sea bass and thought back on my morning and ahead to my appointment with Arnie Roman. In the yacht basin, sails bellied and the fishing boats went out loaded. On the pier, the old men sat in the sun only half watching the bobbing floats on their lines.

The imitation red-head in the reception room told me that Mr. Roman would be free in a few minutes. I sat on a plastic upholstered chair and leafed through a copy of *Nugget*. There were some fine pictures in there; some were up to the trio on that body shop office wall.

In a few minutes a fat and expensively dressed man left Roman's office and the red-head smiled and told me I could go in now.

I went into a gray-carpeted office with dull gray walls and brightly colored drapes and upholstered furniture. It was more like a living room than an office.

Above the desk, there was an expensively framed reproduction of Shahn's "Miners' Wives." Beneath the picture, Arnold Roman was rising to greet me.

He was a big man with blue-black jowls and gray-streaked black hair, beautifully tailored and well barbered. He had come a long way from the two dollar girls.

His brown eyes looked at me warmly. "Mr. Puma. I know you by reputation."

"And I you," I said.

His grip was firm and strong. Black hair curled on his wrists below the French cuffs.

He indicated a chair and I sat in it. He sat down and said, "You've been busy this morning, haven't you?"

"I try to keep busy. I suppose Miss McCrea phoned you?"

He nodded. "And that's why you're here."

I looked past him to the picture above his head. I asked, "Did you ever work in the mines, Mr. Roman?"

"For seven years," he said. "I started when I was thirteen. How did you know that?"

"I just couldn't figure any other way you'd be a Shahn collector. A picture like that can keep a man driving, can't it?"

He looked at me quizzically. "I didn't make the appointment to discuss art, Mr. Puma."

I said nothing more, meeting his gaze and waiting.

He leaned back in his chair and gave me the executive look. "A few evenings ago, you had some trouble with an employee of mine. This trouble centered around a man who was murdered this morning. I don't like my employees to get into trouble."

I said nothing.

"Certain officials in this town are looking for an excuse to persecute me."

"Persecute or prosecute?"

His face stiffened. "Are you trying to be funny, Mr. Puma?"

I nodded. "I guess I missed, huh? Mr. Arnold, there's a bartender who knows me and knew Haskell who will undoubtedly tell the police about your employee with the glass jaw. The police will eventually come to me and I'll have to send them to Miss McCrea and she will lead them to my opponent, if she has any sense left. So why am I here?"

Roman carefully straightened an ebony ink well on his desk. He said casually, "The bartender won't tell the police anything. And I would like to hire you to investigate Haskell's death."

"Why?"

"To clear my employee, if that's the way the chips fall. To pin the murder on him, if that happens to be the way it is. I don't like my men to—engage in outside—activities."

"I see. And why should he want to kill Haskell?"

"I've no idea. I doubt if he did. But he is in love with Miss McCrea and there is a remote possibility he may have gone over to work Haskell over a little and—" Roman shrugged.

I asked, "Did you know Haskell?"

"Not really. Miss McCrea told me she brought him to a party at my house one time, but I don't remember meeting him."

"A famous man like that—you'd remember, wouldn't you?"

Roman smiled. "The last movie I saw starred Tom Mix. I was twelve years old."

I sat and he sat. Neither of us said a word for seconds.

Then he said, "Business must be good, Mr. Puma. Don't you want my account?"

"Yes. Two things bother me. First of all, the police don't like private men investigating murder cases. I've done it before and got away with it, but I've never done it for a man the police don't like. That's the second thing that bothers me."

"Five hundred dollars minimum," he said, "And your regular rate."

"You're talking my language. And if I learn something, I take it to the police?"

"If you learn who killed John Haskell you take it to the police. If you learn anything that might damage me, you had better not."

"There's the bind," I said.

He said nothing, sitting quietly in his chair, staring at me without expression.

Finally, I said, "All right."

He must have known how I would answer. Because the check was all made out. He smiled, and slid it across the desk toward me. "Miss McCrea assured me you couldn't be bought."

"But I can be rented," I said. "I'll get right to work on it."

The name of Roman's employee was Krup. This information plus Krup's address and three separate small photographs of him and his fingerprint card were in the sealed envelope the red-head handed me when I stopped at her desk. Krup, Eddie Krup, age thirty-four, weight a hundred and ninety-six, height five feet nine, complexion ruddy. Kenmore Apartments, Hollywood.

What an efficient man was Arnie Roman. And what did he have against Eddie Krup? There was still time to make the bank with the check, but I decided against cashing it. If things started to smell, I might be glad I still had the chance to return that check.

Was I being conned? Was I being paid off? If I spent a couple of days on a wild goose chase, it would be kind of late for me to run to the police with my story of the saloon fight.

I knew a couple of detectives in the Santa Monica Department; one of them might throw me a bone. I caught one off duty and at home, out in the front yard seeding his lawn with dichondra. He wasn't on the case, but he knew about it. The police had very little, so far. It was the work of a man they were certain and he had used a hammer, but there had been no motive established. Two fingerprints, one of them bloody, were still unidentified.

I thought of telling him about Arthur Morley, but decided that could wait.

He said, "What's your interest in this, Joe?"

"I knew Haskell. I admired him very much before the war."

His smile was skeptical.

"How about the fingerprints?" I asked, "the unidentified ones? You couldn't have checked with Washington yet."

"Not yet. That bloody one should be the clincher if Washington has a record of it."

And if the bloody one was Arthur Morley's, I thought, Washington would have a record of it. All the boys in the service had been fingerprinted.

4.

The *Kenmore Plaza Apartments* in Hollywood was an old building in good repair, located half a block north of Sunset. I was nosing along, looking for a parking space, when I saw Lira McCrea stepping from a Chev Bel Air parked on the other side of the street. She was heading for the apartment building.

I slowed and let her get by before driving on to find a space half a block past the building. From here, I could watch the entrance in my rear vision mirror. It was possible that she was going up to see her monster for an afternoon tryst.

But it was also possible that she was coming here to tell him about me. I waited.

I didn't wait long. The girl came out again less than ten minutes later, and Krup was with her. They climbed into her car.

In my mirror, I saw the Chev swing into a driveway for a U-turn, which would bring them past me. I ducked low in the seat. They turned west at the corner and I followed in the flivver.

They were taking the trip I had taken this morning, to Lincoln Boulevard in Venice. Had Arthur Morley phoned her after my visit to him? I doubted it. She could be coming to warn him about me, or, more likely, she and Krup could be visiting him in order to determine the possibility of Arthur's guilt. Krup had his own neck to consider.

It was an easy car to follow; I gave them a constant three block lead. At the body shop, the Chev turned into the parking lot. I drove past and parked at the curb half a block down.

I walked back on the far side of the street. Through the show window of the shop office, I could see Lira talking to the fat proprietor. Krup still sat in the car.

And now Arthur Morley came out with Lira and they walked over to the car. It seemed like a good time for me to make my entrance; I walked across the street.

I came at the right time. Their voices were rising when I reached the curb and Krup had stepped from the car by the time I got to the lot.

He looked menacing, but I couldn't be sure he was threatening Morley. Possibly, I might have irritated him.

In a few seconds, Morley and Lira turned to look at me, too. I smiled as I came closer.

Eddie Krup said something to Lira, then more loudly to me, "It's a private conference, peeper."

"I'll wait," I said. "I want to talk with Morley." I looked at Lira. "I thought he was in New Jersey."

Her eyes were scornful. "I don't have to tell you anything, Mr. Puma."

"It would have been better if you had," I said. "Because now you'll have to tell it to the police."

Krup said, "Beat it. I know who you're working for and you won't be going to the police."

"Don't make book on it," I said. "I'll wait until you've finished talking with Morley."

Arthur Morley said, "They're through right now, whether they know it or not. What did you want, Mr. Puma?"

"I want to know why they're here," I said. "And I want to know anything else you know about Haskell's death."

He looked at me defiantly. "I don't know anything about Haskell's death. I told you that before and I just finished telling them that. Now I'm going back to work and I don't want to see any of you again."

Krup said, "Take it easy, Morley. We haven't finished."

Arthur Morley turned his back on them and started for the office. Krup took two steps and reached a heavy hand out to spin the kid around.

Here I was, fighting Krup for somebody else again. I moved in, reached my own hand out for his shoulder—and he turned very neatly while I was off balance.

He hooked a clean left into my gut and caught me high on the cheek with a right. I brought over the big right hand from hip level, but it never got home. He tagged me like a professional, smack on the button, and I went down.

Well, you can't win 'em all.

I was drowning. The wave had been too high and the surf board too narrow. I took a deep gulp of the salt water and discovered it wasn't salty.

There was parking lot gravel in my hair and a numbness from my temple to the point of my chin. The sun was out again and I was propped in a sitting position up against the front bumper of a car. The fat proprietor stood in front of me, an empty bucket of water in his hand.

"You could have waited," I said. "There wasn't any time-keeper. I'd have come out of it without the water."

He said apologetically, "In the movies, they always use a bucket of water. What the hell, I'm not the Red Cross."

My shirt, jacket and the upper part of my trousers were soaked. To the left of the fat man, Arthur Morley looked down at me without expression.

"Did they leave?" I asked him.

He nodded. "You've been out for almost three minutes."

I climbed shakily to my feet and rubbed the back of my neck. "Last time we met, he was easy. I guess I was overconfident."

Morley's voice was quiet. "You know who he works for? For Arnold Roman. Man, you're on borrowed time, right now."

The fat man said, "Well, *somebody* has to work around here. Make it as quick as you can, Art; we're way behind." He left.

I said, "You can't think of me as a friend, I suppose? But I could have thrown your name to the law. Really, I tried to play ball with you, boy."

He said evenly, "I can't tell you what I don't know. And I don't know who killed John Haskell. If you want the names of the guys I bowled with, I'll give 'em to you."

"Give 'em to me," I said.

In the office, he wrote down the names of three men and copied their addresses out of the phone book. As he handed me the slip, he asked, "Are you going to tell the police about me?"

"Not yet. Maybe never." I didn't tell him that if his fingerprint was the bloody one, I wouldn't have to tell the police. They'd have him.

I went home and changed my clothes and then phoned Arnold Roman. I told him, "Your boy Krup just won a return engagement. And he seems to be investigating this murder himself. Are those your orders?"

"No."

"And he says he knows who hired me. How could he know that?"

"Did he say he knew it was me?"

"No, he just said he knew."

"He was lying. It was a tactical lie. Stay with it, Puma."

"Right." I hung up.

I wondered if Arnold Roman had lied to me. He, like all the hoodlums who owned Las Vegas, had an air of semi-respectability now. The so-called solid citizens had accepted the legality of Las Vegas and thus by implication accepted the hoodlums who were getting fat off the town. And this trash was coming into Los Angeles and buying into legitimate businesses, adding to their stature.

They were still hoodlums and Roman could right this minute be playing me for a patsy. He might have hired me for that reason. There was a strong possibility that I had made a bad decision.

So what was preventing me from giving him his money back and taking the whole sorry mess to the police?

Nothing was preventing me, really, nothing but my avarice.

I was hanging my wet jacket on a hanger in the kitchen, having decided to have dinner at home, when somebody rang my doorbell. A number of innocent people often ring my doorbell, but I took the .38 from the dresser drawer before going to the door. I kept it in a pocket, my hand on it.

A youth of about twenty stood there. He wore cotton gabardine trousers of a dirty tan and a checked gingham sport shirt.

"Mr. Joe Puma?" he asked.

I nodded.

"My name is Duane Putnam. Can I come in?"

Duane Putnam, indeed. He must have lifted it from an old theatre program. I held the door open wider and he came in, warily, like a cat in a new neighborhood, and stood not far from the doorway.

"What's on your mind, Duane?" I asked.

"Murder," he said.

They get that from TV, these cryptic, monosyllabic answers.

"Whose murder?" I asked.

He took a breath and said, "John Haskell's."

I said nothing, waiting for him to go on.

He took another breath. "I couldn't go to the police. I've had a—a little trouble myself, so I couldn't go to them. But I saw this guy, see, and I had to tell somebody—"

"What guy?"

"The guy that killed Haskell. I mean, I saw a guy leave there, last night, and he was carrying a thing that looked like a hammer, and he was sneaking along the empty lot next to the motel, and—"

"Hold it a second," I said. "Who sent you to me?"

He stared, discomfited. He looked toward the door. Finally, he said, "I was walking along Lincoln Boulevard a little while ago and I saw the guy, the same guy that came out of the motel last night."

"Where did you see him?"

"At that auto glass shop there, in the parking lot. He was with that blonde in the Chev Bel Air. I saw him hit you, so when you left, I followed. The way those guys in the shop talked to you, I figured you were a cop, so I asked them, and they told me who you were."

"You asked them and still picked up my trail? Duane, do you want to start over and make it reasonable this time?"

"Phone 'em," he said. "Right now, go ahead, ask 'em." His face was grim. "Phone the glass shop, go ahead."

"It wasn't a glass shop; it was a body shop," I corrected him. "Sit down. I'll phone them."

I phoned them and Arthur Morley answered. I asked him if Duane Putnam had talked to him about me.

"I don't know what the guy's name is," Morley told me, "but some young fellow came over right after you left and asked if you were a cop. I told him you were a private detective."

"Okay, Arthur, thank you," I said.

I hung up and studied Duane Putnam. I said, "I guess that part of it wasn't a lie. But the rest sure as hell was and you're making a serious mistake, lying about anything as important as murder. Duane, what kind of trouble did you have with the law?"

"That's not important."

"Yes, it is. Are you running from the law now?"

He shook his head.

"All right, then," I said, "I want you to tell the police what you told me."

He shook his head again.

"Be reasonable," I said patiently. "If we hope to convict the man, you'll have to go into court and point a finger. Otherwise, why did you bring me this information? Don't you want the man punished for his crime?"

He nodded. "I already pointed a finger. Aren't you a good enough detective to get the rest?"

"No, and neither are the police. There isn't any kind of police grilling that can break down a man like Eddie Krup. He's undoubtedly been through it all before, time and again. Duane, I insist that you go to the police with me, right now."

For the third time, he shook his head. And this time, he said, "no!"

"Yes," I said, and took out the .38.

His eyes went from the gun to my eyes and he smiled. "You wouldn't shoot me."

"If you try to leave, I will."

Again he looked warily at the door and then at me. His gaze dropped to the gun and he smiled once more. Maybe he wanted to get shot.

In any event, he broke for the door. He'd pegged me right; I didn't even aim the gun. I tried to intercept him before he got through the door, but he was too fast for me. He was nearly out the front door when I got to the head of the steps.

By the time I got to the door, a chopped and channeled '34 Ford coupe was gunning away from the curb in front. I didn't have anything that would catch that, nor could I read the license number from where I stood.

5.

I went back to my apartment and got the dossier on Eddie Krup that Roman had given me. I took the fingerprint card out of the envelope and drove back to the house of my Santa Monica Department friend.

He was still planting dichondra.

There was no name on the card. I gave it to him and said, "Check that against the bloody fingerprint you found. If it matches, phone me, and I'll give you the man's name."

"Why not give it to me, now?" he asked.

"I'm private, remember? P-r-i-v-a-t-e."

"You're also a citizen," he said. "I hope."

"A better citizen than you imagine."

I left him glowering and drove back to the poor man's edge of Beverly Hills. The Chev Bel Air was at the curb; I wondered if Eddie Krup was also there.

Eddie was there all right. Lira McCrea came to the door and beyond her I could see Eddie sitting on a studio couch.

"Now, what?" she asked.

"I came back for the rubber match with your fat boy friend," I told her. "I don't think he's that good."

"Get out of here," she said, "before I call the police."

"You'd better check with Eddie before you phone," I said. "He doesn't want any law here, I'll bet you."

From behind her, Krup said, "Let the slob come in. He doesn't scare me."

She opened the door wider and I came in, Krup didn't move from the studio couch.

"Do either of you know a Duane Putnam?" I asked.

Lira shook her head.

Krup said, "I've seen him play with the Rams. What the hell has he got to do with this mess?"

That's where I'd heard the name. The kid had picked it up from the sport pages. I said, "I don't mean that Putnam. I guess the man who approached me used a pseudonym."

Krup laughed and shook his head. "Dick Tracy. Oh, man, you are a cute one."

"Easy, shorty," I said. "Don't let that lucky punch give you delusions of grandeur. This man claims he saw you leave John Haskell's motel after Haskell was murdered. You were carrying a hammer and sneaking through that empty lot next to the motel."

Lira looked at Krup meaningfully.

Krup was sitting erectly now, interest in his face. "A man or a kid?" he asked.

"Never mind that. Eddie, if you did kill Haskell, you won't get any protection from where you might expect it. And if you didn't, but know something, you'd be very wise to tell me."

"Drop dead," he said. "What'd this Putnam look like?"

I took a card from my pocket. I read off a telephone number and said, "Phone that number and ask if you should cooperate with me."

"That's Roman's number," he said quietly.

"You should know it."

Krup looked at Lira and then back at me. "It's not a private number," he said. "Anybody can look up a phone number. When I get orders to cooperate with you, I will. So long, peeper."

"It's your decision," I said. "You wouldn't want to come outside for a title fight, would you? My vanity is suffering."

"I've got more important things to do," he told me. "Look, if this kid saw me, why didn't he take it to the police? Chew on that and see what you come up with."

"I didn't say he was a kid."

"So long," he said. "Don't lead with your chin."

I didn't bother to answer. I went out quietly.

So, Krup knew he was a kid. So, Lira had taken Krup in her car over to see Arthur Morley. That would indicate the death of John Haskell came from the Morley side of her life, not the Roman side. They were worried, no doubt, and that could mean Eddie was guilty. It could also mean Eddie would get dumped by Roman if enough suspicion for Haskell's death should be centered on Eddie.

For a man in Eddie's line of work, being dumped by Arnold Roman certainly wouldn't enhance his employment chances with other employers in Roman's field. So it could be the loss of Eddie's job that was bothering him, not the loss of his neck.

Duane Putnam . . . In my mind, I heard Eddie's laugh again and I could feel myself blushing. Duane Putnam had seen Eddie Krup leave the motel with a hammer in his hand. With a hammer in his hand. . . . Had there been anything in the papers about a hammer? I couldn't remember.

An item like that might very well be kept from the papers, because it could be a valuable item to use in a lie detector test and its value would be lost if it was an item of common knowledge.

I phoned my Santa Monica detective friend. He asked me to phone back in ten minutes; he'd find out what I wanted to know.

I phoned back in ten minutes and he told me the hammer item hadn't been given to the papers and it had been withheld from them deliberately, just as I had guessed. And it was still a secret and had better remain so or I might wind up working on a parking lot.

"You might, too," I said. "None of us are really versatile, are we?"

"No, but some of us are bright," he said.

I hung up and went out to the flivver. What did I have? This much: the man who called himself Putnam knew a hammer had been used. He didn't want to go to the police. He did want to pin the crime on Eddie Krup.

Now why would he want to do that? Either he had seen someone leave with a hammer or he had left with the hammer himself. But if he was the killer, why had he come to me? His bright move would be to get out of town, as far from this town as possible—unless he had relatives here, or friends who might be suspicious of his leaving. Maybe he was still living at home. Why had I thought he wasn't?

Back now. Why would he want to pin the crime on Eddie Krup?

Two reasons came quickly to my mind, to divert suspicion from himself or from a friend.

And who could his friend be? Elementary, Watson. I only had two real suspects. I drove back to Venice, to an apartment over a four-car garage, the home address the agent had given me.

I went up the outside steps and knocked on the door. I could hear music inside, and it sounded like it was coming from some very expensive hi-fi equipment. It was George Shearing's music.

Arthur Morley came to the door and looked at me wearily. "God," he said. "You, again. Look, Mr. Puma, I've had a hell of a day at the shop and I came home to relax. Can't you give me a break?"

"A man's been killed," I said.

"A lot of men have been killed. I killed over nineteen myself. And got a medal for it. Over half of my platoon was killed and all of them were better men than John Haskell."

"Maybe," I said. "But not better soldiers, I'll bet."

"The war's over," he said. "It's been over for eleven years."

"I'll bet he was a disciplinarian," I said. "I'll bet a lot of you guys hated his guts."

"Whose guts?"

"John Haskell's. *Lieutenant* John Haskell's."

Arthur Morley looked at me doubtfully. "So?"

"Let's go inside," I suggested, "where we can talk."

He shrugged and stepped aside and I came in. It was a roomy and comfortable apartment and I could see the ocean from the western windows of the room I was in. Roomy and comfortable and cheap; that's the kind of place you can get in Venice if you're not class conscious.

Shearing changed to Wallen. This man must love the piano, I thought. I asked, "Got any Tatum?"

"I got all the Tatum there is. Sit down, I'll bring you a beer."

He brought me a frosted can of eastern beer and I sat down in a comfortable canvas and wrought iron chair. He stretched out on what looked like a home-made couch, wide and long and low. To a man who had killed nineteen, the death of John Haskell was probably not very important. Otherwise, I was sure he wasn't completely dispassionate.

"Some life," I said. "I'll bet you have fun, single and handsome and right next to the beach."

"I'm not kicking. What's on your mind, Mr. Puma?"

"A kid," I said. "A kid who calls himself Duane Putnam."

"Never heard of him."

"Not under that name, I'm sure. He probably just gave it to me on the spur of the moment. It's the name of a football player."

"Oh. Why did he give you a phony name?"

"To protect himself. He also told me he saw me in front of an auto glass shop. He meant the place you work."

"We're not a glass shop; we're a body shop."

"I know that, and so did the kid. But he figured, in his story book detective way, that if he made a mistake like that, I wouldn't be inclined to guess he knew you."

Silence, and then, "What makes you think it was a *deliberate* mistake?"

"Any kid that can chop and channel and soup a '34 flivver knows a body shop from a glass shop. This kid also knew what kind of weapon Haskell was killed with."

Arthur Morley stretched and his voice was tired. "What kind was it?"

"I'm not permitted to tell you that. Do you know the boy, Arthur?"

"No."

"Then why should he want to protect you?"

"I don't need protection. I don't know him."

"And I don't think he even saw me in front of the shop," I went on. "I think he found out from you what had happened. Did you phone him after I left? I could ask your boss if the kid was a witness to my knockout. I can do it now."

"You think I'm lying? Why should I lie?"

"To protect him. To protect him from a conviction of murder, just as he tried to protect you from the suspicion of murder. He's a buddy of yours, isn't he?"

"I don't hang around with nineteen year old kids," he said. And then he was suddenly silent and I could hear him breathe.

"I didn't mention his age," I said. "Where is he, Arthur?"

"Finish your beer and beat it. Go to the police with your crazy story. I don't give a damn. I'm clean, *clean* . . ."

I sipped my beer. "The kid must have been eight years old when the war ended. So that couldn't be the reason. He sure as hell wasn't in the war."

Arthur Morley closed his eyes and said nothing.

"The police have a fingerprint," I said. "A *bloody* fingerprint. It's just a question of time. What is the kid, psychopathic or something? Is he your brother?"

Morley's voice was soft. "Did Haskell ever get to you with that pattern kick of his, that pre-determination jag he was on?"

"A little."

Morley sat up. "I need a beer. Then I'll give you a silly pattern to chew on, an eleven year pattern."

He got himself a beer and came back to sit on the edge of the low, wide couch.

He told me the story of Patsy Lankowski, private in the platoon commanded by Lieutenant John Haskell. Patsy was a sorehead and a grumbler, but quite possibly the best combat scout in the 32nd Division and John Haskell knew it. Patsy got all the dirty assignments, but never a rating beyond Pfc.

And home in Waukesha, Wisconsin, Patsy's mother got his growling letters, complaining of the persecution his Lieutenant was inflicting on him, and swearing that if he ever came out of this thing alive, he would look up the good lieutenant and give him the pasting of his life.

And more than once, he had added that if he didn't come out of this thing alive, Lieutenant John Haskell would be to blame, and he wanted the world to know it.

"And Patsy didn't come out of it alive?" I asked.

Arthur Morley smiled. "Sure he did. He's selling insurance in Iowa, right this minute. I just used that name, another member of our sad platoon. The guy who really hated Haskell and really wrote the letters home, his name wasn't Lankowski and he didn't live in Waukesha, Wisconsin. But he had a brother, and the brother reads the letters that had been written to his mother."

"And held a grudge for eleven years? He *must* be psychopathic." I finished the beer. "This man, of course, didn't come out of the war alive."

Morley said, "He died on a patrol. He hadn't volunteered for the patrol. The mother didn't show her other son the letters. But when she died, a month ago, the brother found them."

"And he came out here," I guessed, "looking up the men from his big brother's platoon. And from you, he got the story of the further adventures of Lieutenant John Haskell. And from comic books, he got some distorted ideas of justice and vengeance. Where is he now, Arthur?"

He smiled and shook his head.

"My God," I said, "John Haskell was *murdered*. What kind of man are you?"

"A 32nd Division kind," he said. "Murder is nothing new to us. Where were you when all that was going on?"

"In the 7th Division," I said. "Maybe you've heard of them?"

"I've heard of them," he admitted quietly, "and I apologize."

"And you're a citizen now," I reminded him. "You're not a soldier or a professional veteran or a judge or the swift arm of vengeance. You're a citizen, quite possibly the most important thing a man can ever be."

He shook his head. *"The most important thing a man can be is a friend.* I learned that the hard way. And there aren't enough cops in this world to ever make me anything less than that." He stood up. "I told you this to get you off the kid's neck. I figured you weren't the law and would listen to reason."

"I'm the law," I said. "Sit down; I want to check your closets."

"Why?"

"To see if the kid's clothes are here. He's been staying with you, hasn't he?"

"I don't know what you're talking about," he said. "If you want to look around, come back with a warrant."

"Don't mess with me, Arthur," I said. I started for the bedroom.

He came over to stand in front of the open bedroom doorway. "You're going to have to fight your way in here."

"Don't be ridiculous," I said.

"You've forgotten my sister," he said. "What about her?"

"I'm sorry about her. But a man's been killed. If that isn't important to you, you never learned anything, in New Guinea or any place else. Stand aside. This is the last warning."

"Start swinging," he said, and lifted his hands.

He'd killed nineteen men, but that had been with a rifle. I could have hit him five times while he drew back his right hand. I only hit him once, clean and neat and on the button and I caught him as he fell, lowered him gently to the floor.

I have a lot of respect for 32nd Division men.

And I saw the shadow in the bedroom and then the fury hit me as I came through the door. And this one bit and clawed and used his knees and grunted and used words no nineteen year old should know.

But I subdued him, finally, and dragged him with me to hold while I phoned the Santa Monica Police.

In the neat office of the Chief, Sergeant Koski glowered and chewed his lower lip and the Mayor frowned and the Chief looked at all of us blandly. He was the bland type, fat and smug.

Koski said, "The fingerprint matches. The kid's ready to confess, anyway."

"What's his name?" I asked.

"Lestre Burkholtz. German kid. He's from Eau Claire, Wisconsin."

"And what've you got against Arthur Morley, Chief?" I asked with a sneer.

The Mayor said, "Don't be insolent, Joe. Chief Roeder is simply trying to do his duty."

"That's all I want from him is his duty," I said. "I did mine. I came in with a killer, didn't I? I could have turned him over to the Los Angeles Police; I picked him up in Venice, and that would make him their baby. I brought him here because I thought maybe Arthur Morley would get a break. And I'm staying until he does."

Chief Roeder smiled his smug smile. "Mr. Puma, I run the police department here. And in Santa Monica, we don't toy with accessories to murder. In Santa Monica, we like everything tied up neat and clean."

I looked at him pityingly. I said, "And I'm going to sit in Santa Monica until you change your mind or your district attorney is going to look awful silly in court when I tell the jury Morley wasn't even home when I picked up Burkholtz."

The Mayor said, "You'd perjure yourself? Joe, I thought you were a citizen?"

"I am," I said. "But I'm something almost as important, too. I'm a friend. God forbid I should have to explain that word to a politician."

There was a lot of hemming and hawing and political double talk after that, but it was meaningless and we all knew it. At seven-thirty, Arthur and I stood on the front steps of that big, new municipal building, looking out toward the ocean.

The ocean made me think of eternity which, in turn, brought the late John Haskell to mind. In spite of all that I had recently learned about the man, my feeling at the moment wasn't harsher than pleasant reminiscence.

"Patterns," I said. "What do you think, Arthur? You think the individual can get away from a pattern?"

Arthur shrugged. "Don't know if I get what you mean."

"Skip it," I told him.

"After what you just did for me, I'll go along with anything you say."

I smiled and we went down the steps together, arm in arm.

The Geniuses

Max Franklin (Richard Deming)

June 1957

Even after our explanation, no one seems to understand why we did it. For example, this appeared in the *Star:*

Stripped of its high-flown vocabulary, the statements of teen-age killers Barton Conway and Edward Bolling boil down to the crime being nothing more nor less than a psychotic thrill kill. *The* Star *completely missed the point that our act was an intellectual exercise, you see. They lumped Bart and me in the same class as the juvenile delinquent who carries a switch-blade knife.*

Another thing we resent, or at least I do, is the newspaper attempt to make me seem a kind of stooge of Bart's. They point to Bart's higher scholastic average as proof that he was the superior and guiding intellect. But if the Stanford-Binet test means anything, actually I'm the more intelligent. My intelligence quotient is 163, while Bart's is only 160.

Both I. Q.s rate the designation of genius, of course.

Bart's grades in high school and college were higher than mine because he studied harder. Being able to draw high grades without study, it never occurred to me to work for even higher ones. Besides, Bart is competitive and I'm not. It was important to him to be the top scholar, and it wasn't important to me. I was quite content to be salutatorian of our high-school graduation class, and to let Bart make valedictorian.

Maybe this does indicate that I tended to play second fiddle to Bart, but I was never conscious of being dominated. I simply regarded him as my best friend. Because our superior intelligence set us apart from others our own age, we were inseparable all through grade school, high school and our two years of college.

The newspapers have made a big thing of our failure to enter into campus social life, as though this indicated some psychological shortcoming on our part. We didn't participate in campus events at Rayburn for the same reason we didn't join a fraternity: because we considered both juvenile. But we had a social life of our own making.

Considering our mental attainments, it was natural for the campus intelligentsia to gather about us. It was also natural for the meeting place to be the three-room apartment Bart and I shared, for we were the only members of the group with money enough to afford an apartment. The rest were all from poor families, and lived either in dormitory rooms or rooming houses.

The so-called campus elite hardly ever visited our apartment . . . the athletes, the "activity men" or the fraternity and sorority crowd . . . but we were surrounded by young poets and writers and scholars. It was common for a half dozen or more people to be lying about on cushions in our large front room of an evening, listening while Bart played classical records, or read poetry aloud, or discoursed on anything from ancient literature to the current world situation.

It was at one of these sessions during our sophomore year that the seed for our threat experiment was sown. Six of us were present that night.

Only five of us really belonged, however. The sixth was as out of place in that intellectual society as a harlot in a nunnery.

There was serious-minded Calvin Thorpe, who was majoring in philosophy, and mousy little Annabelle Stang, the hopeful poetess he went with. I had Marge Ridgeway, whom I tentatively regarded as my girl, a beautiful freshman with a golden complexion and a fine mind, for a woman. She was just my age, eighteen, though a year behind me in school.

Bart Conway, as always, presided over the group. He sat enthroned on his red-leather chair while the rest of us lolled on floor cushions at his feet, listening to him expound and watching the play of expression on his thin but sensitive face.

All of us but Herman Groper, that is. Herman was the outsider, the big, blond, over-muscled captain of our football team. He had been dragged along by Calvin Thorpe, who was tutoring him in philosophy in his spare time in an effort to keep Groper eligible for football.

Groper had refused to sit on the floor. He sat on the sofa to one side of Bart's chair with a bored look on his face.

The discussion that night had started with a murder currently in the headlines, but Bart had drifted off into a philosophical dissertation on murder in general.

"A little reasoning would show you that the old bromide, 'Murder will out,' is merely an attempt to deter potential murderers from carrying out their murderous intentions," Bart said. "I doubt that one murder in ten is ever detected."

"Statistics don't show that," Calvin Thorpe objected. "The percentage of solved cases in a city such as New York far outweighs the unsolved."

"For cases diagnosed as murder," Bert agreed. "But what about all the homicides officially accepted as suicides, accidents, or as deaths from natural causes? How many men do you suppose have given their wives a slight push at the top of a flight of stairs, and have had the resulting broken necks diagnosed as accidents? How many poisonings go undetected? How many persons listed on police blotters merely as missing are actually murder victims whose killers have so cleverly disposed of the bodies that there are no *corpus delicti?* The perfect crime isn't merely an unsolved crime. It's one in which the police never suspect a crime has been committed."

Big Herman Groper gave a bored snort. "There's no such thing as a perfect crime. The prisons are full of people who thought different."

Bart glanced at him with a frown. He had been ignoring the football captain ever since his refusal to sit on the floor with the rest of us, and now his expression indicated that he felt if Groper couldn't conform to our ritual, he shouldn't try to intrude himself into the discussion. However, since no one else spoke, Bart decided to answer him.

"That's because the average murderer is a fool," he said. "I could plan and execute a dozen murders without ever being suspected."

Herman Groper spread his lips in a sardonic grin. "Because you're a genius, I suppose?"

Bart's nostrils flared ever so slightly, an indication that he was nettled. No one can match Bart Conway's repartee, and because Groper was a guest, I decided to save him from annihilation by throwing a lighter gaff into him than Bart would use.

I said, "Of course he's a genius. You sound as though that's something to be ashamed of."

Marge Ridgeway did her bit to avert the football captain's devastation too. She asked, "Just how would you go about committing the perfect crime, Bart?"

Glancing at her, Bart's good humor returned. He said lightly, "If I told you, my redheaded doll, you might use the information in evidence against me, if I ever decided to put it to real use."

Herman Groper said, "In other words, he hasn't the slightest idea."

Bart swung back toward the blond athlete, and this time I didn't try to save Groper.

"Don't push me, my muscular friend," Bart said in a soft voice. "I just might decide to indulge in the mental exercise, and use your handsome body as a guinea pig."

Herman Groper ran his eyes over Bart's spare frame and laughed aloud. "I'm trembling in my boots."

Annabelle Stang said, "This conversation has given me an inspiration. I think I'll write a poem about death."

Shortly afterward the group broke up and I walked Marge back to the girl's dormitory. When I returned, Bart was in his pajamas and robe, smoking a bedtime cigarette.

"I think we'll start an investigation of Herman Groper's living routine tomorrow, Edward," he told me. "Suppose you cut class and follow him all day. I'll take the next day, and we'll continue to alternate until we know his exact routine."

"What in the devil for?" I asked.

"So we can sensibly plan his murder."

I looked at him with my jaw hanging. "His murder!"

"As an intellectual exercise only," he told me impatiently. "I don't actually plan to kill him. But I want to satisfy myself that I could, and get away with it."

"Oh," I said. Thinking it over, I decided this was one of the most provocative ideas Bart had produced in some time.

"It would be kind of interesting to plan the big lout's murder, wouldn't it?" I said.

2.

For the next two weeks Bart and I alternated in trailing Herman Groper everywhere he went. Both of us had high enough averages so that we could afford to miss some classes, but this period put a decided crimp in our social life. It was, of course, necessary to suspend the discussion periods at our apartment for two weeks. In addition I had to neglect Marge Ridgeway so much that she finally asked if I were angry about something.

I made the excuse that I was studying hard, but she accepted it rather coolly. As Christmas was approaching, I decided to buy her some exceptionally nice gift to make up for my neglect.

At the end of our two-week investigation we had an hour-by-hour schedule of Herman Groper's routine. He lived an extremely methodical life. He was carrying sixteen hours of work, and he never missed a class. Free periods he invariably spent at the Student Union, and he always lunched at the Chi Phi house, where he lived. Five afternoons a week he spent at football practice, and Saturday afternoon he was either playing in a game at our stadium, or at one of the other schools in the conference.

His evenings followed just as exact a pattern. On Mondays, Wednesdays and Fridays he studied at the school library with a sophomore Tri Delt named Alice Taylor, who seemed to be his steady girl. He always walked her to the Tri Delt house when the library closed at nine, then went straight home to the Chi Phi house just up the street. On Tuesdays he met Calvin Thorpe at the library for tutoring in philosophy, and again went straight home when the library closed. Thursdays he didn't leave the fraternity house at all in the evening.

Presumably because of football training rules he didn't go out socially at all during the week. Both Saturday nights, after the game, he took Alice Taylor to a school dance, but they left early and Groper was back at the Chi Phi house by midnight, again presumably because of training rules.

Apparently he didn't attend church, for on both Sundays he didn't appear from the Chi Phi house until one-thirty. Both times he went straight to the Tri Delt house, picked up Alice Taylor, and they spent the afternoon at a show. They dined downtown afterward, spent a couple of hours at a local student hangout, and were home by nine-thirty.

Bart Conway ruefully summed up what we had learned.

"He doesn't seem to run around with his fraternity brothers at all," he said. "Every free minute he's with this Taylor woman. The problem is that he's never alone. When he isn't with her, he's surrounded by his fellow morons on the football team, or in the midst of fifty fraternity brothers at the Chi Phi house."

I said, "He's alone for a few minutes four nights a week on his way back from the library."

"Yeah, in full view of dozens of students also returning from the library, on one of the best-lighted streets in town. And even if we managed to kidnap him then, he keeps such a rigid schedule, he'd be missed almost immediately."

We brooded over the problem for a while, and finally Bart said, "Herman's the only football player Chi Phi has, isn't he?"

"I believe so," I said. "In fact I'm sure of it."

"Then when he goes home to bed at midnight on Saturday, the chances are he's the only Chi Phi in the house."

"Probably," I agreed. "Fraternity men rarely stay home on Saturday night, and most of the dances last till two. But the house mother would be there."

"And undoubtedly asleep. We could be waiting inside when he came in, force him to leave with us by the back door, and no one at all would see us."

"Force him how?" I asked dubiously. "He's an awfully big man."

"With a gun," Bart said impatiently. "My twenty-two target pistol."

"Suppose he put up a fight anyway?"

"Then we kill him right there and carry him out dead," Bart said.

I emitted a rather uneasy laugh. "You know, we sound as though we really meant to carry this out."

"Don't be ridiculous," Bart told me. "You know it's just an intellectual problem."

There was nothing more we could do in the way of planning until the following Saturday, when we decided to test our kidnap plan with a dry run. I took Marge Ridgeway to shows on both Thursday and Friday so that I could beg off from a Saturday night date. She seemed a little put out, but she didn't make any outright objection.

Both Bart and I had cars at school, but we used Bart's this Saturday night. We parked in the alley behind the Chi Phi house at eleven-fifteen, and waited another fifteen minutes.

We didn't have any trouble getting into the house. Because members come in at all hours, fraternity houses are never locked at Rayburn. We simply opened the door and walked in.

There wasn't a soul on the first floor, although a lamp was on in the huge front room. Tiptoeing up the stairs, we quietly checked every room and found all empty except one. This was the house mother's, who was sound asleep when we edged open her door and peeked in.

Actually we weren't taking any risk by this prowling. It was common for non-member students to wander into fraternity houses in search of friends who were members, and as we both knew several Chi Phis, we had it planned in advance to announce we were looking for one of them if anyone questioned us.

When we were satisfied that the house was deserted except for the sleeping housemother, we took up a vigil at the front-room windows downstairs and waited for Herman Groper to appear. We spotted him approaching the house at five minutes of midnight.

As all we had wanted was to prove the practicality of our kidnap plan, we quietly let ourselves out the back door before Groper could open the front.

When we got back home, Bart said, "Monday we'll take up the problem of disposing of the body."

"Why not tonight?" I asked.

"Because meat markets aren't open at this time of night," he said.

He refused to elaborate on this odd remark. Sometimes Bart liked to be mysterious.

At four o'clock Monday, when I got home from school, Bart was waiting for me with a small, newspaper-wrapped package.

"Let's go," he said. "We'll take my car."

"Where we going?" I asked.

"To experiment in body disposal."

He wouldn't tell me any more, and as I knew he enjoyed keeping me in suspense, I didn't persist in asking for an explanation. He drove straight to the campus and parked next to the Science Building.

As lab sessions ended at three p.m., no one was in the building except a couple of professors in their offices, both of whom glanced at us vaguely and without interest when we passed their open doors. Bart led me to the locked door of one of the chemistry labs, produced a key from his pocket and unlocked the door.

"Where'd you get that?" I asked in surprise.

He grinned at me. "From Professor Jacobs. I asked him if I could do a little special research on my own time, and he handed over a key like a little lamb. That's one of the advantages of being an honor student. Jacobs wouldn't trust another member of the class with a key."

Inside he closed the door behind us and walked to the hood at one side of the room. The hood was simply a sheet-metal awning suspended over a long laboratory bench and vented by a chimney to carry off chemical odors. Smelly experiments and high-degree heat experiments were carried out under the hood.

A portion of the experiment bench beneath the hood was taken up by a small electric furnace. The chamber was only a foot wide by a foot high and two feet deep, but it was capable of generating up to twenty-five hundred degrees Fahrenheit.

It was designed to receive small crucibles of fusible material, not to dispose of corpses. But we used it for the latter purpose. We burned the body of the freshly dressed rabbit Bart had in his newspaper package.

The furnace made an excellent miniature crematorium. There was nothing left of the rabbit except a small pile of powdery ashes. We disposed of the ashes by flushing them down one of the drains in the rest room just down the hall.

"There," Bart said with an air of satisfaction when the last of the ashes gurgled down the drain. "That completes our problem. The muscular Herman Groper has disappeared into thin air."

With a touch of sarcasm I said, "Small for a football star, wasn't he?"

When Bart frowned at me, I said, "I'll concede that you've demonstrated the effectiveness of cremation, but where would we obtain access to a furnace big enough to take Herman Groper's body?"

Bart shook his head in mock pity. "For a supposed genius you can ask awfully stupid questions, Edward. We use this furnace right here."

I gave him a blank look.

"We feed him to it in small sections," he explained patiently. "We dismember him in the bathtub at the apartment and carry him to the lab in small, inconspicuous parcels. We take perhaps two or three afternoons to complete the job."

"Oh," I said in a dubious tone.

Perhaps if I had sounded more enthusiastic, the matter would have ended right there, with Bart satisfied that he had solved the intellectual problem of planning a perfect crime. But we had known each other so long and so well, we were each sensitive to the nuances of meaning in the other's tone. Bart knew I wasn't satisfied with the solution and, being a perfectionist, he wasn't either.

We didn't discuss it any more, but he was silent all the way home and moody during dinner. I had a date with Marge that evening, and when I got home about eleven, he was still brooding.

After watching me hang up my coat, he said, "You don't think we've really solved the problem, do you?"

I said, "If it satisfies you, it satisfies me."

"That's the trouble with a hypothetical problem," he said irritably. "You arrive at an answer, but there's no way to prove it's the right answer."

"We could really kill him," I said with heavy irony.

"Yes," he agreed so calmly, my stomach suddenly lurched. "That's exactly what we're going to do."

As I said, we've known each other so long, we were unusually sensitive to each other's tones of voice. I knew instantly that he wasn't joking. I knew that for his own intellectual satisfaction Bart had decided he had to commit the perfect crime in actuality.

I also knew our leader-follower relationship well enough to realize that while I might struggle against the idea for a time, in the end Bart would have his way. And that I'd help him commit real murder as docilely as I had helped him commit it in theory.

3.

I won't give a blow-by-blow account of my attempt to argue Bart out of his murder plan. It suffices to say that after two days of his countering every objection I made with logical argument, he finally wore me down. As usual when we had one of our rare disagreements, it was his persistence more than his eloquence which defeated me. I finally just gave up.

I recall that at one point Bart said, "It's not as though Herman Groper would be any loss to humanity, Edward. The man's about as unimaginative as they come. And consider the gratification of knowing that we, personally, have overcome the tremendous problem of committing a perfect crime. It will be a contest between our superior intellects and all the mediocre forces of society. How can you even hesitate at such a challenge?"

"All right," I said wearily. "When are we going to do it?"

He emitted a sigh of satisfaction. "This coming Saturday. It has to be then because Christmas vacation starts the following weekend."

Like many geniuses, I have a capacity for single-mindedness once I have reached a decision. From the moment I finally agreed to the murder, I shelved all my previous doubts and entered into the spirit of the thing wholeheartedly.

If it seems unnatural that neither of us had a single qualm of conscience once our decision was reached, you must remember that this was neither a crime of passion nor one for profit. We had nothing personal against Herman Groper. He merely presented an interesting problem, and there was no more emotion involved than if we had been presented with a difficult chess problem.

As our plans were already laid, and even to some extent pretested, there remained nothing to do until Saturday except obtain some necessary equipment. Bart bought some .22 shorts for his target pistol, and he had me purchase a set of meat-cutting tools, including a cleaver. Then we were ready for our great experiment.

Meantime, while waiting for Saturday to arrive, we attended class as usual, and we got most of our Christmas shopping done. For Marge I bought a delicate little wrist watch with a solid-gold case.

Eventually Saturday came.

Again we parked in the alley behind the Chi Phi house at eleven fifteen p.m., and slipped through the rear door at eleven thirty. As during our previous visit, we found no one there except the sleeping house mother. We took our positions at the parlor windows and waited for Herman Groper to come home.

As before, he arrived just before midnight. We waited until he had closed the front door behind him and was heading for the stairs. Then, together, we stepped from the front room into the hall.

"Just a moment, Herman," Bart said in a soft voice.

With his foot on the bottom step, the football captain turned. He looked incredulous when he saw the pistol in Bart's hand.

"Don't make any noise, and do exactly as I tell you," Bart said crisply. "If you think I won't use this, you're very foolishly mistaken."

Groper studied him with narrowed eyes, finally asked in an uncertain tone, "Have you gone nuts?"

Deliberately Bart cocked the gun, and the sound seemed unnaturally loud in the stillness of the big house. Groper's eyes widened.

"I'm not making any noise," he said. "What do you want?"

"Move that way," Bart said, gesturing down the hall toward the kitchen with his pistol.

Groper hesitated, his gaze shifting from Bart to me and back again. Then he paled slightly when Bart allowed his finger to begin whitening on the trigger.

"For God's sake, don't shoot!" he said quickly. "I'll do what you say."

We took him out the back way and got him into the rear seat of the car without incident. Bart sat next to him with the gun pointed unwaveringly at his head, and I drove.

There was no one on the street when we parked in front of our apartment. After I had made a quick check in both directions, and had given the signal that all was clear, Bart backed from the car and ordered Groper to get out. I went first to open the door while Bart prodded our captive ahead with his gun muzzle.

Inside, Groper asked on a high note, "What is this all about anyway?"

"It's an intellectual exercise," Bart told him pleasantly. "Get on into the bathroom."

With more puzzlement than fear Groper followed orders. While he was treating us with a wariness indicating that he suspected he might be dealing with a pair of maniacs, I don't think that at any point he was really in fear of his life. I believe he thought the whole thing was some kind of elaborate and unfunny practical joke.

He discovered it was too late to do anything about it. The instant he stepped through the bathroom door, Bart placed the muzzle of his gun against the back of Groper's head and pressed the trigger.

Even in that confined space the sound of the shot wasn't loud enough to attract any attention from outside. It was simply a sharp crack, as though a medium-sized board had been dropped to the floor from ceiling height. Herman Groper's toppling body made nearly as much noise when it hit the tile floor.

He lay inert, a small singed place on the back of his head ringing an almost invisible dot of blood. That was the only visible sign of damage, as there was no exit wound.

Within minutes we had him stripped and had lifted his body into the tub. Then the real job began.

First we both stripped in order to avoid blood stains on our clothing. Then, with the meat-cutting tools I had bought, we proceeded to butcher the body.

Though neither of us knew much about meat cutting, we didn't have a great deal of trouble because the tools were new and sharp. I won't go into details about our revolting chore, because thinking about it still gives me a queasy feeling in my stomach. It suffices to say that we ended up with ten separate packages, each first wrapped in waxed paper and then with newspaper.

Each arm, divided into two parts, went into a separate package, the two calves and feet into another, and the two thighs into individual packages. In order to have pieces small enough to get in the furnace, we had to quarter the torso and wrap each of the four parts separately. The head made up the tenth bundle.

Spreading waxed paper and newspaper on the floor at the back of our clothes closet, we stacked the ten parcels there.

It was beginning to grow light by the time we had cleaned up the bathroom, had washed our meat cutting tools and had each had a bath. Exhausted, we fell into bed and slept until noon.

Sunday afternoon we began the task of disposing of the *corpus delicti*. We started with the arms, each carrying one package out to the car.

The Science Building was completely deserted on Sunday, of course, so there was no danger of our being disturbed. By dinnertime we had made two trips, and both arms and both calves had been reduced to ashes and flushed down one of the rest room drains.

We suspended operations until the next day then, as we didn't want to risk anyone seeing lights in the chemistry lab and coming to investigate.

On Monday we had to wait until four p.m. in order to be sure the lab would be empty. We got in two more trips and disposed of both thighs, one section of torso, and the clothing Herman Groper had worn when he died. There now remained only the head and three sections of the torso.

Although it wasn't yet publicly known, we later learned that meantime preliminary efforts were already being made to locate the missing man. He had first been missed at two p.m. on Sunday, when Alice Taylor phoned the Chi Phi house to learn why Groper hadn't shown up for their usual Sunday-afternoon date. Both she and the Chi Phi's were more puzzled than alarmed at first, however, and the matter wasn't reported to the police until late that night.

The local police, who had had previous experience with missing students who later turned out simply to have gone on prolonged binges, or to have overstayed weekends at home, did nothing in the beginning except wire a routine inquiry to Groper's home town. It wasn't until Tuesday morning, when the missing man's football coach visited the police, that they began to take a serious interest. They hadn't paid too much attention to Alice Taylor's insistence that Herman Groper's systematic habits ruled out the possibility of the disappearance being his own doing, apparently attributing it to female hysteria. But when the coach insisted the same thing, they began to give serious thought to the possibility that there had been foul play.

They got around to Bart and me Tuesday night.

Meantime we had used Tuesday afternoon for two more trips to the lab, and had disposed of the three remaining segments of the torso. Nothing remained but the head, which we transferred from the floor of the closet to a hat box on the closet shelf, so that we could dispose of the papers with which we had lined the closet floor.

We were wrapping Christmas presents on a table in the front room when our bell rang about nine p.m. Tuesday night. Bart went to the door and came back followed by two men in police uniforms.

One was a beefy, rather stupid-looking fellow who seemed to be merely a patrolman. The other wore the gold badge of a lieutenant, which, except for the chief, was as high as police ranks went in this small college town. He was a quiet-spoken man of about forty with a lean, intelligent face and a slow manner of moving. He introduced himself as Lieutenant Gunderson, and his companion as Patrolman Murphy.

When they had accepted Bart's invitation to sit, Lieutenant Gunderson said, "Have you boys heard about Herman Groper yet?"

We both looked at him inquiringly, and Bart said, "Rayburn's over-muscled football captain? What about him?"

"He's been missing since midnight Saturday."

"Oh?" Bart said, and waited.

"We wondered if either of you boys might have seen him."

Both of us assumed surprised expressions. Bart said, "Why do you ask us? We barely know the fellow. He has fifty fraternity brothers more likely to know where he is than we are."

In no particular tone Gunderson said, "There's some suspicion that he might have met with foul play."

A long silence ensued before Bart said in an ascending voice, "And you suspect us?"

"Suspect is a little too strong a word," the lieutenant said. "Let's say we just wonder if you decided to carry out your brag that you could commit a perfect crime."

I felt the hair rise along the back of my neck. Bart appeared momentarily speechless. When he finally found his voice, it came out unusually high.

"What brag was that?"

"The one you made one evening when Herman Groper was here at one of your bull sessions. You bragged that you were capable of committing a perfect crime, and suggested you might use Groper as your guinea pig."

"Who told you that?"

"Groper's girl friend. Alice Taylor."

I blurted, "She wasn't here that night."

Everyone looked at me, the two officers without expression, and Bart frowningly. Realizing the remark constituted an admission that Bart had made the alleged statement, I slowly turned red.

I decided to let Bart carry the conversational burden from there on.

"No, she wasn't," Gunderson agreed quietly. "But Groper told her all about it afterward. Then, several times recently, he's mentioned to her seeing an awful lot of both of you. He suggested to Miss Taylor that you might be tailing him around for some reason. Seems every time he looked over his shoulder, one or the other of you were just fading behind a tree."

So much for our expertness as shadows, I thought.

"All in all, we figured it might be worthwhile talking to you boys," the lieutenant went on. "Mind if Murphy and I take a look around your flat?"

When both of us merely stared at him, he produced a paper from his pocket and added casually, "On the off chance that you might have some objection, we brought along a search warrant."

4.

I don't know whether my expression changed or not, but my heart began hammering so hard, I was afraid the beat could be heard. If the stupid-looking Patrolman Murphy had come alone, there would have been at least a chance that he would neglect peeking into the hatbox in the closet. But I had no hope that a police officer who obviously knew his business as well as Lieutenant Gunderson would miss it.

If only we had risked a light in the lab just once, *I thought despairingly.*

Bart was saying in an entirely calm voice, "Go right ahead, Lieutenant. But certainly you don't expect to find Herman Groper here, do you?"

Rising, the only answer the lieutenant gave was a shrug. "I'll take this room and the bedroom," he said to Murphy. "You take the kitchen and bath."

With a nod Murphy rose and entered the small interior hall which connected with the kitchen and bath. Bart and I sat and watched Lieutenant Gunderson begin a systematic search of the front room.

After a few moments Bart rose and walked into the bedroom. Gunderson glanced after him, then followed to the bedroom door. My heart went to my throat when I heard the closet door open.

What on earth is Bart trying to do? *I wondered.*

The lieutenant backed from the doorway in order to let Bart re-enter the front room. I looked at Bart in horror when I saw he was carrying the hatbox in his hands.

"You don't mind if we continue with our gift wrapping, do you?" Bart asked the lieutenant casually.

Gunderson shrugged. With a bare glance at the hatbox, he went back to his interrupted search.

Carrying the box over to the table, Bart selected a large sheet of holly paper, neatly wrapped it and tied it with red ribbon. He built an elaborate bow with more ribbon and tied that on.

Momentarily pausing in his search, Gunderson said, "Pretty fancy package. For somebody special?" "For Edward's girl," Bart said. "I have to wrap it because his packages always look as though they'd been kicked down a flight of stairs."

He glanced at me. "How about making out the gift tag?"

I suddenly realized that Bart was enjoying the dangerous situation because it gave him a chance to pit his genius against that of the police. If he hadn't been enjoying it, he would simply have wrapped the package and unobtrusively laid it beneath the table with the other wrapped gifts. But he had to drag out the drama by making an elaborate show of it.

A little unsteadily I got up, went to the table and picked out one of the stringed tags which lay there in a pile. With my fountain pen I wrote, "To Marge, with love, from Edward."

Bart tied it to the package and set the box beneath the table with the other gifts.

Murphy came into the room and said, "How about this, Lieutenant?"

We all turned to look at him, and my heart again jumped to my throat. He was holding the cleaver, bone saw and large carving knife we had used to dissect Herman Groper's corpse.

Gunderson walked over to examine the tools with interest.

"Brand new," he commented. "Now why would you boys need these things in a light-housekeeping apartment? You in the habit of buying beef by the quarter?"

We were saved from having to make an immediate answer by the doorbell ringing. This time I went to answer it, glad of an excuse to turn my face away from Lieutenant Gunderson's speculative gaze.

It was Marge who had rung the bell. She came in breathlessly, started to say, "I'm going to have to catch a midnight train home, Edward. My sister . . ."

She stopped when she saw the two policemen, and looked at me inquiringly.

When I had made introductions, Marge asked, "Is something the matter, Edward?"

"It's about Herman Groper," I said. "He's been missing since Saturday night. These gentlemen are just making routine inquiries of the students who know him."

"Oh," she said a little puzzledly. "I heard he was mysteriously missing, but I didn't know it had become a police matter." She turned to the lieutenant. "Am I interrupting you?"

"We have lots of time, Miss," Gunderson said. "But if you have to catch a midnight train, you've only got a couple of hours. Don't mind us."

"What happened?" I asked. "Is someone at home ill?"

"Oh no," she told me. "My sister's getting married very unexpectedly, and wants me for a bridesmaid. She phoned me at eight tonight. Her fiancé is in the army, you know, and he's been ordered overseas. She got a call from him at noon today that he has a ten-day leave and will be home tomorrow. They want to get married at once, so they can have a few days together before they're separated for so long. I'll only have to miss three days of classes before Christmas vacation officially starts, and my averages are high enough to stand it. Can you drive me to the station?"

"Of course," I said. "Then you won't be back until after the holidays?"

"No. I didn't mean to give you this until Friday, but under the circumstances I'll have to do it now." She handed me a small, gaily-wrapped box and said, "Merry Christmas, Edward."

Turning the box in my hand, I said, "Well, thanks, Marge."

She looked at me expectantly, and after an uncomfortable silence, I walked to the table and reached beneath it for the small package containing the watch I had bought her.

When I handed it to her and said, "Merry Christmas to you, too," I was conscious of the lieutenant's gaze resting on me curiously.

"Thank you, Edward," Marge said, and immediately began to rip off the paper.

"Hey!" I said. "That's not to be opened until Christmas."

"But we won't see each other any more," she said. "I want you to open yours now too."

She finished stripping away the paper, opened the box and gave a little squeal of delight.

"Why, Edward! You shouldn't have gotten anything so expensive. It's simply lovely."

Impulsively she grabbed my shoulders and gave me a light kiss on the chin. "Open yours now."

Slowly I tore the wrapper from her gift, lifted the lid of the small box inside and gazed at the monogrammed cuff links in it.

"Say, these are handsome," I said with a smile I had to force because I was conscious of Lieutenant Gunderson's steady gaze on me. I held them out for Bart to see.

"Aren't you going to give her the other gift?" Gunderson asked in a curiously quiet voice.

If I can only prevent her from opening it now, *I thought desperately.* If I can only get her to take it away with her and promise not to open it till later. Somehow I would be able to think of a convincing story to get it back from her, if only I could get past the crisis of the moment.

Straightening with the package in my hands, I said, "This is just an extra thing, Marge. I want it to be a surprise. Let's save it till the last minute at the railroad station."

"We'll be too rushed at the station, Edward. I still have some packing to do, and it's only two hours till train time."

The Geniuses

As she started to tear the paper, I practically shouted, "No! I want you to save it!"

She gazed at me with her mouth open. Silence grew in the room.

I knew from the ominous nature of the silence that it was hopeless now. While Lieutenant Gunderson couldn't possibly know what was in the hatbox, my near panic had alerted his suspicions enough to make him curious. I knew there wasn't a chance in the world that he'd allow the package to leave the apartment unopened.

Even as this hopeless thought struck me, Gunderson confirmed it by saying in a quiet but definite tone, "I think you'd better finish opening it right now, Miss."

The Kitchen Kill
Jonathan Craig (Frank E. Smith)

September 1957

The squeal came in during my half of the watch, which automatically put me in charge. Stan Rayder and I followed the usual practice of detective teams in splitting our watch, so that one of us caught squeals for the first half and the other for the second. Ten minutes earlier and Stan would have been in charge. As it was he acted as my assistant and I was saddled with all the paper work.

I sent Stan to check out a Plymouth while I picked up a sixty-one from the desk officer in the muster room. A sixty-one is a regular Complaint Report Form, which is made out for all squeals. It is brief and undetailed, but it's the key document of all cases in the department files, and the basis on which everything else is built.

All we knew about the case at this time was that a woman had been asphyxiated by gas, and the address. When we arrived at the apartment building, two radio units were already there. We stationed patrolmen at the front and back entrances and sent a third through the building to tell the tenants to stay in their apartments and out of the halls until we could get to them.

The building was a four-story walkup, and the body was in the one nearest the stairway on the second floor. It looked like the kind of accidental death that could happen to almost anyone.

The girl lay on the studio couch, her arms straight down at her sides and one slim ankle crossed over the other, just as if she'd lain down for a nap. She was about nineteen, a small girl with long, beautiful legs and shoulder-length red hair that was not quite dark enough to be called auburn. She wore only a mist-like chemise and high-heeled pumps, and she had died slowly and painlessly, without even having realized that she was in danger.

The one-room apartment was small but expensively furnished; and the girl herself looked expensive, from the outsize diamond on her right hand to the hand-stitching on her custom-made pumps.

There was hardly any trace of the gas now, and although this was one of the coldest nights we'd had all year, the air in the room was beginning to warm up a little from the body heat of the three people who were there when we arrived.

Two of these were neighboring tenants wearing pajamas and robes. The third was the young man who had discovered the body, a big, bulky-shouldered fellow in his early twenties with glistening black hair and hot black eyes.

When I asked him his name, he said, "Jeff Hutchins," in a preoccupied sort of way, his eyes fixed on the body on the studio couch.

"Let's step out in the hall," I suggested, taking his elbow and motioning with my head at the two neighbor men to precede us.

Hutchins violently jerked his arm free and said belligerently, "Don't go pushing me around, copper!"

"We can talk better out of sight of the body," I said without anger.

"I'm not leaving Helen alone," he said. "We can talk right here."

I reached for his elbow again, he jerked it back and started to take a swing at me. I caught his wrist, swung him around, twisted his arm up behind his back and marched him into the hall on tiptoe.

The patrolman I had sent to tell tenants to stay in their apartments was just coming down the stairs. I said to him, "Put this guy in the squad car and stick with him until he cools off. I'll talk to him later."

I shoved Hutchins toward the patrolman. Apparently his tiptoe walk into the hall had already begun to cool him off, for he let the patrolman lead him down the stairs without objection.

2.

A policewoman named Sue Caiman and an assistant M.E. came up the steps as the pair went down. I'd asked that a policewoman be sent over as we left the stationhouse, because I already knew then that the corpse was a woman, and female DOA's can be searched only by a policewoman.

Motioning Sue and the assistant M.E. towards the open door of the apartment we had just left, I turned my attention toward the two pajama-and-robe-clad tenants.

Neither could tell me much except that the girl's name was Helen Campbell and that she lived alone. Both men lived on the same floor, and had been awakened by Jeff Hutchins yelling for help. They had run out into the hall at the same time, smelled the gas and had seen Hutchins lying collapsed in the open doorway to the dead girl's apartment.

One had dragged Hutchins into the hall, the other had thrown open windows in the apartment and had turned off the gas. Then he'd started to lift the girl, decided she was dead and left her where she was.

I sent both men back to their apartments; then Stan and I looked up the super. All we got from him was a verification that the girl's name was Helen Campbell, that she paid her rent promptly and that she'd never caused a disturbance of any kind.

We went back to the one-room apartment and made a complete search of it while Sue Caiman and the assistant M.E. continued to work over the body. As I said previously, it looked like the kind of accidental death that could happen to anyone.

But it wasn't. Stan and I found enough during our preliminary search to convince us it was murder.

The lab crew arrived before we completed our search, but we were almost through and kept them waiting only about five minutes. When I had told them what I wanted in the way of photographs, I went over to see how Sue Caiman and the assistant M.E. were coming.

Sue had completed her search and was writing data down on her search form.

"You find anything, Sue?" I asked.

She shook her head. "Where would I find it? The kid's got on a pair of shoes and a chemise. There's nothing in the shoes but the label, and nothing in the chemise but the girl." She glanced at the body disapprovingly. "As you can see."

"So that's what it is," Stan said. "A chemise. I never saw one before, outside of a store window."

Stan's a tall, studious-looking guy with a brush cut. He had a habitual expression of surprise, but it doesn't mean anything. He stopped being surprised by things a long time ago.

"Women don't wear them much any more," Sue said.

"Too bad," Stan said.

"It's the kind of thing men buy for women as gifts," Sue said. "About all they're good for is to parade around in, or to stick in a drawer somewhere."

The Assistant M.E. closed the dead girl's eyes and turned to face me. "Pretty," he said. "Just to look at her, you'd say she was the picture of health."

I nodded. "No question about it being the gas?"

"Very little, Pete. The odds would be about a thousand to one. That's where she gets that pink, healthy-looking skin, from the gas. When carbon monoxide combines with the hemoglobin in the red blood cells, it turns the blood a cherry red."

"But it's possible she could have died of something else?"

"It's conceivable, yes. Nothing's ever a hundred per cent certain until after the post-mortem."

"Suppose you were carrying the case," Stan said. "Then what?"

"If I were carrying the case, I'd forget any other possibilities. As I said, it's all but certain she died of asphyxia. Actually, that's a pretty broad term. No matter what one dies of, the real cause of death is always the failure of oxygen to reach the body tissues, particularly the brain."

"How about the time of death?" I asked. "Can you fix it for us?"

He looked at his watch. "It's a few minutes past five A.M. I'd say she hasn't been dead more than a couple of hours. Call it about three o'clock, and you'll be pretty close."

I wrote down the time in my notebook. "How long would it take her to die?" I asked. "I mean, once the gas was on."

He shrugged. "That's hard to tell, Pete. Normally death occurs when about fifty per cent of the red blood cells have been saturated by carbon monoxide. But that doesn't mean too much. You'd have to take into account the cubic feet of air in the room, and the rate of flow of the gas from the burner, and a lot of other things. And then too, if she was under the influence of a narcotic at the time the gas went on, her body wouldn't have required as much oxygen as it would have otherwise, and the saturation might have been as much as eighty per cent. The same thing would have been true if she'd been asleep."

"Any indication she was under the influence of a narcotic?"

"No. There are no needle punctures or anything like that. But that doesn't rule out the possibility. There again, we won't know till I post her."

"How about liquor?"

"Slight trace on the lips. She might have had an ounce, or a gallon. I'll run a test as soon as I get her to Bellevue."

"I think you're going to find out she was stoned," I said.

"Oh? Why so?"

"It figures," I said. "From the way the homicide was set up, she would have to be."

"I've been pretty busy with her, Pete. I heard you and Stan talking about it, but I really wasn't paying much attention. Just what do you think happened?"

I glanced over to where the techs and photographers were still working around the tiny kitchen area. There was a waist-high refrigerator with a two-burner gas plate on top of it, a small gate-leg dining table, and a sink with a food cabinet above it.

"Her killer had a pretty good imagination," I said. "He tried to rig it so it would look as if she'd put a pan of soup on the burner, and then gone to sleep while she waited for it to heat. The soup was supposed to have boiled over and put out the fire, and from then on it would have been just another case of accidental death."

"Did the soup actually put out the fire?"

"Yes. But it also clogged up the jets. It was this real thick minestrone, which is about three-fourths vegetables to begin with."

"I see. But wouldn't the pressure of the gas have forced the stuff off the jets?"

"Sure. But not soon enough to suit our guy."

"Assuming it *was* a guy," Stan put in.

I nodded. "Anyhow, he couldn't wait. When the soup clogged the jets, he tore off a piece of paper towel and wiped the stuff off of them. Not too much of it, you understand; just enough to let the gas out. He was so careful about it that Stan and I looked right at the burner for a couple of minutes before we realized what he'd done."

"We found the paper towel," Stan said. "The guy was so sure of himself that he just wadded it up and stuck it down in the bottom of the garbage. He probably figured nobody could make anything out of a little soup on a towel. He should've looked closer; he'd have seen that he'd picked up a little rust and grease along with the soup."

The Assistant M. E. shook his head. "He couldn't have been very bright, could he?"

"A man's I. Q. hasn't got anything to do with the way he'll act when he's rigging a murder," I said. "If it did, we wouldn't solve as many of them as we do."

"There's more," Stan said. "He got too careful. He laid out a soup bowl and a box of soda crackers on the table, just the way the girl herself would probably have done. But he wasn't taking any chances. He wiped the bowl and the cracker box so clean that there isn't a single print on either one of them. There isn't even a smear.

"And even if you figured it was possible for the girl to take a clean bowl and put it on the table without leaving at least a couple of prints, you couldn't get around the cracker box. Think of the number of people who handled it before it ended up on her table."

The Assistant M. E. frowned thoughtfully. "I see what you mean. You reason that with the girl passed out on the couch, her killer could have taken all the time he needed to make her death look like an accident."

"He almost made it," Stan said. "He just got a little too cocky, and a little too careful. Trouble is, he got cocky and careful in the wrong places."

"We'll appreciate a fast p.m., doc," I said.

"You'll get it. All right to take the body now?"

"Yes. If you come up with anything, leave a message for us at the squad room."

"Will do," he said.

One of the techs said, "All clear back here, Pete."

Stan and I walked back to the kitchen area. While we'd already examined it, we'd had to go easy for fear of smearing fingerprints. Now that the techs were finished, we gave it a more thorough going over.

3.

The cabinet above the sink contained a sufficient variety of liquor and wines and fancy glasses to stock a small bar; there were even a few kinds of beverages and glasses that I'd never seen before. The refrigerator contained an assortment of limes and oranges and fruit juices, a dozen or so bottles of soda and tonic and ginger ale, a huge orchid in a transparent plastic box, and nothing else.

On the table, near the soup bowl and the box of crackers, there was a small bottle of instant coffee and a cup and saucer. Both the bottle of coffee and the china had yielded prints, but the techs had already established the fact that they belonged to the dead girl.

"Nothing interesting except that orchid," Stan said, shutting the refrigerator door. "And even that doesn't mean much. It's been in there at least a week or more. She probably put it in there and forgot it. And besides, it came from one of the biggest florists in New York. They probably sell a couple of hundred of them a day."

I nodded. "Maybe you'd better give the place still another going-over, Stan," I said. "Her boy friend ought to have cooled off by now. I'm going down to see what he has to say for himself."

I went down the stairs and out to the Plymouth at the curb, and told the patrolman I'd assigned to keep an eye on Jeff Hutchins that he could go off somewhere and sneak a smoke for himself. Then I climbed into the back seat with the young man.

"I'm Detective Peter Selby, Hutchins," I said. "I'll be in charge of this case from here on in. You think you've calmed down a little by now?"

He seemed to have. He sat slumped in the seat, his eyes fixed broodingly on the hands folded in his lap.

"I'm sorry about that," he said. "I just blew up, that's all. It was just such a hell of a jolt I didn't even know what the devil I was doing."

"Happens all the time," I said. "Suppose you give it another try. Let's start with how you happened to find the body."

He let his breath out heavily. "We had a late date. For three-thirty. I just walked in and found her."

"The door was unlocked?"

"I have keys to both the outside front door and the door to her apartment." He fished in his pocket for a key ring and removed two keys from it. "Here," he said, handing them to me. "Just in case you want to see if they work."

"You say you had a late date," I said. "You mean she was out with somebody else earlier in the evening?"

"Yes. That is, she had a date with somebody earlier. I don't know whether she went out with him or not. Maybe he just came over to the apartment."

"All right. Go on."

"She said to make it about three-thirty. That's when I got there, at three-thirty."

"Exactly?"

"Yes. I guess I was pretty anxious. I hit it right on the nose."

"How's it happen you didn't buzz her from downstairs?" I asked. "How'd you know the other man wouldn't still be there?"

"I didn't give a damn if he was. If he was still there, she'd just have to get rid of him, that's all."

"You've got a pretty fair temper there, Hutchins."

"Don't get me wrong. I just don't like being pushed around. You're a pretty big man yourself; you know how it is."

"You knock at her door?"

"There's a bell. I started to ring, and then I smelled the gas. I thought I'd never get my key into that damned lock, but I did, and . . . and I saw her lying there on the couch, and all that gas hit me right in the face and I almost keeled over. I yanked the door open all the way and ran inside and opened the window, and then I started to drag her out into the hall, but all of a sudden I got so sick to my stomach that all I could do was yell for help and sort of crumple up on the floor."

"You didn't touch anything in the apartment?"

"I never even got within three feet of her. That gas turned my stomach inside out, and—"

"I didn't mean just the girl. You touch anything else?"

"No. How could I? I never had a chance. A couple of guys in pajamas came rushing in, and one of them dragged me out in the hall. I tried to yell to the other one to do the same thing with Helen, but he went all to pieces. Just kept running back and forth like an old woman. The guy that dragged me out started back for her, but the gas was almost all gone by then, and he said he thought she was dead and that it'd be better not to touch her until the police came."

"What happened then?"

"Nothing. I was still too sick to move, and I guess nobody else could think of anything to do. But somebody must have called for the cops or an ambulance, because you guys started pouring in there only a couple or three minutes after that guy dragged me out in the hall."

"How's your stomach feel now?"

"Physically I'm okay; it's my nerves that's giving me fits." Suddenly he covered his face with his hands and shook his head slowly from side to side. "Why would she do it?" he said. "She had everything. She was so damn beautiful and all—why would she kill herself?"

"What makes you think she killed herself?" I asked.

He glanced up at me sharply. "You mean she didn't? It was an accident?"

There are times when you can't tell whether you're dealing with a killer, or with a guy with a broken heart, and sometimes it's tough to know just how to play it. But you have to play it one way or the other; there's nothing in between.

"You think you could take another jolt?" I asked.

"Like what?"

"It wasn't any accident, Hutchins. She was murdered."

I was watching his face closely for reaction, but it showed me nothing I wouldn't normally expect to see.

"Murdered?" he said, his voice barely audible. "Helen was murdered?"

I nodded. "And rigged to look like an accident."

He moistened his lips, his eyes wide. "Murdered," he whispered. "*Helen,* was murdered . . ."

I leaned back and lit a cigar and studied him in the pale flat light of the early dawn. Hutchins' shoulders shook, as if he'd just become aware of how cold it was.

"I was crazy about her," he said, almost matter-of-factly. "I didn't kill her, Selby. I couldn't have. I couldn't even have touched her, no matter what she'd done."

"Somebody did," I said. "Maybe you can help us find out who it was. But first we have to start with you. After all, you're the one who found her." I paused. "You say you got here at three-thirty. Where were you before then?"

"I was home."

"For how long?"

"All night. I mean from eight o'clock on, till I left for here."

"Can you prove it?"

"How could I prove it? I live alone, in a brownstone. I read until about eleven, and then I set the alarm for three and went to sleep."

"You didn't see or talk to anybody between eight and the time you got here?"

"No. Listen, Selby, I know how you guys think, but—"

"Take it easy," I said. "You don't know how we think. Just concentrate on giving me a picture of this girl. You know of any enemies she had? Can you think of anyone who might have killed her?"

He was silent for a long time. "No," he said at last.

"She ever mention any threats?"

"No."

"Not even any arguments with anyone?"

"Well, not arguments exactly. She and Betty had a few words once, before Betty moved out. But it didn't amount to anything."

"Betty?"

"Betty Dolan. She used to be Helen's roommate, but she moved out a couple of weeks ago. No; it's been longer. About a month."

"Why?"

"Oh . . . Well, I guess you'd say it was over me. I used to go with Betty, see. And then, when Helen moved in—well, I guess I just couldn't help myself. I'd never seen anybody so beautiful in my whole life."

I asked him for Betty Dolan's address and wrote it in my notebook. "Anyone else?" I asked.

"No. And if you think Betty did it, you're crazy. She just isn't the type."

"They never are," I said. "What'd Helen do for a living, Hutchins?"

"Nothing. She had some kind of private income. It wasn't any fortune, but she didn't have to work. I think her folks left her some dough in trust or something."

"She have any family? We'll want to notify the next of kin."

"No family. That much I know for sure."

"You know the name of this man she had a date with last night—the one she expected to be with up until about three-thirty?"

"She didn't say. But I think it might have been somebody named Charles Grantson."

"You don't know him?"

"No. But she's been seeing him quite a bit."

"What'd she tell you about him?"

"Not much. Somehow I got the impression he's married, but that's just about all. She never talked much about anybody. Oh, she mentioned this Ted Joyner now and then, but—"

"Who's he?"

"Some guy that used to be in vaudeville or radio or something. I never did get it straight. Anyhow, she'd known him a long time, from the way she talked."

I knocked the ash off my cigar. "Think hard, Hutchins," I said. "The more you tell us, the easier it's going to be—for all of us."

"I know," he said quietly. "My God, I know."

I talked to him another ten minutes without learning anything more of importance; then I called the patrolman back to the car and went upstairs again to use the phone.

My first call was to the Bureau of Criminal Identification to ask for checks on Helen Campbell, Jeff Hutchins, Betty Dolan, Charles Grantson, and Ted Joyner. Then, while I waited for BCI to complete its search and call me back, I phoned the squad room to report Stan's and my progress to the squad commander and to ask whether there had been any arrests or unusual happenings that might possibly have a bearing on our investigation.

There had been no developments of any interest; and a few moments after I hung up BCI called back to report that there was no criminal record on any of the people I had asked about, and that no information had ever been filed on any of them.

I located the addresses of Charles Grantson and Ted Joyner in the dead girl's personal telephone directory and entered them in my notebook beneath the address Jeff Hutchins had given me for Betty Dolan.

Then, after leaving Stan Rayder in charge of the investigation at the apartment, I took Jeff Hutchins to the Twentieth Precinct stationhouse, booked him as a material witness, and set out to question Grantson, Joyner, and Betty Dolan, in that order.

4.

Charles Grantson, already a very warm suspect, turned into an even warmer one when I learned that he and his wife had checked out of their hotel at two A.M. Grantson had left no forwarding address, and the desk clerk told me that he and his wife had seemed to be extremely upset about something. The clerk was able to tell me nothing more about them than they were both attractive people in their late fifties, and that Grantson appeared to have a great deal of money.

Grantson's description, as given to me by the clerk, was that of a tall, slightly stout man with graying hair and very piercing blue eyes. After I had checked with the bellhop who had helped the Grantsons pack, and with the attendant at the garage where Grantson kept his Cadillac, I gathered from the remarks passed between Grantson and his wife that they had been planning on leaving the city.

I called Communications, gave them Grantson's description and license number, and asked that he be picked up for questioning. The alarm would be broadcast throughout thirteen states and the District of Columbia, and relayed to every station, post and precinct in the city, including a call to Stan and the other police at Helen Campbell's apartment.

There was, at the moment, nothing more I could do about Mr. Grantson. I went out to the Plymouth and drove over to see Ted Joyner.

5.

Joyner turned out to be a small, stooped man of about forty-five with thinning blond hair and alert gray eyes behind shell-rimmed glasses. His apartment was furnished with an eye to bachelor comfort, and against the wall opposite the hall door was one of the most intricate-looking hi-fi outfits I had ever seen.

His expression scarcely changed at all when I told him of Helen's death, but I got the impression that he was making an intense effort to mask his emotions. He was silent for a long moment, and then sank down on the sectional sofa and rested his elbows on his knees, his face almost completely blank.

"A waste," he said. "Such a terrible, terrible waste."

"What was your relationship with her, Mr. Joyner?"

"If you're implying what I think you're implying, I suggest you speak with my doctor. He'll tell you my health has been so poor these last few years that . . ." He shrugged. "We were friends. Nothing more. I met her when she first came to New York. You may have heard me on the radio, even in these days of television. I'm one of the original disc jockeys, you know."

I didn't, but I nodded anyhow.

"I still manage to hang on. A relic of a happier day, you might say."

"You meet Helen through your work, Mr. Joyner?"

"Yes. When her parents died a couple of years ago, she came to New York. It was an old, old story. She wanted to break into entertainment. She was willing to do anything. She had beauty, but no talent. Finally she began making the rounds of the studios, trying to find office work of some kind, even as a messenger. It happens I receive a great deal of correspondence, and I hired her to help me with it."

"Was she still working for you?"

"No. She quit after about four months. I understood she came into some money, but she was never very explicit about it."

"But you continued to see her?"

"Perhaps it would be more accurate to say that she continued to see me. She was, after all, a very young girl, and her parents were dead. I was extremely fond of her, and I suppose she sensed it, the way girls will, and felt that I was someone to come to when she was troubled or perplexed. I don't much relish the idea of being a father-image, or surrogate, or whatever, but I guess that's exactly what I was."

"When's the last time you saw her, Mr. Joyner?"

"About—well, I'd say about a month. Perhaps six weeks."

"She have any particular problem at that time? Anything that might have a bearing on her death?"

"No. That is, nothing at all serious. She seemed to be having a little trouble with her roommate over some young man, but I'm sure that—"

"She give you the details?"

"No. She merely said that her roommate's young man was showing a lot of interest in her, and that her roommate didn't like it. Betty something-or-other. I understood she was quite bitter about it."

"You know a man named Charles Grantson?"

"Grantson? . . . Charles Grantson. . . . No, I don't think I do." He paused. "Such a terrible waste. Helen was only nineteen, you know. A mere baby."

Another half-hour with Ted Joyner brought me no more than I knew already. I arranged for a police cruiser to take him to the Bellevue morgue for an official identification of Helen's body, and then I left to question her ex-roommate, Betty Dolan.

6.

Betty lived in a small, shabby sleeping room on the third floor of a rundown brownstone. The air had an unwashed, spilled-whiskey smell, and neither the room nor the girl appeared to have been cleaned up in some time. But despite her disheveled, lackluster blonde hair and a face that was obviously in need of a little soap and water, Betty Dolan was a strikingly beautiful girl. She had dark green eyes and tiny facial features, and the body beneath the soiled yellow wrapper was small-waisted and lushly curved.

"So Helen's dead," she said, her voice caressing the words. "Well, wonderful. It couldn't have happened to a bitchier girl." She sank down on the rumpled bed, reached beneath it for the fifth of whiskey that sat on the floor, and tilted the bottle to her lips.

"That's the first honest-to-God good news I've had this winter." She put the bottle back on the floor, brushed the dull yellow hair back from her forehead and eyed me narrowly. "So?"

"I understand you and she had some pretty hot words."

"Damn right we did. I got her told, and told hard. The red-haired slut cut me out with my boy friend."

"With Jeff Hutchins?"

"Yeah. With Jeff. God damn him. God damn *all* of them. They'll do you dirty every time."

"When's the last time you saw Helen?"

"Four or five weeks ago. When I moved out on her. Why? You think I'd be nuts enough to kill her lover, a big talking, on-the-make heel like Jeff? I'm glad she's dead, sure. Look, I'm laughing out loud. But if you think I killed her, you got rocks, boy."

She reached for the bottle again, then changed her mind and sat staring at me for a long moment. "It's Jeff you want," she said. "She had it coming and he gave it to her. Now if only somebody would give the same thing to him, I could die happy."

"What makes you think it was Jeff?"

"Because she ditched him for somebody else. She gave him the same brush he gave me. He's a natural-born flip, that Jeff. He just couldn't take it."

"Who was the other man?"

"Some old character named Charles Grantson. A goaty old joker with half a million bucks and a wife with a face that would bust a clock. Helen had been playing him for a long time, but she didn't give Jeff the bad news till the guy said he was going to divorce his wife and marry her. Naturally a guy like Jeff Hutchins doesn't stack up against any half a million coconuts, so Jeff got his little pink slip."

I determined that Betty had no alibi for the time in question, told her to keep herself available until she heard from me again, and then drove back to the stationhouse for another talk with Jeff Hutchins. Either Betty Dolan had been lying, or Jeff had been holding out on me, and I meant to find out which.

7.

In the squad room again, I found a message on my call spike to phone Stan Rayder at Helen Campbell's apartment. I called him, and learned that Charles Grantson had come to the apartment and that Stan had taken him into custody. He had told Stan that he had seen Helen the night before, had drunk with her in the apartment until about eleven o'clock, and had then gone home to his wife. He and Helen had argued about Grantson's decision not to divorce his wife after all, and Helen had threatened to tell Mrs. Grantson of their affair unless Grantson came up with a considerable sum of money. Grantson, so he said, had refused, and had thought he might escape further trouble with Helen by getting his wife out of town immediately.

He had therefore told his wife that they had to leave for Florida at once, to take care of an emergency connected with one of Grantson's business interests there, and that it would be well to leave in the early morning hours in order to avoid the heavy traffic of the metropolitan area. Mrs. Grantson had been reluctant to go on such short notice, but she had finally agreed, and they had started south. However, once Grantson had had time to think things out a little more clearly, he had decided to return to New York, have another talk with Helen, and if possible get her to accept a lesser sum for her silence.

I didn't think much of Grantson's story, and I told Stan to keep him in custody until I had finished talking to Jeff Hutchins, at which time I would go to Helen Campbell's apartment and interrogate Grantson at length.

My second talk with Jeff Hutchins was a waste of time. He had once again become surly and uncooperative, and beyond insisting upon his innocence and calling Betty Dolan a liar, he refused to say anything at all. Finally I gave up, turned him over to the squad commander for further questioning, and headed for the dead girl's apartment.

I never reached it. On the way, I stopped for a sandwich and a cup of coffee; and because of that stop I came to realize something that should have occurred to both Stan and me the first moment we looked into Helen Campbell's food cabinet and refrigerator.

I had bolted half the sandwich and was taking a last sip of the coffee when I suddenly found myself reflecting on the fact that, barring oranges and limes, neither the cabinet nor the refrigerator had contained any food of any kind whatever. Liquor and mixer, yes—and a great deal of it. But no food. The oranges and limes had undoubtedly been meant as ingredients and trimmings for mixed drinks, not as food. There hadn't even been a loaf of bread or a bottle of milk.

And now that my thinking processes had finally become unfrozen, I recalled that the only cooking utensil she had possessed had been the small stewpan which she had obviously used to heat water for instant coffee.

And if Helen never cooked anything at home—never even kept so much as a single slice of bread or a single pat of butter—how had she happened to have a can of minestrone and a full box of soda crackers?

It was, of course, still possible that she *had* just happened to have them on hand. But I didn't think so. I thought the chances were more than good that the soup and crackers had been bought and taken to her apartment for the express purpose of rigging a murder to look like a suicide.

And I reasoned further that, since the soup and crackers would have been bought at an hour when all the grocery stores and most of the delicatessens were closed, the number of places where such a purchase could have been made were few and the probability of the customer's being remembered were good.

I decided that Helen's killer would have been in a hurry, and that he would have bought his necessities at the nearest possible place.

The nearest possible place to the girl's apartment house was a hole-in-the-wall delicatessen. The proprietor told me he closed at ten P.M., that he had sold no minestrone the previous evening, and that the only delicatessen he knew of that remained open after ten was on a side street two blocks away.

I drove there—and learned the identity of Helen Campbell's killer. The proprietor had sold a can of soup and a box of crackers at about twelve-thirty the previous night, and the description he gave me of the purchaser could have belonged to none other than Ted Joyner, the radio disc jockey for whom Helen had worked for a few months when she had been trying to break into the entertainment field.

I phoned Stan Rayder to tell him I would pick him up outside Helen's apartment house.

Half an hour later Ted Joyner motioned Stan and me to seats on his sectional sofa and sat down in a deep leather chair across from us. He looked very small sitting there, and somehow very sick and very old. The gray eyes behind the shell-rimmed glasses looked less alert, less alive.

"Well?" he said softly. "Well, gentlemen?"

"Did you have your own keys, Mr. Joyner?" I asked.

"Keys?"

"To Helen's apartment. We were wondering how you got in."

He shook his head slowly, trying to smile questioningly without quite being able to bring it off. "I'm afraid I don't understand."

"It's just a matter of time," I said. "You can make things a lot more pleasant for yourself if you don't prolong this."

"I still don't under—"

"We have witnesses, Mr. Joyner. Three of them. An old man who couldn't sleep. He saw you go into Helen's building. And two kids. They were in the back seat a car, where they shouldn't have been. The cop on post gave them a reading-out. This morning, when he heard about the murder, he remembered the kids. We've just talked to them. They were having their fun right across the street from Helen's building. They saw you too, Joyner."

Joyner's face was gray. He stared at me unblinkingly.

"So much for the witnesses," I said. "But we have more."

The witnesses had gone down better than I had expected, considering that I had invented them on the spur of the moment. I had, of course, needed a little extra shock insurance to go with the knowledge we actually had.

"We know when and where you bought the soup and crackers," I said. "We know exactly how you rigged Helen's murder, Joyner. We've got everything we need, and we know everything we want to know—except why."

Joyner sat so still, so completely without expression, that it was hard to believe he was still alive. A full minute passed, then another, and slowly his eyes clouded and grew moist.

"I gave her everything," he said, his voice so low that Stan and I had to lean forward to hear him. "I loved her from the first moment I saw her. I gave her a job, and when she got tired of working I kept right on paying her—every dollar I could. I—I liked to buy her nice things. She was just like some kind of beautiful doll, and I liked to dress her up and show her things to make her laugh."

Stan started to say something but I caught his eye and shook my head.

"I never cared for anyone before. I was afraid to give love because I feared I'd be laughed at . . . I was afraid I'd be hurt. But I loved Helen. She was all the world to me. Nothing else mattered at all. And then, when she met this man—this Charles Grantson—she threw me away as if I were filth.

"She wanted to marry Grantson, to marry his money. She didn't want me around any longer. She couldn't stand the sight of me."

He was silent for several moments. At last I said, "Go on, Mr. Joyner."

"What is there to say? I decided that if I couldn't keep her for my own, no one else would ever have her at all. I went over to her apartment to plead with her one last time. I could see the light under her door, and when she didn't let me in, I thought it was because she didn't want to see me. I let myself in. She—she was on the couch, passed out, the way she had been so many times lately. I sat there holding her in my arms for a long, long time . . . and at last I knew what I had to do."

"Had to?" I asked gently.

He nodded. "Yes. Helen belonged to me. I couldn't have borne it knowing she belonged to somebody else."

I glanced at Stan and then walked to the phone to arrange for the immediate release of Jeff Hutchins and Charles Grantson.

As I waited for someone to answer the phone in the squad room I heard Joyner sobbing softly.

"Can't you understand, Officer?" he said to Stan Rayder. "Can't you understand that I had to?"

The Crying Target

James McKimmey

September 1957

Clintock saw the lights coming up fast in the rear view mirror, and a moment later the yellow convertible that had been in front of the roadhouse he'd just left was speeding past him. A hundred yards up the highway the convertible suddenly swayed across the road, then, brakes squealing, ran onto the shoulder and skidded to a stop, bumper resting against a white guard fence.

Clintock, his foot already on the brake, eased his blue sedan behind the convertible, and stopped. He got out and trotted forward. He opened the convertible door, letting the interior lights shine on the face of a pretty blonde girl. It was the same girl he'd seen in the roadhouse.

The girl smiled crookedly. "I just about fixed it, didn't I?"

"You just about did," Clintock said.

"Never drink when you drive," she slurred.

"Never drive when you drink."

"You don't believe in slogans, I take it."

Clintock stood there, examining her. She was in her mid-twenties, well dressed; she had a nice tan and good shapely legs. Her teeth, behind the limp smile, were small, white and even.

"Well," Clintock said, "what now?"

"Now you can excuse me," she said. "I'll be moving on."

Clintock nodded.

The girl started the engine of the convertible.

Clintock reached past her and snapped off the ignition switch. "You've had it," he said.

"You think so?" she said. "You think I'm a little tipsy? The man's a doctor, maybe."

"Where do you live?" Clintock asked.

"We know each other five seconds, and you want to know where I live." She put her head back against the seat and laughed softly "Look up," she said. "Look at the beautiful stars. Isn't it a pretty sky, Mr. Doctor? And—ohh—the trees! Do you like the trees? These are pretty mountains, aren't they, Mr. Doctor?"

"Very pretty," Clintock said.

"What town are we in, sir?" the girl asked.

"Tourey."

"Never heard of it."

Clintock examined the girl carefully. "What's your name?"

The girl looked at him sideways, giggled, then said, "Carol. Carol Adams."

Clintock nodded. "Where were you heading, Carol?"

"San Francisco. I've been in Reno. Do you like Reno—what's your name?"

"Clintock. I like Reno fine."

"Clintock. What's your first name, Clintock?"

"I never use it."

"Clint, then. Good old Clint!"

Clintock nodded once more. "So you've been in Reno, and you're heading for San Francisco, only you aren't going to make it, honey."

"You bet I will."

The girl bent forward to the ignition switch again, and Clintock removed the keys. He turned and walked back to his own car.

"Hey!"

He let her keep calling after him, as he removed his suitcase from the trunk of his own car and the extra suit hanging inside. Then he locked the car and returned to the convertible.

"Move over," he said.

"Like hell," the girl said. "I don't know you."

"Gently now," Clintock said, "or maybe I'll have to get tough."

The girl looked, then smiled. "Good old Clint. I can trust old Clint, can't I?"

"Move," Clintock said softly.

"Sure," the girl said. "Okay, Clint."

She moved across the seat, and Clintock loaded his bag and suit into the back of the convertible, then got behind the wheel. He made a U turn, and headed back up the lower mountain grade, toward the small town of Tourey A motel sign showed ahead, and Clintock pulled in front of the office. Once more he removed the keys from the ignition.

"I could call for help," the girl said.

"You won't," Clintock said.

"I'm a nice girl," she said.

"I know," Clintock nodded.

Then he got out and walked into the small pine-paneled office. He rang a buzzer, and a moment later a thin man with white hair and veined hands appeared.

"Cabin," Clintock said.

The old man squinted outside in the direction of the convertible. "You and your wife?"

"Me and my wife. Only make it two rooms, will you?"

"Two rooms?"

"I snore badly," Clintock said.

The old man turned the registration book. "Sign here."

"I never can remember the license number," Clintock said.

The old man clucked. "Most people can't. It's a funny thing."

Clintock paid for the cabin, picked up the key. "I'll find it all right," he said. And he returned to the convertible and drove into the court.

"I'm all right," the girl said in a small voice. "Really I am, Clint. I'm fine."

"Sure."

Clintock stopped the car and examined the court. There were a dozen cabins, varying in size. The court was shaped like the inside of a horseshoe. Two cabins were lighted, the rest were dark. There were cars in six of the stalls beside the cabins. There was a car with no lights parked at the far end of the U.

Clintock got out and walked around to the other side. His steps echoed, as his shoes crunched through the loose gravel, and then there came the sharp crack, the firey flare out of the corners of his eyes, back, toward where the dark car was parked at the end of the U. A bullet whined inches above Clintock's head, and then there was a second crack, but by then, Clintock had dropped, instinctively, swiftly. He slid toward the convertible, jamming himself close to the front right wheel.

At the same moment, lights flared from the car at the end of the court. There was a roar of a motor, springing into life, and then the wild shriek of wheels sliding against gravel. A moment later, the car careened out of the court and disappeared.

Clintock stood up, staring after it. Lights had sprung on now in other cabins, and from the office, running stiffly, came the old man.

"What's going on? What happened!"

"Nothing," Clintock said.

"There were shots," the old man said.

"Backfiring," Clintock said. "Kids. They were parked at the end of the court."

"I'll have the police on them, disturbing folks that way!" the old man exploded. "I run a decent place." He faced those seven or eight people who had come from their cabins. "I run a real decent place here! Disturbing folks like that! I'll put the police on them."

"Too late," Clintock said.

The old man returned grumbling to his office, while the others retreated slowly Clintock looked inside the convertible; the girl's face was half shadowed, her eyes, only, revealed in the light from over the cabin doorway.

"Let's go," Clintock said.

He kept looking at her eyes carefully. She rolled her head back against the seat. "Noise and everything. So sleepy, old Clint. Gonna sleep right here."

"Move," Clintock said tightly.

He half carried her inside, and she clung to his arm.

"Okay," he said wearily.

And he lifted her entirely then, and carried her to a bed. The cabin was split into two sections. There was an open door between them. The girl turned on her stomach, facing away from Clintock.

"So sleepy, old Clint. You're a nice guy, aren't you, Clint? I'm a nice girl—"

Clintock looked the length of her body She had a firm, young body, wide-shouldered, and full-hipped without being overly full. She wore a good expensive suit, and the stockings were carefully put on, seams exactly straight.

Clintock bent over her, then gently drew a blanket around her. Her purse lay beside her, and he picked it up. He turned toward the lamp and noiselessly unsnapped the purse. He went through the contents slowly and deliberately, replacing each item without change of expression.

Then he opened the small wallet. There was a twenty dollar bill, two tens and four ones. There was her driver's license, an identification card. Her home was San Francisco.

Clintock opened the coin section of the wallet. There were three pennies, a nickel and a dime, and a small worn bronze medal.

Clintock's forehead furrowed. He held the bronze medal up, turning it against the light from the lamp. He wiped a hand lightly across his forehead, and then returned the medal, then the wallet, to the purse, and placed the purse on a bureau.

He turned finally, walked outside and got his bag and suit from the convertible. He looked in the trunk then, and took out the small bag there. He brought that inside, and placed it on a chair beside the bed where the girl slept. He opened it and riffled through it quickly. Then he walked into the other room, closing the door behind him.

He sat down on the edge of the bed, face drawn, heavy shoulders sagging. He unbuttoned his jacket, and removed the gun, a .38 caliber Colt Cobra, from his shoulder holster, running fingers carefully along the barrel. He shivered perceptibly, and then he lay back, looking up at the ceiling, eyes wide, flecked with hate.

2.

The cabin lay in the morning shadow of the mountain. The air was clean and not yet warmed by a sun just starting over the range to the east; smoke curled up from the brick chimney running up the side of the cabin, flavoring the early morning air with the scent of burning fir.

The cabin was large, a rambling-looking structure of rough, unfinished timber. A small creek ran down in back of it. In front were two large automobiles. The clearing in which the cabin rested was surrounded heavily by tall pine and thick, morning-damp bushes. A single dirt road curled away, leading to an invisible blacktop, which, in turn, wound two miles to the town of Tourey, nestling along the lower upgrade of the Sierra Nevadas.

Inside the cabin, in the yellow pine-paneled main room, a thin, hard muscled young man with glistening black hair, sat in a wicker chair, feet up and resting on a thick plank table; the entire room was furnished with heavy informal items; there was a head of a spike buck above the large fireplace; there was a shotgun with a carved stock resting on pegs on the opposite wall.

The young man with the black hair lifted a bottle from the table and splashed an inch of whiskey into a water glass. At the same moment, from the entry leading to the kitchen beyond, came a short man with a thick body and surprisingly broad shoulders, intensified by the shortness of his heavy arms. He wore a dark felt hat which was pushed up and back, faintly indicating the baldness underneath. He was munching a thick ham sandwich.

"What are you trying to do, Jack?" he said to the younger man. "Drink yourself dumb or something?"

"Hell," Jack said. "Drink myself dumb! I had two drinks!"

"You ought to eat something. Nick don't like it if you drink too much. You know that. This ain't a time to get Nick any madder."

The older man's voice was surprisingly high-pitched, soft and whispery.

Jack, the younger of them, removed his feet from the table, stood up, took off the jacket of his sky blue suit, and hung it over the back of his chair He wore a black shoulder holster; there was a Luger inside it. He sat down once more, lifted his feet to the table, then squinted at his black, heavy-heeled shoes. He got a handkerchief from a rear pocket and wiped the shoes carefully, then replaced the handkerchief in the pocket.

"What's Nick doing in there?" he asked the other man.

"Who knows?"

"Hell," Jack said, disgruntled, and he drank some of the whiskey from the water glass.

Al sat down beside the table. "How's the fire doing, Jack?"

Jack nodded.

"You warm enough, Jack?" Al asked.

"Hell, yes," Jack said disinterestedly.

"Cold up here in the mornings."

"Drink some goddamn whiskey," Jack said. "You won't be cold."

"I didn't say I was cold," Al said. "I said it was cold up here. I meant it gets cold outside. It ain't cold in here, is it, Jack? Are you warm enough?"

"I said I was," Jack said angrily.

Al finished his sandwich and wiped his mouth with his hand. "That's good ham, Jack. You ought to try it. You oughtn't to drink too much, Jack."

"You want to fix me a sandwich, I'll eat it," Jack said. "Otherwise, shut up, heh?"

Al leaned on his elbows, looking at Jack worriedly. "Now don't get mad, Jack. You really want a sandwich, I'll fix it—."

But just then a tall rangy man in his mid-thirties appeared from a bedroom near the back of the main room. He was in shirt sleeves, and his hair was rumpled, as though his fingers had pushed through it dozens of times. Still, there was a look of cultivation about him that separated him from the other two. The shirt he wore was expensive. The trousers, though wrinkled, were tailored exactly to his waist.

Al stood up, smiling. "Hello, Nick. How's it go, boy?"

Nick walked across the room to the fire without answering, and stood staring at the licking flames, eyes hard.

"Nice fire, huh, Nick?" Al asked. "You want me to put some more wood on it? Is it warm enough for you, Nick?"

Jack sat there, half-smiling, looking at his newly polished shoes. He finished the whiskey in his glass, then reached for the bottle.

Nick turned around. "Lay off that stuff."

Jack moved his head, cocking it just a little, looking at Nick. "How's that, Nick?"

"I said lay off that stuff."

Jack smiled. He had large perfectly white teeth. "You suggesting or ordering, Nick?"

"I'm telling you. You figure out what it is. Just lay off, that's all."

"Well, now, Nick—"

"Now, Jack," Al said. "You quit for a little, all right, Jack? He ain't had much, Nick. That's a fact. Just a little bit. Ain't that right, Jack?"

Jack laughed softly, shaking his head. "Christ!"

"Maybe," Nick said, coming back across the room, stopping by the table, looking at both of the others, "you don't really get this. This is Bud's older brother. This isn't Bud Clintock. This is Clintock the goddamn cop. There's a difference maybe you don't get. This is no kid this time. This a tough bastard!"

"Tough!" Jack laughed.

"All right," Nick said, face coloring with anger. "You think he isn't! That's a good way to get off dead, do you understand that? You're not dealing with a cheap punk this time. This cop knows everything there is in the book and twice over that."

"I'll fix him," Jack said, "just like I fixed his goddamn brother."

"You fix a lot of things, don't you?" Nick said, his voice rising. "You fixed things last night, didn't you?"

Jack looked up, eyes flickering faintly.

"Well, look, Nick," the short, squat Al said. "Now you know how that was, Nick. We couldn't help it. You know Carol ran off the road that way."

"Goddamn dame," Jack muttered darkly. "What about that, Nick? You talk about drinking. That dame was fractured. If she hadn't—"

"All right," Nick said. "So you couldn't get to him on the road, but how about—"

"See, Nick," Al said, "we were waiting like that about three miles out of town there. We'd of nailed him sure, Nick, if he'd of kept on coming. We done that sort of thing before real good. You know that, Nick. But, see, he stops for Carol, and when he don't come through like Charlie at the bar says he's going to—"

"Maybe Charlie told him the wrong direction," Jack said insolently.

"No, now Charlie told him right," Al said. "Charlie's all right. He done real good, Jack. I checked with him after, and when he says this guy comes in and checks out like the description Nick here gives him, and then the guy asks about where is this Dick Alexander, why, sure enough, he told him right out west of town. No, now Charlie done it right. It was Carol—"

"Goddamn dame," Jack repeated.

"So anyway, Nick," Al said, "it was the light see? We come back down the road toward town when Clintock don't show, and we see him getting into Carol's car and all, and we follow him, and when he goes into this motel to check in, why, we pull into the court, and we got him. Only it's the light. Ain't it, Jack? That twilight, see? You got to use lights, only it ain't completely dark yet. And things are hard that way, ain't they, Jack?"

Jack sat there, mouth grim. He appeared not to be listening. He turned his head, looking out a window.

"So Jack missed him. It wasn't Jack's fault. He's a good shot, Nick. You know that . . ."

All of a sudden, Jack was out of his chair, moving across the room. The Luger was out of the holster and in his hand. He slammed the door open. The Luger cracked.

"There!" he yelled, laughing. "You see?"

"What the hell—!" Nick snapped angrily.

Jack ran outside, the other two following.

He ran across the clearing, to the edge of the timber, and poised. The others came up and looked down at the small rabbit. It lay, still alive, blood oozing from a ripped flank.

"It don't take no shotgun with me," Jack said happily. "Hey, look at its eyes, huh?"

The animal's eyes watched them, fright and panic in them. The animal struggled to move, pulling along its torn hind quarter.

Jack's laughter pealed through the woods, and then the Luger cracked again and again. The bullets ripped the rabbit, splattering blood and fur.

Nick's face had turned white. "Goddamn, you crazy bastard! Do you want to bring up everybody in that goddamn town! How crazy can you get, anyway?"

Jack looked at him, eyes thinning.

"You crazy sonofabitch," Nick yelled, "you get drunk and get picked up by the Vegas cops, and you tell them your name is Dick Alexander. Then you bust out of there and hightail it straight to us, and they damn near get you in Tahoe. You make every goddamn newspaper in the seven Western States. And why the hell did you use that name? Why the hell did you bust Bud's head, while we're at it?"

"Shut up," Jack said thickly.

"What?" Nick thundered.

"I told you to shut up, Nick!"

"You're telling me to shut up? I run this goddamn show, have you forgotten that? And no trigger-happy stupid punk is going to—"

Jack lifted the Luger, his face set like stone.

And quite suddenly, Al, stocky and slope-shouldered, stepped forward and struck the younger Jack on the chin. It was a clean jolting blow, and Jack stumbled back and sat down. His eyes glazed for a moment, and then he shook his head, bringing up the Luger still instinctively in his hand. He half rose. Al swiftly moved forward once more, his left fist arcing into Jack's stomach, his right following accurately, catching Jack hard on the cheek bone.

The Luger came out of Jack's hand this time, and Al kicked it away. Jack rolled with the force of the blows and hit the ground sprawling. He didn't get up.

Al watched him for a moment, and then he bent over him solicitously. "Now, Jack, I'm sorry about that. You know I am. I don't like to do that. But you got to understand. We work together if we cooperate like, you know? Now Nick here is boss. You know that, Jack. We got to do what Nick says. Nick here is smart. We all come out if we do like Nick here says. It ain't like we got nothing to lose, no matter how it goes. That's a lot of money we're after, Jack. You don't want to forget that. Do you feel all right now, Jack?"

And then Nick, face still white, bent forward toward the still prostrate Jack. "Now you listen, Jack. You listen good. What's done is done. Bud stole that money off of us, after we worked pretty hard to get it. He stuck that money somewhere, and now we think we're getting pretty close to it.

"Now we've done it your way before. We caught up with Bud, and we let you work him over to find out where he'd put that dough. Only you broke his goddamn skull first. Now that's over We're forgetting that, but you'd better keep your nose clean from now on. We're going to get that dough, and nothing is going to stop us. Not your lousing things up. Not Bud's older brother. We're going to get that sixty grand. Do you understand that?"

Jack lay on the ground, not answering.

"Can you get up, all right, Jack?" Al asked.

"Get the hell away from me," Jack said.

"Now, Jack."

"Let him be," Nick said. "Come on, Al. Only take his gun."

"Now, Nick, that ain't necessary, is it? Jack'll behave, you let him keep his gun." Nick glared at the younger man on the ground, then shrugged. "Come on, Al." The two walked back toward the large cabin.

"What now, Nick?" Al said.

"We'll talk about it," Nick said shortly.

"How about Carol? It's kind of funny, her getting shacked up that way with Bud's brother."

"Yeah," Nick said. "It is."

"Kind of a what-you-say, coincidence?"

"It really is, isn't it?" Nick said tightly.

"She don't usually go on any bat like that. I mean, Carol, now, she's got class. It don't really figure, her getting tight like that."

"You're thinking a little now," Nick said sarcastically. "Maybe it's about time, huh? Maybe it's about time everybody around here got to thinking, not just me. What do you think about that, Al?"

"Now, Nick," Al said softly. "Jack got you all upset. Everything's going to work out all right. You know me, and Jack don't have your brains, Al. We depend on you like, see? How is it in here, Nick? Is it warm enough for you? Shall I put some more wood on that fire?"

3.

When dawn broke completely, Clintock, the keys to the yellow convertible in his pocket, stepped out of his room into the girl's. She lay sleeping quietly underneath the blanket he'd put around her hours before. Clintock watched her for a moment, then walked to the window and looked outside. The court was silent in the early light. Clintock's eyes roved from one doorway to another. Then he stepped outside.

He walked straight across the court, hands loose at his sides, on out to the blacktop, and then down the road. He walked in steady, even strides until, finally, he reached his own blue sedan.

He drove away from the village. He drove three miles, four. Then he turned off on a small dirt road. He followed it to a dead end. He stared at the empty woods for a moment, then drove back, past the motel, until he reached the roadhouse where he'd stopped the night before. It was closed. Clintock walked around the building and looked at the small house in back. He walked to the door and rapped against it.

A gray-haired woman with a weary face appeared, her body wrapped in a faded brown robe. "Yes?" she said irritatedly.

"The man who runs the bar. Does he live here?"

"Yes, but he's asleep. So was I."

"I want to see him."

"Not now," she said. "You can see him when he opens up. At noon."

Clintock looked back of him, his eyes checking. "Now," he said, turning back to the woman and stepping inside.

"Now look here, mister."

Clintock kept moving inside, the woman backing ahead of him. "Get him," he said.

The woman stared at him in astonishment for a second, then disappeared. A moment later, the bartender Clintock had talked to the night before appeared.

There was an angry frown on his face as he pulled a robe around him. Then he looked at Clintock, and Clintock watched his face pale.

"You remember me," Clintock said evenly.

"Yes," the man said, his head bobbing. "Yes, sure! How are you anyway? What can I do for you?"

Clintock watched the man knot the cord of the robe, noting the man's trembling hands.

"I asked you about Dick Alexander."

"Yes," the man said. "Sure. I remember."

"You told me where to find him."

"I said I thought I knew where'd you'd find him. I—"

"You told me he lived in a house four miles west, and to the right, off the highway There isn't a house there."

"I must have been wrong then," the man said, his voice shrilling a little.

"You must have been."

"Got the direction wrong. I mean, I don't know This guy, this Alexander, he tells me when he's in here where he lives. I must have got it fouled up."

Clintock licked his lips. "I don't think you got it fouled up."

"How's that?" the man asked, his voice going even higher.

"You were waiting for me to come in and ask for Alexander, weren't you?"

"Me? Waiting?"

"You never met a man who called himself Alexander, did you?"

"What are you talking about?"

"Come on!" Clintock snapped. "Spit it out!"

"I got nothing to hide," the man said, whining.

"Alexander's wanted from here to Vegas," Clintock said, voice edged. "The name's an alias to begin with. Now why don't you start telling me the truth."

"I'm telling you the truth, mister That's a fact!"

"How many drinks did you serve the girl?"

"What girl?"

"There was one girl in the bar last night. How many drinks?"

"Why? Maybe two. No, just one. I remember Why?"

"Was she drunk when she came in?"

"Her? Not her."

Clintock stepped forward, moving a hand out, locking steel fingers around the man's arm. The man's wife had reappeared now.

"Who told you what to tell me if I came in looking for Alexander?"

"Nobody, mister," the man cried. "Nobody, honest!"

With his free hand, Clintock suddenly slapped the man's face. The man grunted, taking in his breath. The woman gave a short scream.

"Who was it?" Clintock said, tightening his grip on the man's arm, twisting the man to his knees.

"Don't know . . . what you're talking about . . . "

"I'm telling you—" Clintock said, whispering now, drawing his hand back once more. Then the woman, shrieking once was on him, clawing, fighting.

Clintock let go suddenly, and turned and walked away, his face hard, his eyes black with hate.

He paused only a moment at the doorway, eyes searching ahead, and then he returned to his car He drove down the main street of the town.

The town was old. The buildings looked nearly all to be clapboard. There was a small garage, oil and grease staining the concrete in front, the gas pumps worked by hand. There was a grocery store, a small restaurant. The street ran through the center of the town and the blacktop was pitted; two years before the main highway had cut through here, now the loop of it had been shortened and the town was bypassed by the main traffic. A single car, dusty from travel, passed Clintock's, and moved on out of town. There was a silence, a stillness.

Clintock stopped his car in front of ancient pumps of the garage. Inside the small office, he could see a man in coveralls talking on a telephone. The man hung up. He didn't come out. Clintock got out and walked inside.

"Service is good," Clintock said thinly.

"You want something, mister?" the man said. He was sparrow thin, hands and face greasy. He seemed to be ducking from a blow, without actually doing it.

"I want to find a man called Dick Alexander."

The man's head was shaking back and forth before Clintock had finished speaking. "Not me. I don't know him."

"Maybe you didn't get the name right," Clintock said. "Dick Alexander."

"No, sir," the man said, eyes blinking rapidly. "I don't know him."

"Do you know anything?"

"I don't know anything. Not a thing."

Clintock stood there for a moment longer, and then he wheeled and left. He drove to the grocery store, stopped, started to get out, then did not. He wiped his palms over his eyes. A chill went through him. Then, gunning his engine, he U-turned, and drove back to the motel.

The girl was up; she looked fresh and well-groomed. She had changed to a yellow dress from the bag Clintock had brought in the night before.

"How do you feel?" Clintock asked.

"Shaky. Lousy."

Clintock walked across the room and sat down in a chair, so that his back was against a wall, so that he faced all the windows and the door.

"I've been a cop a long time," he said.

She looked at him. "Cop?"

"I know drunks. You weren't drunk last night."

"You should tell my head," the girl said, lifting her hand to her forehead. "It's splitting—"

"Cut it out," Clintock snapped. "I don't have the time. I don't have the patience."

"I don't know what you're talking about," the girl said, sitting down on the bed, sitting down tiredly, shoulders slumping.

"How do you fit in? That's all I want to know."

The girl shook her head stubbornly. "You're not talking sense."

"You weren't drunk when I came into the bar last night. I could see that. The bartender sold you just one drink, and he said you weren't drunk when you came in. It was an act. Why?"

"Who are you, mister?" the girl asked. "What are you after, anyway?"

"I got shot at twice when we pulled in here last night. You stopped me on the road on purpose. Only the rest of it doesn't figure. I wasn't shot at on the road. And this motel was my idea. You couldn't count on that. What's your tie-in with Nick Brady?"

The girl shook her head.

"You know Brady?"

"I know him," she sighed finally.

"Well?"

"I know who you are too, Clint."

Clintock frowned.

"I knew in the bar. The minute you came in. You look exactly like Bud, in the eyes, in the mouth. You're bigger, tougher looking. You look more certain and confident, but I knew you were Bud's brother."

"Okay," Clintock said. "Keep talking."

"I met Bud in San Francisco. I'm a singer. I was singing in a place on Mason Street. Bud used to come in. He didn't like my singing but we—well, it was one of those things. He talked an awful lot about you, Clint. He idolized you. He said you were everything he wasn't. He said you raised him, practically, when your parents died . . ."

"I said keep talking."

The girl put her hands in her lap, looking down. "He got mixed up with Nick Brady."

"And with Jack and Al," Clintock said bitterly.

"Yes. You know the rest."

"You tell me."

The girl shrugged. "They robbed that bank on Sutter."

Clintock's eyes thinned. "Were you a part of that?"

"No. That's honest, Clint. I didn't know. I tried to tell Bud before it happened that—"

"Okay," Clintock said hardly. "Just keep talking. What then?"

"Bud called me from Sacramento. He said to meet him in Reno in three days."

"And?"

"I did."

The girl was silent then, and Clintock stared at her with black eyes.

"I went to this hotel. His door was unlocked. I walked in. He was on the floor, bleeding. He was—" The girl's face had paled.

"I know how he was," Clintock said, knuckles white. "I saw him in the morgue. He had sixteen lacerations of the face. His right arm and nose were broken. Two fingers of his left hand were broken. There was a double compound fracture of the skull."

"Yes," the girl said, nearly whispering.

"Was he dead when you saw him?"

The girl shook her head.

Flickers of flashing light appeared in Clintock's eyes. His face seemed made of stone. "Go on," he said.

"He gave me this—" The girl's hand reached out, picked up her purse, fumbled the lock open, and drew out the billfold. She got out the small medal. "This."

"I saw it last night," Clintock said tonelessly. "My mother gave it to him when he was ten, just before she died. I've got one like it."

The girl nodded, then said, "I could barely hear him speak. He said money. He said something that sounded like cave. He—" The girl shuddered. "He was dead then. I was scared. I got out, phoned the police without telling them who I was, then left."

The cabin was silent. Outside, the town, the land around, the tall trees clustered up the side of the mountain were still as death. Clintock stood up. He walked to a window, looking out, no wariness in him now.

He turned. "How did you get here?"

"Same way you did, I suppose. I read in the papers about Dick Alexander. I know it was a name Nick Brady had used. I went from town to town. I asked in each place. I asked in the bar here, and the bartender said maybe he could help me."

"They're here then," Clintock said coldly.

"Yes."

"All three?"

"I think so."

"Where?"

"I don't know. Brady came to the bar to see me. I think Al was with him outside. They'd been expecting you, ever since you told the newspapers in San Francisco that you were going to get the man who killed your brother It wasn't Brady who used the name, you know."

"I know," Clintock said. "The description didn't match. It was Jack."

"Yes. He got drunk, and that was the name he thought of."

"What are they doing here?"

"The money."

Clintock frowned.

"Bud took all the money. He was supposed to meet them with it in Los Angeles, but he didn't. He took it all and went to Reno."

Clintock shook his head.

"You don't believe that, do you?" the girl asked. "You think Bud was just taken in by them, don't you? He wasn't, Clint. He knew what he was doing. Maybe you couldn't see the change in him. I could. He helped think up that robbery, and he helped figure out a plan that would give him a chance to get away with all of it."

"You're a cheap liar," Clintock said coldly.

"I'm a lot of things," the girl said. "But I'm telling the truth about this. That's why they beat him up, to get it out of him, where he'd hidden the money. They found him, Clint, before I got to him. Brady is smart. He's got a lot of contacts. I think he figured the possible places Bud might go and told people. And then got word that Bud was in Reno. They went there, and—"

All of a sudden, Clinton reached out and pulled the girl up from the bed. He pulled her into him, crushing her, moving his hands over her, kissing her. He let go of her finally, pushing her away, and she half fell to the bed.

"Cheap," he whispered.

"Animalism is contagious, Clint," she said softly. Her hands brought a handkerchief from her purse and she touched her mouth, the handkerchief coming away stained with blood from her cut lip. "It gets into people. I feel it for you, Clint. That's why I did that the way I did it. It's a hunger for the part of Bud I loved, but never had. It's a lust created out of killing and stealing. I've got lust, Clint, because of what I don't have."

Clintock half turned away, breathing hard.

"You feel it too, don't you, Clint? You liked the way I responded to your lust. You'd like to match it. Do you know why, Clint? Because the animalism is in you too, now. You've let hate grow in you. You've got blood in your eye, Clint. You want to kill and ravage. Ravage me if you must, Clint, but let the other go."

She brought her head up determinedly. She looked at the dark profile of his face.

"Clint, I know what happened. It was Jack who killed Bud. I can see him doing it. Exactly how he did it. Jack is an animal, and maybe he's infected all of us. He wanted that money, and only Bud knew where it was."

"No," Clintock breathed.

"Oh, yes," the girl said. "That's why I'm here, Clint. I want the money too. I want that sixty thousand dollars. Why else would I be here?"

"Bud wouldn't do it that way He—"

"Bud was no good," the girl said.

Clintock turned back to her, muscles flickering along his cheeks.

"Hit me," the girl said. "All right. But Bud was no good, no better than the rest of them, no better than Jack—"

She drew in her breath, waiting, but Clintock's hand did not move. His eyes watched her, steadily penetrating.

"You believe me, don't you?" she asked finally. "You knew that all along."

He wouldn't speak. His eyes were like ice.

"Yes," the girl nodded, sighing. "Yes, but it doesn't matter anymore what you do believe. You want to kill now. You want an eye for an eye. Nothing else makes any difference.

"Clint," she said, looking up hopefully, "I see better than that in you. I see what I couldn't see but only hoped I saw in Bud. I saw that when you walked into that bar last night. Clint—that was why I did what I did. Why I faked the drunkenness. I knew the bartender called Brady the instant you asked for Dick Alexander I knew when he told you where to find Dick Alexander that it was a trap. They were waiting for you. They would have killed you."

Clintock walked across the room, wary once more. He turned, his eyes looking at her impersonally.

"You don't know where they are?"

"No. Do you believe me, Clint? That I'm everything wrong, maybe, but that I don't want to see you hurt, warped? Do you believe that?"

"I'll find them."

"They're waiting for you. They'll kill you."

"They're somewhere near."

"But you don't know where. Nobody will tell you. They've got the advantage. They can hide, and you have to search. They're hidden. You're in the open. Do you want to die, Clint?"

"No."

The girl nodded, mouth twisting bitterly. "But only because you wouldn't be able to kill them then."

Once more Clintock sat down, against the wall, facing the windows, the door.

"There's a map in the glove compartment in my car," he told her "Get it for me, please. And give me that medal, will you?" His voice was edged with steel, as cold and piercing as the quick thrust of a sharp knife into soft flesh.

4.

In the cabin in the clearing, Al poked at the wood in the fireplace. Nick, sitting beside the table, looked up. "Let it go, Al. It's warming up. We'll fry in here, if you keep that goddamn fire going."

"Sure, Nick," Al said, straightening quickly. "Sure, you bet!"

Then the thin, young Jack appeared in the room. His hair had been freshly combed. He wore a fresh shirt. There was a smile on his lips once again.

"Hello, Jack!" Al said explosively. "You feel better now, kid?"

"Sure, Al," Jack smiled. "Sure, fine."

Nick watched the youth carefully, then turned his chair, stretching his legs.

"Sit down, Jack."

Jack nodded. "Thanks, Nick." He sat down.

"We want to stay out of trouble now. You understand that, don't you, Jack?"

"Sure, Nick. I understand that."

"I wasn't kidding you about this Clintock, kid. He's dangerous. And he means business about this. He and his kid brother, they were pretty close."

"Sure, Nick. I understand."

"You know why we can't fool around then. Why we can't take any chances. He's going to come looking for us, Jack. We've got to be careful. We've got to get all the advantages. Do you understand why Al had to bruise you up a little out there, kid?"

"Yeah, Nick. I understand."

Al came up, smiling apologetically "No hard feelings, huh, Jack?"

Jack smiled. "Hell, no, Al. No hard feelings." He looked at the bottle on the table, then reached over and very carefully capped it. "I understand. We got to be careful, all right. We got to get that money."

"That's right, Jack," Nick said. "Now you're talking."

"That's a lot of money, all right," Jack said. "Sixty thousand. How does that split, Nick? I'm not good at figuring. I mean the usual split?"

"Fifteen for you," Nick said. "Fifteen for Al. I take fifteen for myself. And then I put away fifteen to use on operations later."

Jack shook his head. "That's a lot of money, all right. Do you think we're going to find it, all right, Nick?"

"I know we are," Nick said.

Jack leaned forward, smiling. "How do you know, Nick?"

Nick returned the smile faintly "We traced where Bud went this far, didn't we? We found Bud was here right after the robbery, that he was here for two days. Right?"

"Right," Jack nodded.

"Now Carol comes along. Why?"

Jack shook his head. "Who knows? Maybe the same reason the cop comes along. I shouldn't have used that name. . ."

"Maybe," Nick said. "But maybe not. Who was it reported Bud dead in Reno? "

"It was," Al said, "how-you-say, anonymous?"

"But a woman," Nick said. "The papers said it was a woman, phoning from a public booth."

"Carol," Al said.

"I think so. So maybe she knows something."

"How?" Jack said. "Bud was dead when we left."

"Maybe," Nick said. "Maybe not. You can't tell for sure."

"He should have been dead," Jack said irrelevantly, smiling.

"But figure maybe he wasn't. That maybe he said something to her. He wouldn't tell us where the money was. Maybe he told her."

"Is that why she's here?"

"Maybe. Maybe she traced us out and knew we were coming close, and maybe that's why she's here, not knowing what we know or don't know Maybe she's scared we're going to run off with it. Only maybe, too, she's scared to go get it just yet, figuring maybe we'll take it away from her. How does that sound?"

"So," Jack said, "why don't we just kind of get it out of her?"

Nick nodded. "That's what I figured to do yesterday, after I talked to her at the bar Just wait a little to see if she'd go after it, and then if she didn't, I'd just let you, Jack, kind of talk her into it—only being more careful than you were with Bud. But this cop comes along."

"So?" Jack asked.

"You figure it out, Jack," Nick said. "You ever see Carol drink too much when she was working in this joint where Bud used to go see her all the time?"

Jack shook his head thoughtfully.

"Well, Al thought of that, didn't you, Al?"

"Yeah," Al said, head bobbing. "I thought of that."

"So what?" Jack said. "So what does that mean?"

"You thought she was tight last night, when she goes off the road. Well, this girl doesn't get tight. And then it's kind of funny, isn't it, that she goes off the road just in front of this cop, just when we've got him set up and you and Al are waiting to gun him? Right?"

Jack's eyes narrowed. "Yeah, Nick. That's kind of funny, all right."

"So maybe she knew what she was doing, huh? Maybe she wants on the cop's side, to kind of keep us off of her. How about that? How does that sound?"

"Yeah," Jack said slowly "Yeah. You're smart, all right, Nick. I got to hand it to you. But so what do we do now?"

"Wait, kid. Just wait. We got this town in the palm of our hand, do you know that? They're scared of us. They're going to cooperate. When the girl or that cop makes a move, we're going to know about it. This bartender, this joker in the roadhouse there, he runs this town, and he's got the word out. If they don't want trouble, they cooperate. They don't want any trouble. How about that?"

"Yeah," Al said happily, "how about that? How about that, Jack?"

Jack nodded reflectively "Yeah, that's good thinking, Nick. That really is. You're a smart one, all right, Nick. You really are."

"So everything's going to be swell now, huh?" Al said eagerly. "No hard feelings by anyone now, and pretty soon we all get fifteen grand, and fifteen stuck away for the future, like you say. Ain't this nice, after all, Jack? You ain't mad about me busting you a little out there, are you, Jack?"

Jack laughed softly, shaking his head. "Hell, no, Al."

Al put his hand on Jack's shoulder gratefully. And then he said, "Well, me, I'm going out to get some more wood. I chopped it up out there in back yesterday. I don't get cold easy myself, but I don't want you boys should get cold tonight. It gets cold at night, do you know that? Jack, do you want to come along? Fresh air is good for you. What are you going to do, Nick?"

"Get some sleep," Nick said. "Wake me in a little while, will you? I don't want to sleep too long."

"Sure, Nick," Al said. "Do you want to come along, Jack?"

Jack stood up. "Sure, Al. I think I will at that."

Al grinned happily. "I feel good again. Does everybody feel good?" He watched Jack fold his jacket over his arm. "That's right, kid. Take that along. You don't want to get chilly out there."

Outside, a sun was rising toward the middle of the sky, but the chill was not entirely out of the air. A breeze was coming down from the mountain, from beyond where, higher in the range, snow lay over peaks.

"This is good air," Al said, striding along, leading Jack down a small path away from the cabin. "How do you like this air, kid?"

"Fine, Al," Jack said. "Just fine."

"We had air like this back home. When I was a little kid, I mean. We lived in the country. Did I ever tell you that, Jack?"

"No, Al."

"Sure, I come from the country. I'll bet you didn't know that, kid, did you?"

"I really didn't."

"This all reminds me of home somehow," Al said. "Maybe that's why I like chopping the wood and fixing the fire and all like that. I used to do that when I was a kid."

They had reached the place where Al had chopped the wood the day before now, and Al, Jack behind him, surveyed it proudly.

And then Jack said, "Turn around, Al."

Al turned around, eyebrows lifting a little in surprise.

"What's up, Jack?"

The Luger was out of Jack's holster, and he was wrapping his jacket around it carefully, smiling.

"Say, what's going on, Jack?" Al said puzzled.

"You know what I told you back in the cabin, Al? About how I wasn't mad about you busting me?"

"Sure, Jack," Al said, blinking.

"I didn't mean that, Al," Jack said. "I didn't mean that at all."

Al, eyes widening, started to speak, but the first bullet caught him in the throat. He made a wild half-flutter with his arms, and then another slug in the belly doubled him. Jack pumped two more bullets into him as he lay crumpled on the ground, the shots echoing muffledly as the gun exploded within the jacket. And then, eyes bright, lips twisting in a wider grin, Jack began kicking ferns around the inert form.

Minutes later, in a bedroom of the cabin where a shade dimmed the morning light, Nick opened his eyes, looking at a smiling Jack sitting on a chair beside the bed. Jack's hands rested limply on his knees as he watched the drowsy Nick awaken.

"What the hell's up, anyway?" Nick said sluggishly.

"You know that split you figured out, Nick?" Jack said.

"Yeah? What about it?"

"You got to figure that over, Nick."

Nick blinked, trying to plunge entirely back to reality, and at the same moment, he could hear the telephone start ringing steadily, insistently.

Before she'd left the motel, before she'd driven to the roadhouse, and told the bartender that she wanted to talk to Dick Alexander, Carol Adams had stood in the small room of the motel cabin and looked at Clintock.

"You're sure of everything then, Clint?"

"Sure enough," Clintock had said coldly.

"Bud's medal is a St. Christopher medal. There's a Christopher hill."

"You saw it on the map. Bud said cave. The money's in a cave on the hill."

"You know now, then, that I was right about Bud—that he was bad, all bad."

"You want to get started?" Clintock asked, not looking at her. He took out his gun, checking it.

"You don't care about the money?"

Clintock shook his head. "I don't care about the money If you do, you can take it and leave. I won't do anything about it. It means nothing to me."

"Do *I,* Clint? Maybe I won't be getting the money, after all. It's a risk, you know. I could be killed too."

"Stay away from them, when you get near the cave," Clintock said flatly.

"If I can," the girl said. "Otherwise—" She looked at him closely. "You really don't care, do you, Clint? You care only about revenge, about killing. You know your brother for what he was now, and you know this is the way people like him wind up, with their heads cracked open, because they ask for it. But you don't care about that. You care only about killing. Are you any better, Clint? Are you any better than any of them?"

"You'd better take off," Clintock said.

"Sure," the girl said. "So long, Clint. Happy days."

And she had driven to the roadhouse, and now she was waiting, hands trembling a little. A few moments later, the bartender reappeared. "Okay," he said nervously. "They'll meet you. One mile south of town. On the road that goes out from the garage over there."

Carol stood up. "Thank you."

She walked to her car mechanically. She drove out the road that junctioned by the garage. She stopped at the second junction, just a mile out of town. The air was completely still now Not a leaf moved. There wasn't a cloud moving in the sky.

She waited five minutes, ten. And then, suddenly, a hand came in over the window and locked around her waist. She jumped, stifling a half scream, and looked into the face of Jack.

"Hand your purse out," Jack said softly.

She did, and Jack released her hand and opened the purse and ran a hand through it. His eyes flickered from hers to behind her, to beyond, to the woods behind. "Out," he said.

She got out, and he stood very near her.

"Let's go," he said. "My car."

He walked with her so closely that it was difficult to move. "What kind of a guy is that cop, anyway?" Jack asked. "Is he a good shot?"

"I don't know," she said.

"You know where the money is, though," he said, "don't you?"

She looked at him, fright in her eyes. "Where are the others?"

He laughed softly.

She didn't question him further. She got in the car behind the wheel at his command, and he got in with her. He sat right beside her, close beside her. "Okay, honey. Go now."

She drove to the point she and Clintock had picked on the map. "Up through there," she said, pointing. The bank rose, trees stretching upward, old branches cracked from former storms lying across lower limb junctures.

"I'll tell you this," Jack said, "you try anything at all, honey, I don't mind killing today. I've got the feeling for it, you might say. You might say, in an event like you try something, I'd like to kill better than I'd like to get my hands on that dough. Do I reach you, honey?"

She nodded woodenly.

"Then we move again," Jack said, smiling.

6.

Higher up the mountain, a thousand yards up the mountain, Clintock waited.

The cave was down and to his right; he had a good view of the entrance, hidden himself by thick ferns and the foliage of a low-sweeping limb.

He waited, and while he did so, his hand slid out the Cobra from the shoulder holster. His fingers grazed lightly over the metal surface.

In the sky, the sun moved along its highest arc, and somewhere now, a squirrel had begun chattering; a small branch cracked high in a tree, finally giving in to the pressure of the wind that floated above the tree-protected sweep of land below.

That wind did filter down, a few thousand yards away, trembling the ferns around the unmoving shape of a man, a thick wide-shouldered man, who even in death, carried the look of surprise in his staring eyes.

No wind disturbed the fur of what once had been a rabbit. The stiffening of death clotted even the fluffy coat, and the law of the forest was already at work. A string of ants moved purposefully through yellow and red leaves. A small black snake waited patiently.

The law of nature, Clintock thought. The law of reprisal. Life started and was bitten off. Man, in his movement, was nothing permanent, even at best. The hurrying of death was relative. An eye for an eye . . .

Smoke that Clintock could not see now rolled forth from a brick chimney. The flame had died, only red coals down within the blackened shaft remained, only enough heat to billow the smoke upward remained. There was a small snap, like a tiny gun explosion, as the grains of heated wood expanded. And now, across the room, diagonally from the mouth of that fireplace, blood had stopped spilling from the white flesh of the man who lay sprawled across a table, a hand a few inches away from a silent telephone. Death appeared, strangely, like sleep. Shirt and trousers, oddly, still looked expensive and vital to the man, who no longer breathed.

Clintock waited and watched, and then he saw them approaching—down, to his left. He lifted his gun, sighting, eyes cold and deadly.

The girl, now, moved in exact unison with the slim, black-haired Jack. One of Jack's arms circled her waist, and they moved slowly, with difficulty, because of their closeness. Clintock's trigger finger tightened a fraction. The accuracy of a small gun was limited; the target was limited.

So, Clintock thought, even if she dies too.

He felt no tremor of remorse, no emotion of regret. The taste of killing was full in his system now, in his mouth like the bite of a poison herb.

Clintock kept his eyes on Jack, outlining the youth's head, squinting carefully at the profile of chin and nose and forehead. A bullet sent accurately through the left temple, cracking the skull . . .

The girl shifted into Clintock's sights, as the two below moved. Clintock's finger did not release its knowing pressure against the trigger of the Cobra.

Now, Clintock thought, as the girl shifted again, slightly away from the gun sights . . .

And then suddenly, the girl jerked away, tearing from the hard clutch of the black-haired Jack. A sound of angry swearing came up to Clintock, and then, the double crack of Jack's gun. The girl had struck for the bushes now, and Clintock saw her stumble as the gun in Jack's hand jerked, puffed. Clintock, coldly, fired his own gun, watching the gun leap out of Jack's hand. A cry of pain echoed through the woods, as Jack ducked, rolling.

Once, Clintock thought, through the forearm . . .

He waited, watching. Bushes moved now, as the figure of Jack slid slowly back toward where the gun had bounced. Clintock fired just ahead of the movement, and the movement stopped.

Clintock waited, and then finally, the bushes trembled once more. Clintock fired again. Then the bushes moved in the opposite direction, as Jack, forsaking his gun, began his escape.

Clintock smiled. A little further now, he thought, watching. A little further . . .

The terrain opened up just in front of the cave. There was a moment of hesitation, then Jack plunged into the clearing, driving for the protection of the cave.

Clintock carefully fired once more, and the youth half skipped, then stumbled to his knees. He started to get up again, trying to claw his way ahead. He stopped, unable to move fast enough.

Once, Clintock thought, through the left ankle . . .

Jack whirled, on one knee, spreading his arms frantically. "No . . . please!" He began to cry, wildly, pleadingly.

Clintock's mind blanked to nothing but the image of the youth, outlined in his sights. He held the gun carefully, rock-steady. He held the gun and sighted and tasted the hate, the rising jubilation. Alive now, he thought, and then dead so quickly, so certainly . .

And then, suddenly, a slim hand was on his wrist, edging the gun up, out of position.

Clintock turned, blinking. He looked at the girl, at the small scratch above her left eye where a branch had broken the skin. His eyes gazed over her wholly.

"You're all right," he breathed, a surprising exultation going through him, a strangely satisfying exultation.

"Yes, Clint," she said softly.

Clintock licked his lips. "That's fine," he said.

He looked back down at the crying, shaking Jack, motionless now, except for the jerks of his crying spasms.

"Don't, Clint," the girl said.

Clintock was breathing hard now, and once more his hand moved the gun into position.

"I'll go get help," the girl said. "You can bring him in now. You don't have to kill him."

Clintock shook his head, trigger finger pressing once more.

"No, Clint," the girl breathed.

And then suddenly Clintock lowered the gun, sweat prickling his forehead.

Her hand squeezed around his wrist once more, and then she was gone.

Clintock stood up, picturing her moving down, back to the car. She was whole, alive, not hurt. That was the important thing, he discovered, surprised at the discovery.

And then he was moving down toward the helpless, shaking Jack, eyes cold upon the man, but knowing inside, satisfiedly, proudly, that he himself had not killed that day, and would not.

Girl Friend
Mark Mallory (Morris Hershman)

September 1957

"Fourteen years old!" Banner's voice was hollow. He held up the pocket snapshot that had just been passed to him. "A face like a dream, pretty blonde hair and all."

Mill dropped his feet from the desk, swiveled back in his chair and nodded slowly. "An average case as far as I'm concerned. You're going to prosecute it, Mr. Assistant District Attorney, so you might as well get the facts straight."

"What did she do, this girl?"

Mill crossed one foot over the other and rubbed it with thumb and forefinger. "It's quite a story. We had to ask a lot of questions to get the real answers. We wanted to know *why* she did it. Maybe you'd like to know about the why, first." He sighed. "Being a cop is such a rough job on the nerves because a cop can't afford to have nerves."

Mill liked to make little speeches about what it took to be a cop. In the years that Banner had known him, four or five, it happened at least once whenever they met. They weren't close friends; Mill couldn't talk about much but a cop's job. He seemed to have no outside interests at all.

"If you look this over," Mill said, pointing to a number of typewritten sheets clipped together, "you'll get some idea. What you got to know about a girl like this is that it's not all her fault, no matter what kind of nasty thing she did."

Banner picked up the sheets and settled them in his lap. They were in question-and-answer form. The girl's name was Alice King.

Q: How old are you, honey?

A: Fourteen. Fourteen, last December.

Q: What school do you go to, Alice?

A: Marley Junior High.

Q: You get good grades?

A: B's and B-plusses.

Q: Do you have a lot of boy friends?

A: No!

Banner frowned at the pocket-size photograph. "Good-looking kid. Why's she so quick to say she hasn't got a lot of boy friends?"

Mill scratched his foot again, then the back of an ear. He lit a cigar and puffed until it was drawing nicely. "Nothing else she could say. Of course at the time I didn't know it, myself. Don't forget we had just picked her up a little while before."

It had grown dark, and Mill flicked on the desk lamp. In the building, on three sides of them, men scurried back and forth. Outside the window, a pink dot could be seen far away, apparently the bathroom of a private home. Close to it was a larger window with blinds down, and bright light glaring out through a wider slit at the top.

"That kid," Mill said suddenly. "She ought to have been having the time of her life, going to proms and things. At that age, a girl's just finding out that she *is* a girl, and she sure as hell likes the idea."

Banner shrugged, then looked down to the sheet that was now on top.

A: No!

Q: Did you ever have a job, Alice?

A: You mean a job where I worked outside my house?

Q: That's right.

A: Only part-time. I worked in a department store for a while, but the job didn't last.

Q: Why not?

A: They were stingy—cheap, you know—and they kept me working after hours and wouldn't pay me extra for that. My mother said it was practically white slavery. She told them off.

Q: And after your mother told them off, you left the job?

A: I was fired.

Q: What kind of a job did you get then, Alice?

Banner looked up, frowning. "The mother sounds like a louse. Alice doesn't want to talk about her."

"If you ask me," Mill shrugged, "the mother's a good-natured, hearty, heavy drinking, foolish woman. Maybe that's why the kid—go on reading, Ban, you'll see."

Q: What kind of a job did you get then, Alice?

A: In a dress shop, but just about the same thing happened. So my mother said I ought to work for her. She said she'd pay me ten dollars a week if I'd keep the house nice and clean before she-uh, worked.

Q: Sounds like a soft touch.

A: It was okay, for a while.

Q: What went sour?

A: I might as well tell you. Usually, mother kept me away from the house till half-past twelve at night. I'd stay over at a girl friend's place. But sometimes I had trouble with some of the customers. One of them, a Mr. Dail, sees mother twice a week. He happened to come in a little earlier once when I was cleaning. Mr. Dail took one look at me and said to mother: "I'd pay twenty dollars for just a half hour with her."

Q: What did your mother say?

A: She said no. She said she wouldn't let her kid do that. But Mr. Dail, he kept talking about it and after a few minutes, mother said that the rent was coming up in a few days and she was paying more than usual for protection. To the cops, I mean.

Q: So you went into the bedroom with Mr. Dail?

A: Mother said I wouldn't have any trouble. When Mr. Dail and I, the two of us, were finished, she was making jokes about it. All the time we were in there, though, she sat outside sobbing a little.

Banner, looking up, caught Mill's drily amused eyes. He avoided them, stood and walked to the window. The pinkish bathroom light far away had been put out. The sounds of routine police business had increased in tempo.

Finally, after swallowing quickly, Banner asked: "Did Alice King turn pro?"

The cop, openly pleased by Banner's interest, pointed to the sheets. "Read the q-and-a, you'll see." He added thoughtfully, "You know, I don't think you can imagine what the kid was like. Very refined, always smoothing down her skirt. When she asked for a glass of water she tacked on, 'please.' Never blamed her crime on circumstances or said she was victimized. In fact, a good kid. Like your daughter would be, if you had one."

Q: Did you do it with other men, Alice?

A: Sometimes. Mother always told them I was twelve and a virgin. She always charged more money for me than for herself. Up to twenty-five dollars. After it was over, she would give me five dollars for myself. Mother wouldn't let me do it more than twice a week.

Q: How many men would you say you've slept with, Alice?

A: I don't know.

Q: Ten? Is it that many?

A: I don't know.

Q: Twenty?

A: I don't know.

Q: Thirty? Forty? Fifty? Give me a number that's close to the truth, Alice.

A: Fifty, maybe.

Mill said, "You can skip the part where she gives names. The Vice Squad boys have picked up the ones she remembers, and they're in for a bad time. Your boss, the D.A., he'll see to that."

Banner said quietly: "At least I know now what you're holding the girl for. Delinquency. An easy case to prosecute. In her set-up, it could have been something worse."

"It was. It is." Mill looked intently at the tip of his cigar, talked slowly to it. "A hell of a lot worse."

In spite of himself, Banner lowered his head.

Mill added: "Alice King has good stuff in her, as a person. You take the average fourteen-year-old girl and put her in that spot and she becomes like the mother, you know—shiftless, lazy, vain, a stupid slob. Alice didn't."

Banner glanced at the snapshot.

"I don't mean just for looks," Mill said a little impatiently. "There's other things in a kid's life. Alice King kept up her grades at Marley Junior High, even improved them in one case. She started to appreciate ballet and modern dance. She did some dating. Normal, in other words, except for what she did twice a week."

Banner looked a little sadly at the picture. Suddenly he stiffened and set it face down on the desk. He was flushed.

Mill smiled. "Thinking you'd like to jump the kid yourself, I bet!" More seriously he added, "One of the hard things about being a cop is that you can excuse the bad in most people because it's in you, too ... Give me the sheets, will you, for a minute?"

Banner slowly handed them across. The cop turned four pages, his wet thumb driving a crease into every one, then a fifth.

"Here it is. Where she meets Ronald Hutchinson."

Banner's lip curled. "Another customer?"

"Another kid. Fifteen, in fact. I found out a lot about him. A big wheel at Marley Junior High: baseball team in summer and football in winter, editor of the school paper, member of Arista, student president of the G.O. And rich, too. Lot of dough in the family. Old man is president of a chain of supermarkets."

"The kid sounds like a snob."

"No." Mill shook his big head determinedly, and tapped a crown of ash off the cigar. "Nice, healthy kid with a lot of girl friends. A good-looking kid with nice manners."

Q: How did you come to meet Ronald Hutchinson?

A: I went out for the school paper.

Q: Oh, you volunteered to work for it.

A: That's right. I thought I wanted to be a reporter when I grow up, so I took a crack at it. Ron was the student editor. We hit it off, all right. We liked each other. We laughed at the same things and had a lot in common. I always think that's very important with a boy and girl.

Q: Tell me what happened between you two.

A: Nothing did, at the start. I knew he'd want to take me out, but I didn't rush him. He waited two weeks. There was going to be a dance in the gym at school on Saturday night and he asked me to go with him. I said I would.

Q: Did he call you at home?

A: No, I never want boys to call me at home. It can get confusing.

Q: How did your mother feel about your taking off Saturday night?

A: Mother said it was fine, because she wants me to have good times. She doesn't want to interfere with my social life.

Q: That's for sure. So you and Ron Hutchinson hit it off, I suppose.

A: The first date, at the dance, was very sweet. Ron couldn't samba, so a bunch of us showed him. It was a lot of fun. After that, I saw him in school. It got so that we used to hold hands over the lockers in our 'official' rooms. That means the rooms where students do things as a class, you know, according to what the principal wants.

Q: You were dating Ron pretty heavily?

A: We had a few cheap dates, first. We'd meet at the ice cream parlor and he'd buy me a soda and we'd sit and talk. We had an awful lot in common. Once in a while we'd go see a movie and hold hands. Then he'd walk home with me and say goodnight a block from the house. I never let boys call for me at the house.

Q: You didn't mind the cheap dates?

A: No, they were fun. Ron said that the whole town knew about his being rich, so he didn't have to impress girls by flashing a roll. A *bankroll,* he meant.

Q: In other words, you had nothing against Ron Hutchinson.

A: That's right, nothing.

Q: No grudge of any kind.

A: Of course not.

Q: Did you think you were in love with him?

A: I suppose so.

Q: You were serious about him, then?

A: Yes. Almost praying I could keep him interested till I was eighteen, so we could get married. That shows you what a fool I was!

Q: Why a fool?

A: On account of what happened.

Q: How many times a week did you see him?

A: Two, three.

Q: How did your mother feel about that?

A: At first she thought it was very nice and she told me not to give away anything, if you know what I mean. Then she said I ought to be home at nights, to work if I had to. She said expenses were going up and I ought to be paying a bigger share of my upkeep.

Q: How did you feel about that?

A: I wanted to get a job in a store, instead, but my mother didn't want that.

Q: The two of you argued?

A: Yes. I started to get sick when I had to use the bedroom with one of the customers. Sometimes I'd throw up or say that I had cramps.

Q: Tell me about last night—Saturday night.

A: Mother was a little under the weather. She wanted me to stay with one of our customers. The man came in, Mr. Cameron, and I just got sick when I saw him. I started to cry. Mother got angry, but when she saw she was licked anyhow, she told me to go.

Q: You had a date with Ron?

A: We were headed for a party over a friend of his' house.

Q: How about the knife, Alice? How come you took a pocketknife along with you on a date?

Banner caught his breath.

A: My mother thinks it's a good idea to bring one, in case a girl gets into a spot where she needs a little help. Mother isn't like most people, you know, and she always tells me to be very careful when I go out on a date and never go beyond necking. When we're alone, she calls the customers animals. She always warns me that men are after one thing and a girl has to use any way possible to keep—well, you know.

Q: And you believe that?

A: Mother's had more experience than me.

Q: So you took a pocketknife along on every date?

A: Most of them. It came in handy for little things, you know, like cutting open envelopes. I never had to use it to scare off a boy. Not till last night, that is.

Q: Ron made a pass at you?

A: We were at Baker's Lane. You know, a lot of cars stop there for couples to neck in peace and quiet. Ron had borrowed his dad's car for the date. He said to me. "What about it, honey?" He put a hand under my dress and started slowly unbuttoning it from behind. Like one of the customers does, Mr. Strawbridge, that is. Anyhow, I tried to stop Ron. I said: "I'm not one of those girls." And to make a joke out of it, to show I meant it for a joke, I pulled out the pocketknife and said: "Better not." Of course I said it in such a way he was sure it was a joke.

Q: He didn't give up trying, did he?

A: No. He was very calm, very patient, very sure of himself and sure what would happen. Like a customer. Any customer. I was sitting there with my knuckles in my mouth to keep from making a sound. Then Ron fumbled with something in his breast pocket and brought out a wallet and spread it open. He said very seriously: "I hope you'll let me buy things for you, and make life easier for you. A girl and her mother alone always have a rough time," he glanced down at my dress, my best dress, "and I'd be glad to help. The money doesn't mean a thing to me." And all the time he was running a thumb over the bills in his wallet just like one of the customers before he pays. Just like Mr. Dail. The exact same . . .

Q: All right, all right! We'll pick up the questioning later on. The way you're crying, a person would think I'd belted you one. Strike that!

Mill said thoughtfully: "She was in love with rich-boy Ron and, when he offered to buy her, just like one of the customers would, she acted blindly with the knife."

One of Mill's hands stiffened in a fist; he stuck out a forefinger and stabbed it suddenly against his heart.

Banner stared at the finger, then quickly looked away.

Midnight Caller
Wade Miller (Robert Wade & Bill Miller)

January 1958

Nina awoke at midnight, staring, certain there was someone in the bedroom. She turned her head slowly. In the farthest corner, on the chair, she thought she could make out a shape.

It was a man. In the dark he was faceless.

"Who is it?" she whispered.

The shape towered to its feet. She still couldn't see any more than arms, torso and head, advancing. All the moonlight from the window was on her. Such a warm night, she had left the window raised, the blind up. Now she noticed the screening, bellied outward, unfastened at the bottom.

Her shaking hand reached out for the bedside lamp.

Knuckles cracked across her mouth. She kept from screaming.

"I didn't say do that," said the man.

She lay there, trembling. He stood over her for a moment. Then she turned toward the window. He closed it and lowered the blind.

He turned on the bed lamp and she could see him. His face wasn't as bad as she had expected. He looked like a man who had worried a lot, and the lines beside his mouth were deep. The tight controlled way he kept his lips clamped together was somehow terrible, as if someone had cut the muscles so he could never again smile.

He studied her, and worst of all were his eyes, yellow and unreasoning. By his eyes she knew she had no chance of talking sense to him.

She tried not to babble and her voice came out weak but clear. "Is there something special you came after? Money? Clothes?"

He wore no coat, simply a white shirt—not too soiled—plain denim work trousers and plain work shoes.

He didn't answer. She tried to sit up.

He shoved her down again. His hand was strong and sweaty against her bare shoulder.

He said, "Keep lying down. When you let people get up or stand up sometimes they keep growing until they're bigger than you are. You know?"

Nina nodded, wanting to scream. The scream was big in her throat and she thought she'd choke if she didn't let it out.

Suddenly, he sat down on the bed. It creaked with his weight. Slowly, not daring to draw his attention, she moved her legs away from him.

He looked at the size of the bed, double. He said, "You got a husband?"

She nodded.

"Where is he?"

She managed, "Away."

"You expect him back?"

She nodded—too quickly.

"You're lying."

Yes, she was lying. She glanced miserably at the humpback shape of the phone on the other side of the bed, a thousand miles away.

"What's your name?"

"Nina."

He shook his head. "I don't want to call you that. I'd rather call you Marie."

She couldn't follow that but she said, "All right," and he repeated softly, "Marie."

The next door neighbors were coming home from somewhere. Their headlights flashed across the lowered blind. She heard their garage door open and close. She wanted them to notice the loosened screen but they didn't. She heard the wife laugh as they went into the house. Oh, God—would she ever laugh again?

He was staring at her heavy breasts, as if he was watching her heart beat. She had worn to bed a yellow nylon nightgown with lace cups and ribbon straps. He could see right through the lace. She had to say something.

She asked him his name.

To her surprise, he told her. First, he pinched the bridge of his nose, as if his eyes were tired or as if he had been drinking or as if he were trying to reach his brain. "Robert Babcock," he said. Then he added, "But I don't want to be him. I want to be Mike. I'm better as Mike."

"All right—Mike."

"Marie."

She was trying to draw the single blanket and sheet up over her breasts. He noticed and became angry. "Don't do that!" He tore the covers down to her waist. She stiffened with fright.

Then he said gently, "You don't have any lipstick on."

She had cleaned her mouth before going to bed. She touched her lips. The upper one was swollen where he had struck her, but she wasn't bleeding.

He went to the dressing table and rummaged and came back with a lipstick. She raised on her elbow and made up her mouth.

He said, "That's better. You're a very glamorous creature, Marie. You ought to keep yourself up. You're not the kind that would keep asking for more, are you?"

He put his hand on her stomach and she froze inside. She looked at the phone again, then at the window. Next door, the couple were in bed by now, sleeping or making love, not at the mercy of . . .

He ripped the covers off the bed entirely. "Marie with the red mouth." His hand drifted over her hair, tangled with sleep. He touched her ears as if they were jewels.

He rolled up his fist and then opened it. She whimpered and put her hand to her mouth as if she hadn't meant it.

He looked at the cling of the nightgown over the round of her hips. He pushed the hem up her legs so he could gaze at her tight-clasped thighs.

He stood up and began to unbutton his shirt.

Nina saw the dawn against the drawn blinds. He was curled on his side, sleeping heavily, snoring a little. She rolled across the bed to the phone.

She thought about the police. Instead, she dialed the State Psychologist, downtown. Finally, she got through to his private number.

She said, "Doctor? This is Nina Babcock. Yes. My husband has slipped out of the institution again. He's here." She listened, then added, "You'll have them treat him gently, won't you?"

Donald E. Westlake

William Winthrop turned the key in its lock, pushed open the apartment door and stepped inside. Kicking the door shut behind him, he stopped in the foyer and looked at the key in the palm of his hand. He grinned to himself and slowly turned the hand palm downward. The key made no sound at all as it hit the carpet.

Winthrop moved from the foyer to the living room, leaving hat and tie on a sofa as he went by. He walked into the bedroom, tossing his coat and shirt at a chair in the corner of the room as he removed them. Then he sat down on the edge of the bed and put his head in his hands.

He could feel his hands trembling against his cheeks, and was surprised. He felt his chest for his cigarettes, realized he didn't have his shirt on, and walked over to where the shirt lay, on the floor beside the chair. He picked it up, took the cigarettes from the pocket, and dropped it on the floor again. Removing one cigarette, he dropped the pack on the floor beside the shirt, then lit the cigarette with his pocket lighter. He looked at the lighter for a long moment, then dropped that, too . . .

He stuck the cigarette into the corner of his mouth, walked over to the dresser on the other side of the room, and opened the top drawer. He felt under a pile of shirts, came up with a .45 automatic. The gun dangling from his hand, he went back and sat down on the bed again. He dropped the cigarette on the floor and stepped on it.

He took the clip from the handle of the gun, looked at the eight bullets, then put the clip back. He pressed the barrel of the gun against the side of his head, just above the ear, and sat there, his finger trembling on the trigger. Perspiration broke out on his forehead. He stared at the floor.

Finally, he looked up from the floor and saw his own reflection in the mirror on the closet door. He saw a young man of twenty four, long brown hair awry, face contorted, dressed in brown pants, brown shoes and a sweaty undershirt, a gun held to his head.

He hurled the gun at the mirror. The crash startled him and he jumped. Then he lay face down on the bed, his head in the crook of his left arm, his right fist pounding the bed. "Damn it," he cried, over and over, in time to the pounding of his fist. "Damn it, damn it, damn it."

At last, he stopped swearing and beating the bed, and a sob shook his body. He cried, wrackingly, for almost five minutes, then rolled over and stared at the ceiling, breathing hard.

When he had calmed down, he rolled out of the bed to his feet and walked across the room to where his cigarettes lay. This time, after he'd lit the cigarette, he stuffed cigarettes and lighter in his pants pocket, then recrossed the room, past the bed and the dresser and the shattered mirror and the gun on the floor, and on into the bathroom.

With water filling the sink, he took a comb and ran it through his hair, to get it out of the way while he washed. Then he turned the tap off, dipped a washcloth in the water, and scrubbed his face until it hurt. Grabbing a towel, he dried face and hands, and looked at himself in the mirror. Again he took the comb, this time combing more carefully, patting his hair here and there until it looked right to him.

The cigarette had gone out in the ashtray, so he lit another. Then he went back to the bedroom.

Kicking the gun and the larger pieces of glass out of the way, he opened the closet door and looked over the clothing inside. He selected a dark blue suit, shut the closet door, and tossed the suit on the bed.

Back at the dresser, he took out a clean shirt, underwear and socks. From the tie rack on the back of the bedroom door he took a conservative gray number and brought all back to the bed.

He changed rapidly, transferring everything from the pockets of the pants he'd been wearing to the suit. Then he went back to the living room and made himself a drink at the bar in the corner. He gulped the drink, lit another cigarette and went to the front door, to make sure it was unlocked. On the way back, he picked up his key and put it in his pocket.

He sat down, crossed and recrossed his legs, buttoned and unbuttoned his suit coat, played with the empty glass. After a minute, he crushed the cigarette in an ashtray, got up, and made another drink. He swallowed half, lit another cigarette, threw away the empty pack and went to his room for another. When he came back, he reached for the half-full glass on the bar, but his hand shook and the glass went over, shattering on the floor behind the bar. He jumped again.

Leaning back against the wall, eyes squeezed shut, he whispered to himself, "Take it easy. Take it easy. Take it easy."

After a while, he moved away from the wall. He'd dropped the cigarette when the glass broke, and it was still smoldering on the rug. He stepped on it and took out another. He got another glass and made a drink, then went back to the sofa and sat down again.

He was just finishing the drink when the knock came. He was facing the door. "Come in," he called.

The door opened, and the two of them came in through the foyer to the living room. "William Winthrop?" asked one.

Winthrop nodded.

The man took out his wallet, flipped it open to show a badge. "Police," he said.

"I know," said Winthrop. He got to his feet. "Anything I say can be used against me. I demand my right to make one phone call."

"To your lawyer," said the detective. It wasn't a question.

"Of course," said Winthrop. He crossed to the phone. "Care for a drink? The makings are over there, in the corner."

"No thanks," said the detective. He motioned and the other one walked into the bedroom.

"Don't mind the mess in there," called Winthrop. "I tried to commit suicide."

The Best of *Manhunt 2*

The detective raised his eyebrows and walked over to the bedroom door to take a look. He whistled. "What happened to the mirror?"

"I threw the gun at it."

"Oh." The detective came back. "At least you're sane. A lot of guys try to cash in. Only the nuts do."

"That's a relief," said Winthrop. He dialed.

The detective grunted and sat down. The other one came back from his inspection, shook his head, and sat down near the door.

Winthrop heard the click as a receiver was lifted, and a man's voice said, "Arthur Moresby, attorney."

"Hello, Art? This is Bill."

There was a pause, then, "Who?"

"Bill. Bill Winthrop."

"I'm afraid I don't recognize the name. Are you sure you have the right number?"

"Oh," said Winthrop. "Like that. It's in the papers already, eh?"

"On the radio."

"You don't know me, is that right?"

"That's right," said Arthur Moresby, attorney. "Goodbye."

Winthrop heard the click, but continued to hold the phone against his ear.

"What's the matter?" asked the detective.

Winthrop shook his head and returned the phone to its cradle. He grinned crookedly at the detective. "Wrong number," he said.

"How a wrong number?"

"I'm a sinking ship."

"And your lawyer?"

"He's a rat. He doesn't know me. He never heard the name."

"Oh," said the detective. He stood up. "I guess we can go then, huh?"

Winthrop shrugged. "I guess so."

He followed them out of the apartment. They walked to the elevator, Winthrop pushed the button, and they waited without speaking. When the elevator came, they stepped in and the detective pushed the button marked '1'.

On the way down, the detective said, "Mind if I ask you a question?"

"For the insurance," said Winthrop. "I was in debt. Either I paid or chhhhk." He ran a finger across his neck.

"That isn't the question. I want to know why you waited for us to come before you called the lawyer. You had a lot of time before we got there. Why did you wait?"

Winthrop stared at the door. Why had he waited? He thought a minute, then said, "I don't know. Bravado or something."

"Okay," said the detective. The door slid open and they walked across the vestibule to the street. A few passersby watched curiously as Winthrop got into the back seat of the police car.

"I'm twenty four," said Winthrop, as they drove through the streets to Police Headquarters.

"So?" said the detective.

"Seems like a hell of an age to stop at."

"How old was your mother?" asked the cop.

Winthrop closed his eyes. "Do you hate me?"

"No," said the cop.

Winthrop turned and looked at the cop. "I do," he said. "I hate my guts."

Time to Kill

Bryce Walton

Ten Palms, advertised as *A Garden In The Desert*, was originally planned to bring in sick people who hoped to recover, and old people who wanted a healthy, sunny and dry climate to die in.

Many of these people had a great deal of money. The gamblers moved in. Soon there were gilded casinos, nightclubs, a number of tanned girls, and slot machines everywhere, even in the restrooms.

None of these things interested Allan Barton anymore. He didn't go into town so much, but instead he took long evening walks in the dead silence of the desert, watching jackrabbits play in the moonlight, mice and packrats hopping about under the sagebrush.

Sometimes this silence was too heavy for Barton. It reminded him of all the dull years of his life when nothing interesting had ever happened to him. Even the war, because of his bad lung, had passed him by.

Then he would walk a few cabins down the path from his own, and talk with Steve Milton who never talked about himself, but who was always a good listener.

Tonight, Steve's cabin was dark. Evidently he hadn't come back from Ten Palms yet, and probably wouldn't the rest of the night. Steve spent a lot of time in town.

As Barton started to walk on past the shadowed cabin he stepped on Steve's hand. Barton leaned down, then coughed and stumbled back and put his hand against the cabin.

Why Steve's dead, Barton thought in an oddly detached way, dead, with a bullet hole in his forehead.

The body resembled one of those broken sprawled corpses seen in war photographs. The coagulated blood on the face resembled oil.

Barton looked around, feeling that he was being watched from out there in the sagebrush somewhere. He didn't see anything. Voices, laughter, came from other cabins. A guitar twanged.

Barton's thin face was usually taciturn, but now a peculiar smile appeared on his lips. He felt a kind of unfamiliar excitement growing inside. It simply was something that not only had never happened, but never could happen. A sudden feeling of being alive when he had resigned himself to being dead. It was this feeling of danger, genuine danger, breathing down his neck.

The dull years as a kid, the dull years in business college, the dull years with Johnson Belt and Dye Company, the dull years of marriage and the commuting back and forth every day, the dull divorce and his wife marrying an assistant vice-president. It was like all his life he had been a member of the walking dead.

He heard cars droning down the highway toward Las Vegas. A pale dusty moonlight lay over the sand like glass. A small wind whispered in the sage. And oddly, he thought, I ought to stretch it out, make it last a while, like a glass of good imported whiskey.

Who was Steve? Why had he been murdered? Who were these people who had lived around Barton all his life and whom he had never met, never, never even seen, and knew nothing about? These people who were all around, and who lived so far away from his own dull world? Who were these ghosts who lived dangerously?

He turned the wall lamp on inside Steve's cabin. The two rooms had been ransacked, everything broken up, cut open, torn apart, including the mattress and the rug. They had done this after bringing Steve back home, because the place had been neat a few hours ago when Steve had left to go into Ten Palms. Steve was alive then.

Barton wondered if someone had found whatever they were looking for. Was it worth a killing? What was worth dying for?

"A guy's supposed to show here, but he's been delayed," Steve had said that afternoon. "He's a tall guy, and he'll be wearing a gray stetson and his name's Leo Stinson. He's got a room reserved at the Del Rey Hotel. I may not be around, so he can pick the stuff up there."

"What stuff?" Barton had wanted to ask. He hadn't asked.

"And thanks a lot, Al. He may not show at all."

The conversation hadn't seemed important a few hours ago.

On his way in to Ten Palms, Barton stopped off in his cabin and took a stiff shot of morphine, the doctor's remedy for the growing pain in his chest. He put the kit in his pocket before he left.

When Barton asked the night clerk in the Del Rey lobby for his key, saying he was Leo Stinson, the clerk hardly noticed him. So evidently Steve had never run into Leo Stinson, or if he had, it didn't seem that Stinson had been at the Del Rey. The Del Rey Hotel was a second rater on Main Street. The lobby was filled mostly with old people sitting, staring at potted palms and Reader's Digests, waiting for the night to go and the sun to come up one more time.

The room number, 204, was on the key tag. Barton went in and turned on a naked ceiling light. A straight-backed chair, narrow bed, throw rug, bureau, small bathroom, picture of the Vanishing American. Empty, lonely and smelling of antiseptic.

He made a thorough search and found nothing. He started to feel rage, cheated, the show folding before it even got started. And then he heard a squeak behind him, felt a draft on his neck. As he turned, he remembered he hadn't locked the door. Two men entered. Then a woman, who stepped to one side and leaned against the wall. The taller man kicked the door shut with his heel. The woman snapped the nightlock. The younger man stepped nervously toward Barton. His hand stayed under an expensive Shetland jacket. Barton wondered if the nice looking, neat, tanned young man really had a gun under there.

"Feel him down," the taller one drawled, slouching inside an expensive suede jacket. "And watch yourself. This Stinson's supposed to be a really rough boy."

Larry ran his hands insolently in the search, then puzzled, said, "He isn't carrying anything."

"He isn't?"

"Not a thing, Jay."

Jay looked around the room. "Don't even see any harness."

"Maybe he just scares people to death," Larry said.

The woman told Larry to close the window. She had a striking figure under the thin summer dress, wide hips, thin waist, and high full loose breasts. She had long bare legs too, and Barton found himself staring at her body and the molded thighs as she sat down on the creaking bed and crossed her legs.

"Look all over in here for it," the woman said, watching Barton closely. She reacted to Barton's appraisal and her breasts tightened against the low-cut bodice. Her leg began moving nervously back and forth.

Jay started looking everywhere, while Larry watched Barton. And Barton kept staring at the woman's flat stomach, and the long provocative sweep of her thighs.

He remembered all those women, all turning stale over the years, until it turned into dull routine and after that stopped meaning anything at all. His wife coming to bed with him only on specified nights, and performing with all the ardor of an electric toaster popping up bread browned exactly the same every time.

This one would be different, he knew. Maybe so different it would even seem new. He hadn't felt so stirred up and excited about it since he was a sophomore at the Palo Alto School of Business Management.

"Look him over again for papers or something," the woman said.

Larry came up this time with his wallet, and the morphine kit. He threw the morphine kit against the wall and spilled a few meaningless items, including a few dollar bills, out of the wallet.

Larry looked at the inside of the wallet and tossed it on the floor. "He's traveling under the name of Allan Barton."

Barton hoped the bottle of morphine in the kit hadn't broken. If it had, he would be in for some bad pains and that would spoil the fun.

Larry's short vicious jab slammed Barton into the wall. A roaring pain ballooned up out of his chest and burned in his head. The room blurred. He put his hand to his mouth and looked at the blood on his fingers. It resembled someone else's blood.

Jay was leaning out the window and feeling up and down the outside walls. Barton hadn't thought of that. Something could have been taped to the wall outside the window.

Only Jay didn't find anything out there. Jay shut the window again and lowered the blind. Barton wondered how these three had known about the Leo Stinson business. Maybe they had gotten that much out of Steve before they killed him. Maybe they had been out there by the cabin and had trailed Barton into town and one of them had been in the lobby when he gave the name of Stinson.

"We knew your two-timing friend was coming in to pick up that stuff," the woman said. "Steve was watched. We lost him for a while this afternoon and he must have put the stuff in here. It wasn't packaged for mailing, and he couldn't have ditched it anywhere else, not anywhere it would ever do anyone any good. It's here, Mr. Stinson. Or you know where it is."

She watched him with heavy lidded eyes. Her toe moved nervously up and down. She's afraid of me, Barton thought, incredulously. Then he smiled at the idea. It was very amusing. Also suddenly she seemed more exciting and desirable than ever. The bed creaked as she shifted her wide hips.

"Nothing's hid in here," Jay said. "He doesn't have it. It isn't in here. It's someplace else."

Larry hit him again in the stomach. Barton coughed and almost fell as a deadly weakness crept up through his legs. He felt that quivering inside, the feeling that his chest was crumbling like dry clay.

Larry jerked a revolver from under his sport jacket. "I'll get it out of him. I'll chop it out and I'll shoot the bum."

Looking at the gun, Barton couldn't help laughing.

"What the hell?" Larry said. Barton laughed louder. He walked toward the gun.

"Hold it, fella," Larry said quickly.

"I'm going to scare you to death," Barton said. He laughed again.

"Watch it, watch it," Larry said, his voice higher.

"Go on and shoot me," Barton said. He couldn't stop laughing.

"He's nuts," Larry whispered.

Barton picked up the chair by the back slats. "Why shoot me though? Why not use a switch-blade knife, you're a juvenile delinquent aren't you, kid?"

"I'm telling you, you cheap—"

"A shot will bring the police. And if I know where the stuff is, as you call it, shooting me would be stupid. And anyway, if you guys don't get the hell out of here I'm going to heave this chair right through the window. Broken glass, chairs falling down on the main street. You're asking for trouble that way."

"You better shut up, mister," Larry said. He was sweating.

"Ah," taunted Barton, "I dare you to shoot me. Go on, shoot, see if I care."

"I'm telling you," Larry said. "He's nuts." His deep tan seemed to be turning a slight gray color.

The bed creaked as the woman stood up. "He's probably got a load on," she said. "Cool off a little now, Larry."

"I'm going to cool this guy off all right."

"What's your hurry?" Barton asked. "This isn't a proper place to torture information out of someone and then kill them. I don't intend leaving town. I'll probably be around for quite a while."

Larry started to lunge at him but Jay grabbed him by the upper arms and swung him back toward the wall.

"You two get out now," Barton said, smiling. "Or the chair goes out the window." He turned and looked at the woman. "But I'll talk to you."

She studied him with fear and curiosity, then motioned to Jay and Larry. "Outside," she said in a very low voice, "I'll meet you downstairs."

When the door shut, Barton went over and snapped the nightlock, then went over to the bed and pushed the woman back down to a sitting position. The touch of her flesh burned up his arm. She looked at him with eyes full of fear. He reached down and slid her dress up the white length of her thigh. Her hands gripped his wrist. He dug his fingers into her flesh until she gasped.

The Best of *Manhunt* 2

Everything seemed so sharply focused now, Barton thought. Everything was important now. It was as if he had never had it before, instead of as if he would never have it again. Or maybe it was the same thing.

He wiped his mouth with his handkerchief.

"What the hell kind of a guy are you anyway, Stinson?"

"You want to find out I guess," he said. He had never seen one afraid of him before. Passive, accepting, because of fear, and at the same time liking it herself because she was afraid and had to give in. She probably likes, wants to be afraid of it, he thought. Anyway it added something, a special and necessary ingredient. It was a new experience for him.

The bed sagged under his added weight. Her voice was muffled. "You have a big reputation. A friend of mine knew a guy who ran into you up in Frisco. I knew about you even before I found out you were a pal of Steve's. Steve was stupid. You aren't stupid."

"What does that matter?"

"You could really cause trouble. I can offer you five thousand—"

"Just be quiet now," he said, his voice getting thick.

"Don't hurt me," she said in a faint voice. "Please don't hurt me. Steve two-timed me. Maybe you don't know about that . . . we had it all worked out together . . . and he two-timed me. He was going to use it to get the Club. Hell, he would have told Marsten everything just for a slice of . . ."

"Forget all that," Barton whispered. "Forget all that stuff now, you understand? The hell with all that."

"I'll make a deal with you too—only promise you won't—"

She gasped, and then she struggled a little, and after that she lay back with her eyes closed, shivering and then moaning and half-sobbing against his face. . . .

After that he lay there for a while looking at the neon sign bleeding outside the hotel window. It was the best he had ever had, nothing ever like it before. Yet she probably wasn't really much different. She had helped murder Steve, he knew, and maybe that had made it better. He hated her, and she was afraid of him, and there was death in it, and danger everywhere, and blood in it too.

It didn't happen much among the respectable crowd he had known all his life. Most of them hadn't even known they were alive. Because they all wanted to feel safe, safe and dead.

He went into the bathroom and when he came out, she was standing up, adjusting the dress. Her face was damp. She was wiping at her smudged mouth with kleenex.

"Now let's pick up that box and burn it," she said. She was trying to smile at him, but her face did not look happy or anything like that. "Just forget it, that's all I ask. That's all Steve had to do. Knock off Marsten. He was getting ten grand cash to knock off Marsten, and he wanted the whole hog. You can have twenty thousand. You name it. Anything you want, Stinson. But I won't sign over any part of the Club. That's out. Anything else—"

He interrupted. "I want to explain something now."

He looked at her standing in the bathroom putting on makeup.

"You name it, honey," she said, looking at him from the mirror. "But no cut-in on the Club. Steve wanted the works. He would have ground me right out. He said he loved me even, the phony bum. And he gets all that stuff on tape and he's going to let Marsten listen if I don't—what do you want to explain?"

"I'm not Leo Stinson. Like it says in my wallet, I'm Allan Baer Barton. Formerly of Johnson's Belt and Dye Company, but sort of retired now."

"What's that, honey?"

"I'm not connected with Steve Milton in anyway. I just happened to be living out there near his cabin. He mentioned that Leo Stinson might show and that he had a room here. When Steve was murdered, I was curious, that's all. I'm still curious."

She moved past him with a noiseless glide, and opened the door. Her face had a blank look. "I don't believe you. But if it's true—you'll die a lot harder than Steve did."

That could very well be true, Barton thought as he shut the door and locked it. Anyway, it would happen to him under his correct name. He picked up the wallet, replaced the bills and other items in it neatly. He picked up the medical kit and went into the bathroom and gave himself another shot.

The unaccustomed excitement had put a little color under the false tan of his face. He looked rather healthy, on the outside. Looks were certainly misleading. He could do with a little plasma right now. But that was hardly possible. Turning to go back into the other room, he looked at the water-closet. He remembered something from one of the thousands of crime novels he had read, and he lifted the lid and looked into the water.

A packet of water-proof plastic floated in the tank. Barton lay down to rest on the bed. He opened the packet. It contained a roll of recording tape, and a note addressed Dear Leo, and signed, Steve.

The note said:

"I've written several times telling you about making contact with me here at the Del Rey. If you haven't received any of those letters and are reading this because of a tip from a guy out there by my cabin named Allan Barton, he's okay. Don't worry about Barton at all. He isn't interested. Just forget him because he's a sort of an all right screwball.

"Now here's the ticket, Leo. I don't have time to write much here, so this is going to be brief. As you know, Julie Laverne hired me to come in here and knock off Lloyd Marsten. Now here's the score up to this point.

"Marsten's got a hot record back East, and in Nevada no one with a record can own a casino. So the Club Laverne. It's in her name, see, Leo, but Marsten's the guy who cleans up a fabulous profit. She's his mistress. She wanted Marsten knocked off so she not only would own the Club, but enjoy all of its benefits, you see?

"I'm supposed to get a lousy ten grand for this job. But I go along with it. Julie gets me a job bouncing in the Club, and I spot everything in there. Marsten's built up a sweet extortion mill there. Lots of playrooms upstairs, equipped with cameras and hidden mikes. You know, the works. And all these money bags come in here, anything for a good time. They have a good time, and then they get a phone call from Marsten. He puts on the bite. It's good for millions, and the mine's just starting to be worked.

"Turns out this Julie is a pushover for the strong arm treatment. The second day here I was combining a lot of pleasure with business. We went out on the desert for a real good time and I got the whole thing on tape, including Julie talking about how happy she would be soon as I knocked off Marsten.

"I played it for Julie later and she started to crack up. I tell Julie I want everything in Marsten's safe, plus a partnership in the Club. And I think I'm going to come off the winner, Leo. If you're reading this it may mean I never won the spin, but it's sure worth the gamble. Anyway, this may be so-long, pal. And the stuff's all yours. But be careful. It turns out this Julie has some torpedoes around who are real trigger happy. One of them's kill-crazy. A kid named Larry.

"If you need an inside guy for anything, contact Hunky Shannon. He's a flunky who does all kinds of dirty work for Marsten because Marsten's got something on him. Seems Hunky is wanted under another name in Crowell, Kentucky, for killing a girl down there. So you can use Hunky. But watch yourself, Leo. Maybe you'd better call in a couple of guys from Boston."

Barton lay there with his hands under his head looking up at the pale yellow ceiling. So that was the mysterious Steve Milton. A torpedo. The young, blond, good-looking kid sitting in the deck chair and listening to Barton while the two of them sipped beer and talked about sundry things.

Extortion racket. He thought of the people coming into Ten Palms, having a good time, then having to pay out thousands of dollars. Play rooms above The Club Laverne. It was pretty sordid, all of it, from beginning to end.

He thought about all of it, and then he thought about someone named Hunky Shannon. He smiled and stood up. His head felt a little light, and the room not too substantial, but his interest was sustaining itself. He was even anticipating more excitement. Hunky Shannon, and then another run-in with Jay and Larry and Julie Laverne, and Lloyd Marsten. The point was to get up there, right up there above the Club Laverne and see it. See what it was that made people pay out their life-earnings.

He was beginning to see why so many people stayed respectable. Respectable and dull and never knowing they were alive. Even having fun on a weekend was dangerous.

He went into the hall. He remembered there was no elevator. The hotel was cheap and only three stories. He went to the end of the hall and saw the dull surface of a metal fire-escape platform.

They would be waiting below for him, but when he looked out and down into the alley, he didn't see anyone down there. They could be hiding down there. But they were more likely to be down in the lobby. Anyway, he had to get out, and so he started climbing down the fire-escape.

They certainly didn't believe at this point that he really was not Leo Stinson. On the other hand, they might do a little investigating and determine exactly who he was. They still would be likely to watch him, thinking he knew about the roll of tape.

The tape was in his pocket. As he climbed down to the alley and stood there watching for a sign of somebody, he wondered about the tape.

He walked several blocks down a street paralleling Main, then cut back to Main and got into a cab.

"Just drive around a while," Barton said, leaning back. "I've never been here before."

"It's a sweet little town to die in," the driver said. And laughed.

"It sure seems healthy all right," Barton said. "For dying."

"Old folks come here from everywhere just to die right," the driver said. "A couple came in here all the way from Europe the other day. I drove them out to the Springs Motel. All they want is a place to pass away easy and quiet by one of those swimming pools."

"It's a lot healthier to die here than it is in Europe these days," Barton said.

"I wouldn't know about that."

Barton was sure he wasn't being followed. He went into an Owl Drug store while the cab waited. He looked up the address of Shannon, and there was fortunately only one Shannon in Ten Palms.

On the way out to Hunky Shannon's on the outskirts of town, Barton let the roll of recording tape flutter away foot by foot into the night.

As the cab drove away, Barton walked between orange trees toward the front of Shannon's sprawling ranch-type house. The air was heavy with orange blossoms, and the scent of bougainvillea and swimming pools.

Whatever dirty work Shannon had been forced to do for Marsten had certainly paid well. Almost as well as the board of directors of Johnson's Belt and Dye Company. Barton heard the sounds of laughter in the night from neighboring houses, and illuminated back yards, and lawns of dark green devil grass. The smells of barbecuing steaks was redolent. Also, it awakened memories in Barton.

This was so much like the suburban home Barton had once commuted back and forth from daily with clocklike regularity. The home into which he would come tired but looking cheerful if he could. How many evenings had he spent on his knees in the back yard pulling devil grass, or donning the little apron marked "His" and barbecuing steaks in the back yard?

"Tired, darling?" his ever loving wife would ask.

"Tired, but satisfied," Barton would say. "Had another challenging day, another challenge to courage and valor—at Johnson's Belt and Dye."

His daughter would be lying before the fireplace talking interminably to some high school crush. There had been some nice moments. But it never got off the ground and now there was no place to go.

You had to live dangerously. Or you just didn't live. A few cared and they were eliminated.

At any time, he thought as he pressed the buzzer on the Shannon's front door, I could just have walked around the corner and started living dangerously. And I never did until somebody threw a corpse at me, and by then the river was almost down to the sea.

A girl who couldn't have been over sixteen physically, opened the door. She was wearing only a thin negligee. She had a tight pale little face and wispy blonde hair. Her eyes seemed quite old. "What do you want?"

"Mr. Shannon."

He shoved past her into a long, dimly-lighted room so full of green plants it seemed out of doors. The girl swayed listlessly toward him, whining something unintelligible. Barton had seen it while he was layed up in the hospital. In there they were given the stuff to deaden otherwise intolerable physical pain. This girl had been taking it to kill something just as painful but less tangible. She had the dull, glazed eyes of someone whose illusions had already died.

"Baby, baby, what's matter in there?"

"We got company," the girl said dully, looking at Barton as though he resembled everybody.

"We ain't expecting nobody."

"That's right," the girl said to Barton, dazedly.

"We're busy now," the voice called from the next room. "Tell 'em to go way."

"Go way," the girl said.

She turned and almost fell. The negligee opened all the way down and Barton saw the blue bruise marks on her thin boyish thighs. He closed his eyes a moment, then walked past her into the next room, a music room, lots of records and a hi-fi pulsing in the walls. A short stocky man with a pug nose got up from a long furry gray couch and was belting a pink dressing gown around his middle.

"You Shannon?"

"That's right. But it's trouble you're looking for. I said to go way."

He stood on short, wide-spread legs, leaning forward belligerently, squinting little eyes. He seemed to have a driving but frightened arrogance, like a rooster threatened by hawks as he stood with his hands in his pockets.

Barton smiled. Hunky Shannon was funny. They were all funny. Every damned one of them, the whole situation, everything getting funnier all the time.

"How would you like to take a plane trip tonight?" Barton asked.

Hunky's eyes flickered toward the door, then the windows. He stuck out his lower lip.

"Flying ain't safe."

"It's fast," Barton said. "And that's the way they told me to bring you back to Crowell, Kentucky."

Shannon sat down heavily and sweat burst out over his knobby face.

"Marsten," he said. He said it several times. Suppressed fury dribbled out with the words.

"Don't try anything with me," Barton said. "I've got a couple of friends outside. And Marsten will have you extradited anyway. He must not like you."

Shannon leaned back and put his hand over his eyes. He didn't seem to be breathing.

"I knowed it was coming. It's been coming for years. Hell, I couldn't live with it anyway. I've had it. I've had it all the way up. I knew that he would do it one of these days sure."

Shannon jerked his hand away from his eyes and leaned forward.

His face was white. "Listen—I'll go. But let me take a crack at Marsten first. I'll give you ten, twenty grand in cash. Just let me blow that guy's head all over his ceiling, that's all I ask. Twenty grand. I got it stashed right here. Get-away money. You want it. It's yours."

Barton laughed. "I was only kidding, Hunky. I'm not a cop from Crowell, Kentucky. I'm friend of Steve Milton. You know Steve Milton?"

Shannon wiped at his face, and nodded dumbly.

"Well, Steve's dead. Julie Laverne had him shot. He was a friend of mine."

"Then what's the idea—?"

"Just wanted to remind you of how it will feel if and when it does happen to you, Hunky."

"I don't need to be reminded." Hunky didn't sound relieved. He sounded tired. He leaned back again and shut his eyes. Sweat ran down his face. "Marsten will do it. He'll do it pretty soon now. I know it. I got to gun the creep. But then you know too. That damned Steve—he nosed it out of someone over at the Club."

"And I've got a letter written telling all about how you're wanted in Crowell, Kentucky," Barton said. "If anything happens to me tonight, that letter goes to the cops. Otherwise only Marsten and I know, and I've got nothing against you, Hunky. Not if you dig up that twenty-grand for me and take me over to the Club Laverne tonight. I want to get Marsten, or the Laverne woman, and preferably both of them. You're going to show me the safest and easiest way up there, Hunky."

"That's all right with me," Hunky said thinly. "That's good. It's cheap at the price. You get rid of Marsten—then there'll just be you, and I really don't think you'd bother with me any more. Twenty grand—"

"Get it out here now, Hunky. And let's go on over to the Club."

Hunky went out the door, and Barton leaned back and looked into the small flames in the fireplace. The record on the turntable was playing some vague familiar tune he couldn't remember the name of.

He had an eerie feeling that at any moment he would wake up and be on a train heading back out to the suburbs, and he was going over that stock deal, going over and over it trying to figure out why he was bothering to go over it at all.

Then Hunky was coming back in a little wobby on his bowed legs, dressed in flashy sport clothes and carrying a shiny leather briefcase. Barton opened the briefcase. It was full of neatly packaged fifty and hundred dollar bills. He took some of the stuff out and looked at it and dropped it back in the case.

"Let's go now," Barton said. When he stood up, he felt the pain stirring in his chest.

Hunky drove a powder blue Cadillac back toward the Main Street of Ten Palms. As they started down the street, Barton opened the briefcase and started throwing handfuls of fifty and hundred dollar bills and out the window.

He heard incredulous whining sounds come through Hunky's teeth. Finally Hunky half screamed. "Stop it—what you want to do that for?"

"Just keep driving, Hunky. I'm in a hurry." Barton threw thousands of dollars into the night air.

"Jesus—you can't do that. Oh Jesus—"

Hunky stopped saying anything. His shoulders quivered. Barton saw that Hunky was crying. Barton tossed out the rest of the bills and laughed.

After they parked on a lot and started walking down an alley paralleling Main Street, Hunky said. "I get it. You've had it too, right? You've had it. You don't figure you'll be able to spend it anyway."

"I don't know why," Barton said. "Except that it was amusing."

"Jesus," Hunky said.

The Club Laverne was one of the biggest in Ten Palms, bright and gilted in the front. The back of it was dark and smelled of stale garbage as Hunky opened an iron door and stepped inside ahead of Barton.

It smelled worse inside. Barton heard the high distorted pounding of a swing band mixed with abortive jazz, and the shrill wails of a woman singing.

Hunky went up dark narrow stairs that curved to the left. Barton followed him.

"Marsten's no trouble," Hunky said. "But you run into Larry or Jay, you'll be sleeping on a slab tonight."

Hunky walked on up and into a long hallway with red carpeting. A number of doors opened off this hall, and Barton heard laughter, giggles, and other less recognizable sounds behind them.

"Marsten's and Julie's apartment is at the end of the hall. The door at the end there. But Marsten's probably in the play room. Maybe Julie's in there too. I'd take a look there first."

Hunky walked down the other exit, turned left and through a narrow door marked exit. Barton followed him up a narrow iron stairwell and along a rickety catwalk. Hunky slid a paneled door open, Barton right behind him.

It was a small attic room, dark and warm. A square of glass was in the floor between a couple of suspension beams, and over the glass was an intricate camera arrangement. Someone was crouched down there looking through the glass to the floor below. Whoever it was, was too interested in the scene below to be distracted by visitors.

"How's the show tonight, Joey?" Hunk asked softly.

"Great," Joey said. "Marsten's got that real estate guy's daughter down there. He's really giving that kid the business tonight!"

Hunky got down on his knees and looked.

"It's a super production," Hunky said, and Barton heard his voice quivering.

"That's Lifton's daughter, and this'll be worth fifty grand to Marsten."

"At least that," Hunky said.

"That little girl's so hopped up she don't know what the hell she's doing. But she sure is doing it."

Barton saw Hunky's hand raise. There was a gun in it. The barrel came down twice on Joey's head, and Joey rolled over without making a sound.

Hunky turned, and looked at Barton in the dim light. His face was white and shining with sweat, but his eyes were bright. "The Laverne woman's in the apartment I showed you. If she ain't there, she'll be downstairs watching the croupiers. But she's usually in that apartment this time of night. Marsten's right here, and I'm going to take care of him now."

"You've had it," Barton said.

"Yeah, I knew that tonight. It's all over me all the time, and it ain't worth it. Every day what I have to do for Marsten gets dirtier, and it ain't worth it any more." Hunky turned away and looked down through the glass. It must be a one-way mirror set-up, Barton thought.

"You know when I really felt how it had to be for me?" Hunky said.

"No?"

"When you tossed all that greenery out the window. There it went, and I thought, this guy must be screwy. But then what about me, I thought—what kind of a life does a guy live for the stuff?"

"I know how it is," Barton said. "Like living in jail."

"That's right. Now I'm getting out."

A slight groan came out of Hunky as he crouched down and started firing through the glass. The roars seemed to explode inside Barton's head. Flashing lights went off around his eyes as glass crashed. A girl's scream came up from below.

In the mental flash, Barton saw his daughter again—he really hadn't seen her for over five years—but he saw her now. It might have been his daughter down there, he thought. Hunky was shooting at Marsten and didn't care about somebody's laughter down there.

Barton lunged to drag Hunky back, thinking of the girl and when his foot tripped on the rafter, he fell full length and grabbed Hunky's leg and dragged at him. Hunky yelled as his shoulder smashed into the glass. He half turned as the glass gave way. His neck caught on a jagged splinter and stretched out like a fish when someone's pulling a hook from its throat. Blood spurted as Hunky's neck tore and he plunged down out of sight.

Looking down through the jagged framework, Barton saw a huge bed directly under the one-way mirror. The walls were covered with red drapes, the rug was a deep rich red. A fireplace gave out soft flame, and there were several candles burning. Piano blues drifted up through the broken opening with perfumed heat and smoke.

A girl with short brown curls was curled up naked in the middle of the bed. She seemed even younger than the one at Hunky's house. She was staring at Hunky sprawled on the floor in a pool of blood, and at the naked body of Marsten bent backward over the foot of the bed, blood running from his chest and stomach.

The girl was sobbing and making unintelligible noises in her throat. The record player started over again, and then again, playing the same thing twice and Barton sat up there looking at the scene below.

No one entered the room. The music went on. The girl sat there sobbing and moaning in her throat. Her eyes staring wide and fixed. The fireplace wavered, and the candles burned on. And the corpses lay there giving the scene a frozen quality, like some grotesque animated painting.

That room would be heavily sound-proofed, Barton thought. No one outside that room had heard the shots, screams, or glass crashing. The orchestra downstairs had helped too.

She might be my daughter. Somewhere, he thought, my daughter might be wanting to break out the way Lifton's daughter had. Barton smiled, a bit sadly this time. He understood them, all of them. They wanted to get away from the walking dead, they wanted to feel alive. They wanted to live dangerously, get into any kind of world at all where something unexpected might happen tomorrow.

Barton picked up the gun Hunky had dropped on the way down. He went back down to the second floor hallway and started for the door at the other end.

They didn't give you much choice, Barton thought as he stopped before the door. Respectability was dull, and the rest seemed pretty dirty, and you could tire of it in an evening.

He knocked on the door with his left hand. He remembered something about a safety catch, and he moved his thumb on the gun and felt the metallic movement shiver up his arm.

A panel in the door slid open. Julie Laverne's eye looked through at Barton and widened.

"You want the tape?" Barton asked, "Open the door."

The panel slid shut and the door opened at once. Barton walked in past her, with the gun raised. Julie Laverne's body was wrapped in a tight, bright red sheath dress. He glanced at her breasts swaying as she walked sidewise from him toward a fireplace on the right wall. Dimly, Barton realized that she wasn't interesting any more.

"Let's have it then," Julie Laverne said in a tight voice.

Barton walked on past her toward Jay who stood by the fireplace.

Jay jabbed his hand into his jacket pocket. His lips were hanging apart.

"I was only kidding," Barton said. "I don't have the tape. But don't worry about it. Marsten's dead."

The morphine had really taken hold of Barton. He had an eerie detached sensation. His feet seemed to float, not quite on the floor, and the room itself had the look of a dream. The long shadowed room, the fireplace on the right, and the feeling that he was floating toward Jay and the woman beside him.

"But I've got something else for you," Barton heard himself saying. "Something even better. Just what you've always wanted."

"Hold it," Jay whispered. "Listen—"

Barton started pulling the trigger. Jay screamed and rolled along the wall into the corner.

"I told you he was nuts!" Barton heard Larry's voice from behind him. He felt the dull heavy blow in his back, and the sound of the shot. But there wasn't any pain, and the shot seemed dulled and distant. He couldn't feel much of anything. He was too doped up to feel pain. If you didn't feel any pain it was almost as though nothing had happened.

His legs were numb and they didn't seem to want to walk, but Barton concentrated on them and he turned and walked toward Larry.

Larry was about ten feet away, or was it a mile—wavering and blurred like something seen through watered glass. The gun jumped in Larry's hand as Larry backed away down the length of the room. His lips were quivering and sweat streamed down his face.

Barton laughed and walked on toward Larry. Larry backed into the couch. The gun jumped again. Larry yelled. His voice cracked. He fell backward over the couch.

Larry was sliding back along the rug and by this time Barton was close enough and he knew he couldn't miss. He fired several shots.

If I stop walking I'll fall down, Barton thought; so he continued walking in a long circle around the wavering room. He drifted toward Julie and she backed into the wall by the fireplace. She slid down the wall a little and put her hands over her eyes as though hands could ward off bullets.

"It's important. Isn't it important?" he said, and then he was on his face. He couldn't move any more. He never would move again, he knew that. The fireplace moving and dancing between the andirons only a few feet away. It reminded him with a sudden clarity of the fireplace in the living room in Van Nuys where his ever-loving wife had been waiting for him every evening to come home late and tired but smiling from the office. His daughter would be lying here in front of the fire working algebra problems. And his wife would be coming bravely across the room, looking her charming best just for him, holding out a martini to reward him for a courageous day of battle with Johnson Belt and Dye.

Well, he thought, there were some things to be said for all that.

Someone was bending over him, and he never did know who it was.

"Name's Allan Baer Barton, formerly with Johnson Belt and Dye." Barton knew he was laughing again, but he couldn't hear it. "Tell Doctor Linderman—in Los Angeles—tell him—remind him that I told him he was wrong. Six months he gave me—that's all, he said—six months. And here it's been only two."

Absinthe for Superman
Robert Edmond Alter

June 1959

Mason was too young for old sailors' superstitions, as a rule he scoffed at the salty old omens and placed them in a private category he called 'hangovers from the dim days of wooden ships and iron-headed men'. But the moment that he approached the small cargo steamer, Duff, a wisp of foreboding touched him.

The Duff lay in the red eye of the setting moon, at the far end of a lonely wharf. As he approached the ship rose above him, shadowy, antique and forlorn.

Perhaps it wasn't really the ship itself that bothered him, it might only be the solitary figure that stood unmoving on the port wing of the bridge, like a black statue watching the sea with cold eyes. Mason hitched his duffle to a new position on his shoulder and turned away. Behind him the lights of Papette winked and glowed like a cluster of stars.

A floodlight at the head of the gangway suddenly snapped on, making everything except its own circle of yellow, a total black. Mason blinked and momentarily lost his equilibrium. He started up the gangplank as a ship's officer materialized under the glare of light at the rail. It was a chief engineer, a blunt, stocky man, with a homely, worried face.

The chief touched his cap and nodded at Mason. "You the new Second?" he asked in a whisper.

Mason thought there might be something wrong with the chief's throat. "Yes," he replied, "my name's—"

But the chief popped a pudgy finger up to his pursed lips and made a motion with his head toward the bridge. "Softly, mate," he whispered, "the old man's in one of his moods."

What puzzled Mason was that none of the officers in the deck house wanted to discuss Captain Gann's moods. The chief talked in whispers, shrugged and looked worried; the first mate, a rangy, raw-boned, angry-looking man, shook his head and scowled; and Sparks, the only other white man on board, and therefore allowed to live with the officers, grinned and tapped his head, and muttered: "Nuts!"

The Duff cleared the channel in the first pale glint of dawn and put to sea for Nuku Hiva. Within two hours Tahiti was nothing but a wavering thread of black outlined against the pink glow of sunrise.

Mason stood a twelve hour watch and ate three meals with the other officers in the cuddy, but he had still not met Gann. At the beginning of each meal he would pick up his napkin and then ask: "Where's the captain?" but always the negative reply: "In his mood," would answer him.

On the second day, at lunch, he became annoyed with the mystery, and when he heard the inevitable "In his mood" he threw his napkin down and leaned toward the first mate.

"What do you mean? What is his mood? Is he crazy?"

But the chief spluttered in his coffee cup, and threw a look of fear over his shoulder. He stood up, red in the face, and left the cabin.

The first mate scowled after him, and spoke in a short angry tone. "You'll see soon enough. Now let me enjoy my lunch."

Mason began to see that afternoon. He was off duty, and relaxing on his bunk with a dog-eared book, the door of his cabin open in the vain hope that a cooling breeze would find its way in. His eye slid away from the printed page and he saw a shadow laying on the deck.

"What are you reading?" a quiet voice demanded.

Mason looked up with a start and found Gann standing in the passageway watching him. He knew it was the captain, there could be no mistake about that. If Gann had been standing naked before him, Mason would have known him. As it was he wore nothing that resembled a uniform. His trousers were faded denims, his shirt white, long-sleeved and open at the neck. A plain black cap was on his head.

But Mason was interested in his face. The eyes were narrowed slits with glints of callousness, cunning and self-certainty, they seemed capable of looking through flesh and bone and into the minds and hearts of men. His nose was thin, aristocratic. His mouth was a narrow, slitted match for his eyes. Overall there was a satanic quality to the strong face that disturbed Mason.

"It's Mardi," he replied, and as an afterthought he added, "By Melville."

Gann stood quietly in the passageway, his arms akimbo, and seemed to consider the reply with deliberation. He looked up suddenly. "Do you read much?"

"Yes, sir, I do."

"Been to college? Studied literature? Philosophy?"

Mason nodded. "Yes, I have."

Gann's hands fell suddenly away from his hips and he spun on his heel. "Follow me," he said over his shoulder.

Gann's cabin was small and close. A rumpled bunk topped a long louvered cupboard. A deal table, littered with papers and pencils, jutted out from the bulkhead. A battered wall locker, a chest, two portholes, a tarnished mirror and a row of faded books.

The captain flicked a casual glance at Mason. "Look at them," he said.

Mason felt uncomfortable without knowing exactly why. He stepped across the cabin and read the faded titles. In Praise of Folly, The Prince, Ludwig's Napoleon, The Teachings of Friedrich Nietzsche, The Philosophy of Nietzsche, were some that his eye picked out immediately. Show me what you read and I'll tell you what you are, he thought.

Gann was at the speaking tube calling the bridge.

"First," he said, "You'll have to fill in for Mr. Mason for the next few days. We'll be busy talking."

The first mate's voice came back in an angry rasp. "But, sir, we're short-handed as it is!"

Mason turned away from the book rack and looked at Gann. The captain's back had stiffened, and Mason could see the tight knots of muscle bunch up under his shirt. There was a hesitancy between the two men joined by the speaking tube that embarrassed the young mate.

"I said," Gann repeated in a low, deliberate voice, "—you'll have to fill in for Mr. Mason."

Again a pause, and then the muted reply: "Aye, aye, sir."

They talked. The hours ticked away and were lost in the abyss of time without Mason's knowledge. Gann held the mate's interest as though he had caught it in his strong, square hand. He was fascinating, but he was disturbing. He believed in the superman whose god was power.

He gave Mason a bottle of whisky and a glass, but for himself he had a tall platinum flask which held a pale green absinthe that he mixed with water. He sipped his drink and seldom refreshed it. Once he said, "I'd offer you some, but there isn't enough—and it's mine."

Mason said nothing, he was watching him and wondering.

"To strength!" Gann said and held his cup up.

By midnight they no longer discussed philosophy, they argued it. Mason had drunk a great deal of whisky and was at times a little high, at other times somber and weary, but Gann was always animated and intense. The room was thick with the swirled smoke from Mason's pipe and Gann's cigars, and they peered at each other's obscured faces across the littered table and searched for each other's souls.

Gann clutched his cup and said, "Nietzsche says that for the ruling class everything that expresses or furthers the will of the individual is good."

Mason said, "I know Nietzsche, he was insane, he made a fetish out of power. What can it get you? What has it ever brought you? A broken down steamer, four white officers, and seven Kanakas for a crew."

Gann laughed as though he were mocking something. "Perhaps that's all I ever wanted, and it's mine. Here I am king, I'm the power and the strength, no man can say me nay!"

"Be careful, Gann," Mason said softly. "Remember what happened to Ahab when he tried to play God and rid the seas of Moby Dick."

"Ahab was a great man," Gann said bitterly, "but Melville was against him."

Dawn glimmered through the two portholes like a pair of pale, dead eyes. The two men argued on through an atmosphere that was like the interior of a sweat box. Their shirts were open down to the waist, their sleeves rolled up, their expressions sometimes haggard, sometimes angry, sometimes melancholy and weary. They sat now with but inches between their glistening faces.

"At the bottom of everything is the will for power, and all that makes for fullness of life is to be cherished," Gann said.

"There is always the moral concept," Mason replied.

"Morality! Religion!" Gann scoffed, "Pap for the weak. Whereas power—"

"Is an unreality, an illusion," Mason said. "You reach for power and it is gone. If you catch it, you can't hold it."

"Power," Gann said thoughtfully, "is a state of mind."

They stared into each other's eyes for an immeasurable moment, and then Mason began to smile. "In this case," he said, "I'll believe it."

Gann's eyes glittered from beneath his black brows, and Mason sensed he'd gone too far. "Power," Gann said slowly, "is when you want to do something and know that you can, and know that nothing can stop you—like this!" and his hand and forearm arched up and out, like a thick rattlesnake striking, and caught Mason on the point of the jaw.

It had only been a short jab but it lifted Mason out of his chair and threw him back against the closed door. For a moment he was too stunned to even think, then the pain began to spread across his face. He blinked his eyes and looked at Gann.

The captain's eyes were narrowed down to thin slivers of light, his lips were curving into a deep smile. "Now don't go heroic," he said easily, "because I have the strength of ten."

Mason believed him, but the look on Gann's face settled his mind. He came to his feet, lowered his head and charged the sneering face.

A minute later Gann was standing in the open doorway nursing a cut lip, and calling for the steward to come help Mason to his cabin.

Mason slept for three hours and then he woke and sat up in his bunk. He explored different parts of his face, but whatever he touched felt swollen and pained him. He shook his head and reached for his cigarettes. He felt like Don Quixote after the attack on the windmill.

His door banged open and the angry faced first mate stuck his rumpled head in the compartment. "You awake?" He came into the cabin, closing the door behind him, and drew up a chair by Mason's bunk. He studied the young mate's face for a moment and then looked angrier than ever. "The old man do that?" he asked.

Mason nodded. "I asked for it."

The mate snorted, his face showed doubt. "What are you gonna do? Press charges?"

"No," Mason replied. "If I'd planned on that I wouldn't have gone for him. It's too late now. I'll even it up my own way."

The mate snorted again, and looked away. "You won't beat Gann noways, except in a court of law. You know what's been happening since you laid down for your nap? Gann went for the chief."

Mason looked his surprise. The first mate nodded and said, "You know how short-handed we are? It don't bother Gann none, he just tells us to work overtime. He's been workin' the chief about twenty hours a day, but this morning the chief ups an' rebels, says he don't hafta work such long shifts. You know what Gann did?"

Mason shook his head wondering if the chief was laying in his bunk with a battered face.

"He put him on the foredeck chippin' paint for two hours. Stood over him and saw that he did it, every time the chief would stand up to quit, Gann would knock him down. Nice ship you bought a ticket on!" The first mate leaned back in the chair and stared at Mason contemptuously.

"My God," Mason cried, "he can't do that to an officer."

"Go tell him he can't," the first mate suggested. He leaned forward and hitched up his chair, his voice lowered. "I don't know what you're gonna do, but I'm through. I'm relieving myself of duty as of now."

"He won't let you," Mason said.

The first mate drew a heavy forty-five automatic out of his coat pocket and showed it to Mason. "He won't be able to stop me. If he gets within ten feet of me—he's dead."

An hour later Mason heard the first shot splinter through the monotonous drone of the diesel engines. He swung his legs over the edge of the bunk and sat listening. He thought the first mate had killed Gann.

The clump-clump sound of feet running across the metal decks above reached him, then a second shot cracked out, and he came to his feet and rushed for the door. Just as he entered the passageway a third shot sounded, and then a fourth. He ran out of the deckhouse and went aft toward the ladder leading up to the bridge. Ahead of him fled two Kanakas, but the bridge held no interest for them, they fled out across the boat deck to where their mates were swinging out the starboard lifeboat.

When Mason reached the wing of the bridge he paused for a moment at the rail and gasped for breath, then he stepped over the flange of the door and into the wheelhouse. It was empty. But the radio room was not. Sparks was sitting in the gloom, leaning back in his swivel chair, his head laying over on his left shoulder, his eyes glazed and unseeing.

Mason stepped through a thick mixture of horror and sickness and went down to the captain's cabin. The first mate was lying on the deck, on his back, with both hands clasped over his breast. Blood was everywhere. His eyes blinked open painfully and focused on the young mate. "Run for it, Mason," he whispered, "he's gone amuck. He'll get you next." His eyes closed, and for once the angry face looked calm and content.

The shooting began again, sporadic but deliberate. Someone cried out and the sound trembled between the throb of the ship and the crack of the gun. He rushed back to the wing of the bridge and looked aft across the boat deck. One of the Kanakas was lying motionless on the sun-glazed deck, but the boat had been lowered, and the last two natives were just leaping over the side.

Mason turned away, not quite sure what he should do next. Gann was somewhere on the boat deck out of his line of vision. Perhaps there was time to find a weapon. He hurried noiselessly down to the starboard gangway but was brought up short by the sudden sight of the chief's body lying in a deep blue shadow just within the passageway. At that moment he finally realized the spot he was in. The Kanakas had fled leaving four dead men behind them. Mason was alone on a drifting ship with a madman.

"There you are, Mr. Mason, I've been looking for you," the captain's quiet voice spoke from behind him. "You're not still angry about our fight, are you?"

The panic that had been building inside of Mason became complete. For a moment all he could think of was to throw himself over the rail, but he resisted the impulse, took a deep breath and turned slowly around. His lips formed a tight smile as he faced Gann. "No," he said, "I'm not angry."

Gann's face was strangely calm, he was even smiling, but the narrowed slits were open now and his eyes sparkled like two tongues of flame looking for something to devour. The automatic, the mate's automatic, was in his hand hanging idle by his side.

"Run out of bullets?" Mason asked casually.

Gann lifted the weapon up and looked at it. "The gun—" he muttered, and with a quick jerk of his hand he sent it spinning over the side. "I don't like guns, never used one before, but when that fool pointed it at me—something came over me— " He broke off suddenly and smiled again. "Well, Mason, let's repair to my cabin and have a drink."

Mason felt that a weight had been lifted from his chest with the passing of the automatic, but he wasn't going to become foolish now. "No thank you, sir," he said, "I don't feel like one. I think I'll stay on deck for a while."

Gann nodded and smiled. "All right, Mason, I just thought you'd like a drink from my flask, there's a few drops left."

But Mason wasn't being caught that easily. He still smiled but the muscles in his face were beginning to ache from the strain. "Some other time, sir," he said.

Gann moved forward, and Mason stepped backward quickly. "Of course," the captain said, and he stepped through the doorway and over the dead chief.

Mason searched feverishly through the officers' cabins. If he could find a gun he knew what he would have to do; he would go above and shoot Gann down like a mad dog. He held no illusions about what would happen if he tried to meet Gann barehanded, the insane man would tear him to pieces.

Something struck the water on the portside with a solid blow. He gave up the search and went out on the gangway. Drifting astern was the port lifeboat. Gann had cut it loose from the davits. Mason felt sick, he leaned on the rail and rubbed at his face with a trembling hand. He should have jumped overboard with the Kanakas and swam for the boat.

He straightened up, considering. There was still the radio. If he could find Spark's code book and dope it out, he could send a call for help. But Gann was up there somewhere. He would have to wait for an opportunity.

He was in the cuddy eating a chunk of bread and cheese when he heard the heavy watertight door of the starboard passage close. He stopped chewing and listened. A slight rasping noise reached him in the quiet gloom, it was repeated, and Mason frowned. Suddenly he knew what it was. Gann was tightening the dog handles, locking him in the deckhouse.

He heard Gann move off forward and knew that he was going around the deckhouse to block off the port passageway. Good, he wasn't caught yet. He moved hurriedly aft through the galley and out onto the aft deck through the galley service door.

In a moment Gann came along the gangway. He was smiling, he seemed sure of himself. He paused at the railing when he saw Mason standing near the Number Three hatch. The smile seemed to freeze in his face. "Oh," he said, "I thought you were in the deckhouse."

"I know you did," Mason replied.

Gann came down the steps leisurely and started walking toward him. Mason moved away and he followed. They went around the hatches, circled the cargo mast, went up on the fan-tail, around the afterhouse and back down to the cargo deck again. Gann was smiling all the while, but Mason's face was tight and drawn now. Gann had settled down to business.

Mason led the way up across the starboard gangway. He paused long enough to undog the watertight door. He might need that passageway later. They went down on the maindeck keeping Number Two hatch between them, and Mason was beginning to wonder how long this would last. Suddenly the smile dropped from Gann's face and his eyes popped open, glowing with hate. He sprang up on the hatch cover and dashed toward Mason.

Mason turned and fled to the foredeck. He could hear Gann cursing behind him. They went up the starboard side, across the deck and down the port, back across the deck and through the deckhouse. Gann had the agility of an ape, and he was untiring; fear alone propelled Mason.

Certain sections of the ship were restricted to Mason as unsafe. The forecastle, the afterhouse, any of the cabins that contained only one door were definitely out of the question. Gann could trap him too easily.

Once on the boat deck he was nearly cornered. To save himself he went over the rail in a scramble and dropped down to the starboard gangway below. As he stumbled back into the passageway of the deckhouse a well of laughter went pealing after him. It was the sudden laughter of madness. At the sound of it Mason's heart froze and his mind scattered in panic.

He paused in the cuddy and forced control back over his trembling nerves. He couldn't keep this up. Gann would run him down sooner or later, there was too much on the captain's side, and madness was his greatest asset.

He made his way cautiously up to Gann's cabin. He needed rest badly, Gann would have to be tricked. He went past the still form of the first mate with averted eyes and found pencil and paper and started to form a note, then his eye fell on the flask sitting on the desk. He shoved it down inside his shirt out of spite. The note was simple, it said:

Gann, if you want me you'll have to come out in the water to get me. Where is your power now?

P.S. I've taken your flask to keep me warm.

He left the note on the deal table and opened the louvered door of the cupboard beneath Gann's bunk. It was nearly empty, a few old nautical books reposed in a dark corner. Quickly he crawled in and pulled the louver after him. It was possible that Gann would never think to look in his own cabin.

He must have dozed, he opened his eyes suddenly and his heart felt like a giant boulder slowly tipping over a trembling cliff. Gann was in the room with him.

A foot moved near the cupboard, struck something, and Gann's voice muttered, "Damn!" Mason stopped breathing. Gann was moving again, away from the cupboard. Mason wondered if he was looking for his flask. It was impossible to see through the close fitted louvers. He allowed himself a soundless breath and listened.

Paper rustled, and then a deep hush fell over the cabin. Mason waited, wondering. Sweat broke out on his face and dripped from his nose. His armpits turned icy. The cupboard was close and airless, he felt sick, he was afraid he would have to—

Gann screamed, or bellowed. It was a roar of sound that quivered with rage, pain and frustration. It vibrated against the steel walls of the cabin, it burst into Mason's tight sanctuary, and he opened his mouth against it as a man will against concussion. For a moment he almost cried out.

It came again, and through it he could hear Gann's feet clumping against the steel, then the sound echoed down the passageway and faded out of hearing.

Mason crawled out of the cupboard. The first thing he saw was the note crumpled and lying on the deck.

Silently he entered the wheelhouse and looked down on the cargo deck. Gann was everywhere, his cries rebounded against the pale afternoon sky. He tore at the metal, canvas, wood and ropes with his bare hands. Even from the wheelhouse, Mason could see that they were bright scarlet with blood.

Gann plunged down into the forecastle and his cries rushing up after him through the open companionway sounded as though he had broken through the door to Hell. In a moment he was back on deck. His mouth was open, and his lips bloody, his eyes sparkled like specks of glass in the sun. He jumped to the center of Number One hatch and lifted his face to the sky. His voice roared with bewildered fury.

"Where! Where has he gone?" He screamed into the void of nothingness. He waited as though he hoped for an answer, but even to his distracted mind there was no reply. Slowly his clenched fist unfolded and dropped to his sides. His head lowered painfully, and he turned as though it were doubtful if he could, and moved over to the port bulwark. He leaned there for a moment watching the sea, then his head went down on the steel rail, and Mason could see his back tremble.

He realized, after a long moment of no thought at all, that Gann had had it. It might be possible that he could take him now. He slipped off his shoes and made his way down to the port gangway. He hoped that he could find a weapon of some sort.

He stopped suddenly, all his old terror rushing back to him. Gann had straightened up from the rail and was coming aft. Mason ran nimbly to the open door and stepped into the silent passageway. He flattened himself against the bulkhead, watching the square of light.

Gann was coming up the steps slowly, Mason could hear him talking to himself. But something was different. He frowned, wondering, and then realized it was

Gann's voice. It was low, plaintive, almost tearful, it had the curious sing-song pitch of a child. He couldn't make out the words at first, but as Gann neared the door they became audible.

"Superman, Superman, Superman!"

Gann passed the door, his head was down on his chest, his feet were dragging. He didn't look right or left. Mason doubted if he really saw anything.

The sound of Gann's voice floated back, but the words were lost to Mason. He stood in the quiet passageway, buried in the deep blue shadows and repeated the words to himself. He straightened up after a moment; he thought he understood.

He stepped out on the gangway and looked aft. Gann was walking across the cargo deck. Mason thought he must still be talking to himself. Gann went up the steps and out across the fan-tail. He never looked up, he just kept walking. He didn't even pause at the taffrail.

Mason gasped like a sleeper awaking in the atmosphere of sudden shock. The last he saw of Gann were his legs as they flipped over the rail.

Wharf Rat
Robert Page Jones

April 1960

The morgue attendant was a skinny, pinch-faced little guy with horn-rims and a nervous Adam's apple. He peeled back the sheet and said, "It ain't a very good looking corpse, is it, Mister?"

"Not very," I said.

It wasn't. The bullet had smacked him in the forehead, splintering the bone over the bridge of his long nose. The skin around the wound was ragged and burned. In back was another hole, much larger than the first, where the bullet came out.

"Wait 'till we clean him up and wire his jaw together. He'll go out of here looking better than when he came in." Pinchface grinned. "He a personal friend of yours?"

"Not exactly," I said.

I gave Pinchface the two bucks and watched him pull the sheet up over the old guy's face. Then I went out into the hall.

It was a big, almost empty hall, painted green halfway up the walls. The only furniture was a couple of banged-up wooden chairs and a wooden bench like the ones in bus station waiting rooms.

There was a guy on the bench. He was stretched out on his side, his legs pulled up under a seedy topcoat, hugging himself to soak up a little warmth. It wasn't cold. I went over and shook his shoulder and without opening his eyes he said, "Just resting, Officer. Be moving right along."

I shook him hard and he sat up, smacking the bad taste from his mouth. He looked almost as bad as the guy in there on the slab; all bone and loose skin that made his nose stick out. He stopped smacking and said, "Didn't mean to doze off, Johnny Boy."

"It's okay," I said.

The rummy looked up at me. "How about it, Johnny?"

"I'll do what I can," I said.

"I knowed you would." The rummy got to his feet and we started down the hall. "Pesk was a right guy, Johnny, not like the rest of the bums along the wharf. Pesk had a family, he did. Worked hard, kept himself clean. You should have seen him around the boats. Peck could work them engines as good as anybody."

"Yeah."

We went down the steps to the street. It was a little after six A.M., and the sun was up, but it wasn't hot yet. I said, "You sure the old guy was killed?"

"That's the legend, Johnny."

"The police say he knocked himself off."

The rummy shrugged, as if in shrugging he could resolve some problem that bothered him.

"You got anything else?" I said.

He glanced over his shoulder and said under his breath, "The word is you should talk to Hiram Moon on this one."

"The boys think Moon was involved?"

He gave another shrug and looked down the street again.

"Here's a buck," I said. "Get yourself some breakfast."

"Gee, thanks, Johnny." He took out a little notebook and a pencil stub so short the lead seemed to start out of the eraser. "I keep a record of who I owe. That way it ain't so much like a handout."

"Forget it," I said.

"No, sir. A loan is a loan." He wrote deliberately in the notebook, wetting the pencil lead with saliva. "You just get the man what done this to old Pesk."

"I can't promise anything," I said. "Tell the boys that. I'll do what I can, but you tell 'em I can't promise anything."

"I'll tell 'em," he said. He gave his hat a little tip, like an old time song and dance man, and grinned at me through rotten teeth. "I'll tell 'em you're on the job boy."

Lieutenant Julian Flack is a tall, red-faced cop with big hands and feet and an aversion to work. He poured coffee from a hotplate on the windowsill in his office and said gently, "Goddamn you, Chance."

"Julian." I made a clucking sound with my tongue. "What would your mother say?"

"You should know by now I never had a mother." He rummaged through his desk drawer for another cup. "And don't call me Julian. Coffee?"

"Black."

He came back to the desk and slid my cup across. "Now then. Just once more. Tell me just once more why we can't have a little trouble in this town without you sticking your nose in."

"Because," I said, "I have a very inquisitive nose."

Flack pointed a big-knuckled finger at me. "I'll tell you one thing, Chance. If I had a mother, she sure as hell wouldn't allow me to associate with private detectives."

"So get rid of me by telling me what I want to know."

He spread his hands in a helpless gesture. "Look, Chance. Frank Peskin was a bum, a rummy. Who knows why a guy like that knocks himself off. One of his buddies found him propped against a piling at the end of a wharf. There was a hole in his head, made by a .38 caliber bullet lodged in the piling. The condition of the wound, the position of the body, indicate the wound was self-inflicted."

"You made a paraffin test?"

"You know that a .38 probably wouldn't leave any traces that could be detected by a paraffin test."

"You make one?"

"You know we made one."

I looked at him. "Well?"

"I told you. A .38 probably wouldn't leave any traces on the firer's hand." He relaxed a little. "There were powder burns on the guy's face, and the skin around the wound was torn. That means the gun was pressed against his head when it went off."

"What gun?"

"*The* gun." He took a can of condensed milk from the desk and stirred some into his coffee with a pencil. "What's the matter with you?"

"You got it?" I said.

"Got what?"

"*The* gun."

"I'm warning you, wise guy." Flack's face turned red. He rose halfway to his feet and sat down again. "Peskin's body was discovered less than two feet from the edge of the wharf. The gun could have slipped from his hand into the water."

I took a sip of my coffee and made a disgusted face. "You got any sugar?"

"This ain't the Ritz." He handed the can over. "Kill the taste with a little cream."

I said, "What about Hiram Moon?"

"What about him?"

"Peskin worked for Moon. That's enough to warrant an investigation. You know that."

"Why? Because Moon isn't the town's leading citizen?"

"Because he's the town's biggest crook."

Flack took a deep breath and let it out slowly. "You're way off base, Chance, trying to tie Moon in on this thing. If you've got any sense you'll leave this one alone. I mean *alone,* understand?"

"*Julian.*" I made the clucking sound again. "Don't tell me Moon has his thumb on the department, too. Not while Julian Flack is still on the force."

Flack leaned back in his chair and grinned wearily. "I'm telling you, you're wasting your time. Moon is clean. We've checked that. You go sticking your nose in, and he hurts you, there's nothing we can do."

I got to my feet. "Just the same, I think I'll do a little checking around."

"Meaning Moon, eh?"

"Maybe. I'll stay out of trouble."

"Sit down."

I grinned at him. "Some other time, Julian."

"Goddamn it." His voice was the same, but I could tell he wasn't kidding. "Sit down."

I sat.

Flack said, "You got a client on this thing, or you just trying to make trouble for me? So help me, Chance—"

"No client. But I wouldn't make trouble for you," I said. "Let's just say there are some interested parties."

"I know." He pointed the finger. "Chance, you're a sucker for every wharf rat and rummy in town. Why don't you get some clients with money?"

"I've got money." I grinned. "Besides, the gentlemen in question are my best source of information. It pays me to do 'em an occasional favor."

"They think the old guy was murdered, eh?"

"Like I said, they're my best source of information."

"It's funny," Flack said. "That bunch could tell me the color of my Aunt Flossie's underwear. But whenever I have 'em brought downtown they clam up like it was a few days before Christmas."

"That's because you don't know how to communicate with them," I said.

"Yeah. Well, if I find out they're withholding evidence, I'm going to rattle their heads together." Flack sipped his coffee. "I'm going to level with you, Chance. We're already working on this thing. Don't get me wrong. Chances are the old guy did knock himself off, but there are a couple of things that don't fit."

"Like what?"

Flack's face tightened. "I've got the autopsy findings here," he said, tapping a stack of papers on his desk. "They agree with the preliminary report made by the police doctor who accompanied the ambulance. The old man was shot in the forehead, about two inches above the bridge of the nose. That's pretty high up on the forehead. The skin around the wound was burned—indicating a contact wound."

I held an imaginary gun against my forehead and squeezed the trigger. "Seems like an awkward way to shoot yourself."

"Exactly. Considering the position of the hole in the back of his head, and the trajectory of the bullet, it barely seems possible. Of course, he might have pulled the trigger with his thumb . . . but that doesn't make much sense either."

"You think somebody pulled it for him."

"I don't think anything, yet. You remember that." He scratched his head. "If Ben Sharber knew I was even talking to you, he'd throw a fit."

Sharber was the District Attorney. I said, "You telling me to lay off?"

"You know I can't tell you to lay off. I'm not even sure I want to. If it was homicide, and Moon had anything to do with it, it might not be a bad idea for you to stir things up a little. But just remember that the police are convinced it's suicide."

"You got anything else that might help, anything that points directly to Moon?"

"No. But I'll give you some good advice. You scare Moon too much and he might bounce you around. This guy's big, Chance. He owns a couple of state legislators right down to their bunions—and he enjoys playing things rough."

I was insulted. In my crepe-sole shoes I'm slightly over five feet five . . . and nobody bounces me around. Nobody. I still have a few muscles left over from my college days, and I carry a gun. I figure the gun adds immeasurably to my stature.

"I'll watch it," I said.

Flack went into his desk again, took out a fifth of bourbon, and poured some into his coffee. He grinned. "Wanna cheer yours up a little?"

"No thanks." I got up, "I'll keep in touch, Julian."

Flack's grin disappeared. "Don't call me Julian. And watch your step. I got enough trouble without having you turn up dead."

"Yeah," I said. "Then how come you tried to poison me with the coffee?"

"Goon, beat it."

Hiram Moon made most of his dough during the war. As a smalltime politician, he held a couple of minor city offices, and even ran unsuccessfully for Congress once. When that didn't work out he took the money suckered out of a lot of private citizens and sunk it into certain "investments." They paid off—big. Now he owned a good chunk of the San Diego waterfront—a fleet of sport-fishing boats, three of the big new tuna clippers and a popular sea food place out on the Point, a five-mile-long blade of land that shelters the bay.

The sea food house was a big, barny place, painted red, with a big neon sign in the shape of a lobster suspended up over the roof. It was built halfway out on a plank wharf that extended maybe four hundred feet over the bay.

I started there.

Inside, I climbed up on one of the wooden bar stools and waited for my eyes to become accustomed to the dark. A couple of tourists wearing loud Hawaiian shirts and two-dollar yachting caps sat in one of the leather booths against the far wall. They chatted over tall drinks and shot occasional glances at the stuffed Marlin over the bar. The sun was up full by now, and it was hot.

"I'm looking for Hiram Moon," I told the bartender, a big guy with puffy, freckled forearms.

"Moon?"

I nodded.

"What you want with Mr. Moon?"

"Business," I said. "It's personal, so why don't you just tell me where I can find him."

The bartender said, "You want to tell me your name?"

"Nope."

"It's a hot day," he said. He shrugged, put a slice of lime in some juice tongs, and deliberately-squeezed juice into my glass. He dropped in a sprig of mint and slid the glass across. "Why don't you enjoy your drink and run along."

"The weather's bad for your disposition," I said.

He grinned.

"It's the kind of day everybody should relax and take things easy." I put a five spot down on the bar. "Come on, where do I find Moon?"

He put his face up to mine. When he opened his mouth I could see the piece of meat hanging down in the back of his throat. "Listen, shrimp. Anybody have any business with Mr. Moon, I know about it first, understand? Now drink your drink and beat it."

I could feel the muscles around my mouth twitching. I don't like it when people call me shrimp.

"You fat bastard," I said.

He wasn't really fat. Most of it was muscle, but I was too mad to worry about that. I grabbed a handful of greasy hair and pulled his face forward. With my free hand I snatched up the juice tongs and fitted them over the end of his nose. Then I squeezed. "Where's Moon?"

He couldn't answer me right away.

Tears came to his eyes and his lips popped open a couple of times, but no sound came out. He tried jerking his head loose and the tongs damn near amputated his nose. It was pretty gruesome. I even began to feel a little sorry for the guy, but I figured he might kill me if I let go of the tongs.

He tried sticking it out.

He reached down under the bar, scrabbling around frantically, his face purple. I gave a little tweek on the tongs, and his hands shot back into view, palms flat against the bar. Tears ran down his cheeks and mixed with the blood dripping from his nose.

"You want to be pleasant?" I said.

One of the guys in the booth giggled faintly.

It wasn't funny.

I squeezed the tongs.

"Yeah. Yeah." He tried to nod. "Jesus. Anything you say. Only let go, will ya? For Christ's sake, let go."

I swallowed.

I began easing my grip on the tongs, gingerly, testing his reaction.

There wasn't much reaction left.

He picked up a bar rag and began mopping his face, pouting, a tiny piece of lemon peel protruded from one nostril.

I stuffed the five spot into his shirt. "Where do I find Moon?" I said.

He dug out the five spot, looked at it, and crammed it back in his pocket. Then he looked at me for a moment, "Around the side and up the stairs."

"Thanks," I said brightly. I went back out on the wharf.

It was the middle of the afternoon, but the neon sign over the door was on. It read: *Sen Food. Regular Dinners. Cocktails.* Water slapped at the pilings beneath me.

The building took up nearly the full width of the wharf. In back, facing the end of the wharf where Peskin's body was found, was a flight of stairs that led up to a door marked *Private.*

When I knocked, a little pear-shaped guy with no hair and a pimple on the top of his head opened the door a crack. He had a can of Schlitz in his hand. "Yeah?"

"I'm looking for Mr. Moon," I said. "The bartender said I'd find him up here."

"Who's looking?"

"Tell him, Johnny Chance."

He looked at me skeptically. "Who's Johnny Chance."

"That's me." I grinned at him.

"Some other time, shorty. Mr. Moon is—busy."

It hurts my pride when people call me shorty. I reached out and put a little pressure on the door. "I guess you didn't hear me good."

A voice said, "Let him in Charlie. He sounds very nice."

The voice sounded very nice; it was like hot candle wax sliding down the neck of a bottle, warm and sultry.

"Thanks." I didn't wait for Pimplehead to object, but gave the door a shove and walked inside.

Out of the corner of my eye I caught a glimpse of Moon seated behind a desk on the other side of the room, but only a glimpse, because even the corner of my eye couldn't stay interested for long.

She was draped over the arms of a pink modern Danish chair, a tall, honey-haired blonde with soft, luminous, nearly-black eyes that went all the way with the sexy voice. She wore a yachting outfit; a sleeveless sweatshirt and a pair of thin cotton shorts, bone-white against tanned, full-calved legs that were so long they seemed out of proportion with the rest of her. All of her best parts seemed out of proportion with the rest of her—rounded hips and pencil waist and firm breasts that jutted almost shockingly beneath the sweatshirt.

"Hello," she said brightly when I walked in. She squinted at me curiously. "Hel—lo."

"I'm Johnny Chance," I said.

"You can call me Marty."

"Marty?"

"Uh-huh. My father had his heart set on a boy."

I muscled my eyes up from the sweatshirt. It was an effort. I said, "He must have been bitterly disappointed."

"Crap." Pimplehead still had a grip on the doorknob. I figured he must be Charlie Visser, Moon's partner. I took a good look, filing his features away in my brain.

"Don't get excited," I said. "I'd like to talk with Mr. Moon."

"I'm Moon." Moon tapped a knuckle on the desk. "The babe you're drooling over is my wife. This is Mr. Visser. You got business with me?"

"I'd like to ask some questions."

"What about?"

"Frank Peskin," I said.

"The rummy?"

"That's right."

Moon didn't say anything right away. He took a can of beer from a bucket of ice on the floor and popped it open. Then he leaned back in his chair, sizing me up, pulling absently at the beer.

He looked heavier than I remembered from the pictures I'd seen in the papers. Most of it was in his face, and in a thick bulge of purple fat that puffed over his collar. He had slack, unhealthy-looking skin, and there was sweat on his face.

"You a relative of Peskin's?"

"No." I looked at his face, watching for a reaction from eyes that were like marbles pushed into a lump of moist bread dough. "I'm a private detective. I'm checking a few things concerning Peskin's death."

Behind me Visser said, "A private dick, eh?" He giggled. "I thought maybe you was a jockey."

"Don't mind Charlie," Moon said good-naturedly. He wiped some of the sweat from his face, "How about getting to the point, Mr. Chance."

"Okay. Peskin was found at the end of the wharf last night, with a hole in his head. You know that, naturally. My client wants to know how come the hole."

"The police seem to think it was suicide."

"They do," I said. "My client doesn't agree."

"Your client, eh?"

"That's right."

"Who's your client, Mr. Chance?" He grinned.

"I'm sorry. I can't tell you that."

"Crap."

"Shut up, Charlie." Moon leaned back in his chair. "Chance here is just doing a job." He leaned forward again and said slowly, "But, Chance, you should be careful about coming in here and throwing your—ah—weight around. You want to ask a few questions, fine. You just want to throw your weight around—that's something else."

Visser giggled. I figured it was at the remark about my weight—after a full meal I push the scale up to around 130—and I said, "Listen, Fink. You keep interrupting and I'm going to pop that pimple on your head. Moon here can tell me what I want to know."

"Apparently you didn't understand," Moon said. He tensed up for a second, then relaxed again, and took a swallow of the beer. "What's to tell? Peskin was an old guy. Maybe he was sick. Who knows? As far as I'm concerned, he got fed up with the rat race and pulled the cork. Bang. One squeeze and he had no more worries—like in the spray deodorant ads. Simple."

"Too simple," I said. "Peskin wasn't the kind to knock himself off."

"Maybe. I wouldn't know."

"He worked for you."

"A lot of guys work for me. Look, Chance, I'll make it easy for you. I know from nothin' about Peskin's death. The old guy worked around on my boats, keeping the diesels in shape, earning, a few bucks for booze. He's been around the wharf for as long as I can remember. So he knocks himself off. So what? If you're smart, you'll leave it that way."

"I'll leave it," I said. "For the time being. But I'll be around, Moon. If the old guy was killed—I'll get the man who did it."

Moon got to his feet and leaned over the desk. He brushed at the sweat on his face and said, "Drop in anytime, Chance. Always glad to be of help. You a drinking man, Chance?"

"No, thanks," I said.

"Too bad." He popped another can of beer. "It's a hot day, eh?" He held the can in a toast.

Visser opened the door for me, grinning, and followed me out onto the landing. "Chance."

"Yeah."

"You're kind of little to be talking as tough as you were in there. You know that?"

I didn't answer him.

"You ought to watch that mouth of yours." He had a raspy voice that rubbed my nerves like a cheese grater. "Mouthing off like that ain't healthy. Sometimes just asking questions ain't healthy. You get me?"

I stared at him.

"If I were you, Chance, I'd stay away from the wharf and from Mr. Moon and from *everything*. You get me?"

"Crap." I said it the way I'd heard him say it. Then I started down the stairs.

I shouldn't have turned my back. I heard his foot drag across the plank landing, but I didn't make it back around. I grabbed for the railing, but it was no good. The foot caught me in the small of the back, and shoved.

I woke up sick. For a minute I just sat there with the odor of old fish in my nostrils, gulping big lungfuls of the ocean breeze, wondering whether I had enough strength left to make it upstairs.

I didn't.

I barely had enough strength left to pull myself up on the first step. I was still sitting there, hurting in every bone in my body, when the door at the top of the stairs banged shut. I felt under my arm for my .38 and swung around in time to glimpse the nut-brown legs and the flouncing sweatshirt and the cotton shorts that were so tight they pulled into a little V in front.

From where I was sitting, the effect was superb.

"Goodness," Marty bubbled. She sat down beside me. "You fall down the stairs?"

"Oh, brother," I moaned. It seemed like a shame, all that lovely skin and no brains.

"Charlie said you fell down the stairs." She giggled, blonde hair swirling round her face. "I'll bet he tripped you. Charlie's nasty."

"Charlie's a real bastard," I said.

"They're all bastards," she said. "Charlie and Hiram and the whole lousy bunch around this wharf."

"Hiram know you're out here?"

"He doesn't even care. He'll sit up there all afternoon, until he runs out of beer, and then he'll come get me and undress me with those fat hands." She made a face. "It's the price I pay."

"For what?"

"For this." She pointed with her long fingers. "For all of the money it brings. Hiram's a very successful man. He's a pig—but he knows how to make money."

"That's important to you?"

"More important than anything in the world." She said it matter-of-factly, but I knew she wasn't kidding.

I said, "You make your husband sound like a pretty ruthless guy—capable of almost anything."

She pulled her black eyebrows together and looked at me. "He's capable of murder, if that's what you're not quite saying. But he's also very smart. I don't think he'd go around killing people just for the fun of it."

"You can't think of any reason why he'd want Peskin out of the way?"

"No." She said it haltingly. "Questions over?"

"Anytime you say." I grinned.

"Let's talk about something else." She squirmed a little, only in the tight shorts it looked like a lot. "Let's talk about you. Are you really a private detective?"

"Uh-huh."

"How interesting! I don't think I've ever known a real private detective." Her lips parted slightly, exposing rows of even white teeth that rubbed almost imperceptibly together, as if she wanted to bite on something. It was a peculiar, fascinating gesture that somehow went with the throaty voice and the slight, Southern accent. "But aren't you awfully small? I mean, I always thought private detectives were big, mean-looking men who chewed gum."

"I don't like gum," I said.

"You're not mean looking, either." She pushed a strand of hair from her face and said softly, "You're sort of cute, really. I'll bet you can take care of yourself, too. I mean, I'll bet you can handle most men twice your size."

I said glibly, "Two or three at a time. Sometimes, when they gang up, I bite their limbs off."

She gasped, "Oh—" She thought that was wonderful. "I'll bet you do, Johnny."

She was a strange girl. She got to me, got under my skin in a fascinating way. I could feel the sweat collecting on my face. It made me uncomfortable. I said, "I'd better go—before Charlie comes out and tries kicking me *up* the stairs."

"Oh—" She smiled, moving her teeth in that odd way. "Just when we were getting acquainted. You haven't even seen my boat."

"You're a sailor, eh?"

"Uh-huh." She pointed to what looked like a hundred thousand dollars' worth of sailboat at the end of the wharf, a white-hulled sloop with the name *Marty* lettered across the bow in gold. "It's all mine."

"Nice," I said.

"There isn't another one like it." She leaned forward. "We'll have to go for a sail sometime."

"I'd like that," I said.

"I know you would." She raised one of the black eyebrows in an arch.

I smiled and got up, bracing my feet, and said, "Thanks for the information."

"You're not really going to leave me?" She lay back on the steps, running slender hands over breasts that would have been ridiculously large if they had been hands or feet or anything but what they were. As it was, she looked deformed in the most wonderful way imaginable.

"Got to," I said.

"Oh." She pouted. She pouted all over. "That's too bad."

"Yeah." I grinned at her, "Too bad."

My apartment is in the Sea Cliff Apartments in La Jolla. For three hundred and fifty dollars a month, plus a repeated promise not to disturb my neighbors by having licentious parties and disporting myself generally, I am able to put on a lavish front of the type that spells success to my clients. It gives them a sense of security—plush, butter-coloerd carpet, expensive furniture, a view of the ocean—and makes my exorbitant fees seem less exorbitant.

In back is a garage where, for an extra fifty bucks a month, I park my Corvette and stack old copies of *Nugget*.

I parked.

I had made several stops along the bay-front after leaving Moon's place, bars and hangouts where a few bucks might buy a little information. Nothing. It was after midnight, and I had run out of capacity before running out of bars. I was beginning to feel the drinks and my brain was turning like a roulette wheel. Inside, jumping around like the little white ball, was the thought: *nobody wants to talk about Fran Peskin.* Then I thought: *the hell with it. Nobody ever wants to talk about a guy that's dead.*

I got out of the Corvette and was reaching for the handle on the overhead garage door, when a voice behind me said, "Chance."

I froze, my hackles standing up like toothbrush bristles.

There were a couple of guys there in the alley. They were bigger than me. Hell, almost everybody is bigger than me.

"Who?" I said pleasantly.

"You're it," one of them said. I wondered what he meant by that. He was a big up-and-down character with holes in his face, as if his skin had been gnawed by a rat. His pal was about the same height, only thinner, with hair that stuck out all over and a broken nose. The thin one was grinning as if something was about to be very funny.

I had a feeling I wasn't supposed to enjoy the joke.

"Sorry. My name's Alfred," I said conversationally. I lowered the door. "Alfred Humphrey—"

"You sonofabitch," the big one said. He spit the words out, lips tight against his teeth.

I started to circle around, slowly, so that my back wouldn't be against the garage door. I was scared. I opened my mouth to say something else as a fist slammed into my face. It hurt. It split my lip and brought blood rushing into my mouth. I spit some of the blood at ratface and hit him in the stomach, hard, right where he lived. Then I ran down the alley.

Ratface caught me.

He doubled my arm up behind me, twisting my hand up high, and spun me around just as the skinny one came racing up. I lifted my knee and he ran into it— groin first. He went down on his hands and knees and I kicked out at his face with my foot. I missed. I tried to get at ratface, but I couldn't. He gave my arm an upward twist, shooting a stab of pain through my shoulder, and held me. The pain made me dizzy and I shut my eyes.

Ratface put his face up to my ear and said conversationally, "That wasn't so smart. When you don't stand a chance it's best just to hold still and take your beating. Sometimes it ain't so bad that way. Now you've got Patty mad."

Ratface held me until Patty got to his feet. He was right. Patty was mad. He let me know it by digging out my .38 and busting me across the cheek. Then he slipped the gun into his pocket and went to work on my stomach with his fists. He talked pleasantly while he hit me, the moist grin spread across his face like an infected sore.

"How you like that, Big Daddy?"

Wham!

"That feel real good, Big Daddy?"

Wham!

It didn't. It felt more like somebody had stuck a cherry bomb in my navel and exploded it. Each time he swung his fist I tried to suck my stomach up inside my chest. Pain throbbed through my brain, and my breath came in short gasps.

He was enjoying it. His face seemed to waver and change shape before me, as if I was seeing him through muddy water, but the grin remained the same. He kept on grinning.

After what seemed like a long time I realized that the blows had stopped. I was lying on my back in the alley, my head making like a roulette wheel again. The taste of blood was strong in my mouth. When I got to my feet a stab of pain in my stomach bent me almost double. I leaned against the fence that ran parallel with the alley, trying to clear the fuzz from my brain.

It took me a full five minutes to make it up the stairs to my apartment. I took it a step at a time, pausing every few steps to rest. Mrs. Hollenbeck, who lives in the apartment below mine, opened her door a crack when I passed her landing. She looked at me curiously, grunted, and narrowed the crack until only one eye was visible. I leered at her and she banged the door all the way closed.

When I got upstairs I didn't try to undress or clean the mess off my face. I didn't even take off my shoes. I just flopped face down on the bed, grabbed a mouth full of the spread to ease the throbbing in my jaw, and slept.

It wasn't completely light when I woke up again, but the foggy, half-light that sometimes lingers along the coast in August. I got up and put some coffee water on and got under the shower. Pain leaped through my stomach and my head felt like a coconut that had fallen from a tall tree.

I soaped my face, carefully washing away the caked blood, wondering whether I should try to shave between the cuts. When I had toweled off I worked through a cigarette while I drank some of the coffee. I began thinking about Frank Peskin, wondering why a guy like that would kill himself—or get himself killed. I thought about Hiram Moon, too, wondering why the rummies around the wharf had hinted that he might be involved. It didn't seem likely that he'd have any reason for wanting Peskin out of the way, but I'd never known the wharf rats to be wrong.

The punks in the alley were Moon's boys. That much I knew. Why they were there, why the rough stuff, I didn't know. Unless the beating was Moon's way of scaring me off. Only that didn't make much sense either. If Moon was really involved—and I hadn't uncovered any evidence to suggest that he was—he'd have better sense than to sick his apes on me.

I thought: the hell with it. Let the police handle this one. There's nothing in it for me if I get involved.

I drank some more of the coffee and made a call to a client in San Francisco. I told him I'd fly up in a day or so with some information he'd asked for, then I went in and shaved.

I'm not sure when I made up my mind. Maybe it was when I got a good look at my beat-up face in the mirror. Maybe it was plain curiosity coupled with the fact that I had some time on my hands. After a while I just got dressed and left.

Julian Flack had said that Peskin was living with a daughter out in the beach area. I called him for the address and headed out there. The house was a neat whitewashed frame job in the 1700 block on Peacock, about a block from the ocean. I parked the Corvette out front and rang the bell. It was a little past 8:30 A.M. I rang again.

I wrote a note on one of my cards, asking Miss Peskin to get in touch, and pulled open the screen so I could slip it under the door. It opened.

Before I had straightened up, before I got a really good look, my stomach told me she was beautiful. The first thing I noticed were her eyes, soft, light-brown eyes that looked almost golden under dark brows that arched up slightly and then tapered back over clear temples. When she looked at me the eyes had an innocent expression.

"Well?"

"I'm sorry," I said. "I didn't mean to stare. You're Miss Peskin."

"Yes."

"I'm Johnny Chance," I said. "I'd like to ask you some questions."

"What about?"

"About your father."

She looked at me. Her face got very sober for a minute, and then she said, "Of course. Please come in."

I walked past her. The place was small, but it had a warm, cheerie look about it. There was a lot of yellow in the room, in the ruffled curtains and in some of the furniture. Off the living room I could see a spotless kitchen also done in pale yellow.

There was a pot of coffee perking in the kitchen. Real coffee. The aroma reminded me of a little store I used to know in Newark as a kid, where fresh coffee beans always spilled out of a grinder into the window. It was the only street in my neighborhood that didn't stink.

"I was just about to have some coffee. Would you like a cup?"

"Some coffee would taste good."

She came back from the kitchen pushing one of those low serving trays you get with green stamps. On top were a couple of cups and a pot of steaming coffee.

"Were you a friend of my dad's?"

"I knew him only slightly," I said. "But I have some friends who thought he was just about the greatest guy who ever lived."

"You must mean his friends around the waterfront." She smiled with even white teeth. "Frank was one of them, really. He drank too much and he would disappear with them for days sometimes—but he was different, too. He had a real understanding of their problems—maybe it was because he had the same problems—and he tried to help them whenever he could. He could never keep any money, because there was always a buddy who needed new teeth or a drink."

"You called him Frank?"

"He was my stepfather." She sipped her coffee. "I think that's the reason I've always been sort of tolerant of—the way he was. You see, he took on quite a handful when he married my mother. I've got seven sisters, Mr. Chance. That's a lot of women for one man to contend with. My mother died shortly after they were married. He took it very hard. It broke his health completely, and he was never very strong after that."

"He raised one very attractive daughter," I said.

"Thank you. He really tried."

"You lived here alone, just the two of you?"

"Yes. I have a job, as a waitress. It's not very glamourous work, but the tips are good. With the money Frank was able to pick up working around the waterfront, we made out okay."

"Miss Peskin," I said. "Did you know of any trouble that your dad might have been in?"

She looked at me, puzzled. "No. There was always some minor thing—an unpaid bill or something—but never anything serious. Why do you ask?"

I hesitated, and said, "When you heard that your father was—dead, did you have any idea his death might not have been suicide?"

She looked dazed for an instant, and then snapped right out of it again. "Why, no, of course not. Why should I think such a thing?"

"I don't know," I said. "It's why I asked."

"Who are you?"

"I'm sorry," I said. "I'm a private investigator. I should have told you that."

"You said you were a friend of Frank's."

"I knew him casually." I paused. "That made me his friend. In many ways he was a very strong man. I don't think he would take his own life."

"But why?" she said. "Why would anyone want to kill a man like Frank?"

"I don't know," I said. "I was hoping you might be able to tell me something that would help. Was he in any trouble with his friends, or any of the people he worked for?"

"No. Nothing that I knew of."

"How about Hiram Moon?"

"No. Nothing."

"You're sure?"

"Please," she said. I thought she might cry. "I just don't understand all this. Frank was a sick old man. He would have died anyway before very long. Why would anyone want to kill him? It just doesn't make sense."

I took a slug of my coffee. "I'm sorry. About all the questions, I mean. I shouldn't have come barging in here like this so soon."

"It has been kind of a shock," she said. She settled down a little. "Perhaps if you could come back later, after I've had time to think."

"Of course." I got up and she walked me to the door. "If I've upset you, I'm sorry."

"It's all right."

"Your dad was a nice guy, Miss Peskin." I felt foolish and headed for the car.

I had some breakfast in the beach area and drove downtown. On the way I went over the whole thing in my mind. There were only two sides to it. One: the old guy knocked himself off; I should quit wasting my time. Two: he was murdered; the evidence is all there.

I figured he was murdered.

What I couldn't figure was why. Why would Moon—or anybody, for that matter—knock off a harmless rummy like Peskin?

In a town scared half to death of a man like Hiram Moon, there's one source of information that isn't afraid to talk. The city newspaper.

I decided to give that a try.

I spent most of the rest of the day thumbing through soiled copies of the *Union* in the morgue. I wasn't sure of exactly what I was looking for, but I figured that if there was anything in Moon's past that shed any light on the subject, I might find it in the paper.

I was lucky.

The story ran the day after Rome fell to the Allies, June 5, 1944. It was shoved in among the news from Europe, a short, one column story under a mug shot of Victor Pompero.

I remembered reading about the Pompero thing. What I hadn't remembered was the names of some of the others involved. The story refreshed my memory. It said that Pompero, a small fry in the L. A. rackets, had fallen over the side of a fishing boat during rough weather off the point. It also gave the names of the other members of the fishing party: Sidney Potter, owner of a bowling alley and fight promoter; a Mexican businessman named Armando Perez; Hiram Moon, businessman. All three men admitted to the fact that there had been liquor on board and that, despite the rough sea, they felt partially responsible for Pompero's death. The skipper of the boat had been too busy fighting the swells to even notice that Pompero was gone. The skipper's name was Peskin.

At 9:45 I turned into the drive at Moon's place on the point and stopped about a hundred feet from the house. It was a big, sprawling place with a wall around it, crowded by hundred-year-old eucalyptus trees. French doors opened onto a tiled patio in the rear. I crossed the patio, my feet making a faint tapping noise on the tile, and slipped inside. The room I was in opened onto a larger room that must have been used for entertaining. There was a piano and a few car loads of fancy furniture and a bar long enough to accommodate a room full of thirsty sailors. Light seeped under a door on the other side of the room. I walked over and pushed it open.

Moon was in there.

He stood behind a desk roughly half the size of a boxing ring, a big .45 in his hand. When he saw who it was he put the gun on the desk and sat down again. He said, "I didn't hear you knock, Chance."

"I didn't," I said.

"You should have." He nodded toward the .45. "If I was the nervous type, I might have killed you."

There was money on the desk, lots of it; more money than I'd seen in a long time. It was separated into stacks. As he finished counting one of the stacks, Moon riffled it with his thumb, like a deck of cards, snapped an elastic band around it, and placed it aside. He said, counting, "You're a persistent man, Chance. I like that. Your manners could stand some improvement though. Next time, I suggest you try the front door."

I said quietly, "All right, Moon." He looked at me, snapped a band around another stack of bills, and smiled. "What's on your mind this time, Chance? Still hot on Peskin?"

"Hotter than you think," I said.

"Okay. You start it."

"Vic Pompero," I said. I watched him close, waiting for a reaction.

"Pompero?" He took a cigar out of a box and bit the end off.

I dug out the clipping and dropped it on the stacks of bills. I said, "Why don't you give me the straight story, Moon?"

"Pompero, eh?" He still had the end of the cigar in his mouth. When he spat, the tobacco caught on his lip and hung there. "You know what I think, Chance? I think you're out of your mind."

"Maybe."

"The police tried to pin the Pompero thing on me fifteen years ago. They couldn't. What are you trying to pull, anyway?"

I said, "Think about it, Moon. There were four people left on that boat after Pompero went over the side—four people who knew what really happened out there."

"Go on." He licked his lips.

"Where are they now?" I said.

"You're telling it, Chance." He leaned toward me, his face nasty. "But you'd better make it real good, sucker. I don't like accusations, understand? You start making statements you can't back up, I might get angry."

"I figure what I got to say makes sense," I said. "Let's add up the score. First of all, Sidney Potter gets knocked off in the war. A few years later Perez gets it in an automobile accident in Mexico. Now Peskin takes care of himself. That leaves only you, Moon, with only one story about what really happened on that boat."

He didn't react. Not the way I expected. His face went slack, and perspiration popped out on his neck, but he wasn't scared.

He said quietly, "You're crazy, Chance."

I said, "Not this time. It's too good, Moon. There isn't a D.A. in the country that would pass it up."

Moon said, "Answer me this, shrimp. How come I waited so long? If Pompero's death wasn't an accident, and I was afraid Peskin might run off at the mouth, how come I waited fifteen years to get rid of him?"

"The old man was sick," I said. "He didn't have much longer one way or the other. Knowing that, maybe you figured you couldn't keep him quiet any longer."

Moon got his cigar going and grinned at me through the smoke. "I like you, Chance. That's why I'm going to straighten you out before I toss you the hell out of here. For one thing, Pompero's death was really an accident. I can't say I was sorry to see him go, but I didn't kill him. That should make the second thing pretty obvious. I couldn't have any reason for wanting Peskin out of the way."

I looked at him. There was still no hint of fear in his eyes, no hint even that he was disturbed. It bothered me. I said, "If you didn't kill Peskin, somebody's gone to a lot of trouble to make it look as if you did."

He said thoughtfully, "You got real evidence that Peskin was murdered?"

"Enough to send you to the gas chamber."

He chewed the cigar. His eyes narrowed and he said, "Who'd want to pin a rap like that on me?"

"Who'd stand to gain the most?"

"Nobody. That's just it. Nobody."

"Visser?"

"What do you take me for? Anything happens to me, Visser would be out on his tail in a week. Why else do you think I take care of all this myself, Chance?" He indicated the money on the desk. "I control everything, understand? Nobody's got a string on my business, nobody."

I thought about it for a second. That's all it took. "You're wrong."

Moon's face got pink. I think he got it too. "You bastard," he said.

"Your wife," I said. "With you out of the way, she gets it all. Everything."

For an instant I thought he might go for the gun. He came all the way to his feet, eyes narrowed to angry slits, but even through the slits I could see the hint of doubt, "You bastard—"

And that was the end of the conversation.

That was also the end of Moon, He died with his mouth open, about to call me another dirty name, but the only sound was the explosion of the gun behind me and the dull smack as his head bounced off the desk. For an instant he stared up at me from the blotter, a neat hole parting one eyebrow, and blood running out onto the stacks of money. Then he slipped down behind the desk and was gone.

I turned slowly, fear eating its way up my spine.

Marty was standing just inside the door, her small hand clutching the gun that had made all the noise. Her small, red-tipped fingers looked very fragile against the blue steel.

I said, "You must want it bad."

"I do." She came a step closer. She wore a low-cut blouse of some gold material and a pair of black, skin-tight pants and gold slippers with little tassels on the ends. "All of it."

"But why this way?" I said. I swallowed. "You were his wife. It belonged to you anyway."

"That's Where you're wrong." When she spoke her voice was tight. She shuddered. "As long as he was around, none of it was mine. You can't own anything with Hiram, only be owned. I didn't want it that way. Not with him; not with that pig."

"So you killed a scared old man and tried to make it look as if Moon did it to get him out of the way."

"It will still look that way." She looked at me, smiling. "Only it doesn't make any difference now."

"You killed the old man." It made me sick.

"Yes."

"You bitch."

"He didn't know. He was an old man, Johnny." Her eyes widened slightly. "He was asleep, Johnny, just sitting there on the end of the wharf. I walked out there and held the gun against his head and threw the gun in the water. He didn't know."

"Then it was you who sent Moon's boys to work me over."

"Yes." She said it matter-of-factly. "I didn't know the police would think the old man killed himself. When they did, I thought the whole thing would turn out wrong. Then you came around asking questions. I wanted to make sure you didn't give it up."

"I didn't," I said.

"Maybe you should have. Now I'll have to say you came barging in here and accused Hiram of poor Peskin's murder. That seems like a reasonable accusation. Hiram reached for the gun on his desk and you shot him."

"And you shot me."

She smiled. "Too bad."

"You're developing a real taste for killing."

"I wonder if I really am." She licked her lips, pressed her teeth together. "I'm sorry it has to be you, Johnny."

"You've made a mistake, Sweetheart. You can't kill me with the same gun you used on Moon."

It pulled her up short. Her breath sucked in and she looked at the gun in her hand. It was enough. As soon as her eyes shifted I grabbed the .45 on the desk, jumped sideways as I pulled the trigger.

I was lucky.

She fired, but it was too late. The bullet caught the edge of the desk, gouged out a hunk of mahogany, and slammed into the carpet behind me. I went down on my knees and watched as her body jackknifed four or five feet against the far wall. She lay on her back, her eyes open, the long legs spread obscenely against the expensive carpet. Most of her jaw was gone.

I didn't even feel her pulse.

I waited for Flack and gave him the story in bits and pieces while he yelled at me. It was okay. Flack is always yelling at me.

The Safe Kill

Kenneth Moore

April 1960

His name was Ramey and at forty-four he had the shoulders of a football player, the neck of a boilermaker, the chest of a wrestler and the integrity of a Kansas City gigolo.

On this hot Friday evening he stood in the middle of Tony Spaino's office holding his hat in his hand and looking very much like a schoolboy waiting to be punished by the principal. He felt beads of perspiration break on his forehead and run to catch in the corners of his eyes. He licked dry lips and wished he had enough courage to light a cigarette.

Spaino, healthy and prosperous behind a polished desk which sent back the bright reflection of the overhead lights, peeled the plastic wrapper from a cigar and waited for his bodyguard to come forth with a platinum lighter. While the bodyguard held the lighter with a steady hand, Spaino studied the man in the center of the office. "How long have you been in this section?"

"Three weeks, sir," Ramey said, then realized he shouldn't have said "Sir". It cast Spaino in the role of the superior.

"Why were you transferred from the old section?"

"I killed a man," Ramey said.

The swivel chair creaked under Spaino's weight as he leaned back and nodded slightly. He made a nice appearance: a tall, heavy man in his mid-forties, with a clean shaven olive face that glistened in the light. The expensive Italian suit was so well tailored it exposed only a slight trace of a paunch acquired from years of soft living.

"You know about Joey Keener?" Spaino asked.

"The whole city does," Ramey said. He was beginning to relax now, and a smile twisted the corner of his mouth.

"Joey and I used to be friends," Spaino said, "But now we don't get along so well. Joey thought he'd like to take over part of my organization."

"I know the tale," Ramey said. "He tried to gun one of your lieutenants, but an innocent bystander got in the way. Now that Joey's been identified, the cops are working overtime to find him. He's just a punk, but he knows enough about you to put you in the death house. The cops figure if they sweat him long enough he'll testify against you to save himself."

"And if he's knocked off, they'll know I did it or had it done," Spaino said. "Either way I'm on my way to the death house."

"Interesting situation," Ramey said.

"That's why I sent for you," Spaino said. "I've got ten thousand dollars that says you can help me."

He snapped his fingers. The bodyguard moved forward, placed five one thousand dollars bills on the glossy desk. "Take it," Spaino said. "Half now; half when the job's finished."

Ramey looked at the money for a long time, then shook his head. "You're the gambler. Not me."

Spaino's eyes narrowed. "What's that supposed to mean?"

"I want all of it now."

Spaino relaxed and Ramey could hear him exhale across the room. "Give him the rest of the money, Elwood."

The bodyguard placed five more one thousand dollar bills on the pile. Ramey reached over the desk, folded the money and put it in his pocket.

"Remember, I can't be connected with this in any way. If the cops even suspect I had anything to do with it they'll find some way to burn me for sure."

"Don't worry," Ramey assured him. "You'll be in the clear."

Spaino handed him a slip of paper. "Here's the address. My boys traced him to this spot."

Ramey studied the slip of paper. "What's he doing?"

"Waiting. Trying to decide whether to run or take his chance with the cops." Spaino chuckled lightly then, probably his first chuckle in days. "He's almost in the same predicament as me. If he runs, one of my men will get him sooner or later. If he goes to the cops, he stands a good chance of getting the chair."

"You can relax," Ramey said. "I'll take care of him."

"It has to be tonight. If my boys were able to trace him, it'll only be a matter of time until the cops manage to find him."

"Tonight then."

Ramey turned and walked out of the office. He went down a flight of stairs to the alley and got in his car. He drove six blocks to an all-night drugstore, went inside and bought a box of envelopes and a stamp. Inside a telephone booth at the rear, he addressed one of the envelopes with his home address and stamped it. He took the bills out of his pocket, placed them in the envelope. It was a necessary precaution. He couldn't afford to have the money found on him in case he had to go downtown to police headquarters to sign a statement. Some smart cop might take it upon himself to suggest a search.

He left the drugstore and dropped the envelope in a corner mail box. He climbed into his car, studied the address again. He checked his watch, saw that it was half past midnight. He kicked life into the motor, pulled the car away from the curb.

The address was a shabby six floor hotel on the city's southside, situated in the middle of a block of gray and black granite buildings. It was typical of a place where a man like Joey Keener might hide. It was a neighborhood where a man could pass unnoticed for months and buy anything if he had the price.

Ramey parked a few doors away from the building and walked to the front entrance. The clerk was dozing behind the desk in the lobby. Ramey went inside, spun the register around on the desk and checked the name assigned to room thirty-seven. He knew Keener wouldn't be using his real name, but Ramey wanted to appear professional for the benefit of the clerk, who now yawned and climbed to his feet.

"Sorry, no vacancies," the clerk said.

"Give me the key to 307," Ramey ordered.

"That's Mr. Scott's room."

Ramey's jacket fell open, exposing the .38 holstered under his arm. "The key," he said.

"Sure, sure," the clerk said. He dug into the pigeonhole for the key.

"How long has this Scott been here?"

"A couple of days," the clerk said. "A week maybe."

Ramey pointed to a chair. "You stay there."

The clerk dropped into the chair, his mouth hanging open. "And don't try to warn him on the house phone," Ramey said over his shoulder as he turned.

"No sir," said the clerk.

Ramey took the stairs three at a time. When he reached the third floor, he dug his .38 from the holster and walked softly down the hall toward the room. He put his ear to the door of 307. Hearing no sound from inside the room, he put his shoulder to the door, felt the lock snap under his weight.

Joey Keener was at the bureau pouring himself a drink when Ramey came through the door. He spun suddenly, and the glass and bottle shattered against the floor.

"Easy, Keener," Ramey ordered, leveling his gun on the other man's chest.

Keener gave one fleeting glance at the gun on the bedside table across the room. "I wouldn't try it, Joey," Ramey cautioned. "I could drop you before you went two steps."

Keener raised his arms. "Who are you, mister?"

Ramey walked around the shabby room, noted the overnight bag on the bed. "Looks like you were getting ready to take a trip," he said.

He picked up the gun from the table, balanced it on his palm. "Nice gun," he said. He pointed it, pulled off two fast shots in the direction of the doorway. He looked at the holes for a moment, then nodded. "They should do nicely."

"What's the pitch?" Keener asked. "And who in hell are you?"

"Spaino sent me," Ramey said.

"Spaino. He's crazy if he thinks he can get away—" Recognition suddenly crossed his face and with it came fear. "Say, aren't you—"

Joey Keener never finished. Ramey pulled the trigger of his .38 twice and watched the bullets tear into Keener's chest. The little man's body slammed against the wall. He stood there a moment, his body supported by the wall, his fingers laced across the bullet holes in his chest. Then he slid slowly to the floor and collapsed in a heap.

Ramey put away his gun, took a handkerchief from his pocket and wiped his prints from Keener's gun. He bent over the body, placed the gun in the limp hand. He put the dead man's fingers through the trigger guard, pulled the trigger and then kicked the gun aside. He lit a cigarette and went over and sat on the bed to wait for the police.

"Christ," swore the lieutenant. His name was Bland, and he had been trying to nail Joey Keener and Tony Spaino for months. He stood in the middle of the hotel room and watched the deputy coroner complete his preliminary examination.

"I tried my best," Ramey said. He pointed to the bullet holes in the door. "But he put up a fight."

"I wish there had been some way to take him alive," Bland said. He looked down at the body. "There goes my last chance to get a case against Spaino."

A reporter pushed his way through the crowd into the room. "How about a story, Lieutenant?"

Bland gave him the story, speaking slowly so the reporter would get all the facts. The reporter jotted notes in his notebook. "Off duty policeman kills wanted man resisting arrest," he said. He turned to Ramey. "Should make a nice headline, Sergeant."

Ramey's face turned sour. "Can I go now, Lieutenant?"

Bland nodded. "Yeah, Sergeant, but you'd better report to headquarters first thing in the morning. The captain will want to talk to you."

Ramey nodded and pushed his way toward the door. The captain would probably raise holy hell and even suspend him, but Ramey wasn't worried. He had ten thousand dollars now, and it was just possible that Spaino could find another job for him in the future.

A Question of Values

C. L. Sweeney, Jr.

June 1960

I suppose that every older man with a young and beautiful wife asks himself these same questions sooner or later. Sooner or later he awakes one morning and sees his wife lying there beside him, sees her young and warm and desirable there in her sleep, and for no reason at all a little sliver of panic suddenly forces itself into the back of his mind.

He hurries into the bathroom, turns on the light and hopefully examines himself closely in the mirror, searching for a reassurance that is not there. He sees instead a man no longer young, grey flecks in the stubble of beard, white in the hair at the temples, and eyes pouched and tired.

And then the panic sharpens unreasonably and the questions begin to flood into his mind. Will a younger man try to take her away from me? Who will he be? What will he look like? What will she do? What will I do? These—and a thousand others like them.

For most men these questions need never be answered, simply because, like most things we worry about, the event never occurs. For others, like myself, the questions are forced on them and must be met.

When the time comes, however, some of them will obviously answer themselves. For example, what will he look like? There was no longer any reason to wonder. He sat across from me now, a young man of about her age, handsome, almost pretty, soft like his expensively tailored cashmere jacket, soft like the skin on his beautifully tapered hands, strangely out of place here against the worn books and racked guns and roughly hewn logs of my hunting lodge.

"Really," he said petulantly, looking about the room with obvious distaste, "I don't see why you should ask me to drive up to the top of this Godforsaken mountain."

"I'm sorry," I said, "but I've always found that I can think better, clearer somehow, up here at the lodge. The mountain air perhaps, the clean scent of the pines. I thought we could make our decisions more intelligently up here than in some crowded bar in the city."

"Decisions?" He flicked at an invisible spot on his cashmere lapel. "There was only one decision to be made. That was hers and she made it. She's leaving you. That's all there appears to be to it."

I leaned forward in my chair. "But *has* she really made that decision?" I asked him. "Does she know you well enough as a man to decide that she can love you better than she has loved me?"

"I don't follow you," he said, his voice sulky, bored.

"I'm suggesting," I said, watching his delicate hands, white against the dark oak of the table, "the possibility that she doesn't really love you, the possibility that she is only temporarily infatuated because you are a rising young concert pianist and because she has always loved music. I'm suggesting that perhaps she is in love with your talent, with the artistry in your hands, not with you as a man."

His lip curled disdainfully. "That's ridiculous," he said.

"Ah," I said, "but how do we know? That's one of the questions which must be answered."

He looked at his watch and yawned. "Really, if this is all you have to—"

"No," I said, "it's not all. There's also the question of what I will do about it."

"What you will do about it?" He shrugged. "And what do you think you can do about it?"

"The choices are simple," I said. "I can let her go or I can refuse to give her a divorce and keep her. On the other hand, the decision between these choices is much more difficult. You see, it's not easy to give up the woman you've adored for almost five years."

He shrugged again and smiled. "I wouldn't know," he said.

"No," I agreed, "I suppose you wouldn't, and yet I want you to understand exactly how I feel, appreciate the importance of this decision to me." I thought for a moment and then my eyes stopped and steadied on those soft, white beautiful hands of his. "Yes," I said slowly. "Yes, I believe that's it. I believe that losing her would mean as much to me as, say, losing one of those hands would mean to you."

He winced involuntarily and pulled his hands back into his lap.

I laughed. "I'm sorry if that upset you," I said. "I was only trying to draw a comparison."

He cleared his throat, moved uneasily in his chair and looked at his watch again.

"So there we have it," I said, before he had a chance to speak. "She has a question to answer and I have a question to answer. And yet, oddly enough, neither of us can come to an intelligent decision until we know how your question will be answered."

"Question?" I watched him closely. A few tiny beads of perspiration were beginning to form along his brow. "I'm not aware of any question I'm supposed to answer."

"Ah," I said, "but don't you see? That's just the point. Of the three of us, you're the only one who has no question to answer, no decision to make, everything to gain, nothing to lose. It offends my sense of fairness."

He started to get up. "Really—" he said.

I stood up with him. "I'm sorry," I said. "I'm afraid that I've been a poor host, moralizing to you like this, not even offering you a drink." I went to the cupboard and took down two glasses. "Surely you'll at least have one with me now before you go."

He hesitated for a moment, then, "All right, just one," he said, "just one for the road."

"Just one for the road," I agreed and went to the heavy ring holt in the floor in front of the fireplace and tried to lift the trapdoor. "I keep my liquor in the little cellar under here," I explained and pulled on the ring again, tugging at it this time.

He had moved over to watch me and I looked up at him. "I haven't opened it for some time and it seems to be stuck," I said apologetically. "Perhaps you'd—?"

He knelt down and grasped the ring with me, his right hand against my left. "All right," I said, "all together when I give the word." I put my right hand into my hip pocket and removed the steel handcuffs. "Now," I said. He strained upward and I snapped the cuffs tight, one about his wrist, the other through the ring. Then I stood up.

He looked at the cuffs and then at me, his face suddenly pale. "'What is this, a game?" he said tightly "Are you crazy?"

"No," I said "or at least I'm reasonably sure that I'm not. I'm merely trying to illustrate what I was saying before, that of the three of us you alone have had no question to answer, you alone have been spared the pain of a decision."

I walked to the mantle over the fireplace and took down a heavy hunting knife and balanced the point thoughtfully on the tip of my forefinger. He watched me, fascinated at first, then little sounds like whimpering beginning to come from his throat. I laughed. "Don't worry," I said, "I'm not going to harm you. The decision will be entirely your own." I held the knife out to him, handle first, but he only stared at it, refused to touch it, and so I drove it into the floor beside him, where he could reach it when the time came.

"They'll find me here," he said. The whimpering had become more distinct. "They'll miss me. They'll come looking for me."

"Yes," I said. "Yes, they'll come looking for you, but in the meantime you'll have already made your decision and then perhaps she and I will be able to make ours."

I turned my back to him and went to the corner and took the can of kerosene and began to soak the walls, the books, everything. I felt his eyes on me and heard the rising panic in his harsh breathing but I didn't look at him again until I had tossed a wad of burning rags against one wall and watched the flames leap to the ceiling.

I went to the door then, opened it and turned. I saw him through the eddies of smoke, on hands and knees, choking, sobbing, frantically digging at the wood about the bolt with the knife.

"It's no use," I said. "It's four inch oak and the door has been bolted down."

He stopped and looked at me, the sobs rising to a scream. "Don't leave me, I'll burn, I'll burn."

I shook my head. "Not necessarily," I said.

Slowly then his eyes left me and went to the gleaming knife in his left hand, to the white wrist imprisoned by the steel cuff. Finally, realizing, eyes wide with shock, he looked back to me.

I bowed slightly. "Your question," I said and closed the door and got into my car and drove down the mountain to the broad highway leading into the city, never looking back.

Shatter Proof
Jack Ritchie (John G. Reitci)

October 1960

He was a soft-faced man wearing rimless glasses, but he handled the automatic with unmistakable competence.

I was rather surprised at my calmness when I learned the reason for his presence. "It's a pity to die in ignorance," I said. "Who hired you to kill me?"

His voice was mild. "I could be an enemy in my own right."

I had been making a drink in my study when I had heard him and turned. Now I finished pouring from the decanter. "I know the enemies I've made and you are a stranger. Was it my wife?"

He smiled. "Quite correct. Her motive must be obvious."

"Yes," I said. "I have money and apparently she wants it. All of it."

He regarded me objectively "Your age is?"

"Fifty-three."

"And your wife is?"

"Twenty-two."

He clicked his tongue. "You were foolish to expect anything permanent, Mr. Williams."

I sipped the whiskey. "I expected a divorce after a year or two and a painful settlement. But not death."

"Your wife is a beautiful woman, but greedy, Mr. Williams. I'm surprised that you never noticed."

My eyes went to the gun. "I assume you have killed before?"

"Yes."

"And obviously you enjoy it."

He nodded. "A morbid pleasure, I admit. But I do."

I watched him and waited. Finally I said, "You have been here more than two minutes and I am still alive."

"There is no hurry, Mr. Williams," he said softly.

"Ah, then the actual killing is not your greatest joy. You must savor the preceding moments."

"You have insight, Mr. Williams."

"And as long as I keep you entertained, in one manner or another, I remain alive?"

"Within a time limit, of course."

"Naturally. A drink, Mr . . ..?"

"Smith requires no strain on the memory. Yes, thank you. But please allow me to see what you are doing when you prepare it."

"It's hardly likely that I would have poison conveniently at hand for just such an occasion."

"Hardly likely, but still possible."

He watched me while I made his drink and then took an easy chair.

I sat on the davenport. "Where would my wife be at this moment?"

"At a party, Mr. Williams. There will be a dozen people to swear that she never left their sight during the time of your murder."

"I will be shot by a burglar? An intruder?"

He put his drink on the cocktail table in front of him. "Yes. After I shoot you, I shall, of course, wash this glass and return it to your liquor cabinet. And when I leave I shall wipe all fingerprints from the doorknobs I've touched."

"You will take a few trifles with you? To make the burglar-intruder story more authentic?"

"That will not be necessary, Mr. Williams. The police will assume that the burglar panicked after he killed you and fled empty-handed."

"That picture on the east wall," I said. "It's worth thirty thousand."

His eyes went to it for a moment and then quickly returned to me. "It is tempting, Mr. Williams. But I desire to possess nothing that will even remotely link me to you. I appreciate art, and especially its monetary value, but not to the extent where I will risk the electric chair." Then he smiled. "Or were you perhaps offering me the painting? In exchange for your life?"

"It was a thought."

He shook his head. "I'm sorry, Mr. Williams. Once I accept a commission, I am not dissuaded. It is a matter of professional pride."

I put my drink on the table. "Are you waiting for me to show fear, Mr. Smith?"

"You will show it."

"And then you will kill me?"

His eyes flickered. "It is a strain, isn't it, Mr. Williams? To be afraid and not to dare show it."

"Do you expect your victims to beg?" I asked.

"They do. In one manner or another."

"They appeal to your humanity? And that is hopeless?"

"It is hopeless."

"They offer you money?"

"Very often."

"Is that hopeless too?"

"So far it has been, Mr. Williams."

"Behind the picture I pointed out to you, Mr. Smith, there is a wall safe."

He gave the painting another brief glance. "Yes."

"It contains five thousand dollars."

"That is a lot of money, Mr. Williams."

I picked up my glass and went to the painting. I opened the safe, selected a brown envelope, and then finished my drink. I put the empty glass in the safe and twirled the knob.

Smith's eyes were drawn to the envelope. "Bring that here, please."

I put the envelope on the cocktail table in front of him.

He looked at it for a few moments and then up at me. "Did you actually think you could buy your life?"

I lit a cigarette. "No. You are, shall we say, incorruptible."

He frowned slightly. "But still you brought me the five thousand?"

I picked up the envelope and tapped its contents out on the table. "Old receipts. All completely valueless to you."

He showed the color of irritation. "What do you think this has possibly gained you?"

"The opportunity to go to the safe and put your glass inside it."

His eyes flicked to the glass in front of him. "That was yours. Not mine."

I smiled. "It was your glass, Mr. Smith. And I imagine that the police will wonder what an empty glass is doing in my safe. I rather think, especially since this will be a case of murder, that they will have the intelligence to take fingerprints."

His eyes narrowed. "I haven't taken my eyes off you for a moment. You couldn't have switched our glasses."

"No? I seem to recall that at least twice you looked at the painting."

Automatically he looked in that direction again. "Only for a second or two."

"It was enough."

He was perspiring faintly. "I say it was impossible."

"Then I'm afraid you will be greatly surprised when the police come for you. And after a little time you will have the delightful opportunity of facing death in the electric chair. You will share your victims' anticipation of death with the addition of a great deal more time in which to let your imagination play with the topic. I'm sure you've read accounts of executions in the electric chair?"

His finger seemed to tighten on the trigger.

"I wonder how you'll go," I said. "You've probably pictured yourself meeting death with calmness and fortitude. But that is a common comforting delusion, Mr. Smith. You will more likely have to be dragged . . .."

His voice was level. "Open that safe or I'll kill you."

I laughed. "Really now, Mr. Smith, we both know that obviously you will kill me if I *do* open the safe."

A half a minute went by before he spoke. "What do you intend to do with the glass?"

"If you don't murder me—and I rather think you won't now—I will take it to a private detective agency and have your fingerprints reproduced. I will put them, along with a note containing pertinent information, inside a sealed envelope. And I will leave instructions that in the event I die violently, even if the occurrence appears accidental, the envelope be forwarded to the police."

Smith stared at me and then he took a breath. "All that won't be necessary. I will leave now and you will never see me again."

I shook my head. "I prefer my plan. It provides protection for my future."

He was thoughtful. "Why don't you go direct to the police."

"I have my reasons."

His eyes went down to his gun and then slowly he put it in his pocket. An idea came to him. "Your wife could very easily hire someone else to kill you."

"Yes. She could do that."

"I would be accused of your death. I could go to the electric chair."

"I imagine so. Unless . . .."

Smith waited.

"Unless, of course, she were unable to hire anyone."

"But there are probably a half a dozen others . . .." He stopped.

I smiled. "Did my wife tell you where she is now?"

"Just that she'd be at a place called the Petersons. She will leave at eleven."

"Eleven? A good time. It will be very dark tonight. Do you know the Petersons' address?"

He stared at me. "No."

"In Bridgehampton," I said, and I gave him the house number.

Our eyes held for a half a minute.

"It's something you must do," I said softly. "For your own protection."

He buttoned his coat slowly. "And where will you be at eleven, Mr. Williams?"

"At my club, probably playing cards with five or six friends. They will no doubt commiserate with me when I receive word that my wife has been . . . shot?"

"It all depends on the circumstances and the opportunity." He smiled thinly. "Did you ever love her?"

I picked up a jade figurine and examined it. "I was extremely fond of this piece when I first bought it. Now it bores me. I will replace it with another."

When he was gone there was just enough time to take the glass to a detective agency before I went on to the club.

Not the glass in the safe, of course. It held nothing but my own fingerprints.

I took the one that Mr. Smith left on the cocktail table when he departed.

The prints of Mr. Smith's fingers developed quite clearly.

The Old Pro
H. A. DeRosso

December 1960

It seemed rather strange and chilling to him because he had never contracted for another man's death before. But it was something that had to be done and he could not do it himself because he wanted to remain clean. Direct involvement, if discovered, would destroy all that he had built these past few years. He might even lose Loretta and she meant too much to him to risk that. So he made a long distance call and entered into the contract.

"Mike? This is Burn. Remember me?"

"Burn?" Sargasso's voice over the phone sounded as coarse and rasping as it had always been. "Oh, yes. It's been a long time. Four years, isn't that right?"

"About that."

"How's retirement?"

"Good. Never had it better. Until something came up."

"Oh? Is that why you're calling?"

"Yes. I was wondering if you couldn't refer someone to me, a-an engineer experienced in removing obstructions. It's a ticklish matter and I need a good man. You know of someone like that around?"

There was a short silence. Then from Sargasso's end of the line there came a soft, grating chuckle.

"Is something funny?" he asked with a touch of anger in his tone.

"In a way, yes," Sargasso said. "I mean, you of all people—" The chuckle sounded again.

He flushed in the privacy of the phone booth. "Well, do you have the man?" he asked testily.

"Sure, Burn, sure." Amusement still lingered in Sargasso's voice. "You were always the hasty one. Take it easy. When do you want the engineer?"

"This weekend. Sometime Saturday. At my place out at Walton Lake. I'll have the job all set up for him. Can you get him up here in that time?"

"Now, Burn, you know I always guarantee results." The humor still teased in Sargasso's tone. "Well, luck."

"Thanks, Mike. So long."

The line clicked dead at Sargasso's end before he had even started to hang up . . .

The name on his mailbox spelled Ralph Whitburn. He had a comfortable home here on the edge of the small town with a nice view of the curving river that was the boundary between Wisconsin and the Upper Peninsula of Michigan. Beyond the river stretched the vast, second-growth forest. He had fallen in love with the view the first time he had seen it. He enjoyed the cool green colors of summer and the tartan hues of autumn, he even enjoyed the bleak look of winter with the trees standing dark and dead among the silent snow. It was so far removed from the squalor and stench of all the cities he had once known.

This was the good life. He could hear Loretta humming in the kitchen. The aroma of cooking was pleasant in his nostrils. He stood on the lawn and watched some swallows wheeling and darting not far overhead in their swift pursuit of summer insects. Yes, this was the good life and he was not going to let anything destroy it. That was why he had contracted for a man's death.

"Chow's ready, Ralph."

His eyes feasted on Loretta as he sat down at the table in the dining nook. She was tall and red-headed with a pert, saucy face spattered with freckles that also spread over her bare shoulders and arms. She was wearing halter and shorts that set off her good figure, which was high-breasted, lean-hipped and long-legged. Once he had thought that love was an emotion he would never experience but that had been before he had met Loretta.

This was the good life, this was true contentment.

"Is something wrong, Ralph?"

He looked up with a start, surprised that he had revealed anything. Loretta was watching him with a half-frown, half-smile, green eyes clouded with puzzlement and concern.

His lips twisted into a smile that felt awkward and forced to him. "Why do you say that?"

"You look—preoccupied."

"Do I?" He laughed. "The approach of middle age when muscles grow flabby and the skin sags and—"

"Oh, stop it, Ralph. I'm serious." The frown was very pronounced on her forehead now. "Something's been eating you lately. What is it?"

He sobered and the great solemnness came over him again and the needling of a dark and futile anger. "It's nothing, Loretta. I swear it's nothing."

"Well, if this is how 'nothing' affects you, I'd hate to think how you'd be when something big and serious pops up."

"I've been thinking. You know, about expanding the plant. Wood products are selling very well. I've been trying to decide between enlarging the existing plant and building a new one, maybe over in Michigan."

She was staring at him in a strange, examining way, "Funny you never mentioned this to me before. Are you starting to keep things from me, Ralph?" She tried to say the last lightly but it did not quite come off. There had been a catch in her throat.

He got up and bent over her and kissed her cheek. "I'm just a little down, Kind of tired. A weekend at the lake will fix me up."

She hugged his arm and looked up at him with shining eyes. "I was just going to suggest that. Why don't we go out there tonight? You can stay away from the plant tomorrow, It's Friday and the business will get along without you for one day, I'll start getting ready now."

She rose to her feet but he put a detaining hand on her arm, "Saturday's soon enough. And, Loretta, this weekend I'm going out there alone."

She gave him a long look. Then her mouth smiled but the eyes said she was just pretending. "You mean what the Hollywood people call a trial separation?"

"No, no," he said hurriedly, "nothing like that." He took her in his arms and held her very tightly, thinking that this was something he would never allow anyone to break up. "There's something I've got to thrash out alone. I wish I could explain to you, Loretta, but it's something I've got to do by myself. I'll miss you every minute I'm at the lake. Believe me."

"Ralph," she gasped, "I can't breathe." She leaned back in his relaxing arms and caressed his cheek while she smiled up at him. "Old and flabby?" she teased, "Another minute of that and I'd have had to go see a chiropractor."

"Then you don't mind my going alone?"

"Of course I mind, but I bow to your will, master." She kissed him fervently. "I'll miss you, too, you big lug. Very, very much."

He buried his face in her hair. This was the good life, he thought. Nothing, no one was going to take it from him . . . He had always liked the solemnity and quiet of the forest. There was something restful and soothing in the isolation, the lack of the sounds of machinery and motors, the absence of the hurry and bustle of the cities. The only intrusion from the outside world was the occasional snarl of an outboard motor out on the lake but even this was not overdone for he had selected a far end of Walton Lake on which to build his cottage. There were no immediate neighbors. He had come to these north woods for seclusion and here at the lake he had it.

He found the waiting hard to take and this was unusual for he had always been a patient man. The thing he disliked most about the waiting was that so many doubts and uncertainties were forming in his mind. He realized these were foolish fears for the man Sargasso sent would be efficient and capable. He knew how these killers operated. They entered a town or city as strangers, studied the habits of their quarry, decided on the best means of liquidation, did so and departed. They were the professionals who very seldom were apprehended and if they were never named their employers. He knew that very well but still he could not keep a feeling of anxiety from creeping over him. There was too much at stake, he had too much to lose, that was the reason he worried so endlessly.

He tried fishing to while away the time. He got his boat and went out to the center of the lake by the island and on his third cast hooked a wall-eye. But his heart was not in it and he played the big fish carelessly and impatiently and lost it. He started the motor again, intending to cruise about the lake, and with his mind on other matters almost wrecked the craft on the treacherous rocks that lurked just beneath the surface of the water at the south end of the island. He swerved the boat barely in time and as he looked back over his shoulder at the place where he could have torn the bottom out of the craft the idea was born.

He could feel his heart begin to pound with an old excitement. Then he remembered that Sargasso was sending someone and that whoever it was he would have his own ideas. So Whitburn filed the thought away, somewhat regretfully, telling himself he could not become involved directly. He had to stay clean.

Heading back to the cottage, he saw the car parked beside his convertible. A strange tightness gathered in his throat, a sensation of uneasiness almost akin to panic, and he wondered at this for he had always prided himself on his iron nerve.

He told himself to relax. The matter would be in capable hands. No one was ever delegated by Sargasso unless he were thoroughly competent.

The stranger was standing on the small dock, watching the boat come in. He was on the short and chunky side. He wore a gay sport shirt and tan slacks. The head was round, the face chubby with small, hard eyes staring out of thick pouches. The graying hair was clipped short, giving him a Teutonic appearance.

"Burn?" he asked. The voice was soft, almost gentle.

"Whitburn. Been waiting long?"

"Maybe five minutes."

Whitburn tied the boat to the dock and stepped ashore. The other was watching him with a patent curiosity.

"I didn't catch your name," Whitburn said.

"Mace." There was a silence while the small, granitic eyes went on measuring Whitburn. "I understand you have a-an engineering problem."

"Come inside," Whitburn said. "I've got some cold beer."

This was rather unusual, Whitburn was thinking. It was a new experience for him, this outlining the matter and arranging a man's death. It had never been quite like this before.

"I don't know how to begin," Whitburn said. Mace smiled thinly. It was an expression of patience as well as amusement. "Take your time. Tell it any way you like." Whitburn took a sip of beer. It seemed without taste, he found no pleasure in it, and told himself angrily to stop acting so damned childish. He had seen his share. Why should this appall him? And he told himself it was because he had never trusted anyone, only himself. That was his creed. To that he attributed survival and the good life he was now enjoying.

"There's a man—" he began and then had to pause, searching for words that were not there. Mace watched him, smile widening slightly, and Whitburn knew a touch of resentment. He remembered Sargasso's amusement over the phone. Was this the same? It couldn't be. Mace seemed to sense his thoughts and the small smile vanished. Mace took a deep swallow of beer.

"He'll be coming here this evening," Whitburn went on after a while. "After dark. Not exactly here but to the island. You noticed it, didn't you, the island? He comes there every Saturday night. I want this to be the last time."

"Blackmail?" Mace asked in his quiet voice.

Whitburn leaned forward in his chair, somewhat angered. "What did Mike tell you?"

"Mike? Oh, you mean—Nothing, Whitburn. You know how it is. He just acts as an agent. You know, like agents who book actors? He sends us where there's work for us. You know that."

"Why did you say blackmail?"

"You mentioned a man you don't want coming around any more. I've found it's almost always blackmail. Something else, a guy can run to the cops. Blackmail, a guy has something to hide, he can't have the Cops nosing around. Anyway, that's what I've found. Don't you agree?"

"You know the man?" Mace spread his hands. "How would I? Brief me."

Whitburn could hear the leaden thumping of his heart. That sense of anxiety would not leave him. If he could only be sure that there would be no slip up. Mace looked competent. All of Sargasso's men were competent. Failure sealed their doom, there was no such thing as a second chance. But if something did go wrong and he was implicated, there would be small comfort in knowing that Mace would pay for his bungling. The good life would be gone, most likely lost forever.

"His name is Cullenbine, Earl Cullenbine," Whitburn said. In his ears his voice sounded dull and flat. "He used to be a police reporter with underworld connections. Blackmail had always been a sideline with him. The last couple of years he's been giving it his full time. He came up north last November to hunt deer and recognized me. At the time he didn't let on but he came back this spring and hasn't let me alone since."

He looked down at his hands and saw that they were clenched tight. He forced them open and became aware that a trickle of sweat ran down each cheek. It was warm outside and some of the heat had penetrated into the cottage. Still he cursed silently and asked what had happened to his iron nerve?

He glanced at Mace and thought he caught the vanishing of a look of amusement on the man's face. But it could have been only imagination. He was as jumpy as a wino after a month long binge.

"You want it on the island?" Mace asked.

"That's as good a place as any. It'll be night and there shouldn't be anyone around. There's no one living on the island, not even a shack. During the day sometimes fishermen pass by there but very seldom at night."

"Fine," Mace said, nodding. "Fine."

"I don't want you to think I'm trying to tell you how to do your job but would it be possible somehow to make it look like an accident?"

Mace smiled the amused smile, "I imagine it could be arranged."

"I mean, without a weapon. That is, without something like a gun or a knife. It would be a dead giveaway otherwise. I don't want you to think I'm trying to tell you just what to do but I don't want to be connected with it in any way. You see, I'm alone at this end of the lake. If a weapon is used, naturally I'll be questioned on whether I saw or heard something. Perhaps I might even come under suspicion. I don't want that."

He felt a little foolish talking like this. It was so strange for him to be the one saying these words.

"Relax," Mace said, the smile still on his face. "I'll fix it just the way you want it."

"I suppose I better describe Cullenbine to you."

"I've just thought of something better," Mace said. "Why don't you come to the island with me? You can make sure it's Cullenbine then. No chance for a mistake that way."

Whitburn was silent, unable to find anything to say. The feeling of anxiety was stronger than ever in him and he could not understand why it should be. Tension and suspense had never bothered him before.

The Old Pro

Mace laughed softly. "If you're squeamish, I'll wait until you've left the island. After all, you do want to make sure it's Cullenbine and not someone else I might mistake, don't you? This way there's no chance for error. Like I said, I'll wait until after you've gone from the island. You won't have to watch anything."

Whitburn remained silent, thinking.

"You said you're the only one at this end of the lake. So who's to see you going to the island with me? You do want to make sure it's Cullenbine, don't you? Chances are he'll be the only one to show up on the island tonight but you never can tell. I just thought, you worrying so much about something going wrong and all that, you'd want to be positive it's Cullenbine."

Whitburn sighed. "All right, Mace."

Mace glanced at his wristwatch. "What time do you expect him on the island?"

"About ten."

"Good. Is there a place I can catch some sleep here?..."

Frogs had their choral groups scattered along the shore of the lake and in the ponds in the nearby forest. Something flew past not far overhead on softly flapping wings. Stars glittered brightly. The surface of the lake looked black, like the underground river of the dead.

They got into the boat and Whitburn used an oar to push the craft away from the dock and into deeper water so that he could drop the outboard. The motor caught on the first try and he kept the throttle barely open, easing the boat toward the island with as little sound as he could manage.

"This how you make your payoffs?" Mace asked. "On the island?"

"Every Saturday night."

"Didn't your wife ever get suspicious?"

"Sometimes I'd fish offshore in the afternoon and then cruise around to the other side where she couldn't see me go ashore. We had a place where I'd leave the money. Sometimes I'd come here at night, like now, and hand it to him in person. I'd vary it from time to time. Loretta never caught on."

Saying her name put a tightness in Whitburn's throat. For you, Loretta, he thought, I'm doing all this for you and the good life we have together. I'd never have got into this otherwise.

"Why didn't you ever take care of Cullenbine yourself?"

"I—That's not my line."

Mace laughed, a sound barely heard above the purr of the outboard.

The island loomed dark and brooding in the starlight. An owl hooted softly. Whitburn eased the boat in to shore, cutting the motor and letting the craft drift the last few yards. The prow grated gently against gravel and he stepped out into several inches of water and with Mace's help pulled the boat halfway up on the beach.

He stood for a few moments, staring out over the lake, wondering if anyone had seen him and Mace Crossing to the island. Only the black water appeared. There were no sounds other than the glee-clubbing of the frogs and the soft lapping of the lake against the shore.

"He'll be on the other side of the island," Whitburn said to Mace and started walking.

He led the way with Mace several steps behind him. They took a roundabout route, following the shore line for this was easier going than plunging through the timber that was choked with thick underbrush. Even so, Mace, who was more accustomed to walking the uncluttered and smooth cement and asphalt of the cities, stumbled a couple of times over the uneven earth and sponge-like ground littered with debris that had been washed ashore. His curses were angry and vicious.

Mace was breathing hard by the time they reached the southern end of the island. Whitburn's breath, too, had quickened, from his exertions and a strange, uneasy excitement that he could not quite fathom. Mace caught up with Whitburn as he paused to study the darkness ahead. Finally Whitburn saw it, the faint, pink glow of a cigarette as the smoker inhaled on it.

He started ahead again, aware that Mace once more trailed him. He could understand Mace's difficult progress for he himself tripped and all but fell over a piece of driftwood. Then he made out the tall shadow standing there, watching them approach.

He should have known how it was when Cullenbine evinced no surprise that Whitburn was not alone. Cullenbine stood there quite calmly, inhaling on his cigarette. The night concealed whatever expression there was on his lean, sallow face.

"I see you got here, Burn," Cullenbine said.

Whitburn felt his throat constrict. Something shrieked a warning in his brain but he realized that the alarm had come too late. Like an amateur he had let Mace stay behind him all the while. He turned and saw Mace standing a few feet away. Even in the darkness he could make out the black shape of the pistol in Mace's hand.

Cullenbine chuckled. "Have you finally got it, Burn?"

It was too late for recriminations and reproach. He had grown soft these past four years, he had lost that fine edge, that intuitive sense that had always served him well. He had lost all that and his life in the bargain.

Loretta, he thought, and for the first time since he had been a child he could have wept. Once more he said her name to himself and then put all his mind to what was at hand.

"I guess I read you just in the nick of time," Cullenbine was saying. "I didn't realize how fine I had drawn it until Mace told me that you had called Sargasso, too, but only after I'd done so. Mike has a sense of humor, don't you think, Burn? I mean, sending Mace up here to both of us?"

Whitburn became aware of the calm, hard beat of his heart. This was more like it had once been. He was beginning to feel some of the coolness, the detachment he used to experience. Maybe it was coming back. Maybe he had not lost it after all.

"Who did Mike tell you to serve, Mace?" he asked.

He sensed Mace's shrug. "Mike said it was up to me. He told me to figure out if you'd gone soft, if there was nothing worth salvaging about you. I never knew you when you were one of Mike's boys, I was with another organization then, but he said you'd been his best. But then you got married and went in hiding up here in these woods. He said if you'd gone soft to take you and you are soft, Burn, like a creampuff."

"I have the priority, Burn," Cullenbine put in. "After all, I called Sargasso first. You were a mite too late. I figured you were tired of paying me and were about to do something about it. But I thought you'd do it personally. After all, I wouldn't have been the first man you'd have killed. But like Mace says, you went soft and called Sargasso, just after I did. I figured I wouldn't have a chance against a professional like you which is the reason I got in touch with Sargasso. Anything else you'd like to know?"

Whitburn stood there, silent. It was as though he were already hearing the earth thudding down upon his coffin.

"Good," Cullenbine said. "No sense in dragging it out, is there? Mace. Do me a favor. I'd rather not watch."

"You're the boss," Mace said. He motioned with the pistol. "Start moving, Burn. Back the way we come. I told you I was going to do it like you wanted it. An accident, you said? That's how it'll be." He walked on wooden legs, hardly conscious of the pain when he barked his shin against a piece of driftwood. He walked like a beaten man, shoulders slumped, feet dragging. Mace stepped in close once and jabbed Whitburn hard in the back with the pistol.

"Faster, damn you," Mace snarled.

Whitburn's pace quickened then, after a while, began to slow and drag again. They were well away from Cullenbine now. Only the night was there, and the inanimateness of the island, and the frogs chorusing and the water lapping against the beach.

Whitburn had angled close to the edge of the water. He paused when he felt a stick of driftwood and stood with one heel poised against it. Mace's curse sounded softly and Whitburn sensed the man moving in to jab him again with the pistol. Whitburn kicked back with his heel, sending the piece of driftwood hard against Mace's shins. Mace swore as his feet tangled and tripped him. He fell heavily, cursing sharp and loud. The pistol roared as he dropped but the bullet went wild.

Whitburn was on Mace instantly. A hard toe against Mace's wrist sent the pistol flying out of numbed fingers. They grappled, rolling into the water. With a fury he had never known, Whitburn got a hold on Mace, forcing him face down into the water. Whitburn's knees dug into the small of Mace's back, his hands never for an instant relaxed their iron grip.

Mace thrashed and kicked and tried to roll, he tried swiveling his head to get his mouth out of the water but it was just deep enough to thwart his efforts. Whitburn held him until Mace's movements weakened and finally slackened and were still. He stayed as he was on Mace until he was sure Mace would breathe no more.

He had never known rage and hate when killing until now. The realization came to him as he was walking back to Cullenbine. But then, Whitburn told himself, this was the first time he had ever been personally involved with his victims. All the others had been detached objects for whom he'd had no feelings. They had merely represented a job he had to do. They had never been a question of survival.

He had Mace's pistol in his hand as he came up to Cullenbine who was waiting, smoking calmly. It was not until Whitburn was almost on him that recognition, shock, then horror came to Cullenbine.

"Burn," he cried, voice harsh with surprise and terror.

Whitburn motioned with the pistol. "Start walking, Cullenbine. You're going to join Mace . . ."

He had the good life again, without the worry and fear of being exposed for what he had been. It was never better than it was now with Loretta. He bought her a Thunderbird for her birthday and in return she became *more affectionate* and satisfying than ever before, Yes, he had the good life again.

The deaths of Cullenbine and Mace had not created too much of a stir. They had been found drowned at the south end of the island, among the treacherous rocks. Cullenbine's boat had been found there, too, with the bottom smashed in where Whitburn had run it onto the rocks. The deaths were officially written off as accidental.

One day his phone rang and all the joy ran out of him and he was just a shell, hollow and empty, as he heard the coarse, rasping voice from the other end of the long distance line.

"Burn? Mike. How goes it?"

He had to run his tongue over his lips and swallow before he could speak, "All right," he managed.

"You handled yourself very well," Sargasso said. "They never tumbled, did they? Accidental drowning." Sargasso chuckled. "I always said you were the best. That's why I hated to see you go into retirement. Didn't a taste of it make you hungry for more? You want to come back, Burn?"

"No, damn you, and listen to me. What was the big—"

"You listen to me, Burn," Sargasso snapped. "I just wanted to know if you still had it. If you couldn't handle Mace you weren't worth taking back."

"I'm not coming back. I—"

"Listen, Burn, Listen good. You got a wife, huh? Good looker, huh? *She* wouldn't be such a pretty sight after she'd caught acid in her face, Get what I mean, Burn?"

Something sickening formed in his stomach. He could see the good years begin to fade.

"There's something in Vegas," Sargasso went on when Whitburn didn't answer. "Something real touchy. It needs the best. That's you, Burn."

"No." He tried to shout it but it came out as a barely audible whisper. He was not sure whether Sargasso had heard it.

"Maybe you'd like to think it over," Sargasso was saying. "I can give you twenty-four hours. No more."

"All right," he said in a dull voice, "I'll think about it."

"Fine. See you, Burn." The line went dead at Sargasso's end.

He stood there with the receiver in his hand, staring with unseeing eyes at the view he had once enjoyed so much. He could think it over but there was only one answer Sargasso would accept. And the Vegas thing would not be the last. There would be another and another and another until he eventually bungled and had to pay the penalty.

Finally he stirred and placed the phone back on its cradle. The sound that made was the requiem for the good life . . .

Retribution
Michael Zuroy

April 1961

"You're quite sure?" The president of the Chowder Falls National Bank stared unwaveringly at the auditor, his face expressionless. He was a large man whose features and bald head seemed formed out of one solid chunk of stone, unsoftened by the rigidly brushed and trimmed hair at the sides. The neat nameplate on the desk before him said in black and gold letters: Augustus Prescott, President.

"Quite sure," said Mr. Tunney, the auditor, matching Prescott's unemotional tone.

"Your figures show that something over forty thousand dollars is missing?"

"Exactly forty thousand, two hundred and eleven dollars," said Tunney, as though reading from a balance sheet. Tunney was a crisp, spare man with cool eyes behind rimless glasses. One could not picture him in anything but rimless glasses.

There was a silence. When Prescott spoke again, it was with a heavy deliberateness, as though he intended to make absolutely certain of one point before going on to the next. "Your audit also proves that one of our tellers, Robert Dorp, took the money?"

"That's right."

"There's no question about it?"

"None."

"Seems to me," said Prescott, "a difficult thing for an audit to pinpoint the crook. Is that evidence conclusive enough to stand up in a court of law?"

"Absolutely." Tunney left his seat alongside Prescott's desk and strode to a long table, on which were spread out ledgers, balance sheets and work sheets. "These figures prove beyond the shadow of a doubt that the shortage originated with Dorp. Any C.P.A. in the country would agree with that."

"I don't want to prosecute the man unless we're certain."

"I repeat, this evidence is indisputable."

Prescott let out a weighty sigh, crossed the office and opened the door slightly so that the two men could look out at the banking floor. Dorp was at his cage several windows down, serving a woman depositor, smiling pleasantly. He was tall and lean with dark hair that held a trace of a curl.

"Fine-looking man," said Prescott.

"Yes. Attractive to the ladies."

Prescott and Tunney exchanged glances. "Too damn attractive," said Prescott.

Both men fell silent, wrapped up in their own thoughts. After a while, Tunney asked, "How's your daughter?"

"Eh? Oh, coming along, thanks."

"She still doesn't realize that you know?"

"She doesn't and never will, if I can help it. They call me a hard man, Tunney, but I'm soft when it comes to my daughter. I'd never hurt her—and I'd make anyone who tried to hurt her sorry."

"I'm sure," said Tunney. "By the way, how did you find out?"

"She confided in a girl friend of hers. The friend thought I ought to know."

"You are not one to advertise your feelings,"said Tunney, "but I know how you felt. I know that you worship the child."

"Don't get me wrong," said Prescott savagely. "I wouldn't stand in her way when the proper time comes and the proper person. I don't go for this father antagonism towards the lover, and I don't expect her to remain a virgin child forever. But she's barely sixteen now, and not ready for life. What happened to her was just a rotten seduction."

"Do you think she sees it that way?"

"I think she's beginning to feel that. There's a humiliated, shamed look about her. She's hurt. I think she's feeling that she's been used and discarded. You know the romantic illusions of a young girl. Instead of the adoring prince her lover's turned out to be a rutting goat that stayed for a few encounters and has gone looking for other females in heat."

Tunney nodded sympathetically. "She'll get over it. Time, you know."

"At her age it'll leave an emotional scar." Prescott lit a cigar and brooded over the smoke for a while. Then he shook his head, as though to shake the thing from his mind, and inquired of Tunney, "How's the wife?"

"Oh, all right, I suppose. She's at her mother's."

"Yes, of course."

"I don't feel that I want her at home just now."

"Yes."

"Give us both a chance to calm down, you see."

"What are your intentions?"

"I suppose I'll take her back. I think I can forgive her in view of her attitude."

"Oh?"

"Yes, she begged me for another chance. Swore that this was a temporary insanity, that the scoundrel was so persuasive that she couldn't help herself. She's considerably younger than I am, of course, and hot-blooded. But she claims she loves me and has never been unfaithful to me before, and never will again if I take her back."

"I see. And how did you find out?"

"I walked in on them."

"A shock, eh?"

"You can imagine. I'd finished an out-of-town audit unexpectedly soon, and decided not to stay away another night. It was a long drive home, and well past midnight when I arrived. I didn't want to disturb Ann so I was quiet. I was about to step through the bedroom door when I realized what kind of sounds I was hearing. I couldn't believe it. I waited, listening to the relentless sounds and to Ann's soft crying which I hear all too seldom myself. My eyes grew accustomed to the darkness, and the moonlight came through the window. I saw Ann's naked form and glazed eyes and bared teeth. I saw the man's lithe, animal body, and in that instant I admit I envied him his youth and strength. It was only afterwards that I grew furious.

"I didn't know what to do. I backed away and left. I'd seen the man's face clearly in the moonlight, and I decided I could take measures later. Ann, of course, I sent packing the next day."

"And so he remains unaware of your knowledge?"

"Yes."

A long silence ensued. Finally, Tunney broke it. "What do you intend to do with the whip now?"

"The cat-o-nine tails? Keep it as a curio."

Tunney grimaced. "Nasty-looking thing. You could kill a man with it."

Prescott permitted himself a frosty smile. "Yes, I could. However—what about your gun?"

"I'm getting rid of that. I won't have any use for it now, any more than you'll have for that whip."

"In my opinion," said Prescott slowly, "it's extremely fortunate that we happened to begin exchanging confidences over a drink. Had we not uncovered the similarity of our situations, one of us would be in trouble now."

"Yes, and awful trouble. I would hate to be facing a murder charge."

"It's much better this way."

"Much better. Do you think he suspects anything?"

"Not a thing."

"Yes, he's a handsome fellow," said Tunney. "Real ladies' man."

"Well, let's get on with it." Prescott took a key from his pocket and unlocked the bottom drawer of the desk. He brought up two packages of currency and two shiny half-dollars. "That adds up to your figure. Twenty thousand, one hundred and five dollars apiece in bills, and a half-dollar apiece to make up the odd dollar."

The men pocketed the money.

Prescott said, "Once more, you're positive you've set up the audit to prove Dorp guilty beyond a doubt? No loopholes?"

"None whatsoever. These figures are incontestable. Remember my standing."

"Fine." Prescott puffed at his cigar. "Personally, I think he's getting off easy. I think we're being pretty fair."

"Under the circumstances I think we're being very fair."

"Well, might as well call the police."

He reached for the phone.

In Memoriam
Charles Beckman, Jr. (Charles Boeckman)

June 1961

Everyone in Hesterton knew that Wilber Minetree was dying. In a town of five thousand souls, a thing like that gets around.

It was the main topic of conversation at the post office, one of the early morning meeting spots of the downtown business set.

The nature of Wilber's illness was analyzed; the fact that this one and that one had seen Wilber only a few weeks ago "looking the picture of health" was noted with a shocked clicking of tongues and shaking of heads.

Then it was unanimously agreed that Wilber had been a fine, upstanding citizen during his tenure of life, that he had promptly discharged his debts, paid his taxes, voted the straight Republican ticket, made a success of his job, and belonged to the Elks lodge.

"Of course he owed it all to Hortensia."

This statement was also seconded and accepted with no dissenting vote.

"Why, I knew Wilber back in grade school," one of the main-street business men offered. "He was tardy every day of the year. Never got to a class on time in his life."

This little human flaw in Wilber's character was agreed upon fondly by other friends of the now almost deceased.

"Fact is," the spokesman ventured further, "I guess if he hadn't married Hortensia, Wilber would have turned out to have been a bum."

Now this was going a bit too far. Even though it was probably true, it showed remarkable lack of tact. There was a disapproving clearing of throats, shifting of feet, and a few dark looks.

Mort Fowler, owner of the Serve-U grocery store, who had made the faux pas, looked embarrassed and drew back into the crowd.

There was a moment of silence. Then one of Wilber's colleagues at the Farmer's First National Bank said, "Well, you do have to give Hortensia credit, though. She's been the making of Wilber Minetree."

There was a general agreement to this observation.

The fact was that most of them had known Wilber since childhood and they knew that Mort Fowler had been right. Without Hortensia, Wilber would indeed have turned out to be a bum. Though, it was in pretty bad taste to point this out with the poor man on his death bed.

Before Wilber got married, he'd never been anywhere on time in his life. He blissfully overslept every morning, was fired off innumerable jobs. Alarm clocks were totally ineffectual with Wilber. At the time he met Hortensia, he had been reduced to racking up pool balls at the Downtown Recreation Hall and Domino Parlor.

It was a matter of record that a startling metamorphosis had taken place in Wilber after his marriage. Fortunately, Hortensia was a strong willed woman, a fifth grade school teacher who was a few years Wilber's senior. She had a matronly bosom, a slightly brassy voice, and the hint of a mustache. But she was just what Wilber needed. She spoke to Alex Craine, president of the Farmer's First National Bank about a job for Wilber. It was in keeping with her nature that she would want her husband to have a position of dignity in the community. Needless to say, working for the Farmer's First National Bank carried more status than racking up pool balls.

It was with considerable trepidation that Alex Craine put Wilber on at the bank. Please don't misunderstand. Alex did not dislike Wilber. Nobody in Hesterton actually disliked Wilber. He was one of those happy-go-lucky, affable slobs whom everyone liked. It's just that you didn't want him working in your place of business.

But Hortensia was extremely persuasive and to escape the frontal assault of her personality, Alex had agreed to give Wilber a job in the bookkeeping department at ninety dollars a month on a trial basis. He felt justified in lowering the bank's personnel standards in this manner on the grounds that, with a clear conscience, he'd probably be able to fire Wilber after the first week.

He was extremely surprised to find Wilber reporting for work the next morning precisely on the stroke of eight. "Shocked" would perhaps be a more exact description of his reaction. To the best of his knowledge, it was the first time in Wilber's life that he had ever appeared anywhere on time. Not only that, but Wilber's shoes were shined, his suit pressed, and his shirt starched. "Good morning, Mr. Craine," Wilber smiled affably.

This was the start of a satisfactory relationship between Wilber Minetree and the Farmer's First National Bank that continued for thirty years. And not once during that period of service—let us repeat—not once, was Wilber Minetree ever tardy, nor did he miss a single day of work. There were times, it is true, when bets were laid among the employees of the bank with rather startling odds. The time Wilber dragged himself down more dead than alive with influenza, and the morning after the Elks Christmas dance when Wilber had been more lit up than the thirty foot Christmas tree down on the square.

But he always greeted Alex Craine on the bank steps at eight A.M., with his "Good morning, Mr. Craine," even though somewhat weakly on the two occasions mentioned above.

Of course, no one knew, but everyone guessed what struggles, cajoling, threats, and tears Hortensia Minetree went through in order to keep Wilber punctual. There was some rumor as to the use of force, but this was probably malicious gossip.

It was, however, public knowledge that all the clocks in the Minetree home were set a half hour ahead, that a strident and somewhat brassy voice was often heard in the early mornings issuing from the Minetree house and carrying the length of the block, and that on many occasions, Hortensia, herself drove Wilber to the bank and literally led him up to the bank steps by the arm.

But through her untiring efforts ("relentless," while being, perhaps the more exact nuance, is somewhat unkind), Wilber had escaped his destiny as the affable town bum. He held a respectable position for thirty years with the bank, advancing to the post of first teller. He and Hortensia bought and paid for a comfortable though not pretentious home. They raised two children, a boy and a girl who were now both married and had children of their own. And Wilber had even once been elected water commissioner of the city.

Hortensia had indeed succeeded alone. So she phoned Mrs. Schien, canceling her services for the evening, and when Miss Redding left, Hortensia settled herself alone in Wilber's room beside his bed, to await the end.

Wilber's breathing became more and more shallow. The quiet hours of the night ticked slowly away. Hortensia glanced at the bedside clock from time to time, remembering with a fond and tearful smile that it was still set a half hour ahead. At times she dozed, her head nodding forward.

It was during one of these catnaps that Wilber yawned and sat up.

Hortensia came awake with a startled jump.

"Hello, Hortensia," Wilber smiled affably. "Where am I?"

Hortensia's mouth opened and worked, but for the first time in her life nothing came out.

Wilber looked around, bright-eyed, but slightly befuddled. "Oh, I remember. I've been sick, haven't I?"

Hortensia was still too stunned to utter a sound. Wilber had been in a coma for three days. He hadn't spoken rationally for a week. Now he was sitting up clear-eyed and in full possession of his faculties.

"H-how do you feel, Wilber?" she finally gasped.

"Me? Oh, I feel fine. Only I'm awful hungry. You got something in the house to eat, Hortensia?"

She groped her way to her feet, clutching at the chair for support.

"Some cold roast beef maybe," he said, "or a drumstick. And a bottle of beer."

She stumbled out of the room toward the kitchen.

"See if you have any of those good homemade pickles of yours in the refrigerator," he called after her.

She fumbled blindly at the refrigerator. Wilber had rallied. The doctor said that, on rare occasions, patients in Wilber's condition did rally, though he hadn't thought it possible in Wilber's case. Hortensia remembered when Leona McPhail's husband had been in that coma last year and not expected to live the day out; he'd rallied unexpectedly and hung on for a whole month. And old man Marreth who fell down with that stroke on Main Street. The doctor said he wouldn't live until they got him to the hospital. Well, that was two years ago and the old geezer wasn't any more dead than the doctor.

Hortensia was too upset to pay any attention to what she was doing. She automatically got some food on the tray and started back to Wilber's room. But her mind was swimming with the monstrous inconvenience that this unexpected turn of events had caused. Everything had been so well organized and timed. Now Wilber had thrown a monkey wrench into the plans, throwing everything into a hopeless snarl.

It was too late to stop the relatives. By now they were on trains and airplanes converging on Hesterton. By tomorrow night the house would be swarming with relatives. Why, they might have to hang around for a week or more now, waiting for the funeral. They'd eat up a fortune in food, and her son would lose important time from his job in South America, and her daughter's husband might not have that much emergency leave from his army post in Germany. The florist had already wired for a huge order of flowers due to arrive tomorrow. They'd be completely wilted and ruined. And the obituary in the Advocate. Good heavens, she'd forgotten about that! Mr. Seelingson was starting to print the paper tonight. It would be too late to take that   out now.

Completely distraught, she brought the tray into Wilber's room and put it beside his bed. He smiled at her good-naturedly. "I sure am hungry, Hortensia."

"Lay back down, Wilber," she said distractedly. "You'll tax your strength."

Obediently, he settled back against his pillow. She picked up another pillow, clapped it down firmly over his face, smothering him.

He struggled weakly. "Lie still, Wilber!" she panted. "For heaven's sake, if it weren't for me, you'd be late to your own funeral!"

Bugged
Bruno Fischer

August 1961

I know you're in the room, bug. I think in the wall. You must've heard me and Floyd talking, so you know how we're trapped.

Bug, do you hear me? You're our one chance. Bring help.

A second car just pulled up behind the trees. Four guns now, but they'll take their time on account they know how straight I can shoot. If I was running this from their side, I'd wait till dark before moving in. There's time to save me, bug.

I don't mean too much time. Could be there's hardly any time.

This is all the thanks I get from Lew Angel. Did I wish him anything bad? All I did was for his own good. Sure, me and Floyd Finch were looking out for our own good too. What hurts Lew hurts us. Like they say in Washington, D.C., we're a team.

I mean were.

We came up from nothing together, me and Lew and Floyd. It wasn't easy. You take a city like this. It isn't Chicago or even St. Louis, but it's a city. Let a guy be five times as smart as Lew Angel, he doesn't climb to the top of the rackets without he has help. My kind of help. Even Floyd's kind.

Many a time I saved Lew's life. And when somebody big needed cooling, who did Lew depend—

Well, never mind about that.

Fact is, I was a lot more to him than his muscle. More than his bodyguard. I was his pal. All of a sudden, does this mean a thing to him? Nothing! On account of a dame.

Out there they're not starting to make any move to close in. I'm at a window talking to you, bug, while I'm watching them among the trees. They look like they're talking things over.

A school teacher. Those are the worst kind. A kindergarten teacher, no less.

There's Lew Angel, so big in town he can get hot-looking dames by the dozen by reaching out for them. Who does he reach for? Who's he been dating two, three times a week this last month? Esther Hunt.

I don't mean she's bad-looking. It's just that if you stood on a street corner with nothing to do, you'd hardly bother giving her the double-o as she walked by. Kind of small and very quiet. And no idea of fun.

Tuesday night I found out what Esther Hunt was doing to Lew.

We picked her up at eight o'clock at her run-down, walk-up apartment house. Usually Lew liked to drive, but when she was with him they sat in back, leaving me sitting alone in front like I was nothing but a chauffeur. And they held hands like a couple of teenagers. This was all he was ever getting out of her, holding hands and a good-night kiss, and from the looks of her I didn't think he'd ever get more. Go figure him. For this he had to become the big wheel in the rackets?

She dragged us to see Shakespeare, no less.

Lew's dates used to be pleasure. Hot spots and parties. If we went to the theater you could see something you could laugh at or stacked dames with hardly any clothes on. With Esther Hunt, Shakespeare! And the time before a symphony concert. And one afternoon I got sore feet tagging after them in the municipal art gallery. What a guy will do for a dame!

But you know something? This Shakespeare isn't as bad as he's cracked up to be. The play was about a Scotchman name of Macbeth and how he and his missus knocked off the king so he could become king. Just like in real life. Like right here in our own town when Yank Sands was top man in the rackets and Lew was moving up and one night me and Lew—

Never mind.

I was talking about Tuesday night. The show was over and me and Lew and Esther Hunt were moving up the aisle when a guy in front turned around. It was Allen W. McGoldrich, the new D.A., who one of the reasons he got elected was he promised the voters he'd put Lew Angel in jail.

McGoldrich said sarcastic-like, "So it's true what I hear about you, Angel, you're on a culture kick."

"This is against the law?" Lew said.

"No," McGoldrich said, he touched me under the left shoulder where I wear my clip. "I see you're dressed for the theater, Willie," he said.

"I got a license for it," I said.

"I'm aware of that," McGoldrich said. "My predecessor in office was rather lenient, wasn't he? This resulted in him becoming a much richer man than I ever will be. I could have your gun license if it was worth the effort." He turned a smile to Lew that was full of teeth and said, "I'm after much bigger game than a mere henchman."

By this time we were all at the end of the aisle. We went one way and McGoldrich the other way. And I remember how Esther Hunt looked after him. Her eyes were the best thing about her, great big brown eyes, and now they were twice as big.

I don't mean she didn't know till then what Lew's line of business was. Everybody in town knows, even kindergarten school teachers. But I think this was when she started seeing something she hadn't seen before.

From the theater we went for a drink. Not the kind you think. She had no use for the hard stuff. So help me, we had to go to an ice cream parlor.

As we were lapping up ice cream sodas, which I'm not crazy for, she looked at me across the table with her big brown eyes. "Willie," she said, "have you really got a gun?"

"Just kind of insurance, Miss Hunt," I said.

She shivered and said to Lew, "Must we always have him along with us?"

"Don't you like him, honey?" he said.

"I go out with you, not with both of you," she said.

Lew sipped his soda through the straw and didn't say anything. So I said, "I see your point, Miss Hunt, but a guy in his position is like the kings in the play we just saw. Everybody is looking to knock them off. You don't want it to happen to Lew here, do you?"

"Of course not," she said.

"So that makes the both of us," I said.

"I hate having it to be like this," she said. And looked like she was going to bust out crying.

Lew took the straw out of his mouth and said, "Scram, Willie."

"But—"

"Leave the car," he said. "Take a taxi home. Now beat it."

He was the boss. I finished the soda and left them there at the table sitting practically on top of each other. But I didn't go home. I had my responsibilities. For one thing, Augie Pitcher was getting ideas about moving into slot machines, and he'd have no trouble at all if all of a sudden Lew Angel stopped living. I got me a cab and sat in it down the street from the ice cream parlor. When they came out and drove off, I was right behind them.

They went to her place. I paid off the cabbie and leaned against the faded brick wall of the building. After a while I got tired and sat in his car. Waited better than two hours. It was maybe two-thirty when he came out, and her having to get up early to teach school. On his face he had a look like a little league kid who had just hit a home run.

I figured this time he'd gotten a lot more off Esther Hunt than a lousy good-night kiss and I was glad he was no longer wasting his time. The way he was feeling he wasn't sore I hadn't gone home like he'd told me to. Got in the car like it was a cloud and I drove him home to his swank apartment house.

"Come up for a nightcap, Willie," he said, speaking to me for the first time.

"You bet," I said, this being my first chance to get the taste of the ice cream soda out of my mouth.

Lew Angel doesn't pour it out of a bottle and give it to you. He has to mix it up first. He was standing at his bar in his living room, putting God knows what in the shaker, when I said, "I think maybe I ought to sleep here nights for a while."

"What's the matter with your cottage?" he said.

"Nothing's the matter with it. But what with Augie Pitcher . . ."

"We can forget about that," he said, shaking the shaker. "I'm getting out of the rackets."

"You're kidding!"

"I'm dead serious, Willie. This week I start pulling out." And turned around and poured into a couple of glasses.

I looked at his back that's not more than half as wide as mine. I said very slowly, "If I didn't know you, Lew, I'd think you were scared of Augie Pitcher."

"That lightweight!"

"Then it's the new D.A., McGoldrich."

"That do-gooder! He can't touch me." He handed me a glass, and a sappy look was on his face. "Drink to Esther and me, Willie. We're getting married."

I didn't raise the glass. I said bitterly, "So she talked you into it?"

"Well, we discussed it tonight in her apartment," he admitted. "Willie, she's a wonderful girl. Nothing like the cheap broads I've been messing with all my life.

She's the first girl I've wanted to marry. She's got class, Willie. Brains. Refinement. And she loves me."

"No dame is worth giving up all you have," I said.

"What have I got?" he said. "This isn't a real home. There's no loving little woman in it and no kids. Willie, I'm a man without dignity. I'm merely a glorified hoodlum."

"That's not you talking," I said. "That's the kindergarten school teacher."

"And I'm not getting any younger," he went on. "I've made my pile. Enough for us to live on the rest of our lives. Though, as Esther says, a man should do useful work, so I'll look around for some kind of business. Strictly legitimate. In Florida or California. We'll buy a nice house in the country with a swimming pool and have four kids. Two boys and two girls." He was still way up on that cloud. "I'm thirty-six years old," he said, "and it's getting pretty late in life. Like Macbeth said in the play tonight: 'Tomorrow and tomorrow and tomorrow creeps in this petty pace from day to day.'"

When a guy like Lew Angel not only goes to see Shakespeare but starts reciting him, you know there's no hope for him. So at last I raised my glass and drank to their happiness, his and Esther Hunt's. But there was no taste in it for me.

I got a good look at all four of the guys among the trees, bug. Know 'em all real good. Lew's boys of course. Like I am—I mean was. Maybe one reason they're waiting is for Lew himself to show.

Bug, are you bringing help?

This set-up is perfect for them, this cottage in the hollow without another house very close. Guess you think it's a funny place for a couple of bachelors and all like Floyd and me to live instead of tight in the city. But me, I like to fool around growing flowers, and Floyd can't stand the noise of traffic and kids yelling and other people's televisions blaring. Besides, there's all the privacy you want for bringing dames to.

But this isn't about any of our dames, Floyd's or mine. It's a dame I wouldn't give two cents for, but was wrecking our lives. Esther Hunt.

I came home Tuesday night and Floyd was right here in this living room working on the books. I mean Wednesday morning on account of by then it was close to four o'clock. Lew is a guy never leaves a loophole in his tax returns to give the government a chance to put the hook on him, and it being close to income tax time Floyd is working day and night on the books and tax forms and all those headaches.

I mean was. Floyd has kind of lost interest in his precious books. Right this minute he's in the kitchen crying like a baby. What can you expect from a bookkeeper?

Well, I came home around four A.M. and told Floyd about Lew going to marry this Esther Hunt and retire. He was hit as hard as I was.

He took off his glasses and blinked his watery eyes and said in that whinny voice of his, "What'll become of me?"

"The same thing as will become of me," I said. "We'll become a couple of unemployed bums. How much dough have you in the sock?"

Floyd gave a very sick laugh. "Minus about two grand. The horses haven't been running right for me,"

"And me," I said, "I haven't drawn a decent hand in poker in months."

I got a bottle out from the cabinet and we sat drinking at the table and telling each other how black the future was for us. We weren't just Lew's bodyguard and Lew's bookkeeper. We were big men in the organization, and Lew paid us real good. We had real respect in this town, I tell you. But Lew turns straight and we're nothing but a couple of working stiffs on the labor market, scrounging for every lousy buck. This was a very soft life, except for Floyd at income tax time.

"There's only one thing to do," Floyd said after a few drinks. "We got to sour her on him. We'll tell her all about him."

"She reads the newspapers."

"I said all about him," Floyd said. "Things only we know. The real dirty stuff. You go to her, Willie, and tell her."

I shook my head. "No good. He's promised her to quit, and there's no dame more devoted to a guy than a good woman reforming him. This goes double for kindergarten school teachers." I reached for the bottle that by now was close to empty and said, "Let's turn it around. Sour him on her."

"You have an idea, Willie?"

"Yesterday I ran across Deuce Melody on the street," I said.

"And who may he be?"

"Deuce Melody is a con artist," I said. "A very handsome guy that slays the ladies, especially the elderly ones, by having dimples in his cheeks when he smiles. I met him two, three years ago in L.A. where he hangs around on account of that's where most of the suckers live. We were in a poker game together and after the game he fixed me up with a hot little redhead to kind of make up for all the dough he won off me." I took a drink. "Well, Deuce Melody was driving through town yesterday when the transmission of his car went. They said it'll take two days to fix it. He's never been here before. Lew doesn't know him and he doesn't know Lew. He wouldn't know whose girl Esther Hunt is. He's our boy, Floyd."

"Are you thinking, Willie, he can make time with her?"

"Not a chance," I said, "even with his dimples."

"Then what are you getting at?" I told him, and behind his thick glasses his watery eyes got scared sick.

"I don't like it," he said.

"You got any other idea how we can hang onto our jobs?"

Floyd emptied the bottle and said, "No, I haven't."

So next day I went to see Deuce Melody in the motel outside of town where he'd told me he was staying. I could've left a message for him to meet me in a ginmill where I could've been comfortable waiting, but of course I didn't want we should be seen together in public. I had to hang around three, four hours before he showed. Then I slipped into his cabin after him.

"My car will be ready in an hour," he said. "Nothing doing in this crummy town. I figured I'd be on my way."

"Is a chance to pick up an easy hundred bucks nothing doing?" I said.

"What is it, a divorce case?" he said. "Will I have to come back here to testify?"

"You can leave right after and never come back," I said. "Better that way. It's just that a pal of mine wants to get dirt on his girl friend so he can pull her off his neck without her raising hell. One hundred bucks."

"Tonight?"

"Tomorrow night, I'm hoping."

Deuce pushed his hand through his curly hair. "To spend another night in this ghost town it will cost three hundred."

"Two hundred."

"Is she pretty?" he asked.

"A knockout. But this isn't for your pleasure."

"Pleasure is where you find it," he said, showing his dimples. "It's a deal."

The breaks are with me next evening. Yesterday evening that was. Lew and Esther Hunt didn't have a date on account of he wasn't wasting any time getting out of the rackets. He had Floyd Finch over his place going over his books with him so he'd know how big a bundle he could retire with, and later on he was going to have Augie Pitcher and other wheels over to break the news to them. So the coast was clear and at six-thirty I was ringing Esther Hunt's doorbell.

Timed it exactly right. She was finishing dinner she'd eaten by herself. Her place was a tiny two-room dump, but kind of neat.

"Seeing you and Lew are getting married." I said, "I came to make sure there are no hard feelings between us."

"There are certainly none on my part," she said. "I never disliked you. Only what you represent."

"I'm glad to hear this, Miss Hunt," I said, "on account of I'm going on the straight and narrow too."

"Why, that's wonderful, Willie," she said.

"Let's have a drink on it," I said.

"I don't drink whiskey," she said. Which I knew she didn't. "But I was about to have coffee. Will you have a cup with me?" Which is what I'd hoped she'd say.

She poured the coffee. While she was in the kitchen getting some cake to go with it, I emptied into her cup the powder I'd gotten from a druggest pal. It wouldn't hurt her any. Anyway, not by making her sick or anything.

Also while she was gone I snapped the catch on the door lock so it would be unlocked.

You know something? It wasn't so bad having a cup of coffee with her. I mean this was the first time we were alone together and she had a very sweet way about her. But what the hell, I had my own problems.

When pretty soon she started to yawn and get sleepy-eyed, I got up and said good-bye and left.

I phoned Deuce Melody at his motel where there was a private phone in each cabin and told him everything was under control and to start out in fifteen minutes. I waited in a doorway across the street. Deuce showed in forty minutes, this being about what I'd figured it would take him. I watched him go into Esther Hunt's building, then got in my car and drove over to the block on which Lew Angel lived.

I didn't go up to his apartment. Went into the corner drugstore and dialed his number. By then it was eight-thirty. Augie Pitcher and the others would be there already for the meeting. Floyd was also still there, giving himself an alibi.

I made my voice sound thin and high like an old lady's. I said, "Is this Mr. Lew Angel?"

"That's right," Lew said. On the wire I heard the buzzing of voices of the others in the room with him.

"Mr. Angel," I said, "right this minute your girl, Esther Hunt, is carrying on something scandalous in her apartment with another man."

"You're nuts," he said.

"She looks like such a nice girl," I said in that cracked old voice, "but such carrying on. I mean all the time men coming and going in her apartment. Right this minute."

"Madam, who are you?"

"Never mind my name. I live in the same building with Esther Hunt, and I feel it my duty to let you know how she's two-timing you."

"Madam," he said, "You're a lousy liar."

I could hear it was quiet in the room now, like they were all listening. I said, "You can insult me all you want, young man, but you can go there and see for yourself."

And hung up.

I stayed in the phone booth a couple minutes more, then walked over to the front of the building like I hadn't a thing on my mind. Lew was coming out in a big hurry when I got there. This was my alibi.

"Willie," he said when he spotted me, "where's your car?"

"Right over there," I said.

"Drive me to Esther's place," he said.

He didn't say another word all the way, just sat in my car staring straight ahead. I'd hardly stopped the car in front of her house when he was out of it and running. At the street door he stopped and came back slowly.

"Maybe you'd better come up with me," he said.

"Is anything the matter?" I asked.

"Maybe nothing," he said. "If there is—" He massaged his face all over with his hand. "I don't want to kill her. If I try to kill her, Willie, don't let me."

I'd just as soon not have gone up there with him, but what could I do? I tagged after him up the two flights of stairs. He stood at the door a little while, just stood there, then moved his hand to the bell. Didn't ring it though. Instead turned the knob and the door was unlocked on account of I'd made sure it would be. Both for Deuce Melody and for him.

He barged across the tiny living room and threw open the bedroom door. Then stopped dead like he'd come up against a wall.

I didn't go all the way with him, but I could see past his shoulder into the bedroom. Could see the bed and Deuce Melody sitting up in it in his underwear shirt. With a kind of silly grin on his face and the dimples punching deep holes in his cheeks.

Esther Hunt was in the bed with him. Out to the world like she'd been since before Deuce had come up and taken her dress off her and put her on the bed. She looked like she was peacefully asleep. Which was what she was, that powder I'd Put in her coffee having done it.

The whole thing lasted two, three seconds. Lew didn't have to worry about killing anybody. I didn't have to worry either, though up to then this was what I'd been worried most about. Lew was too dead inside to do anything but turn around and walk out of there.

I drove him back to his house. He got out without saying goodnight. Maybe he didn't even know I was there.

I had one more thing to do. I drove to Deuce Melody's motel. He'd just got back from Esther Hunt's place. I paid him off and told him who the guy was who'd stood in the doorway. Though he hadn't known what Lew Angel looked like, he'd sure enough heard of him.

"My God, Willie," Deuce said, "you double-crossed me. He'll cut my heart out."

"Not if you keep your trap shut," I said. "And if you don't lose time getting out of town."

"I knew the minute I lost my transmission in this dump there was nothing good about it," he said.

I went home to the cottage and got out a bottle. Pretty soon Floyd arrived. He was a happy man. He said when Lew got back to his apartment the first thing he did was kick out Augie Pitcher and the others that were waiting for him to go on with the meeting. He'd changed his mind about retiring. Which was no surprise to Floyd hearing this.

We shook hands and between us killed the bottle. Celebrating.

This was on account of we didn't know about you, bug. And you were here all the time.

So you know most of this anyway. Guess I'm on a talking jag. I always talk a lot when I'm nervous.

I found out about this afternoon, bug.

I came back to Lew's apartment from an errand and found Esther Hunt with him. School was still on, but she'd walked out on her kindergarten kids to try and explain about last night. Said it was all news to her, he thinking she'd been in bed with a guy, till she phoned him at lunchtime and heard it from him. Said all she knew was she'd fallen asleep very early and when she woke up she'd still been alone. Said there couldn't have been any guy with her.

A likely story.

"Throw the bitch out," Lew said to me.

I put my hand on her arm, but gentle-like. She threw her shoulders back and marched to the door with her face like a cake of ice. You know, I felt a little bit sorry for her. But what the hell!

"Serves me right, Willie," Lew said when I came back. "I was old enough to know all dames are tramps."

"Live and learn," I said.

A couple of hours later Allen W. McGoldrich, the D.A., came up to the apartment. He was carrying a kind of square case by the handle.

"To what do we owe this pleasure?" Lew said sarcastic-like.

"I have something here that will interest you," McGoldrich said.

He put the case on the table and took off the top. A tape recorder. We didn't say a thing watching him plug the cord into an outlet. Then he snapped a switch and the spools started turning and I was listening to my own voice. And Floyd's.

On the tape was everything I and Floyd had been talking about in our cottage the night I'd come home and told him Lew was going to get married and retire. How we were going to hire Deuce Melody and fix it so Lew would have no more use for Esther Hunt.

But you know. You were right in the wall listening, bug.

I mean you have to be in the wall on account of you're not anywhere else in this cottage. I'm no beginner. I know the cops and the D.A. are all the time bugging houses and apartments of guys like me and Lew Angel. One of my jobs is to go over Lew's apartment every few days to see if it's been bugged. Found a bug only last week behind a picture. Went over my cottage too, but found nothing.

This leaves inside the wall. Put there while I and Floyd were away. With electronics and all, these days you don't even need wires. A tape recorder can be a mile away recording every word we say as long as a bug is somewhere around.

And there was the tape on Lew's desk repeating all our words. And Lew just looking at me. And McGoldrich smiling that smile of his full of teeth.

McGoldrich was playing the old D.A. game. If you can't beat 'em, make 'em beat themselves. Get 'em to fighting each other. Afterward clean up the pieces. A smart cookie, that D.A.

Lew kept looking at me.

I was safe as long as McGoldrich was there. But after he left! Me, I had no hankering to hang around.

I slipped out of the apartment while the recorder was still going. I shouldn't have stopped. But I figured I had a little time to warn Floyd and pack my clothes and get the few bucks I had stashed away in the cellar.

Floyd got the hysterics when I told him. I was all packed and ready to go, but then I had Floyd on my hands. I couldn't get him to move, he was so scared. Should've left him, but what the hell! Then I was going to leave him, but when I opened the door the first car was pulling in among the trees a couple of hundred feet away.

Got me the box of cartridges out of my valise and my gun hasn't been out of my hand all the time I've been talking to you.

Talking is good for me when I'm like this. Quiets my nerves. Floyd is nobody to talk to. I can hear him bawling in the kitchen.

Now Lew is out there. I just saw him. And it'll be dark soon. There's not much time.

Of course the first thing they did was cut the telephone wire. So I can't call the cops for help. It's up to you, bug.

You got me into this. Now get me out.

I hope there's a man at the other end and not just a tape recorder. A man who heard me and will send help before it's too late.

Bug, for God's sake, are you listening?

Interference
Glenn Canary

October 1963

He saw her when she came down the stairs, but there was nothing special that he noticed about her at first. He had been waiting for the train, leaning against the post and reading his paper. The girl stood near him and looked up the tunnel. He glanced at her again and then folded his paper and watched her. Her face was pale and she was sweating and biting her lips. He thought she was sick and he started to speak to her, but then he decided not to.

There was something wrong with her appearance, too, but it was a few minutes before he thought of what it was. She had no purse.

He crossed the platform and dropped his paper into a little basket. He could hear the train coming. When he turned to look at her, the girl was leaning forward, looking down at the tracks. He walked over and stood beside her. The train came around the curve and he could see the green and red lights on the first car. He looked at the girl. Her lips were moving as if she were whispering to herself.

The train came into the platform area.

The girl threw herself forward and would have fallen on the tracks, but he caught her arm and hung on. She tried to pull away but the train passed them and stopped. The doors opened.

Neither of them said anything. Finally, the girl slumped slightly and relaxed and he let go of her. The doors closed on the train and it started moving. They stood beside each other and watched it go.

Then she turned to look at him and said, "You didn't have to do that."

"You were trying to jump."

"What makes you think that?"

"You were scared and you don't have any purse." That was all he could think of to say. "I was watching you."

"It's none of your business."

"I know it's not, but I had to stop you."

"It's none of your business what I do."

"I know."

"Leave me alone then, Go away."

"Will you try it again?"

"That's my business, too."

"I saved your life. That makes me responsible for you, doesn't it?"

"Don't talk like a David Susskind play."

"I didn't mean to sound that way."

"It's none of your business, but it's not funny."

"I know it's not funny."

"Leave me alone," she said again. She stared at him as if she expected him to argue with her and then turned and started running toward the stairs.

He went after her and caught her arm. "Wait a minute," he said. "I can't just leave you now."

"What are you going to do, call a cop?"

"That's what I ought to do."

"I'll tell him you're a masher."

"Would he believe that if I were the one who called him?"

"I could call one myself."

"Go ahead."

For a minute he was afraid she was going to cry. "All right," she said. "What *are* you going to do with me?"

"I don't know. I never saved anyone's life before." He smiled at her. "What's your name?"

"Peggy."

"Peggy what?"

"You're not going to know me that long."

"My name is Alan Johnson."

"So go away Alan Johnson and let me alone."

"We could have a drink somewhere and talk it over."

"Why don't you go back to work instead? "

"I don't have a job right now."

"Then why don't we jump in front of a subway train together."

"Is that what's bothering you? Don't you have a job either?"

"Oh, for God's sake," she said. She pulled away and began walking up the stairs. When he followed her, she turned and said, "I wish you'd drop dead."

"Let's have a drink first," he said, "and then maybe I will."

She kept walking, but she said, "All right, anything to get rid of you."

When they left the tunnel and came up onto Madison Avenue, they passed a policeman. Alan knew he ought to stop and tell him what had happened, but he didn't want to do that. He knew they would take her to Bellevue and once he had visited a friend there. He didn't want the girl to be locked in it.

She turned into the first bar they found and he followed her. They sat in a booth and he ordered whiskey for her. He thought it might act as a sedative.

"Listen, Peggy," he said and then stopped and lit a cigarette.

"What's the matter?" she asked. "Can't you think of anything properly paternal to say to me?"

"I guess not."

Her hands were on the table and she had them clenched. She looked down at them and opened them slowly as if she were surprised to find them closed. "I'm sorry," she whispered. "You're just trying to help. You don't know what you're doing."

"Who does?"

"I don't want any help, Alan Johnson. You don't know anything or you'd just leave me alone."

"I don't think you know what you want to do."

"Now you sound like a caricature of a psychiatrist."

"What am I supposed to sound like?" He felt a little angry with her, but he didn't want to show it.

"I don't know. Why don't you do an imitation of a bus leaving town?"

The waiter brought their drinks. "Take it," Alan said. "It should make you feel better,"

She drank the whiskey quickly and put down the glass. "Are you satisfied now?" she said. "I'm calm, You've done your duty."

"Why don't you tell me about it?"

"Because I don't want to."

"You must have a reason for wanting to kill yourself."

She shook her head. "I don't want to kill myself. I only want to be dead."

"Is there a difference."

"Yes. I'm afraid to kill myself, but I'm more afraid of what will happen if I don't."

"What will happen?"

"I'll probably be killed."

He started to laugh.

"What's funny about that?" she said.

"It doesn't make sense,"

"Yes, it does."

"And this whole thing is so silly. Here I am." He couldn't stop laughing.

She stood up. "You're right, this is silly. I'm leaving."

"Then I'm going with you."

"I'd rather you didn't."

"But I haven't finished cheering you up yet."

"You can't cheer me up."

"Beautiful girls can always be cheered up eventually."

"I'm not beautiful."

"Sure you are. And I haven't even *begun* my act yet."

"You'll have to do it outside on the sidewalk."

"All right, but I'll probably get both of us arrested for being drunk."

He followed her outside after he paid for their drinks and she said, "What do we do now?"

"That's up to you," he said.

"Why don't you go to a movie?"

"I don't want to. In the dark I couldn't see your beautiful face."

"I want you to leave me alone."

"No," he said. "Not till I'm sure you're all right."

She started crying. "Please," she said. "Please go away and let me alone."

People were looking at them. Alan was embarrassed and he wanted to just walk away, but he thought it was a good thing she was crying. He took her arm and made her come with him.

"I feel like such a fool," she said.

"You don't look like one. If that train had splattered you all over the station, then you'd look like a fool. Now you just look unhappy."

"I wouldn't have cared then."

"How do you know you wouldn't? I read in the paper a while back about a man who tried to commit suicide by jumping in front of a subway train. The train didn't kill him, but it cut off both his legs. His only problem before was that his wife had run off with another man. Now he'll be in a wheelchair for the rest of his life."

She surprised him by laughing. "I thought you were going to cheer me up," she said.

"Do you think it's funny?"

"Of course, don't you? They say most suicides are caused by a desire for attention. He should get plenty of it now."

"Is that why you tried, to get attention?"

"No."

They turned off Madison Avenue and went toward Central Park. "Why did you do it?" he asked.

"Why do you want to know? What possible difference can it make to you why I did it?"

"It won't make any. I just think it might help you to tell me about it."

She stopped beside a bench. "I'm going to sit down," she said.

He sat down immediately and smiled at her when she sat beside him and crossed her legs. "Why don't you try telling me?" he said.

She asked him for a cigarette and after she lit it, she said, "I wanted to be an actress once."

"Did you?"

"Doesn't everybody?"

"I don't think so."

"Well, I did. I came up here right after I finished my freshman year at Ohio State. I thought I just had to come to New York or I wouldn't be able to live another day."

"And you couldn't make it as an actress?"

"I don't know. I tried for a while. I was even in an off Broadway show, but I didn't like the people or the work. So I gave it up and became a secretary."

"Did you like that?"

"I didn't dislike it. I worked for a nice man and he paid me enough to live on."

"That sounds all right."

"It wasn't bad, but I was lonely."

"Everyone gets lonely sometimes."

"I know that, but I couldn't seem to get to know anyone. I never even had any dates because I never got to know any single men at the office."

"Jumping in front of a subway train is no way to improve your social life."

"Then I lost my office job and couldn't get another. The company I worked for closed its New York office and took all the executives back to Chicago. So I finally took a job in a department store, selling dresses. And I met a man there."

"You see?" Alan smiled. "It can be done."

"He was a floorwalker and we used to go out together, but we had to do it secretly. The store had rules about floorwalkers and salesgirls. If they had found out, he would have lost his job, so we had to pretend we didn't know each other at the store. But we had fun together." She stopped and crushed her cigarette.

"And you had an affair with him," Alan said softly.

"Of course I had an affair with him," she said. "I was lonely, I told you, and he was the only friend I had."

"What happened then?"

"Then I found out he was married. No one ever told me at the store because I wasn't supposed to know him except in a business way. I used to avoid even looking at him, so no one ever told me."

"How did you find out then?"

"He told me. Last night, at my apartment, he told me he was married and he said his wife was getting suspicious of all the time he spent away from home. He said he thought we should break it off."

She began to cry again. Alan touched her arm, but she pulled away.

"You'll get over it," he said.

"No, I won't," she said. "I won't ever get over it."

"Yes, you will. Don't you know these things happen every day?"

"Not like this. They don't happen like this."

"Sure they do. And people get over it."

"Why don't you just leave me alone? "

"I can't now. I want to help you."

She stood up and said, "Take me home then."

"All right," he said. "I'll do that."

They took a taxi to her apartment. He paid the driver and followed her into the building. She rang for the elevator and they rode to the fifteenth floor where she lived. They didn't talk to each other. She had stopped crying, but she wouldn't look at him.

At her door, she said, "You don't have to come in."

"I think I'd better."

"I don't want you to."

He took her key from her hand and opened the door. He pushed her in ahead of him. "I'm not going to hurt you," he said.

"I don't want you in here," she said. She was frightened.

"I won't hurt you," he said again. "I just want to help you." She laughed and he said, "It's not as bad as you think."

"Come here," she said. "I want to show you something."

The dead man was lying on the bed. He was wearing his trousers, but his shirt was on the floor. The butcher knife was so deep in his back that none of the blade was showing. There wasn't much blood, but the man's body was waxy and he lay in a bent position as if he had tried to get up and then had died and hadn't had strength enough to lie down again.

"I told you," she said.

Alan thought it was odd that he didn't feel anything as he looked at the man. He turned and walked out of the bedroom.

Peggy followed him. "Why don't you cheer me up now?" she said.

"Why did you do it?" he said.

"Because I wanted to," she said. "That's a good reason, isn't it? He didn't just come and tell me he was married, he came and spent the evening and then he told me. So I wanted to kill him and I did."

"You ought to call the police."

"No."

"Then I will."

"I'll tell them you're involved."

He looked at her and she was staring at him. He thought she was going to laugh. "All right," he said. "All right."

He left the apartment and rode down in the elevator. He felt weak and when he was out of the building, he stopped and breathed heavily before he started walking away.

A woman across the street screamed and then he heard a heavy, chunking sound behind him.

The girl lay across the hood of a parked automobile. The metal was smashed in and one of her arms had gone through the windshield.

The woman across the street was still screaming.

Alan turned and began running away. At the corner, he stopped and leaned against a street light, panting. A man passed him and asked, "What happened up there where that crowd is?"

"A woman jumped in front of a subway train," Alan said. Then he laughed until he was sick.

Also Available from Stark House Press, starkhousepress.com . . .

The Best of *Manhunt*
A Collection of the Best Stories From *Manhunt* Magazine

Foreword by Lawrence Block
Afterword by Barry N. Malzberg
Edited and Introduction by Jeff Vorzimmer
ISBN: 978-1-944520-68-7 $21.95

Made in the USA
San Bernardino, CA
08 May 2020